From the mid-century glamour of New York to a quiet village on the Italian Riviera, this beautifully written literary novel follows a man who searches for the truth of his own identity in a world of beautiful, broken things.

In the late 1950s, Peggy Drexler-Leighton is a well-known face in high fashion. But as the decade turns, she finds herself sidelined by an industry that has little room for maturing women. Following a sudden tragedy, she and her young son, Walker, retreat to their Pennsylvania roots—only to find that 'home' is a place of shifting expectations and difficult truths.

Decades later, we follow Walker to Italy, living as an ex-pat on the Riviera, where he finally seeks to define himself to himself, navigating a life of unusual pairings and hard-won independence. His quiet existence is disrupted by the arrival of his cousin, Lydia, whose presence brings more than just a conflicted memory of home.

As Walker witnesses the increasing strain on Lydia's marriage—dragged into the personal and professional drama of their lives and those around them—the tension reaches a fever pitch. Private resentments become public tragedies. When the local peace is shattered by a series of shocking media events, the ensuing news coverage turns an intimate family struggle into a spectacle that predicts the onset of global witness that the world-wide internet will soon deliver. Walker is forced into a life-altering reckoning, finally confronting the cost of acceptance and the reality of a planetary view that make it almost impossible to look away.

The Green Pear is the second book in 'The Harrisburg Trilogy.' Below you will find praise for *The Blue Orchard,* the first book in the Trilogy:

"In what could be a modern classic, poet and fiction writer Taylor takes an unblinking look at abortion in America many decades before Roe v. Wade. Introducing Verna Krone as she's arrested in her home in 1954, Taylor then transports readers to her poor Pennsylvania beginnings…before long, Verna begins working for Dr. Crampton, a well-to-do African-American doctor who performs illegal abortions…. In this powerful, vivid debut novel, Taylor parses issues of race, power, and religion in unflinching terms while believably inhabiting the mind of a conflicted woman. (*Jan.*)"

—STARRED REVIEW FROM *PUBLISHERS WEEKLY*

"Taylor is a master storyteller, and his novel is riveting, substantial, and unforgettable."

—WALLY LAMB, AUTHOR OF *SHE'S COME UNDONE*

"A work of overwhelming tenderness, unflinching veracity, delicacy, and restraint. I was engaged and moved from start to finish by Jackson Taylor's storytelling art."

—PHILLIP LOPATE, AUTHOR OF *NOTES ON SONTAG*

"This novel re-creates wonderfully a time, a place, and a circumstance in American life that drove women and men alike to break a law that could never—and will never—be obeyed. I found myself stirred repeatedly."

—VIVIAN GORNICK, AUTHOR OF *FIERCE ATTACHMENTS*

"Through fiction, Jackson has coined the phrase 'the image before the image, before the truth, a reference to the masks of social media wherein one group of stereotypes is traded for another."

—CLYDE HERBIE

"The Blue Orchard is a classic, a great American novel that will astonish and quicken dead and bored parts of our hearts. If Jackson Taylor never writes another word, he has made his mark with *The Blue Orchard.*"

—SAPPHIRE, AUTHOR OF *PUSH*

THE GREEN PEAR

JACKSON TAYLOR

BRONSON & CARL

The Green Pear

Published by Bronson & Carl
Crown Lodge, Chelsea SW3 3PP, London, England.
Contact: Andrew Hanges, BronsonandCarl@gmail.com

508 West 26th Street, Suite 4D, New York, NY 10001, USA.
Contact: Catherine Walker, BronsonandCarl@gmail.com

www.bronsonandcarl.com

First edition, revised March 2026.

Book design by Alan Barnett, www.alanbarnett.com
Cover art by Tom Cocotos, www.cocotos.com
e-book design by Robert Henry, www.righthandpublishing.com

ISBN paperback: 979-8-9888036-0-7
ISBN hardcover: 979-8-9888036-2-1
ISBN e-book: 979-8-9888036-1-4

For Rita Andreopoulos, Paul Cocotos
& Dino Sotococo

TWILIGHT

· · ·

In those late summer afternoons, my mother would arrive at the playground dressed in pumps, pearls and pastel sheaths cut so simply they could only be expensive. Making a television kind of cameo-appearance, she'd then cheerfully tend me for an hour or so, enabling the nanny to take a break. With her fine wardrobe, mother was rightfully perceived to have just come from a modeling job, and often other mothers and nannies lingered on the benches as though beauty-pageant judges, waiting for what might be their only chance to behold a real-live Breck girl in the flesh. While they sat eyeing her poise, I felt my own body and personage gladly fade into the background, becoming invisible, proudly invested in the certainty that people could no longer see me. If my presence did gain sudden notice, or as they say in film—pulled me into focus—the illusion would stall, and I'd be forced to double-down on my invisibility, hiding from the stares that too often went looking left to right—comparing her looks to mine.

In an odd premonition, my mother once noted how the jetliners flying around our globe with ever more speed and frequency, would one day instill a feeling of being *other* in many people. At the age of nine, I did not yet really understand what that meant, but in a faint way, I felt her mention of the sky and its travelers was aimed at me—assumably as a kind of guide, guard or even forewarning. Maybe she thought to predict so many of us would soon be in motion, could form a kind of alliance, recognize some larger phenomenon, perhaps leading me to trot more assuredly alongside a tribe of dislocated others.

It's been said that all imagination is based on memory, so, with that in mind, let me continue to recall how in a short time our family finances began to contract making nannies unaffordable. It was then that Mom began to accompany me to the park alone, always after sundown, wrapped in the last of her furs, a soft honey-colored mink, trimmed in beige leather. I'd leave her on a bench to go run around the illuminated fountain in Washington Square, and when it was time to go home, I'd know from the tear streaks on her powdered face that she was still grieving—not yet over the loss and promise that had been my glorious stepfather Coleman Gordon.

• • •

At nine, I'd believed Mom and Cole had been brought together magnetically by the forces of undeniable romance. All through my youth the words of Cole's proposal were repeated. Reportedly he told her: "I can't promise you happiness, or bliss…can't promise you wealth or rubies. All the promise I hold is a chance for love…and an interesting life." And interesting it was. Her beauty could hush a room, as could his, and together their contrast dazzled. When they spoke to each other their formal diction seemed witty, theatrical and elegant, the intelligence suggesting the kind of desire that defied opposition, especially those cutting critics claiming sexual congress between races to be but a perverse erotic twist. The worst of them predicted unions such as theirs would sooner or later prove certain facts to be self-evident. Make no mistake, the marriage between Peggy Leighton-Drexler and Coleman Gordon did indeed mix an emotional high-ball, poured with a double dose of spirit, yet they claimed to enjoy the strength of such proof.

In 1963, marriages between races remained illegal in half of the fifty states; the words "I do" spoken between a couple holding even mild contrast in pigmentation disavowed by many on both sides of the aisle. Even the minister who performed the ceremony expressed concern when they'd met the man in his office the week before the ceremony. "Don't you want to pause and pray over such a grave decision?" They shook their heads. "We appreciate learning from one another," they said, thinking they could, even when the lesson plan wasn't one they fully understood—or ascribed to.

Discovering their determination, the minister soon gave way, even grinning as he complimented them on the *anti-establishmentarianism* of it all. Years later, the couple still giggled over that long inchworm of a phrase—using it to jest many a difficulty they encountered.

Their wedding was fair-sized, performed before me and a circle of their closest friends—writers, musicians, actors—all of it staged at The Little Church Around the Corner on East Twenty-ninth Street in Manhattan. With vows taken, three hansom cabs brought down from Central Park carried the main wedding party up along a mile of Fifth Avenue—still then a two-way street—before turning onto East Fiftieth headed for the Waldorf-Astoria Hotel. My mind's eye can still see the bright weather that September day, the glamorously statuesque bride, pink and freckled, nestled in the arms of the lean and fit, butterscotch-brown groom, the carriage riding behind the clopping hooves of the chestnut horses, strangers on the sidewalks stopping to stare in astonishment.

At the hotel, sumptuous roses graced the dining tables, shades of peach and pink, freshly cut in Garden City that morning, arranged and delivered by a posse of Greek brothers from their flower shop on Sutphin Boulevard. Their niece Arité, was a friend of Mom's, and when I look at photos from that day, she appears in many of them, exquisitely dressed and bearing a strong resemblance to Maria Callas. Her floral family was experienced in delivering to the hotel, for three months earlier Arité's sister, a woman so beautiful she could have also been a model, had alongside her own well-polished groom, held her wedding reception there, which Mom had attended. In fact, the first song danced between the newlyweds, *Speak Low*, played by a nine-piece orchestra, was also borrowed from that earlier wedding. Only for this occasion, Cole asked a friend, Renee Guerin, to sing it for their guests, and she did so expertly, having once understudied Mary Martin, the singer who first introduced the song.

The room was glowing while Ms. Guerin performed, and the bride and groom danced, light reflecting off the polished brass of the doorways. The song's haunting melody and bittersweet warning of lost time—gave a moody tone, with an even greater edge brought by the contrasting epidermis not only of the honored couple, but also many of their guests. At that time, different complexioned people were not prone to mix socially (in many places they still don't), though typically and by necessity Cole seemed more practiced at this than Mom.

Afterwards, waiters in gold braid uniforms moved about the room—pouring champagne from big green bottles, corks popping as the wine was kept in flow. Over the years I've often wondered how the hotel handled the affair. Did the old waiters or some hard-hearted head of catering feel the need to demonstrate a kind of contempt? I can imagine a relish tray artlessly put down, a water glass left unfilled, a canapé tray passed in gruff haste. Or as employees of a grand hotel with visitors from all corners of the earth, did they pride themselves on unflappable courtesy, perhaps being in service too seasoned, or blasé, or even too-damn-tired, to give a shit? Sadly, there's little else I can recall about the day, for apparently I fell asleep before the foie gras left the kitchen, and it wasn't long before the nanny brought me home.

• • •

It also wasn't long before the act of marriage between two races lodged its complaint. In devotion and attractiveness, Cole and Mom certainly complemented one another, and they seemed intellectually simpatico, or was that accord just an act? Another myth? A failure of memory? It seemed finding common ground made for a grand life, or so they insisted, and as the Waldorf wedding had been meant to prove, it was indeed a grand life. Yet, maybe the Irish were accurate in noting two parts to that saying—a more bitter and back-handed Celtic completion: It's a grand life—*if you don't weaken.*

And the naïve couple though not weakened, were often bruised and caught up short through social misunderstanding, which could polarize them as judgements came flinging from either side. Yet, in a strange paradox, the challenges also drew them nearer, at least until some chaos disunited them once more, sometimes propelling them into awful emotional distance. Over the years they fought, made up, fought, made up, elation following sorrow, sorrow following elation, with many a promise pledged to simply try harder.

And pigmentation itself was often the least of what challenged them, frequently it was cultural difference that lent the most trial. Different people hold different notions of what it means to 'earn good money', or what 'good money' should be spent on. They differ on what it means to 'get ahead,' or 'be successful,' what a 'good neighborhood' is. There are wide variances in the choices for dress, hairstyles, music, automobiles, nightclubs, how women or men should convene, or even what someone means when they say they want 'to party.'

Additionally, as the facts of their marriage became more widely known, career gains for them both stagnated. Why should a nervous national magazine editor, or some stressed backer of a Broadway musical, risk hiring anyone who might bring unnecessary trouble? Was the dream that Mom and Cole held worth that price? Must've been. But under such cloudy circumstances, it wasn't surprising that most marital spats began to increasingly involve money. Mom earned more than Cole—until she didn't. And Cole, as a featured dancer could earn well enough, while also carrying the prestige of Broadway, until new stage shows grew slimmer, opened and closed faster, the months between them growing longer and longer.

When Mom and Cole were at their peak I had a nanny. Later, when bank accounts were overdrawn, they'd argue: "It's your turn to take him to the park," or "It's your turn to stay home with him." On certain occasions when attending me interfered with something special Cole wanted to do, he'd outplay her ace by saying: "Well, he is *your* son." That phrase could sting Mom, not to mention me, and she'd rage on over their financial hardships. Yet, they nonetheless remained united in each other, both stubbornly needing to believe they could escape opposing bias, which might leave either one of them feeling guilty, or even worse—that either of them might in fact be—*the other*.

A decade later, a psychiatrist I was seeing said something that brought to mind Mom's long-ago comment on jet-travel, which I had amidst adolescent melancholy never forgotten: "The number of people with an opposing dislocation like yours is increasing. The feeling of *otherness* is a new cultural norm."

My reply held rancor. "I thought therapy was supposed to comfort—or help a person resolve? That's like saying if enough people grow lonely and commit suicide, then suicide is simply a daring new fashion!"

"Ah! I can see I've touched your trauma place," the therapist said, seemingly pleased with the accomplishment.

"Human feelings aren't fads."

She went on to speak in a bemused way, noting how trends in emotional conformity upset many people. "*Especially* those needing to see their *otherness* as something profound."

Not sure if this was a dart aimed at me, or at suicidal people, or if it was simply a general remark, I went on to change therapists the way others change socks. In my sessions with many practitioners, I reported and repeated dreams of myself as a fractured body lying in the road, or standing at the edge of an abyss gazing out over some vista, wondering about all the other lost and invisible mammals like me.

I also began to ponder if claims about heritage or genetic connection were even important. By the time I got to college, my feeling of strange indifference had grown. There I read what Emerson wrote on self reliance—and how no one could own the entire landscape—a note that mirrored the bible when Abraham learns that only God can confer ownership. And besides, I came to think—at the end of the day we all came from somewhere imaginary—like outer space—and furthermore who the hell cared?

I also began to notice how those stressing historical origin usually sought to claim either prideful pedigree, or some mournful violation. Was it God's will to divide us in this way? I came to believe: in pain we are all connected. More than one therapist assigned me the status of personal trauma, but I soon reckoned they probably said this to all who came through their door. In my college coursework, amid the daily discussions on global diaspora, my mouth clamped shut. No way would I discuss equanimity, identity, or conformity, telling myself it was only because I wasn't about to let anyone see my otherness as needing to be recognized. But the true caution, a truth I was unwilling to speak—was the fact that I'd never met, and knew absolutely nothing about—my biological father.

• • •

In the years since, especially through my work as an editor, I've heard many people express feelings of otherness, a secret realm of transience and invisibility, like the wind or an electric current, some admitting sadly that they've never even encountered a book with a character like them. As a reader, it astonished me to realize how I saw myself in practically every character I'd ever read—including the ones I didn't like. Reading might not hold the first-hand experience of, say, touring or aerial flight—yet books formed in me a profound and intimate connection to my own species that might not have otherwise been possible.

As an editor, I also came to see how frequently the language of literature urged through unfathomable advice, things to be shown rather than told, bowing to the suasions of cinema. Further bending pressures came from agents or marketers who said while characters could express murderous violence or other maladaptive behaviors, they shouldn't be otherwise controversial—assuring offense to no one—and therein appealing to as many readers as possible—such neutralizing restrictions placed in hope of protecting the corporate employees, the house brand and adding some gain in sales. But if our invisible selves can't be imperfect, conflicted, delusional and blunt in a truthful telling of our human complication—then how on earth can other strangers see us?

• • •

Two months after the wedding President Kennedy was assassinated, and Mom told me later she and Cole felt New York subvert its elegance overnight. While Lyndon Johnson advanced his plans for a great society, the streets introduced grim metal gates rolled down over their shop windows, cars parked at the curb increasingly vandalized or stolen, all reactions tense, forming a brutal new urban backdrop for vicious and regrettable public displays of intolerance from many sides. More than a few old birthrights were being challenged on both ends of the spectrum, some lamenting the halcyon days of old were fading, with others voicing that such a past was mythical—any changes too slow and small in coming.

Sometimes on a Sunday, we'd drive out to the North Fork of Long Island to have dinner with Cole's family, and there Cole's younger sister and I would play chess. Marvene was a few years older than I, and so it took every ounce of skill possible to try and win the game from her. Meanwhile Grandma Gordon liked it when Cole and Mom showed their determination to make a good marriage, both acting like an advertising poster for the Peace Corps saying: "We can do this!"

And they were indeed doing their best to negotiate forward through the mounting money struggles. Mom and Grandma Gordon were fond of each other, and the older woman made it clear that her family valued the tenets of Christianity. "Jesus don't care nothing about color—and we follow Jesus," she said, pre-establishing her views in case the subject of race came up—as it often did. Too bad so many others in the world didn't agree.

In the Spring of 1968 Martin Luther King was assassinated, and in June Bobby Kennedy was also slain. The times they were indeed tragically changing. The war in Vietnam grew more divisive by the week, and as the summer sweltered on with more American cities burning in riots, one of the crueler money fights in our family took place. "My sense of being a man is being diminished," Cole seethed. And then, as if hit by a divine thought, he announced it was time for him to move to the West coast. Mom saw right through the plan, and accused him of picking the fight. "Crying over your lost manhood was just a trick…an excuse to ease your guilt," Mom steamed. "And sure, why not go West…go join all the other shiftless junkies out in California."

"I'm not some flower-*kid!*" he objected.

But Mom's rant continued. "You'd say anything now just to dump me…not to mention Walker." Like most children, my attention sharpened at the sound of my name being used like a poker chip. I sat stunned at the idea of our separation.

Mom did all she could to bargain on with guilt, but Cole had made up his mind. A week later he was gone, and his instincts proved right; he had barely stepped off the plane when a lucky break came his way. A new television pilot had been accepted—about a groovy sleuthing trio—and in re-development was being re-cast. As a sign for the times, the producers had decided to cast inter-racially, making one of the three players a Negro. Cole was chosen to play the part.

His instincts had proven right, and that night he phoned the good news and Mom urged me to pick up the extra telephone receiver in the kitchen so we could all be on the line together. Cole was so grateful that his life was taking a turn for the better, but then he broke down. "I need you here, Baby," he said. "It don't mean a thing without you." Hearing that, Mom began to cry. As usual, too young to comprehend what their constant agony was all about, I nonetheless grew sad at the emotion breaking through their voices, and in a moment was also crying along.

"All for one, and one for all," Cole wept. And I listened as once again they pledged to learn from their old mistakes, restating a willingness to persevere through the world's prejudicial stereotypes of hate that were so affecting the household's harmony. I felt important to be included in their phone call, as it seemed they needed me to witness their devotion. We bonded as any musketeers might, swearing to sword-fight our way through all social obstacles. As with so many couples from different backgrounds, I can look back now and see how Mom and Cole were also trying to prepare me for a life of normalcy—as if that could be chosen.

One week before Thanksgiving, Cole signed the kind of juicy acting contract that would make him not only rich—but also a household name. For Christmas he sent us two first-class plane tickets, with some sleek eight-by-ten glossy photographs, face smiling, his name printed at the bottom over the logo of the Quinn-Martin production company. Mom taped one of the photos on a kitchen cabinet and his astonishing presence gave us exciting energy. For the first time in ages Mom seemed relaxed, her face and eyes wide open. Wherever we went people commented on how well she looked, and many of her friends indicated they would do all they could to help her find new modeling work. When I came home from school, Mom and I began to spend hours going through our possessions and weeding out things that were no longer useful for a life of utopian prosperity in California.

In mid-January, a few days before our departure, Coleman's new Lincoln-Continental met another car head on while traveling along the Pacific Coast Highway. The cops said two cars speeding over sixty-five miles an hour had fatalized the crash, both drivers pronounced dead at the scene.

Mom received the news by way of the New York City Police Department—who had been informed by the police in Los Angeles. They sat with her for a good twenty minutes, leaving only after she'd phoned Grandma and Grandpa Gordon out on Long Island to break the terrible news about their only son.

Cole's body was shipped home—and we buried him in the small Greenport cemetery at the end of Third Street. For the rest of the nation, it was an historic day of inaugural activities; President and Mrs. Nixon limousined down Pennsylvania Avenue, passing a few spots where they were pelted with stones, thrown by angry anti-war protesters—until they arrived safely at the White House, where they would take residence. We experienced none of that governmental transition, instead we stood bereft, weeping with a smattering of dancers who'd once worked with Cole on Broadway. Inside the nearby family church we congregated, as Cole's sister Marvene sang: *What the world needs now is love sweet love*, tears streaming down her smooth, round cheeks.

After the service, at the graveside, the Gordons demonstrated the good faith they believed in, shaking hands and hugging Cole's many friends who'd traveled all the way out East to honor their son. It was off-season and none of the larger restaurants were open, not that many of them would have been very eager to accommodate our mixed group anyway, so everyone was invited back to the house. But the gypsies, many of whom were scheduled to dance in shows that night, were already climbing back into the cars they'd borrowed or rented in Manhattan. "Now, now, let's not be sad," Grandma Gordon called out over her tears. "Cole's gone to walk with Jesus!"

Back at the house, Grandpa Gordon placed his arm around Mom's shoulders. "Cole adopted Walker when you married," he said. "And so, Greenport remains your home too." He explained how much they respected Cole's decision to be my father, the only one I'd ever known. "We intend to honor that commitment." With those words Mom fell apart.

The next morning, we huddled in the Gordons' car waiting for the train back to New York. "Always good to be an early bird," Grandpa Gordon said, pouring hot coffee from his work thermos into dixie cups. The newspaper on the front seat declared Nixon the new president, holding his arms up and waving two fingers on each hand, a gesture he'd appropriated from the peaceniks, showing solidarity with them while also declaring an energetic readiness to finish the war in Vietnam. Before boarding the train, we stood on the platform and hugged one another good-bye. Mom took the opportunity to address the Gordons. "I hope you know how much I appreciate your offer to come live here," she said. "But Walker needs the continuity of his school…and I need to find work while I still can."

"We aren't going anywhere," Grandma Gordon said, her voice sounding like a song over the train engine. "You change your mind…you come right back out here. Just take the train to the city if you need to pose for something." Mom smiled and took my hand to board. "Now don't forget what I always told you," Grandma Gordon called: "Jesus don't care nothin' about color…and neither do we!"

* * *

Harrisburg, Pennsylvania

Back in New York, the last of our savings dwindled. To pay rent Mom borrowed on credit; she also bought gin. I easily comprehended her upset, as our circumstances had indeed changed for the worse. And should, by chance, anyone glance down from the windows of the apartment buildings that neighbored Washington Square, they'd spy the attractive, slightly-inebriated woman crying alone on the dark bench, her son, a short distance away, playing chase with the arcs of light and shadow cast by the streetlamps. Sometimes, I'd leap and empathetically race through the twilight towards her, the pale skin on her face glowing smooth as porcelain, and with the insensitive radar of children who intuit adult things, I'd ask what happened to my real father. Her replies were always stunned, cryptic and vague, claiming the man who'd sired me had gone a-wandering, a rootless phantom, though once when she'd had quite a bit, she admitted he was out there somewhere on a hunt for other women. As Mom drank ever more gin from a small silver flask kept in her purse, I asked fewer questions.

Finding an antidote for extreme grief is difficult, and financial challenges can in times of mourning be accompanied by rash decisions. Our lease at number fifteen West Eleventh Street expired and Mom did not renew it. By then, the last of our good furniture and copper kitchen cookware had vanished. Mom's friend Arité, accompanied by her sister, were among the friends who came by to check on us, but Mom gave strict instructions to the doorman, to tell all visitors we'd gone to Europe.

A few days later, Mom forfeited the apartment, and came to pick me up early from school. Turns out, contrary to what she'd told the Gordons, she could indeed pull me out of school early—if she really wanted to.

In the way of an Irish gentleman, our doorman piled our suitcases into the cab, and he sincerely wished us well. At Pennsylvania Station, an announcer wearing a conductor's uniform and cap sat in a glass box suspended over the newly rebuilt waiting room. He called cities like horses at the track or boxers in the ring, vowels lengthened, in nasal New York-ese, a sound from days gone by, certain syllables accented: *New*-ark, *New* Jersey, *Wil*-mington, *Del*-aware, *Balt*-imore, *Mary-laaand*. Then a dramatic pause before the last phrase dipped low only to rise in crescendo: *A-a-all A-board!* That urgent call of conductorial experience, sounding through the hall, stirred in all who heard it, the thrill of imminent departure.

After the Hudson tunnel, watched through the window of the train, the backs of crumbling factories appeared, probably vacant since World War Two, first Newark, then New Brunswick, then Trenton, acres of failing industrial structures, metal window grids hanging bare, their panes long shattered by brick-throwing vandals. We pulled out of Philadelphia along the main line, and the scene changed to the backs of large stone houses.

Mom's manner grew jittery, over-explaining what we could expect to find in our new home. I was shocked to realize we were not on an excursion—but permanently moving. By the time we hit Lancaster, it was clear Mom needed a drink, and when we disembarked in Harrisburg, she politely questioned the man behind the newsstand about reasonable lodgings. He handed us a flyer for discounted rooms at the Senate Hotel, then with sudden nerve Mom asked where some gin could be purchased for her sick uncle. One brow lifted before the man gave directions to a nearby liquor-store. Our taxi paused long enough for her to jump out and buy a top-shelf pint. She got back in and took a few swigs, complaining to the driver of a mysterious toothache.

The Senate Hotel, an old, brown-sandstone structure standing beside Market Square, had seen better days, and as we approached the front desk to check-in, a buckle in the burlap backing of the torn carpet caught Mom's heel, causing her to stumble. A gray-haired porter hurried over, eyes and cheeks creased in concern. "Steady, now."

"You'd never guess how nice this place used to be," Mom said.

"Yes, ma'am. The Senate was the sun, moon, and stars of political life!"

"Republican life."

"Yes, ma'am. Not many left who know them days. For more than forty years the whole state was run from that big table in the back bar."

Mom nodded. "A small group, to be sure."

"Yes, ma'am. You know it!"

Upstairs, a door was unlocked to reveal a hotel room as shabby as the lobby, wooden lathing visible where someone had once punched a hole in the bathroom wall. After the porter left, we sat on the bed and sulked at our prospects. Then, as if she'd found some great purpose, Mom opened her train case and took out our toothbrushes. "C'mon!"

She showed me how to turn on the bathroom light by pulling the short, beaded chain on the china fixture, and then standing side by side we opened a tiny tube of free mint toothpaste, and began brushing our teeth.

"We can't loaf around here all day," Mom said, suggesting we go out to get some food. After a cheeseburger and fries at a luncheonette off the square we strolled through Capitol Park, then explored nearby streets, Boyd, Susquehanna, Reilly, Logan. Mom's head shook over and over at the sight of entire blocks boarded up, here and there a whole house completely burned. "What in God's name happened here? This used to be a nice neighborhood. Decent working people." It was clear our long walk was depressing her, and we finally returned in defeat to the Senate Hotel.

On the afternoon of our second day Mom rallied again, and laid out my best clothes: a serge jacket, pants with a navy and white woven check, and a striped tie. She dressed with equal care in a suit of aqua silk and shoes of beige calfskin, her hair teased and sprayed. Using her eyebrow pencil, she dialed the rotary phone, and spoke in her gliding, courteous television voice, requesting the front desk call the Keystone Taxi Company. "And please ask the dispatcher if we might have a newer car." The receiver was cheerfully put down in its cradle and Mom pulled me close. "A cab! A cab! My kingdom for a cab!"

In the lobby, an enormous spray of peonies and carnations she'd ordered from Stephenson's florist waited, and Mom asked the driver to load the arrangement into the trunk. He seemed baffled at her command, and by the way she stood looking his vehicle over. "Not as new as I'd hoped."

"Where to…*your majesty?*"

"Palmyra. To pay a family call."

The driver nodded. From the backseat, her white-gloved hands brushed, then re-brushed the sleeves of her mink. A face powder-compact snapped open, and carefully studying its gold framed mirror, she drew a fresh line of lipstick, blotting it with a tissue. "You were but a baby last time your grandmother saw you. Now you're all grown." She checked the edges of her lashes. "Grandma wrote a few weeks ago to say she's been diagnosed with a weak heart, so it's important we make this a calm visit. Good chance she'll want to help us with some money."

The fertile Dauphin County farmland passed outside the window, dozens of black-and-white cows watching us roll by. I thought of how bad it must be to have one's heart weaken. In the town of Hershey, we turned down a sideroad that wound beneath a huge roller-coaster rising up over the tree line. "This amusement park is where I learned to swim. Back then in winter they had ice-skating too. When our prospects improve, I'll take you."

In Palmyra, the driver followed her directions, at last pulling up along the curb of a red brick house. We got out.

"This is my childhood home," she whispered so the driver couldn't hear. "A style of house called a foursquare." A curtain fluttered in the downstairs window. "Somebody has seen us…I hope it's Mother."

My tie was straightened, then re-straightened. The door opened and my grandfather emerged, planting two very well-polished shoes on the porch's walnut planks, a tan sweater patched with leather at the elbows lending him a careful look. The taxi man hurried to open the trunk, removing the gigantic floral arrangement. Grandfather called out to the man in a stern tone: "Driver, don't you dare bring that here! Now, just take her and that boy back to wherever you got 'em."

Mom found her courage. "I won't leave until I see my mother." She spoke with an angry, emotional force I'd never heard before. "You've no right to deny us…me or her…or any of us!" Her carefully made-up face remained defiant in staking a claim to her own mother, the lone link in all our biology. "It's only fair she get a chance to see Walker. He's nine now!"

My grandfather's cheeks pulsed like a man who knew he'd pulled a winning poker card. "Well, missy, finally come home to see your mama."

I felt Mom take a deep breath. "I won't stand for it. I've put up with this bullying for too long. You've no right…"

An epic battle between father and daughter resumed. "So I'm a bully, eh? While you show up here all high and mighty, demanding to see a woman you've ignored all these years?" The light and clouds reflected off his black-framed glasses. "All right, missy! You go right on. You go see her. Just have this hired jockey drive your butt out to Grand View. She's buried there. Died four days ago. Greta tried to phone but your line was disconnected."

The driver and I walked Mom back to the car, holding her up by the elbows.

•   •   •

We lived underwater, creeping bleakly about our tiny hotel room like lobsters in a holding tank. The room's faded curtains and bedclothes suited our low, blue mood. On one wall our suitcases sat stacked, forming a pedestal for the extravagant and ungiven gift of browning peonies and carnations. We'd attempted to leave the flowers at the cemetery, but the caretaker interfered, saying that size and type of container weren't allowed. Mom looked him up and down with steel. "In New York, they'd never uphold such crap."

"Well, this here ain't New York, lady."

She'd carried the overdone flowers back to the car, and then later walked with them through the hotel lobby, the porter offering a pitiful look before scrambling to help. "Seems our lives add up to nothing but a growing list of losses," she said, through her tears.

"Yes, ma'am," the porter nodded. "My own mother died last year."

That porter became our lifeline over the following days, a man paid to procure takeout—chicken chop-suey, five-and-dime hot dogs, grilled tuna melt sandwiches, or burgers and fries. With both Cole and my grandmother dying so close in time, Mom remained caught between two funerals, two cemeteries, two kinds of grief.

But after a couple of days of overpoured gin, she somehow repaired once more. With new determination, she got up, did her hair, and put on a cotton dress. When she was ready, I ran to get her fur coat and gloves. "No mink today, sweetheart, or they'll gouge us."

"Who?"

"The landlords."

I put the fur back and brought her raincoat instead. Together we left the Senate Hotel to try and find a more permanent home. Our first stop was again the park grounds of the capitol building where we tossed our leftover food scraps to the birds. "Why can't we live in New York?" I asked.

Her replies were short. "Too expensive. Too far. Please stop!"

My other complaint centered on my grandfather. "He's the meanest man ever." Mom explained a sharp tone can for many become a bitter custom. I didn't know if she meant for him or me. But my point of view remained fixed; his orders to the taxi man were for *that boy* to be returned, and these words were not erasable.

We left the park and headed North. "My goodness…even the midtown section has toughened," she said, as we trudged around. "Tenants must be leaving in droves." Inspecting various decrepit apartments, Mom mustered all her vanquished charm to impress each prospective landlord, faking hope and optimism for my sake.

Almost a week passed before we finally came upon a cheap place, at the corner of Woodbine and Fourth. A lighter-skinned black woman named Rosetta Wilkins owned the building and lived downstairs. Tall and lanky she wore her hair in close-cropped curls that were permed into place.

She looked anxious as Mom deliberated on whether the apartment would be right for us. The shabbiness of the living room was deepened by the presence of an enormous couch, its cushions upholstered in a sage-green, leaf-cut fabric, with two wooden arm rests carved to resemble heads of long-necked geese, their faces curved down to the ground, an eye drilled on each side, any varnish long worn-down to grain, "Must've been piped and stuffed before the Great Depression," Mom whispered, only half-joking. In the efficiency kitchen, Rosetta showed how a wobbly gate-leg table with an enamel top, and ringed by four mismatched wooden chairs, could be positioned to hold an electric fan up by the window. "With this turned on the room has a constant Summer breeze."

One of the bedrooms had a cedar wardrobe, missing the door panel on the left side, a piece of cardboard tacked in place to keep the moths out. There were two beds, both with lumpy mattresses, which must've accounted in no small part, for why the place had such low rent. Turns out, Mom and Mrs. Wilkins then recognized one another from their days on the district swim team when they both were young. They stood laughing and reminiscing about coaches and teammates they'd known at their respective schools. "I can't get over how it feels like providence that we should now run into each other after all this time," Rosetta kept repeating. "My Lord…Peg…I think you'd find my home *more* than satisfactory for this fine young man." Mom feeling pressured to not offend a friend, finally agreed to sign the lease, and Rosetta's hands clapped merrily, elbows akimbo, bracelets jangling.

• • •

Rosetta Wilkins and Mom quickly deepened their friendship. At night, tucked into my lumpy bed, I'd hear them in the kitchen punching triangular holes into beer cans or uncorking cheap wine. Sometimes, after they thought I'd gone to sleep, the metal hangers would scrape the closet's wooden rod, coats pushed and pulled, voices in whisper as they bundled up, chuckling as they went off to a neighborhood bar a few doors down.

The speed with which Rosetta appeared in our lives felt nothing short of miraculous. When Mom was caught short, Rosetta would step up with a dollar or two, and even gave me school lunch money. One evening, after they'd had a few, I overheard Rosetta ask Mom about why she hadn't just settled back into Palmyra. "People saw me as the long-absent daughter returning to her folks…a homecoming that should've been something to celebrate. But I was late…four days…too late to see my mother alive one last time."

The story cut through Rosetta's curiosity. "But you'd just come into widowhood!"

"Didn't matter."

"But you're a prodigal daughter…comin' home!"

"But I missed the sick bed…the burial. No way to live that down…not after *my* past."

Rosetta slammed the icebox door. "That's Palmyra for you…and every other damn narrow-minded town around here. Always judging. God forbid if them bible-thumpers sense any sort of passion in a woman…they turn that word against us as if we wanted to screw the devil! 'Stead of standing up for us…they attack. Stamp out a woman's natural desire by calling it promiscuity!"

"Poor Walker never got to see his grandma. In fact, the only time she ever got to see him, he was still in diapers. Not that he remembers. My mother worked part-time at Seltzer's. And to avoid my father we met her there at the factory instead of at the house."

"Think I remember her…wasn't she a secretary there?"

"No, that was Vicky Hinkle's mom. My mother worked as a slicer…she'd collect all the puckered end-pieces of bologna and put them in clear bags to sell at discount. They had a real outlet too, not one of those phony ones. Somewhere, we used to have a photo of that visit…she in her white uniform and hair net… Walker on his blanket…spread on top of the employee picnic table. Wish I could show it to you…but with all this moving a good many of our family photos have gone missing."

Not long after that talk, Mom started going out alone, and I'd be left with Mrs. Wilkins. She was always extremely kind, offering sticks of gum, and once buying me a black plastic comb at the drugstore to be kept in my back pocket. Usually, we would sit in her apartment watching police detective shows, her voice talking loudly, whenever it suited her, predicting how dangerous situations in the script would resolve. I once asked her where Mom had gone, and she explained with great glee how over drinks and dancing to a jukebox at the neighborhood bar, Mom had met a man named Russell.

"Single gals all over Jefferson are losin' sleep over the way your mama's nabbed the only decent bachelor…the only good catch…one of the few who can provide, or ain't already saddled to some swayback wife! He does everyone's taxes around here, and knows all there is to know about rockets and space. Lord've mercy…if he gets going on that stuff, why, he can talk the ears off a brass monkey!"

As night wore on, her talk often grew tougher, as if she were speaking to a grown-up. "This old house is all the savings I got, and I'll be damned if I sell it for ten cents on the dollar!" She frequently repeated how determined she was to ride out Harrisburg's hard times, and how in the meantime, our lowliest of rents at least covered her utilities, fuel bills, and taxes. "But, baby, even the rats on this block are out looking for something better!" She laughed, showing a chipped tooth on the side of her mouth.

Later, when Mom came home, I'd listen from bed as she told Rosetta of her evening out, and how Russell, as a professional man, always paid for the drinks and dinner. That chivalry didn't go unnoticed for he also insisted on paying

Rosetta an hourly wage to be my sitter. "Man's either a patsy or sent from God!" Rosetta laughed.

Sometimes when they were out, Rosetta and I would sit at the kitchen table and she'd let me take a sip of her beer. "Russell's real steady. Doing taxes is good money…and he likes your mama's New York ways!" She grinned, the chipped tooth visible through her sly smile. "Only problem is he can't quit talking about Sputniks and them guys that walked on the moon! He didn't like it one bit when I piped up and said they oughta take the money out of rocket fuel and use it to fix our streetlights."

A month later, Mom invited Russell over for some chicken-corn-soup, one of his favorite meals, and I studied his double-chin and moustache as he ate. His skin was shiny, a deep burnished brown, that complimented his pale blue dress shirt. He asked if I was looking forward to school in September, and what books I liked, and he was respectful and polite, though not really all that interested in me. Rosetta was right, he did like to talk about the men who had walked on the moon, continuing on even after the table had been cleared and the three of us sat back down to play Parchesi.

That evening, after Russell left, Rosetta came in, and Mom quietly reported on the evening. She then told us both that Russell had invited us to live with him. I was stunned.

"He inherited that house from his mother," Rosetta said. "And the upper end of Jefferson is more than a bit nicer than the lower end." Rosetta looked suddenly sad and stared at a spot on her whiskey glass. "I sure hate losing the rent," she said, and got up to wipe the rim on a dish towel. "But feel worse about losing you."

"I know," Mom said. "And I feel bad about needing to break the lease. Especially after all you've done."

"Since you asked with such courtesy, of course I agree," Rosetta said, tipping the bottle to top off her whiskey. "You're not the kind who try and tell the landlord what's what—to skip off in a flash like low-class trash."

"I don't want to leave you in the lurch. I'm also going to pay an extra month—in addition to you keeping the deposit."

"It's astonishing how you can tell the content of a person's character by how they uphold their signatures on a lease."

"Russell is honorable that way."

"Well, that's rare around here. Man like that is rare. He's not only telling you his worth—but yours too!"

"He understands a lot…law and finance. His character enjoys being honorable. That's why he's so successful."

"Well, who knows? The next tenant to sign up here might be a millionaire. Might pay double. Even *triple*!"

At the end of the month, Rosetta helped us pack as we prepared to vacate her dilapidated house. "I'm happy for you…so very happy," she said. "I really mean it. I'm so happy for you."

Our possessions were few, but on moving day, Russell drove over in a metallic-brown Plymouth. He spent a great deal of time explaining how he'd bought the car at an amazing price, from an estate auction of a deceased tax client. He then loaded our suitcases and we climbed in for but a short distance of only a few blocks. Rosetta was right—he'd inherited the three-story house from his mother. For a hundred years Jefferson Street sat too close to the railroad tracks, and thick coal smoke from the locomotive engines blackened that street's windowsills, sprinkled soot over the wash lines, and left shadowy clouds on the pink linings of people's lungs.

Russell's mother bought the house with money earned by catering weddings, selling life insurance, running numbers, while saving her tips as a waitress at the Plantation House Restaurant. On an oak plate rack in the dining room, a tinted photograph taken when she graduated from high school, stood by itself. "In the *honors* program at William Penn," Russell said when he noticed me looking at it. "Known far and wide for her baking. Every Sunday she'd haul a layer cake to church. Had a fine sideline in wedding cakes, birthday cakes, graduation cakes. Everyone loved 'em."

One Sunday, a few weeks after we took up residence, Mom pulled me into the dining room, and under that very plate rack told me Russell was going to be my new stepfather. I was shocked. "Why can't we go back to New York?"

"We live here now, honey. Don't you like it? Russell's real steady."

"I don't want to live here. Why can't we go back?"

"Walker enough of that question! And for God's sake, stop asking it in front of Russell!"

In the corner cupboard, I stared at a set of gold dishes reflecting the window light. The delicate china dinner service had been the prized possession of Russell's mother, used only on Christmas and Easter. "You can't marry him!"

"Don't say that, sweetie. We'll all get along! You'll see. You'll come to like him."

"Why can't we go back?

"Stop it!" Her face, which at one time had gained her so much success, now showed strain. "Don't you see? There's no way any of us can go back!"

Later, to try and cheer the day, she asked me to help her scan Russell's record collection and pick an album to play. I chose what had become our favorite for the moment—*Black, Brown and Beige*. She loaded the disk onto the hi-fi, then pulled me close to dance in the living room, as if Ellington's orchestra was all that we needed to resolve our disturbance.

At lunch, we sat at the kitchen table, and I watched her pepper and salt a tomato sandwich, the bread already slathered with mayonnaise. Dividing it on the cutting board, she handed me my half, then took the other adjacent one. I bit into the bread but it caught in my throat. There was too much upset in me to swallow properly.

"Come on, Walker. You're dining without heart. If you don't smile, you'll give me a headache."

"You always have headaches," I said, and tried to take smaller bites, counting how many times I chewed.

. . .

Against unfavorable odds, Mom soon found part-time employment at a dress shop downtown. On the day before she was to start, she came to my room after breakfast. "I've a surprise for you."

"What?"

"While I work, you're going to meet your cousin Lydia. She's agreed to look after you and let you swim with her at the Central Y."

To get downtown Mom preferred our walking route to go through what some people called 'the better neighborhoods.' First, we'd head West in the direction of the river then at the junction of Wiconisco Street, we'd turn South by the Polyclinic Hospital. There she, more than once, motioned to the parking lot. "When I was a girl, a rose garden grew here. It had a long reflecting pool like the one on the mall in Washington. In June, people came from all over to admire the roses, and your grandmother would even bring me all the way from Palmyra to see blooms of every color."

"What happened?"

"What always happens *honey-chile!* They *paved* paradise to put in a parking lot. Many consider that to be progress. In the old days there were fewer cars because men and women rode on trolleys, but they were torn out before I can remember. Buses replaced them, moving slow and horrible, Russell calls them ghetto mass transit. The government wants it that way so people have to buy vehicles, and nowadays, if you're in town in June, you hardly know if it's rose season."

We turned down Third, past some nice homes. Mom changed the subject, talking about my cousin. "Only thirteen and already studying cosmetology. Could do worse, I suppose. Her family lives in Wormleysburg, on the other side of the river."

"Do they have a lot of worms?"

"What a question! No more than other places. I don't know where the name came from." As we approached Schuylkill, the great limestone building of the Kesher Israel Congregation stood, where a woman in sunglasses bent over her car to unload something. She reached to adjust a headscarf knotted under her chin, protecting an enormous confection of lacquered hair. Balancing a cardboard box on one knee, the woman glared as we passed, then slammed the trunk lid shut, supporting the underside of the box with both hands. I kept turning to watch her lug whatever it was up to the handsome building. She paused before reaching the doorway and in a harsh voice called down, "You're in the wrong neighborhood, dearie! We don't need painted doxies uptown."

The woman disappeared. We walked on, my feet lining up to the stripes of the crosswalk. "What's a doxy?"

"Someone with impeccable taste."

At the YMCA, a plump girl stood beside a skinny boy in a plaid shirt. Seeing us, they threw their cigarettes into the shrubbery. My cousin Lydia was a few years older than me, and she not only studied cosmetology but smoked. "You didn't take the bus?" she asked, in a voice almost rude.

Mom held her hand up to shield her face from the sun. "In our house, we take pride in exercise."

Given Lydia's abundant figure, noting our contrasting fitness seemed a tactless point. Lydia ignored the remark. "This here's Buddy," she said. We shook hands, and I tried to match Buddy's firm grip. I then spied his name written on Lydia's notebook with a heart around it. Later, I learned he was close in age to Lydia, but had been held back a year in school. He made small talk, noting how this year the horseflies outnumbered previous summers. Before Mom left, Lydia and Buddy nodded their assurance to look after me, and it was also clarified that Buddy's mother would give me a ride home. Mom kissed me on the cheek, then hurried off to her job. Now that my transportation home had been arranged, I suspected she'd probably meet Rosetta Wilkins after work.

Inside the Y, Buddy led us to the men's locker room, and we changed into our swimsuits, hanging our clothes in the metal cages. Buddy explained with no small pride that his father was a chemist who'd invented a profitable epoxy glue. "What's your dad do?"

"Mine's a movie star," I said.

Out at the pool, we rejoined Lydia. "Say…is his old man really in the movies?"

"None of us knows much about any of it," Lydia said. "Or anything about what they did in New York." She saw the look on my face and suggested we all count to five and jump into the pool, deliberately diverting any more questions. A strange new family connection stirred in me. Being placed under her wing somehow felt like safety.

For the rest of the afternoon, I stayed in the pale-blue water. They didn't really watch me, but sat quietly chuckling on some chairs by the vending machines, reading limericks that Buddy had written in his notebook. At one point she massaged his shoulders and they whispered to each other. At another point I heard her say: "Promise me you'll never get fat!"

Later, we showered and put on our street clothes, and Buddy showed me his notebook. It was filled with all kinds of poems. "I write 'em all the time," he said. "If my well don't run dry, I plan to be famous one day."

We emerged from the lockers, where Buddy's agitated mother stood waiting in the lobby. "Can you imagine that girl working the desk had the nerve to tell me that I'd need a family membership! Can you imagine…to check on my own son! I'm about to complain to the manager." She glanced over her shoulder and lowered her voice. "Whole country's being overrun by dark impudence." She then grew more flustered, seeming unaccustomed to much challenge in life. It was then decided, after looking at her watch, that no complaint would be lodged after all, and we left the building.

Lydia had described Buddy's mother as a proud horsewoman, but to me she appeared less proud than a horse, and much more nervous. At a parking meter down the block, her polished emerald Oldsmobile sat with its front wheels wedged to the curb, in a way that Cole used to say might let the air out of the tires. Her grievance over the YMCA's decline continued. "Demolishing the Negro Y was stupid. The old Central is now completely overtaxed."

"Who tore it down?" Buddy asked.

"Who? Well, how should I know. Who does this kind of stuff? The government…the state…some reformer. They wanted to widen the road…all of them a bunch of thieves!"

At Market Square, we dropped Lydia by an idling silver transit bus, scheduled to cross the Susquehanna on its way to Wormleysburg. Buddy's mother gripped the wheel with two hands, much tighter than Russell or Cole ever had. By the time we arrived uptown, I saw through her disdaining eyes, how shamefully run-down everything on Jefferson Street appeared. No wonder Russell, Rosetta Wilkins, and our neighbor Mrs. Braxton worried so much about working families disappearing, no buyers for the houses, banks putting up high chain-link fences. Though no paint was flaking from Russell's square columns or banisters, my pride as we pulled up sank nonetheless. Even his stringent upkeep failed to hide the oldness of the gutters and downspouts which matched the decay spreading over the rest of the block.

Buddy's mother softened as she reached into her pocketbook and handed us each a Hershey bar. "I'm sorry, I meant to give these to you earlier… to energize you after the swim. Who knows, maybe your grandfather made this one?" She smiled as I thanked her, then waited for me to go up the stoop with my key to open the door. Once I'd stepped inside, they waved good-bye. "Be sure to tell your family hello," she said, rolling her window up all the way and reaching back to make sure her car door was locked. The sedan then pulled away, headed uptown toward what I'd been told was a large modern house, close enough to Fort Hunter that Buddy could sprint there.

• • •

Russell sat in the dining room, drinking coffee with another man, the table between them spread with receipts. He peered over his glasses, as if boys my age were something to be found in a circus sideshow. "This here is Mr. Leftwich," he said, and as if seeking to impress me with the caliber of his clients. "Mr. Leftwich owns a funeral parlor." Leftwich seemed surprised when I offered to shake hands. "A boy with manners," he said, with wonderment. "Well, I tell you, courtesy in life opens many doors."

"Walker, recite for Mr. Leftwich what I coached you."

"What?"

"The Apollo missions!"

"Oh. Yes sir." I began with the fire that killed the first three Apollo One astronauts. "The next five missions were unmanned, to test for safety."

Russell interrupted. "I taught him Roman numerals! Go on, Walker, tell him who manned Apollo Seven."

"Flight number seven…or V-I-I…resumed human spaceflight."

"Well, tell who commanded it!" I froze at his impatience and my mind went blank.

"Oh, for heaven's sake! Mr. Leftwich is going to think you have a numb-skull!"

"No! He's done just fine," Leftwich said. "Just fine." He then put his hands on his knees, stood and hiked his gray pants up by the belt. "Now, where'd my hat go hiding?"

"At least finish your coffee," Russell said.

Leftwich found his hat and then sat down again, this time keeping it on his head. "Righto. But just another minute. Then I gotta keep moving…only popped over to drop off the envelope."

"And no worry, not to worry. We can bend these numbers."

"That's what you said last time."

"But you gotta scrape up some more expenses…" Russell tapped the envelope with his fingertips.

"I don't want no audit again."

"Well, then generate more receipts. Write 'em yourself if you have to. With receipts we can prove anything."

"Can't be caught cheating…not again."

"It's not cheating, it's interpretation."

I stepped forward and said to Mr. Leftwich it was an honor to meet him, and he gave me a wry quizzical look. "I return to you the honor."

"No need to bow so low, boy," Russell said.

Upstairs in my room, I fumed. Why do so many grown-ups like to give pop quizzes to kids in front of company? If the kid freezes like I did, the company always feels uncomfortable, or they take pity on the kid and say something encouraging that can only belittle. I felt diminished. It would be hours yet before Mom would come home and start supper, and I began to grow anxious realizing how another afternoon was about to dissolve into pitiful boredom.

I'd have to hide out in the basement, read comics on an old slip-covered couch, or play darts, as Russell's frugality didn't permit a television. But to head downstairs with Mr. Leftwich still there was a risk. It might prompt another grandstanding challenge on space travel. So, I did nothing but lie on my bed listening. Their voices carried up through the heat grate, and my ears perked up when Leftwich mentioned a shooting…"Only seventeen…seven times…twice in the head… viewing tonight, funeral tomorrow. His mother howled and hollered how everyone ought to see what the world did to her child, and she's right. But his head was gone…we have to keep the lid down. So young…'nough to make you sick."

Russell had read about the violence in the newspaper and so knew all about it. "You know it as well as I do, Horatio. Jobs for our kids are being eaten by minimum wage…and then with these damn drugs…forget about it."

I tip-toed out into the hallway, opened the door to the attic, then silently climbed up the wooden stairs to my less-than-favorite hideout. After pulling the light bulb string, I lay supine on the dusty floor in the pool of light, feeling the weight and measure of the house beneath me.

From time to time, I could still hear them talking, Russell now back on UFOs, boasting he'd seen dozens. "Gotta watch the sky close…the rewards come best in the middle of the night. Then you'll see how the government lies…saying spacecraft are secret missions sent by the Russians! That's the only kind of alien they understand." I felt the air pressure shift as the front door opened and knew by that sound Mr. Leftwich was departing.

The afternoon stretched on. My play made itself into invisible games and dreaming plans, and avoiding the fears preying on the solo balance within myself. Mom was to blame. Her choices had brought this.

I must've dozed off, for when I looked up, the small attic window was pitch black. Just beyond the pool of light, I imagined spiders multiplying everywhere. My stomach heaved. I jumped up, skin tingling, and once the light string was pulled the darkness expanded into a vast ocean, now infested with sharks and electric eels fifty-feet long. An un-swimmable rogue wave rose up to block the path between me and the stairs. Shuddering, I sank down them as fast as I could to escape, desperate to find an adult to whom I could cling. My death race brought me to the dining room where Russell sat alone reckoning someone's income. In humiliating terror, I approached, wishing this tax-man had but even a fraction of Cole Gordon's warmth.

Russell glanced at me, then went right back to the books. "What? A boy of nine still acting like a baby?"

"I'm gonna be ten."

"Even worse…and you'll soon be eleven. Whatcha' got to whine about? Food on the table. Roof over your head."

To have my fear spurned was more than I could bear. I grew up on the spot, forcing a big smile, then making a timid attempt to pretend my agony was but only playacting. Abandoning any hope for comfort, I went to my room to wait out the shame.

. . .

September arrived, and the secretary in the principal's office instructed Mom to supply verbal answers for a registration form while she typed them in. I stared down at the starched crease in my new school pants and felt a sense of prosperity. A question about race came up, Mom, perhaps inspired by Ellington, told the woman I was beige.

"I can't type that…that's not a category!"

"Then put sallow…or olive." The secretary had a small chin and it dropped. "You must be joking?"

"Freckled? Gray? None of us is truly anything."

The woman grew curt. "This form has to be filled out exactly as defined."

I could see Mom getting agitated. "Requiring these generalities is an insult to any number of people. And what the hell difference does it make?"

I already knew this exchange was going to make life at the school more difficult. Mom was using me to illustrate some point I didn't yet understand. Already we weren't popular people, and the cool mood in the principal's office now frosted over so that we stood in slush. "Why can't you just fill it in like everyone else?" the frazzled secretary asked.

Mom instructed me to go out into the hallway and find a drinking fountain. I obeyed, and didn't hear the outcome of my recorded race. But throughout the day I felt certain teachers look at me with curiosity. Did I imagine it? Or had the secretary informed the whole world that my mother wanted me to be beige?

That night, Rosetta Wilkins dropped by and from my bedroom, I heard Mom complain to her that it was growing more difficult to shelter me. Rosetta must've been upset for her voice was loud. "These people don't understand what motivates your choices. And I gotta tell you…I don't either! I mean, why buck some bitch in a school principal's office? Why stir all that drama? Unless you yourself might want some attention."

"Rosetta! How can you say such a thing? I hope that's just the wine talking. I'm not out there trying to make some clumsy social declaration. I'm trying to gain acceptance for my son! We can't even go to a restaurant together!"

"Just because you say you love Russell don't mean people are gonna roll over and accept it. They see you as gloating over something in an uppity way. That old secretary's probably never seen a white woman stake a claim against her own skin. And a Revlon girl to boot? That's beyond comprehension!"

"It was Breck."

"No matter, they'll always beat you down for thinking you can make your own rules. And they'll punish you even more for being too beautiful…and for gettin' loved up every night by a virile black man. It's called *envy*, baby, and that ain't doing Walker any favors."

"I won't be beaten, and neither will he. Decent people are out there." I held my breath at the tinge of heartbreak under her defense, a sadness not to be overcome.

"Can't educate the entire world," Rosetta said. "Or uphold some silly debate. Sometimes you gotta let sleeping dogs lie."

"You've no idea how bad it's gotten. When Russell and I go anywhere, they glare and grimace…their faces positively cartoon-like! Total strangers see me as trash, the type who sexes her way across color lines. They cast Russell as some kind of pimp. What's worse, if Walker is with us, they act out even more. Like hostility is some sort of recalcitrant birthright."

Rosetta's chair creaked. "Hope you'll forgive me for saying this, honey, but you sound like a mouse caught in a trap who suddenly decides she don't like cheese after all. You're like someone having to prove something, needing to think of herself as upholding some noble cause."

. . .

Somewhere along the way, Russell discovered Mom had a fondness for the color blue, and while she worked at the dress shop, he began a project to paint every room in the house that color. Each day she returned, as did I, to find ever more walls freshly rolled in blue. But the shade he'd chosen held a deep, greenish-aqua tint, much too gloomy for Mom's subtle taste. Russell proudly admitted the odd-colored paint had been on the clearance table at the hardware store. Discounted pricing only further hindered appreciation for the hue and made a bad bargain worse. The more determinedly Russell painted, the more oppressive the house showed itself to be, even to him.

After a few weeks of living in the darkened rooms, he goaded Mom for her opinion, perhaps ready to be petted with some kind of praise. Mom told the truth, saying that while she more than appreciated the effort, the color was ugly. Gently, she asked if he might be willing to change it, and that a bone-white paint would freshen the whole house.

Her response frustrated him. "I didn't take you for a woman who likes white!" he said.

"Russell! That's pejorative, and you know it!"

I didn't know what the word *pejorative* meant, but by the tone of her voice, I knew it was awful. Running to the doorway I shouted: "You don't know what she likes. You don't know *nothing*! You'll never know!"

The heat of my reaction stunned us all. We stood staring at one another. "Walker," Mom reprimanded. "Have you forgotten all I taught you about respect for elders?"

"I ain't no elder!" Russell said. "Not yet. But I do spend every damn day doing nothing but trying to make you happy." I was made to apologize and then ran to my room in tears. Later I overheard him say, "That boy'll always be *betwixt and between*." A few days later the paint miscalculation had cooled, and Russell, as Mom had asked, spent more money and another month of workdays on a ladder with a brush and roller, until the walls and trim of each room reflected the color of an egg. Every shell lightened, except mine.

• • •

Braving the city of Harrisburg as a family, we grew ever more restrained. But one Sunday, Russell announced the Penway was showing an art-house feature, which he thought Mom would enjoy. The theater was newer, and located out on the hill section of town; it had no balcony, just nicely cushioned seats on the main floor where we could sit absolved from the worry of disrespectful people dropping candy, popcorn, or worse onto our heads.

As we walked to the show, Russell spoke the names of every family whose house was now abandoned, boarded up, their windows broken. Arriving early, we purchased tickets, then to kill time, strolled over to Reservoir Park to see the sun begin to set. We didn't linger long, for Russell insisted on punctuality, saying it played a major role in getting ahead in life. At the traffic light waiting to cross back over State Street, a bow-tied man in a convertible pulled up and yelled over to us. "You people won't be happy till the whole damn world's mulatto." The light went green and his foot was already on the gas. Mom turned to Russell, mouth aghast.

Russell spat with disgust. *"You people?"* He then forged on to cross over the street to the sidewalk on the other side, his stride an aide for trying to regain a modicum of composure. "The news prints its biased head-lines, agitates us to divide the working class," he said trying hard to sound measured. "In the years since they shot Dr. King, that cruel act has disrupted the sum of many people. If the workers of every race united…the wealth-hoarders would awake to a rude surprise!"

"The news doesn't report what's standard," Mom said, trying to align with Russell's attempt at rationality. "Millions arrive safe to work each day…but the two who crashed their cars are the ones who get reported."

"Yet every criminal with a Negro face is sure to get his picture printed in the paper…no matter how small the crime."

"They print other faces too," Mom said, hoping a bit of balance, even if not equal in measure, might soothe the situation. I thought about how the bow-tied man reminded me of the woman who'd once called Mom a doxy. This was indeed more evidence that we as a joined group provoked anger, and it showed my schoolmates held no exclusive right on bias. Our being together left us unequivocally despised all over town.

A crowd had formed a line waiting to go into the cinema. Russell went to the end of it then leaned back on one heel, fingers of one hand resting casually on his hip, continuing with his rational act, trying to suggest a cool ease. It astonished me when he placed his other free hand on my shoulder and whispered: "With no interest in cooperation, conflict and bad happenstance fracture us all."

"What's a mulatto?" I asked, looking squarely at him.

He answered under his breath: "Chess sets who mate."

"Russell! Hush!" Mom lowered her voice so the others on line couldn't eavesdrop. "He means children born to people of different backgrounds…parents like us…who smile at everyone as we get together and try to love one another right now."

• • •

Each day after school, the old sense of loneliness overtook me as I'd relive the newest humiliations, often involving being tripped or pushed in the hallways as I went to class. I'd hear faculty remark to one another about the remnants of the old systems breaking down. How shocked they'd been to see crinolines and collared shirts, cede to despicable bell-bottoms, hot pants, long hair, and tie-dyed tee-shirts. Then one day female teachers were liberated, permission suddenly granted for them to wear pantsuits, the younger ones wearing mini-dresses.

One long-time chemistry teacher stood in front of our class still wearing a sweater, matching cardigan, and pearls, she lamented: "Wouldn't you girls at least want to comb your hair?" The students laughed at her quaint obsoletion.

Buddy wore the first pair of hip-hugger pants I ever saw, and when he went down the hall, the way his loose walk moved the patch pockets against his small, rounded butt made me envious. I vowed to emulate him. I began to carry a notebook just for poems like he did, hoping that like him I'd be seen as a poet who was just another ordinary guy. In my poems, I imagined what the older girls might see in Buddy's walk, or what tender things he might write to them.

I knew my lines were scribble compared to his, often quite crude in their sexual depictions, and I crossed many things out, and didn't dare show them. I tried my best to imagine what words he might say to hold Lydia, but inside myself, the feelings were not cool. I was always tending some upset or other, while nothing seemed to bother Buddy.

With Mom working more hours, I now traveled by myself to swim at the Y. The anxious glances and rude remarks we'd heard in the better neighborhoods Mom preferred to travel, made me nervous. So my route stayed back along Jefferson, where foreclosure notices, curled by rain and sun, hung tacked to many doors. I studied the flowerbeds, given over to creeper vine, waist-high ragweed, and thickets of thorn. I'd heard Russell tell Mrs. Braxton that nature was our main intruder, and this thought brought apprehension. There was no way to win.

At one house, I often came upon a pair of chained-up dogs sunning themselves, and when they saw me, they'd jump up, growl, snap, and bark. To escape their ferocity, I'd jog, soon sprinting as far and fast as I could.

Sometimes I'd wander around the farm-show complex on Cameron Street, staring up at the limestone animals sculpted to border its red brick roofline. On days when a farm show committee was in session, a side door would be propped open, and I'd sneak in and tip-toe past the meeting room, where a group of business leaders sat alongside some red-necked farmers hashing things out. I'd continue on until I could enter the enormous dirt ring, walking around and imagining all the animals to be gathered there come January.

One day, as I ran down the street to another barking dog sprint, I hurried to reach the Y, my torso wet with sweat. There I saw Cousin Lydia standing out front and quickened my jogging pace, excited at the idea of getting out of hot street clothes for a leap into the pool. But even from a distance, by the way she handled her cigarette, I could tell she was in a fury.

I drew near. "What's wrong?"

"Buddy can't swim here. That's all."

"Why not?"

"Parents. They say he can only swim up there!"

"Where?"

"The Country Club."

"Why can't he swim with us?

"Plain as the nose on your face."

"Huh"

"The way your mother sashays around town with that guy."

To discover Mom might be the cause of Buddy's removal was a terrible shock, and his banishment was deeply upsetting. There must be someone in charge to whom I could object, but I didn't know where such a person could be found. With my clothes stowed in the locker, I rejoined Lydia poolside, and swam listlessly, following her in a lane shared with many others. Having the pressure of blame on me, was like a price on my head, and it slowed me down, more than one swimmer splashing on by in annoyance. After twenty minutes, I again followed Lydia as she climbed the ladder out of the pool, and sat drying off. The exertion of having fiercely lapped seemed to have calmed her.

Back in my street clothes, I waited in the lobby until Lydia finally emerged. "What took so long?"

"The bathroom. It's so well-scrubbed. Whenever I'm in a nice one, I look straight into the mirror and try to see the future. In my head I give award speeches. I get cheered by the audience as I receive a ribbon from the White House. Sometimes I'm awarded a prize, like from a newspaper, for say helping a cripple kid with his tray in the cafeteria, or reading books to people who are dying."

"You get awards every time you see a nice bathroom?"

"Sure. Why not? Can't do that in our crummy bathroom at home."

We walked out of the Y and strolled up Front Street, selecting a bench that faced the river. She smoked, and together we watched a small flat-bottomed boat navigate between rocks. "Feels bad not to have Buddy here."

"They're trying to keep him away from me...his mom's jealous."

"Of what?"

"Me, of course! I might take him from her. She can't stand that he writes poems just for me. Some women get scorched over that kind of attention. Just ask your mother!"

"Okay, if you say so, I will."

"No, don't ask. And don't you dare tell her what I said about Russell, or people not handling it. My Dad is disgusted one minute and then he yaks on and on about how great she was in the old days, her picture in *The Patriot*...all dolled up to sing at the Copa. He says she was *piss elegant*."

"The Copa?"

"The Copacabana. A famous club. Once I get my beauty license, I'm going to New York to dance there. And I'll go to all the other fine nightspots too."

We lingered on the bench, and she changed subjects, going on about a new hair perming process she'd been learning in cosmetology class. "I tell you, won't be long before hairspray goes the way of Brylcreem." She changed subjects again, holding up a magazine for teenage girls, featuring photographs of young singing stars. "That's Bobby Goldsboro. I saw him in concert. What a dreamboat! A chorus of angels joined him for the song about the wife who died? I just cried and cried! I still cry whenever it comes on the radio. Especially if we're in the car. Can't help it! Can you imagine loving someone that much and then they just go away? Imagine, every time he leaves that house, the tree she planted reminds him of her. That's how I feel about Buddy."

That night I asked Mom about the Copa.

"It was a ludicrous job…I can't sing. None of us girls could! They hired us to dress up the place for a few nights. They wanted it to seem classy, like the Empire Room at the Waldorf, or the Persian at the Plaza, which was up the street. So, we stood around in rented evening gowns with instructions to look adoringly at the singer."

Russell looked up from the paper. "What singer?"

"Julius La Rosa."

"Never heard of him."

"They gave him the big build up…tried to get women to be mad for him."

"Did it work?"

"I guess, for a while."

• • •

We hadn't seen Rosetta Wilkins in some time, and I could tell Mom felt happy when she stopped by one evening. "Is Russell in?"

"No. Tuesday is Elks."

"Good. I'm in no mood to be badgered. Have him interrupting all the time. Asking how many we've had."

They sat in the kitchen using the opener to puncture beer cans as they talked. "Walker's been assigned to read *The Diary of Anne Frank* for school. Has to write a book report. Imagine…whole family in hiding…a young girl being persecuted. She died in a death camp. Yet, in that poor girl's diary, she still believed all people were good."

"And did that save her ass?"

"You don't understand. I absolutely must agree with her. I have to believe in good, or I'll go insane!"

"The question becomes what *good* is?"

"You know. Decent. Moral. Kind."

"Those are just words when people act like animals. I've known from birth life is stacked against me—and for other black women. And men too for that matter. What's good is not to let them turn you into something you don't want to be. To prove people wrong."

"Is that how you describe good then?"

"I don't know. Finding ways to resist the animals. I mean ways that don't hurt anyone. I suppose that's what everyone would like to know how to do?"

"That reminds me of a story. One I heard years ago. A willowy model I used to work with told it to me. She was part Japanese—that ancestry on her mother's side. What she described took place during the second-world-war, her grandmother and young mother were rounded up and sent to a camp for Japanese-Americans. The camp was converted from an old army barracks in the Arizona desert. And when the grandmother, a refined lady from the city of San Francisco, saw there were no partitions between the latrine's row of toilets, she refused to use them. After a day or so, necessity finally forced her to enter, but in an act of passive resistance she sat on one of the porcelain bowls with a brown bag over her head."

"Wouldn't catch me hiding in a bag like that."

"That's all she could do."

"I'd want to look 'em right in the eye while I went. Now, I'm not saying many people can't be good. They may be decent. And most of us if our backs are to the wall can be both. But you hold no idea to how the whole thing works. Believing in good don't always smooth the road. Too many people are still mean as rats."

At that point I stopped listening for in my mind what Rosetta said made sense. I could measure it by what I was sensing about myself. At school, Buddy's homeroom was just down the hall from mine, and daily I'd raise my hand for permission to get a drink of water from the hallway fountain, hoping, that in passing his door, I'd catch a glimpse of him. At assemblies, he was one of the boys who carried the flag, and seeing him hold such tremendous responsibility to our nation, his impression on me grew stronger. I persuaded Mom to buy me a pair of gym shorts like the kind he wore, red stripe running down the side. If I could just find the right look, I might be ignored by the boys who frequently slammed my head into the lockers, or punched me in a kidney if I dared bend to tie a shoe. I never reported these incidents. If I *were* to admit such things at home, I worried Mom would storm the school. And going to the principal would also only add to the school's notion that it was my presence bringing the nuisance, that any disturbance reflected the negligent way they thought my mother was raising me.

When the ugly group of older boys gathered in the boy's room and tried to stuff my head into the stinking toilet to make a *swirly*, I fought back, and that seemed to make an impression. But walking home, a bottle was thrown from somewhere, and it shattered behind me. I pretended not to notice, to act casual, walking laid-back like Buddy might. Turning to look, could bring eye-contact, and an ensuing fight or chase. I kept my gaze down and acted distracted, but turning slowly, as if searching for a lost cat. I'd gone a good distance down the block when I saw the bully trailing me. Slightly older, he was certainly rough, but I didn't know him. He picked up a broken piece of glass and with expert aim threw it across the street in my direction. I felt the glass sting the skin of my elbow, just below the cuff of my summer shirt. The wound stunned. He smirked, and I continued home, blood trickling down from the nick in my arm. No one had ever drawn blood before. To justify his crime, he chanted: "*White-mama-shacking-with-a-taxman-black.*" It was a relief to then see him turn up a side street, like most bullies, disappearing before he could be tagged.

I lied to Mom, saying I'd cut my arm on a chain link fence. She told me I should be more careful, but must've intuited something, for the next day Russell took me out to the backyard to give me lessons in self-defense. He explained the workings of a left-jab, a right-hook, the one-two to the chin. He seemed ridiculous to me, his heft dancing to show how I ought to keep my feet in motion.

"C'mon, now! You not even trying!" I swung wildly, fearful that I might hurt him. "There ya' go. Don't let them motha's lick you!" At the end of our spar, Russell looked at me with disappointment. He knew as well as I did, that as a fighter, I didn't stand a chance.

Not wanting to endure more of Russell's self-defense lessons, I kept quiet about school. Who knows, in the case of another *swirly*, Russell might even require that I learn to scuba dive.

More kids whispered the hallway chant as I walked by: "*White-mama-shacking-with-a-taxman-black.*"

. . .

That my mother and Russell were perceived to lead some kind of wanton, lust-fed lives amazed me, as Russell was so square. He treated Mom in a manner his mother might have approved of, complimenting the impeccable ways she presented herself, the nice dresses, the set hair. That this kind of flattery could capture her heart irritated me, and only made life more unbearable. I bristled while weighing my growing independence.

Lydia's birthday fell on the first day of Autumn, and at Bowman's Department Store, Mom helped select a bottle of cologne as a gift. She nixed the more expensive stoppered-crystal bottles I favored, opting for a subtle brand she thought enhanced Lydia's burgeoning maturity. Once we'd paid, I begged Mom to take me to the shoe department and buy me a pair of desert boots, and I sulked furiously when she claimed we didn't have the extra money.

I presented the perfume to Lydia and lied, saying I'd heard it was Bobby Goldsboro's favorite scent, that he liked jasmine and spice.

"Really? Where'd you read that?"

My lie expanded. "In a magazine…LIFE." I changed the subject and said I'd written a poem in her honor. As I read my tribute out loud the realization of how wrong it all sounded came over me. But I ignored my instincts and went on until the last line finished. She looked at me as if seeing me for the first time, then took a drag of her cigarette. "That sounds nice, Walker. But for God's sake, I'm no kissin' cousin!"

Recognizing I'd expressed some kind of romantic adulation that only Buddy should make, brought the full shame to bear. I closed my notebook and lied again, saying that I was only practicing on her for when I had my own girl.

"Thank goodness. I thought I was going to have to hit you with a stick."

A few weeks later, Lydia handed me a gift wrapped in paper printed with miniature clown faces depicting Emmett Kelly. "But my birthday is three months away."

"I know. But it's something we need now. We both can use it."

Inside a sleek box, snug in its velvet mold, a switchblade lay. She picked it up, snapped it open, and pointed it. "Let's carve our initials on that tree." She cut first, two sets, hers intercrossed with those of Buddy. "Haven't seen him except in the hallway for over a month."

• • •

When my real birthday did finally roll around, Lydia was invited, but her dad said the crime in Harrisburg was too dangerous at night. So, seeing my disappointment, Mom and Russell sang with more than usual cheer, while he played on his mother's out-of-tune piano. Mom then doled out slices of coconut cake, and Russell presented me with a rolled-up magazine tied in string, a special collector's edition on astronauts, this one all about the life of Alan Shepard. "Now," Russell said. "There's a man to look up to!"

"You look up at everyone in space," I said.

Russell caught my pun. "That's cause they're up in space!"

Mom's birthday gifts were practical: dress shirts, socks, a pair of cuff links, and three books: *Flags of the World, America's Historylands,* and *The Pharaohs of Egypt.* There were also a pair of desert boots, the very ones I'd begged her for, and identical to the pair I'd seen Buddy wearing. I spent the rest of the evening reading, engrossed in the story of King Tut's tomb, pretending my room was a chamber under the sand. At bedtime, I emerged from the tomb in my new boots to make an educational presentation to Mom and Russell, rehashing all I'd just read, explaining how Howard Carter was a great archaeologist in charge of the expedition to find the tomb. "Did you know Egyptian civilization is five-thousand years old?"

Russell stared. "Oh, Africa's old, all right. By the time them slowpokes from Europe lit their first fires, Africa had already lived through centuries of civilization. Probably more than five thousand years…but if we calculate that and divide five generations for every hundred years…that comes to two-hundred-and-fifty generations before Europeans ever got their butts out of their damn cradle."

"I'm sure it's more complicated than we'll ever know," Mom said.

"The claim to have then founded civilization only allows the riches stolen from Africa to be justified."

"Aren't you always the first one to go on about how nobody owns the land?" Mom challenged. "You even say that about the Indians."

"Many American ignoramuses think it all started here," Russell said. "To bypass history is to ignore law, commerce, agriculture, religion, cooking, even burying the dead. I'm talking human origins! But I can see you'd rather think about another drink than listen to me talk true history."

"Now, that you say that, I don't mind if I do."

   . . .

Buddy was absent from his home room class, and Lydia soon learned he'd been transferred to a private school, presumably up closer to where they lived. Meanwhile, a new boy came to join my homeroom, and I found him oddly fascinating. Sensitive and obliging, he had polished dark skin, and the vulnerability of his character made my stomach twist. From the moment one saw Ronny Wilding, it was clear that he was a boy born to suffer.

Each morning, his mother turned him out in freshly ironed shirts and spotless slacks, but by the time he was half-way to school, the other boys would circle like jackals, knocking books from his hands, his sweater tossed in the dust. "What's a matter, Ronny? Can't you speak?"

His face, angled sideways, eye lashes aflutter, brought a bashful smile to the corners of his mouth. Then in a voice soft as talcum powder, he answered. "Nah…I can speak." The boys would howl, and usually pushed him down, boxing the sides of his ears. His eyes remained clear and wide, expressing a nervous sincerity, mixed with shock over the punishment he'd done nothing to provoke, except vary in some degree from the point where other boys felt comfortable.

At recess one day, someone smeared dog feces on his lunch bag. He made no comment but gently stooped to gather leaves to wipe at the folded brown paper his mother had packed so carefully. One of the more vicious boys named Kyle Latsha, ran over and kicked Ronny in the hipbone. He fell sideways, eyes blinking, face perplexed, not fighting back with anything but a haunting, passive endurance.

"Better quit," another boy called. "Someone's gonna tell." Like sleepwalkers awaking from their own unconscious vice, the pack grew worried. Had they gone too far?

That afternoon, I found myself in the boy's lavatory as they once more gathered around Ronny. It was his turn for a *swirly*, dipped in the same toilet where my head had once been. I knew this round of Ronny's abuse was harsher, and coming fast and furious because earlier in the day, his very passivity had made a gang of bullies feel afraid to be bullies. This new attack was meant to show their fear had been conquered. They flushed the toilet, then pulled him up out of the water like a catfish. Head dripping, gills heaving, he looked in my direction as if to plead mercy. When Ronny saw no aid would be coming forward from me, he looked off in another direction.

That night I lay in bed reliving the shock of Ronny's beseeching look. Although I'd not participated directly, I'd also not stopped anything. How pathetic to recall even the small pride I felt to have been included in such an awful group, and to also feel inside myself that a boy of my lowly station had only been permitted to witness Ronny's misery to further humiliate him. The truth was to avoid standing out, I had stayed close enough to the group to seem to belong, but far enough to fool myself into thinking I wasn't complicit in the cruelty. How many people throughout the world pass their days in just such a safe and sad end-zone? My shame at such cowardice hit me with an ugly truth, as the linings of my nostrils began to burn: as long as the boys were picking on Ronny, they weren't picking on me.

. . .

The sons of Mrs. Braxton stood on the sidewalk dressed in their Sunday best, ready for their weekly march to the Capitol Street Baptist Church. I awoke to the sound of Russell speaking outside the window, his voice holding a grand moral tone: "You boys look like a credit to the race!" Gazing up at my dingy blue ceiling, I wished someone would say that to me, that I too could fulfill a responsibility of some kind.

Later that week, I came home to find Russell drinking coffee with Mrs. Braxton. She had our phone book open on her lap, and was running her finger down the pages to count all the august families of Harrisburg who'd moved: "Boas, Caldwell, Cameron." She noted those who'd gone to pioneer the West Shore, or East toward Hershey, and still others, like Buddy's family, who'd gone North towards the Country Club.

"Where's Mom?" I asked.

"At the Emerald…where else?"

Mrs. Braxton chimed in without looking up from the phonebook. "Them girls do like to party!"

"Yup," Russell said.

"It sure relaxes 'em."

"Yep."

As Mrs. Braxton continued her citation of names, Russell returned to the top subject of his profession: *taxation.* "In '51, close to a hundred thousand lived here. Now, twenty years later on, and a quarter of the population has flown. The fat-cats move their big houses to cheaper acreage, robbing the commonwealth of the city, the schools, the fire department, the police, and the public works. And what do the politicians do? Jabber, jabber, jabber. Then they move away and join 'em."

"Damn right!" Mrs. Braxton agreed. "All civic engagement this…and urban renewal that…meanwhile the capital goes to seed. Old rich families don't like taxes wasted on people like us. Come Winter, them oaks and maples will drop branches through the roof slates of all them abandoned houses, snow will powder the inlaid floors, and soon all those walls will fail."

Russell drained the last of the coffee from his cup. "And the banks don't do a damn thing! They just foreclose and put up more chain fencing."

"You know, maybe we *too* oughta go down to the Emerald?" Mrs. Braxton said, and gave a wink.

The idea seemed to suit Russell fine. He turned to me. "Walker, mind the fort. And do some more homework."

I nodded, and went to my blue room, lying on my bed, reflecting on the month of schooldays just passed, and how there was no halt to Ronny's intimidation even with the many strident teachers about. I'd recently overheard one from their ranks discussing *me* with another teacher. "Keeps his grades up… despite the home situation."

The other teacher replied, "You can just imagine what *that* must be like."

The rest of the afternoon was lost to reading about Alan Shepard, only to discover I was nothing like him. I'd never have a yearning to launch a rocket. Perhaps Russell wanted to encourage me to believe maybe I could? But that very notion seemed to mean he saw some lack in me. A lack of something that needed encouragement. The whole enterprise of pity made me shudder with embarrassment. I was no hero. Declining to defend Ronny Wilding proved I'd '*always be betwixt and between*' and certainly no credit to any race.

• • •

Rosetta Wilkins and Mom had recently decided they should treat themselves with more respect, and to progress from cheap beer and wine to Screwdrivers and Manhattans, which Mom usually supplied. They also socialized earlier and earlier in the evening, their gossip centered on other women at the bars, how so many of them lost themselves to getting fat or hitting the bottle too hard. Whenever their voices turned to whisper, some tale of peril was a certainty, and my ears would grow alert to the shift. "…left her broke and knocked up…"

"After everything else…?"

"She'll abort…not so easy…"

Mom's future began to frighten me. I sensed Russell, no matter how approving or safe he might seem, could never save her from herself. If only some method to restore her confidence could be found, something that might lead her back to some kind of control. But granting such a wish remained beyond my reach. Often Rosetta, showing a zeal for maudlin therapeutic psycho-drama, coaxed Mom to admit how grief-stricken she still was over the death of Coleman Gordon.

"I'm still only just now reckoning it. Oh, Rosey…"

"I know, baby. You're a woman with hard luck."

One afternoon, when the trees were blowing hard outside the window, I heard Mom whispering about Cole's Pacific Coast crash, how a young blonde had been in the passenger seat.

Rosetta whispered back: "Dead?"

"I never asked."

"Nothin' worse than a trashy blonde. I don't remember. You mighta told me already…but I don't remember. Was Cole Walker's real dad?"

"Walker uses Cole's last name. We married. He adopted him." Even to my ears Mom's reply sounded too vague.

"What happened to his real dad…did you tell me this already?"

"I did not." Mom remained quiet. "He's also dead."

"You lost both of 'em?" Ice swirled in her glass. "No sirree…you never told me that. I'd have remembered *that*. Honey, you've been through more than women should have to stand. Sooner or later…let's face it…we all get the call to meet our maker…and meanwhile we sit here hoping our departed loved ones are in a better place…and all that crap. But Lord! Your mother died as well! Peg… it's just too damn much!"

"Please. Let's talk about something else."

"You're still a real looker…why don't you just go back to modeling?"

"At my age? Those chances gave way years ago."

"Nonsense!"

"The modeling racket drops you down the ranks fast. First you go from editorial, the slick expensive magazines, to department store ads, then ever lower catalog brands…then sales pamphlets for knock-off dress shops. In wedding books, the fat paycheck goes to the teenage bride. My age is the wedding basement…mother of the bride…or that divorced, worn-down aunt with the frosted hair, selling the jewel-colored cocktail dresses. No wedding ring or cake for us…we eat only crumbs."

"You had your losses too young…and your mother…"

"Please stop…" I came into the room. Mom stood instantly. After fixing her belt she emptied Rosetta's ashtray.

"How about we all go out for a walk," she said.

• • •

The Italian Lake reflected the sky beneath a statue of dancing girls that stood fountained in the middle. Circling the path around banks of clipped shrubbery and perennials, an older woman approached us. She wore brown fox fur clipped to the padded shoulders of her jacket. Mom and I had seen her before, often on a stretch of sidewalk near North Fourth, and we agreed she must live nearby. We never spoke to her, but something about eyebrow pencil and lipstick set on aging skin disturbed Mom. Was this her future? After the woman was out of earshot, Rosetta put great energy into dissecting her outdated style. "Ankle-strap shoes! A netted hat. She must've rolled them bangs on hair rats. No one's done that since the end of the war…even the Andrews Sisters now have pixie cuts!"

"Maybe she likes old-fashioned things," Mom said.

"That kind of pancake base is turned from wide cream sticks…no one but strippers use that crap anymore."

"That gal's no stripper."

"Might've been? Though I never saw her anywhere."

"We see her all the time." I interrupted. "Her face is painted like faces in the Egyptian tombs. I think she's beautiful!"

Rosetta, tipsy from cocktails, let out a howling laugh. "Well, at least this here boy knows a mummy when he sees one!"

To me, our neighbor was a work of art and I dug in. "But she is beautiful!"

Rosetta's laugh grew more obscene. "Probably lives under a pyramid!"

"Don't mind," Mom said to me. "Walker, you go right on finding whatever is beautiful to you. And understand something else…never think something is beautiful or not beautiful based on what other people think. Base it on what you think."

"Your Mama's right." Rosetta dabbed her eyes with a handkerchief. "Don't mind me. This old hen is just jealous of that gal's plumage!"

"Russell, I want you to question any critic you meet."

"I'm not Russell, I'm Walker!"

"Right. I meant Walker. You question, Walker. You question whatever the critics out in this damn world devalue. Also question what they praise. What they fawn over. What they bow down to. A mink coat. A fancy car. Someone's name in a headline. A young face in a magazine. And especially question this crap if it's in print!" We continued up Third Street, reaching the glass block doorway of the much-favored Emerald Street bar. "Walker, run along home, now. We'll be back shortly."

She handed me a dollar for ice cream, and I headed up the street, newly disturbed not only about what to think, but about Mom, and about the woman in the park. Her outdated makeup I thought was so beautiful, now suggested something sinister. I could imagine some kind of fear in the way her plain face must each day exercise such great effort to express an image no longer there, the stylized face of her youth, that other women now laughed at.

• • •

For English class, I wrote a poem comparing the neighbor woman to Howard Carter's discovery of the Egyptian mummy. The teacher was new and very young, and she appreciated the poem's references to history. After class, she called me aside to say her extracurricular teaching assignment was to lead the school's club for public speaking and recitation. "You read so well…I'd like you to join." Caught off guard and too surprised to say no, I agreed.

For the next few weeks, I stayed late every Wednesday preparing for a countywide meet, an event that included all the local school districts. For my published work, I memorized a passage of Thoreau, and for my own writing sample, I worked to improve and polish my recitation of the poem about the neighbor.

The auditorium of the hosting school was a two-hour ride away, and on the yellow school bus, the hope that Buddy might be there with a poem grew. Sure enough, upon entering I spotted him, looking glowingly spoiled and handsome in a navy suede jacket with a sheepskin collar. I went over and said hello, pulling the adjacent wooden auditorium seat down. He looked at my desert boots, which matched his exactly, and he immediately got up. "I can't sit here," he said.

"Why not?"

"We don't go to the same school anymore." He walked back to the last row and took another seat. In my chest, a swarm of stinging hornets built their gray nest.

Students from the younger grades read first, so that meant I'd read in the group just before Buddy. My hands were clammy with nerves, but somehow when my turn came, I managed to present the Thoreau passage and then read well my poem about the outdated neighbor who seemed like an Egyptian mummy.

An hour later Buddy's turn came and he went down the aisle toward the stage with an ease of movement that I still longed to acquire. He didn't try for grace, but was just a smooth ordinary guy, with dark bangs hanging in a healthy shine above his brow. His athletic stride and the way his pants clung to his hips as he walked, left me in awe. But now I also found myself hating him. I hated him for that comfortable ease, an ease which I couldn't match.

For published work, he read *A Talk with a Tax Collector,* by Vladimir Mayakovsky, a poet I'd never heard of. When he finished, he raised his fist and the auditorium sat baffled. His own poem was about a hunting trip taken with his dad, and how they'd managed to bag a deer up in Potter County bringing it home lashed to the hood of their car. He looked handsome up there, wholesome even, as he described the blood dripping over the car's paint job, drying on the chrome fenders. I hated him for that hunting trip, the better school, the better house, a benign and appropriate father who provided well, for knowing who Vladimir Mayakovsky was.

At the end of the event, prizes were announced. A cheerful girl from Shamokin Dam won first in her age group with her ode to helping her grandmother plant narcissus bulbs in Spring. Nothing scary in that. I placed second in my age group, and Buddy in the same group, was awarded but an honorable mention, any honor diluted by the fact that over twenty such mentions were made. He rolled his certificate and stuffed it in his back pocket then marched out in a huff, slamming open the push bar on the exit door. I overheard one teacher say to another that his graphic depiction of blood was unnecessary. When our yellow school bus pulled away, for a moment it passed by his, our windows side by side, and I saw him, slumped in the back seat all alone.

• • •

Grandma Gordon heard about my prize from Mom, and called to express her pride at how well I was faring. Her musical voice over the phone reminded me of her perpetual mirth. "With the school year done, why not have your mother bring you out to Long Island? We're still here! Haven't gone nowhere! Love to see you!"

Mom, sadly blaming work, said such a trip wasn't possible. But several days of my pleading finally allowed a travel plan to develop, one that proposed letting me go to Greenport by myself. Russell surprised us when he agreed to drive me as far as New York City. No doubt, standing in as their son's replacement, he wanted the Gordons to think well of him. For their part, the Gordons decided Cole's sister Marvene would ride the Ronkonkoma line down the middle of Long Island to fetch me at Penn Station.

The first words out of Marvene's mouth were: "Don't you dare call me Auntie! I'm not much older than you are, thank you very much!"

"How old are you?" Russell asked.

"Eighteen."

"You're not," I said.

"Well, I will be. And now if we're quick, we could go up to the street and drink a cup of coffee," she said. Russell liked the idea, his curiosity about the wonders of the big apple visible. I could see he liked Marvene's energy and deportment, and I couldn't believe my luck that the plan had all worked out and we'd been able to meet up in New York!

Marvene already held a round-trip fare, but she stewarded us to a ticket window so a ticket could be bought for me. Russell asked Marvene how much her own ticket had cost, then he made a big show of taking out his wallet to reimburse her. Marvene wasted no time accepting. Russell never mentioned the idea to pay her way had been Mom's. My ticket was also paid with money Mom provided; that wasn't mentioned either.

As we ascended the escalator, I suggested we try the Chock-Full-of-Nuts on Thirty-third, and I was thrilled to find it was still there, and that I'd remembered where it was correctly. "Try the nut bread with cream cheese," I said, and my knowledge of the menu stunned Russell. I didn't say how that sandwich was a favorite for many a nanny, or that I myself had never eaten one. The place was jumping, and though the sandwiches arrived fast, a scant few minutes remained before our departure.

"I must obey the instructions," Marvene said, wrapping her sandwich in a napkin. "They said: *Collect Walker and be quick about it.* So, we must go!"

Russell chuckled. "Walker…you like a baton passed in a relay!" Marvene shook Russell's hand, said goodbye, then pushed me out the door, leaving Russell behind at the coffee counter to wait for the check.

The same train that had brought Marvene in, now took us back in the other direction. Ninety-three minutes later we reached Ronkonkoma, where we changed for the old, slow diesel engine that was still in use along the North Fork run. In Greenport, Grandpa Gordon stood waiting to meet our train, after giving me a big bear hug, he took my bag. We started walking away from the station toward Seventh Street, Marvene carrying her own bag.

At the house, Grandma stood on the smoke-free side of the grill, turning ribs. "Don't I get a kiss anymore?" I went over and hugged her with enthusiasm. She kissed me about ten times until she burst out laughing.

Dinner was served with macaroni and cheese and some greens. "I made banana pudding," Grandma said. "It was Cole's favorite."

"Mine too!"

That night, I slept in the same wallpapered room Cole himself had occupied as a boy. A bookshelf displayed his collection of baseball cards, beside a stuffed bear, a stuffed dog with a mouse hat, and a cheerful green plush snake curled in guard around a bowling trophy. An early photograph showed Cole as a boy in tap dancing class, and a glossy headshot showed his smooth skin and amber-green eyes glowing in the artificial light of a photographer's studio. Beside it there was a playbill for *Gypsy,* autographed by Ethel Merman; other framed publicity photos showed him dancing onstage in musicals, doing the gym mambo in *West Side Story*, smiling as he tapped in the chorus behind Diahann Carroll, and in one photo he stood among four guys gathered around Pearl Bailey for a nightclub act. That club was where Mom's eyes had first set sight on Cole. I knew the story well, Mom had known the director from an Oldsmobile industrial she'd once done in Detroit, and he'd brought her along to a cast party afterward, where she'd introduced herself to Cole, telling him how exciting she'd found his dance movements. By the time the gig left New York for Las Vegas, they were dating.

Years later, Cole took Mom and I both to see Miss Bailey in another show and then brought us backstage to be introduced. Miss Bailey winked her thick lashes, said I was a cute rascal, and added a public aside: "And I hope you come back in a few years when you're grown up!" Another publicity photo was signed by Buddy Hackett and Karen Morrow, from a show set in Coney Island that showed Cole dressed as a hot dog vendor, with a half-folded apron and black bow tie, kicking his legs up beside a big crystal ball.

Centered among the memorabilia, in a place of honor, was a photo of Cole with Mom, arms around each other's waists, taken from the carriage on the day of their wedding. They looked younger than I knew them, and I studied his face, then hers, perfectly framed by the teased Breck-girl hair. It was obvious how captivating they both were, and how their union possessed an excitement that I could still feel. On the far wall hung his final Quinn-Martin career photo, dressed in a doeskin sport coat, costumed to play the suave and ultra-cool detective. Mom and I once owned a copy of this one as well, taken only days before he died. That this vibrant and attractive man was no longer here made the room feel solemn as a tomb, a place of sadness, yet strangely illuminating. I fell asleep on his bed, reliving his memory.

In the morning, after a breakfast of pancakes, eggs, and bacon, we took a boat out to fish for fluke. I studied Grandpa Gordon, watching how he baited his hook, noting the brand of his coveralls, how he carried a small metal-trimmed wooden ruler folded in his side pocket, a pencil for marking things tucked behind one ear. We ate the fluke for dinner and afterward went to the AME church for Bible study and choir rehearsal. Again, I noticed Grandpa had changed to nice clothes for church: dress pants, a yellow cardigan, and a shirt of blue button-down Oxford. I noted the neat, modest way he read the Bible, and later sang his short solo. I knew he had some kind of job helping transport people around the Riverhead Hospital, and could imagine him doing his work with the same modesty.

The next day at the grocery, I watched Grandma Gordon in the same way, cheerfully counting coupons and balancing her checkbook as she waited in the check-out line, thin elbows leaning onto her cart. The cashier, an elderly woman with cropped gray hair and glasses on a chain, greeted her with smiling familiarity. Grandma wasn't impatient like Mom, and showed no hurry as the woman took her time punching the pale green keys on putty-colored register.

It astonished me that here in Suffolk County, just as back home in Dauphin County, the choice spot on the wood paneling beside the manager's office, was reserved for an artist's rendering of the late president. These creamy pastel tributes had to have been nailed into place sometime before the assassin's bullets turned them into mourning portraits, with customers not wanting to see them taken down, never forgetting how they'd seen their first lady forced to climb across the back of a bloodied limousine to clutch at her husband's skull fragments, or how her small son had been coached to salute his father's coffin. In the Harrisburg Weiss market, the president's high-styled wife sat in profile beside him, a triple-strand of pearls around her neck, both peering off toward the checkout lanes, as if to guarantee the honesty of every transaction. At the Greenport IGA, the president's famous pouched eyes looked directly at us with assurance as if to say: "You Gordons, as well as any members of your large family, can feel free to shop here at any time."

. . .

After supper, Marvene announced the movie *Showboat* was being broadcast on television, and she and I tuned in with fascination. At the end, as the broken Julie emerged from the shadows of a dockside warehouse, blowing a kiss to the showboat as it went on down the Mississippi without her, Marvene's tears rolled down her cheeks. My eyes welled at seeing that while hearing the orchestra's soaring final notes. We both tried to hide our tears as Grandpa Gordon came walking through the living room.

"I see old tales of tragic miscegenation have you both in their grip?"

"Can't help it," Marvene sniffled. "It's so sad…I know…of course it's concocted…but the characters suffered so."

He turned to me. "And why're you crying?"

I wiped my cheeks on my sleeve suddenly bashful to be caught. "I can't stand to see Marvene cry. I feel sorry for you…I mean so sorry…for what you people have had to go through."

They looked at me, bewildered, and after a beat Grandpa Gordon said: "Every civilization on earth has practiced some kind of slavery and you are included in that." He then advised us both to question all stories of sad mulattos, and the downfall of poor souls who try to pass. "Even a king acts to pass as something, sometimes just as a person of humility. Never forget you too are now a Gordon." He then recited from memory a letter Paul wrote to the Galatians about there being neither slave nor free man, that all were one in Jesus. "So, you see, son, you're not responsible. And while we may be few shades darker than you, we are not without power."

Marvene turned off the set and pulled a tissue from the box. "It's still sad."

His tone turned sharp. "Yes, and we all know the sad stories of old Negro women who live in shoes and have so many children they don't know what to do. But we do have new stories. We're doctors, engineers, entrepreneurs, we curate art and write influential books. Slavery is being written out of our future. And while parts of the old story might be true enough, we must also invest in the variation of other stories, for in that variety, we can be fully realized and ever more truthful."

A few days later, Marvene accompanied me once more on the train back to New York. To leave the Gordon house felt gut-wrenching and tore at a soft, hollow place in my emotions. Arriving at Penn Station in the frenzy of rush hour, I thought if only we could stop time in the corridors, disperse the crowd, then head by train downtown, then I could show Marvene the neighborhood where Cole, Mom, and I used to live. But once more, only an hour stood between trains, so we simply waited for a payphone to call Mom, assuring her Marvene would escort me to the right platform, and that I'd be in Harrisburg by five o'clock.

• • •

Back on Jefferson Street, I talked endlessly about the Gordons and all the fun there, especially on the fishing boat. "You that keen on fish?" Russell said. "Then one day we'll drive down to the Jersey Shore. I got some cousins out by Asbury Park."

The Summer wore on, but no beach trip appeared. Because I'd mentioned watching *Showboat* with Marvene—Russell grew more prone than ever to want to go see the movies. One night during a heat wave, while he and I dried the dishes and Mom washed, out of the blue he suggested we go down to the Rialto. "Let's get out of this hot soup and sit in air conditioning."

"You mean catch whatever's playing?"

"Sure! Who gives a hoot, long as we keep cool."

The Rialto stood in midtown, and while the place wasn't segregated, we sat up in the dingy balcony where the air conditioning barely reached, most of the cool air hanging on the lower level. Halfway through the film, a tense chain gang drama, its spell was interrupted when the sprockets of the film jumped their gears and the hot lamp of the projector melted the acetate; a cancerous white light flashed across the screen. A fuse popped somewhere and then the whole place went dark, the air conditioner whispering down before shutting off. We sat on the taped-up velvet seats, our forearms sticking to the wooden armrests and listened as people began to talk. It took ten minutes to get electricity back, and when it did, we could hear the re-spliced film clickety-clack its way through the projector, to shine once more from a square hole right behind our heads. A moment later, the reel broke again, blowing another fuse. Beat from sitting in the warming darkness, the audience grew insolent. Some guys down below started catcalling, hollering complaints about prices and then shouted all manner of vulgar things. The whole place started booing. A bunch of teenage boys riled loose, and began tearing at the seats with box cutters. In more pent-up anger, fistfights swung loose, and screaming people soon were stampeding for the exits.

"Let's get off here," Russell said. We followed him, and with stealth he pressed us through the bottlenecked crowd. Out in the steamy night, the asphalt on Third Street was still soft from cooking all day. Then down the block, we heard plate-glass windows shattering, as people began racing by holding arm-loads of clothing and small appliances.

"Midtown's getting looted!" Russell said. He kept us moving, but at the corner of Boyd and Susquehanna, Mom spied a hysterical teenager crouched by a car fender among a pile of stolen shoes and several cardboard counter displays holding bottles of nail polish. The girl's face had a thick triangle of glass lodged on her right cheek, and an unstoppable flow of thick red blood was soaking her pretty summer dress. Drawing closer, we saw her upper gum had actually been penetrated, the knife-like shard sunk clean to the bone.

"Don't move," Mom said. "We'll get you to the hospital."

The girl screamed through a mouthful of blood. "You white bitch—git away!" Russell lifted his palm to calm the girl, but she screamed even more, blood dripping from her mouth. "Git that bitch away!"

More people arrived, staring with astonishment at the wound, which led to stupid comments and advice. After half-an-hour, the ambulance finally arrived. The Polyclinic medics got out, approached, and we backed away. None of us could believe our eyes. The medics held guns, which one of them, a young man with a fresh-scrubbed face, kept trained on the crowd. We hurried away. "Damn," Russell said. "Never thought I'd live to see the ambulance needing to be armed."

• • •

In the days that followed, the riot upset any equilibrium the capital city still tried to claim. Overnight, the price of houses sank all over town, more and more homes put up for sale. Russell talked endlessly with Mrs. Braxton about the disaster. "Things can only get worse."

The injured girl's outburst had hit Mom like a two by four. How could her exemplary life and longing to help have brought this reaction? She remained dazed. Like many, she kept wishing for a way to turn the page on the horrible night. I began to notice a new habit. When Russell wasn't around, she'd bring down a coffee can stashed at the back of her closet and sit counting the nest egg inside. "How much?" I asked.

"Not enough," she said. "But maybe one day it'll put you through college."

"Can't we go back to New York?"

On a cold night in December, just before the holidays, the dress shop employing Mom caught fire and burned to the ground. The police report said faulty Christmas lights had caused the blaze, but *The Patriot* quoted more than one official who held suspicions of arson. With no job, Mom began drinking even earlier in the day, Rosetta at our place so often that Russell said we'd soon have to charge *her* rent. Sometimes in the late evening, Mom sat hunched over the table, speculating that if the fire had been arson, it could've very well been on account of her.

"No proof," Russell said. "Fearing prejudice casts worry where there may be none."

Over Christmas, Lydia accepted an invitation to come over and help decorate our tree, but her father stipulated she could only come in the daylight, and even then only if someone picked her up and gave her a ride home. We set dinner for one o'clock, and it was decided Mom would be the better choice for the Wormleysburg pick-up. Russell proudly chose to prepare baked ham, collard greens, and mashed potatoes and Mom was about to leave, but in the last minute, Lydia's dad phoned to say he'd given it some more thought and given the danger of riots, he didn't think it a good idea for his daughter to be roaming around in Harrisburg even in broad daylight.

"What a stupid man," Mom said as she hung up the phone. "It's not even noon and he's drunk as a skunk." She tried to shrug it off, but for the rest of the day seemed like a woman struck by a bolt of lightning, a direct hit that had scorched her belief in things changing for the better.

During these anxious ruminations, my thoughts began to separate from hers. The dingy blue paint in my bedroom brought me to realize, good or bad, a certain strength came from facing ugliness. Suddenly, the world around me was yet again revealing its own unvarying and merciless accuracy.

The weather grew colder and after the new year, Mom got lucky when a new job came her way, assisting with custom upholstery and drapery orders at Goldsmith's, the best furniture store in town. But Harrisburg's decline, the pall of crime, and the dwindle of its population, kept slowing city commerce. Russell calculated twenty-five percent fewer people meant proportionately fewer sofas and dinette sets would leave the store.

The shadows under Mom's eyes deepened, and because in the magazines the models all looked like Twiggy, when the weather warmed again, she became obsessed with losing weight. "Thin is in," she and Rosetta Wilkins would say, trying every trend and slimming regiment: grapefruit extracts, fasting on carrot juice, and high colonics at the beauty spa down in the basement of Mary Sachs Ladies Shop. On one occasion, I overheard Mom speaking with a doctor on the phone to discuss being injected with sheep serum.

In July, as the heat rose up, Russell talked again about a trip to the shore, but now for just the two of them. Mom said she wasn't *bathing-suit-ready*, and Russell said it sounded like she was fishing for compliments. I felt disgusted when I saw how his admiring words regarding her figure brought her around. At first I was furious not to be included in their planning, thinking Russell must've figured out how much less it cost to take two to the Jersey Shore than three. But then I learned that they'd made plans with the Gordons for me to go out to Long Island, and I was thrilled.

The Gordons extended another jubilant welcome. An uncle from Wyandanch drove out for a picnic with Maisie, his latest girlfriend accompanying him. She was a dark-skinned woman in a blonde wig and she lived up-island in Patchogue. Uncle Sturgis was almost comic the way he jumped up to fetch her drinks and a big plate of barbecue. She held her glass with her pinky raised, flashing a ring with a single large pearl the size of a quarter, a garish piece of jewelry, to be sure, and something about that kind of showy behavior made the family extremely polite. They passed cornbread, and later pieces of homemade lemon sheet cake with cool smiles. Marvene told me in the kitchen that everyone knew Uncle Sturgis still had a wife in Wyandanch.

At one point, Uncle Sturgis called me over and motioned to a folding chair beside him. "So, how's your mama doing?"

"Fine."

"When you get home, be sure to tell her old Sturge was askin' for her."

That evening, after they'd gone back to Wyandanch, my cousin Joel spat and said how disgusting he found Uncle Sturgis. "That man's got no right to bring such trashy whores round here."

Grandma Gordon appeared and brushed some crumbs off a side table. "And what makes you think you're so special?" she asked. "We *all* God's children." She disappeared from the room before anyone could even change the subject.

That Sunday, I came down with strep throat, the sky outside hung dark gray, the wet trees bent to the grass in the heavy downpour. Grandma Gordon put a roast in the oven, with onions and carrots, asking me to keep an eye on it, as illness prevented me from going along to church. After pinning her waterproof hat into place, Grandma put an LP of hymns onto the turntable, 'to provide some spirit of the Lord.' *Didn't it rain children, rain oh my Lord! Rained for forty days and forty nights without stopping. Noah was glad when the rain stopped dropping.*

Alone in their house, I'd rise from bed coughing, check on the roast, then move to the hi-fi, lifting the needle from other gospel songs and setting it back to re-play *Peace Be Still.* I listened to the song over and over, holding Cole's headshot to my chest. How I wished we'd been blood relatives, that I'd been born with him as my real father, or at very least could look as handsome as he did. The Gordons returned from church at one o'clock and sat down to a tender chuck roast dinner, a small bowl of beef-bone broth brought to my sickbed, the only food I could swallow.

The fierce storm, and convalescing from strep-throat, delayed my return to Harrisburg. By the time I'd recovered, trains were running again, and my stomach held the familiar knot that tied whenever I had to say good-bye to the Gordons. In Harrisburg, stepping out at Market Street station I made it to the curb out front just as Russell pulled his Plymouth in. He swung around the drive, almost running me over, then rolled down his window. "You don't look sick."

"I'm better now."

"Get in, kid. Your mama will be glad to see ya."

I placed my bag on the backseat and climbed into the passenger seat next to him. "Boy, old Doria was some storm, wasn't she?" I had to agree.

Back on Jefferson Street, our house was bone dry, but Mom wasn't. A tumbler of vodka splashed on her dress while she tried to dial the phone.

"Who you calling, baby?"

"I don't know...?" Russell took the phone and dialed, placing a most courteous call to the Gordons, letting them know I'd made it safely home.

. . .

Drastic alterations began to affect Mom's appearance. Unlike our neighbor in fox furs who styled backwards through time, Mom and Rosetta lunged forward, thighs bared in short skirts, calves clad in suede boots, bypassing any restraint or good taste. Rosetta dyed her hair flame-red, giving a green tint to her caramel skin; Mom teased hers up in a long flip, dyed Priscilla Presley black, lips a new pearl-bisque color, eye lids now lined with kohl and glued with thicker lashes, giving her face a washed-out look that required ever more concealer under the eyes. The worst part of this 'mod' fashion was how already it was something of a fading fad, younger women foregoing 'mod' for a more natural look. I cringed to see Mom leave for work in the morning wearing a glossy chartreuse vinyl miniskirt, as if she were twenty and not forty-five.

The absurd daily starvations also continued, only a fifth of vodka for nutrition, to wash down a surreal cloud of painkillers, stressing her already disunited nervous system. In the school library, I read a book on mammals that explained when caught in fur traps some gnawed their own limbs to escape. I thought of Mom, feeling cornered by advancing age, manifesting a similar self-destructive panic. At one point, she tried to read the Bible for a few days, and I think she saw herself as a female Job, quietly taking umbrage with God, demanding to know why even in narcotic bliss, the sense of life's underlying torment was never far.

Rosetta was relieved when Mom's biblical phase passed, saying people who've enjoyed freedom from religion, needn't suddenly enslave themselves in it again to cope with challenges. No, I thought sarcastically, better to disappear into booze and pills. Being seen with Mom in public, in her transcendent, groovy threads, left us objects of ridicule, making it even harder to navigate the hellish sidewalks, where vulgarities continued to fly from both sides of slavery's polarity. I grew more and more leery of being seen with her.

Russell also let it be known he wasn't crazy about her *get-ups*. She told him to mind his own wardrobe. She'd no sooner said it than a romantic sense of remorse overcame her. "Living with a woman like me," she said, beginning to weep, "separates you from your own culture." I'd never heard anything like this from Mom before, and it felt like a slip. Previously she'd have believed our separations, if noted through pity, would be racist.

Russell noticed it too. "People say things like that when they wish for some kinda credit," he said. "Or a tax break. Some kind of moral exception."

"Well, what if I am some kind of moral racist? What I really wanted to say was how lucky Walker and I *are* to know two worlds."

Russell would have none of it and sneered. "Hell! I've only ever known two worlds." He grew angrier. "You think your nod of compassion towards me, for what you perceive to be the penalties of darkness, will somehow make you noble or set apart."

Mom's voice grew enraged. Increasingly, she was becoming a woman unable to gradate or contain emotions, especially her strange contrition. "Christ almighty! I don't want that!"

"Well, talk about separating me from my culture is bullshit. Pure sanctimonious bullshit. I wasn't born in Mozambique. I'm American just like you."

"Don't you dare speak to me in that tone! You can be sure, *mister*! I too have seen plenty from both sides that wasn't heroic."

"What's that supposed to mean?"

"You know damn well. Your *dear* churchgoing Mrs. Braxton! She maintains plenty of biases, and you don't say a word to reprimand her!"

Russell paced the dining room floor, his tread so heavy the glass in the cabinet holding his mother's dishes rattled. "She may be against the greed and sneak of *wealthy* folks! But she's earned that right! Hasn't she?"

"What about her smug derision toward other neighbors? Those on the dole? Those not attending church as often as she? Like me! I get so tired of hearing the two of you sermonizing like deacons on a soapbox."

"Oh, you tell it, sister! Who's sermonizing now?"

"Everyone's got a bias or two."

"She's still an upright woman!"

"Oh, yeah? Just get her started on how many children the Mexican apple-pickers coming through town to work have! Or get her going if she sees someone on welfare buying liquor or grass."

"She tells it like it is!" Russell said.

"Well, to hell with that. Tell her to go tell *that* to the mountain!"

"All people hold some bias. Maybe she's suffered more than her share of consequences. You ever been turned down by an insurance company? Banks? Landlords? Job foreman? Complete strangers?"

"As a matter of fact, I have."

"Well, you certainly have no trouble getting a barman to bring you a drink."

"Russell!…How can you! Walker, right here!"

"Should've thought of that before opening your yap! Truth is…you're turning into a lush!"

"How dare you? How dare you speak to me that way! I'm not some slutty fool. You think all women are children or a kind of chattel. That we only masquerade as adults."

"I'm the fool. Busting my ass to earn a living so you can run amok."

Mom's overly-made-up face twisted, then lowered with the tears of spurned misgiving. I grew aware that in her folly she was trying to reckon with something that somehow connected to my own pitiful tears—and the pitiful apology I'd expressed to the Gordons after watching *Showboat*.

• • •

A few months later, Goldsmith's fine furniture gathered its employees in the main showroom to discuss an essential staff cutback. No small share of the blame fell to Hurricane Agnes, another storm, one with astonishing fury. The Susquehanna had flooded downtown Harrisburg, putting the prime business district under seventeen feet of miserable roiling water. To honor seniority, the Goldsmith staff was told, last in, first out. Mom was a latecomer so she was out. Mom grew distraught. "I can't let Russell pay for everything," she said. "I've got to find work."

Russell had predicted the worst, for after the floodwaters receded, he took me along as he drove his Plymouth up and down every passable street. The city's oldest and most luxurious homes on Front and Second had taken the worst of it, the governor's mansion also hit hard. Russell looked at the beautiful, water-logged furniture stacked on the ruined lawns and muck-caked curbs. "Now you'll see rich folk flee for sure." And true to his prediction, it wasn't long before even the venerable Goldsmith's, despite its belt-tightening cuts, was forced to close, leaving behind its long-held spot on the square.

It was Labor Day weekend, school about to begin, when Russell, leaving to keep a tax appointment, pulled me aside on the stoop, and spoke in a tone low and confidential, as if man-to-man. "You need me, I'll be in Carlisle. The home of a family named Byers. Here's the number." He handed a slip of paper to me, as if honoring me with some kind of high responsibility. "You need me, be sure to call." What was he worried about? Why would we need him?

Soon as he drove away, Mom hurried to bring down her coffee can of savings, stacked the bills, and put them in her purse. Our bags were pulled from the spare-room closet, already packed! A call to the taxi company announced we needed to be taken to the train. The car arrived and we piled our bags in and headed for the railway station. After only a few blocks traffic came to a standstill. The driver lowered his window to inquire about the situation. "Can't cross downtown," a cop said. "All streets below Fifth are closed. Cameron Street's your only way."

"But we have a train to catch!" Mom called from the backseat.

The cop leaned his forearm on the doorframe to get a better look at the face of the racket-maker. "Lady, no one's getting through. In a few minutes, they're blowing up the Penn-Harris Hotel."

"What?" Mom was now a nervous wreck. "Who'd do such a thing? First we had the flood, now this. What's next? Famine? A plague of locusts? Driver, how could you not have known? Or in these snarled streets are small fry like us your biggest catch!"

The man did not reply, but detoured East where we eventually reached Cameron Street. It was also choked. And what the policeman said was true. As we sat waiting beside the farm show complex the windows of our taxi shook from the blast of dynamite detonating a mile away. And so it was, the city's finest hotel, once its social anchor, and center of its catered life, a twelve-story brick and limestone structure, flew through the air as dust.

Bumper to bumper, we finally reached the overpass at the back of the station, and it seemed as if the city of Harrisburg were itself conspiring to challenge the last of Mom's resolve. Our train departed without us.

"Next New York-bound…ninety minutes," the ticket agent said.

"Used to be a train for New York every half hour," Mom said.

"Yeah lady, and Calvin Coolidge used to never talk!" With disgust, he went on to explain how the mighty Pennsylvania Railroad had been forced into bankruptcy, even after having torn down its magnificent station in New York to balance the books. "Besides, it's Labor Day."

"Well, it's a national disgrace," Mom said.

"I completely agree. Government now runs these rails just like it's Moscow!"

"And that waiting room is too filthy for decent people to sit in," she said.

"A lot of people go across the street now to wait at *The Alva*."

We hauled our bags up the alley to the restaurant. Mom knew the owner and when she saw him, she cried. "Oh, Donato! What's become of the world? Everything's getting blown up!"

He assured us that although there was now a bomb-sized crater just two blocks away, the ill-planned explosion unintentionally wrecking some additional buildings, he still had fist-sized meatballs for us. She ordered a soft drink with ice for herself, and while I twirled spaghetti, she took the flask from her pocketbook and poured alcohol into her soda.

"Are we trying to run away from Russell?" I asked.

"Course not," she said. "We're setting him free. I don't want to weigh his shoulders down."

I somehow knew Russell was not the reason we were in flight. The real weight was on her shoulders, admitting how diminished her own life had become. After completing the spaghetti, my body grew tired of waiting and slumped sideways in our booth, exhausted by another day of drama.

• • •

I awoke to find Russell sitting nearby. Somehow he'd managed to find us. In my jacket pocket I searched for the slip of paper with the number in Carlisle. It was gone. Russell whispered soft words to Mom, and Donato came over and also spoke in a hushed voice. "Look, Man, I have other customers. Just get her out of here." Donato went back to his own booth beside the cash register, where he sat alone, computing a spindle of the evening's guest checks, pausing only to glare impatience and irritation in our direction.

Russell stroked Mom's once lustrous hair, her bleary-eyed face leaning into the vinyl upholstery. "I was leaving because I've failed you," she sobbed. "All the love and good I wanted to bring to your life has spoiled."

"Now, now," he purred: "I don't need your help, sugar…It's you who needs mine."

If that night of the riot had once shifted something in Mom, knowing she'd tried to run away, now shifted something in Russell. As the weeks passed, he grew kinder toward her, and began asking me thoughtful questions about what I might be reading. He vacuumed, shopped, and cooked most of our meals. Omelets were his specialty, with fried potatoes, crisp and golden brown. Recalling my talk of fishing with the Gordons, after school he once brought the three of us to fish at a pond out near Linglestown, where we brought home two trout. Russell cleaned the fish and fried them up, and we ate together at a table that he had set.

A few weeks later he bought me a baseball glove, and playing catch in the backyard, he tried to teach me how to throw curveballs. Whenever I dropped the ball I'd pause to admit: "I'm not very good."

"Don't fret. Takes practice. Anyone can improve anything with practice. You're a boy with a good heart. That's where habits really count, *son*." He'd never called me that before. In October Russell and I raked leaves, and before helping him mow them to shreds, which he said would add nitrogen to the grass, he gave permission for me to jump in the great leaf piles. Quite a bit of red and gold remained yet above our heads, and when the breeze blew more leaves fluttered down to join those already stuck to the pavement. In the morning, Russell left for Carlisle to do taxes for the Byers, and in the afternoon I hurried home from school to rake the backyard to surprise him. At Russell's house, the front screen door hung open, the wooden one behind it split with a crowbar. When I pushed at it, I felt warm heat escape from our house and meet the chilly air outside. This was not going to be good. I knew something in me was about to be called upon to see things I didn't want to see, to go places I didn't want to go. In the kitchen, Mom's body lay resting on the floor of the pantry.

I held my breath. I didn't want to leave her there asleep, yet we needed help. Running next door, no matter how hard I hit the aluminum storm door, Mrs. Braxton did not answer. Was the danger still among us? In panic, I knocked on Mrs. Howard's door. Again, no answer. Finally, the mailman saw me moving distraught between the two stoops. "Everything okay?" he asked.

At the postman's gentle knock and request, Mrs. Howard finally opened, and hearing what was amiss, agreed to let me wait in her living room.

The police arrived but I couldn't speak or answer their questions. My hands felt numb. I couldn't feel my tongue.

"In shock," one of them said.

Mr. Howard arrived, probably called by his wife. "None of this kind of trouble belongs in a Christian home," he said. "You're welcome to handle this situation out in our garage, but for the sake of my wife and family, I think it best if you'd leave our quarters."

The police caught up with Russell at the Emerald Bar. I didn't want them to find him, but they did. He'd gone there after Carlisle to meet a client and had only taken a cup of black coffee. They confronted him. "Sure, we bicker from time to time," he said. "Most couples do."

I heard later that he cried like a baby when they said Mom was gone, and he denied what they accused him of. In order to put handcuffs on, the arresting officer, whose name was Lembur, had to smash Russell's face repeatedly against the edge of the zinc bar. All of this was told to me within the hour, as if Russell's take-down would bring consolation. But I already knew his nature would never permit him to resist arrest, nor would he ever have harmed Mom.

• • •

Officials came and went all evening, and as it grew cooler we left the Howard's garage and came to settle inside Russell's dining room, his mother's gold dishes gleaming over our heads, Mom still lying under a cover in the kitchen having just posed for her final photography session. They would not let me near her.

The hours drifted by in a chasm of despair with increasingly stupid questions being asked. All I could do was shrug. I heard whispering in other rooms. Then somebody I did not know explained that as my mother had not designated Russel to adopt, I'd become a ward of the state. The Milton Hershey homes were mentioned as a source of where I might be placed, as was Carson Long military academy. Finally, a government woman with blue-silver cat-eyed glasses drove me along a highway for more than an hour. "This tragedy must be accepted as God's will," she said. My brain fogged and I hated her for saying this killing was God's idea. We arrived at a huge and hideous red-brick building, somewhere I did not recognize, and the lady driving said it was an offshoot of the Quincy orphanage.

The woman in charge, whose beefy frame seemed stuffed into her navy dress, a ring of keys around her neck, ordered cookies and warm milk be brought from the kitchen. Left alone in her office, the television on, sounds of a quiz show filling the den, I looked away from the frenzied contestants with their forced excitement, to the pattern on the wallpaper, rendering rust-colored woods and pastoral cabins trailing smoke, each scene framed by acorns. Mom had promised to buy me new shoes, and now everything in our entire universe had simply ceased to exist. *I'm sitting here among total strangers. How can that be possible?*

An announcement echoed in the hallway, time for lights out, but I hadn't yet been assigned a bed. The woman in charge came back and spoke to me as if hard questions pronounced emphatically would bring forth answers. I tried to comprehend the things she was asking me, but my tongue still had difficulty forming even simple words. She shook her head in perplexity, then ate several of the cookies from the plate I hadn't touched. She left me alone again, saying she had to make arrangements for where I was to sleep.

The ten o'clock news came on, the top story a brutal murder in North Harrisburg. A gurney was being pulled outside, and all at once the camera pulled back and I saw it was Russell's front door, and it was Mom's body zippered inside the body bag, wheeled right out to the curb on Jefferson Street for all to see. It stunned that the beautiful model Peggy Leighton-Drexler was no more. How could this be? My mother's voice—now silenced forever? I grew upset and couldn't grasp the truth. The matron entered just as my own photograph flashed on the screen. She called over her shoulder to a night watchman, "Bill, come quick! Will you!"

The man left his desk and entered; she told him that I'd been watching myself on television. "Now we'll have no more of that," the man said, and quickly shut the set off. "I can see we're going to need to keep an eye on you!"

My mind raged at stupidity. This wasn't my fault. It wasn't me who left the television set on. I got shown to a bed, and seeing Mom rolled onto the street, my exhaustion and the stress of grief took me right out.

That night I dreamt of an aqua swimming pool, with Buddy and Lydia lowering the backs of their lounge chairs and giggling, while I swam alone, only to sink—drowning. Buddy finally strolled over to the ladder buck-naked, then climbed down into the water to make rescue. Pulling me to the edge of the pool, he magically brought me out of the highly chlorinated sea and onto the tile surround. He gave me mouth-to-mouth resuscitation and at one point put his fingers down my throat to dislodge a bloody wedge of glass. I bit down on his knuckles, releasing an enormous serpent. Buddy's head shook as he cried out to Lydia that I wasn't going to make it. I awoke drenched in sweat and found that I'd also wet the bed, something I hadn't done since I was an infant.

I cleaned myself up, found a pair of fresh underwear in the suitcase someone else had packed for me, and left the wet pajamas on the floor. I tried to go back to sleep, but my mind felt injured, replaying the way Buddy had in real life once refused to sit with me at the poetry meet. Later, I began to cry in my pillow at the thought of where Mom's dead body might be. In the morning, I awoke with perfect recall of the dream and my bitter tears. And I hated Buddy for his unfeeling ability to leave. How could he not come to save me from drowning sooner?

I hated Buddy even more, when the matron came in and saw I'd wet the bed. She called the cleaning janitor right away, and ordered him to come and take the spoiled linens and pajamas to the wash house. Out in the hallway, I heard him ask her why he had to be doing laundry before breakfast. She told him my sheets were wet, because I'd had an *accident*. He chuckled and said: "That happens to a lot of us young bucks. If you got the time…I could show you how it all works?"

"Don't start that first thing in the morning, or I'll call your wife right now."

"Go ahead. She won't care. She likes to see a man and woman having a good time. You can tell her all about us."

The woman giggled. "What's got you all fired up this morning? You're just too fresh!"

I then realized the man had mistakenly thought I'd had a wet dream and my shoulders cringed in shame. For a moment I wondered if all this horror was really still a dream. But no. I was still in the strange room, with more strange wallpaper. The clock then slowed down, time itself sublimating to the stillness that comes from being grief-stricken. My history, so indelible in my imagination, felt like some kind of mistake, that if I just lay back down motionless and didn't move, not let myself give into any muscle activity, perhaps things would still return to normal.

A bell sounded and the hallway beyond was filled with a cacophony of children as they ran to wash, dress and go to breakfast. Someone came and fetched me. Everywhere I went children followed. They seemed to know more about Mom's murder than I did, questioning the facts openly, citing details culled from some news source and local gossip. They soon took it in stride that I couldn't speak, and couldn't form even simple words.

Death brought each moment an excruciating dose of dread, as if being forced to take some important exam for which I hadn't studied. No appetite, too little sleep, and I kept asking myself why hadn't I taken more time to pay attention—to really see the body lying twisted on the floor of the kitchen? If I'd only had more time, time enough to get used to it, time to touch her skin to comfort her while she was still warm, time to say good-bye, then maybe I could grapple with it. I longed to revisit the details.

The children quickly developed a habit of speaking on my behalf. "No. He don't want *cold* cereal he wants *hot*. No, he ain't gonna feel like listening to no piano recital. His Ma's just been *killed*." Their honest fascination was preferable alongside the staff's matter-of-fact pretense that all would simply smooth over if one would just make up one's mind to accept things as they were doled out by life.

One afternoon, a disagreement began among a group of children over the rotation of the planets. A fistfight ensued, and though I was not involved, a punch landed so hard to my ear, that I was knocked out cold. The matron on duty had no choice but to bring me to the wellness clinic. The nurse revived me, looked at my chart and grew concerned. My body weight had dramatically declined, and she noted my general health and mental well-being also seemed to be deteriorating, so much so that she contacted the state and sounded an alarm. Though I never learned that woman's name, I will always remain grateful to her, for she was the catalyst that got me transferred out of that wretched place.

. . .

My new social worker was a large, husky man, who wore gray pants with a built-in belt, combining two elastic tabs at the side of the waist that could be expanded daily as needed. I'd only ever seen such pants advertised in the back of the t.v. guide. Escorting me to the beige sedan, his walk tilted side to side over the brick pathway. The suitcase containing my few possessions was gingerly placed in the back seat, then he got behind the wheel. "Feel free to call me Jerry."

We drove in the direction of Harrisburg, and he talked at great length about how important it was for boys to learn and practice self-confidence. "I can help you if you need. I think you'll do fine as you're a nice-looking…very nice-looking."

We wove through traffic and when we turned onto Jefferson Street, I grew elated at the sight of Russell standing at the foot of his porch steps; a velvet string circling his head to hold a navy-blue eyepatch into place. When he smiled, quite a few teeth were missing and as a result when he wasn't smiling his cheeks looked sunken. Despite these physical changes, he was still good-old Russell. He placed one hand on my shoulder and squeezed hard to fight back the tears. His house had already passed state inspection, and I now saw Russell was not about to invite the social worker inside to do any more snooping. The necessary paperwork for my transfer was signed in the winter chill, on the stoop. Only after Jerry drove away, did we go into the house.

Passing beyond the entrance I noticed where the doorframe had been repaired, the new piece of wood and putty-filler still unpainted. It was tax season, and papers were stacked in folders on the desk. In the kitchen, a tuna casserole was brought from the oven with a dish of collards. I learned later social services had advised Russell to serve me a hot meal as soon as possible and to remove every photograph of Mom, or us. He complied. There was no trace of her anywhere.

Outside the kitchen window, the unopened buds of late Winter floated on the pear tree. "How you holding up? You look glum. That orphanage can't be no home. I begged those Quincy people but they wouldn't let you come back here on account of the money they get from the state. But no matter, when you stopped eating, I got Leftwich to get a white lawyer to write them, and accuse them of negligence. That sure worried them." He chuckled and his hands tremored slightly as he spooned out the casserole. "Mrs. Braxton made this. The greens are for you. Too stringy for me. Them cops have made a mess of my choppers."

I told Russell how the house had been on the evening news with Mom being taken outside, and that I was scolded for watching a television set that the matron herself had left on. Russell was incensed. "Why do so many people collecting their pay from some bad system develop cottage cheese for brains? Then they blame you to boot? That's rich."

"Did you see it?"

"Heard about it. No television in lock-up." I lowered my head and took another bite of the casserole. "How do you like it?"

"Good."

"When you see Mrs. Braxton be sure to make a fuss. She worked hard to make that for us. Got it?" I nodded. "And now listen up, tomorrow they're putting you in a brand-new school, out near Colonial Park."

"Do I have to go?"

"I'll say you gotta go or they'll throw my ass in jail: a car is supposed to come pick you up. And you better march straight 'cause they'll be spying all the time to make sure I'm not killing you."

Just after eight the next morning, instead of a school bus, the beige sedan appeared. "I hope you didn't forget me? Do you remember? I'm Jerry." We drove away with him explaining that to chauffeur kids to school was not something he usually did, an exception was being made for him to pick me up himself only because it was my first day. Apparently, he'd convinced someone in social services. "I told them we hit it off. That it would mean a lot to you if I showed up and took you myself. That it would be appreciated by you. I hope that was okay?"

I nodded.

"How did last night go?"

"Fine."

"Were your teeth brushed? Did you use the toilet."

"Yes."

"Get to shower?"

"Yes, sir."

"Did anyone stand there to watch? Or were you left alone?"

"I don't need to be watched."

We arrived in the suburbs outside of town and he pulled in alongside an empty football field and turned off the engine. "Do you have your comb?" I showed him the one Rosetta Wilkins had once bought me. "Here. Give it. Let me help." I sat still while he began to comb my hair. "You're a nice-looking boy, and I want to help. We should get to know each other better." He patted my hair, tickled my ear, and put the comb back in my hand and held it there. "You're nice-looking. Unusual. It's good if you put your best side out there. Know what I mean?"

"Yes, sir."

"I know how lonely it can get. So, if you need something, or just want to talk, or whatever, you can call me anytime." He took my notebook and wrote a phone number on the cardboard backing. "That's my home number. I don't give it to everybody. You need old Jerry for something, you just call, and I'll drop everything day or night. We can have dinner or go bowling. Whatever you need. Does that sound good?"

"Yes, sir."

He started the car again and we drove a couple of blocks to enter the school's parking lot. He pointed out the entrance of a plain modern building, and sat watching me as I got out. Before going inside, I turned to look back, and he gave a small salute.

I found the principal's office and she came around her desk to greet me. "As it's February, our school year is well under way," she said. "So, I'm going to walk with you to class."

We entered a room, enduring the stares of the other pupils. The teacher, a thin woman with her hair in a French twist, introduced me to the class.

The school was new, calm, and orderly, and the day passed without incident. The pleasant teacher treated me with considerable deference.

Every morning and afternoon thereafter, a sedan came to pick me up, driven not by Jerry, but a series of older men and women, who seemed to all wear raincoats and rarely spoke except to give a curt greeting. My arriving by private car was noticed, and made me seem important and unapproachable. As the Spring weather grew warmer, I'd return home and then go for long walks among the budding trees around the Italian Lake, lingering in hope to catch sight of our former painted neighbor clipped into her fox furs.

One night, Russell accidentally broke a glass in the bathroom. I found him leaning up against the wall, whole body shaking. "These damn seizures. Don't be scared. It will ease-up in a minute."

"What causes them?"

"Don't know. Ever since they hurt my head." I followed his instructions and helped him back to bed.

"Leave those glass shards alone. I'll get them in the daylight when I can see better."

• • •

A few days later, at the breakfast table, Russell put two bowls of oatmeal down. "I've said it before, you're a boy with a good heart. And to show you I know it, tomorrow after breakfast, I got a surprise for you."

"What kind of surprise?"

"Ask me no questions and I'll tell you no lies. But we'll need an early start!"

At dawn, Russell stood in his boxers pressing his pants on the ironing board, and once he was done getting dressed, he checked himself in the mirror carefully. We drove downtown, parked and I followed him as we entered an appliance store. The salesman studied Russell and his eyepatch with suspicion. My mouth dropped open when Russell said we'd come to buy a Motorola television set. He told the man it was his wish to bypass black-and-white and go straight to living color. After reviewing the displays, we decided on a model, they came to an agreement on cost, and the salesman wrote up the sale. But Russell discovered too late that he'd figured the money in his wallet wrong and was seven dollars shy of the price. The salesman called the owner over. The man was very pleasant, in fact, overly sincere and courteous, as if it was important for him to treat us with the understanding that we were among his finest customers.

"Sadly, I can't give credit for something that's not a necessity," he said. "And a bit extra will still be needed for an antenna, and the labor involved to hire a man to hook it to the roof. But tell you what I can do, is give you a very nice deal on a very good black-and-white set."

Russell handled the situation with aplomb. "I appreciate the offer," he said, projecting his personal worthiness for such a top-of-the-line product. "But I promised my boy color. His mind's made up. It's color or nothing. We shall return with the extra funds."

Excited by any prospect of television, and afraid we'd never return, I interjected: "It doesn't matter. I'm okay without color!"

"Nonsense. Nope, nope, nope," Russell said. "A promise is a promise!" We left the store and walked down the sidewalk.

Russell's inability to have completed this simple transaction suddenly infuriated me. Why hadn't he planned better? He had allowed us to enter a store unfortified, shopping as if on a wish and a whim, and now, along with being judged, we'd left without our goal. Publicly assigning his own preference onto me for the expensive color set felt like an excuse for his own failure. I sensed something in myself grow inconsolable and wanting to punish him for showing such weakness. "*I knew* we couldn't get a television like *normal* people."

"What?" Russell stopped cold. "You better check yourself, boy!"

For him to witness what seemed to be my mounting fury exposed our weakness and my privileged point of view. "Why couldn't you just get the money right?"

Russell's mouth twisted in a rage I'd never seen before. "What the *fuck* do you know about it?" The curse shot through the air and cut me to the quick.

I stood stunned. He'd never used such language in front of me before. The episode at the store had affected him more than I knew. All at once, I felt shame. My childishness had fostered no comprehension or compassion for how difficult things might've been for him. Especially with an eyepatch and missing teeth. Showing financial lack was humiliating, but for a professional, a tax man no less—it simply had to scorch. On his own, Russel probably would've weathered it, but my petulance bore too much witness. As a brat, I'd failed to understand how he had to process his world.

We moved closer to the car. He got the keys out, and his hands shook. "When I told them crackers you wanted color…'stead of following my lead, you undercut me!" His voice was like a hammer on wood.

"I didn't."

"Don't you sass me. Get your ass in that car, 'fore I find me a switch."

"You touch me and I'll scream murder. They'll beat your other eye out. You'll go to jail! I'll tell them how you cheat on people's taxes." My words sounded their threat. Russell looked at me with disgust, our newfound fondness for each other stalled. But how could I ever know or articulate my real fear: that I might *lose* him once more.

We climbed into the car, his hands still shaking as he shifted and began to turn the wheel. After driving several blocks, we both cooled. I grew forlorn. He began to explain how all week he'd been picturing the two of us leaving the store grandly hauling the set home. I grew deeply ashamed at how his sweet plan had been ruined.

When we got back to the house, I tried to make myself useful, cleaning up the kitchen and bringing the laundry in from the line. I folded the towels, and put them away in the linen closet. There I found our missing photographs, still in their frames and tucked in a box at the back. I looked at Mom's face and felt sick; an old card from Arité was stuck to the back of one that read: *Please call me*, she pleaded, the word *call* underlined. With care I put everything back as it had been, so Russell wouldn't know, too timid to suggest the pictures of us be returned to their rightful place.

In the afternoon, Russell came and stood outside the door to my blue room, asking if I wanted to play catch. "I'd rather read," I said, and kept my head down in my book. My remorse worsened.

• • •

The next afternoon after a lunch of tuna fish sandwiches, Russell fiddled with the transistor radio, setting it up on the drainboard of the kitchen sink, the only place in the house that got decent reception. I went to my room to read, and for the next hour could hear him gently touching the dials, struggling to try and get a clear station between static. Finally, he stopped, coming upstairs to say he couldn't get anything and was going over to Horatio Leftwich's house to watch the ballgame. He tried to coax me to go along, but still not over our tussle, I stubbornly said I'd rather finish my book. He stood in the doorway, his one good eye working hard to fathom all the ways he might persuade me, then finally he gave in, and soon the front door could be heard shutting quietly behind him. After Mom's murder, and with the state so involved in my care, I thought for sure he'd not concede, and I was honestly now disappointed to be left behind in the house alone. I knew then that Russell was tired of fighting. By the time he returned home I'd fallen asleep and did not hear him.

Later that week I finally learned why Russell had been so hell-bent on wanting to buy that television. He knew Hank Aaron was set to play in Atlanta where he was predicted to break Babe Ruth's home run record, hoping for us to watch that historic baseball game in vivid color. It was now Thursday, three days later, and I'd just come home from school when Russell appeared holding what at first I thought was a book. But as he pulled out a handle, it turned out to be a portable cassette player, borrowed from the chef Joseph Randall. "He's got a cousin that works for the Union-Times newspaper—and that son-of-a-gun drove all the way up from Jacksonville just to throw a party and deliver this recording. Chef's been cooking all day…and I only borrowed it so you could have the chance to hear it. It's gotta be back soon…or they'll come looking for it!"

Out of habit, Russell pulled two kitchen chairs nearer the window by the drainboard, too excited to reckon that unlike the transistor radio, the cassette player didn't need to be near the sink to get reception. "Now, sit down Walker," he said. "And I'm gonna play something for you like you never heard before." Once he was convinced that I was settled and taking his mission seriously, he lifted his index finger like a sorcerer and very firmly pressed down the play button. The tape wound silently and then all at once the kitchen was filled with the sound of the Fulton County Stadium in Atlanta. "Now just wait," Russell said. "Hear that crowd? That was Monday night. And Henry Aaron is coming to the plate!" A few seconds paused like an hour, and then Aaron did indeed come up to bat at the plate, and in recorded time the voice of Vin Scully announced that the crowd was giving Aaron a standing ovation. "We couldn't get this broadcast here. Only the Dodgers network had it. But Randall's cousin taped it in Jacksonville—and then imagine that damn devil drove all night to bring it up here to party…I mean imagine!!"

One man's devotion, and passion, to want to toast to the news of history riveted me. Scully announced the first pitch—*a lowball*. The crowd was booing. I could feel the pressure building in my chest. Then quickly, on only the second pitch, a heart-stopping crack of the bat and Scully's measured, silken voice rose up with feverish excitement: "It's a high drive into deep left center field, going up, over, and into the stands." And then Scully stopped talking, just stopped cold. The crowd went wild. Russell and I couldn't look at one another. We sat fermenting in the juiced emotion of the crowd, a new state of shock, fans screaming in madness, hollering like nothing we'd ever heard. And still Scully stayed quiet, not one word spoken for a whole half-minute. His genius knew to let the fans take it—simply cede ownership of the airwaves to let the people of baseball roar and roar. For us in the kitchen, our imaginations entered their own private ballparks. As listeners we too grew lathered, as if taking a rocket ship to another galaxy—experiencing first-hand a living flight to the moon!

The cheering escalated. Fireworks could be heard popping over the night sky of Atlanta. Aaron must be rounding the bases. And then Scully's voice resumed. And he spoke not just as a poet but as a statesman, not only for sports and its fans but for all eternity. "It's a wonderful night for Atlanta and the country and the world…because a black man in the Deep South is getting a standing ovation."

That language of triumph gave me goose bumps. I suddenly knew with these sounds—the crack of that bat—something not only in America but inside ourselves was changing. Russell sat, enraptured, staring into the cassette player watching the tape wheels turn. His one good eye had gone glassy. Scully described the way Hank Aaron's mother and father ran out across the grass to meet him at home plate, and how when Mrs. Aaron hugged her son, she hugged him for all she was worth. Perhaps she too couldn't believe this moment had happened in her lifetime. Hearing such love described was beyond comprehension. I knew we were both thinking of Mom, her photographs still lying upstairs in the dark of the linen closet. I also knew our terrible challenge of one another had ended, and with no hesitation I rose up to hug Russell.

"Damn, *son*," he said, tears streaking down his dark cheeks. "I'd so wanted us all to see that."

"It's okay," I whispered, my voice choked. "Can't we just play it again?"

* * *

Russell's seizures grew to become part of our everyday routine, until a day in September when I returned from school to find yet another social worker there, a tall, gray-haired man with eyeglasses that darkened in the sunlight, and a navy overcoat that swung behind him whenever he turned.

"Russell had to go away for a rest. So, I packed you a bag. You've been chosen to go live on a farm with a nice family."

"What? Well, I'm not gonna go. I want to stay with Russell."

"Now, don't you act so ungrateful. These are good country people you'll be living with…salt of the earth. You're very lucky."

"But I want to stay here with Russell."

"Don't be a fool, kid. That man ain't your pappy."

"Then I want to talk to Jerry."

"Geez…I wouldn't. You'd do well to steer clear of *that*…you hear me?"

"Yes, sir."

● ● ●

The state agency denied permission for me to visit Russell, so I remained tethered in another new home, a farm owned by a family named Weaver. They sought to be considered as compassionate, adopting, mission-work types, but I bristled at their emotionless, overly practical voices, the hush of patience on display whenever they explained in great detail that which was usually pretty obvious. "Bringing a young man from the city to Lancaster County, with another school system, are steps God has intended to shield you."

Gazing out over the wintery farm, watching a lone forsaken gray-brown bird poke through the barren ice, my whole being felt a futile link to that small, wretched creature. I remembered Mom saying feeling *other* would one day become quite an ordinary experience—was this what she meant? No, this was all about grief, loss, wretched sadness.

The house had no indoor plumbing, and in the evenings, unwilling to use the chamber pot hidden in a commode, I'd grow agitated, getting up from bed to pace. One such night, Mr. Weaver heard my footsteps and pulled a rocker into my room so he could sit and pray with me. "I don't give a shit over what you and your God pray on," I seethed. "Your damn religious quotes don't matter either. Not one shit!"

Mr. Weaver gave me a dismissive look, and left the room with his rocker, leaving me to face an unbearable silence. If I ever did decide to speak to God, I'd demand to know why in his name did my mother have to die. I'd also demand to know what the state had done with Russell.

I snuck into Mr. Weaver's study the next day to see if I could find anything. The only books in the room were an enormous bible, clad in leather with silver hinges, and a ledger where farm expenses and income were recorded. I opened the desk drawers and came across a folder bearing my name: *Ward of the Commonwealth of Pennsylvania* printed in blue ink, making permanent my new identity. The file made no mention of Russell, only that I'd been removed from *a less than satisfactory home.*

Fury toward prayer turned to fury toward devout people. When Mrs. Weaver came upstairs to clean with two of her girls, I shouted at them: "Where is Russell?" Her voice attempted a firm, but cheerful sound. "Last we knew he was getting treatment at hospital. Maybe the Veteran's hospital? Was he in the service?"

"No."

"Well, they say it's a nice place…men come from all over to rest there."

"I told you he was never in the service."

Her face looked startled and she bowed her head leaving me to study the top of her white bonnet. "Oh, well then. He must be some other place."

"I wanna go see him."

She lifted her eyes and appraised me sternly, while I studied the knife-straight part in her dark hair that divided her skull into two neat halves. "I want to see him," I repeated, this time more loudly, to show I meant business.

To outdo my theatrics, she let her manner display its own anti-dramatic determination. She brought herself up to full height, then opened the hallway window, and hollered down through the cold morning air. "Mose…can you come in here…?"

We met Mr. Weaver in the kitchen, still in his leather milking apron, his face clouded by impatience at having to be pulled from his chores. He saw Mrs. Weaver had deemed a man's strength was in order, and he listened to my demand. His head lowered in prayer, then lifted. "Maybe once Summer comes one of us can take you," he said, almost in a whisper. "But we'll have to wait."

"Wait for what?"

He looked at the floor. "Well, for school to end."

I stared at the wall. How could he and that dumb cluck Mrs. Weaver be so stupid as to think I'd ever go back to school again? Hell! Let the cops or the principal himself throw me in jail. Let them go back and retrieve my books and jacket from the old school locker. Why has no one already done that!

"Hell! Hell! Hell!"

The state agencies were called in and they ruled alongside the Weaver's God, and so off to the Mennonite school I went. The bus driver, a tough, white-haired lady named Milly, let me pester her to explain the geography of the area. "Let's see…your farm lies on the West side of the Lititz borough…closest intersection…Temperance Hill…that puts us about an hour from Southeast of Harrisburg…with Lebanon about an hour to the North."

· · ·

Mr. Weaver came in one morning not long after, and sat down at the kitchen table where I was eating porridge. "The trial of the man who killed your mother begins today. The state thought you should know in case anyone brings it up. We will now pray that you will find forgiveness for that man's soul." I contemplated the remark, and as he prayed watched his lips move in reverential pity. "No one on this farm has any time to take me to see Russell, yet you always find time to pray. Pray, pray and attend church, and ever more church."

After school the next day, I told Milly I had an errand to run for the Weaver's and she dropped me in Lititz. I went straight to the newsstand and stood reading one of the newspaper accounts. I learned the crime was being proven in court using Mom's plain wristwatch as its main evidence, the timepiece had been found in a hock shop, its proprietor pointing across the courtroom to identify the weeping and remorseful man who'd sold it.

"Hey, squirt…you gonna buy that rag?" A slack teenage boy hired to mind the store took obvious pride in addressing me in that smart-alecky, derogatory way—a tone unusual around Lititz. I ignored him. "Wanna read for free? Go to the library."

I nodded, left the store and went over to Broad Street, where after asking a few people, I found the library building at the corner of Marion Street. Inside the periodical room, lay a treasure trove of newspaper editions.

By then most area accounts reckoned the crime involved a typical break-in, the ensuing murder simply a case of entering the wrong place at the wrong time. Some were quoted saying the murder had little to do with Mom, while others noted how she'd made *uncommon* choices in her life, held *outspoken political opinions*, and a few even inferred that a fateful come-uppance might be her *due*. From the Harrisburg paper, I learned the killer had confessed how prior to the night of the crime he'd never heard of Mom, and knew nothing of her *unusual ideas*. In one of the news articles, I read Russell was reported to be at the State Mental Hospital in Harrisburg. The news crushed me. Now, I'd never find a way to see him.

In the days that followed, the Weaver family went on praying, went on working. They seemed to enjoy making even the smallest events in their lives, a cracked egg, a spider in the butter crock, or a moving weather vane, have some connection to God's will, as if they knew the mind of God. I ignored them and in the days that followed went on reading every day at the library. Mom's trial moved toward conclusion. The verdict was quick, the jury finding the tear-streaked thief guilty. The man would be sent to Rockview penitentiary, forever trapped in the worst thing he'd ever done. And even without any prayers, for some reason I did pity him.

That evening, the Weaver's farm found its lane clogged with dusty cars driven by journalists on the hunt for a good sob-story. Their by-lines depended on up-to-date photos of my thirteen-year-old face, to be captioned in print: *murder victim's son.* The Weavers seemed to relish having their mettle as foster parents tested, and they and their four children actually did a gallant job of protecting me. One of the girls even drove a herd of thirty cows over from the barn to act as a barrier to the house. Sitting inside, I looked out through the pane of a window to the crowded scene below.

A few weeks later, and the story wasn't a story anymore. I could go about Lititz unbothered, odd glances coming my way, but no questions. At the library I'd been able to learn that the State Mental Hospital stood off of Cameron Street, and now if I could only find a way to get there. One afternoon Mr. Weaver came in and stomped the mud off his boots. "Have something to discuss with you Walker," he said, and sat me down, folding his hands on the table, yet another somber expression on his face. From his back pocket he pulled out a section of *The Harrisburg Patriot.* "The mailman come by and gave this to me…he thought we all ought to know."

I began to read, and soon learned in horror how a gang of inmates at Rockview had shanked the man who had murdered Mom to death. Reportedly, he'd been killed in full view of the guards. Much was being made over the fact that the attackers had been of different races, as if such unity demonstrated a new kind of social advancement. I sat astonished.

"I'm guessing we ought to brace…" Mr. Weaver said. "Likely be another round of circus coming our way."

The response was mild, as only a few lone reporters showed up this time, from different publications, along with a news crew from WTPA in Harrisburg, probably drawn by the hope that I might emerge and express some juvenile joy over the vengeful stabbing, or better yet, confess a miracle of healing, telling how Jesus now stirred in my sorrowful breast. The Weaver farm was indeed photographed, as was my school, but I remained hidden—I remained silent. No one would ever find out Mom's departure from my life had begun long before her death.

. . .

In my mind I rejected the farm geography as my home. The Weavers continued plying me with tough-love pity, but numb and speechless, I no longer cared. They were so forgiving, and in time I conceded to their wishes, learning to help with chores. After all, I drank the buttery yellow milk from their Guernsey cows, ate warm apple dumplings made with fruit from their orchard, and buttered biscuits milled from their wheat, with honey from their hives.

And yet, despite my acquiescence, the weeks and months of the calendar collapsed together like a poorly engineered bridge. Morning blended into night, night into dawn, no variation, the movement involved in daily physical activity done by rote. I sensed Autumn come and go, the landscape disappearing into one long blizzard, Christmas somewhere in the middle, then a New Year, then another March with another interminable biting wind. After class, I'd wander along the railroad tracks until I reached the Wilbur Chocolate factory. Eventually a Weaver kid could be spied in the distance, coming to look for me, then ever so gently herding me home like one of the stray cows. Everyone realized my compromised nerves-everyone but me.

And then somehow, I began to notice geese return in patterns of horizontal flight. I'd walk all the way to Lititz Springs to watch them splash-land in the rill running through the park. In time, other birds began chirping as they built nests, and I noticed the smell of lilacs, then rainwater dripping from the new leaves of the sycamores, and eventually the fibrous pull of blue chicory flowers rising in stubbornness along the railroad tracks. Soon the weather grew hot, and on a day in late June with the school year concluded, Mrs. Weaver received a letter that excited her. "It's from your Palmyra aunt…she and your grandfather want to take you to the shore!"

I'd not forgotten how the old man had stood on his porch and rejected Mom and her gift of flowers, calling her *Missy.*

"No," I said. "Not going."

Mr. Weaver paused and rubbed his beard. After a bit he explained. "Walker, we all need to turn our heart over to trust the Lord…let bygones be bygones. The Hershey factory is a generous employer, and your granddad's toil there has brought forth bounty, allowing him to spend his holiday at a nice place…a seashore. This is part of God's plan…he knows a change of scenery will do you good."

"No. It won't!"

My resistance was ignored. Instead, a family prayer was called, and that effort indeed confirmed, contact with my family was God's will. No further appeal was granted.

. . .

Inside the small cottage that the old man had rented in Rehoboth Beach, I remained silent in his presence. Aunt Greta was the one who after breakfast brought me to the sea, standing guard in the sand on the Delaware shore, as I waded out counting the cycles of waves. In the evening she took me to the boardwalk, paid for me to ride the roller coaster and bought me a soft ice-cream or a machine-spun cotton candy. On most days, at about noon, the old man would join us, unfolding his aluminum chair at waterside, sitting with his back pressed into the yellow webbing, his afternoon spent painting daylilies, beach roses and hydrangeas.

"Imagine!" Aunt Greta gushed when we were alone. "A year since he last held a paintbrush…yet that eye for detail…sharp as ever. Like another Audubon!"

At supper, he complained that some berries she'd served were too tart. She apologized several times and carried the bowl back to the kitchen saying she'd cook them down to make jam. I saw his preferences were notable, and if that's how he spoke to his sister, I could only imagine what life had been like for my poor mother and grandmother.

On more than one occasion, my grandfather mentioned boot camp and basic training. "When we made our beds, a quarter had to bounce off our blankets," he said, inferring that the same kind of discipline would surely help shape me. But always a shadow seemed to fall over the subject of the service. I finally worked up the nerve and asked if while fighting had he felt brave?

"Tales of bravery are but bull for the infantrymen. Leaders alter the record to flatter themselves. I was in Italy. The losses up from Monte Cassino…for me…the atrocity of a slaughterhouse. After such unnecessary sacrifice…no one wants to admit how many heroes join the military simply because they were failures in civilian life."

He saw I didn't understand. "I only hope you won't ever have to face combat." Did he mean because I'd never be up to it? He didn't wait for my reply because he saw none was coming. After a while the subject shifted to Mom. "I'm sure for you there was no easy time in it. But maybe now you've come to understand how her choices were poor. She was led too easily down the garden path. Her dealings low…improper."

"But she was good," I objected. "She believed all people were good. Every night before bed, we said prayers…every morning she'd pray by her own bedside too."

"Praying don't prove nothin'," he leaned back in his chair. "The Whore of Babylon probably prayed, probably on her knees pleasuring men at the same time!"

"Please!" Aunt Greta said. "Let's not speak with vulgarity."

"None of you has lived long enough. One day…you'll see."

Alluding to Mom's sad end seemed to have added fuel to justify the old man's point of view. He saw my fury and his voice took on an unexpected tone. As if he thought I was suddenly old enough to understand something about the world's curse. "At the Hershey plant, I been the butt of too many jokes. You'll never know the many times I suffered on account of her. Those guys rib and make fun all day long…said my daughter followed me into the business of making chocolate."

I put down my spoon. "Mom was good. Mom was *very* good."

Aunt Greta smiled kindly, and told me I could excuse myself from the table. In my room, I longed to scream, but instead swung rage at the window curtains with a fist, while the fear that a boy my age might still be spanked, brought even more rage. Meanwhile, I could hear Aunt Greta whispering in the kitchen. "Not fair to blame the boy…we said we'd help build his well-being."

I heard the old man growl. "Just shut up! This was your idea."

"I won't. He's your *only* grandchild…my only nephew. They're desperate for us to help him."

In that moment I knew that I'd only been invited because someone had gotten to Aunt Greta. The state social workers? The Weavers? Greta probably agreed to try and reason with the old man to make it happen. How could it have been otherwise? I felt intense shame. Screw it! No matter what that old coot said, I knew Mom was good. I knew that fact in the way children through osmosis comprehend the private patterns of their parents, including certain tendencies, their regrets, their wish for lost dreams, lives unlived and unspoken, often gone because of having children.

On our last day I walked Aunt Greta to the post office. "You know, every year he used to send me one of his cards…painted on watercolor stock. This year, like you, I've come along for the first time. But I'm still sending this card to myself! That way when I get back to Hummelstown, a souvenir of our trip will be waiting for me in the mailbox. Won't that be nice!"

"Sure," I said. Aunt Greta showed me the card, painted with wild looking beach roses, then paused, as if seeming to catch something regretful within herself. "Walker, he only gave me one card. But if you like I'd gladly send it to *you*?"

"Naw, you keep it," I said. "If I wanted a card, I'd have bought one." Though I knew she would have sent the card to me in a second, I could sense she was also very relieved not to have to part with it.

Not long after I returned to the Weavers, another familial invitation was extended. In what could hardly be a coincidence, it seemed the Gordons had also suddenly decided to track me down. They'd even somehow filed with the state to request permission for me to visit them out on Long Island. Secretly, it was a thrill to be found, and when questioned, I tried to persuade my social worker that such a trip was important.

"Are you saying for your sanity and well-being?" the woman coaxed. "Saying the right words will help me fill out the report."

"Yes," I nodded.

• • •

In Greenport, while dinner was being prepared, I suddenly lost the happy mood, and sat at the kitchen table feeling my nerves grow shaky, desperately wanting to hide how bad I felt, and yet needing to have someone notice, to belong somewhere, and to hope for a permanent rescue. With little coaxing, I blurted out my anger, telling them what the old man had said about Mom being in the business of making chocolate. Grandma and Grandpa Gordon remained focused on their tasks: she shredding cabbage for coleslaw, he sorting mail. They made no comment, made no ill remark. I then shared stories about the old man's service in Italy. They nodded and said we must find compassion for that experience—a cruel slaughterhouse for working-class men.

When Grandma Gordon called Marvene to the table, a platter of fried chicken was put down. "Tonight, Walker in honor of your visit, you will be served first," Grandpa Gordon said. "Would you like white or dark?" Large bowls of creamy coleslaw and potato salad were then passed, me getting the first serving of each. While we ate, they continued to ask questions, especially curious if I liked living with the Weavers. "I hate them. I hate farms. I hate going to that school…everything's bout the Hebrews, Cain and Abel."

"Those lessons won't hurt you none," Grandpa Gordon said.

Marvene cleared the dinner dishes, and afterward Grandma Gordon put down a homemade cushaw pie and began to cut it into wedged sections. She winked at me. "I had some pralines left from the holidays, so I chopped them up to add some crunch."

Over dessert, the Gordons allowed me to go on and on, sharing all my disappointments and dislikes. Once the pie was polished off, Grandpa said we should discuss my future. "We want everyone to know we still embrace the idea that Cole, in marriage to your mother, accepted all the natural duties to be your father."

"We don't like hearing you're unhappy," Grandma Gordon added. "We should probably consult with your Aunt Greta about what other options you might have."

Grandpa Gordon nodded. "We might also want to ask Russell too."

"They won't let me go back to Jefferson Street. Russell isn't there. They locked him up because of his seizures."

"We understand. But we just want to be sure that everyone feels included. We've been told the injuries to Russell's eye plague him very badly, so he can't handle any extra responsibility right now. But we can still let him know."

Grandma Gordon put her arm around me. "None of this has been easy, and because of that, how'd you feel about coming to live here in Greenport?"

"No. I want to live with my Mom again…in New York." They both looked down at the rug.

The next day, a local woman was brought in for consultation. She worked as a guidance counselor at the High School, and her husband owned one of the pizza restaurants in the village. We met there over slices of sausage pizza, and in what was either an argumentum or a curse, the woman thought my opportunities would be limitless if a wager could be placed on my getting into a private school somewhere. The next day, she came to the house. I sat at the table, working a jigsaw puzzle, listening to them trying to hatch plans for my future. The neighbor helped the Gordons develop application essays. "Most private schools need minorities," she said. "We'll stir that…and orphan pity…get compassion to pay."

• • •

A baroque series of moves began, kept largely hidden from me, wherein a pro-bono lawyer was brought in to help the Gordons petition the Commonwealth of Pennsylvania, allowing them to become my legal guardians in New York State. There were no objectors, but for reasons not declared, that permission was denied. The guidance counselor persisted, and through her efforts, the Gordons managed to retain a civil-rights lawyer. He, working for peanuts, approached the man who had directed an industrial for Oldsmobile that Mom had once done in Detroit. This was the same man who'd brought Mom to the party on the night she first met Cole, and who'd written a very nice letter of sympathy to the Gordons, saying if there was ever anything he could do for them, to let him know. The guidance counselor had discovered with glee that the director also served on the board of a private school in Connecticut, and together they re-petitioned the state of Pennsylvania to transfer my residence to the school's home state. The New York legislature agreed to the transfer—provided it was only to attend a private school—not a taxpayer funded public school. In some kind of miracle—perhaps based upon the sorrowful nature of my application—and the director's influence—and simply to make the problem go away—the Gordons became my official guardians—the school in Connecticut granting me free tuition, room and board—and parties in agreement signed on the dotted line.

In the Fall, Marvene traveled with me across Long Island Sound, once more acting as a kind of family ambassador. Mrs. Curtis, Director of Admissions, met us in the circular driveway of the admissions building, and behaved as if we were long-forgotten friends. During the course of our talk, she eventually cut right to the core: "I understand a while back you lost your mother under difficult circumstances?"

"Yes. Ma'am"

"I am sorry. And now you are thirteen."

"Yes. Almost fourteen."

Marvene stayed in the background, like me, practicing politeness. Our awe of the place was palpable, as was her envy as we toured the campus, planted with neat hedges of azalea and crabapple. "Our student body is international," Mrs. Curtis said. "They've come from all around the globe." She escorted us to a well-appointed, yet quaint, guest lodge where Marvene was told she'd stay.

My campus dorm room smelled of new paint, and that evening Marvene and I lounged there. Her eye, keen as ever, had spent the day surveying the school, her disdain at its many rich children visible. After she'd had a chance to relax, her talk grew blunt. "They're all so square!" she said defensively. "Square and snotty. Out East, our school plays field hockey with rich brats like these. East Hampton kids…and boy, they too are square. So square they never even heard of James Brown!"

Her assessment made me uneasy. I so longed to remain in union with her, but I excused myself to go into the bathroom, where I sat on the edge of the tub and pressed my face into a towel without making any sound. When I emerged, Marvene's renewed critiques of my classmates brought more discomfort. The next morning, at breakfast on the terrace of the student café, she read to me quietly from the alumni newspaper, a story about how many high-ranking colleges accepted large percentages from this school. "Face it, baby. You've been drafted as a private into an army of generals."

That remark felt like a lash, and I sensed more than a tinge of resentment. "Look, Marvene, we both know this school only accepted me out of orphan pity. Some people simply burn with the need to show that kind of do-goody-ness."

"Well, you're handsome and can almost pass." She saw through my feelings, and softened, maybe sensing she'd gone too far. "Walker, who knows? Maybe this rich jailhouse is God's goodness protecting you at last."

I appreciated her attempt to not only see my isolation, but to steer me past blind depression. Still, I was relieved when she left the next day. I needed to navigate this place alone. Walking around the orderly campus, I soon realized that nowhere among these fine stone buildings would I likely find a conversation that challenged me the way hers would. That night, I sat looking at the lit-up windows of the library, before it the campus green stretched with its border of boxwoods dark as poison. Why was my life always so damn complicated?

Despite her vitriol about privilege, which only I was privy too, the school psychiatrist deemed Marvene's visits would do me good, and so the administration organized and funded her to come on a regular schedule, the first weekend in every month. She also made a special trip over on my birthday, and I could not wait to see her, running over to the campus guest lodge to make sure the room was reserved.

At dinner, a large cake was brought into the dining hall, and I asked Marvene to cut it. Turns out the kitchen had specially prepared the cake at her request. All the staff came out of the kitchen and sang "Happy Birthday," and we sliced through the white cake layered with chocolate buttercream to share with everyone. Later, in my room, Marvene gifted me a pair of felt slippers Grandma Gordon had embroidered with my initials on the toes. I put them on, and tried to hide how my feet had grown, the sizing of the slippers already too small.

Marvene's critiques rarely varied from their sharpness, and remained a way for me to see and accept her version of truth, something most of the campus wasn't ready for. "Civil rights were fought for Negroes born in America," she informed me. "Yet families of slaves going back centuries are stuck in rat-infested projects, or working stupid clerical jobs. Meanwhile, these fat-ass brats are sent here from Liberia, or Nigeria, or Haiti, or wherever the hell they're born, sent by rich parents to grab what's 'posed to be our opportunity. And we're supposed to smile, say shucks, and be grateful for all the gains."

"You sound like Russell."

"Well, Russell is right! And I'm sure your Mama would agree too."

Marvene was more than a little proud that her family had never taken welfare. "But that don't mean with my background, I'd be welcome here at this school—let alone Harvard. They only want people of color who were born silver-spooners."

"Russell used to say students from abroad come here better trained. That foreign education was still colonial and therefore superior to ours."

"Damn right!" Marvene stood and went to the mirror, dipping her finger into a tiny pot of cherry lip-gloss which she applied. "Foreign born kids still got uniforms and punishment. We ought to bring back paddles. Spank some butt."

"No one is gonna spank me."

"Even Uncle Sturgis says affirmative action should be reserved for descenders of cotton workers—not some Johnny-come-lately's. And the rich parents of these pikers are probably politicians or own some kind of corrupt corporate factory."

"I've learned a lot of them are children of mogul dynasties in the Caribbean. Czars with their own mining camps, pineapple plantations, or some fat-cat concrete monopoly."

"Exploiting cheap black labor!"

"Yup. Some are said to be rich oil suppliers, or high African muckity-mucks. We can't fathom the wealth. Parents beyond mega-rich."

"I believe you. And boy, what pity I feel for all the housekeepers getting dropped off."

"See 'em every day. Rich parents send maids to clean the dorm rooms."

"How nuts is that! These brats oughta learn to clean their own damn rooms. Not let servants be brought in like dogs, or some low-paid chain gang. And your being here only helps hide the crappiness of our own public schools."

"What?"

"You being here probably lets some clerk check a box. Claim some damn minority credit for having Negroes. I bet they call you inner-city! Face it, baby, you're a token, and one who carries no threat of black power. No militancy, what-so-ever!"

"So, I never picked cotton. Have you?"

"These kids from Africa or the Bahamas never picked it either. And your Mama? She'd *never* picked a rose…though she wanted the world to think she understood picking…ignoring her own whiteness!"

"Don't say that."

"Okay. Sorry."

"Uncle Sturgis used to say that. He used to annoy her. Saying: 'Hey, *Breck* girl…How you gonna raise that child?'"

"He shouldn't have done that."

"It was pejorative," I said, proud to show my hard won vocabulary. "But Sturgis couldn't help himself. Whenever he saw Mom, he'd ask her if she was going to raise me as black or white. She knew it was a trick question to mock her."

"I remember. He used to grin and say: In America it only takes one drop… there's only *one* answer."

"And she just played along."

"Along with what?"

"I don't know. Not for me to say." Our rapport came to an end. Marvene's strident talk suddenly felt dangerous.

• • •

At some point, the school recognized that I might be enduring another bout of depression; they prescribed some pills and made me attend psychological therapy. They also made any student social gathering on campus mandatory.

I stayed in bed one Thursday, knowing full-well a mixer was under way. The house monitor knocked on my door: "I have specific instruction to bring you," he said.

"Who wrote the instructions?"

"Dunno? The dean?"

I forced myself to get dressed and went to the social hall, but made up my mind that on no account would I mingle. A girl with a bleach-blonde afro offered me some cookies. "Where you from?"

"New York."

"What your parents do?"

"My father's a diplomat."

"What country?"

"They move him all the time."

"What kind of diplomat?"

"For legal reasons I can't discuss his work." The girl looked at me as if I'd just been doused with napalm. At the drink table I poured a soda and another girl with a red face and pale blue eyes came over and introduced herself. "Yetta Wildenstein," she said. "I only came to the slammer last week."

"Slammer?"

"This shithole…this friggin' adolescent prison. Third one I've been to."

I nodded and grew tongue-tied, observing how she and Marvene both used the metaphor of lock-up for the school. Yetta told me she came from the Riverdale section of the Bronx, and it was obvious that she was more worldly than I.

"Have you been picked for a sports team?"

"I didn't try out."

"Have you been asked to join any other clubs or activities?"

"No."

She'd looked at me and said: "Well, what are we? Chopped liver?"

Though secretly relieved to be excluded from extra-curricular activities, Yetta assumed I'd been ostracized. Somehow, I felt a kind of camaraderie in that. In the weeks that followed, she and I began to meet in the library to study together. Most of the other students avoided us. Yet, in our cocoon, we encouraged one another to read—and read we did, sometimes a dozen books a week. Yetta began to urge me to ponder more deeply. "What worth does any infant have in this world if it's seen only as a Jew, an Arab, or black and white. Is no in-between allowable? And, what's race but some other characteristic, like long legs, baldness, green eyes."

Through the library window I saw the girl with the blonde afro walking hand-in-hand with another girl across the campus green. The other girl was much darker in complexion, and yet they'd somehow copied the same hairstyle. If hair-color can be dyed, without repercussion, why can't race be equally mutable? After all, what am I? I asked in my own head. Chopped liver? Quietly, and to myself, I came to realize that Mom had given me the false sense that we belonged to a special tribe of chameleons. I already knew well how darkness could lighten or deepen depending on a situation or environment. With Marvene, the Gordons, and certainly Uncle Sturgis, black was a positive thing. With Mom's father, it was deeply negative.

A few days later, while in the throes of this paradox, Marvene came to visit. She and Yetta took one look at each other and decided they were enemies. Yetta soon disappeared, and I now felt guilty to be spending time with Marvene.

I didn't let on, but I was hurt when during this visit Marvene negated all my suggestions for things to do, even the movies and bowling. She seemed strained, irritable, somehow more aloof. On her final afternoon we sat on a stone wall by the rowing lake with nothing to say. I finally could not stand it anymore. "Marvene, what's wrong?"

She looked off across the water and watched the captain of a crew give instructions to the team holding oars in a boat. "Nothing, I'm good. But you have new friends. You don't need these visits anymore."

"Of course, I do. Your presence here is like an elixir."

She turned and looked at me with a smirk. "That don't sound like Walker."

"What?"

"Your diction….elixir…you speak all *lofty* now."

"Well, like the kids in the projects, I'm a product of my environment."

Marvene's look discredited my regrettable reply. "Sounds *stuck-up* to me."

The next day Marvene departed, and no matter how I tried I could not erase the cut her criticism had gouged across my heart. I found Yetta in the library, and she too glared at me.

"What is it?"

"You never said your family was black."

"Does that matter to you?"

"I just didn't get it."

"So. What difference does it make?"

"Forget it," she brought her attention back to the book in her hand.

In the following days, we continued to meet and study for our final exams, but somehow our personal discussions never resumed. At night, I lay in bed, my fists curled in anger to have lost both of my only confidants in such a short span of time.

The cruel school year finally ended, and my classmates were packing up for Summer holidays, dashing off to places like Geneva, Ibiza, Hawaii, or to bake clams at some family compound on Martha's Vineyard. Yetta went to visit some family members in Haifa. Meanwhile, the Gordons were urging me to cross the sound and come to Long Island for the Summer, but for the first time, Aunt Greta also beckoned, inviting me to spend the season with her in Hummelstown.

I told myself to ferry across Long Island Sound from Connecticut and back to see the Gordons ate too deeply into everyone's wallet, not to mention the overcharging car service needed to shuttle from school across Connecticut to Bridgeport. On the Long Island side, someone would have to take off work, then drive all the way to Port Jefferson to pick me up. I half-heartedly looked at the train for an alternative, but the route involved a whole day's travel, first down to New York, then a walk from Grand Central to Penn Station then a transfer to the Long Island Railroad. In truth, Marvene's criticism of my manners and way of speaking weighed on me more than I could admit, and only later did I come to recognize how my hurt was matching her resentment by choosing Aunt Greta and Harrisburg over Greenport.

• • •

Aunt Greta's house was small, and made even smaller by ruffled lampshades, needlepoint pillows, collections of teapots, floral-painted cups, and potted snake plants standing in their saucers. A neighbor man would often stop by after work, and bring us plates of food from a restaurant where he worked as a cook. To his credit the man saw my restlessness. "You know our restaurant has an opening for a dishwasher," he said. "We sure could use a fellow like you."

The Progress Grill stood out beyond the hill section of Harrisburg. My job consisted of bussing tables, running food orders, washing dishes, and when the joint got really busy, even taking an order or two. The frenzied kitchen served light fare: grilled crab cakes, roasted vegetables with angel-hair, large salads of apples and spinach, an alternative to the region's famous calorie-rich Pennsylvania Dutch cooking: pot-pie, scrapple, meat pudding, and pig-maw.

Dishwashing was the hardest task, but also my favorite. I imagined myself like Orwell in Paris, hidden from customers in my private tiled chamber, steam rising through the green plastic glassware racks, used flatware dropped into a pan of dirty dishwater, then I'd thwack the plates of leftover food against a hard circle of rubber built into the drain board, a patron's unfinished portion falling to the trash can below. Despite *The Progress Grill's* lighter fare, whenever I bagged and carted those heavy black trash bags of waste to the dumpster, I began to realize how nowadays unprecedented numbers of people on our planet died not from famine but from overeating.

I had applied for the job to earn cash, but I also wanted to escape Aunt Greta's pitying eyes, as well as those of her three cats. I soon took every shift the place was willing to offer. Aunt Greta seemed to understand my long hours, when I explained that even paltry sums of pocket money would give me an advantage at a school where many attended with unlimited credit, thoroughbred horses and matching python-skin luggage.

While I did dishes, I frequently pondered how Russell might be doing, and would think about our life on Jefferson Street, which now felt like a hundred years ago. One afternoon I went to a payphone, and dialed the State Mental Hospital in Harrisburg, only to be told Russell had been transferred. They said they'd get back to me about where he'd been sent, but as I had no phone number that I felt comfortable leaving, I said I'd call back. I never did.

That Fall, I returned to Connecticut with my own spending money, going into town for a movie, buying books, and getting some new clothes whenever I felt like it. The Summer had long passed, and I still often carried a nagging feeling of guilt that I'd not gone to visit the Gordons, not even for a weekend, especially after all they had done for me. I longed to see Marvene, but she wrote to say she couldn't accept my invitation to visit for a while. A new job at a bank in Mattituck occupied most of her time, as did a new romance with a young man who worked for the post office.

It was ironic how the Gordons, by placing me in private school, that bastion of privilege, had also brought about our separation. Marvene's retreat required me to face sad facts, like it or not, and regardless of what Grandma Gordon taught about all of us being God's children, we were now separated by class.

I also used the logic of limited resources to avoid any further tracking down of Russell, but I felt no small amount of worry and concern that my diction might sound stuck-up to him now as well. In mid-November, Aunt Greta came to visit me at school for family weekend, staying in one of the rooms at the over-night guest lodge. "What a lovely place," she said, looking out over the campus. "So many different backgrounds, all living in harmony." I could see from the sarcasm forming in my brain, that the wall of class was beginning to divide us as well. It was during that visit, she confided the old man was being treated for stomach cancer. "I fear he's not long for this world."

Good, I thought to myself without mercy. Good. Aunt Greta looked startled when I offered no response, merely asked if she might like another cup of coffee, saying I'd be glad to get it from the cafeteria line.

At the end of her guest weekend, Aunt Greta stood on the train platform and handed me a large brown envelope. "I tried to give these to your mother once…she asked that I keep them for you." Inside, the bigger envelope, a small pale blue envelope held a fifty-dollar bill. "I'm sorry we've not been able to help you more," Aunt Greta said. I then pulled out a large flat box, and saw they contained dozens of hand-painted floral postcards, sent to her over the years by the old man. "One of the few things people agree on is that blossoms are beautiful," she said, her voice sounding weak. At the bottom of the envelope, a blurry photograph sat in a cardboard frame. Aunt Greta took my hand. "When she married, your mother gave me that for safekeeping. We believe this picture to be of your biological father."

I stared at the man's unusual features, his green eyes reminding me of my own.

"My birth certificate says 'father unknown.'"

"Yes."

"Who is he?"

"We don't know. We never met him."

"Nothing of his background is known?"

"I can't remember. I wish I could. I think she once said he came from a place called Corfu? That his family was forced to go to live in Egypt? At some point, they were made to leave there too. I know she said he grew up in Paris? I'm afraid none of these places means much to us."

"Corfu is an island off of Greece and Italy."

"I'm sorry Walker, you know so much more than I do. I'm not really up on world geography. And Lord knows, I certainly, wouldn't dream of ever going so far away myself. I mean not to somewhere we never heard of. I thought Delaware was a big trip. Yet, I suppose if any of us could dig back far enough, we'd discover that as people, everyone in the world is related to everyone else. Isn't that what really matters?"

Aunt Greta carefully placed the postcards back in order, then returned them to the brown envelope, before handing the package over to me. "These were my summer souvenirs, and now they belong to you." I thanked her with a hug, and tucked the envelope under my arm with a reverence I hoped she would appreciate. She boarded the train and in a minute it began to depart. I found a bench, opened the envelope again and found myself staring at the man's photograph, unable to pull myself away from the youthful but shadowy face suggesting so many similarities to my own.

Book Two

TIGHTWIRE

• • •

Levanto, Italy—1994

On the Cinque Terre that fat July, they came to tour the magic show. Their arrival coincided with my thirty-fifth birthday, and while Lydia shamelessly claimed the celebration to be the very magnet that had pulled her to the Riviera's azure coast—we both knew this was bullshit. Still, all evening she carried on her ridiculous charade, acting as if my little dinner were some swell, unparalleled event. In truth, she'd only deigned to descend on the Cinque Terre to use it, making our village a secure and temporary base for her show-biz ambition. If I hadn't provided this convenient opportunity, I'd have probably never heard from her again.

"You have a trophy life," she'd gushed more than once that first night, fawning over me in a way that kept me checking to be sure my wallet hadn't been stolen. What a fool I'd been to arrange a property rental for her and Buddy, and even more foolish to have chosen the house standing directly adjacent to mine, as our two houses shared the terrace between them. That arrangement diminished privacy, all our comings and goings visible to one another. The neighbors who owned the place, a pleasant pair of Swedes, lived in Oslo most of the time, and were delighted to have renters who weren't simply strangers, but cousins of mine. Still in my mind, Lydia and Buddy after fifteen years of absence, were strangers.

Yet, the longer they remained, the more our enjoined architecture revealed the puerile strain of their marriage, its untenable toil and strife, with carousing marital fights that spilled out into summer's heat, over-broiling love, patience, not to mention the restfulness of our garden. Their arrival to my birthday celebration was now eight months ago, and this was hardly the first time I'd been roused in the middle of the night, shorn of sleep, teeth still in grind, accosted by the absurd proximity of our communal terrace. Tonight, my bedside clock glowed past two in the morning, and the loudness of their voices certified the guzzle of martinis, a whole pitcher full, perhaps two, with any accompanying jubilation long vanished. I rose from my bed only half-awake and moved a chair to sit by the window.

The conflict surged, Lydia's voice yelling this time: "You don't know nothing! Why...I've seen more celebrities...up close than you'll ever. They get there... where they are...by sheer will."

Buddy sounded back. "Will?... *Will?* Sounds like a *cowboy's* name! Yes! That's it! Will, that hung, young cowboy adored by so many *older* actresses!" His ridiculous, drunken mockery found its mark.

"You bastard! That...doesn't...stupid...make even sense. Why can't you just support me? Other people...are attracted...they exalt me! But you? Never!"

"Exalt? Ha! Ha! Exalt? What're you, a *deity?*"

She cursed him, as he probably hoped she would. "You want me to apologize for breathing!"

After eight months, I'd grown tired of their scorn, expressed in that horribly twisted corkscrew known as *marital jest*. But what bothered me most was how quick and often I found myself an unwitting mimic of their sarcasm, even in private thought. At first, it had been enjoyable to hear American voices, the language of childhood holding unmatched nuance, no matter how well another language might be mastered. Most early conversations develop in families, schools, maybe even via long-forgotten strangers, those voices will influence us forever. And likewise, a sequestered community of expats dig a similar communal well of speech, sound, pattern and thought, from which all in isolation drink. How often had I recently heard Buddy use a phrase uniquely mine? And to recognize my own phrases echoing back through the filter of his voice was suffocating, particularly as he often aped the dumbest disquisition I'd made, a bit already smugly borrowed—or stolen—some silly tenet on poetic verse retained in memory, only to years later be vomited up as knowledge.

I cringed to realize that such reverberations also came from me, that I too was prone to repeat something spoken by someone I'd known, another friend, perhaps another Italian neighbor, and certainly Roberta. She was a fine raconteur, with many winning phrases that later I heard myself replicating in whimsy. Yet, isn't that influence at least one aim of comprehension? Of literature even?

But conversation with Lydia and Buddy was a familial vacuum, and so our talk, talk, talk, repeated even quicker, developing a mimetic circle to echo opinions, lobby ideas, even sling arch phrases—not to mention our most appealing and appalling theories—until after a few months of insular and daily exposure, we all began to sound more and more alike. As with pre-school children, we simply could not eliminate the cross-pollination of our shared language.

And while the terrace's joint public space made us steer clear of things like nude-sunbathing, we couldn't find a way to cloak naked opinion, or worse, hide those bald, untutored things expressed beyond a speaker's sphere of knowledge. And how many times had I heard Buddy counsel Lydia in a pedantic way?

Saying that she ought to relish her newfound role as a *magician's assistant*, I'd secretly agree with him, despite it being clear that Lydia loathed the magic act. I grew increasingly self-conscious of my language absorption, especially when in the very next breath Buddy might say the act was 'her last chance to roll the dice in celebrity's crap-shoot.'

And so tonight, like on other awakenings, I simply sat back and listened, an unflinching nocturnal creature, thinking, oh, what a terrible day it is when you discover you're no longer interested in your partner's point of view, nor they in yours. And if finances are involved, as was the case with them, any return to living solo could involve years of fighting to avoid paucity. But I'd climbed out of my marital soup. Why couldn't they climb out of theirs?

"I'm…*me!*" Lydia shrieked. "You keep trying to change that!"

"Oh, give me a break…Why don't you just go and nail yourself to a cross?"

"No need! Not with you here to swing the hammer."

"Oh, boohoo! Boo-*you!*"

A glass shattered. "Now look what you made me do!"

"I made?"

Tonight's conflict had started stewing the day before yesterday, when the magazine *Hearth & Table* accepted an article Buddy had pitched, wherein Lydia would cook triangles of pasta in Liguria's famed walnut cream sauce—a dish I'd introduced them to. Something about that opportunity had shifted their balance of power.

I recalled the joy in Buddy's voice, shouting into the receiver of the old black phone in the alcove off the Swedes' foyer. His fervor had carried across the terrace. "Let me be sure I understand…are you giving us the green light? I see! Well…well, well there…that's swell!" The call ended and he shouted up the stairs. "They're giving us the green light!"

Through the pane of the window, I saw Lydia jumping up and down. "The green light! The green light!"

"Just you wait, baby, I'm going to make you the next Julia Child!"

It was clear, prior to this, Buddy had been languishing in the wings, supporting more of her drama offstage than on. And what a numbskull. Couldn't he see she abhorred any notion of him as her Svengali, the patron of her success? Buddy's grandiose prediction, brought my impatient foot to tap under the counterpane. How could such jubilation have turned into this acrimony so quickly? I watched him pass by the screen door with a broom and dustpan. "Don't you *dare* clean up after me!" she shouted. "I don't need your milquetoast tolerance…It's *my* glass!"

Her hyper-loud theatricality obviously aggravated him, but I'd also seen that *very* quality bring him pride—in the same way, his magazine writer's byline, brought her status. And yet, they were two crabs in a bucket, each pulling the other back from some kind of gain. And how frustrating for her to witness the simplicity by which the writer's art can practice, needing but a cocktail napkin and a crayon, books by poets who barely left their beds, lining the shelves in the great libraries of the world. Her art, on the other hand, required physical exertion: rehearsals, stages, scenery, scripts, auditions and, of course, *backers*.

The contrast between their two artistic efforts, built insult. "Writers are a parasitic class," she'd say. "You sit around on your asses all day, imagining grand ideas." By the time Lydia claimed to have discovered this grotesquery, she declared it was too late for her to run. "I was stuck like a chipmunk to a glue board." Often, Buddy, worn down by tending such a temperamental wife, would needle her back. Or he'd bait her by saying: "The actor's art can but *interpret*—writers and visual artists *originate*."

Their arguments sometimes grew so blistering, I'd long for reprieve, and begin to itch for the soothing touch of television. Normally, I aligned with those who despised the twinkling box, saying it married too many images, hawked too much product, hi-jacked musical sincerity to stir unearned emotion, and stupefied love with sentimentality. And it was true, the tube's simple-minded persuasions lowered the standards of language, leaving even well-trained actors to blather bad scripts. And television also left a viewer with no tactile experience, no practiced skill, and yet, despite all these torments, tonight, listening to a real-life conflict, I longed to be held in the arms of colorful fantasy, to ache the blue-gray emotions not of real people but of players in hollow rooms, trussed in bright costumes, wigs glued in place with fixatives, the painted faces pretending artificial problems. I felt a particular longing for those maladaptive commercials: the amazing gratitude shown a new floor wax, a new cold pill, a fabled foot spray. I even craved the sardonic expressions of those make-believe wives, who rolled their eyes on cue as the affable actors cast to play husbands, returned home in shiny, well-lit, sports cars.

Across the terrace, Lydia now passed by the doorway, carrying the dustpan in the opposite direction. Who needs television when such unbridled drama plays right outside the window? A few final moments of badgering, and the lights on the Swedes' house went out, leaving no resolution for their play. Loneliness descended, that terrible, occupational hazard for voyeurs. In the dark, all alone, the well of sadness that refilled every night was felt. I sensed the stone of our village walls cooling down, crickets pulsing their metronomic count in match of the well-patterned heartbeat on the dark side of the planet.

• • •

My eyes opened, squinting in watch, trapezoids of sunlight moving millimeter by millimeter across the bedroom floor, revealing all that was uneven in the graining of the wood. The herringbone shone in the morning sun, and overhead, the glow also reflected off the coarseness of the chalky walls, plastered centuries ago to build not a house, but a stable for mules. I knew this intimate early morning mood wouldn't last, and that soon I'd be moving through another day, a ghost among ghosts. Rising from bed, I went to the basin and combed my hair with cold water, then for comfort dressed in one of my softer shirts, the chill inside me warming as I made coffee, readying to busy myself with life's many distractions.

From the terrace, I went up the pink marble steps, passed through our wrought-iron gate, then walked up through the village to take the local bus down to Levanto. Once on board, my mind replayed last night's bout. For Buddy and Lydia, a sickening pattern had emerged, a sugar-sweet honeymoon phase, soon followed by mounting irritation, impatience, then distemper, until fierce barking inevitably led to some cruel and violent bite. Afterwards, pity, regret, a short-lived forgiveness, and a new phase of honeymoon stickiness launched once more the entire cycle. Other people's conflicts fascinated me, but only if they didn't show tedious patterns revealing a calibrated or even secret pleasure. Once I saw that Buddy and Lydia had become predictable, with the cycles moving faster, I shifted into my avoidant mode.

In adolescence, a therapist assigned to me once tried to explain how my empathetic vibrations were over-wrought from trauma, and that given my circumstances, emotional dysregulation could be expected. "You suffer periods of disassociation," she said, noting how a history of my type could be found in literature—sympathetic characters, often orphans who suffer early loss. She said most often they lack root, or certainty, and suggested I read Dickens, *The Secret Garden*, *The Wizard of Oz*. Though I may have an overly developed soft-spot for such underdogs, I told her I found no identification with those characters, nor did I want the pity they wrought from readers. I also refused to accept any psychiatric label applied to me, finding myself too functional, even if I might be overly cross and too acerbically guarded.

But then there were the flashbacks, splitting me in half, often replaying the many questions put to me time and again—which I still could not answer: What

Mom had been wearing the day she was killed, if she'd fought with Russell, or had I seen anyone who might be the suspect? Somehow having Lydia in proximity once more brought these buried questions back to life. On some nights I dreaded going to sleep because of the intrusions. And the memories remained incomplete, in ever so many pieces, fragmented, warped, the past and present frequently merging. Meanwhile, time kept its pace, distancing the present from the scramble of the past, only to merge them again, leaving me to pretend horror could be controlled or overcome, that I could delay or deaden a somewhat quick response to anger, or ignore the burning in my nostrils, or the press of dread in my chest or stomach when an unexpected reflex pulled, thinking I was still present when a fog would cloud my brain, the muscles around my eyes and mouth squinting, wincing, and smiling falsity.

The bus lurched down the mountain, the driver blowing the horn at the many offending vehicles blocking his way. We halted often, with an abrupt jolt, usually to pick up passengers; at one particular curve we braked for an elderly woman clad in black. Local legend held that years ago an infant born to her was stung by a bee and died. Her grief never abated, and she never stopped mourning. Every driver knew to halt for her, and open the folding door, so she could climb up the two steps. Most days she didn't need a ride, just merely wanted to see who might be on the bus. I thought the woman was lucky to have so many people recognize her pain, her black dress and stockings a signal to telegraph her mournful state.

Today her inquisitive eyes scanned each of our faces as if we were in a police line-up, yet she displayed no recognition, or disappointment, or satisfaction. Was she looking for her lost child? She turned to exit, as was her custom, and the driver gave her a nod. As we drove on, the woman stood looking toward the horizon, as if dumbfoundedly indifferent to our departure. It was a familiar act of *incoscienza*, the stock local response, honed through centuries of enduring moldy bread, bugs in the millet, and molars cracked in rot by the age of twenty-five. People here learned the hard way not to wax *poetica* like those ridiculous Romantics. These hard lives measured themselves against centuries of Ligurian cemeteries full of skull, femur, vertebrae, and the uncertainty of dead children. As Russell had taught me long ago, every hundred years leaves behind five generations of old bones, every thousand years, the carcasses of fifty generations.

Our bus continued winding downward, and I thought of all the buses I'd taken over the years while traveling obsessively around the world. After college, I left America for Portugal, then took jobs in many other places: Singapore,

Tokyo, Auckland, Athens, Berlin, Madrid—enough towns (and buses) to learn I'd never belong to any of them. In hindsight, I think my journeys sought to prove the world was safe, identifiable, predictable. And yet, once my travels lasted long enough for me to see myself as worldly, I discovered not merely the cultural variance of our complicated species, but also the astonishing human similarities that we all shared. And yet, even that insight, could not erase my split of otherness, I refused to play that static, orphaned, hero-archetype. I held no record of speaking out for justice or worthy causes. Whenever opportunity gifted the chance to display such virtue, I slunk away.

Navigation of the earth can be a quest. At first, one feels like a citizen of the globe, but a traveler who stays in motion too long, eventually discovers that an accompanying uprootedness can in time disquiet the body; the experience of absence for me was uncannily familiar. Then after years of prolonged movement, my losses seem to suddenly intensify, leading to a strange kind of loneliness, a self-haunting that felt like death. Unlike Dorothy and her celebrated return to Kansas, my childhood homes had evaporated. In response I told myself it was essential to learn how to carry the notion of home inside of me. But this interior home, an extremely private place, often remained as mysterious to me as a truck housing a carnival sideshow, and I frequently lied about myself—even to myself—in order to keep what I could not face concealed.

The bus pulled into the square, and I disembarked. Our region of Italy is one of the most beautiful landscapes on the planet. As a resort town, our narrow streets offer the typical array of toplofty hotels, eateries, and bars. On the Riviera, so many come from somewhere else, and as a result, not being born an Italian left me with fewer feelings of isolation, for my kind of face blended easily with the Mediterranean swarm. And after seven years of living in Levanto, I considered myself a faux-local, knowing which shops rolled good ravioli, which baked supreme pine nut cookies, which sold the best savory basil and tomato pie.

It was Summer's high season, and even ersatz locals like me took to the sidewalks early, conducting our commerce in haste before the visiting masses awoke from their rented beds, to roam about with touristic encroachment. I continued on toward Levanto's promenade, its concrete mass running alongside the Ligurian sea, a line of crustaceaned rocks shining wet and brown in the morning sun, the temperature already warming. I took a deep breath of briny air to nourish my seafaring spirit.

Ambling onward, I decided to follow a less familiar backstreet, passing a small shop making fritters in the window. A sign leaning up in one corner of the display asked an enticing question: *How much of life is given over to food?* I smiled. Was this question on food a feature of what it was to be human? I thought of other categories one could ponder, other missions on which our daily lives might be spent? Work? The pleasantness of a house? The writing of poems? These for many seasons seemed like the answer, but Lydia's intrusion back into my life had re-introduced an all-too-familiar sense of being frightened. This feeling went alongside the involuntary gut-wrench of emotion, something I'd worked hard to escape, thinking it could be escaped. But any tranquility, any safety even, now felt fleeting, the terrors of the past having never been overcome, having never traveled anywhere beyond them.

A young couple approached and politely asked if I'd take their photograph. I obliged.

"Do you live here?" the woman asked.

"Yes." I nodded. "Where are you from?" I asked, focusing the lens.

"Moscow."

In the three years since the Soviet Union collapsed, certain Russians had begun to mint money, that wealth allowing a love affair with the Riviera to resume, an Italian or French villa a commodious place to escape Moscow's frozen Winter.

"And where do you come from?" the girl asked.

"My mother's people are from County Cork," I said, accommodating their curiosity with an involuntary surface engagement.

"You don't seem Irish," her mate said, perhaps not knowing Spaniards had once roamed Ireland, that Romans had roamed England, or that Neil Armstrong had once walked on the moon.

"Raised in America."

"And your father?"

"From Albania," I lied.

Why do we as strangers so often want to know the origins of others? What province, what borough, what neighborhood? Italian? Jewish? Armenian? Travel has taught me our entire planet is obsessed with origination, perhaps a human need to place ourselves among others. And how often have I too questioned others. Just now I'd also asked from where this couple hailed. Perhaps, as a courtesy, I ought to explain the broadness of my background to them? But no, why tell strangers?

"Do you know which direction we face?" the girl asked.

"South. If you charted a direct line down a map, you'd scrape the coasts of Corsica and Sardinia and then head straight into Africa."

"Have you been to Africa?"

I shook my head. "I once went to Tangiers but that doesn't really count. It was a detour from a Spanish holiday, crossed back and forth from Algeciras with but two nights between."

How Russell would've loved me to tell them that even Italy's antiquity was no match for the ancient continent to the South. As Browne taught: 'There is all Africa, and her prodigies in us.' But as I traveled and matured, I came to recognize how much of Russell's associations might be simplistic utopian fantasy. Not all Egyptians were Pharaohs.

"Your eyes change with the color of the light." The Russian girl smiled. "At first they looked topaz, but now they shine more green!"

I grew self-conscious and handed back the camera. Thanking me, they continued on in the opposite direction. Did they imagine we were now friends?

· · ·

At a favorite café, I ordered espresso and watched the weekly flea market unpack along the quay. The scrappy vendors reminded me of undertakers, in control of the bridges that span acquisition and loss, their mercenary tolls paid in departed treasure. Many spoke French, so perhaps some kind of a permit allowed *brocanteurs* to trade across the borders? In high season, the trees are thick, and they shaded the street, where two men were passing along. Both wore striped shirts, linen shorts, and sandals typical of the Riviera, with a seeming preference for the same barber. I brought out my notebook to write.

What might the erotic desire for a twin be—the pleasure of sameness? Losing—or finding oneself in the comfort of joint mimicry? It's said butterflies look for mates that resemble themselves, so why not people? And why shouldn't couples resemble one another? Over time, they eat the same meals, raise the same children, shop the same stores, swim the same lakes, fret the same guilt, pay interest on the same bills. Thousands of conversations, questions and opinions shaping the brain—just as our families of origin do.

One of the men browsing antiques paused to stare into the mirror of an armoire. Why not simply gaze at his companion? Now both peered into the silvered glass, becoming quadruplets. I returned to my notebook to write on the subject which I knew I'd been avoiding:

Most men, whatever their predilection, would condemn any thought of bromance. They'd call it absurd, a delusion. My publisher says potential marketing ensures romantic books remain binary—this or that. But such genres seem too narrow to accommodate a human's full sexual range, except poetry, of course—which he says doesn't sell anyway.

Yet why shouldn't experiments be encouraged? To believe our nature, the nature of self, is unchangeable is probably delusion or dangerous.

An elderly man wheeling a wooden cart came over to show it loaded with ornate rococo dishes. He pulled out a floral platter inscribed in gold for an anniversary. "Five hundred lira," he said. "Good price. Whole set."

I stupidly attempted humor in Italian. "Imagine what that couple had to go through to earn those." He stared at me in befuddlement. "I mean…every plate and saucer, a crawl through a ditch."

He nodded, then from a pocket pulled out an orange handkerchief to wipe perspiration from his face. "Couples who arrive at the golden jubilee still in love…they deserve to be celebrated."

"You mean…more than couples who arrive with acrimony?"

"Ha," he chuckled. "You raise a good question…are happy lives superior?"

I felt my shoulders shrug. "They might *think* so."

"After the honeymoon comes the work. This means to rediscover the good in one another."

"What you say might be the very art of marriage! But you see…I'm blissfully divorced. So, I can no longer imagine such devotion."

The man's face struggled. Then the idea that one could have an ex brought a smile. "You ought to write a book and sell it to all the honeymooning couples!" He chuckled at his own teasing wit, then tucked the orange handkerchief back in his apron pocket, tipping his hat and wheeling along.

The waiter came and I ordered another coffee, and baked eggs topped with parmesan and pesto. In my notebook, I added a few sentences about the man with the cart of dishes, when I felt a presence at the table. I looked up to find Roberta standing before me, skin aglow, bright hair loose and half-unpinned. "What a nice surprise!"

With no insistence, she pulled out the table's other chair. "I'm shopping for the Pasadena people. This couple changes plans the way we change lira. And speaking of lira, it never ceases to amaze how rich people so often show private pride in penny-pinching!"

Jasper earrings danced at her neck, and the lilt in her voice still held the subtle memory of Oklahoma, a southern sound soothingly pleasant; as with the arrival of Lydia and Buddy, I'd noticed an oddly increasing affinity in myself for the syntax of other native Americans.

Roberta ordered a bowl of soup with summer squash and explained she was trying to teach the Pasadena clients to cultivate imperfection. "I tell them flaws make life interesting. But most Americans hate patina."

"Money for flaws? A new wrinkle in plastic surgery?"

"No puns, please! Don't forget, if you marry a shrink, witty Freudian connections are an everyday endurance. As for flaws, I sometimes repeat Hans: *Perfection is but an invitation for nature to destroy!* I cringe to hear myself paraphrasing his maxims: *If décor's too tight, rooms become like many people—uninviting.*"

"Decorating is its own psychology."

"Oh, my God, yes. Months of work, everything artfully in place, then the owner announces a move. Or a whole house is made uniquely beautiful, but the owner prefers to live in the den, or worse, descend to the rec room to ride exercise bikes, or more often drink hard liquor from a subterranean wet bar. Many women prefer to do their drinking in the she-shed. It's funny, but I think some people don't really feel comfortable in a beautifully appointed room. Yet as clients they all demand them."

"But why?"

"Easy. To show other people an illusion."

• • •

After lunch, we strolled the flea market, pausing to study objects once new or energetically sought, now abandoned. "Those teacups," Roberta said. "That jewelry, the stack of clocks, the sun-warmed linen, all are taken from rooms that once connoted the illusion of permanence."

"Permanence?…an odd phrase."

"And junk dealers are their own breed. I mean how much effort the business of hoarding requires. Rich buyers deal with that same loss of freedom."

"So, the flip side of dearth is excess?"

"Exactly! Poverty and wealth. Both extreme time-wasters. Both prisons. And the very fact that these waylaid estates now get carted from town to town, means that as tokens for life everlasting, they've already failed someone."

"It's like Pompeii. Or Egyptian tombs. Expensive trophies wrestled from the stiff fingers of their original owners."

"Yes. Each item *here* probably represents a stroke, a heart attack, a cancer. And of course, in time, we'll all be parted from our own soup plates, our own silverware, our own collection of the world's great books."

"Not to mention old toasters and adding machines! The broken things we can't part with."

"On a deathbed, I wonder how many people wish they'd grabbed for more?"

Roberta lifted a piece of linen and looked closely at its weave. "Most probably wish they'd grabbed for less? Leaving surplus frustrates many wealthy people. A lot come to realize how wealth made them a target of envy. So many say they can no longer trust."

"Over-spending won't stave off dementia, will it?"

"My problem *too* is surplus—a whole warehouse full! You know how expensive storage units in Santa Margarita are. I've got to get these Pasadena people to at least take a farm table or a credenza."

We stopped at a waist-high cardboard carton holding hundreds of loose photographs. "Imagine, a box full of people all once worthy enough to stand before a camera," I said.

"Yes. Now strangers meeting strangers in a box of anonymity." She raised a handful and the glossy faces shuffled against one another. Lifting the lid on a box of slides, she held one up to the sky. "How many boxes of these have I been hired to put into storage? The unidentified ghost children, a baby's first steps, that trip to the Grand Canyon, the mermaid show at Weeki Wachee. Sometimes the owners narrate: 'Oh, that's us riding donkeys in Jordan, camels by the pyramids, eating *authentic* Iranian in Berlin, here's that glorious woman who sold paper masks on a street in Katmandu!'"

"I suppose the hope is authenticity? I mean not to remain tourists?"

"The lives I deal with are mostly inauthentic. Women and men who hit the golf course or exercise class six times a week. The lazy going off to places like Alabama to buy ass implants on the cheap. Some study art, some fatten in French cooking classes. Some work jigsaw puzzles. I fear I'll end like that. A pupa dreaming of metamorphosis. Maybe that's why I've had so many lovers, of late Eligio, among them."

What I knew of continental affairs was that married lovers were presumed, but rarely mentioned. How provincial that idea of multiple lovers made me feel.

At a stack of albums, we opened a leather-bound book, its black and white photos held in place by small corner squares, men standing in tailored suits, hair slick with brilliantine, women with Marcel waves pressed beneath hat brims, Spring dresses darted with quality's fit. On the back of a wedding photo a fine green ink scripted the name of a photo studio in Prague. What became of these long-forgotten people posing between the wars? And what of the shop? The camera? Did any of them survive?

The woman running the stall approached. "That one has something special." Her delicate fingers pulled a slim envelope from a secret flap along the spine. Inside a packet of photos showing the same young men, only naked, a single strong key light defining form.

"Any comparable photos of the women?" Roberta asked.

"If there were, they've gone missing," the woman said, before moving to help someone else. We studied the nude anatomies, the gymnastic musculature, the genitals. Over sixty years come and gone since these men had posed, so vigorous and proud, the unclad flesh forever in its prime, like heroic figures painted on old Greek vases.

• • •

In the parking lot, an elderly man with a red-veined nose stood beside Roberta's car, acting as if the vehicle belonged to him, a ruse for the traffic police. It was an absurd charade, as everyone in town knew the orange Bentley belonged to Roberta. She handed the old man some money, and he deferentially bowed, kissing each bill, saying they'd enable him to support one of the town's formidable churches. She laughed at the ridiculousness of that. Her dog, Apollo, waited in the car and began excitedly licking our hands as we got in. Roberta started the engine and pulled back from the curb.

Moving to a peculiar village, where Roberta had already been living was a bit of luck for both of us. It delighted her to have another American available for cocktails or dinner, and for my part, I was grateful to have such a seasoned guide to explain the do's and don'ts of daily life among a somewhat insular and prideful group of Italians. Roberta owned a grand, ancient house—one of three such residences—among the fifty or so other pastel dwellings—all of us hanging from the side of a cliff above Levanto.

Now at the edge of town, we drove uphill and on one of the mountains in the distance I could actually see our village. We paused at a wide, cobble-stoned bluff with a breathtaking view of the sea. The motor was left to idle as we stepped out. Before us lay gallons of glittering water, a phosphorescent body, stretching far and away, and at our backs the formidable mountains rose. I felt the metallic taste of salt on my tongue, it seemed to hang in the air, then, as if on a breath from long ago, I heard and felt the voice of my long dead mother: *Romantic landscapes allure, but better to ache through not belonging than to fool ourselves into thinking we do.* More than twenty years since her killing, and still that gentle use of inclusive pronouns brought an involuntary shiver to my shoulders.

Roberta sensed my absent drift. "You alright?"

I tried to form a convincing smile. "Sure." How does one explain a life gone by without taking a lifetime? I turned toward a cliff in the distance. "I was just thinking how all the world's money moves like water, evaporating here, collecting over there, sometimes drought, sometimes dripping with excesses like stalactites in a cave."

Roberta gave a suspicious glance then followed my gaze up the mountain where an imposing villa stood amidst a meridian crown of Cyprus. "The Agnellis command that."

"Yes. I know."

As an heiress, Roberta had been trained to spot money, her eye particularly keen to note places where wealth intersected delusion. She was the first to laugh at her own eccentric education: several seasons at a Swiss boarding school, a stint in Brighton where the costly tuition granted attending ladies official use of '*the Roedean O,*' a British vowel so embarrassingly grand, Roberta wouldn't dream of sounding it. Her final degree in communications came from a Seven Sisters college, a diploma she claimed held the same usefulness as confederate money. 'Only thing worse,' she'd say, 'would be having one of those silly teaching degrees—whole classrooms of children compromised by the notion that a teacher need not master an academic subject.' Even Buddy agreed, saying why keep teachers ignorant, by focusing only on methodology? His conspiratorial mind thought voiding the teaching profession of true academic accomplishment left young teachers less able to abandon teaching for other lines of work.

Roberta continued to stare up at the villa. "People always think they'd like to do what the Agnellis do all day…I mean sit around in a commanding house, graciously hosting parties, ordering servants about."

"I heard the Duke and Duchess of Windsor stayed there."

"Poor Wallis and her lost king. They fought a revolution against the crown… the church…jealousies of entitled women…not to mention men. They defied the monarchy only to ossify in their own palatial prison."

"The royals sell their brand like soap."

"In England some defend it, saying that manufactured lore is of great benefit to ordinary people."

"I disagree. Royal propaganda turns the public into buffoons, thinking they can't live without royal speeches, laughable dowdy hats, a belief that gold-coach spectacle is an important heritage."

Her eyes twinkled. "I never suspected you for an anti-royalist, Walker."

"A mere pragmatist."

"I secretly envy those able to follow the ways of many, members of an orchestra for example."

"Ah, and here we differ. For I think of Hitler youth, and then alas—no joiner I."

"One day there might not be anything to join."

"Yes, we'll shift back to feudal systems, global corporations overtaking the borders of every nation and re-writing law."

"People always assume a government they've come to know will always be the one they have."

We returned to the car and drove back down to sea-level, following along the underside of the elevated promenade, its structure supported by a tall set of arches reminding me of stadium bleachers. Arriving near the train station we turned, inching along a street racked with postcards, straw bags, and olive-embroidered tablecloths. From the doorways, shop owners glanced with come-spend smiles.

At block's end, several necks craned to watch Roberta spin the wheel for a tight turn. "Italians are car crazy," she said. "Orange paint on an English make fascinates them. Hans wants me to get a plainer car."

"You know how opposites attract. Maybe you keep it just to *repel* him."

"Thank you, Doctor. I think you've found the root of all my problems."

"I'll send you my usual bill."

"In Brighton, while reading Jane Austen, I learned of the dangers that face young women with yearly incomes. So many rich schoolgirls I knew married husbands, who once relieved of financial responsibility, regressed into immature boy-men."

"The Swiss are certainly less showy."

"Say what you will, at least Hans's fingers weren't dipped in honey hoping to stick to my money. His concerns were more proprietary—what I should wear, what purse to carry, what running shoes are right for the gym. I mistook control for care. Still can't believe I put myself under his spell for so long. Now, of course, our *gemütlich* period has expired. Telling me how to wear my hair is out of the question."

"Speaking of definitude, Lydia and Buddy were at it again last night. That same discordant tango. Sharing the patio, I can't help but hear every time their well-worn record skips on a pitiful scratch."

"Walker, why can't you, in God's name, just tell them to scram? They never stop upsetting you."

"I keep thinking of my mother. She once said: *where the sea and sky join together you'll find a thousand shades of blue.*"

"I don't mean to hound, Walker, but are Lydia and Buddy all that's bothering you? You seem distracted. Back there on the cliff, you looked a million miles away."

"Just life, that's all." A church bell sounded the noon toll.

"Shit. I'm late for my appointment. Pasadena people don't like to wait for mere tradespeople."

I asked Roberta to drop me at the square and when she drove away, Apollo, paws up on the back seat, gazed with worried eyes from the back window. Was she off to meet *Eligio*? Even in silent echo the name intrigued while also making me jealous.

I drank a beer at a waterside café, and seeing the sky darken, hurried to the flea market before the storm. Passing the mirrored armoire that hours earlier had so mesmerized the two identical men, I now couldn't resist peering into the spotted glass myself. Did I really look so tired? I slid my palms to smooth my humidity-thickened hair. It bounced back fuller than before.

Down the quay, the vendor with the photo albums was rushing to unfold a plastic shower curtain with which to cover her wares. She pardoned her inability to let me shop as the rain began in earnest. I helped anchor the corners, then bid adieu to run for shelter.

. . .

In Torino, my publisher, Malcolm Rinaldo reviewed my assignments, developing the calendar so I would receive my fair share of new acquisitions. As a poet, I often felt ambivalent about editing books that didn't interest me, and Rinaldo's taste in literature often mystified. I did my best to hide it, aiming my knocks at the translations, the ill-used adverbs and prepositions, looking for governing pronouns and governing tenses, but I think Rinaldo sensed my reticence. He held tremendous respect for poets, and frequently sought my opinion when a book was being considered for contract. I tried to admit my preferences honestly, for if he bought the title, I might be one of those poor souls assigned to edit, translate, or write the English introduction.

During the course of our meeting, various colleagues came in and went out, mainly those handling contracts and marketing. When pending projects came up, against my better judgment, I brought up the idea of Lydia and Buddy doing something on Italian cooking. "She really is a good cook. And her husband is trying to make her the next Julia Child."

Malcolm looked at me with patronizing eyes. "Child may be a star in America, but *French* people don't buy her books...or even give a *merde* about them. We Italians are just as chauvinistic. An Italian home might have one cookbook, say *La Tavola*, but American housewives will have fifty, and most of the people still can't cook. At least nothing of quality. Easy to sell that kind of thing there. As an Italian, you couldn't compel me to read what an American makes of my *own* cucina."

"A television thing is in development... her husband is in talks to figure out ways to market it."

"Hmm. I suppose if he succeeds a link-in could sell well the book whatever the content. It needn't be truly miraculous."

"I think that's right."

"And, if we don't do it, someone else might."

"I can assure you; she is interesting."

"She'll have to be a genius to get anyone in Italy to watch. Italian cooks are proud, fussy not to mention protective. The greatest skill can't compete with national pride. The United States and Britain love Child because they know nothing about food. As publishers, our consideration must always assess if something will work continentally. Then at what scale. In what languages. Any doubt...and it's best to pass."

"Hazan has certainly proved popular."

"For those who like *science* in their stew! The recipes are way too exacting... go to the market on a *Thursday*—buy a rabbit of *only* medium size—raised *exclusively* on clover—look for one with blue eyes and a loping left ear! Ridiculous!"

"It sells."

"It's selling fantasy...but not cooking. I mean good luck finding *that* rabbit in America. Or for that matter, *any* rabbit."

"Yet, the book is a huge success there."

"And I just told you why. Of course, I'm not saying we couldn't try. But first I'd have to know if she has something to tempt Italy with...unusual techniques? Powers to appeal to our varied palates? And you know as well as I do, what plays in Milan might very well *not* play in Calabria."

"I see your point."

"Again, I'm not saying we couldn't try it. Let's discuss it again in the future."

I nodded, and our meeting was over. Ordinarily, during my business visits, Rinaldo took me to dinner, often dining with various authors passing through Italy. But he and his wife were celebrating their wedding anniversary, so he arranged for me to spend the afternoon with Marco, a new book designer. Over lunch, Marco told of a private dinner party he was attending that night and invited me to join. "They're book people. I'll call to say I'm bringing you."

Glad to not be sitting alone in my hotel, I gratefully accepted. After work, we traveled to a rotund villa on a hillside with a splendid view. Our hostess, a pedigreed Argentinian, displayed a house where books, syntax, and syllogism were a fetishistic devotion. We dined at a table with several literary intellectuals. Across, was seated a young woman from Philadelphia who'd just finished a fiction degree at Iowa. Already she had a contract for her unfinished book.

"My editor says there's no sin so great as not signaling to a reader where a work of fiction is going! So, I'm working to indicate that."

Other voices joined in. "But that implies there's always a pattern. Copying that which came before."

"We must know the history of our field," said the man who'd brought her to dinner. He wore a ponytail coated with coconut-scented oil, and a paisley scarf tied at his throat. Last Summer he'd published a biography of Borges.

"Doesn't everything depend on imitating what came before?"

"How can one encounter true originality? I mean the novel idea?"

The salon full of erudite bookworms seemed to intrigue the young woman, and not sensing any danger, she worked the table and began to tell of her youth, a childhood spent in the Germantown neighborhood of Philadelphia. Her account was vivid, an enclave of strong-willed neighbors living in an area of historic but rather run-down houses. The woman then confided how there were frequent upsets at home. She went so far as to say she was the survivor of a dysfunctional family.

The man with the ponytail who brought her, winced, but did not stop squeezing lemon juice over an enormous grilled fish. The woman from Philadelphia sensed immediately that she'd made some kind of mistake. Any doubt vanished when the publisher of a British satirical magazine stopped scraping artichoke petals across his lower teeth. Through a mouth full of green mush, he repeated the words *dysfunctional family* as if they were being viewed under a microscope. As a publisher of satire his life had been spent parsing usage with exactitude;

poking popular clichés for him was sport. Then with great precision he asked: "And just what *is* the *function* of a family?"

The man winced again, now jabbing a fork into the half-lemon, to disrupt the pulp. Whatever childhood agony was imprinted on the young woman, the critical, questioning looks, deepened the pain. Her eyes darted, their luster gone, as if she'd just traded places with the grilled fish lying before us now having its backbone removed.

The man adjusted his paisley scarf, then sniffed as he cut the fish into portions. "I see the point," he said. "If one makes it out of infancy, then hasn't the function of a family been bestowed? I mean, from whatever family might enfold one?"

"Well said," the publisher agreed, selecting another artichoke petal. "Why allow our families to be taken hostage by yet another Oprah-esque bromide?"

Having been punched in the gut by a pair of linguistic pugilists, the young woman took her blows in silence, discovering what she probably already knew: cruelty wasn't merely a function of a dysfunctional family but the whole world.

I felt the familiar desire to want to rescue the woman, but as my mother's son, I knew public defense or compassionate understanding might only add to her failure. Rather than grandstand, patronize, or appropriate her agency by shining my own goodness, better to do nothing. The woman's face remained stricken, transformed from someone youthfully naive, once thinking her story to be of interest to others, now finding herself to be someone growing bitter and world weary. She spoke not a word for the rest of the meal, and no one asked any more from her. Still, her injury roiled my head with involuntary empathy.

And just what *was* the function of a family? After dinner, Marco drove me back to my hotel, and having had a bit too much to drink, he suggested that if I happened to be lonely, he'd be willing to come up to my room for a while. It wasn't the first time a married Italian man had shown sexual variance towards me. It seemed to be something the culture permitted, provided it remained clandestine. The idea did flatter, he was attractive and somewhat younger, but I knew Marco to be not only drunk but married, and if he wasn't up to including his beautiful wife, then why relive a one-night stand every time I entered the Torino office?

To avoid giving a direct no, I pretended his offer was a joke, and that I found his sense of humor to be amusing. In my professional and affable retreat, I declined to mention how awful I'd feel cheating on my fantasy lover—Eligio—especially as even to imagine that, meant I might be cheating on Roberta, my closest friend.

. . .

As a result of the trip, my desk now held three new manuscripts. I read for more than an hour, grateful to be back in the village losing myself in work, stopping only when the Swedes' phone rang across the terrace. The device, an old black rotary model, hung in the alcove off the Swedes' hallway and Buddy shouted up the stairs that he'd get it. A conversation began, and I heard the name "Mr. Garafallou" repeated several times.

At dinner a short while later, he and Lydia sat flush with excitement. As always, they took the first share of cold cuts before handing the platter off to me. "The producers want in on the televised stuff. And of course, they need to raise bank. And so do we."

"It's time to sell the salons. I don't want to go back."

"One of the television consorts I've met with suggested travel inserts for existing venues."

Buddy also reported his negotiations with the editor of *Hearth & Table* magazine. "The guy's jazzed over the walnut cream piece. Said he'll send one of his best photographers from New York. He detailed circulation numbers, claiming a sagging readership. I told him, look man…Italy sells! He heard me. Now, his production team is moving at an unheard-of pace. Get this, thanks to yours truly, we'll be in as early as the issue after next! And if that rag moves, they might go for a series! I told him our phone's ringing all the time with offers."

Lydia looked annoyed to have his knife gesture at her. "No, it's not." She lit a cigarette.

"Please, my dear. I do deserve some credit. As I told Phil, food articles are an ingenious way to promote the magic show. Italy is many people's *numero uno* fantasy. Oh, and…hey Walker. Were you able to pitch the cookbook idea?"

I recounted a more positive version of my Torino conversation. "The publisher is very interested. But a good point was raised. What will compel Italians to watch an American making their dishes? And on the way home I thought of a solution, simply incorporate some real Italians."

"Already thought of that. *Hearth & Table* is especially eager to shoot photos of Lydia, and I'm going to add Pina in. An American cooking alongside an old white-haired Italian? Well, what viewer wouldn't want to dream it could happen to them? Seems to me, to gain market share, all we gotta do is keep putting them both in the kitchen."

"Great," I said. "But will Pina agree? She's territorial. Took three years before she'd let me even walk through the kitchen if she was preparing something. And even then…she still turned her back. Sharing the secrets of her cucina is a trust that must be earned."

Buddy looked at me with new determination, eyes glowing like furnace coals. "With Clinton in the White House, folksy living is in. And since no one wants to eat what they eat in Arkansas…Italian food fits the bill! The timing is right to snag the peasants. And I can make it funny. Italians *love* comedy."

. . .

At dawn, I heard Buddy on the terrace, calling out the arrival of a taxi. Lydia's heels came clicking down the stairs, to cross over the patio, before climbing the marble steps to the roadway. She was headed to another out-of-town gig, in a magic show they'd yet to let me see.

Not wanting to be trapped with Buddy all day, I rose, dressed and snuck up to the parking lot, managing to catch the early bus. I could've gone to meet Roberta for coffee, but she usually slept in.

At the familiar curve, our bus braked, letting the woman with the lost child climb aboard. Today, she surveyed us as if we were heads of lettuce at a produce auction. Our bus then continued angling downward, stopping a dozen times for schoolboys and men and women carrying boxes and market bags.

On the final hairpin turn, for a heart-stopping moment, the rear tires swung dangerously close to the road's edge. Why hadn't I bought life insurance? Once the streets leveled out, our speed increased, and a moment later I was disembarking on the square. Not sure of what to do with myself, I bought a newspaper and ate a breakfast panini, then decided to go to the cinema to improve my Italian. The film involved a savage murder, and I listened wearily while a pair of insipid detectives ran around ferreting out the case. Any fascination with the criminal mind had ceased long ago; the criminal mind for me felt predictable, always the same. And yet so many entertainments fed a gluttonous appetite for murder and violence.

Emerging from the cinema, I found the sky overcast once more, the palms swaying, their tops greened from a season of plentiful rain. A week had passed since Levanto's last flea market, and returning to the photo vendor's booth, I attempted my own act of *incoscienza,* casually locating the album with the hidden packet of naked bodies posing in Olympic strength.

The vendor recognized me and saw past my indifference. "You must like?"

"I guess what strikes me is that there isn't a trace of self-consciousness around the mouth or in the eyes of the men."

"People posed more natural then," she said. "The camera hadn't yet stolen innocence."

To buy the album was a temptation, but it bothered me not to discern if the life depicted in the hidden pictures was public or private? I doubted purchasing something intended for private viewing would exacerbate my own secrecy? But it could? For whatever reason, the thought of Roberta seeing the images on my coffee table made me wary. Better leave the dead figures for some other necrophiliac to procure.

A fine mist began to descend. The vendor smiled as I once more helped cover her stall in plastic. "*Déjà vu!*" she said.

A stiff breeze whipped off the sea's chilly waves, making a walk through town with an umbrella impossible. I shopped at the vegetable stalls for some wet onions, then hit some shops for other groceries, before running with soaked feet to catch the bus. Halfway up to the village, the mist converted once more to rain, and droplets of water streamed down the foggy windows. It irritated me that I'd wasted most of the day simply to avoid Buddy. Especially as concentration on work had become more difficult of late, sleep often a restless tangle of sheets, dreaming of Roberta dancing with Eligio.

Dancing, that respectable way to test someone's physical capacity for rhythm. I thought about how the great discos of New York were mostly gone, and I resented their shuttering. For three years, I'd danced there nightly, the strobe-scaped beat miraculously pulsing loneliness and personal sorrow away. In the discos, I saw how long-held puritan repression had yielded to the urges of the patrons. It was there that I first heard people say *everyone's bisexual.* But as in other historically cautious times, a plague had challenged that expressive freedom and its candor, returning the full scope of sexuality back to the default: all that was forbidden, taboo, prohibited, decadent, inhibited, repressed, condemned, and secretly exclusive.

In the clubs, the most attractive men, the most sexually alert, the most versatile, the youngest, the most obedient, were first to die. Married bottoms were also particularly stricken, their need to hide, shamefully unveiled, the full range and spectrum of their desire exposed. Men on the down-low heard the churches of their youth deliver the sermons of olden times, the epidemic restoring condemnation, human sexual history narrated with cause-and-effect scorn, wherein to seek sexual pleasure without procreation was sin. As a curious onlooker, I wasn't touched by the disease, and my envy of those with a license to explore, converted to feeling glad I'd not been possessed with their allure.

In the daylight hours, funerals replaced affairs, eulogies for the beautiful men, and women abducting many potential partners; fantasies, once featuring any number of bodies moving every which way, parties of two, three, four, or more—all possibilities permitted across lines of race, sex, and age—now grew lonely. By night, newly adopted standards for safety chilled desire. Far fewer claimed versatility—that term no longer aimed at everyone as it had been in the seventies; the antics of ambidextrous heroes—Bowie, Reed, Baldwin, John, Jagger—or Donna McKechnie's marriage to Michael Bennett—now in hindsight appeared like aberrations, somehow dated and reckless.

Many who felt natural in such libertine attitudes mourned the joy and popular acceptance that the disease stole, but to note the plague's sparing of the sexually impenetrable was frowned upon. Also unkind, was to mention how the epidemic scared many effete men into pretending they could be tops—even absurdly dominant tops. Only the cruelest mentioned how the plague often spared the ugly, the avoidant, the wall-flowered, the prudish, the impotent, the shy, stunted or the voyeuristic people like myself. To speak such fact showed ingratitude, and was in part unspeakable because many uncharismatic survivors were now ordained by necessity to become representatives advancing a seriously political fight.

Might I have married because of the plague? Was it a secret hope to assure a healthy normalcy? Did I think marriage was worth the price if it would stave off an early death in the corporal world? Was I hasty? Did I ignore my struggle to sublimate to her emotional moods—the inanity towards anything she couldn't control? In hiding from the plague did I in playing a good husband allow myself to transform into the perfect patsy?

The bus reached our village, and I disembarked. Inside Roberta's courtyard, the rain pooled, reflecting the grand portico against the sky. Annoyingly, Pina answered my knock, saying the Signora had gone to Santa Margarita. I thanked her and walked on alone to my house, imagining how at this very moment, Roberta and the mysterious Eligio might be in a dimly lit bed somewhere making love.

•   •   •

It took ten days for the new *Hearth & Table* contracts to come through, and soon after the Swedes' kitchen and our adjoining terrace hosted a circus of tripods and cameras. Buddy placed a small voice recorder on a shelf, then ran around with a 16mm camera filming anything that caught his fancy. Lydia, apron tied at her waist, waited by the counter, dusting her hands with a thin film of flour. Pina stood working a mortar and pestle, arguing in Italian that chocolate sauce had no place on a chestnut cake.

"Please," Lydia said to me. "Can you translate her dialect? Tell her we've no choice."

To negotiate magazine politics with one's housekeeper is disagreeable. Pina was a lone wolf not interested in any pack, and it had taken years for her to begin to accept me. Now, because of my cousin, her singularity returned. I was sacrificing my acceptance to explain: "The chocolate manufacturer advertises in every issue. They dictate a chocolate dessert must follow the Ligurian pesto."

Pina shrieked. "This chestnut recipe is five-hundred-years old. One couldn't get cacao then!"

"Tell her to quit yapping," Lydia said. "We're also baking plum tart. Tell her to focus on that."

There was a loud greeting as Roberta entered, and the sight of her leaning on Eligio's arm startled me. I felt an enormous disappointment envelop my body. From the back, I reviewed Eligio's contours, shoulders square with downy hair along the nape of his neck. Given Roberta's rigorous aesthetic, one would expect a more dashing gigolo, or at least one easier to despise. The eyeglasses, the thin hair, that small chin all surprised me. They suggested no gloss of romance. His ordinariness actually made him more compelling, and I felt the poorer not to have known him sooner. Upon introduction, I realized he flirted with men as well as women, and I pretended not to notice.

Buddy began to dole out costumes, and handed me a fuchsia vest. "Today's shoot oughta hit newsstands by April or May, so the magazine specified citrus shades." I buttoned the vest, while watching Eligio don a shirt of hideous lime-green silk. Roberta received a sweater set in pale-blue cotton. We stood staring at our ridiculousness, when Mr. Garafallou entered. As producer of the magic show, he'd allowed himself to be the last to arrive, tipping his homburg. A rounded back wore a great plaid raincoat, and his face carried the most distinct set of eyebrows I'd ever seen. At times they overshadowed his eyes.

After more introductions, Buddy handed him an anorak of pale orange. Garafallou disliked it at once. "What fascists magazine people are." He objected even more to the face powder coming around, his nose patted for shine. "Quit now, or I'll look like Quentin Crisp." Buddy finished him off, grooming the eyebrows with a toothbrush until they swept out like fantastic wings.

"Thanks to these outfits," Lydia said, "some mom in Ohio will read the article and insist her family also dress like Easter eggs!" I noticed a new habit, where her voice amplified its proclamations, an implied exclamation point placed at the end of each sentence.

An hour later, and the photographer, sent from New York, stood on a step-ladder, his camera clicking as Lydia sifted chestnut flour into a pottery bowl chosen for photographic charm. Pina had by then conceded to the chocolate sauce, but only if it were placed in a pitcher as an option not a requirement. "Hold that desk lamp for extra light," the man barked at Eligio. "And Lydia, give your expression some theatrical excitement."

"Be careful, or she'll start mugging for the camera," Buddy said.

The plain batter was poured into a greased pan and put into the oven. "Now just go on," the photographer said. "Prep the second dessert, or we'll be here all night." For better composition, he asked Lydia to change places with Pina. Once more Lydia sifted flour into a well-chosen bowl while Pina cut cold butter into chunks on top. "Okay, ladies, tilt your torsos and slow your movements." The camera clicked as they blended pinches of sugar, salt, and ice water. Once the dough was lightly mixed the bowl was set into the freezer to chill and Lydia insisted a smoke-break be called. The photographer agreed, but he kept working, moving a plate of plums to capture the chalky blush on their taut purple skins.

Buddy asked to look through the man's viewfinder. "I prefer you didn't," the photographer replied. "It's finicky." Denied use of the apparatus, Buddy pretended to busy himself with the tiny voice recorder, placing it on the counter. "Talk into it," he told Pina. When she finally recognized the device's purpose, it fascinated her. She began to speak, converting her village dialect into formal Italian. "Thoughtful cooks recognize one another through certain evidence: the way an olive is pitted, an onion chopped, or knowing how to handle knives…the slicer, the boner, the parer."

"Never knew her voice could sound so gentile," I whispered to Roberta. "Like a senex."

"Or a nun explaining things to children."

The photographer loaded more film as Buddy watched his every move. "What always makes me holler, is a sojourn down to Rome. Have you been?"

"Planning to go," Buddy said. "Got a ton of books on the history. I get the ones with loads of pictures."

"Well, you haven't been to Italy if you haven't seen it. Get yourself down there, man!"

"We intend to," Buddy said, his reply voicing a strained but energetic cheerfulness. "We're also in discussions to secure other parts of Italy. It's not easy to work all the scheduling into our budding *superstar's* itinerary."

The photographer's concentration on the camera showed he didn't really care about Buddy's reply. He announced it was time to prep the plums. Again, the women assumed unnatural postures to capture light. "Splendid. Splendid." The camera clicked. "Keep talking as you cut and pit the fruit."

Roberta chimed in, "Venice is also fascinating."

"Just avoid the rainy season," Garafallou said, coming up to inspect. With the plums sliced, Pina brought the cold dough from the freezer and placed it on a marble slab. Still using formal speech, she narrated how to flour a wine bottle, using it to roll back and forth. With the right flatness in the dough achieved, she lifted the crust into the tart pan, her leathery fingers pinching the edges to crimp in a rustic style. The camera clicked. "Lydia, help her! Dust your hands with more flour." She stuck out her tongue. The cameraman clicked.

"Hey what's the name of that French brandy?" Buddy called out.

Lydia scratched her nose with the back of her wrist. "You mean Armagnac?"

"Yeah. How do you spell it?"

"How should I know? You're the poet. Look it up."

Pina pulled the oven door open, placing the unfilled tart shell to bake beside the cake. The aroma of chestnut wafted through the kitchen. The camera clicked.

During the next break, people were beginning to tire, and Pina lifted a wicker hamper and extracted a bottle of homemade limoncello. Her unexpected hospitality beguiled, as she distributed small glasses to us. The photographer followed her, camera clicking. "Is it true you understand English?" he asked.

It took Pina a beat to realize the man was addressing her. Her solo defiance grew visible, and she muttered something about him being released from a lunatic asylum.

"Don't be fooled," Lydia said, in a snide aside. "That old broad gets more than she lets on."

Opening the screen door, the photographer focused his camera on a pergola of small grapes. "They look like green pearls! Pina? What variety?"

Pina's dialect returned. "Framboise. The Swedes brought them from France. They'll ripen but never make a wine. Like all things French, they ferment to poison."

"Some say Italian wine brings madness!" Eligio joked.

Pina's eyes glared disdain. "No solid Italian man holds such sniveling attitudes toward wine!"

"Signora! Don't discount me for a little jest. Each Fall, I help Mama make our wine!"

Garafallou returned from a phone call. "Lydia my dear, in all this baking frenzy I forgot to mention news about our little magic show. Three new bookings have been arranged. One near Milan!"

Lydia's smile turned into a smirk. "Milan? I see. Well…hopefully you'll continue to book us as far from the center of town—or anything of human interest—as possible."

"The show is not a tourist junket."

"Perish the thought."

Garafallou tipped back his glass. "Perfectly tangy-sweet!"

Pina shrugged. "There is no other way."

The chestnut cake and the browned tart shell were brought out of the oven and set on the cooling rack. At the photographer's command the two women moved in slow motion stirring custard in a saucepan over a low flame. Once Pina decreed that it was the proper consistency, they worked quickly to spoon the mixture into the tart shell.

The photographer leaned over them on the ladder. "Fill it slower." Pina and Lydia obeyed, slowing their movements, as if caught in a magnetic force field. "Go even slower. Lydia, I want you to layer the plums like they're heavy stones."

Buddy, out of sorts to no longer be art-directing, paced slowly back and forth on the sidelines. Garafallou noticed and took pity, pouring him a fresh shot of the limoncello. "You know, wonderful foods can also be found in the Piedmont, Emilia-Romagna, and further South. You could go to Sicily."

The pastry was returned to the oven. Lydia followed the photographer's instructions, scraping the wooden spoon against the sides of the saucepan, then bringing the remnants of custard to her lips. The camera clicked.

"You know…I have a house in Corsica," Garafallou said. "Plenty of room! I invite any and all of you. Buddy? Lydia? Roberta? Can your husband get away from Zurich? We could all share expenses!"

"He's a shrink." Roberta tilted her head demurely. "He can't just take off." I realized that with Eligio here, the idea of Hans seemed absurd, and in my mind I saw how traveling together might ruin the trip for everyone. There was no need for us all to run like a pack of lathered mules to France, Corsica or any other damn place.

The kitchen grew oppressively hot. I opened the kitchen door and went out onto the terrace, startled to see Eligio was following me. The two of us stood staring down at the terraced garden, at a small green pear tree glowing in the sun. "It's hot in the kitchen," he said. I agreed. Eligio motioned up behind us. "Look at that sky. I'll be hiking in the mountains just above here in a few days, part of my quest to look for clues in the tunnels. The view from up there is like standing on a cloud. Perhaps you'd like to join me?"

The suddenness of the invitation caught me off guard. My heart began to pound. "Sounds great. I mean, like fun. But wouldn't I just be in the way?"

"Nonsense," Eligio said. "The only proviso is that we wear long pants. The bushes are dense."

Could I again be imagining? Was his tone flirtatious? Could Roberta overhear us? I glanced at the door. How could I possibly be finding her lover attractive? It felt like committing a felony. In the discos, I'd danced with many a provocative man, but we rarely left the dancefloor, and even in that fluid world, I'd never felt this heightened degree of pull. Did Roberta study him this way? Eligio's eyes met mine for a second, yet failed to clarify anything. He deftly changed the subject. "Can I ask how you ended up living here on the Cinque Terre?"

"A publisher in Torino, one I'd freelanced for, offered me a job and I leapt at it, mainly because it came with a promise that said I could work from home. With my employment secure, I came down here and bought a house."

Buddy burst through the screen door, Lydia on his heels. Eligio looked at me and raised a scrutinizing eyebrow. Was this meant as a comment on the quarreling couple, or an expression of something else? In a manner I hoped unnoticeable, I shifted my stance, increasing the distance between my body and his.

Lydia and Buddy settled on a lounger, she massaging his shoulders, before lowering her hands to the back of his waist. "You used to be so thin." He brushed her away. She stopped, hands mid-air. "I was trying to be sweet, but I see you prefer castor oil." She unfastened her hair, twirled it, and then pushed it back up again, readjusting a rhinestone clip.

Pina used her elbow and hip to open the screen door bearing a tray of coffee. Under her arm she also held a bottle of mineral water, preserved cherries settled at the bottom. The photographer followed, camera clicking. "Red cherries! Great color!" The photographer wiped his lens. "Lydia, let's hustle while we have the light. Go in and get the cake."

She leapt up and came out, carrying out the chestnut cake as if it were a religious icon. "Who wants to watch me cut?"

The photographer began to shoot. "Okay gang. I want you to gather like at a birthday. Lydia don't put it down yet. Let me catch you holding it." The camera clicked.

"No one touch a thing," Buddy said. "Wait till he gets it." Under pictorial consideration, the cake was eventually placed at the center of the table, and Lydia picked up the knife. On the photographer's count of three, she slid the blade in ever so slowly, forming wedges, then lifting them one by one onto porcelain plates. The photographer moved the gravy boat holding the chocolate sauce closer.

"Gotta get a good shot of that!" Buddy said. Lydia leaned in to him. "Your ear looks like a big pork chop," she said, and bit at the edge for the camera.

"For God's sake! Will you quit it?"

Lydia scowled, then turned without a word and went back inside. The malignancy of their union, laced with barbs and comeuppance, was more like the rivalry of siblings. The photographer ignored them and focused the camera on Eligio. "So, you're Italian?"

"Yes."

"Live in Levanto?"

"Chiavari."

"Keep talking. What line of work you in?"

"I study art." The photographer reached to brush Eligio's hair back. "Keep talking. What kind of art?"

"Hidden treasure. My mother told me how before the war, Levanto sometimes hosted Benito Mussolini. Legend has it that he secretly used the train tunnels to hide not only arms, but also paintings."

"Museum stuff?"

"Yes. Renaissance works."

Lydia returned carrying the tart, her manic mood had shifted, displaying no residue of her previous ire. Once more, following orders, we gathered around the tart. The camera clicked. "There! That's it! Lydia, pretend you're having an orgasm!"

"That's easy," she said, her mouth exaggerating an ecstatic expression. Buddy looked away.

Garafallou sensing trouble tried to distract. He edged closer. "Buddy, do you think we can get Eligio to explain what the tunnels might reveal? I mean, what he hopes to discover? Devotion?" Buddy looked perplexed.

Eligio saw that it was wise to play along. "What I hope to find is maybe something more like…let us say…people's endurance? The role that art plays in wartime? Or how for many it becomes a symbol, worth risking one's life for?"

Roberta's hand came to rest on his shoulder. "Eligio discerns which stories of hidden loot are lore, which are fact. He gives lectures."

"Where do you speak?"

"Genoa. Sometimes the *Accademia Ligustica* invites me for a special panel."

Garafallou looked impressed. "Fine old place."

"I've read poems there," I said. "And felt lucky to be asked."

The photographer called to Pina. "Signora, start passing plates and cups."

Garafallou took his, a cup in one hand, the saucer in the other. "I was just thinking how a strong link connects the work of art and science. Buddy don't you think writing like science uses imagination to invent and test." Buddy agreed, still looking confused, as Garafallou continued. "Of course, the occupations are also divergent, the way astronomy differs from astrology…law from philosophy…theology from faith."

"Well, perhaps art and science are also both sacred?" Eligio said. "That's why the story of the tunnels deserves proof."

"You mean to confirm the lengths people are willing to go in order to honor art?" Garafallou turned to me. "Poetry has to exact similar effort. Wouldn't you agree, Walker?"

"I can admit to being but a cipher. One frightened by self-doubt."

Buddy lifted his glass in my direction. "Here. Here. All we can do is scribble the stuff down, brother. Otherwise, our dreams turn to dust."

Pina forced a cup into my hand. "By the time *he with the camera* gives the order to pour, the coffee will be cold." Her voice in dialect dripped with sarcasm. The photographer looked at her with irritation, and commanded she commence at once.

"Does anyone still think poetry matters?" Lydia asked.

"Oh, it matters," Garafallou said, spooning sugar. "If it doesn't…then why in totalitarian regimes, are poets so often the first to go to prison? Because poets dare to tell the truth. And they do it memorably and succinctly. They express the moral conscience of the people!"

"Fascinating," Eligio said. "And I must agree."

Roberta leaned in. "Mr. Garafallou. You produce plays. That's also an art."

"Currently, I produce magic! In fact, I'm guilty of bringing this lady to Italy."

Lydia swiped her finger along the side of the knife to scrape custard. "You certainly didn't bring me for the sake of art."

Garafallou ignored her. "Walker, your poetic pen must follow in that great tradition. I mean the ordinary soul intensified…to speak pure truth."

The photographer interrupted. "Please! Stop talking. Concentrate. Pretend you're in a focus group. Deliberate the sweets. Act like you are savoring the sour plums, the sweet cream, the warm crust."

Garafallou nodded chewing and chewing. He traced a fingertip along the rim of his plate then poured some chocolate sauce on top. "Our palates have certainly evolved in five hundred years."

Pina pushed the gravy boat away. "Chestnut is too delicate for chocolate."

Buddy began to laugh. "Some recipes are best left to memory. My slice is as dry as dust."

Responding to his jibe, Lydia dropped her plate to the table with a thud. "All right. So, we won't put it in the fucking magazine. But then we *won't* have a fucking dessert with fucking *chocolate*." Any doubt about the difference between marital jest and anger vanished as she stormed back into the house.

. . .

A growing stack of brown envelopes cluttered my desk. I tore the top one open: a first chapter, the manuscript's author building a timeline of minutia about Proust. *The past is but an invention, a collection of moments curated for meaning.*

I sensed the timeline of my own life drag, but I continued reading all afternoon, sometimes stopping to count the number of envelopes remaining. On a whim, I rose and pulled the chaise away from the wall, sliding it across the floor until it sat beside the glass door to the balcony. Why hadn't I thought of this before? From my regal eagle's nest, I could work in a horizontal position and not have to get up whenever I wanted to observe the patio. For the next hour I studied the Proust manuscript, and sought to develop an introduction not too biting. "Intros aren't critiques," Malcolm Rinaldo loved to say. And if my intro became too critical, I'd be lambasting the taste of my employer.

The Monterosso hike with Eligio was but a few days away. Anticipating this brought many questions. Ought a man confess to a tease, the possibility that there was no intention of pursuit? I pulled over a mason jar filled with pencils and began to sharpen them. Contemplating eros and ethics with someone improbable like Eligio made no sense. Was this desire the added risk of an erotic triangle? Maybe secret yearnings remained safe that way? The mystery of intention remaining unsolved? The true risk was in betraying Roberta. Even to dwell on the possibility felt morally caddish. And why should a gigolo be the first man worth the bother of a sexual self-audit?

I quit work for the day and caught the next bus down to town to have a swim. As I approached the salty water, the clouds bloomed fantastic overhead. Let us not forget that a human's first hope ever was the sky. A radiant haze over a calm ocean can still enthrall the planet with its luminous brilliancy, as it has done for far more seasons than Shakespeare, Dante, Borges—or even Eligio. I dove into the golden reflection rising to lap back and forth perpendicular to the shoreline. How our family used to love water. And at fifteen, Mom's lithe swimmer's build and her unusual beauty brought a ladder to climb. Before turning twenty, the great eyes of the age—Horst, Green, Avedon, Stern—had all photographed her. Horst said her mystery dared his camera to find it, and he knew mystery was the thing which most captured the heart of another.

I stayed in the sea for almost an hour. Later a sense of boredom about what to do next brought anxiety, and led me to stroll the main shopping street of Levanto, though there was nothing I wanted to buy. At one end, I noticed an unfamiliar set of stairs leading to some terraced gardens, and I decided to explore them. Near the top, an elderly woman, clad in somber black with a faint floral print, stood sweeping. Like the poor bee-stung baby's mother, this woman too appeared to have been stitched to these byways from swaddling cloth to midnight shroud. The traveler is always under scrutiny from those who never leave home, and so I smiled. Her face turned to the yellow wall, preferring the close-up sight of stucco to an American so forward in his ways. Perhaps for this woman, ex-pats connoted yet another plague, wallets stuffed with too much money, suitcases with too many clothes, and luncheon baskets weighted with champagne but no turnips from the garden. Maybe she worried I'd pen a postcard describing her in pre-feminist cliché: *Passed another withered crone today sweeping the corridor of her confinement.* There was no way to assure her that I'd never put *that* line on a page.

I continued on and soon found myself on a narrow street I'd never traveled before. At a cobbled bend, stood a small, pale house, a garden on three sides. The kitchen window was propped wide, and from a whitewashed ventilation hood streaked with soot, I saw a beautiful leg of lamb hanging from a piece of twine tied to its shank bone. A hefty cut, eight or nine pounds, not especially young but not mutton either, it smelled delicious. Just then an elderly hand came into view and gave a nudge, and like a trapeze artist, the meat wound hypnotically round and round. When the leg finally slowed, it paused, glistening in midair, hot fat sputtering onto the embers. Then the roast began to unwind ever so slowly in the opposite direction. After a while the mysterious hand was seen again squeezing the juice from a lemon. Today, cooks would probably prefer to dial an oven, or fiddle with an electric rotisserie's pointed hasslers, but this leg was cooked with unimprovable technology—the plainest of holy trinities: fire, string, a single nail, all of it set into motion by the human hand.

I resisted the urge to knock and invite myself in to dinner, and instead, continued to the next alleyway that led back down to a more familiar side street. After this fantastic spy work, my appetite stirred, and at a Salumeria window, I searched for some savory meal to carry home. As I neared the train station, I felt the need to urinate and decided to use the public restroom down by the tracks. Its large vestibule led to a dim alcove, floor-length urinals forming a giant horseshoe pattern on three sides, with two men standing in one corner. They seemed unnaturally quiet, the stillness holding charged a tension, something furtive being telegraphed. Sensing myself as an interrupter, I nervously veered toward the stalls. The first was locked. The second had a trash bag over its bowl. The third stood filthy with excrement and lacked a door. Feeling foolish, I returned to the porcelain wells, as far from the other two as possible. We stood unmovable as boulders, the corroded plumbing between us. By sound, I appeared to be the only one making water. No, these men weren't buttoning up to move on, they stood their waiting ground for me to leave.

I glanced in their direction, and in corporeal engagement they both stared back. Fast as the speed of light, I turned my head back forward, my scalp tingling, then pulled by hypnotic curiosity, with nerves a-jangle, I engaged them with one more glance. They checked, then rechecked me, perhaps to verify that I wasn't a policeman in plain clothes…or perhaps to see if I wanted to join? The younger, in his early thirties, face set with pale eyes, lifted his striped shirt. German? Danish? Cock-proud, he stepped back. The other man, older, with goatee and cap, had a darker shade of skin. Moroccan? Algerian? His eyes launched a tennis match between the man's massaging foreskin and me. Defiantly, he dropped to one knee, pressing the violet glans against his lips. *Corpus spongiosum*—public fellatio—an ancient act found in public toilets around the world.

Avoid notice. Even Christ witnessed prostitutes and venery. Did he feel this same illicit thrill? Did he know guilt? I faced the tile wall. Think of Gerard Manley Hopkins, his daily written confessions recording impure thoughts and acts with Jesuitical introspection, his painstaking notes recording his masturbations and fantasies, the body a vessel for impurity. Known for rigorous honesty, his pages referred to men as beautiful and dangerous. To repress homosexual encounters would likely have been unbearable for a man with his cataloging impulse. He'd have found a way to diary physical deeds, even if in code.

And what about *these* men? Met before? Did they claim to be straight? Straight-acting? Straight-looking? Top? Bottom? Versatile? Highly acrobatic? So many labels. I allowed another look. The younger man pressed his palm to the back of the older man's neck, forcing the throat to take more. On his finger, a thin, pale strip of skin revealed where a wedding band had been. Then something I'd noticed many times before—racial differences could meld easily if a chance for sex were drawn.

The younger man's fervor pulled back, breathing suddenly labored, fingers compressing several strands of semen onto the dirty floor. Instantly he disengaged, pulling on a tissue roll he'd brought to hastily clean his genitals. The kneeling elder masked his sudden loss by offering an inquisitive glance in my direction. My trance held me spellbound. He rose and came to stand beside me, the interchangeability of his partnership astonished. A warm hand placed itself on my left hip, and the magnetic fascination switched off to leave sudden revulsion. I pushed away, determined to be the first man out of iniquity's den. I secured my trousers in the vestibule, and hands shaking, fumbled some coins into the dish at the attendant's empty window. Back on the street, walking at a good pace, nerves still jittery, a clinical feeling overtook me, a constriction of mood, the need for a good scrub.

*   *   *

Once at home, I sat in a hot soaking tub for an hour's worth of somber ablution. Leaning back on the padded headrest my mind evaluated its associations. Such ruminations, their sources unproven, certainly weren't science, and yet if clouds can get born again and again, as they did during my swim, sun rays teasing through the torn edges, then why not ourselves? Did my anonymous encounter with those men manifest a lonely forewarning of my own future? Did it connect to my infatuation with Eligio?

If I hike with Eligio, might sexual sameness also be my future? I've dated few men, but might there be a time to form such a union more permanently, one day morphing to mirror one another? In literature there were stories of pansexual characters, but none seem to express what I was experiencing with Eligio—a male pas de deux—one where both protagonists still engaged in passion, and even lust for women.

The next morning my longing to swim continued, but an attempt at the sea was cut short once more as heavy rain began to fall on the surface of the water. The foul weather scrapped other errands as well, and I huddled under the awning of a shoe store, sidewalk streaming, the striped fabric overhead dripping water as it pooled. The collecting canvas began to sag, then gave way, buckling from the awning's metal frame, gallons of rainwater cascaded down around me. Desperate, I ran toward the wide-open doors of an adjacent church.

After drying off as best I could, my towel annoyingly damp, I placed myself in a wooden pew in the second to last row. Of the parishioners present, all three were women, and none looked under the age of sixty-five. I'd often read statistics that a great number of the world's faiths were in decline, people even claiming that their societies were advancing toward a post-religious culture, science and modernity replacing or outgrowing ritual and superstition. But just wait until people grew frightened, by war, or crime, or famine, or plague, and while many might lose their faiths under these pressures, most, like migrating birds, flocked back to nest in some form of mysticism, hoping to pray their terror away.

At the altar, a priest with thick, dark hair climbed to test the lectern's microphone, reciting the opening lines of the Lord's prayer in Latin. I understood the cadence better than the words, but it sounded noble. Another pair of elderly women entered, wrestling wet umbrellas, and after adjusting the volume, the priest left the podium and walked down the aisle, stopping to shake hands with the smattering of worshippers, who bowed their heads as he welcomed them. Reaching my row, he spoke to me in Italian. "Bad weather has made you a convert?"

I smiled. "Yes, afraid so."

The priest realized I was American. "What city?" he asked, his English charmingly shy.

"All over. My early years were spent in New York, Philadelphia and Pennsylvania's capital—Harrisburg. I've lived on the Cinque Terre for the past seven years."

"Seven years! In Levanto?"

"Yes, but I've never been inside this church as I'm not Catholic."

"In my father's house, all faiths are welcome. I'm Padre Vincenzo. Only here a short while myself. I come from Brazil."

"Brazil! Well, how on earth did you end up here?"

"I seem to be too liberal for my own country, so they sent me over to be near the Vatican hoping to breed acquiescence, or at very least conformity. Some of my peers say that I deserve to be fitted for a straitjacket." He chuckled with gusto. "My expansive vision irritates them. Someone must've decided the best thing would be to bury me here in the provinces. I guess they'll keep trying to figure out other outposts to hold me until the day comes when they just kick me out altogether!"

"Well, I don't want to keep you, Father. You must have a lot to look after. I imagine priests are overworked? Needing sleep?"

"Oh, I'm not one of those grown bitter by the demands of my calling. It was my choice to professionalize my faith. And if no clocks tick in a casino, why should they chime in a church?"

"I see your point. But I assure you I'm not here to be a burden."

"You needn't be in trouble to speak with me. Meeting people from other places actually cures me of a frustrated wanderlust!" He paused and then changed his tone. "I'm about to make myself a cup of tea before the service. Maybe you'd like to join me while you dry out?" Padre Vincenzo appeared to be an ideal movie star version of a priest, and I easily accepted the invitation.

In his office, drinking a cup of hot chamomile, he asked about my family. Avoiding details, I explained the story of my divorce, my work as an editor, and how I found academia an ill-fit for creative people. "Yet they still sometimes hire me to deliver talks."

"What brought you to live here?"

"Sad memories. Things beyond my control. I didn't feel right in America." His empathy broke through and I went on to explain something about the condemnation of my mother, the men she chose to love, our ostracization, how many shades of skin there were among us. I then for some reason revealed what I rarely spoke of—her untimely death.

"I'm sorry." The priest's eyes showed compassion.

I thanked him. "America is trying to grow out of its conflict over race. But there's still too much Montague and Capulet. That divide is one reason why I left."

Padre Vincenzo seemed to admire my honesty. "One day DNA will expand our convergent links. That will alter everything. As for otherness, we often find blessings outside our assigned culture. And perhaps living in exile, people embrace or gain something not possible in their own country? Just look at me."

"And nowadays so many clergy in their forties or fifties say they're burned out. They create whole psychological programs to manage their suffering. They hate it when I poke them and say good luck getting a real job. I mean, might not a plumber in his forties or fifties also feel burned out? And which job is worse? Tending to the poor and sick, or breaking your back by lying under a sink to weld someone's dirty pipes? And yet, we allow little self-pity to the plumber. We say, my goodness, man. What do you think life is? A holiday?"

I told the padre about my American visitors. "They're struggling to make meaningful work for themselves in television. And yet their presence here is complicating my life, dragging the past in like a sack of rocks." His face softened with understanding.

It was then that I realized I had no real need to talk about Lydia and Buddy, and segued to what I really needed to talk about, starting with the two men I'd witnessed at the train station. Padre Vincenzo nodded appearing agreeably human. "An age-old question," he said. "Is the natural man bad? Many would want you to believe so…to control others through morality."

His forbearance persuaded me to bring up the subject I'd felt even more in need to speak of, but how awkward to confess to a lovelorn priest my well-populated world of fantasy paramours, especially my growing attraction to Eligio. "I label him a gigolo, but he really isn't. As far as I know, he takes no money. But he allows himself a mysterious sexual freedom that fascinates me. In fact, the very thought must sound deranged to you? Like a man struggling with an opiate. And yet I'm attracted to know this area within myself."

Padre Vincenzo looked at his mug of tea but said nothing.

"I feel shame for my bluntness. As a priest, I imagine you're now bound to say such attractions mark the end of our species…that AIDS dooms us to perish…or you'll quote Leviticus."

"Well, your luck today is finding a priest, perhaps one of but a few Catholics in all of Italy, even the world, who has no wish to burn you at the stake!" Padre Vincenzo chuckled at his own hyperbole. "If the attractions you describe are deranged, then the priesthood too might also perish. But I better hold my tongue, in case the walls are listening! As I told you, I'm already marked as *persona non grata*."

"I hear what you say. At least, I think so."

"What I mean is…nunneries and monasteries, like prisons, hold many curious love affairs. Not to mention divinity schools, seminaries, even catechism centers. Any of these can act as socially acceptable gathering places to hide sexual confusion…or to draw those who wish to avoid sex altogether. And if these places *aren't* drawing those with sexual aversion…then they run an alternate risk of attracting those with forbidden yearnings."

I nodded. "My own doubts might belong there."

Padre Vincenzo took a sip of his tea, and after consideration, continued. "Well, I believe at a certain point in life, gender is meaningless. But in admonishment lies control. Many orthodox sects use restriction as a way to maintain spiritual, financial, even architectural wealth. It's easier to repress evidence of normalcy, calling a romantic pull between devout followers—sin. As for the book of Leviticus…blasphemy there is punishable by death, yet we rarely kill people who swear. It also states animals can't be slaughtered outside a temple. Leviticus asserts that childbirth generates impurities, and that sprinkling blood offers atonement, yet most of us don't view birth as impure, or sprinkle blood anymore. The shedding of Christ's blood is the permanent replacement."

"Father, let me be honest…I've never read Leviticus."

"Neither have most! Yet despite the incongruities, Christians and non-Christians love to quote Leviticus as a weapon against sex. Why not also cite how it forbids relations with a menstruating woman. Or a neighbor's wife. Leviticus claims eating oysters, shrimp, scallops, mussels, clams...also birds of prey, to be unholy. And the vegetarians get roused that Leviticus deems meat a *sanctified* meal. It's also sinful to crossbreed livestock, or plant seeds of different varieties in one field. Your American Indians with their squash-bean-corn planting combination would fail here."

"When it comes to Leviticus, we as humans are all indigenous! Even the conquerors are indigenous? My belief is that God ignores human claims that separate us by geographical claim. Did you know Leviticus also says wearing cloth blended from two textiles makes one unclean. And one must also refrain from picking up sticks on a Saturday! In ancient days, extremists demanded expulsions from the tribe for these infractions, and sometimes execution was practiced. But the bigger question is...might not intolerance itself be the true crime? To reference biblical passages as governance can put us in a very narrow box, especially if there are sticks to be picked up on a Saturday!"

"Padre, that's astonishing. And yet many human minds open through poetic verse. I mean, psalms and parables can navigate life."

"Yet, how many feel guilty for pursuing some kind of physical pleasure or attraction? Often those who've withheld these impulses, can't abide that some other human animals have pursued such pleasures with no apparent consequence! They only know pleasure must have a price. And often—that pleasure-price is procreation."

"Devout procreation also has a price? Procreation!"

"Children can be a challenge to one's youth. And those who've paid that price...sacrificing themselves in parenthood, can often feel betrayed by leniency toward sex. To say pleasure itself is natural somehow robs their sacrifice of marital justification, even civic status. And many who've denied themselves pleasure can become persecutors...often the most cruelly self-righteous. But tell me, might not poets be susceptible to this kind of blind sanctimony as well?"

I laughed. "We would be wise to bypass and ignore how often poets sermonize! Present company included."

At that, Padre Vincenzo quickly glanced at the wall clock and put his tea mug down. "Speaking of sermons, it's my turn. I must hurry! But please...return any time. And in parting, let me add the most important question to consider: It's not *whom* you love, but *can* you love?"

• • •

Before going to dinner, I put on a crisp new shirt and selected a bottle of wine to bring to Roberta. It surprised me to find her still in her bathrobe, initials monogrammed lavishly to one side of the lapel. The confident look that usually distinguished her was absent.

"I apologize for not being dressed."

"Everything all right?"

"I'm a hopeless case. Today my little Don Juan told me that he's adding someone new to his list."

"A list?"

"Yes. Or should I say a stable? Like most polyamorous jerks, he enjoys boasting. I used to think it European sophistication. Now I think it's just cruel."

I tried to suppress a fear that the added name on Eligio's list might be mine. Or could it be someone else? Maybe more than one?

In the kitchen, a pair of branzino were brought out from the refrigerator. "Vescovi just brought these. Marvelously fresh!" She dredged the fish in flour and placed them in a skillet of hot oil. "Of course, I'm a hypocrite. I keep a husband while expecting Eligio to remain true."

"Have you discussed it with Hans?"

"What for? Ours is a marriage in name only."

"Is there something particular that draws you to Eligio?"

"That's difficult. I guess Hans has something to do with it. The Swiss are so reserved, and he's a shrink to boot. His cultural and professional need is to distance himself from discussions of personal things. Eligio, being Mediterranean, is very expressive, which, Hans would classify as pagan."

I uncorked the wine, and Roberta maneuvered a second sauté pan, its copper lid clattering on the counter. Her stove was an Irish cooker, a luxury imported by the previous owner, a member of Irish parliament.

"God knows, I must sound totally naive," she said. "But Eligio's attention and focus toward me as a woman is intoxicating. I don't know that he fully gets my point of view, but he at least pretends to value it. I can talk about anything, and he remains agreeable."

Instead of the expansive formal dining room, Roberta and I preferred eating in the kitchen at a tabletop that pulled out like a drawer. Perched on stools, we toasted, and began to eat the delectable fish, our entire meal seeming to center on talk of Eligio.

"A hustler is in truth, a kind of hypnotist," she said. "This one is not the brightest, and way too shallow, but he gives me the sense that I'm the center of his world. If it's a scheme to make his narcissistic prey dependent on him, it works. I mean, just look at what a mess I am today. I feel injured. Yet I know the rules—have from the start. But, girls like me need to be kept comfortable. Trials aren't for us. It's not that we can't *handle* trials, we just don't *want* to. We long for ease. And we don't really crave the men who can be bought, and always look for men who can't be bought. And yet if they can't be bought they don't usually find rich girls like me very interesting."

"You are being very hard on yourself."

"I've been given many toys in my life. And have tossed too many aside without even unwrapping them. Now I must pay."

"You are a psychological curiosity."

"Don't be glib. Not now, when I have my hair down."

"What do you really want?"

"I want everything. I want it all."

"But that's the same as saying you want nothing."

The telephone beside the refrigerator rang, she answered, and a noticeable change came over her face, the angle of her chin shifting downward. My interest in her caller was noticed. "I'll take it upstairs," she said. "When I get there would you hang up the receiver?" A small box of vanilla sponge cakes was placed before me, and she hurried out. I held the phone to my ear, but the person on the other end made no sound. I heard Roberta say she'd reached the bedroom extension, and I placed the receiver back onto the cradle. Was it Eligio? Hans? Someone else?

. . .

Our mealtime was definitely now ended, so I rinsed and stacked the plates, feeling that wearying, morbid, all-too-familiar isolation. Waiting in a house where the owner is invisibly present can stir awkwardness. One hopes not to mishandle a precious vase or be caught sitting in the wrong chair, the body politely on guard for when a hostess might suddenly reappear. Pouring the last of the wine, I left the vanilla cakes unopened and wandered into the living room. A set of bronzed mirrors lined one wall, doubling the space, while the far wall held built-in cabinetry of dark-wood, the glass doors dangling fat purple tassels from the keys. Inside the shelves housed art and decorating books stacked horizontally, the kind of volumes that dress up a coffee table, or people present to each other to indicate their participation in culture. Three sets of patio doors had been propped open by stones, allowing humid air to breeze over the velvet furniture, the curtains billowing like sails on a boat. Above it all, the ceiling glowed under a luxurious glossy-pink lacquer, like the inside of a shell. I stepped out into the vestibule, and under a time-darkened fresco, a small table held a picture book: *Levanto, Gateway to the Cinque Terre*, a deliberate and generic choice aimed at an idle guest or irritated friend waiting out some phone call. I sat on the staircase and opened the book. Must be the lover. Hans would never keep her this long.

The town, nestled atop an incline, dates to ancient times, where a prominent thirteenth-century castle still commands, once the region's most important defender. And in the season when undulating swells curl in from the South, the oceanography forms some of Italy's most superb surfing.

The editor in me longed to red-pencil the text to omit the local guide sincerity, and how lazy to use a French adjective in a book about Italy. Yet people invested in such silly tourist publications all the time. I turned the page and studied a photograph of Levanto's bay, said to possess an unusually buffered ocean floor. Defeated by abandonment, and feeling too anxious to sit by myself any longer, I returned the book to its place on the table, and left Roberta's house.

· · ·

Reaching the front of my own house, I opened the small gate and came down the pink marble stairs to find Buddy and Lydia on the terrace, dinner dishes still scattered between them. "Take a nightcap," Buddy said, and reached for another glass. He poured stiffly from a half-empty bottle of Scotch. Lydia stared trance-like into the flame of a candle, then whispered as if in contemplation to herself. "I can't do magic very much longer…too many things go wrong."

Buddy handed me a drink and indicated an empty chair, then swayed in her direction. "Baby, when people see the show…they don't even look at Phil."

Lydia turned to look at me as if for sympathy. "Now these rats want me to do both—magic and cooking!"

Buddy gulped from his glass. "Not a chance! I'll see to it. Soon you'll only do the cooking thing. I spoke to Garafallou today, he says the pilot is gonna sell. Once the deal is set, you'll never have to do magic again. We'll break the contract. Say you've had an exhaustive breakdown. Whatever it takes."

"Oh, Walker." Lydia reached into her bag and pulled out a handbill printed on thick, shiny paper. "Would you just look at this!"

I brought the flyer over to the light and studied the image of a man wearing a turban standing beneath a superimposed proscenium arch: *Phil Filbertson and the World Beyond Twilight!*

Lydia lit a cigarette and took a furious puff. "That son-of-a-bee has printed thousands of these. Can you imagine, I'm not even mentioned? Not anywhere except the back, as an afterthought."

I turned the handbill over to see a hot-pink sticker had been affixed: *Special assistance by Miss Lydia.* She watched my face for reaction. "Special assistance! Miss Lydia! Sounds like I work in a *massage* parlor!"

The back of the flyer also featured old publicity photos of Phil, standing in front of Caesar's Palace in Las Vegas, arms linked with other magicians for a group photo: Blackwell, Orson Welles, Nicky Mococo, and the Amazing Kreskin. Other shots showed Phil posing with Debbie Reynolds, Eartha Kitt, and Eric Clapton. A telephone number for direct dial tickets was printed along-side another odd photo of Phil shown dining on a yacht with Christina Onassis.

Buddy showed his irritation. "Probably a deckhand or an oarsman! At the Sands, I heard he dealt blackjack!"

"No doubt wearing that same moth-eaten tux." Lydia snatched the flyer away. "That idiot thinks he's heir to the throne of Siegfried and Roy, or Doug Henning. But he can't rise up the ranks because he's stuck with me…Miss Lydia, the shrew!" Her eyes began to well with self-pity.

Buddy put his arm around her and looked at me. "Phil rejected the new name I came up with. *Sophisticatto!* Isn't that great?" I nodded only to console, but it embarrassed me to see them wish to represent themselves as sophisticates. Buddy stood proud. "I even wrote a subtitle: *The rhythm of sophistry!* Isn't that great! It's better than *Beyond Twilight.*"

I pointed recognition at him with my finger like a cap gun. "Yes…yes. Amazing!"

Lydia opened her purse and drew out some tissues. "I'd be so proud to tell people I was in a show called *Sophisticatto.* But no…that Albanian dictator refuses! Why I'd rather say I work in a chicken factory!"

"Don't you worry, baby, the Beetle is making progress with the television folks. The right director will catch up with you. Then you'll kiss doing tricks with that little con-man goodbye."

Lydia took a swig of her drink. "I'm not getting any younger."

"The pilot's gonna sell. You'll rocket to the moon!"

I stirred my drink and took a sip. "By the way, have you two decided when I can finally buy a ticket and see this thing?"

"No buying!" Buddy hollered. "You'll be comped! In a few weeks we'll be opening in a new space, only an hour from here. Our first local venue! By then the bed-bugs will be out of it. Over the next few days, we're going to change the whole look of the show. Phil's about to find out what special assistance is all about! You'll see! We don't want you to come, until everything is fixed."

TWIXT & TWEEN

• • •

The draft of my introduction to the Proust manuscript sat on the desk. Many writers and editors, like hermits or monks, rely on nocturnal habits to work, but tonight, even if I had a monk's devotion to text, that wouldn't rally me. Get busy, I told myself, but instead, decided to ready myself for bed, unable to stop worrying that I should've been more patient with Roberta. Climbing between the sheets, I felt guilty knowing my departure from her house was accompanied by a hope to stir regret, that my absence would cause her some corresponding pain. Oh, why hadn't I just waited for her telephone call to end? Was I really that consumed by jealousy?

I dismissed the psychiatric theory of pain as a pleasure. Pleasure is the only motivator—the truly great carrot. But what of those men exchanging favors at the urinal? Did pleasure or pain motivate them? They'd acted prurient and conspicuous, exhibiting more compulsion than pleasure. Susceptibility to arrest must add obvious danger, as might the gloom of the men's room. Was the kneeling man a bug chaser—in mortal danger for his thrill? Perhaps fear and vacancy develop some hidden kind of fetishized desire?

As a boy in Harrisburg, I'd read newspaper accounts of Capitol employees going to tryst at lunchtime in the men's toilets of the State History Museum. And in the 70's, *The Patriot* reported quite a few people were soliciting at the rest stops on the newly built interstates. Vice squads arrested many men in the midst of same-sex action, including quite a few married men. On Interstate-81, near the racetrack, thousands of taxpayer dollars were used to pay for monitoring cameras, trying to stem the volume of truckers and other motorists seeking to get off with one another. Reading newspapers, I'd learned all sorts of people held the capacity for a full range of impulses, including murder.

As Padre Vincenzo alluded, history has recorded the natural durability of like-sex attraction, particularly in the daily life of prisons, boarding schools, warships, or the pup tents of the armed forces. For many, daily terror and being lost within isolating systems beyond control, seem to stir longings in people to bond with other people they might never ordinarily consider—anonymous bunk mates or a fellow draftee huddling in some sleeping bag. Lonely people who are in a frightening situation need the touch of other lonely people, a most important human impulse, stabilizing mental health, often tended just until dry land can be rejoined for the kind of comforts they can only get in port.

But my longing for Eligio carried no excuse, no war, no loneliness at sea, no incarceration, it must therefore reside in some other recess of my brain. So far, it was only fantasy. Like so many men, I'd not met or yet realized the man who generated enough electricity to cause me to permanently redefine my physical precincts. A loud rapping on my bedroom door scattered my thoughts like buckshot.

I opened the door and Roberta stood on the threshold, a fawn-colored trench coat tied at the waist, worn only to traverse the chilly distance between our two homes. "Walker, please, may I come in?" She unbelted the coat and removed it. Her low voice pleaded tearfully. "Please, I'm so sad. May I sleep in your bed?" The moonlight from the window illuminated her nightgown turning it into a sheer concealment—all gossamer and silk.

• • •

At dawn, the first crest of sun brought deep shades of maroon that soon lightened to violet, then to orange, until the entire sky turned beige, with long navy shadows stretching over the wet grass. I sat alone eating a solemn breakfast gazing out at the sea. I'd never surfed, but the fantasy of balancing on a formidable Italian wave was a pleasant thought. It was easier to think of surfing, than to accept myself as a man whose erection hadn't cooperated. I blamed wine and exhaustion, embarrassing misfortune, but more likely a guilt-born anxiety had brought about my fumble in the dark, born over my pending fantasy hike with Roberta's lover. What made me think I had what it took to manage sexual intrigue?

It was after ten o'clock before Roberta finally joined me, wearing my robe and carrying my mother's scrapbook. "Hope you don't mind…you know I love to look at this." I nodded and hid my disapproval. No mention was made of last night, and for distraction I described the dawn-breaking colors she'd missed. She didn't seem to care and instead studied the magazine clippings pasted in the scrapbook. "I've heard models in those days did their own makeup."

"True."

"Lydia said you and your mother lived in Harrisburg for many years. I always thought you were mainly in New York."

"Mom grew up in a town near Harrisburg. We didn't move back there until I was almost ten. Later I moved from Pennsylvania to a school in Connecticut. But none of it is Lydia's business. What else did she say?"

"Nothing. Just that it puzzled people to see your mother come back. Apparently, she'd done everything to get away?"

"It was desperation. My first stepfather died. We went broke. So that's why we went there, and Harrisburg is also where she found a new man."

"Lydia said it was a rebound thing?"

"Who says finding someone new to love has to be a rebound thing?"

"Gee, I didn't mean anything."

"Sorry. Guess, I'm touchy over it."

"I don't mean to pry."

"Life in Harrisburg often made me ashamed."

"Ashamed? Over what? Your mother was a beautiful model."

"In that city, we were refugees. I felt shame over Lydia too." I pondered my sudden willingness to divulge my past, perhaps I needed to offer it up as a kind of recompense for last night's disappointment, or maybe use it as a plea for compassion. "*Okay. Here goes.* It's complicated. I mean, because of the men, the kind of men Mom took up with. Maybe Lydia told you? You see…Mom preferred… or was attracted to dark skinned men."

A matter-of-fact composure overtook Roberta's face. "She did mention it." I knew the calm mask from a lifetime of seeing people wear it. An expression that I'd come to call the *progressive's reflex*—an initial surprise or even shock quickly converting to pretend it was all no big deal. A kind of pretend blindness, that would eventually give way to a faux kind of puzzlement. Then the questions begin. They'd want details of our suffering. Sometimes there'd even be prideful references to other racially diverse people they'd known.

Roberta arrived at this faster than most. "Oh…so then your stepfathers were *both* black?"

"Mom used to speak in bizarre nuance—say *more pigmented.* In childhood, I can hardly recall questioning anyone's origin. Too young to consider shade. My first stepfather adopted me. I knew no other dad. He and she were mine. I was theirs. We all loved one another. That's all I knew."

"But your biological father then…he wasn't white?"

"I know very little of him."

"Not a big deal. I mean, what difference does it make? Lots of people come from unexpected backgrounds…I mean, so what?"

I knew what came next. The drill was all too familiar. Racial curiosity would soon reveal itself, dozens of small glances in my direction, a quick steal when Roberta thought I wouldn't notice, her scanning of my every feature for miscegenate clues previously unnoticed or hidden. "You must see me as confused?"

"Of course I don't! But you are baiting me! When I was at Roedean, I went to a Spring dance with a boy from Pakistan. My first French kiss!"

"You're right. I was baiting you. Sorry."

For diversion, Roberta held up the book of clippings. "Just look at this. Here she's in Mainbocher. This page, Madame Grès."

"She never wore clothes like that in real life. I mean, over the top stuff. But she did take certain pleasure in wearing gloves. She was quite elegant, and I think some resented her because of that—especially certain women like Lydia. I think she cast her own crassness in part to contrast Mom and still does. If you want to understand something of what I'm trying to explain you should look at this." From an envelope at the back of the album I pulled out a wedding photo of Mom and Cole taken at the Waldorf.

"Oh, my. How beautiful they were. And you do resemble him."

"Not really. I told you he's not my real father."

"Oh. Right. I'm sorry. Look, I hope it is okay, but can I ask about your real dad? I mean, biological."

"Sure. But I know little. Whenever I asked Mom she'd simply say he died. They never married. I never met him."

"Then he could be anyone?"

"You mean even someone with more pigment?"

"You're baiting me again."

"Sorry. But I am quite olive-skinned, too much so, or not enough so, for some to feel truly comfortable or certain. In New York, when I was young, I don't recall the question coming up. In Harrisburg, because local people knew my second stepdad, it came up all the time. My mother's relationship with him put me under suspicion."

"But wasn't your first step-dad, the dancer, a darker man?"

"Yes, but Russell was much darker than my first stepdad."

"Did Russell become your dad?"

"Sometimes. He tried. And I was quite fond of him. I saw it was Russell's darkness alongside Mom's lightness, that could make some people crazy. Also, sexual freedom for women earned harsh judgment in those days, and hers had a racial component. So, forget it. Her own father never got over it."

"You knew your grandfather?"

"Yes. He lived in a brick house, bought just after he returned from World War II. A habitual man, the kind who trimmed his privet hedge every Thursday, and on every Saturday, would walk the push-mower in a different direction after someone at the hardware store said it was better for the grass. At the Hershey factory, he sculpted hot metal molds to shape specialty chocolates for holidays."

"Can I ask what happened? I mean…how your mother died?"

What relief it was to see Signor Vescovi in the lower garden, stepping over the small boxwood border. He sported a Tyrolean hat, and from his belt a pair of recently hunted rabbits hung, forepaws tied, their pelts brushing against his leather britches. In approach he tilted the rifle against his shoulder. "How abundant the feast grows with the aid of a gun."

Roberta averted her gaze from the gun and the rabbits. "More amazing is how much food the table can hold without a gun!" The old man was puzzled. She explained: "Arugula, tomatoes, honey, bread. I think in Greece they call plant-eating *hortaphagos*…can't think of the Italian."

He nodded. *"Ah bene, bene. Vegitariano."* His eyes swept down to the magazine clippings where mother posed in evening clothes. He began to move around the table to see them right-side-up.

"Does it bother you to pull the trigger?" Roberta asked, standing up to tap the gun. I appreciated the great subtlety she employed to distract him. I knew she was protecting me, and yet I felt additional relief in that our scrapbook séance had ended and would remain between us.

"The gun is fast. In traps, they stay injured and in pain."

Roberta gathered dishes, and I admired how casually she closed the scrapbook and placed it under her arm.

The kitchen door opened and Pina, as if having heard Vescovi, came out to mark her territory, placing a fresh pot of coffee on the table with great emphasis. Signor Vescovi pretended not to notice and simply gazed off toward the yellow hills as though a most peculiar rhinoceros had just appeared. Pina, having staked her claim, snatched the dishes and took them back inside.

"What is it with the two of you?"

Vescovi shrugged, unperturbed. "Family matters. We nurse old wounds." He too knew how to distract, and changed the subject by gesturing toward the olive groves on the hillside. "The first tree was planted by a Benedictine monk in the twelfth century. *Taggiasca* are the best in the world. In olden days, mules climbed the cliffs to deliver tools, food, and passengers, and take olives to press the green oil at the mill. Liguria alone had thirty mills. To live up here was thought to bring one closer to the gods. This terrace was a barnyard, your house home to many beasts. Now the mills stand empty but for rats. We choke in dust when the ugly diesel truck comes to take what we grow to the factory." His voice faltered, his eyes misting. "All in one man's lifetime."

We'd heard this tale before, its emotional sincerity still enchanting, but today it was interrupted by Lydia's nasal voice, heard coming through the filigreed door across the terrace. She was shouting something about an adapter for a hair dryer. Her loudness grated. When excited, Italians could be loud, but in our village, secrecy was generally valued over volume; suddenly I held new appreciation for the quietness of the Swedes. And yet I could only imagine how difficult it must be for Lydia to perform her daily beauty rituals in the tiny bathroom's stone sink, square block of soap pushed aside, oafish husband in the way. Who wouldn't grow shrill or shrewish?

Pina reappeared with a small pitcher of warm milk. Signor Vescovi collected himself, patted his ribcage, and announced it was time for him to go home for lunch. He tipped his hat and returned down through the garden, once more stepping over the boxwood. Pina muttered something unintelligible and went back indoors.

"How peculiar people are," Roberta said. "Every village the same: always a wedding, always a funeral, always a feud. You'd never suspect they were cousins. Years ago, I heard some conflict went down. She and Vescovi haven't spoken since."

"Pina is Anglican. But Vescovi is Catholic, right?"

"I think she converted for her husband. Vescovi dislikes church. A proud atheist, he laughs at those who sit in pews and confess to being human."

• • •

At breakfast the next day, Lydia wore a slim dress the color of dark cocoa, cloth-covered buttons running down one side. Buddy wore a tee-shirt printed with the logo of a bar on Martha's Vineyard. Coffee was poured, but Lydia declined.

"Butterflies in your stomach?" Roberta asked.

"Bats."

Buddy reached for a thick slice of bread and spread it with creamy butter. "Applause must pay its price."

"Like to see you get your ass up there."

He pulled his chair closer to the table. "No one's begging you."

Recrimination crossed my face, but too late for me to hide its disapproval. Buddy noticed, and my person was now placed under his suspicion. I passed him some gooseberry jam.

"I'm especially nervous today," Lydia said. "We're addressing stage business that's not working. That's always a fight."

"I'm sure you'll handle it," Roberta said. "We can't wait to see you on stage!"

"I don't want you there until all the changes are made. Oh, I wish Pina had left some orange juice. I could maybe drink that."

I got up, went to my kitchen, and returned with a carafe of juice. "Fresh squeezed."

"Oh, you're a lamb. It smells marvelous!"

Buddy watched her pour. "Too much citrus can turn acid in the stomach. At least eat some toast with it." One couldn't ignore how often Buddy and Lydia viewed each other's world through the lens of dismissal. Perhaps his convenient form of control was perfected to keep her exhaustive self-focus in check? He continued unabated. "Lydia, you haven't gained an ounce. People are gonna think you're turning anorexic."

Lydia kept her focus on me. "Beetle will be there today. To discuss new bookings." She continued on, and I felt my concentration drift, brain split between two frequencies: on one side her droning monologue, on the other, thoughts that led to the dizzying elevator drop that was Eligio. Out beyond, the sunlit aqua water sparkled above the unusual contours of the buffered ocean floor, nature's gift for superior surfing. My peripheral hearing sensed Buddy mention my name and I had to catch up. He said: "Finally, I have time like you do, Walker. After all the years spent in the classroom…I mean…now there's time for my creative stuff…for writing."

Lydia innocently sipped her juice. "And when do you expect we'll hear some new poems?"

"Don't you worry!" Buddy said. "I'm a worker. I support myself."

"Well, I'm the last one who wants to see creativity blocked," she said. "I support art. But if a day came when you said you didn't want to do the poetry thing anymore? Well, I'd support that too."

Buddy ignored her. "Hey, Walker, maybe you can have a look at my new stuff? Give me some free advice?"

"I'm never sure what to say about other people's poetry."

"Just critique me, man! Hold nothing back. Let it rip. That's what Ginsberg did. After Alan, I cherish criticism. He said I should be like a glass of water, clear and nothing to hide. But my new stuff might be too self-referential, too inward-looking. Still, as Ginsberg said, tackling political shit shows chops. But I'm not one of those writers who enjoys the tragedy of others. Still, I'm planning to do something on the Gavin Cato thing. But I need to do it in a way that doesn't look like I'm running around saying *look at me, look at me, I'm a social justice hero!* I mean, who wants credit for mopping another man's floor? I don't. At the same time, I don't want to be dull either."

"I wouldn't worry," Lydia said. "Many modern books are dull."

"Got that right," Buddy said. "And Walker, I'm sure you've seen this too. Faculty meetings? Where some dumbass gets up to praise the thinnest work by a colleague. Hey everyone! Our Olga just finished her paper on Slovakian bowel movements. Or today we celebrate the erotic poems of our very own Dr. Lipschitz! She's over forty, but traveled all the way to a fertility shrine in the Yucatan—so *empowering!* Or even worse, are those pathetic ones left to plead for themselves, bragging how their *Ode to Gandhi* poem got selected for print in the coupon shopper."

Roberta sat up. "I just remembered there's a parcel waiting for me at the post office. If anyone wants a ride to town—better hurry." Eager to bypass the bus, we all accepted and rose as a group to clear the remaining dishes.

*   *   *

Fifteen minutes later, we stood in the parking lot beside the orange Bentley. Roberta designated me driver, and perhaps to keep the bickering low, she sat in back with Lydia. Apollo debated which gender to side with and curled up on the back seat. As I held the wheel, winding down the mountain, Buddy, in the passenger seat, continued to excrete a narrative mastered over time, claiming total indifference to seeing his poems in print. "Publication for me, is not a *primary* goal," he said. I could tell his modesty was being used as a vainglorious shield, and my ears were pulled into another of his self-righteous circumlocutions. "The hacks in our English department come right out and say publication is too hard for them. They beg minuscule grants to attend bullshit conferences in crappy towns at crappy hotels where they read crappy bullshit papers."

"Isn't presenting to one's peers important?" Roberta asked.

"Ha! They're lucky if ten people are in the room! And usually, they just imitate some trend. Tenure guarantees their dead wood can rot."

I tried to calm him with agreement. "I'm afraid many colleges have become palazzos of mediocrity. Especially in the way they interpret English as a Social Science."

"At a religious school, you oughta see how many delude themselves. They mask their desperate atrocities, claiming prayer guides them. The forgiveness of their faith becomes a way to get away with savagery."

"I can't see why you let them make you so angry?" Lydia asked. "I mean, then you let them win."

"Some skip half the shit they're supposed to go to. Lame excuses. They walk around campus with yoga mats, claiming their stretch class is a medical need.

One guy wrote the entire faculty to say he had to miss a faculty meeting to show his girlfriend support, saying she was an alcoholic who'd that morning been bitten by a dog. Can you imagine! And the noblest excuse of all? Simply say, 'I gotta pick up my kids.' Any problem with kids becomes a saintly excuse, parenthood granting workplace negligence a special pass."

"You get too riled up," Lydia said. "If he's not careful, the resentments will kill him."

"Sure, I'm riled. In English departments, our literary heritage gets taken over by fat, lazy slugs who sit in dirty sweatpants all day and watch movies. They absolutely fetishize film! I'm sorry but film is not the same as literature. Don't you agree Walker?"

"The truth is few professors know how to measure literature on the basis of merit anymore. They only learn to discuss text through the biographical or class background of the writer. They don't realize that to study through that lens is really social science."

"I think I understand what you mean. You mean lack of excellence. Only the latest fads! These academic clowns, script themselves to the accepted positions of their school. They adopt the thinnest scholarship. Many publish only anthologies. Then they update them every few years, and *that* constitutes their major output!"

Buddy was on a roll, and I could see he did not fully understand what I meant by literature being studied as a social science. Roberta joined in. "May I ask something," she said, trying to act as a soothing voice of reason. "Might not screenplays be the drama of our time?"

Buddy rebuffed her. "Films depend less on writing than camera trickery, lighting and music. And most of them are crap!"

"Roberta has a point," I said. "Let's not forget Pliny wrote three hundred plays, but only a fraction remain. Maybe some of the lost and found ones were crappy?"

Buddy swept his hands back through his hair in frustration. "In our school, you oughta see how many don't like poetry. Guys especially. They say it's hooptedoodle. Too fancy. Too hard to get."

"It's always been that way in the States," Roberta said. "American men believe it shows strength to pretend no comprehension of art. Coarseness becomes a defense against culture. America does a poor job of educating most men. Stupidity gets to claim education is only for the fey. In other parts of the world, the poorest farmer can recite poems."

Buddy stared out the window. "Our farmers recite scripture. And being familiar with poetry is out of fashion. Besides, most poets have been sucked into postmodernism. The obtuse poems get too abstract for most."

"From all the manuscripts I read and edit, I've realized good literature is almost always self-evident. You just know it when you see it. But the good stuff is infrequent. And like the books of the Bible, some are simply better than others."

Buddy snorted. "The bible has the world's largest publicity department. Churches! They keep it on the bestseller list! Poets hold no commercial value. Poets don't write potboilers, mysteries, romances, or business books. Gathering blurbs and expressing our kinship to one another is all we get. And blurbs are just name-dropping bullshit."

In the rearview mirror, I saw Lydia wipe her sunglasses on a square of felt, then hold them up to the window. "Like the rest of us," she said, "poets *too* have to sometimes press their noses to the grindstone."

Buddy did not let her interrupt his rant. "I've heard you say it many times Walker. A poet's readership is invisible. Except guys like Ginsberg. He had a whole den of fans, usually sensitive boys."

Lydia chimed in again. "Looking for their daddy to sex them?"

Buddy ignored her. "Hey, Walker, did I ever tell you, I was at Naropa when Alan was there? Burroughs too? Burroughs knew me, called me by name, chatted me up all the time. You had to wade through his fans. I was there the night his son coughed up blood!"

In my head, I sounded a response and was about to voice it when Lydia placed her hands on Buddy's headrest and leaned forward to be closer to our ears. "Mentioning Ginsberg and Burroughs, in fact any famous names …isn't *that* a kind of blurb? Or brag?"

Buddy didn't flinch. "Many greats never get published in their lifetimes. Walker, you can back me on this."

It was now my turn for the violin solo I'd been playing ever since our string quartet formed. But wait, was I first or second violin? And if Roberta was the viola, then Lydia had to be the moody cello. Lydia made no effort to hide delight at noticing the quagmire Buddy had backed himself into. "That must mean there're also many *un-great* who also go *unpublished.*"

"Hey, lay off will you! Don't I support your shit?"

Lydia's face became a deadpan mask. She'd won by getting his goat.

"Being noncommercial has value for poets," I said, determined to ignore their drama. "It frees us from the deforming pressures of the marketplace. We can say whatever we damn well please."

• • •

The car passed between two stone pillars, each holding a brass plate etched with the name *Belacqua*. Having the name on both columns made one say it twice. Ahead of us the roadway curved through the well-clipped hotel grounds, the smell of shade wafting through the trees. Occasionally a glimpse of the sea opened, becoming wider, until at last we arrived at an enormous villa. "Phil stays here?" Roberta asked.

"This used to be someone's private house," Buddy said. "Eighteen bedrooms. The proprietor owes Beetle a bunch of money from a card game. As producer, Beetle works down his winnings by making the guy put both him and Phil up."

"Why do you always call Mr. Garafallou *Beetle*?" Roberta asked.

"His eyebrows?" Lydia said. "Like the hairs on a giant beetle."

A valet hurried over to park the Bentley, and Roberta knelt to put Apollo on a leash. Inside, Buddy greeted the *portinaio* as though they were old friends. "I know the way," he said, passing the old man's desk and leading us down a hallway lined with green moray silk. At a set of leather-covered doors, edges studded with brass tacks, he pulled one open and we entered a grand ballroom with pale gray walls topped by a frosting of white plaster. The soft decor, I thought, must make a delicate backdrop for weddings and other splendid occasions.

At one end, a man plunked notes on a grand piano. Upon seeing us, he lowered the lid and rose to his feet. "Ahh…a place of beaut-ee for one of beaut-ee!" He went to Lydia and extended a pair of pale, thin hands, exaggerated in a manner that reminded me of pantomime.

"Oh, knock it off." She crossed to the wall and threw her handbag on a chair.

Our host turned to us. "Welcome one…and welcome all. Welcome to *Belacqua!*" He shook our hands and repeated his name to each of us. "Ph-eel F-eelbertson…Ph-eel F-eelbertson…Ph-eel F-eelbertson." His strange, embroidered speech squeezed his vowels and sounded comic, reminding me of old werewolf movies on late night television. As a boy, I stayed up late to watch them, and for days after, went around imitating Maria Ouspenskaya, the gypsy intensely warning of the full moon's danger. Phil's baroque manners swept his arm to the far corner of the room. "I believe you already know our mee-racle worker, Mee-ster Garafallou!"

Garafallou nodded. "*Enchanté.*" But he stayed in his corner, still as a bison, wisely letting his star command the scene. Phil recited the hotel's amenities: herbal spa, lap pool, dining room. "Every night at the buffet, under a three-ton chandelier, our chef sharpens his knife to carve a great b-eeg steam-ship round of b-eef."

Lydia interrupted. "You're the one who always whines we never start on time. Let's get going." Phil offered no rebuke, but jokingly wagged his finger in her direction. Roberta and I took our cue, exchanging a few too many *arrivedercis* as we exited.

. . .

Tiny ravioli laced with marjoram and a liter of local red wine made a fine lunch at a sidewalk restaurant, Apollo at our feet, gnawing at the bone of a veal chop the owner provided. The topic of the charmingly ghoulish Phil Filbertson soon gave way to the bizarreness of Buddy's conversation during our strange car ride down to the village. "I agree with him on one thing," I said, "the mediocrity of many colleges. I did not want to stoke him, but I know for a fact, each year, dependent on tuition, these terrible mid-tier schools graduate a high percentage of clods whether they earn commencement or not. They must graduate the clods just to keep their academy doors from closing. Lately, there's also a trend for totally mediocre colleges to actually bribe states into letting them become universities! There's no end to how low it can go."

"Probably all backed by middle-class tuition-paying parents?"

"Yup. And neither they nor their children can recognize college is meant to advance critical thinking, and they're the kind of folks who can't afford to breed aristocrats, so they tell their kids to take marketing or accounting courses thinking that's the ticket to advancement." Once again I could feel Buddy's thoughts and ideas merging with my own. "They come for what amounts to vocational training, or to party at Spring break. Colleges have adapted to this, eliminating rigor, and handing out expensive certificates that make dumb promises about job placement."

"And yet they still call it college."

"Or now university!"

"And does that explain how a guy like Buddy could earn a doctorate?"

"PhDs are often sold like cemetery plots. And Buddy's a full-time professor. On a paid sabbatical! While I'm but an occasional guest lecturer, who must edit books written by others to earn a living."

"Did your parents go to college?"

"Mom was always working. Though she did like museums and thought they offered more than many colleges. My first stepfather, Cole, went to Howard for a while. He only did a few semesters there, and then left to study theater in New York."

"That's interesting. I mean…museums being an alternative."

"In New York Mom often took me to the Met or the Frick. We also went to the zoo in Central Park. I'd gaze at the monkeys in their cages, see lemurs, bobcats…snakes. She'd kneel with a small brown camera, clicking, at me. My face now the subject—not hers. By nightfall, back at home, the nanny would be there, and Mom would peer at her thin gold watch, kiss me good night on the upstairs landing, then hurry away to dress for cocktails, dinner, perhaps even to see my stepfather in a play. The nanny would prepare my dinner, and at bedtime would read to me. I was already prone to words."

Roberta smiled. "And so, you became a poet and an editor, sandpapering text for a living."

"Yes. They say people measure themselves against those closest to them. For status, I mean. When we were young, I would mimic Buddy. And lately I've been wondering if there might be some way for Buddy and I to still spur each other on? Yet, I resist, as more and more I find us all sounding like an echo chamber. We can't seem to avoid mimicry. Buddy even sounds like me when he says here in Italy his poetic impulses have re-awakened. In youth, Buddy had the head-start writing poetry. But over time, his writing sought visibility through magazine bylines or even working in advertising for a while. Now, however, he refers to such things as dumb scratch."

"It would be nice to see him find an alternative to tending his wife's stage-struck fury." Roberta noted the way Lydia and Buddy seemed to cope with life's disappointments by ranting at one another.

"He claims to be trapped by his wife's career, the banality of working at a religious school as well. He certainly doesn't belong there."

• • •

After lunch we drove to the post office where Roberta spotted the familiar red-faced man. She waved at him and he came running over. "You need me, Signora?"

"Yes, I have to park illegally." Without hesitation, the man said he'd stay with the car, and stood nuzzling Apollo's ears through the open window.

Waiting in a line lengthened by postal bureaucracy, we soon realized—he who holds the parcel holds the power. Roberta used our time in line to once more make me the topic of discussion. "I keep thinking about what you told me, and it shocks. I mean, that at such a young age, people actually noted your race so blatantly."

"Don't all children have to account for their physical appearance in one way or another? After Mom died at least I was no longer assaulted. Her death made me a figure to be pitied. But there were some who knew my family history, Buddy's mother even, who still might accuse me of passing. Grandpa Gordon used to say a person must adjust their step to the dignity of the burden being carried. I think he said that just to brace me. And yet, no matter how trying my experience, I never had to withstand the scrutiny he did."

"I don't follow."

"Taxis stopped for me. They often wouldn't have stopped for Russell...or any of the Gordons. I could go to any shop for a haircut without worry. I've never been redlined or denied insurance. Both my stepfathers had to contend with these things."

"Do you think your mother was in love with Russell? I mean the same way she loved your first stepfather?"

"Physical rapture between my mother and Cole Gordon was electric. Russell on the other hand was quieter in romance. I always imagined he would rather crunch numbers than kiss; his true excitement seemed to be found in declaring income, taking deductions, or gazing up into space."

The customer ahead of us finished, and after taking a healthy, restorative pause, the clerk finally signaled her readiness to receive us. Roberta handed the woman her postal receipt. She scrutinized it with official indifference, then disappeared somewhere in the back. Eventually she returned, carrying a shoebox wrapped in brown paper. Roberta shook the box. "It's from Oklahoma. Mother sent it."

I too shook it. "Something in pieces... a puzzle?"

"Maybe!"

We strolled back to the car, and despite last night's problem of my weak function, I sensed with both Hans and Eligio absent, Roberta was glad to have me at her side. It was reassuring to see I could still be ordained to stand in as a paramour, even if but one who disappoints.

At the car, the red-faced man stood crestfallen. "So sorry, Signora."

"Sorry for what?" Roberta glanced into the Bentley's empty backseat. "Oh, not again! I hired you to watch!"

The old man lifted his eyes. "Forgive me, Signora. But the dog is like Houdini."

Roberta opened her purse to extract some bills. "Here, buy yourself some more brandy."

"Signora, you needn't pay."

"I must. Next time you'll do better." She got in, started the car and slowly backed away. "Apollo adores hide-and-seek. Probably eyed his chance with that old wino the minute my back was turned."

"Still, that man does not deserve to be tipped."

"You've lived here long enough—you know the drill. It's always essential to tip, or else run the risk of it getting all over Levanto that you stiffed a local. Ex-pats can *never* say or do repudiating things. Not overtly, and certainly not within a local's earshot. That man may be a drunk pauper but he holds the pride of an Italian nobleman. He'll defend his honor no matter how low his station. And to let him know we felt *obligated* to tip—is *worse* than not tipping him at all."

"I guess it's better to be stiffed than insulted."

"For him anyway. And if I let him know I was tipping when I didn't want to, and did so because I thought him some kind of hobo, why he'd be so offended the entire town would be told what a bitch I'd been. And people here would remember this insult for the rest of their lives. *There she goes…the arrogant prima donna! Flinging insults at we who are born of this earth.*"

*   *   *

We drove along a narrow street and at every intersection whistled up the side alleys. Roberta knew the breed and mix of every leash-less mongrel that came running. I was impressed. "Have you ever noticed how stray dogs outnumber cats?"

"Dogs hold the towns, cats the hills," Roberta said, as though it were a civil war.

The streets grew more crowded, and at the next corner a young woman dodged into the road. Roberta tapped the horn and the girl stared as we floated by. A corpulent man in a pair of petit point driving slippers crossed next. "Probably a business baron on holiday," Roberta said.

"What makes him want to press fat, swollen feet into such frail footwear? Why he's a pachyderm in toe-shoes!"

"The choice shows defiance. It's his rebellion. Denying facts because he can. Too much money breeding a compulsive need to prove his will, or that he deserves the very best."

"The taming of the shoe," I quipped.

"Ha! But too much money can also awaken feelings of scarcity. It's easy for the competition of capitalism to make the rich feel poor no matter how much they have. Soon the whole point becomes to advertise oneself: the best table, the best view, the biggest yacht, an entire artificial service industry of luxurious ideals meant to reinforce that as emperors, these titans are not naked, but have closets full of ermine robes. Affording slippers spun in silk neurotically validates!"

"Or denies one's gout! Yet even crooks and drug dealers can buy expensive handbags. Or sports cars. Even art can be sold to anyone."

"True. And the real art of living is not to buy things, even rare things," she said, "but to make things. The magic of creation. That's why in a crowded room, the good poet or artist has more stature than the tycoon."

"I'm not sure about that."

"Then why do the rich invite artistic-achievers to sit at their purchased event tables? And why do you think so many buy and hoard art?"

"Portfolio diversification?"

"Well, there's that. But most buyers have proven they can make money, or inherit it, or hire someone to make it, but they can't create art. Money is common. Art is rare. So, they grow proud in demanding their name be put on some plaque in some museum, loaning or donating that which has been ostentatiously bought. Proximity and ownership to art makes them feel like they are its creators."

"Remember how Buddy said academics, behind their jargon, hold little notion of quality."

"The rich can be predictably similar. Unsure of their own taste or expertise, they rely on hired advisers like me. We lead them to what they should like, what they ought to covet, what they then buy. They follow the status of the pack or the herd."

In the town center we slowed. "Speaking of herds," I said. "I find all this increased tourism vexing."

"Until we want to visit somewhere ourselves!"

"True! So many people claim they travel to relax. Yet, the stress and ennui of tourism affects their behavior."

"It's in the walk. The gait of a tourist lacks purpose—no job to get to, few true destinations."

"Unless they're about to miss a plane. Or rushing ahead to see something before the rest of their group. Then they're quite funny!"

"Most will never see what's hidden behind these Riviera walls. Or the places where the world's private wealth really congeals."

"But is that worth seeing? I say things like that out of nervousness. And then I hear the voice of my grandmother in my head—saying what makes us think we're so special? "

She kept her eyes on the road as we passed a bearded young man guzzling wine from a jug tied to his backpack. "This guy majors in the sport of unabrogated drinking. What makes him so special is an intensive survey of alcohol in as many towns as his train pass permits."

"When I was his age, I used to go to discos. But when Buddy talks about how in the late seventies he backpacked all over America on a dollar a day, I admit envy. He has that over me. I don't know why, but since they've come to Levanto, it feels like more and more things I comment on are coming from Buddy's perspective."

"You're certainly more traveled than he is."

"But *his* might have been the greater pleasure. Even though we're the lucky ones who get to live here."

"Well, I certainly don't feel *Italian*," Roberta said solemnly. "I wish I did. I have this great love of Italy, and I really enjoy pretending to be an Italian. I mean, I can feel so happy when I'm with Italian friends, listening to them talk, watching them cook. And I hope through their generous exchanges, I've adopted some kind of Italian sensibility. But at the end of the day, I will always be American. Buddy, and even these tourists are in some way closer to my own tribe."

As we arrived back down at water's edge, along the brown stone beach, some Eastern Europeans were unfolding a portable camping table from a silvery cocoon. Proceeding along to the back of the promenade, our car pulsed in the shadows. There beneath the fringed branches of a date palm we finally spotted Apollo, legs splayed, tongue panting. Roberta leapt from the car and went to him, kissing his snout, even as she began to reprimand.

Apollo licked her hands for pardon, but that remorse couldn't disguise the mischievous pride in his canine eyes, tail wagging a slow switch of delight, how for even but a brief moment, he'd eluded domesticity's subjugation. Above us, standing on the elevated promenade, several men were looking down, captivated by the sight of a woman simultaneously scolding and stroking a beast. Some naughtiness in their own past perhaps revisited the men, the lips of one parted, as if Roberta represented a volcano under the ocean, the nefarious divide between hot and cold. How often in the celluloid marriages of Italian cinema were this fire and ice staged? Steam billowing up to rude hissing slaps, then tears and kisses to stoke the flames of prowess.

Roberta lifted Apollo, and sauntered back to the car. Does ignoring the attentions of men allow a woman to harness power, or lose it, I wondered? Opening the rear door, she leaned in, spine and pelvis tilted, gingham pants straining their seams. She spread a towel to protect the upholstery, her body seemingly a wild voluptuous challenge.

Back in the driver's seat, she noticed my expression. "What?"

"Did you see the men up on the promenade looking at you?"

"No, I didn't." Our car pulled away. From the side mirror, I gazed back at the promenade. The men were leaving.

"For a moment, I thought they were going to whistle at you."

"They'd never dare do that. Not here. If Italian men do try that sort of thing, it would be toward younger women in the big cities. Levanto only has six-thousand people. You know how small this town is. Everyone knows everyone. Those men know we live here—and their wives do too! We live here most of the year, so by paying property tax we're considered at least on some level to be one of them. Besides, I'm over thirty-five!"

"Important to keep good reputations."

"I'm not kidding. No man in Levanto would ever behave overtly sexual toward me. And they'd certainly never wolf whistle—though there are days when I wish they would! You know, once, when I was in Rome, some drugged-up misfit made lewd, hectoring signs with his hands as I passed by to catch a train. If Hans had been on the scene, or you, or any other male presence, he'd never have dared to be so brash. Anyway, a couple of very young, baby-faced policemen were standing nearby and saw the whole thing. One marched over to the man and called him out in no uncertain terms. The other hurried over to me and said, '*Signora*, please forgive.'"

"Did you tell Hans?"

"Hell no! That'd make him feel emasculated. More likely, he'd blame me because I wasn't born a natural blonde."

* * *

When we re-entered *Belacqua's* ballroom, we found Lydia and Phil Filbertson continuing their face-off. Seeing us enter, both glanced down at their watches as if choreographed, then without missing a beat, returned to their abuse of one another.

Lydia noted too few bookings in the promised grand hotels. From the sidelines Garafallou listed the shows now set for Antwerp and Bruges, with one still pending for a resort on the coast of Belgium. "Almost had a ski lodge in Chambéry," he said. "But they had a warm Winter. Low snow means low francs for summer floor shows."

"These bookings are crap," Lydia snapped. "Why even bother?"

Garafallou remained calm as a magistrate. He stated that his interest was in finding venues worthy of her art.

"Liar! There's no art here, and you know it."

"Very well, if you prefer. Shows from abroad tend to do well. And with only two cast members, magic costs less than mounting a musical. Those take at least ten people who can sing, not to mention musicians and music royalties."

"That's insulting."

"No, my dear. That's show business."

"What about the television stuff?"

"Working on it, night and day."

"Night and day!" Phil's voice echoed.

Lydia turned toward us and winked, then looked back at them. "To get a break, I mean, to appeal to television, we must reinvent ourselves. Our only chance is to grab attention. We need a new look."

Phil's demeanor turned to outrage. "A new look? And who are you to say? Maybe you want that we should also grow horns?"

"Don't talk to me that way, you nitwit!"

Garafallou came over and stood beside us. "See how passionate your cousin gets! Oh, her fire reminds me of the great Magnani!"

Comparing real people to icons of the screen was a dubious practice, but Garafallou saw something in Lydia's bearing that indeed conjured the beloved Italian actress. Maybe it was her self-assertion, including a comic pique and imperious irritation, a kind of attitude that back home I'd observed more often in black women than white. The manner was almost comic and defended them against tough jobs, wayward men, the judgments of other women. "And did you know the real Magnani?" Lydia asked.

"Of course!" Garafallou replied.

"How? By sitting in a scratch house with the rest of the lice?"

Garafallou smiled. "See, that is funny! Something in the tone, that fire. Uncannily Magnani."

"Well, I'm sick of parading around in this bustle. Tying on a fat keester so you boys can get off on some hottsie-hottentot fantasy."

Phil wagged his finger. "You keep blending starlight with house dust."

She glared. "Don't talk to me about dust! That vest looks like it's a casket lining."

"This is real brocade!"

She turned to Garafallou. "You're the producer. Make him change it. All of it! The cravat, the spats, those ridiculous pinstriped pants!"

Phil began to shout. "And what will we wear? Pee-jamas?"

"This act is turning me into one of those crazy women who stand on the window ledges of downtown hotels threatening to throw their babies. And for God's sake, cut your hair! I can't look at that ponytail another second!"

Phil's face registered fury. His hand lifted to protect the hair tied at the nape of his neck. "You're no Magnani," he snarled. "You're a Delilah!"

"If you don't stop, I'm gonna throw this baby!"

Garafallou neared. "One of the reviewers said the bustle shaped you into a femme fatale."

"That wasn't a real review, and you know it. Phil paid the guy off!"

And then, as if an imaginary referee was blowing his whistle in her head, Lydia stopped cold. Calmly, she folded her hands across her body, and cast her eyes down toward her feet. Her tone shifted, as if she were another person. "Look I'm sorry," she said, sounding suddenly smooth and silky as a politician's wife. "I've not had enough sleep."

Buddy rose like a defense lawyer. "Let the lady rest!"

Garafallou wrung his plump hands. "Oh, my poor dear. Yes, why don't we take a break?"

"We started late. That's our handicap."

"No. We began on time!"

"I don't mean rehearsal. I mean we're starting late in show business." Like a horse whisperer she then artfully suggested more tickets would sell if their look were fresher. "We could still be retro, but later…say, fifties Las Vegas. Him, a box-cut tuxedo. Me, stilettos, sequins, feathered hats."

Garafallou grew serious. "Finery costs…no profit in a show with too much stitchery."

"The changes needn't cost you a dime. Fabric and sparkle can be got on the cheap. I can sew the costumes myself."

Phil grew furious. "Th-ees kind of swank is for country clubs! Parading around as M-ees Dior would undermine m-ee-stique!"

Garafallou wet his lips. "Now, Philly. A bit of freshness might stimulate. After all, Victoriana and Land of the Pharaohs have all been done."

"Everything could be sewn by the day after tomorrow," Lydia said. "And while we're at it, might we throw in a few jokes? Poke some fun at magic?"

Garafallou stood chewing his lip. "People do flock to comedy."

Phil's face grew red with anger, his odd vowels sounding even odder. "Mag-ic ee-s no joke! E-egypt stands as the most symbolic time and place."

Lydia lifted her hands toward heaven. "See what I gotta put up with?"

• • •

Belacqua's sumptuous bar became our waiting room, and while Roberta and I sat on heavy brass stools sculpted to resemble monkeys, a red velvet seat balanced on each head, we studied old photos of celebrities adorning the walls, trying to identify the famous faces. The bartender spoke in soft English. "The Riviera was elegant, no? A fine place for entertainers?"

Roberta stared at a picture of Anna Magnani. "I've never seen a Magnani film," she confessed.

"Oh, you must go!" the bartender said. "Your American writer Mr. Tennessee wrote parts just for her. This photo is from *Bellisima*! She signed it when it opened here. "

Buddy entered and the bartender looked askance at the casual dress. It was obvious they'd met before. Buddy, despite the Martha's Vineyard tee-shirt, postured like someone just off a polo field in Buenos Aires. Seeing our drinks close to empty, he insisted we try a Pimm's cup. The bartender lifted his nose, as if dealing with an imposter, and then nodded in cool formality. Buddy seemed indifferent as to how he was being perceived, and slid one of the heavy brass monkey stools over the carpet.

"They're still arguing. That bastard doesn't appreciate what she brings. She's the one who makes the act." Our drinks appeared and we toasted. "They could play top supper clubs if those jerks would just use the name I came up with. *Sophisticatto!* But no, Phil won't allow it!"

I took another sip. "Does the world still have top supper clubs?"

"These bozos said she'd play before the crowned heads of Europe. Live in five-star hotels. But so far, it's been mostly cruise ships. I mean, what could be worse than magic at sea?"

Roberta smiled. "No magic at sea?" She lifted her drink and smiled.

"When Lydia walks out onto that stage, you'll see who brings the magic.

And as for Beetle? You ever see a guy more crooked?"

"He seemed to like the new costume idea," Roberta said.

I took a swig of my drink. "But sewing men's formal wear? Where on earth did Lydia learn to tailor?"

"Oh, she can't sew," Buddy said. "The box-cut tux was bought in New York. In fact, all the costumes came with us. That's why we've so much damn luggage. She's only claiming to sew to lure the Beetle. As you can see, Walker, Lydia's tastes haven't changed." He gestured to the room's elaborate fixtures. "She likes this kinda stuff! Gilded furniture, candelabras, caviar. Her salons look like Liberace's pad. And this junk costs dough! We've had to put the Westport shop up for sale."

"Are the salons flagging?"

"We're not minding our stores. We're not doing hair. We're in Italy!" Buddy called to the bartender to bring us shots of whiskey chasers. "This fiasco will take us belly-up. High and dry!"

"I didn't realize. I guess clients don't like being palmed off?"

"You kidding? Women get nuts over their hair. Many are going elsewhere. Not to mention those already gone on account of Lydia's lessons and auditions. One acting coach isn't enough—she has to have three! The first told her to train in the classics. He got her cast in *The Merry Wives of Windsor*, a dreadful production at a community center out in Forest Hills. They had cash problems. So, guess who ended up footing five grand! And her with no ear for Shakespeare."

"Lydia seems more contemporary," Roberta said.

"Yeah, but then some dude cast her in a modern piece. Played a sociopath in a nut house. It was wretched! I stood in the wings till I couldn't stand it. Waited it out in the dressing room. Watching naked actors change costumes was more entertaining. And the reviews? Horrendous! Even the terrible agent she'd worked so hard to get dropped her."

"What about soaps? Commercials?"

"Crap! And ninety percent of the jobs in Hollywood are cast with the kids of producers and directors. One guy, whose hair she cut for free, threw her a bone: a national ad for a resort off the coast of South Carolina. That led to a spot for a local car dealer, and then one for a Pocono motel, where she sat in a bathtub made to look like a giant glass of champagne. Then she was a murder victim on some police detective shit. All of it brutal third-rate stuff." He downed a shot of whiskey and Roberta saw him eye her glass.

"Go ahead."

He took her drink and his head snapped back. Roberta put her hand on Buddy's shoulder. "Her employees must be excited for her."

"Ha! Inside every hair salon sit hundreds of men and women who once nursed theatrical ambitions. When she got into doing commercials, we saw how that's also true in the makeup trailers and wardrobe rooms, and even for those behind the cameras and lights. No matter how great these wannabes thought themselves, their appeal to an audience was nil. Graceless, nervous, or just plain bad, to make ends meet they ended up in crew jobs—technicians, prop handlers, key grips, script supervisors, Teamsters, and, of course, *hairdressers*. A bitter, hard-boiled and cliquey lot, they sit around all day trading war stories: the time Demi Moore tripped on a cable, the time Aretha Franklin smeared her orange lipstick eating ribs. They say, 'I was on the Pepsi gig the day Michael Jackson burned his hair! I once saw Brooke Shields's titties! I looked up Connie Steven's skirt.' Like circus bums who sweep up after elephants, they talk crap all day long. Cynicism is for them a drug, and yet they refuse to give up show business! So, when one from their ranks, tries to step out of the shadows to persuade the world they've got talent, well, it better be chockablock. Otherwise, an avalanche of shit falls."

"Does the magic show stand a chance?" Roberta asked.

Buddy ordered another shot. "Not in the rat holes they've booked. Now, you both know I'm not the kind of guy to run his wife down. I'll defend her to the grave. But the beauty business is no joke. We're on the verge of financial ruin! Most of what my old man left is gone. We've spent down principle!"

Alcohol untied the last strings of indiscretion. "I don't mean to be unkind, but am I supposed to just wait for Miss Lydia to finish wrecking our lives? We sleep in the same bed, but I don't even know who she is anymore. On the occasions when we're not too tired to make love, I tell myself to enjoy it, but there's no joy. She's so disdaining you'd think she had a golden vagina!"

Through the haze of liquor, Buddy looked as though he might cry. "It's all always moving too fast or too slow." I tried to look at him with compassion, but from my own divorce I learned that when people tell you unpleasant things about their spouses, it's best to run for the hills.

"Maybe she'll retire," Roberta said, her speech also showing signs of booziness. "You'll go off and have a family? You already had this paid sabbatical. You've gotten to travel to one of the most beautiful parts of Italy. That's more than most people get!"

"It's not enough," Buddy said. And the flip side of his boosterism once again drew a less than flattering portrait of his wife, noting that beneath her artistic ambition lay a gargantuan iceberg of delusional desperation.

A couple of businessmen entered in natty suits, sized up the scene at the bar, then took monkey stools as far from us as possible. They removed and carefully folded their jackets as only Italian men can. Buddy continued. "Lydia doesn't want kids. Says she's got too much talent to be a soccer mom. I'm only saying…I mean, I'm telling this only to you…she better watch her step! I aim to win my own place in the hall of fame!"

I rose up off my monkey stool. "Buddy! Poetry isn't a career. It's a *calling*."

Roberta agreed. "You can't expect to be fawned over like an actor."

"Poetry can't provide a living…like selling insurance." I felt my toes go numb, my socks and shoes confessing to each other they'd grown apart. "Besides, who knows which poets stand the test of time. Some voices will make it out. Others won't."

Buddy traced my idea. "Well, I sure as hell don't plan to teach at a Bible college the rest of my life. I'm not even religious. The Bible isn't even a real book. Ta Biblia! An anthology stuffed between two black covers, written and rewritten by tons of people. It's been retyped, xeroxed, censored, re-censored, and still folks look you in the eye, to say God's talking in there. Ya gotta laugh. People ignore how much editing God took!"

"Truth telling has a price," I said. "And just imagine, out there somewhere right now, people are writing great things that we'll never know. Imagine Whitman and Dickinson, alive at the same time…"

Roberta furrowed her brow. "They grew up together?"

"No. I mean her poems weren't even frigging found until the very end of Walt's life, thirty years after she died! Yet they were contemporaries, lived through the same time period, but imagine…Whitman never got to read her!"

Buddy's eyes shone glassy as he slapped the bar. "Yeah…so! So what? Fifty or a hundred years from now, and some mysterious pages come blowing out from under some sand dune, toppling us. A bunch of damn wordsmiths are right now working in secret! And we'll all be dead. And who the fuck cares? Oh! Another writer died today! Hooray!"

Roberta struggled to straighten herself in her chair. "Who died?"

"All of us! And anyway…who wants to sit beside the creeps that get chosen? Lousy ass-kissers following the other cows into the big barn to get milked by some master's deciding hands. Curdled in the same compilations…picked by the same dung-sniffing editors. Photographed in *The Times,* posing all prim and proper in front of saltbox cottages—proud of their ivied garden."

"Ivied?"

"Yeah! The whole lawn! Nothing but fucking English ivy."

"Ha!"

"And let me ask you something else, my friend. Why is it…that so many elites who hold the poetry world hostage…hail from some hard-ass place in New England? If they're not scribbling shit, they spend their afternoons getting pruned on a Salem dunking stool!"

"Ha!"

"Well, I say, screw New England! As wretched a place as any ever conceived. And screw that bitch of a rigged club too! Run by a bunch of snobs. No offense to you, Walker."

"None taken."

Buddy howled even louder, his bawdy self-delight gasping for air. I held up my hand. "Buddy, please…*Sotto voce!*"

Buddy pounded the bar laughing hysterically. "Ha! What cod fish! The rich posers. They govern the Academy but can't spot a phony. Can't! And never could!" He looked around with a sudden conspiratorial air and calmed, voice lowering to a half-whisper. "Do you think any of them might be here?"

"Who?"

"Might that prick of a bartender be taping us?" Buddy's face twisted in slow motion. "Just my luck…this fucking place is a world of surveillance." He lowered his forehead onto the bar.

Another group of men entered and started moving tables. They spoke French, and from what I overheard, seemed to be from Paris. Two were unzipping narrow jackets, two held small dogs, and our watching them only seemed to encourage their clannishness. Voices arched, they laughed a little too loudly, as city people might do when they're trying to act comfortable in a country setting. Buddy lifted his head, and we both studied a man applying tinted powder from a small case. The man looked right at us and puckered. I looked away.

Buddy spoke to us using his loudest stage whisper. "Place must be a magnet for 'em,"

"Buddy please!" We tried to quiet him, and he struggled to keep his bearings.

I tried to assess the situation. I knew Levanto was a conservative and small provincial town, but I found it hard to believe that a Parisian man in an expensive city jacket would feel any threat from a drunk American like Buddy. It was all too bizarre. But who knows? Such encounters could lead to serious fights. Buddy, a foreigner, might not realize the danger of his own recklessness.

But wait! Had that man really applied tinted powder to his nose? Or had I imagined this? I took a closer look and saw that the men were older than I first thought, and the powder box was really snuff, and the jackets had hoods, the kind worn for skiing, and their fur trim had only looked to my eye like small dogs. The men had probably just come in on the train from the snow of the Alps.

I checked and rechecked the scene for clues. Buddy dropped his head back onto the bar once more, and then like a child, he began to blubber. As most diplomats will tell you, whenever someone starts to cry in a bar, it's time to find the exit. I signaled the barman for the check, but as I tried to straighten my legs, the unexpected pull of gravity's inebriation landed me on the floor.

• • •

On a bench by the sea, not far from the spot where we'd found Apollo, another dawn broke. How I came to be there, I did not know, let alone what happened to the others. A raging hangover left the muscles in my chest weak. I inhaled fresh air, my lungs stiff. Rousing myself, I hailed a taxi and rode up to the village, recalling some of yesterday's long afternoon under the influence. On the terrace, I found bread and soft-boiled eggs tied in a cloth napkin, but I could not eat. By my third cup of coffee, I was sobering up.

From below, unseen, I watched Lydia step out onto the balcony. She leaned against its elegant forged-iron railing, her head was wrapped in a damp towel. As Sontag wrote, in the most beautiful women there is almost always something masculine, just as in the most attractive men there was almost always something feminine. Both Anna Magnani and Lydia brought that to mind. Now looking up to study her, so fresh after her morning bath, all artifice seemingly rinsed away, a certain brutal and unapologetic beauty remained. The Ligurian mountains and the overcast clouds seemed to have joined in sacred love to parent her, thereby granting her dominion over the entire valley. The light of the sky brightened our terrace, but I remained in the deep-blue morning shade, a grotto of darkness hiding me like some deep-sea creature, one so captivated by this nymph, that I'd risk my life to guard her.

Lydia looked down. "Walker, my God, what're you doing down there! We've been looking everywhere for you!"

Buddy, hearing my name, hurried out of their kitchen and came toward me. "Last night you could barely stand! We tried to help you, but then you bolted like a lunatic! This morning we knocked and knocked on your door. You okay, dude?"

"Yes, sorry…I don't remember much. But in God's name why are you both up so early?"

"Another friggin' rehearsal! But what a blast we had yesterday! We gotta do it again real soon!"

A short while later they hurried back out, bid me farewell then rushed up the stairs to meet their taxi. I went inside and ran a hot bath, and after a long soak, sat on the chaise by the window. From that angle, I could see Pina cleaning the kitchen of their house. At the end of the counter, she lifted the lid on a plastic pail of vegetable peelings, then carried them outside to the compost bin. Before tossing the scraps, her free hand reached in and extracted the tops of some fibrous blue leeks. She folded these stems and placed them into her apron pocket. After tossing the rest, she put the bucket down, and in order to neatly coil the garden hose she bent, the hem of her apron lifting to reveal a beige slip trimmed with ivory lace. Village women her age usually wore more somber shades, was this undergarment her rebellion? She straightened and went back inside to the kitchen, filling the sink with sudsy water. If Pina were someone who operated less mysteriously, I'd lose interest. But her idiosyncratic behavior, even while just running water, fascinated. Had she heard the recent battles in that kitchen? Was last night's drunkenness louder than usual?

I sat on the chaise, intending to outline my introduction to *The Galaxy of Love*, but I heard the screen door open and shut. I glanced down to see the patio table being wiped. Then a metal chair was pulled, and it shocked me to see Pina settle into it, wrinkled hands smoothing her hair back to the bun pinned at the nape of the neck. She studied the sea, eyes squinting. I knew those born to this region, often lived in small houses facing the back sides of a mountain, and by mid-morning their homes stood in shadow. Only foreigners could afford the sunny, larger homes with views of the water. Pina's eyes lowered in a prayerful pose.

Down in the garden, a trio of yellow butterflies formed a small cyclone, swirling up above a patch of herbs surrounding some tall cardoons. I followed their twirling ascent, up and up, past the purple-blue artichoke heads, parallel now to the mighty vine clinging to my drainpipe. It was then, at the top of our outdoor stairs, that I spied the four Italian women from the village, gazing down at our patio through the iron gate. To behold a servant sunning herself like a lazy cat on the property of her employer, as though the property belonged to her, was a great find, particularly if Pina was that servant. One woman shouted: "*La* Signora c'è?"

Pina's eyes snapped open, and she leapt to her feet like a bantam prizefighter. *"Sta zitto!"* she shrieked. The women howled with laughter at her thinking she could tell them to shut up. What joy to ruffle her so completely, merely by having asked if the lady of the house were at home!

Pina waved her fist. *"Contadina!"*

The women defended their dignity of being peasants and hurled some insults down, while Pina continued her own charge. *"Ignoranti! The only learned man in the village was my husband!"*

The women made remarks I couldn't decipher. The invective must have been comic, for one laughed so hard she doubled over, face flushed and gasping. Satisfied with their day's wages, the group moved slowly onward, skirts in sway over round calf muscles hardened from a lifetime spent in climb.

Pina now hid in the deep shadow of the kitchen door-frame. Her wrinkled hands holding a sweater of soft lavender angora, which I recognized as one that Lydia had left on a chair. Pina brought the garment up to her old cheeks and pressed her face into it. How desperate she must feel. Was she longing for her dead husband, the nonconformist who left her the only converted Anglican in a village of Catholics? Was she crying because a woman her age ought to be able to warm herself in the sunshine without ridicule?

My involuntary empathy wrenched, and longed to go down and comfort her. But Pina's pride would be outraged. I could just hear her say a man who spies on a woman now thinks he can be a saint!

For a moment a weird fantasy flashed through my mind, what if I were to go down and tell her the story about the Japanese-American woman that mother had once modeled with, the one whose grandmother had put a brown-bag over her head in order to use the toilet. But how absurd—an American man of Irish and partially unknown origin, raised by various dark-skinned stepfathers, living in Italy amid a garden planted by two Englishmen, telling an exiled Anglican in a Catholic village in Liguria about a Japanese-born American from San Francisco who protested poor latrine facilities in the Arizona desert? Ridiculous to think such a story could comfort! And yet how many moments in my life had felt so ridiculously dissonant, globally and geographically extreme, seemingly impossible to weave together except by way of fantasy, fable or circus.

Pina lowered the sweater, and her pink tongue swept across the toothless part of her gums. Her expression shocked. She hadn't been crying at all, but laughing, her merry eyes seeming to enjoy the memory of her contentious encounter with the village women. I watched in awe as she draped the sweater on the chair exactly as it had been before. Then her shrewd senses detected my presence, and whatever thoughts had so amused her, instantly vanished. Her gaze shot up the drainpipe. Too late. My movement in the window was spotted. Having privacy stolen twice in a row was too much. Like a hare hidden in a meadow, but facing exposure from the sudden cut of a scythe, she bolted. Wherever she hoped to escape, I imagined her hand pressing down into her pocket, fingers tracing the lines of the tough blue leeks salvaged from the compost.

Book Four

TARANTELLA

• • •

"Ready to hike?" Eligio greeted me in the parking lot with a gentlemanly kiss to each cheek. Was this intended as a flirtation? "Kissing men in Italy is an old-fashioned way to greet," he said as if reading my mind. "But I'm something of a traditionalist!"

"I suppose more Italian men are following global ways now."

"Sadly, we rarely anymore express platonic affection toward male friends by touch, it waned after the war. When hugging, most modern men will but place one arm around the upper back to pat it. Before this generation, male friends frequently walked holding hands, or strolled arm in arm, or shared Vespa rides. In that context, two men simply enjoyed the physicality of each other's company."

"I've seen some policemen still riding like that."

"Yes, as partners in duty it can be unavoidable."

Eligio and I wasted no time striking out on the road inclining above the village. I nervously noted the things catching my attention about the wildflowers and the weather. At an overgrown spot beside the road, he bent back a giant fountain of cardoons, their cut, silvery leaves concealing a hidden bank of stone steps invisible to the average passer. "The old rabbit hunter showed me these."

"Vescovi?"

"Yes. If we climb, they'll lead to the tunnel." He tilted back the thick stalks, and I took hold of them, following his lead. Beyond, some of the steps were cut right into the rock, wide enough for but one foot, while other places were stacked, and so steep a lunge was required. Unaccustomed to being the follower, I imagined how the youth of ancient Athens must have felt reportedly following the learned men. I quickly censored my thoughts. *For God's sake, this is not Athens, and you're no youth. It's also not a Thomas Mann novel, no creek of ashes—Eligio no Aschenbach. And you certainly are no angel-boy!*

We were but male companions in sensual attraction. Yet we didn't follow the pairings of lifelong friends, or of rivals, nor did we portray Herculean machismo, or mirror the renderings that were simply pornographic. Try as I might, I couldn't recall any other examples in literature to match this. Surely there must be something of a similarly amorous nature, perhaps in Forster? Lawrence? Coward?

Half an hour of climbing and our necks and shoulders grew heated with warmth from the sun. Eligio enjoyed leading, and my will gave in. Panting, we spoke haphazardly. "The challenge of climbing this landscape," he said, "Must be the cardiovascular secret of those peasants in newspapers…celebrating birthdays at one hundred and ten!"

I could only grin and nod.

Our trail rippled across the mountain, zigzagging beautiful contours, first North, then South, left to right, our heart rates and blood pressure pounding. On either side of us, rows of grapes stretched. The flinty soil an unlikely place to seed wine's fertility, yet somehow the stubborn green tendrils, wired between posts, grew a luscious harvest. The view widened as we rose. The altitude must be affecting me for some dizzying remnants of my hangover were felt. I was most grateful when, at a slender summit, Eligio paused so we could drink some water.

Maybe to appear entirely comfortable, I put my reserve aside and brought up Noel Coward, telling of a trip I once took to Jamaica. "Near Port Antonio, the house of the English playwright had a view like this. It'd been turned into a museum. An elderly man led, explaining he'd been Coward's valet. He even showed me the bathroom, saying, 'Here's where Mr. Coward fell and called my name for the last time.' I was the only visitor that morning, and the valet insisted we walk across the lawn to the edge of a cliff. 'On this exact spot,' he said, 'the Queen Mother stood looking out at the ocean. She said: *Mr. Coward, you've the best view in all Jamaica.*'"

Eligio glanced at me with amusement and I suddenly chastised myself. How could I let my nerves turn me into such a chatterbox? "I'm sorry. As an editor I ought to resist frivolous stories…especially those with too many queens."

"But I like it," Eligio said. "When you talk your thoughts and words make pictures. Maybe this has also to do with our notice of one another?" A feeling of intoxication overtook me. How delightful to sense even the subtle admittance of some attraction. *But beware…admittance to an idea doesn't grant it a passport! Eligio is Roberta's paramour…not yours. You have no permission to touch the damp place between his shoulder blades where his cotton shirt clings.*

"If we rest too long, we'll lose our edge," Eligio said. "Let's go on."

Back on the steps, Eligio's thighs, at eye level, revealed fine curve and form and I forced myself not to stare. We climbed on in syncopation, my lanky frame a contrast to his fuller one. Exertion honed a trance, one weighted leg lifted, then another, our eardrums soon pounding out the iambic pentameter of a beating heart. The burn of calf tissue and lung strain reduced our talk to a few grunting phrases, and I imagined us posing objectively naked side-by-side, like in the photographs at the flea market.

Do ordinary bodies make their owners better lovers? Eligio's rounded form was preferable to me over some buff, iron-pumping zealot, or worse, those who pretended indifference to a gym while displaying abnormally ridged abs. Perhaps the ordinary, even the ugly, is more enduring? *A nice body never hurts*, Mom used to say, *but beauty can be quick to flaw.* She warned that good-lookers could be both greedy and stingy, and that true attraction lay in the mind. Was she referring to *herself*? I'd never know. What I did know was that Eligio could've dropped from outer space, with green skin and antennae, and I'd still be drawn. In these days of plague, a genderless Martian might even be quite a sensible choice.

One step, then another. Higher and higher. Up and up. On the mountain plateau, we paused again, this time resting on a bench assembled from planks and twisted branches. We drank more water, a breeze cooling our foreheads. Below us, the sky on the horizon merged into the blue sea. On the eastern side, a tanker inched along like a snail, the weight of heavy, viscous crude-oil filling its insides, yet nonetheless a vessel floating on fathoms of water. It moved over murky and deep despair, riding above the invisible repressed seas, and all the dark liquids trapped beneath the floors of the world's oceans.

From this height, it all appeared otherworldly. *The intensity of attraction brings giddiness. Govern thyself. Be discerning. He accepts impulses from many. Remain immune to his profligacies. Let him troll the woods, the waterfront, the bordello, even the matrimonial bed. Let him stir lustful craving with his charm. Let him be the one to resist or seduce.*

"I suppose to write poetry depends on conjuring such lofty views, no?"

"Sometimes altitude can be a spectacular perch," I said, appreciating Eligio's associations. "A point-of-view like looking from an airplane. Before airplanes, cliffs were the only way to gain this bird's perspective."

"I think you poets do more than simply see…your words can offer the very feeling of elevation."

"Especially if something has been worked long enough to show the *lie* that one has been telling oneself…that's always a thrill."

"You actually search for the lie you tell yourself?"

"That discovery can be a great moment…a benefit of truth's energy, to express my version of the truth."

"Amazing…you poets! Writing of all that's meaningful and essential for the human soul. You then press that fruit of witness…and distill it."

"Here among all these grapes, alcohol is an apt metaphor."

"The Gulf of La Spezia used to be called the gulf of poets. Petrarch and Dante wrote here. Byron used to swim in the grotto at Porto Venere. Shelley lived in San Terenzo before he drowned."

"You seem to know more about English poets than I do…I also know very little about Ligurian poems. I'm ashamed to have read *only* Montale."

"Try reading Cigala…Grimaldi…a contemporary author, Claudio Pozzani."

We repacked our bags to begin our descent over the ridge. Preoccupation made me careless, my left foot stepped out and met an air-void, the sole of my shoe lurching out from under blank space. Eligio spun in concern. A cascade of small stones tumbled down to infinity.

"I'm okay! I'm okay."

He made sure I was steady, then marched on, downward, faster than we'd climbed, a pair of nomads descending some lost pyramid. Eligio unzipped his jacket and tied it around his waist. Something connective yearned beyond expression. It seemed we could go on no longer, when the gravel bed of the train track appeared. "We're now almost at sea level," Eligio said. Having our destination realized brought a sense of joyful accomplishment. Eligio raised his arms in victory, the pits of his shirt soaked, he then hinged down from the waist, hands resting on his knees. I followed his example and also bent at the waist, both of us gasping for air. What relief to breathe through a racing pulse and feel the blood pressure normalize. Heartbeats slowing, we lowered ourselves to the silty ground, replenishing our bodies with more water. Eligio propped his backpack by his feet and tore open a small package of cookies. I reached to take one, but atmospheric tension blurred my eyesight, and for a moment, my hand grasped yet another air-void. I forced myself to focus on the pack with its bold red lettering, took a cookie, then readjusted my vision toward the shifting pattern of green leaves swaying in the breeze.

"Is anything the matter?"

I echoed his phrase in my head. *Is anything the matter?* Allowing my sight to restore, I inhaled. If only he could read my thoughts, the way a metal detector scans below the surface of a sand dune, its clicks leading not just to shrapnel, but a gold Spanish coin or a fine pocket watch with a pearly face. But I'd learned young how regret in life emerged mostly from fear and parsimony. "My feelings seem jumbled," I said, my voice sounding low in my head. "I'm afraid…to arrive at the grave sadly bitter to have wasted…the chances of life."

Eligio looked bemused. "I thought people only said those kinds of things in movies."

I smiled, wanting to say more—more about the altering realities of our world. Eligio understood. "You sense inside you…that things of this moment are terribly complicated?"

It wasn't easy to let the blackboard of my mind chalk words which a good many men would rather die than utter—some, in order not to say them, might even kill. I nodded. My lips, teeth, and tongue fought silence to shape vowels and consonants. At last, my vocal-chords aligned and words came. "I was wondering if you…if you…well, if you might be willing to let me touch you?"

Eligio drew back.

"It's alright. You can say no. I'm sorry…it's quite embarrassing. You can say no."

Eligio looked off into the distance and took his time answering. "I will think it over."

The idea remained hanging in the air. We sat still, faces gazing up at the morphing clouds. The request for even an unrequited gesture left me to sense just how resistant to realization my own fingers felt. Whatever the outcome, humiliation was a small price to pay to avoid stirring the burden of regret.

"We might simply be in the midst of a boy-crush," he said quietly, studying the voluminous white billowing shapes against the sky.

If this were true, that we simply stood in the midst of a juvenile equation, did that mean no solution or response was necessary? For a split second, I saw the way attractions built their own logic, feelings of romance for others moving like the clouds. I insisted no shame upon myself. "I'm trying to find my footing. But I can't. Or rather, I won't. I'm not a boy…and feel too old for crushes."

"American men find brotherly love to be forbidden. It distorts their sense of manhood. Yet you remain a man even if you want to touch me."

Courage failed and I admitted not having slept well last night. "I drink too much lately…might be the anticipation."

Eligio nodded. "I'm trying to decide what will happen and why."

"All I know is I'm drawn. I want to touch. Because when you touch something living, it touches you back."

Eligio's expression deepened. Slowly he got to his feet and waited for me to stand. He motioned for me to face him. Had we become warriors, wrestlers, monks, schoolboys, prisoners? It simply didn't matter. Backpacks between us, Eligio reached across time and space to take my hand, and he gently placed it above his heart. "Move it wherever you like."

I hesitated, recognizing this expression to be as rare as rare can be. Nerves opened toward mystery. My palm moved to the right. Then I felt his ribcage. The musculature of that frame with its solidity so similar to my own, lacking a woman's softness. Eligio placed his hand on my shoulder and pulled me into an embrace.

. . .

No longer a man stored under plastic to hang among the mothballs, my hope had traversed across its risk. An undeniable calm descended, the seep of liquid into porous stone. Our chance had been taken, and now we were free to walk along the rails and explore the arching stonework comprising the tunnel's entrance.

"Looks like this track is still in use."

"Oh, yes, they use it all the time."

"I'd no idea. I thought the tunnels had been abandoned."

"*Al contrario.*" Eligio untangled more thickets as though disabling a landmine, the thorny canes arching down into the weeds. In the undergrowth, he found smaller bushes holding berries encased in a glassy black skin. Shared experience enchanted the physical world. "Currants. The French make cassis or jam. We make gelato. They dislike hot weather. The leafy canopy helps."

"America had many native currants, but they were thought to host a disease afflicting white pines. The lumber industry banished them early in the century. Whole logging crews dispatched into forests to poison them."

"A tragedy."

"Americans prefer mostly cultivated fruit."

Eligio turned on the flashlight, and we moved forward into cool and musty air. After a hundred carefully counted steps, the stone walls on either side widened to reveal small cell-like spaces piled waist-high with gravel.

"To foil the Germans," he explained. "Arms could've been stashed in such pockets. Liguria was luckier than other regions. It was spared the bombing and destruction of the South, or the mountain fighting like in the Alps."

"My grandfather was at Anzio. The experience forever haunted him. Once while on a vacation at a beach, he sat painting watercolors, and when I asked him about the war, a long moment passed before he could answer."

"Most people deny having supported Mussolini or Hitler," he said. "Many lie even to themselves. In the beginning, the compromises were probably small. History shows that early attempts to negotiate with a bully often make the bullying worse."

I pulled the flashlight from my bag and tested its bulb. "You make such good points," I said.

"I agree. Resistance is complicated. Communists say there's nothing more dangerous than teaching a person to write their own name."

"Hannah Arendt thought our most reliable moral compass are the words 'I can't.' Saying these words is fine. But it's writing them. By that I mean it holds them down as they were intended, and stops the adaptation of memory and our more flexible ears."

"Incredible! More and more, I see why you decided to become a poet."

"I didn't really decide to become a poet…I simply discovered I was one."

Eligio clicked the flashlight to a higher setting. "Look, if I point the beam straight ahead, the track running beneath us is lost in the dark. Are the rails still there? And our starting point, the sunny mountainside behind us, is that perhaps now completely nonexistent?"

"And are any of the books stacked in the libraries of the world real, if we don't read them into meaning?"

"Oh, you stir a great failure in myself. Why haven't I read more? Why haven't I read everything? What a responsibility our eyes must bear to not forget the old poems, the old stories, even as we seek out what's new."

We pressed on. "Is it true that in New York rats dwell not in the tunnels but in the stations?"

"Wouldn't surprise me. People drop banana skins and pizza. There's no other food down there."

Another chamber revealed itself, almost gothic in its height and grayness. Here the rock cutters had carved out an even deeper space. "It's bone dry," Eligio said. "Suitable for storage."

We stepped into the chamber, and a rush of frigid air instantly chilled our summer-damp faces and necks. Eligio surveyed the great ceiling with the light beam, bird-whistling to test the cavern for echo. We sat to rest. I felt contentment in the spooky space, unable to recall a time when I hadn't known this man. In the cone of the flashlight's battery-powered illumination, his smooth-shaven face looked asymmetrical. Yearning to feel my own body and have it connected once more; I quietly asked the question burning inside. "Can I touch you again?"

Silently, he rose to his haunches, and motioned me close. Our arms tightened in this, our second embrace. Now my emotions accelerated, long dormant feelings surging. Before I could contain them, pent-up sobs burst free. Like the boiling of an electric kettle, the aching expressed out like clouds of steam, jaws wide, lips agape and wet, the intensity of losses magnified. My mental health wasn't in question, but the intimacy of embarrassment felt astronomical. Eligio held me in my suffering, and that tenderness stirred arousal. What attraction Eligio felt, if any, was still unknown to me, but all that was deep and bitter in me felt its compression release. My uncontrollable shame soaked his shirt, and yet a peculiar, timid joy flitted alongside the fall, the sense of being alive. A deep rumbling began to sound.

"That's the train," Eligio whispered.

"What should we do?" I sputtered, but did not move.

"Do? Why nothing. We're not lost." He clicked the flashlight off. The roaring expanded into the void, shadows stretching long on the cragged rocks. Against this rapid advance, I held Eligio and he held me. The deafening noise opened a new wound of excruciating pain, decades of strained muscle held fast so that I would appear strong and fine. A sudden withdrawal now wrenched my chest and I let my throat wail. The train's headlamp flashed as it went by. Intense darkness followed, then the ghostly green glass of passenger windows clicking along, each offering the briefest sense of the people inside, like space ships headed out to the black hole of the universe. The final car passed, leaving a shocking vacuum of black dust.

Still locked in Eligio's arms, our ears still ringing, my last burst of sadness shrank. "When they get to Genoa," he whispered, "some dignified lady will locate the stationmaster. She'll report that she saw two men hugging in the tunnel. He and his colleagues will offer her bemused courtesy, and some professional attention, but no one will believe her."

. . .

It was after three when Pina, irate and bellicose, scolded us on the terrace. "Vitella baked for lunch and not a soul here to eat it!" In my best Italian I explained the return of the others to be imminent, and how cold roast was quite enjoyable. She grunted with disgust and wouldn't be consoled. Eligio tried to help, one Italian to another, but she'd not forgotten his recent flippancy about making wine, and departed in a dismissive huff of hand waving and muttering. The platter of sliced meat smothered in the tuna sauce was found in the kitchen. Famished, we brought it out, poured wine, and cut bread. Eligio's elegant handling of silverware brought a balletic distraction to the dizziness of our intimate adventure, the climb, the surreal dark mountain tunnel, the excessive emotion, all of it feeling intensely dramatic and already a lifetime ago.

In the ensuing quiet of eating, he sensed my nerves. "It must cause concern that I am Roberta's lover and she is your friend?"

I nodded. "Yes. I think of that."

"She's hardly a child."

"I also worry what Hans would say."

"People rarely sit their spouses down to calmly explain they'd like to explore another person. Deceit allows the pursuit of pleasure, without forfeiting whatever comforts and convenience a married or settled life allows. Stirring pain in a spouse is not, for me, an act of pleasure. One follows rules or deception spreads gangrene."

"Rules for infidelity?"

"Of course. Many balk…but I insist. And yet I'm not interested in being a guide. I've no more patience, particularly for men curious to play but wanting to maintain the illusion of straightness. Often guys who think they are straight think that automatically makes them irresistible subjects of sexual idolatry for men who prefer men. I also grow irritated with guys pretending intense mystification at having even the faintest attraction toward their own gender. Just *whom* are they trying to convince?"

"I'm afraid I'm more in tune with those types."

"Why not a man who seeks to exemplify infinite freedom?"

"My publisher once took me to lunch at the home of an American writer, Gore Vidal. Maybe you've heard of him? His house hangs on a cliff below Ravello."

"Yes, I've heard of him.'

"Mr. Vidal stated that any and all desire—was *natural*. He explicitly said, letting oneself experience variety, brings a more accordant view."

"What does he mean by accordant?"

"It seemed clear at the time. I now regret not having asked."

"From what I know of him, he's a man who likes daring himself to walk through checkpoints?"

"Yes, and being perceived to cross intellectual borders in broad daylight validates him. But many in the last decade have died seeking what he defined as natural."

"Do women in their *Rubyfruit Jungle* permit more leniency? Not that desire can't cause them suffering too. But even a woman testing her own sexual freedom—can still loathe allowing an equal experience to her man. Do you agree?"

"AIDS has rattled everyone's notion of what's natural or simply allowable. In America, and I suppose here too, men must uphold a rigid image."

"Most opposites hold changeable, or should I say varied, middle zones. Italian men have been libidinous for centuries. Many engage in varied sex but prefer to forget."

"An American man, if he's perceived to be *a man,* can't publicly admit to testing that border. Not with another man. Not even once."

"Same in Italy. We still claim to be a country of Catholics. The most ridiculous pretense I ever heard was that it's easier to procure free sex from a man than a woman, as if that thrift were virtue."

"Ha! The cost of paternity suits is certainly minimized."

"Yes. And I've known many Italian men who cruise for quick sex only to adamantly state they hold absolutely no such desires within themselves. If their variance were made public, they'd feel so threatened they'd likely shoot someone, and they'd certainly rant more denial. But just as you didn't decide to become a poet, most did not *decide* to become variable. They simply discovered they *were.* But they must beware. Many religions will turn the natural man into sin."

"And what do we call those people willing to run an alternate route outside of their marital bed?" We answered in amused unison. "*Simply natural!*"

In the kitchen, I reached for the silver moka pot. "Here, let me." Eligio took the pieces to assemble them as though coffee were an Italian business. Measuring espresso from the sack into the metal disk, he added a teaspoon of sugar, something I'd never done. "If we add sugar now, the granules caramelize." He placed the pot on the stove. "I've heard people say living by rules gives a kind of freedom, yet most rules leave me feeling constricted."

"Especially in love."

"But Walker, in divorce, perhaps your rules of marriage were violated?"

I caught myself realizing that in Eligio's company, any topic seemed possible. That thought made me decide to mirror his libertine frankness. "Yes, that's true. In my early twenties, the girl I engaged to marry cheated on me. After such cruelty in a fiancée, I should've never married her. But I was stupid."

"Who was the guy?"

"Some jackass she'd known back in high school, now a policeman. I believe she chose a cop to sadistically flaunt a poet's polar opposite. She simply thrived on the drama of sleeping around, sometimes with married men. And she also relished the act of spite. I now believe these situations were meant to compensate for a time when she felt powerless against men. In conflict, she usually grew cold, even violent. And in divorce, the same kind of perversity painted me as the arch villain. She never owned her part, that it was *she* who was more hostile…and the first to cheat."

"Self-delusion can protect people from themselves."

After the coffee pot gurgled to announce our brew, Eligio lifted it from the stove, poured, and suggested we carry our cups outside, standing beneath the brilliant green leaves hanging from the pergola. We sipped the espresso with appreciation, while at the same time noting the elegant contours of the valley below.

"From here the road looks like a snake baking in the sun."

"Yes," Eligio said, his smile showing good teeth. He turned to study my small garden planted with figs, clementines, and small un-ripened pears. "It's a perfect blend of wild and tame, more English than Italian. Deceptively difficult to achieve!"

"Actually, English actors once lived here, and they planted the whole thing."

"Actors up here?"

"A Shakespeare troupe. Their producer was Italian. He summered in the house that's now Roberta's."

"As an Italian, I shouldn't say this, but I, like many, hold the opinion that the English are the true gardeners."

"You mean Capability Brown, and all his earthworks? Getting nature to outdo nature?"

"Yes. Precisely. Transforming an entire landscape is much more difficult than lining up fountains, statues, and urns." Eligio's face changed as if he were working a puzzle. "May I tell Roberta about today? I mean, about the tunnel?"

"No!" The force of my objection stunned. "Can't we wait? I mean we're just getting to know each other. Under scrutiny…this'll feel like we're in some kind of Noel Coward play."

He read the look of terror on my face. "I don't know those plays, but you mentioned him before. Free love is very difficult. The longer we wait, the more time will be added, only lending to more injury. So far, you and I have little to report."

"I really need to think about this."

"You must think about what you're admitting. Remember no one decides, we simply discover."

"Yes. I know. And truth can cauterize hurt."

• • •

We finished our coffee just as Lydia and Buddy appeared from the roadway opening the wrought-iron gate at the top of the stairs. Signor Vescovi walked behind, carrying packages and a market bag. "Put them anywhere," Lydia said.

Buddy reached in his pocket and handed Vescovi a tip. "This army marches on its chiffon!"

Vescovi looked perplexed.

Buddy tried to explain. "Sequins? Glitterati?" His fingers moved in midair as if tinkling keys on a piano.

Lydia stood stretching the small of her back. "He doesn't get English, you jerk!"

Vescovi glared at her, then haltingly said, "Good night, lady…and gentleman!"

Buddy whooped. "See! He gets something!"

When Vescovi was gone, Eligio offered wine, but Buddy held up a flat palm. "Gotta use the can first." He did a little dance that accentuated his thickened legs, then ran inside.

Removing a compact from her bag, Lydia rubbed a finger over one eyebrow. She recounted how that afternoon a local man had stopped her at the market. "He'd seen the magic show…told me I was better than my partner!"

Eligio's face held an expression of either awe or repulsion. My crude cousin, the heroine of every story she told, forever presenting her life as uber-amusing. When Buddy looked at his bride, did he still find her recognizable? The mounting diatribe of her vinegary nonsense made a caricature, one stippled with feathers, beads, and an artificial laugh. But under that overbearing persona lurked the pudgy and profane teenager still enrolled at the beautician's academy. As a youth, I hadn't yet parsed sarcasm as the weapon of the weak, and her witty and irreverent abrasions were mistaken for power.

"The little son-of-a-bee wants more rehearsal! Says I don't care about quality. I say quality? This show's so cheap it oughta play in a button factory!"

I glanced to see Eligio's reaction; unfortunately, Miss Lydia, shrewd beautician that she was, caught the glance and perhaps our chemistry. If I dared hold anything private, her invasion would soon try to break into even my most protected places.

Her blue eyes bored like lasers into my body, as I tried to fortify myself, hoping she could feel the strength of my vault, built for perpetuity. But our history and shared pool of genes exposed us, and privacy felt futile. I smiled. Her brittle laugh, and the suggestive tilt of her head, let me know she was indeed peering into my soul. Hoping to hinder further investigation, my mind conducted a war with ethics: how well could I lie? Half of the veal roast, the two plates we'd eaten from, our two wineglasses and coffee cups remained in view. Should I clear them to hide that we'd taken lunch alone?

Buddy returned. "Did she tell you about Portofino? Tickets are selling like hotcakes! Garafallou is capitalizing with two more bookings, one at a military base near La Spezia, the other a higher-end hotel near Monte Carlo. He's close to a deal in France."

Lydia lit a fresh cigarette, gesturing in the air for emphasis. "Who wants to play a military base?"

I laughed. "Bob Hope?"

"And Buddy, would you *please* stop telling people my army marches on chiffon?"

Buddy was unfazed. "I'll stop when you stop."

I felt relief that her criticism was now focused on him.

We all turned to find Roberta calling from the top of the stairs. "No one told me there was a party! I had to hear it from Pina!"

Buddy went to the steps. "Why you'd never be left out!" Eligio leapt up and went to kiss her hand. An ancient voice spoke irrationally in my head: *What am I, chopped liver?* Buddy poured Roberta a glass of wine.

Like a parrot snatching at a sunflower seed, Lydia's glance suggested she was about to purloin my private life. This would be retaliation for what I was hiding. She placed a hand on her hip in a pasty, movie-star gesture. "Eligio did Walker ever tell you that his mother was a model?"

Eligio turned to me. "Was she really?"

"Let her tell it. If she can."

Unable to resist the spotlight, Lydia balanced her cigarette on the rim of an ashtray. "You see, my grandmother worked at Pomeroy's, a department store in Harrisburg, Pennsylvania. And every Wednesday, her sister, Walker's grandmother, came in by bus from Palmyra. The pair ate lunch at Caplan's, a drugstore soda-fountain. Right, Walker?"

"If you say so."

"One Spring, 1950 or 51, a portrait photographer working on consignment passed through town. He set up a backdrop and camera in one of the front sidewalk display windows. People stood on the pavement watching other people get their portraits taken. *Right?*"

"Wasn't born yet."

"Grandmother worked at the notions counter. Since she believed young ladies liked soaps, thread, and ribbon, her niece, Walker's mother, was invited to remain there in that cheerful department. Her mother took the elevator up to housewares to buy vacuum cleaner bags, and as soon as she was out of sight Walker's mother was rushed into the photo window. As a store employee, my grandmother got a discount and the guy behind the camera grew bewitched by the contours of the young face. Walker's mother couldn't have been more than fourteen or fifteen years old? Months later, a fashion editor in New York phoned and invited her to pose. The guy had talked her up. Isn't that true, Walker?"

"Couldn't tell you."

Lydia looked triumphant as any town crier. "Well, her father blew a gasket. Refused to let her go! It was weeks before her mother prevailed, reasoning the money could go for college. So that's the sanitized…I mean edited version of how Walker's mother, in a matter of months, became a star of the fashion pages."

Pina came out and with a damp cloth, began to wipe the table around Lydia's ashtray. Lydia gestured in a dismissive way she'd learned here in Italy. "Lady, please! *Scuzzi!* I'm in the middle of a story!"

Pina glared and went muttering back inside.

Lydia paused. "What did that old bat say?"

I shrugged. "Wasn't important."

"Come on! Couldn't have been nice."

"Just nonsense…"

"Tell me."

Roberta broke in. "She said 'dalle stalle, alle stelle, alle stalle.'"

"What's that mean?"

"Loosely….'from the stall, to the stars, back to the stall.'"

"Is that a kick at me? Does that old broad think I'm a mule? She does, doesn't she?"

Eligio smiled. "Old village women delight in being contrary."

"It's that converted barn we rent. She doesn't know we can afford more. That there's no need for this cheapness."

"Pay Pina no mind," Eligio said. "Here on the Riviera, these villages are secrets kept by savvy Italians from Genoa and Milan. They're by no means second best." He moved to pour more wine, and I noticed how well his pants fit, and resisted a ridiculous impulse to reach out and touch the seat of brushed cotton fiber.

"Roberta doesn't live in a barn. Why can't we get a house like hers? One down by the water."

I moved my chair closer to the table. "Anyone in-the-know knows…that the places by the water are corrupt and overpriced."

"And my house costs a fortune to maintain," Roberta added. "A wreck when I bought it."

Pina returned resentfully bearing a plate of cheese and sliced pears. Vengeance suddenly overcame me. "Hey Buddy, tell Pina how someone said Lydia looks like Anna Magnani." Pina, hearing her name, looked for explanation. "Go ahead, tell."

Lydia's face was startled. "No don't!"

Buddy grinned. I feigned innocence even as I jumped in to translate. Hearing Lydia compared to the great Magnani, Pina looked at me as if I'd just birthed a calf. "Not possible," she said. "Anna's eyes were deeply dark, this woman's light. Anna's teeth…large. This woman's small."

"But an essence of something?" I prodded. "The stance? An air of humor? Peevishness?"

"Anna was never peevish! She suffered malcontent from loving unfortunate men."

"She says you're both distinct."

Lydia was all ears to my obviously warped translation. Any satisfaction was short-lived, for I saw Eligio's disapproving face and was embarrassed to have adopted the kind of ugly tactics Lydia might employ, in front of him. Before I could amend my action, a circus calliope began from somewhere across the valley.

"That's the village of Santa Merici!" Eligio said. "Their church festival begins tonight." The electricity was switched on, and glowing white bulbs now dramatically outlined the frame of the belltower in the distance. The volume of the music swelled, and cheers could be heard.

"Can't we go?" Lydia asked.

"It'd be a good hour to get there," Eligio said. "It only looks close."

"Is it safe?" Lydia asked. "I mean, the road—at night?"

Eligio looked incredulous. "Is any road truly safe?"

Buddy came over loosely clutching a beer bottle. "My wife's got a zany fear of heights. Gets jittery as a monkey."

"Stop putting words in my mouth. I'm not jittery. Let's go!"

● ● ●

Darkness doubled our travel time. Each turn up the neighboring mountain, widened our view of the sea in the distance, the moon mirroring to fracture the dark water. On all sides the mountain pine trees leaned in, barely rooted in the soil, brushing their inky branches over the Bentley's roof. One moment the temperature was sultry and full of brine, the next dank with that well-known subterranean mountain air pressing fog onto the window glass.

The village marker of Santa Merici appeared, vehicles lining both sides of the roadway. At an open spot we parked, and stepped out onto a bed of soft pine needles. A stream of other merrymakers went joyfully by toward an archway in the distance, and we followed them. Walking through, we stood in a large open square, sausages and chestnuts on portable grills smoking the air, the bulbs on the church bell tower we'd seen from across the valley glowing in the haze. At the far end, a wooden platform housed a calliope, a man and woman in folk costume accompanying on neck-strung accordions, wrinkled fingers pressing the pearly buttons, while pushing and pumping the bellows. Two girls came to stand on either side, lifting red violins to their chins. Through old teeth with matching gold bridgework, the elders smiled as their youth joined in measure.

Couples circled the platform in a foxtrot, round and round, leather shoes sanding the planks of the wooden dance floor. The men wore starched shirts and dark pants, the women cotton dresses or straight wool skirts topped with knit pullovers. Lydia leaned on the railing. "I love it…whole town knows the same steps!"

Across the valley's dark abyss, I tried to identify which pin-cluster of lights on the mountainside might be our village. "Do me a favor," I heard Lydia whisper to Buddy. "Ask Roberta to dance."

Buddy grew irritated. "Can't you and I dance first?"

"I mean *later*. Who knows if Eligio even dances?"

"He's from these parts. Why wouldn't he know what they dance?"

Buddy was right, and I enjoyed hearing him bristle at being cast as the dancing husband, an interchangeable figure spinning on a marital cuckoo clock. The song ended and the townsfolk clapped, rosy faces full of cheer. They began to trade places, the stairs crowded, some coming down others going up. A four-four waltz began, and Eligio asked Roberta to dance. Buddy's grin had a great deal of gloat in it. Lydia, in disgust at his sense of vindication, walked off, pocketbook dangling on the crook of an elbow like Mama Roma.

Buddy signaled, and we ran in pursuit toward a row of gaming kiosks. Mercifully, she stopped at a booth where tin ducks swam in a loop waiting to be shot. Lydia threw money down, grabbed an air rifle, pressed it against her shoulder, aimed, then pulled. The force shook the ducks, but none were hit. Unencumbered, their circular swim continued, powered by a boy on a stationary bicycle. On the third pull, Lydia struck a green-headed mallard. "Bulls-eye!" the boy yelled, pedaling faster. The fallen duck circled to the upside-down part of the loop, passed a rubber wedge, then reset, springing back to life.

"Finally, a legitimate resurrection," I joked. That made Buddy smile despite his mood. Five rounds later, urged on by the pedaling lad, the requisite number of ducks finally slain, Lydia walked away having won a small stuffed camel. "Anyone want a grilled sausage?" Buddy asked. We declined and watched him walk to the vendor. Lydia read my thoughts. "Funny how out of all of us, he's the one to put on weight. He was always so skinny."

We studied him as he waited for the grilled sausage, the curve of his backside looking positively equine, all rump and gallop.

Lydia hugged the camel to her body. "So, what's up with Eligio?"

"Huh?" The question shattered our truce.

"You can't fool me…"

"What? What're you talking about?" My surprise exaggerated into ridiculous proportion.

"Looks like a fancy three-way? Don't worry…I won't tell!"

Buddy returned with sausage and bread stuck on a skewer. I felt myself try to hide how shocked I felt over the directness of her query. We meandered back toward the calliope. At the platform, Buddy finished the sausage and asked Lydia to dance.

"Oh, for God's sake, wipe your hands first." He tried to use the paper napkin wrapped round the empty skewer, but it was greasy, and he tossed it in a metal barrel, wiping his hands on his pants. She hesitated, then passed the stuffed camel to me. Soon on the platform, they went gliding by, Lydia leaning back to catch my eye, her preening yet again meant to illustrate how hers was indeed a champagne high-life. I waited by the wooden railing like a rube. Ignoring the dance, I looked instead at the brilliant clouds etching the black sky. Someone once said life's most sublime moments almost always occurred while standing alone. Could that be true? God knows I'd never asked for this celibate life or to mishandle present opportunities, and yet I accepted any and all blame for it.

The waltz ended, and they stood bickering. Something must have shifted, another romantic tempest begun. They came closer to the exit stairs. "Felt like I was dancing by myself." I heard him say loudly. "Oh, fuck off, will you!" she shot back, oblivious to the looks of the crowd. Embarrassment crept up my neck. To wait out the disagreements of quarreling couples takes deliberate stoicism. Toy camel under my arm, I dug my hands into my jacket pockets.

Buddy pushed his way down the steps. "Come back here!" Lydia shrieked as the calliope began to play an Italian folk tune. She began rushing against the crowd to keep up with him. "I'm sick of apologizing for who I am!" she screamed. "Other people exalt me. Why can't you?"

He turned for a face off. "What are you? A deity? No. A big nobody! Any normal woman would prevent her husband from dancing with other women. Not you!" They walked on toward the arch leading back to the car. I looked up and saw Roberta and Eligio still dancing.

THROATLATCH

• • •

Portofino, Italy

An enormous painted figure of Phil Filbertson stood guard on the roof of a refitted warehouse on the outskirts of the port. The eyes, underscored with green tint, blazed below a turban lit with miniature lights that twinkled on and off, a dark cloak featuring a huge gemstone painted on one shoulder surrounded by a gold braided knot. An accompanying sign cut from plywood announced: *Teatro Commedia!* Laughing people stood crowded by the front entrance to have their picture taken beside a life-size cutout of Phil, this one constructed of thick cardboard. His right hand held a magic wand that pointed to a placard reading: *Phil Filbertson and the World Beyond Twilight!* On his upper thigh a large pink sticker announced: *Special assistance by Miss Lydia.*

Buddy greeted us at the door, his face twisted with anger. "We've threatened to sue over that. I mean, the damn thing is practically pasted on his groin."

Roberta patted Buddy's shoulder. "I'm guessing Lydia's quite upset?"

"You know it. As a consolation Garafallou has demanded Phil wear the box-cut tuxedo. And still, she looks like she's about to tear flesh. Well, that bastard better watch his step! He's about to be royally upstaged."

"What do you mean?"

"Tonight, she's gonna take off. Play it for laughs. High time too. We're taking control of this flea circus once and for all!"

An usher came to seat us, and once we'd crossed the threshold Buddy scurried off with but a quick "*Ciao!*" We took our seats and gazed up at the mighty metal beams supporting the roof, its walls hung with gigantic Egyptian medallions, emphasizing an ancient world about to unfold. The theater could hold more than a thousand, and we knew tonight was sold out, each row filling with patrons under the excitement of anticipation. In the program, Lydia's biography named and thanked all of her acting teachers. "Too many Svengalis," I whispered. "Implies they're a mercenary lot."

"I don't follow."

"Her earnest, gushing gratitude suggests the show is tangible proof that all the classes she's paid to attend have been worth their fees and time."

"I see. By that logic, playing awful cruise ships, where mediocrity frames the walls of every stateroom, must then also represent their teaching prowess?"

"Exactly. Over-enthusiasm in an eighteen-year-old can be forgiven. But at her age?"

We spotted Garafallou pacing the back of the house, counting heads. The aisle seat beside Roberta sat empty, and I suggested we might be able to move over. "That's for Eligio," she said.

"Oh. Is he coming?" That fact disrupted my equilibrium. Now I could only pretend to study the playbill. Some Egyptian-sounding music began to be piped in, swelling until the house lights started lowering.

Eligio arrived just in the nick of time, a swashbuckler plunging into his dark seat, amid the familiar thrill of theatrical hush affording no time to acclimate. He kissed Roberta's cheek hello, and leaned across to whisper some cordiality to me. The curtain began to rise, hot stage lights warming our cheeks like sunshine. Phil stood dead center, unblinking, a small portable table at his side. The sharp lines of the box-cut tuxedo granted his unwashed crust no forgiveness, and delivered no trace of the dreaded country-club swank. I imagined Victorian mystique lent a better disguise. In truth, Phil resembled a mortician, one just back from embalming something left outside for too long.

He let the applause go unacknowledged, standing in perfect stillness without blinking. The hall quieted. He moved quickly to produce a deck of cards. Some instructions were skillfully mimed to people seated in the front row, directing them to draw a card without looking. They brought the choices up close to their chests, waiting for Phil, in deep concentration, to speak slowly, his Italian as strangely-accented as his English. The efficiency and timing impressed, as he guessed every number and suit; the crowd applauded. A few more well-executed but perfunctory tricks followed, and then the deck of cards was smoothly tucked away. A clear glass wand appeared next. Phil held it up, and its color changed from yellow, to green, then blue to purple, then red. I glanced around and saw people staring with rapt attention. On cue, the wand released a white smoke. With each puff, Phil repeated the word, "Sha-la-mar-ee!" The acoustics exaggerated his stiff Albanian-Italian accent. Many stifled chuckles at the odd conjuring sound, especially in its repetition. "Sha-la-mar-ee! Sha-la-mar-ee!"

And then something strange occurred, Phil's earnestness took deep hold, as if the audience as a whole suddenly decided to forego cruel amusement, relinquishing their free will. The theater entered a weird, communal, hypnotic trance, sitting spellbound as Phil wove bizarre magic through a series of well-practiced tricks. His fluidity is what wore them down. How eager people seemed to want to suspend rationality, to feel the pull of an illusional mystery. More than thirty minutes passed, enough time to allow the rhythm of these various warm-up tricks to cast a complete spell, the whole routine gliding along to eradicate all resistance. There was no doubt, Phil was in control. I leaned over the armrest and whispered: "Exceeding my expectations."

"Unbelievable," Roberta agreed.

In awe at the crisp timing employed to fold up the portable table, we startled when his soothing precision was interrupted, by the beat of a pre-recorded drumroll sounding from speakers. Moving left of center, Phil gestured grandly toward a crushed velvet curtain at the back of the stage. He converted to English to speak over the suspenseful drumbeat, conveying excitement even to those who spoke no English. "And now, with no further ado, joining to assist m-ee— the one and only M-ees Leedia!"

We applauded madly as the velvet curtain parted revealing Lydia holding a pose on a small platform in a spectacular silver dress. The spotlight switched on, a hot flash to illuminate her flawless ivory complexion with its violent red gash of crimson lipstick. People gasped at the contrast. A man several rows back bellowed, "Phantasma!"

Lydia batted her thick theatrical lashes, waiting for the hall's applause to abate. Only then did she step down from the dais, her elegant high-heeled walk so sleek in its choreographed grace. The silver sequins of her dress crackled and sparkled like sunshine on a lake and Phil came to meet her, extending his arm. The audience *ooh-ed* when he bent to kiss her hand through its long black velvet glove.

Roberta and I turned to one another in disbelief, then leaned forward not to miss a thing. Buddy had been right, her physical presence did indeed upstage Phil. I dared not breathe, the stage glamour holding me enraptured, as she lit an incredibly long wooden match, ever so gracefully lifting the flame to meet a cigarette dangling from Phil's mouth. He puffed, and the cigarette somehow vanished from between his lips. A murmur ruffled the hall. The smoking cigarette reappeared from inside his mouth, and a spontaneous applause broke out. "How does he not burn to a crisp?" a captivated woman behind us blurted out in Italian. We watched with scrutiny to try and detect the trick, and its many variations. Each time the smoking cigarette heightened our excitement as it reappeared from a different place. In a final gesture, Phil allowed the cigarette to magically appear between Lydia's velvet fingers. She puffed on it. Impossible! The audience clapped joyously to be so fooled. She continued to puff, and the hall grew achingly quiet, held in elated concentration. All at once the butt vanished, then reappeared, Phil now holding it. He took the final drag, tossed it down and pressed it into the ground with the toe of his shoe. The hall erupted in cheers, thrilled to have been smitten by the mysterious unison of the pair.

In the next trick, Lydia extended her gloved arms, and Phil placed a wide champagne glass on the back of each hand. The glasses were filled from a hefty over-sized champagne bottle. The crowd's murmuring could be heard as the liquid in each glass disappeared, and then somehow re-appeared. Phil lifted one glass to Lydia's crimson lips, and she took a sip. "Dom Perignon—1929", she said, her first spoken line. She winked. The audience *ooh-ed* with appreciation for her and the rare vintage.

Phil returned the glass to her extended hand. He poured again, and the riveted crowd watched like eagles as he took the second glass and brought it to his lips. He sipped, sipped again, she winked, batted her eyelashes, and the glass disappeared. The audience grew wild. Lydia made an elegant curtsy. Phil bowed. By their smooth union onstage, you would never know they despised one another.

Another drumroll and Phil returned to center. Again, his comic broken English added amusement. "Thee-s next moment has not been seen by any Occ-ee-dental person since the famous V-ee-netian explorer Marco Polo saw ee-t on a trip to I-ndia." He paused as a voice from the speakers translated his words into Italian. He gestured even more grandly. "M-ees Leedia…let us pro-ce-eed!" Lydia did a sudden comic double-take, one eyebrow shooting up. The audience chuckled at her reaction to his stilted command. Phil looked clearly vexed and waited for seriousness to restore.

"New stuff?" Roberta whispered.

I shrugged, unable to pull my eyes away from the careful maneuvers. Phil was uncoiling a piece of heavy rope across the length of the stage, and it really was quite funny to watch Lydia's expression as she displayed more mockery. His gestures, goaded by her corrosive comic glare, grew correspondingly precise. The audience recognized hi-jinks in the making, and thinking it part of the act tittered in a manner Phil clearly didn't appreciate. It seemed to me he knew Lydia's condescension would lend derision to his magician-ship and under her incredulous reactions their efforts might soon appear to be merely hoaxes.

Roberta leaned in. "Treats him like Ricky Ricardo."

"Yup."

The snickering grew louder. Phil paused dramatically, waiting for the house to return itself to politeness. "Plee-ase people!" But even the many p's sounded funny coming from him. He continued to straighten the rope, and every few seconds a different member of the audience let an unrestrained guffaw break free, and then more laughter followed. Phil persevered with dignity, and just when boredom at watching the rope preparations began to stir restlessness, the long piece of jute shot straight up into the rafters disappearing behind a transom. The surprise and speed of it all astonished us and a mad applause burst forth.

Good performers, like good politicians, will hold a fickle mob in the palm of their hand, and Phil was showing he had some of that instinctual skill. Through clever feats of magic, he by-passed the crowd's pre-dismissal of him and went on to triumph. Disrespect and snickering now had to be re-considered, and the audience seemed ashamed at how only minutes earlier their power had united against Phil. They as a group had wished failure upon him, and now their crazed applause displayed a kind of penance for their too facile abandonment of *Twilight's* magician. Lydia detected the shift. The mystery of his magic was trouncing her crass comedy. I could tell his success was unnerving her plan, eyes squinting, concentration disrupted, her glittery entrance suddenly seeming not grand but diminished, irrelevant, unsustainable. Terror flashed over her face, followed by a static fix. I recognized that look: *Danger!*

My jaw-bone clenched. I knew with that look, impulsive self-doubt and insecurity were flooding her brain. That look always marked a transition to reck-lessness. Lydia delivered her next line with a sarcastic bite, but an over-bearing pretentiousness infected her tone. No wonder Phil was furious. He tossed a large metal ring in the air. Lydia strained to catch it on her gloved forearm, her venomous face wrenched to broadcast how criminally overqualified she was for these maneuvers. But somehow her stage superiority had stopped being funny.

The precision of their unity evaporated, replaced by a ridiculous and disdain-ful type of playacting. The audience sensed it, but they were not privy to know the source of what was behind the scene—nor could they ever know her pain— that youthful vulnerability, that young girl coming from green spigots and grotty tiles, wishing for more, wishing for better, making award speeches in the mirrors of public restrooms, that young girl in love with Bobby Goldsboro, and shamed by a father who after dinner walked around the house with his pants unbuckled, saying he needed to let his 'guts breathe.' How could these strangers know the grotesque disappointment and pain that were the source of this woman's comic defense? Try as I might, it was impossible for me to disassociate her arrogant stage manners from that overweight Wormleysburg adolescent, trying so hard to escape her crude meat-packing childhood, the meager Friday paychecks earned but for Kielbasa and potatoes. As a teen, cruelty had filled her dating life, yet she regaled us through biting humor to savage a slew of mediocre boyfriends, each anecdote justifying her stoic vengeance. Back then she delighted us with tales of her own cheating, bragging of trysts with the married bosses at restaurants where she'd waitressed. These painful memories flashed through my mind, and I saw all the nights she and Phil must have trooped around from town to town, earnestly playing it straight for any frat-house, shopping mall, or child's play-party that would hire them.

Playwrights advise clowns never to do more than is written down for them, and as the act wore on, Lydia illustrated why. Working ever harder to swim upstream for laughs, I saw her old man with his pants unbuckled appear within her. My stomach grew queasy. Too bad the audience held no key to source the trauma lurking under her psychological defense. By now she truly wasn't funny—just excessively crass. Her impertinent vanity deepened the crime. Even the sequins of her dress seemed to tarnish and tire. Out of breath, she seemed unable to ace even trivial duty. She flubbed a line, her voice over-pitched, milking the error like in an under-rehearsed school variety show.

Lydia's attempted coup to overpower Phil was a dismal failure. With no intermission, and no chance to regroup, doom blossomed irreversible. My elbows ached from how hard I was pressing the armrests, and I grew ever more disturbed. Phil began to toss the foot-wide rings across the stage directly at Lydia. She lunged, dark, velvet gloves jutting in rapid movement, like the necks of two black-swans, fiercely pecking at the rings as if for breadcrumbs. She missed a ring and it clanged to the floor. Pride and perfection quashed, her subterranean fracture widened. Had Phil purposefully thrown it off to punish? She grew clumsier, bending down in the tight dress to pick it up. Though managing to catch all the remaining rings, her efforts began to look dim-witted, and the ruthless clang of metal against metal felt mechanical and puny.

"Can't save her," Roberta whispered.

"Nope."

During the next sequence, she accidentally dropped a loving-cup, revealing the trophy was not made of gold or even metal, but hollow plastic. To retrieve it, she again had to crouch in the tight dress, this time her rear end bumped a scenery panel, the canvas rippling up to shred any last trace of elegance or illusion. The audience laughed. Some laughed harder still. Her complexion went from pale to waxy. How would Buddy ever sustain his cheery boasts of her talent after this? Married couples have seismographs, and like me, he must have sensed her disaster seconds after the unscripted comedy began.

"A drag show now," Roberta whispered

"Yup. Pathetic."

Another recorded drum roll, and Lydia hurried to the far side of the stage. A lit sword was handed to her from the wings, and like a well-practiced revolutionary, she bore the flaming weapon, but her high-heeled walk wasn't intended for haste, her pointed shoes now tip-toeing, as if in fear of slipping on a newly waxed floor. The judicious among us grieved lower into our seats. My stomach churned on. Phil glared. He then grabbed the fiery sword, and turning in profile, plunged it down his throat. The tendons of his neck strained. After a pause, his mouth released a brilliant, fiery, volcanic display. The skin around Lydia's features went slack, then she made a gagging expression.

"She's got a run-of-the-tour contract," I whispered.

Phil turned to the audience with a scripted joke, saying that the fire had *warmed* his throat. There was some cheering and claps. Strangely, the madness of Lydia, her condescension and lack of restraint continued to work to Phil's advantage. The tricks were paltry and base, but his persistence revealed an attractive quality of spirit. The crowd began to root with strange compassion for his enduring determination.

He took center stage. "And now, lad-ees and gentlemen, for our finale, we bring you the *pièce de résistance!*" He paused and waited for the voice-over from the speakers to translate his words into Italian.

I felt a sudden lurch of hope as Lydia looked to be recovering, but then a large sarcophagus was pushed in from the wings and she walked slowly to meet it. Sadly, one of the castors caught a floorboard and the monolith tottered. No, it was not carved of mighty granite, but something more akin to Styrofoam. A stagehand wearing a headset scurried out, to steady the artificial mass and keep it from toppling onto Lydia. Marching with impatience, Phil went and swung the paint-chipped door open. Lydia leaned on his arm, removed her heels, and stepped inside, her hips and thighs looking thick as they pressed into the sides of the sarcophagus.

"Bustle would've been more flattering," Roberta whispered.

"Yup."

The lid closed, and as the mummy's coffin turned, my mind spun too, weighing what future Lydia might have—if any. Should she still want to perform, she'd likely be typecast as over-emoting harridans, neurotic witches, and what Roberta defined, a drag queen's stylized female competition.

How was Eligio taking it? The illumination from the stage shadowed his jaw. Sensing my gaze, he turned and our eyes locked. A shocking animal sensation stirred. I snapped my head back to the performers and forbade my eyes to turn and look again. My pulse raced, a parrot on a unicycle, vision blurring, focus softening, the heat in the theater rising as it does in a mid-day desert, the stage becoming a mirage. In only partial comprehension, I saw Lydia's feet wiggling, some metal sheets slid with purpose into the Egyptian box. Then, somehow, she was being pieced back together and the next thing I knew she was stepping back out onto the stage, and stepping back into her shoes.

The sound of applause cleared my head. During the curtain call, Phil did his best to feign admiration as he presented her with a bouquet of feathered flowers. Their compressed wires sprang open and Lydia brought them to her nose, pretending they held fragrance, the full brunt of her ignominious degradation illustrated by the seedy fakeness of the petals, their bright edges gray and frayed from nights of being tossed backstage among the greasepaint and flea powder.

The houselights went up and the aisles grew clogged, people putting on their jackets, the whole nightmarish thing bloody over. As hostess for the after-party, Roberta said she had to dash.

"But, wait," I replied. "Aren't you going backstage?"

"I hate funerals."

"Roberta, they comped us! Come back…even if but for a second?"

"I can't. Or surely, I will cry. Seeing my tears will be awful for her."

Eligio looked at me with eyes full of pity. "As a cousin, I imagine you must go?"

"My stepfather was an actor. I know the drill. My cousin has just been drawn and quartered. I must go. Poets learn to accept silence, but actors? Actors perceive it as excruciating criticism. No art demands more response. Claps and bravos are all there is to counter the nerve-wrack. That's the theater."

Eligio held Roberta's coat as she eyed the exit. "Look, I'll heap plenty of praise at the party."

"I reckon for the privilege of leaving, hosting the after-party is worth it."

"I will compose myself. Be ready and waiting to cheer her at home."

Buddy came rushing up the aisle. "Stunning, wasn't she…I mean, what an entrance!" His speech was taken straight from the good husband's handbook.

We stared at him like three blind mice.

Eligio spoke first. "It was clever…and so amusing!" I envied his tact.

"Yes, we were just saying how awfully amusing it was!" Roberta caught the gaffe in her backhanded praise, repeating that as hostess she couldn't come backstage. Buddy said he understood. "But Walker, you'll come back, won't you?"

"How can I not?"

Roberta took the chance and made her getaway. I watched Eligio follow in obeyance, now to occupy *my* passenger seat in the car beside her.

• • •

"The acoustics went wonky," Buddy said leading me backstage. "And the new comic bits will need adjustment to settle in."

Near the dressing room, not wanting to swing a wrecking ball, I practiced words in my head to express support. Luckily, Garafallou was a producer who knew his after-show job. His tight pocketbook couldn't let even a trifle fold, and his abiding shrewdness understood backstage drama could do more damage than even a bad review. "Oh, what fun we've had tonight!" he said, taking me by the elbow. "Lydia look! Your cousin has come to worship at your feet!"

I congratulated her, and we hugged, but her eyes held the stultifying look of a slaughterhouse calf, one just gutted, a humiliation too horrible to imagine. Garafallou fought to keep us from tripping over her defeat by employing a frolicsome effervescence. "Oh, what fun! And more fun is just beginning!" he said, voice thick with cream. "What fun!"

I placed my arm around her shoulder. "You've always had a penchant for comedy," I said. "And now we all look forward to celebrating over dinner!" She smiled, mechanically, as she must've been told to do. But then her eyes began to well.

"Tears of joy are to be expected at a triumph," Garafallou interceded. "And what fantastical mountain peaks lie ahead!"

Lydia dabbed at her lashes with a tissue, her features becoming a mask. "Walker is it true you're driving back with us?"

"Plenty of seats," Garafallou beamed. "There's always a space if you're a member of our star's royal family!"

A few more guests came through the door, and Garafallou hurried to lavish his madcap boisterousness onto them. I kissed Lydia's hand, then stepped out into the hallway so they could greet Lydia unencumbered. In the distance, Phil stood alone by an open garage door in the holding area, a fresh cigarette between his lips. I went to him and offered my congratulations.

He grimaced. "To pree-tend pleasure not received…insults the inner compass." He brushed ashes from the sleeve of his jacket.

"Fair enough." I smiled, leaving him to enjoy his smoke.

He called after me. "Walker, perhaps you can tell me-e something?" His voice rose too high at the end of his question. "Has your cousin always been this ee-mpossible?"

I gave the question a moment's thought. "Yes. She has."

• • •

Levanto, Italy

A dress of dark velvet, scooped at the neckline, emphasized the soft slope of Roberta's shoulders. But as soon as I entered it was clear by her face that something was wrong. "Hans is here." Her voice stayed low. "Never dreamed he'd come down tonight. He never comes this time of year."

Her irritation shifted to warm welcome as Garafallou came chattering through the door. "Oh, there's nothing like an after-party! As producer, I live for these times!"

"I'll take your hat. And where are the others?"

"Lydia and Buddy stopped by their house so she could change. And Phil, a perfect gentleman, sacrificed the event so Walker could have his seat in the car. No amount of pleading would sway him. He drew his sword and knighted Walker without hesitation!"

"The bar is set out on the terrace…go, pour yourself a drink." Roberta then called after him. "If you don't take it neat, Eligio will be along with ice."

"Where's he getting ice?" I asked.

"Vescovi."

"Vescovi has ice?"

"You know, a huge freezer full of rabbits!" Roberta moved around, nervously arranging tangerines, chocolates, and little silver dishes of pistachios. I could tell she'd already had a bit of wine. "Can't believe Hans came down during allergy season. There's some plant that blooms this time of year…always gives him a rash."

Garafallou popped back to join us, swirled a drink. "I must tell you what magnificent furniture you have!" He brushed a hand over an armchair. "Fine furniture has to be one of life's great assurances."

"It will all end up at auction someday." She moved a vase. "Hans hates flowers close to the edge."

"You know, this house seems very familiar. I think I've been here before. Could it be that a producer named Bene Piccolo once lived here?"

"I've heard that name. Was he Florentine?"

"Yes! After the war, he and I collaborated to stage Shakespearean plays for Italians. A very poor living, I might add! In those days the house was a worn-down pile. It's been completely transformed!"

"A member of Irish parliament lived here before me. They put the real money into fixing it."

"Well, as I said, it wasn't this well restored when he resided here. After the war, money was so hard to come by. You've done wonders."

"Don't forget," I chimed in. "She's a decorator."

"Well, well, who'd imagine I'd once again be standing in the house of Bene Piccolo! Such memories! Each week, the famous visitors, French, English, Portuguese. The American writers, Baldwin, Hemingway, the film man De Sica. We would all stay up talking and drinking. Such stamina!"

Roberta thanked him for the compliment and patted his hand.

"You know, half of Shakespeare's plays are set in Italy. So, Piccolo used to bring an English troupe over here, a theatrical company founded and run by another actor, Francis Leicester. They all stayed in this very house…up late reciting their lines…but one night Piccolo got tired of constantly listening to them, and to English words, so he purchased a couple of old mule stalls, and persuaded the actors to convert them. That way they'd have their own residence."

"I live in one of those stalls," I said. "We share a charming terrace!"

"What! Another coincidence! I can't stand it!" Garafallou tossed a couple of pillows aside and seated himself on a low sofa. "Hard to get to these villages back in those days. But so cheap! And Italy more tolerant for the ways of actors than England. In the fifties, in Britain, their kind might still go to prison! But here! Such sunny freedom!"

A few more moments of reminiscences followed, and then Roberta and I made our way to the kitchen. Her whispering resumed. "Should've never mentioned the party. Hans is so irredeemably transparent. Takes great pleasure in supervising."

Pina entered, grimaced in our direction to mark her territory. We left and went out onto the terrace. At the far end, in Roberta's all-white garden a long table was set before a small trickling fountain. "Hans being here is sure to guarantee no one will have a good time."

As if hearing his name, Hans shouted from inside, "Who opened that flue?"

"Shit!" Roberta said. Her beautiful dress flowed behind her as she rushed indoors. The fire was indeed blazing too high. She picked up the poker and pushed at it. Hans was already padding down the stairs in slippers, face half coated with shaving cream, neck and arms tinted with calamine lotion.

Roberta spoke nervously. "I'd hoped that the aroma of lamb would waft through the house. Walker told me about a leg of lamb he'd seen roasting in a window. He'd never got to taste it so I wanted to recreate that."

Hans snatched the poker and maneuvered the vent. "Fire is no play toy!"

Roberta's face became a smooth, unreadable sculpture. Her quiet grace brooked something in my bloodstream.

"I must recount a humorous story," Garafallou said. "A grease fire in Natick, Massachusetts. It nearly ruined a family's Thanksgiving. An entire box of bicarbonate had to be dumped on the old bird. The turkey, like me, simply too fat for the oven! Once extinguished, we cooled it, rinsed it, and ate every morsel! Never saw wings so large or so well done."

The fire now under control, Pina arrived like the tardy servant in a *commedia d'arte* play. Hans handed her the poker. "I must go up to complete my toilet."

Garafallou smiled at Pina. "I recall seeing you here as a young girl, when this was Signor Piccolo's house!"

"Perhaps," she shrugged. "I care for many houses. Have done so for fifty years."

He began to recount for her the story of the Thanksgiving fire. "*Uno grande festival Americano d'autunno!*" She paid no attention and headed back to the kitchen. Garafallou took her snub in stride, and with an index finger, brushed a mighty eyebrow.

• • •

Entering the party and just learning Phil had bailed, Lydia rolled her eyes. "Good!" Roberta helped remove her wrap, and we stood in the double-height foyer as Lydia showed off her pleated dress. "I've developed a complete distrust of magicians. Like those attention-starved people who stroll around showing off exotic pets. Ferrets under hats, parrots on shoulders, chihuahuas in handbags."

"I knew a tattooed man in Marseille," Garafallou said. "He promenaded with a python round his torso. When you play there, maybe we'll look for him. If he isn't dead!"

"When I lived in Miami, a guy I knew on Lincoln Road biked around with a white hen in the basket. It laid a single fresh egg every day."

"Walker!" Garafallou said. "Is there any place on earth you *haven't* lived?"

The dimmers on the foyer lights turned higher, and we all looked up. Hans stood in the brightness of the upper landing gazing down, as if he were about to deliver a speech. He was now completely shaven, the top and sides of his gray hair trimmed flat like a brush. He wore a shirt of silvery-beige silk, cut too high in the armpits. He descended like a duke and went straight for Lydia. "I'm afraid as host I must beg forgiveness for missing your triumph."

"You didn't miss a thing."

"And where is Mr. Phil Filbertson?"

"He bailed."

"Bailed? Such a pity. I did so want to meet him. I hear he used to photograph celebrities. That he has personal acquaintance with film stars?"

Lydia pushed a hand through her hair. "No, he doesn't. He just stalked them with a camera."

"Untrue!" Garafallou said. "Phil has rubbed elbows with many elites. He and I have known one another for years, and he asked that I let you know he'll provide complimentary tickets on any night you might be free. He insisted! Generous to a fault, that one—"

Lydia interrupted. "They arrested him for stalking Jeanne Moreau!"

"Oh, now, that's been widely misrepresented!"

"It went to trial!"

"A sandbagging! He'd simply been to a party, where actors and executives were caught in beastly romps, bent on ignoring the law. He put public figures on film *flagrante delicto*! Can't always have fame on one's own terms, you know!"

Hans's face was a map of curiosity. "What was the charge?"

"Ancient history. Who remembers?"

"There were orders of protection. They forced him out!"

"Lies! Voting rigged by irresponsible lawyers."

Lydia sneered. "Spoken like a spin doctor."

"But even a minor setback can become a bright spot for one's future. You see, a travesty of law restored Phil's true passion—*magic!*"

"Bullshit."

Garafallou put his full gaze upon Lydia. "And when that day comes, my dear, when sadly you'll have to leave us, we'll be forced to search high—and low for your replacement." His phrasing paused in all the right places.

Roberta broke the tension and guided us into the living room, offering Lydia some wine. "No," she said. "I fear it's a beer-drinking night." She eyed Hans. "You know, there's no such thing as magic once you know the formula."

"A formula?" Hans asked. "For magic?"

"Yes. There are three parts. First the pledge. We show something ordinary…

deck of cards, martini glass, a cigarette. The second part is the turn. You take the ordinary and make it do something weird like disappear. The third is the hardest. Something has to be brought back. That's called the prestige."

Garafallou interrupted before she could reveal any other elements of illusion. "Oh, how the time does pass! Last week, in Paris, running late! My watch keeping time with the station tower. I had to run across the Boulevard Diderot and barely made it. Unlike driving an automobile, on the train our thoughts travel free. Did you know the Côte d'Azur express used to be called *Le Train Bleu*! And a speeding bullet it was! Today that elegance is gone, but still the cars pass through the most unified agrarian scenery imaginable. Old mustard and lavender fields so artfully planted. Great curtains of purple and gold!"

Eligio entered, holding up a green patent-leather ice bucket. "Hey! Party-people! Who wants ice?"

"Iced drinks?" Hans said. "No. They shock the digestion. They're not healthy."

Eligio blinked. "But it's a party, and I was sent out for ice. And Americans, I'm told like it."

"Born ice-lovers," Lydia said, her voice deepening with flirtation.

"Apollo loves to lick snow," Roberta said. "We went skiing once in the Alps, and he ate an entire balcony of snow." She led Eligio around the living room where his fingers gracefully lifted tongs and clinked cubes into any glasses that wanted them. "We must go easy on it," he joked. "Vescovi is going to bed!"

•　•　•

At the table, Buddy photographed the lamb roast, a platter of fried cod, and a bowl of sautéed greens. He shared news about a food story in the works and passed consent forms around the table. "Please, everyone, sign so that your faces can be considered." We all took our turn with the pen; only Hans declined citing professional reasons. Garafallou turned to him. "I've been told you're a psychologist."

"Psychiatrist."

"Nothing more noble than the helping professions!" Garafallou said.

"His success rate is extraordinary," Roberta said. "In most cases resolutions occur in a very reasonable time."

"What's the secret?"

"Hans smiled. "It's in the Swiss character."

"Can't imagine the Swiss speaking of personal things," Garafallou said. "Even in therapy."

"True." Hans agreed. "Getting past appropriate discretion is a good part of the job."

Buddy gestured with his knife. "I did a bunch of talk therapy in college. The shrink insisted I talk, talk, talk! Meanwhile, he kept his own yap shut. Just sat there and took notes. To this day, I've no idea who the guy was that I was talking to!"

"An interesting point," Garafallou said. "I mean, if the therapist is a role model for mental health, wouldn't the patient be encouraged to practice that same behavior? Be taught to listen emphatically?"

"Ha!" Lydia said. "If the sap on the couch followed the shrink's lead, they'd both sit there like dummies. They'd never analyze anything!"

Hans looked strained. "You're wondering why clients are encouraged to exercise behavior different from the therapist?"

"Yeah," Buddy said, reaching for more potatoes. "Why not just follow the guy who's the normal one? But it can't be easy when payday depends on the habits of a bunch of neurotic people. I mean therapists have mortgages too. I'm just saying, if therapy succeeds, then the patients ride off into the sunset. They never come back. A business model for the poorhouse."

Hans grew visibly agitated. "Swiss health insurance is compulsory. There are always new patients. It's all regulated."

"What Hans means is that unlike in America, there's no financial incentive for long treatment. Physicians are paid through insurance. In Switzerland, we also have deductibles—*La franchise*."

"All day long just listening to strangers blather," Lydia said. "Hans, does it ever feel like your own life is slipping through your fingers?"

Hans waved a piece of celery. "Well, it is not as entertaining as *magic*."

Buddy reached across the table for one of Lydia's cigarettes. "Stop mooching. Get your own." Buddy laughed, ignored her and lit up. "They say the only difference between shrinks and patients is that shrinks always show up."

"And who are *they*?" Hans asked.

"I dunno?" Buddy said. "Comedians?"

Lydia snatched the cigarettes back. "But Hans-y. I'm serious now. What about love and romance? I mean, having a client getting attracted to you? That must be like the holy grail!"

"That would simply be attraction transference."

Buddy moved his cigarette to his left hand and with his right served another helping of potatoes to his plate. "They say old Freudie sure rounded his bases.

I mean, all this transference stuff. That all certainly must've helped him score!"

Lydia chuckled. "Or at least solve boredom?"

Hans spoke at them with great precision. "I admit some days, listening is a chore. But the nature of the profession is to give oneself away. To provide the patient with what they never had."

Lydia gave him a sly look. "Hey Hans-y. You yourself ever have someone want to follow you along Freud's path?"

Hans glanced at Roberta, and his voice sounded with utter contempt. "And if I said yes? Would you feel violated? Or perhaps satisfied?"

Lydia laughed. "Gee, not sure. Let me get back to you."

Hans gripped the table, and I saw his knuckles were white. "Transference is not an issue in my practice. I deal mainly with children. Preadolescent and preconscious of their own sexuality—or mine."

Pina opened the door from the kitchen and with her usual surly manner asked Roberta if the plates could be cleared. To spare further interrogation, Garafallou moved his chair over to sit beside Hans, wherein the two men started a separate conversation. I tried to eavesdrop, but they spoke in French.

Lydia, at the other end of the table, began reciting for Eligio a list of her favorite beers. I could only decipher some of Hans's French. He was agreeing to some general dislike of mass media: "*...passivité n'en poursuite pas therapeutique?*" Garafallou suggested he and Hans move to occupy some lounge chairs by the window.

Eligio interrupted my concentration. He wasn't obsequious, but he did somehow charm. Was it his odd humor and funny references, the way he gestured with his hands? No. His true generosity, was the courtesy of listening. As Hans might agree, to listen is perhaps the most transformative power people have. What a great seduction—personal interest.

Lydia noticed our chemistry was making it difficult for her to launch into one of her caustic leitmotifs—fame, fashion, weight gain, eyebrow plucking, or the old days at the Mudd Club. She rejected another offer of wine. "I want beer! More beer! With ice! Hey, Walker, remember how my father put ice in his beer?"

I nodded, unwilling to be snagged as her supporting cast. Buddy reached forward to take some olives from a dish and bluntly asked Eligio what besides art did he do for a living.

"Mostly, I remove dirt from old canvas."

"Don't let him fool you," Roberta said. "He may as well have a PhD in fine art!"

Eligio demurred. "In Italy, people who might posture that they have degrees in art are as common as marble ashtrays!"

"He's promised to clean the fresco in my foyer."

"Anyone with patience can do it. It only takes water and a rag."

I tried to focus intently on hearing a new point Garafallou was making. "Television has opened the minds of the world for betterment. In the imaginations of millions, the iconography of cinema supersedes the church." Not able to translate his French fast enough, I could only catch bits of Hans's reply: "develops an *over-entertained* spectatorship…dull and inert…idles too many hands…distracts…weakens critical thinking…deepens depression and neurosis."

Lydia swirled her glass and her voice grew artificially refined. "I love art. No, I mean it. I absolutely love it. I mean…I could just be looking at it all the time." She swirled her glass. "I just love it…almost as much as I love icy beer." Another pattern in her was noticed: interjecting comic chaos to win attention.

Eligio smiled. "Art is of course important."

"What about you Walker? Do you love poetry the way I love art?"

To avoid annoying her, I answered. "Yes. I suppose."

"And why?"

I paused. "Justice. By that I mean I believe consideration for what's beautiful inspires people to seek justice. When I first read that concept, I stood up from the chair. At last, I knew my purpose."

"Yes!" Eligio said. "And that is *why* I restore art."

Lydia stared at us. "I don't get it."

"What's to get? I mean throughout time, don't you think art has been an aid to justice."

Buddy spat an olive pit into his hand. "So, you're saying art helps justice? Hmmm. Well, if that's on the beam, then even the silly art made by children should be able to persuade the court to uphold itself?"

"Perhaps. The desire would be to preserve what's best in the human animal."

Pina interrupted, placing a cheese board on the table with a thud. As we began to pass it around Garafallou and Hans rejoined us. "Hey Hans-y," Lydia said, crumpling her empty cigarette pack and insolently tossing it onto the table. "What about wife-beaters? Can they be cured?"

"Men who strike women? They can usually be helped most in a group. With one-on-one exchanges they're too self-involved, too guarded to form a meaningful relationship with the therapist. As members of a group, they eventually hold each other accountable. But one must also be sure that the woman isn't violent herself. Or provoking violence as a weapon to ensure the man becomes the guilty party."

Lydia stared across the table. "Hey Hans-y…should I see a shrink?"

"I've no opinion there."

"What about you? Do you see one?"

Her inanity finally hit its mark. Hans bristled. Roberta saw it and patted his arm. She replied for him. "We went to couples therapy once, but disliked the therapist." Hans muttered through clenched teeth. "This is no one's business." Roberta ignored him. "And I myself have over time gone to maybe six different therapists, each for six months or so."

Lydia enjoyed Hans's discomfort. "So, were you cured?"

"Of what?"

"I dunno…whatever brought you?"

"A really cool woman from Detroit helped me most," Roberta said. "She called herself a non-therapy therapist and thought if therapy lasted for more than a year, something was wrong."

"*Too* prescriptive," Hans said. "Different people need different things." His tense jaw bit a cracker and chewed. "Trauma treatment can take years."

Lydia rummaged in her handbag for a fresh pack of cigarettes, maintaining the belligerence of her tone. "Hans-y. Have you ever seen a successful union between a shrink and a patient?"

"Not often. Most people can be drawn more eagerly toward experiencing pleasure than facing pain. And over time the empathetic interest of a listener can redirect the pathways."

Garafallou looked thoughtfully at the platter of cheese in front of him. "A therapist I once met on a train told me all therapy is power based."

Hans glared. "Do you suggest I want power?"

Garafallou was startled. "Oh. Not at all. Sorry…I didn't mean to suggest anything."

Lydia lit and exhaled a stream of smoke up into the night. "But I wonder. I mean, do you…do you…in counter-transference, ever yearn?"

Hans's face contorted. "Enough! Why must Americans always assume the therapist is the deviant predator? It's disgraceful! Go anywhere on the globe, and you'll find more often it's patients who stalk therapists!"

Garafallou agreed, piling some brie onto his knife. "I've some friends in Holland who say it's a particular problem there."

Lydia folded her hands and leaned her cheek down on them to rest her head on the table. "My mother said beware any man who wants you to lie on his couch. And we should all stay away from the Danes!"

Buddy stabbed some green olives with a cocktail fork. "Danes aren't Dutch."

"What?"

He popped olives in his mouth and repeated his comment. "Danes aren't Dutch."

"Shut up. Stop picking on me. You know I'm not good at geography."

Now I noticed how the use of scorn was becoming a frequent mask for ignorance. If Lydia couldn't dominate a subject, she'd trivialize it. Irreverence provided a defense for any arena where she felt inadequate.

Eligio folded his hands and placed them on the table. "Perhaps all any of us really needs are the kind words of a mother?"

"He's right," I said, charmed to hear family substituted for professional help. "That alone might be the function of a family."

"Depends on the mother," Hans replied.

"Or the father," Buddy added.

"And do you then believe your families murdered your souls?" Eligio asked.

"This talk of killing is ghoulish," Roberta said.

Hans looked stern. "You mean each man kills the thing he loves?"

"I do not fathom it," Eligio said. "I've no wish to kill my own. My mother is a wonderful, beautiful lady."

"And what about you Walker?" Eligio kidded me good-naturedly. "As another American, have you had your share of therapy?"

The question startled. "Yes, in adolescence."

Eligio chuckled. "Well, what now! Too many stones thrown in the schoolyard?"

"No. My mother died suddenly. Counseling was mandated by the court."

"Oh." Eligio apologized. "I spoke in jest. I didn't mean to pry."

Buddy glanced at Lydia, realizing a bad topic had been introduced. "Walker's mother was very young. We couldn't have been more shocked or heartbroken."

No one at the table had the nerve to ask more questions. And Lydia seemed too planked to try and grab on to narrating the tragic story of my life. Garafallou steered an empathetic course, saying his father too had died young. "And such things can bring anyone to both Lourdes and therapy."

"Yes," Hans agreed. "Certain tragedies do more trauma than others. People often need help at these times, to seek an end to hunger, or lack, to find some absence of pain."

Lydia lifted her head from the table and now found it impossible to contain her intimate knowledge. "Walker's mother was murdered! I mean…in cold-blood!"

I felt my temperature rise at her grabbing that chance for theatricality. Garafallou looked mortified. "Oh, I am so deeply sorry."

In the nick of time, a tray of miniature orange soufflés arrived, puffed like voluminous clouds. Everyone focused on the ceramic cups but Hans. "My bed calls," he said standing up. His manner let it be known that he was done engaging petty, small minds, who through drink became armchair psychologists.

"But we haven't served coffee yet," Roberta said, utilizing social propriety to challenge his Swiss stubbornness. Hans ignored her and nodded good night in a way to let it be known that even to drink coffee with us was now beneath him. Roberta's expression became a map of inscrutability, her gentle face once more gone to stone.

. . .

Thunder awoke me, outside a torrential downpour was underway. Flush with fever, a new strain of erotic malaria pulsed through my veins, a force like the water streaming off the clay tiles and sluicing through the roofline gutters. I'd been dreaming, and like Gerard Manley Hopkins, the forbidden-self visited me in sleep, fingers of both hands clawing up patches of green moss, the earthen crust soon crumbling away to reveal an even deeper labyrinth. In this dreamscape of eros, men and women lay stripped and moaning, writhing within niches and upon catwalks, arched in pleasure, bejeweled fingers nakedly indulging gratification, aroused for whatever might still be lusted for. Was I awake? Still dreaming? My journey included a rainy walk along slick stone walls thickly grown with blue sedum, and then on through a wooded wetland, the path leading to a subterranean cave of ferruginous stalagmites.

Out over the black sea, a bolt of lightning lit the sky. Through the window, in a brief flash, I saw the universe illuminate, a dark mass suspended over a dark abyss known to us as ocean. I got out of bed and went trance-like to my bookshelf, moving a green and white agate chess board. Behind it, stood *The Book of Phrase and Fable*; and behind that, I found the familiar brown envelope. Inside were my grandfather's watercolors, along with the old photograph Aunt Greta had given me. On the daybed by the window, I lay back and studied the man's face.

In a complete reversal, tonight I saw no resemblance whatsoever between his features and my own, and sensed no imprint. How can we recognize a stranger

we've never known? I put the photograph back in the envelope, and turned to
the blooms, each watercolor, with flowers their only subject.

In hindsight, it saddened me that I hadn't complimented the old man during that Summer I'd accompanied him and Aunt Greta to Rehoboth. Instead, I'd
openly complained to her that we couldn't *buy* postcards like other people, the
kind spun from metal racks on the boardwalk, with roller coasters, bikini clad
girls, or the giant rooftop sign advertising Dolle's saltwater taffy.

On a whim, I rose and went to the wall, thumbtacking the old man's water-
colored cards in a line by order of postmark, the first dated 1949, the last 1975.
As a collection they formed the timeline of his creative life. The storm continued
sending bolts of lightning, split seconds that shocked my vision with the electric
color of the cards, an intense beauty, the petals, especially those of the later fluo-
rescent blooms, that last psychedelic advance, the borderless edges suggesting,
like tonight's thunderous clouds, the old man's inner tempest.

• • •

A day at the beach in Levanto had sounded grand in the aftermath of the party,
but a morning hangover made it seem less ideal. Shielded from the sun by an
umbrella, I waited on the terrace for the others to appear. If tried, the urgent
force of a pen could usually bring me around, so after drinking a Bloody Mary to
bypass a headache, I opened my notebook and scribbled to collect my thoughts:

I feel like the perplexed ancients who consult the prophesies of hempseed.

This with my virgin hand I sow: who shall my true love be, the crop shall mow.

*Is this attraction to E. misplaced—merely a way to justify timidity? A way
to engage R.? H. probably knows. I've heard erotic three-ways are like tea-
bags—reused, they brew ever weaker cups of tea. But E.'s tea has tannic
strength. And what about the Padre's point—that gender becomes meaningless? Is gender a subversive set of judgments—a landscape within the scope of
humanity. How much of American character relies on our notion of a dangerous frontier? Fighting something human that is unfamiliar? A treacherous walk on a rope bridge staked over an incalculably grand-canyon.*

I put the notebook down. Across the valley in the morning light, each village hung like a pastel fairyland. I sensed someone watching me from behind

and without turning, I knew who it was. Eligio called from the iron gate, already entering and coming down the stairs. At the table, my excitement grew as he pulled out a chair. "Hans has just decided to go to the beach with everyone else, so, I must defer. It wouldn't be proper. I wanted to let you know in person."

"But the beach was your idea!" Surprising fury wrenched my gut. How could Eligio simply toss the game? I quickly caught myself and adopted an indifferent tone. "That Hans is certainly the spoiler."

"There's something else I must say," Eligio said. "Please allow me to apologize for talk of killing families last night. Roberta later explained your mother's death."

"Not to worry. Obviously, you couldn't know."

"Had I known, I certainly wouldn't have spoken as I did. Not of something so tragic. I'm full of remorse. If something like that happened to my own mother, I'm sure I would simply go crazy."

"I appreciate the apology, but you did nothing wrong."

"Thank you for being so gallant."

"Oh, by the way, since I last saw you, I read about an ancient garden near Rome, surrounded by a *bosca*. An inspiration for Capability Brown."

"Yes, now that you say that I remember hearing of it. The place was bombed in the war. A doctor acquired it in the fifties, but I hear preservation is ongoing."

"Perhaps we've both been too quick to dismiss Italian gardeners!"

"To their credit, Italians often recognize they are but stewards to the land. At least some anyway. To maintain the earth's beauty is to them a value to be upheld, and they often conclude that landscapes belong to everyone."

"The world's developers ought to legislate along such social ideas. In America, most believe the land is theirs alone to exploit for profit forever into eternity. Vistas are easily stolen, or overbuilt with too big or too many houses. So many farms destroyed. If you take one-hundred acres, divide into quarter acres, that's four hundred lots. Most houses nowadays want at least two and a half baths, meaning no less than twelve-hundred toilets on one hundred acres with endless traffic, and highways. Yet any request for preservation, say build multi-storied apartments or villages on only ten of the acres, leaving the other ninety free for birds and foxes and raccoons, or to grow food, is said to interfere with the individual's promise of freedom."

"In Italy, or I should say in the more beautiful parts, many seek to preserve the unity of view, as a gift to the eyes of future strangers. Yet we too fail. Have our share of ugly warehouses and trucks. We must face facts about industry and modern necessity."

"Then I guess the question becomes, why must a warehouse be ugly?"

"Beauty costs more?"

"Does it?"

"Always."

"But it may be worth the price."

"I hope so. Maybe we can meet again to discuss this further." He stood to leave and noticed my notebook. "Are you writing poems?"

"More of a journal really. And some stuff for work. I'm developing an introduction to a book on Proust. I'm also preparing to deliver a lecture in Genoa in a few months."

The idea of a public talk engaged him, as I'd hoped it might. "Is it open to anyone?"

"Yes. Roberta and Lydia plan to attend. You'd be most welcome, but I'm warning everyone, I have yet to come up with a dignified subject."

An awkward pause widened. He lingered, then smiled. "I do look forward to it."

I watched his graceful legs climb the stairs to the street.

• • •

Hans dropped us at the private beach, and Roberta wasted no time in negotiating arrangements with the manager, a bronzed man in his late twenties, who to bulk up his biceps, gripped both ends of a yellow towel looped around his neck. The fellow seemed to take seriously the dual role of beach attendant and seducer. A few minutes of bargaining and a deal was struck that both could live with. For the rest of the Summer, we held exclusive rights to six wooden chairs slung with blue and white fabric. The chairs, set in pairs, were side-bolted to round cocktail tables, each of the three tabletops skewered with an umbrella like three toothpicks through three olives.

At the back of the beach, a wooden cabina completed the deal; it stood among two rows of identical structures, a plank walkway down the middle. Each alternating cabin was painted either bright blue or white, and at the far end a warm open shower sprayed onto a concrete slab. "Our shed is *Palermo 36*," Roberta said. "It will preserve dignity, and avoid toting wet gear all over town."

She changed into a polka-dot suit, her full bodice pleated with perfect folds. Buddy went next, the fabric of his baggy-trunks decorated with silk-screened iguanas. The bronzed proprietor, his own micro-briefs a bulging neon contrast, smirked when Buddy walked by, for the iguanas seemed to be dancing on his backside with each step. Lydia emerged last, in a one-piece tied at the neck, and to hide her thighs from the lewd man with a toothpick stuck in the corner of his mouth, she maneuvered a large straw hat the way a lady of burlesque might move a feathered fan.

Hans returned, already complaining that the sun irritated his rash. He wrestled one of the cocktail table umbrellas to the side for extra shade, and after slathering his jowls with another layer of pink calamine, wrapped his head in a Turkish towel, looking a bit like the invisible man.

The color of the sea had shifted to shades darkly indigo, the waves curling in at calf height. Buddy waded out past them to deeper waters. Lydia met him there and they sank into the saline buoyancy, her wrist draped over his shoulder like a piece of carved ivory.

With Eligio absent, the day was already excruciating. To make matters worse, Garafallou arrived, his beachwear consisting of white linen trousers and a navy blazer, Phil, at his side, looking more cadaverous in the bright light, wearing dark shorts with sheer support socks.

"Our investor in Monaco has pneumonia," Garafallou said. "To get him to write a check we must wait for his lungs to clear."

"He's nine-t-*two*!" Phil emphasized, sinking into the chair on the other side of my cocktail table.

"Change into your swimsuits in our cabina, if you like," Roberta said.

"Heaven forbid!" Garafallou said. "I'm like an old patriarch of the Greek church, my body must remain shrouded!"

Hans stood and offered Garafallou his chair, then made an announcement. "I've decided I must head back to Zurich at once." He turned toward Roberta. "I'll taxi to the train. You keep the car."

None of us said a word to dissuade him. In fact, the very idea of his departure brought giddiness. Lydia and Buddy returned, dripping wet, just as Hans walked off.

"Know what we should do?" Phil said. "Ask the waiter to bring us a deck of cards."

"Sure! Play poker on the beach!" Buddy agreed. "Find out who's King of Italy!"

"I've no talent for gambling," Roberta said. "Count me out."

Lydia cut through merriment like a knife. "You heard her. NO cards!"

Phil, perturbed, flagged the waiter and instead ordered two bottles of Pinot Grigio.

"The week's receipts are strong," Garafallou said. "Probably enough to encourage new bookings. Places these days want proof that something sells." He noticed a manuscript on my table. "Is that some author's new book?"

I nodded.

"The ability to read and write separates us from all other living species," he said. "People proclaim the wheel is a great invention, and it is, but it's nothing compared to those little squiggles of ink!"

"Yes. Truly the world beyond twilight," I said.

"They conjure that it was Greek stonemasons who developed this alphabet. And only in order to track tombstones. If that's true—then it was a *working-class* of people—not nobility—who made writing democratic."

"I suppose I always imagine some king's edict saying 'bring me an alphabet of only twenty-six letters.'"

"The genius is the brevity!"

"Yes, those twenty-six shapes are simple enough to be memorized by children, yet capable of building the world's greatest lexicon. And if that code gets passed on, the characters retained, we can continue to commune across the centuries."

The waiter could be seen hurrying back toward us from a restaurant built under the promenade. He carried a tall standing ice bucket with some stemmed glasses.

"Imagine! Symbols cut for cemeteries eventually overtook more complicated systems of writing, requiring armies of scribes penning hundreds of complex characters."

We watched the waiter uncork the wine and Phil approved it. Once it was poured the waiter offered a food menu, and Buddy, after quick deliberation, took the man's suggestion, ordering a large salmon salad to be prepared for seven.

Lydia gazed into her compact, stroking the bridge of her nose, then dug in her tote bag for a vial of tinted sun-lotion. "Hey Buddy, what was the name of that Brazilian guy? That used to hang around the Mudd Club?"

"The one who wanted you to do him on the fire stairs?"

"No! That was Pedro. And that was at CBGB's."

I suspected Lydia, hoping she might impress Roberta, was about to trot out her exuberant tales of nightlife in the big city.

"Alfred?"

"Nah. Amador!"

"Oh, I'd forgotten that one. Had terrible teeth. Remember?"

"You called him a termite."

"Wanted to be a journalist. On the dance floor, he tried to unhook my bustier. I slapped his hands. I'd bought it on Eighth Street that very afternoon. A hundred bucks at Patricia Fields. Wasn't about to see it thrown to the crowd."

Her acerbic display of status through curated memory continued until the waiter returned, this time carrying a large tray and a foldable stand. A bowl of warm potatoes was dressed in green oil, with shallots, capers, lemon, and chopped egg. The last thing added were slices of smoked salmon. After tossing, the waiter portioned the salad onto seven plates, each receiving a chunk of crusty bread. Buddy ordered another round of wine.

* * *

Talk of the past continued long after all our plates had been wiped clean. I decided to work and remained upright reading the acquiring editor's notes, but as the waiter came to claim the dishes the remainder of our group stretched out like lizards in the sun. I tried to block out the lazy conversation, but Buddy and Lydia kept introducing new topics, now droning on to list things that made most Americans fearful: *Germs. Body Smells. Lawyers.* My eyelids drooped. *Street Cameras. Taxes. Insurance Companies.*

Forget work. I put the papers aside and lowered the back of my chair. *Oh, sleep, beloved from pole to pole.* How annoying for Hans to run off after sidelining Eligio. I closed my eyes and tried to focus on the cries of circling seabirds, but Buddy's voice could not be entirely ignored. "Our Prez used to say we've nothing to fear but fear itself. Now they scare us…infringe upon our liberty. It was Reagan who dismantled the banking regulations to pay for his Star Wars… Politicians say they want to keep children safe…Just a ruse to expand the military complex."

"Can't wrap children in cotton batting." Garafallou held his wine up to the light then fingered a small gnat from the glass. "They've survived wars, caves, wigwams, igloos."

"More resilient than we give them credit for," Lydia agreed. She called the waiter, this time to bring champagne.

"The real problem is race. And history shows how too much largesse—concentrated on too few—has always made for hate."

And this from a man who'd lived much of his life on his father's money. I grew drowsy listening to such ridiculous simplifications. A cork popped. For distraction, I tried to recall passages of poems I knew by heart from my days in the high-school recitation club. "*Gunga Din*." Silently, I began to recite. How many lines could I still retrieve? *You may talk o' gin and beer when you're quartered safe out 'ere.* "Everyone quivers at taxes. My French friends go into fits. Our angel with pneumonia is French and he receives substantial reductions by residing in Monaco." *But when it comes to slaughter, you will do your work on water, an' you'll lick the bloomin' boots of 'im that's got it.* "Protecting riches demands the rich distrust even their most trusted workers. Insecurity grows with money, and they treat those workers like shit, trying to demonstrate how hard it is to be rich. Of course, working in daily inequity, often creates swindle, perhaps in powerless retaliation." *It was Din! Din! Din! You 'eathen, where the mischief 'ave you been?* "I ran into a guy from the States I once went out with. He said Sicily is the place where people get free houses if they fix them. He bragged how he planned to take one, live in it for free, but never fix it. Imagine announcing a cheating scheme so openly. How unattractive. And of course, he'd no gumption to do it." *If we charged or broke or cut, you could bet your bloomin' nut, 'e'd be waitin' fifty paces right flank rear.* "That red-headed girl doing mushrooms at Babyland. Later we both lost our rabbit-fur jackets!" *I shan't forgit the night when I dropped be'ind the fight, with a bullet where my belt-plate should 'a been.* "A terrible heroin habit. He wrote that song called 'Mr. Hurl.' Once we stopped taking him to rehab, he was dead within a year." *An' 'e guv' me 'arf-a-pint o'water green...* "He often argued that Betsey Johnson and Johnny Moke were shoe geniuses—but for different reasons. He said *both* of them beat Manolo Blahnik hands down. I said bullshit." *It was Din! Din! Din! 'Ere's a beggar with a bullet through 'is spleen...* "Titties in corsets obsess men. That's why you and Phil insist I push mine up." Roberta interrupted, her voice astringent. "But today we have choice." *Stinking water? Colonial War? Injia's sunny clime?* The lines of Kipling evaporated.

Lydia felt the harsh shift in Roberta and to hide her shock at being challenged, she obligingly concurred. "You have a point. Yes...we're not like Japanese girls with bound feet."

Buddy chimed in. "Chi-n-ese."

"What?"

"A custom in Ch-ina, not Japan."

"Whatever! Oh, must you hound me? You know I don't get geography!"

I couldn't take their sharp inanity another second. Before anyone might stop me or try to join, I slipped on my pants and quickly reported I was taking a walk.

• • •

The waterfront made a good, hectic place to take exercise, every stride more vigorous beside the docked boats bobbing up and down. "Hey, you!" a man shouted as I passed the marina gatehouse. "Buy the last ticket for a ride?" I shook my head. On a sloop below, a dozen pleasant-looking people sat waiting, and then a quest for adventure awoke in me. Hurrying back, I learned the boat was set to tour some cliffs for two hours. Though I'd left no message back on the beach, on a lark I purchased the last ticket.

The captain welcomed me with a life vest, pointing to the remaining empty seat opposite a young man with a pair of attractive women on either side. His face looked familiar, and I suspected the three of them to be American. From the dock, knots of all sorts came undone, ropes flung aside. Our vessel sputtered back, a flock of seabirds eyeing us from the pilings.

"This is Honey, and this here is Jill," the man said.

Both women smiled. One, tossed a thick wave of long hair over her shoulder, the other I saw was with child. She extended her hand to offer some strawberry licorice. I declined.

"You sure? It's really good." She told me how they'd been traveling in Europe for months, and how difficult it had been for her to find the chewy strawberry candy. "Somebody from Arizona brought this over." At her urging, I finally accepted a strand, and she watched carefully as I bit into the red confection.

All at once it flashed on me where I'd seen the guy before. In shock I stopped chewing. The train station urinal. The two men. He was the one getting serviced! My startled expression must have registered, for he flashed me a profligate grin.

Heart pounding, I chewed faster on the licorice. Astonishing. His audacity displayed no shyness or shame—yet the memory of his sexual act joined us in a compromised and unalterable history. The engine of the boat throttled open, its noise mercifully preventing the possibility of further talk. I watched the land recede and felt a growing derision for the man—not for his action but for his lie. At the same time, I was curious to understand more about them and how they functioned. Who were they?

Our boat motored out along the coast for a quarter of an hour, and I noticed the man's hand now glistened with a wedding band woven from two strands of gold. The ring introduced new doubts.

Some consider oral acts not to be perfidy. Therein, conveniently, all fellatio is free, at least for the receiver. *If rings get yanked off, do erotic exchanges not count?* Where had I read that? I wondered if the hidden nature of this man's sexuality might also inform my own notions of truth.

The engine cut; our boat slowed toward some rust-colored cliffs. Now that we could hear ourselves again, the man began to chat about a business enterprise he was in, selling amino acids blended with berry-flavored powder. "It comes in a convenient packet and gets stirred into water." The man claimed the concoction improved physical stamina. Had he detected some private worry for my libido? Was he preying upon that? One of the girls fished into a macramé bag and offered a pamphlet. It listed a corporate address in Provo, Utah. The powder's price was high, much more than simple arginine capsules cost.

"Clients order this miracle through the mail," he said.

I practiced politeness, telling the trio I didn't take supplements. "Well, all I can tell you is, everything has consequences." The man put his arms around both women. "I feel like a million. Energy to spare!" The two women sat seemingly contented to be bookends for his weighted volume. Then I noticed how all three wore wedding rings. Could the man possibly have married them both? Might they even be sisters?

To keep my cool, I looked away. Were these three fugitives from some extremist fringe group? Were they breaking laws to practice polygamy? Did these women have any inkling of this devil-man's private carnality? Did they accept all his tumescent acts unconditionally?

The boat rounded a rocky promontory, and though I'd hoped to avoid the man asking anything personal of me, he suddenly inquired about my line of work. I paused with great hesitation. His gaze was hypnotic. "Editing stuff," I said. His puzzled eyes seemed to delve deeper into me and through additional questions he pressured me to stupidly confess that I also wrote poems.

"Poetry. Wow! That's bitchin'! Jill, Honey, run and get your autograph books! This man's a poet!"

"No… stop. I'm *not* famous."

"You look famous. Maybe you just strive to project a low status?"

"They say being a famous poet is like being a famous mushroom. Besides, I believe most ordinary people, given paper, pencil, and a bit of time, can work to scribble something poetic."

"I believe you. And you know why? 'Cause on the side, I'm also a life coach! I too help people perform miracles." The man's gaze continued to intensify, as if he were convincing me to join him as a brother in darkness. His voice lowered with sincerity. "I love poetry," he said. "In school we read Longfellow, Hart Crane. But the rhymes of the gospel hold more importance in my life. Singing hymns in a choir used to make me cry. That is, before our church changed."

"Changed?"

"Too much grabbing for growth. Too much grabbing for wealth. Too much unaccounted tithing. Ridiculous religious clothing. And every fifty years or so, shifting our deeply held beliefs. Yet we who remained faithful to the original doctrines get left high and dry."

"I just heard a professor at a religious college complain about how much editing God has required."

"Exactly! I mean, did God get it wrong? Did he change his mind? The prophets claim God spoke to them. They talk as if they know the mind of God. But is growing the biggest church God's will—or theirs? I'm suspicious whenever someone stops being human to claim they know the mind of God. That means lying, and crawling on your belly, and bending covenants. Church is not a corporate system, so how many men does one need to grab? Is it normal to crave ever bigger numbers? Size only proves power, not worth! I tell my girls, to persuade is to crusade. Proselytizing for growth is a terrible sickness! And colonizing through baptism leads to but one dirty game. Advertising!"

"Sometimes," Jill said, checking her long hair for split ends, "I wonder if we should even give out sales material for the berry powder."

"That's different. I've told you. That's business, darlin'. That's not coaxing someone to sell their soul."

"The question is, did Christ attract or promote? Fishers of men has a big meaning. I mean…not every fish wants to be caught, right?"

Honey smiled. "At least no one makes us wear headscarves."

Jill looked directly at me. "Right now, back home, eighty to ninety percent of our churchwomen are hooked on antidepressants."

"Well, you sisters take no drugs! My girls aren't depressed! When they get to heaven, they won't be on some cloud, wondering where to get their prescriptions filled! We're a family. Do everything together. Well, almost everything!" He grinned.

Did the man mean sisters literally, or a church's figurative siblings? At a loss, I asked the women to what they attributed the high rate of depression.

"Not enough equality," replied Jill, mouth full of red licorice. "Or power."

"Too many in-family marriages," said Honey. "The men of our church think we're better off popping pills. They've made all kinds of charts to explain it. They try and keep us super busy: potlucks, sing-alongs, childcare, chores."

Jill agreed. "But just cause some women *don't* take the meds, doesn't mean they aren't depressed!"

The man pulled his shirt over his head. "The deacons demand a kind of soldierhood, even as they chuck our deepest beliefs." He patted Honey's stomach. "But the future of our faith is right here. And who knows? That baby might enter national politics one day, might be the president who saves the nation by a slender thread!"

"Might even be a girl!"

Against my better advice, I decided to ask a constitutional question. "Wouldn't you want to separate church and state?"

"To hell with that. I mean, seriously! Both church and state have already betrayed us. There's not one church that isn't for power or big business!"

"Which is why freedom from religion is so important."

"You mean *of* religion?"

"No. The Constitution says *from* religion. Explicitly says *from*."

The man stared at me. "I always thought it meant we could choose whatever religion we wanted."

"Nope. Given the history of the world, many people don't want to be governed by a religion at all."

The man shook his head. "I guess that's because churches get all them tax breaks on the land they own?"

"A friend of mine works at a bible college. He often raises that question. Wonders why non-believers, have to pay the church taxes of believers. Says church-goers actually get a big satisfaction out of that legal swindle. They mistake the tax break as a kind of spiritual advancement for their cause."

"The bigger the church, the bigger the swindle."

"But they do provide social services."

"If that's true, they sure do a lousy job. Especially when it comes to mental health. Or housing the homeless. Or jobs."

"Unless you're keen to work in a thrift store."

"Ha! Our deacons go running all over kingdom come if there's a hurricane, and the politicians suck up to the deacons, to gather them church votes. And meanwhile, all these tax exemptions keep rising. Churches invest in property, demand more tax breaks; they become more and more like governments. Only, unaccountable. Just like it was in Rome."

For a moment I heard the voice of Russell. How he would agree. He used to love to point out that we are not guaranteed freedom *of* religion—but freedom *from* religion. He loved to say it was only a small word but that it changed everything. And he was right. It was amusing to now hear a closeted religious nut, make almost the same point as Russell. "The entire philosophical framework ain't about choosing where one might want to pray, but being clear that it's essential to keep a separation of religion from state, which can at any time turn to a crusade. Churches easily become opponents to government or states claiming to uphold law and fairly spending everyone's taxes. Our American forefathers fought a revolt against England. They saw the dangers of having a King or Queen be granted divine rights because they conveniently head up some church. Same with the Vatican, or the other damn religious dynasties on this damn planet."

The boat drew ever nearer to the cliffs, passing between some other tour boats anchored at various points, the heads of their passengers tilted up to watch daring boys take turns jumping down into the water. The captain turned the engine off and urged us all to try a swim, perhaps even a jump. I undressed, and the two women looked disappointed to see I already wore my suit. They watched me roll my pants into a cylinder, staring as I rose to stow them. I hurried down the ladder, dropping into the water to shield myself from their unrelenting watch. Soon, they too eased off the steps, paddling in circles while their man swam over to me with the broadest of strokes.

"Hey…wanna jump?"

Looking up at the cliffs, I already felt queasy. "No. Fear of heights runs in our family."

"It's easy," the man said. "Just follow me." He called instructions to the two women. "Jill, I want you and Honey back on the craft. We'll catch you in a little bit."

"Can't we just swim awhile?"

"No! I told you! Get out now!" His commanding voice carried across the water. Once he was secure that the women were in obeyance, he motioned me to follow and we swam toward the rocky base of a cliff, pressing our upper bodies flat against its ledge to pull ourselves from the water. I felt as foolish as the women might, to follow the commands of this man. He talked about an enormous lake in his home state. "Fresh water used to flow all the way down to Mexico. But it was dammed. Now whole stretches of Mexican land aren't farmable. Too much water being held *El Norte!*"

"Does the law let them hoard water?"

"People from our neck of the woods prefer not to discuss it. They just boat and swim and admire the beauty. They'll tell you every beautiful place has a flaw or price, that even Zion knows inequity. Most prefer to say, to practice damming is God's will. If you want the truth, just read the Mexican Water Treaty, my friend. It's all there."

We scaled the rocks. The man went on about his lost faith, how for years he observed the grinning faces of the deacons as members handed them their tithing envelopes. "No report or account on how that money gets spent! No public books! No mention of which members get handouts, which don't. Yet they make a practice of counting and recording everything we attend or do."

At the first set of ledges, he looked over the side. "This is for pussies. Let's go higher." Against my better judgment, I followed. At the tallest point, he judged the distance to the water to be that of a five-story building.

"Just look Satan in the eye, my friend," he said, motioning me to the edge. "Now, I command thee—stare down! Breathe through your fear! See how all of us are *one*."

I'm dealing with a lunatic. A madman. Yet, like an acolyte, I wanted to obey. The water below sparkled, and our boat crept farther out to lend us space. The two women could be seen onboard, untangling their wet hair.

"Confidence comes after you do something, not before. A running jump is best. But be sure to point your toes. When you hit the water, pull the life-jacket down with both hands, otherwise your arm sockets can dislocate." He turned and motioned me back toward some dry brush. I reluctantly did as he commanded, and he, ever the slippery con man, leaned in, speaking once more with his low, confidential tone. "You know, it isn't fair for you to judge me. As men, we're wired the same. When I look at you, I see the mix, just like me. I'm part Cherokee. What're you?"

"None of your business."

His grin was lurid, a prowler on the cover of a dime-store novel. "You just don't want to be pegged!" The man reached forward and pulled the back of my head, planting a naked kiss on my open mouth.

Horrified at the warm, wet tongue, I recoiled, but my fists met air, the man was gone, over the cliff with a victorious rebel yell.

I wiped my lips with rubbing force. Below the ledge, a white plume of spray was already contracting. He bobbed to the surface, hair seal-slick, legs pumping like a bullfrog to reach the boat, he climbed aboard and then gave each woman a kiss.

"You nut!" I shouted horrified. "Have you ever heard of AIDS? This isn't the free-swinging sixties!"

Sound travels upward. Too bad. The nearby tourist boats couldn't make out my rant either. I knew his kiss was the penalty for having witnessed his promiscuity in a public toilet. Though I hadn't judged him, or abetted him, what he couldn't stand was that I hadn't joined him. Here on the ledge, he was trying to regain power by linking me to his secrets, getting me to collude with him in a hidden place with no bystanders. The religious folk who spent their lives trying to rewire sexuality would have a field day with this guy.

Below, the women knelt, drying his legs with an orange towel. Had they never heard of auto-immune disorder? And yet, as a trio they seemed more in tune with one another than many couples I knew. The man looked up, raised a fist at me, and gave another yell. The captain turned too, gazing up with anticipation. I saw three other vessels draw near. One speedboat sounded its horn, then another, then the captain of our boat sounded too. My boatmates began to clap and whistle.

Why on earth had I come here? Why on earth hadn't I jumped first? Yet to hobble weak-kneed back down the trail in dizzy defeat felt worse than jumping. Stepping back like a fool, every fiber in my body resisted the order to leap. "Crazy fucker," I spat out. "Dog in heat! Flaunting your berry-flavored libido." I screamed as I ran over the edge.

Toes pointed, my body sliced through the cool water, torso pulling down in the grip of weightless gravity. I'd remembered to clutch the bottom of the vest and now felt my hands let go. Bubbling like a fish on a hook, my course reversed, calves, feet and legs sensing no limit, the vest and the air in my lungs pulling me upward, I breached the surface, bobbing and gasping in dazed natation. The boat neared and the captain slowed the engine. I breast-stroked to the ladder and found my footing.

The polygamist extended a hand. Back on board, he slapped my back, unaware of my fury. "Well, here's a guy!" And I saw once more that he was the type of man who was least aware when forcing his power over others.

The captain brought coffee. "You're pale. I didn't expect you'd jump from so high. I once saw a college girl from another boat split her skull from so high. Her brains floated on the water like gray breadcrumbs."

"That's cause people don't point their toes!" the polygamist said. "Their bodies spin midair."

"The human body is mostly made of water," the captain replied. "When like hits like molecule, people rupture spleen, liver, kidneys, heart. Others break necks and spines."

"Weren't you scared?" Honey asked.

"Terrified."

The polygamist showed his irritation. "Fear of destruction is an important part of doing manly things. All the good of life lies beyond that fear."

Honey began to cry. "Oh my God! If something had happened to you…I'd be alone with the baby."

"But, I'm fine, darlin'. For me, just another baptism!"

My rage returned and intensified. "People have a right to know beforehand how dangerous something is. Louganis, Olympically trained, hit his head on the diving board! Has he now been delivered beyond the fear?"

"Take it easy, man! If I'd warned you too much, you'd never have pulled the brass ring."

I decided to escalate the man's trial. "Part of risk is knowing how to measure it. Otherwise, it's just recklessness. And stupidity! Imagine your beautiful child being left without a father!"

"Oh my God," the expectant mother wailed.

"Now quit!" the man ordered. "You're upsetting Honey!"

• • •

When our boat returned to the dock by the promenade, it was after six. I discovered having survived the cliff jump brought none of the promised euphoria. No satisfaction. No inclusion. No epiphany. And no word left with my friends to explain my long absence. But I found them right where I'd left them, stretched out on the beach or in the striped chairs, in soft evening light.

"Did you just get back?" Lydia asked, sun-reddened.

"Yep."

Buddy roused, and he sent an empty wine bottle spinning with his foot. "Where were you?"

"Went down by some cliffs and fell asleep."

Lydia fumbled for a white pill, downing it with warm wine. "At least you found some shade."

Phil woke and looked at his watch. "WOW! W-ee must be going."

Garafallou opened his eyes. Seeing Phil already leaning over to lace his shoes, he pulled himself out of the chair, pausing only for a moment to slowly bend his stiff knees. "Philly, wait now…I'm coming." After packing they made farewells, and then ambled off, like Laurel and Hardy, a lopsided pair. Once they'd climbed the steps back up to the promenade, Roberta turned to the rest of us and announced she was going to make a frittata for dinner.

"Let me do it!" Lydia said, lighting a cigarette. "I know a great way…and we can eat on our terrace."

We gathered our own belongings and went to the car. By the time we'd returned to the village, the last glow of fiery orange sun cast long shadows across the cobbles. Lydia went straight into the kitchen of the Swedes' house and began dicing potatoes, grating cheese, and sautéeing leeks. Over a large bowl, ten eggs had their shells cracked open, their insides whisked and poured into a hot skillet. Watching her deftness. I realized she really did have skill in the kitchen.

Just as it went into the oven, Pina entered with a kettle of soup. She glared at the messy counter and protested in her strangest dialect. "My job is to prepare at least one meal a day!" Lydia managed to convey to the old woman that tonight it was she who *needed* to cook. Amazingly, Pina comprehended that, and even appeared to respect it, but she insisted on helping and stood at the sink washing the arugula.

"Hey Walker," Buddy said. "Got any Scotch?"

"Yes." Eagerly, he followed me across the patio, where I pulled a bottle of the liquor from the cabinet. A copy of my first book of poems lay on the coffee table and he spied it. "Can I borrow that?"

Before I could reply, it was tucked under his arm. We returned and poured drinks, settling into the couch like two sunburned pensioners. I pretended to read a supermarket circular; an advertisement delivered every week though we'd told the postman many times that we didn't want it. Using my peripheral vision, I watched Buddy read my poems. Most of that first book held reverent intentions, poems that ruminated on Mom's belief that our bodies were but reliquaries of skin and bone, vessels of flesh intended to house the inner-self. The later poems were elegiac, attesting to Mom's body having ceased to exist. The collection's final poems spoke to unanswered questions about the origins of my own body.

Turning a page, Buddy's brow furrowed. To have my poems read by someone who actually knew Mom was moving, yet to have them scrutinized also irritated. A familiar streak of pettiness revived and seethed in my mind. No communication for decades, now drinking *my* whiskey, after a few months in Italy, and he acts as if a steadfast friendship has held—as if some significant childhood bond joined us.

He splined the book open to reach for his drink. "Just finished the one with the naked models—*breasts and buttocks bouncing—suspended by rubber bands.* That's hot man! Did you actually witness that?"

I shrugged. "Mom knew lots of models who liked to undress. *Posing libertarians* was her term for them. She thought their unwarranted nakedness held conceit."

"Still can't get over it," Buddy said. "Must've seen some wild stuff!"

"Not that wild. Mom gave none of the worship the culture gives to models. In her mind they all simply worked in advertising."

"I can see that," he said. "Especially this line: *Being assigned a popular body, faces no decision, none of the effort of learning carpentry or neuroscience.*"

Roberta came and stood by the credenza behind us, gently turning a fragile old globe. I watched her fingers touch the curled, glossy edges of peeling continents, then trace down the papier-mâché mountains running between the fractured spherical lines of latitude and longitude.

Lydia drifted in from the kitchen, wiping her palms with cream. She held her hands up. "Too long on a beach and I dry up." Having the appreciation of my poems hijacked to discuss dry-skin was annoying. Lydia gestured to the large blue and white plaid in the upholstery on the couch. "Roberta, you said this material is more Swedish than Italian."

"Yes, I think so."

Buddy raised the book into the air. "Gotta love any poem that compares a woman's body to a cathedral! And what about this? *The cycles of ovulation, menstruation, birth: lunar in force, mightier than the elegant massing of stone.*"

"A dress can be like a cathedral," Lydia said. "Especially the stuff by Dior or Balenciaga."

"That kind of couture is beyond me," Roberta said. "It's contorted. Some homosexual's fantasy of femininity." The suddenness of strong denouncement stilled the room, just as her remarks about corsets had done earlier at the beach. The tone brought alarm.

Lydia looked stricken. Her face went through a process, that eventually chose to adopt a cloying sugar coat. "Well…I mean, we all prefer Chanel." But then her acquiescence could not be sustained and she delivered a dash of salt. "But Roberta, your bathing suit today, with all the underwire and pleats…doesn't that conform to some Swiss guy's fantasy?"

Roberta looked perturbed. "The designer is a woman. I've met her. And my breasts certainly weren't pinched between whalebone."

"No, no, of course not. All I'm saying is, to follow any fashion can bring a lot of discomfort, and yet life is made exciting by it." I had to admit, Lydia practiced a willful backstroke against the current of Roberta's pedigree. "Just ask Walker about the clothes his mother modeled."

"She found fashion abhorrent," I said. My voice came out stronger than I intended.

"Maybe she didn't get to choose what clothes she had to wear?" Lydia said. "But surely, to be a model? One must love fashion!"

"Mom always said fashion was deadly. That it is the cause of the banal."

"Fashion? The cause of the banal? Hmmm…I don't even know what that means."

"Mom believed a free woman released some kind of pheromonal evidence—a pulse accelerator magically pumping adrenaline that stirred inner beauty. She thought true beauty relied on freedom, not oppressive perfection. But true beauty relies on some other law, asymmetry and certainly imperfection. I was young, but she tried to teach me using music as an example…with its sequences of opposing but complementary sounds. She also pointed out any architecture with an unusually intuitive proportion, or an oddness combined with symmetry. Compositions that endured, she said, not just by their presence…but by the loss one feels when they've passed by."

Roberta nodded. "You mean what we feel when we realize something might end?"

"Exactly. The dread of loss…life itself…old manners struck down…old trees hit by lightning…aging huts burned or sold or demolished…losses sensed as immeasurable."

Roberta nodded. "Your mother was right. Anyone contemplating beauty must also measure loss. Beauty, to endure, must maintain something imperfect. Lately I think the fad is conceptual kookiness. Models staring like blank-eyed zombies. It's embarrassing. Even suggests women have mental illness."

"Yes. Crazy has become an aesthetic. Mom called it psychotic solicitation. Presenting madness as power. The fantasy of an unreachable woman. Print technology giving her a glamorous controlled space…implying a fake form as a living paradigm."

Lydia's face had the look of someone dropped from a seaplane to be encircled by sharks. Roberta and I certainly delivered enough bite to high fashion to cost her an ankle or an arm. Still, she swam on and defended fashion. "Look. If you'da been fat as a teenager—like I was, nice clothes would mean more to you too. In high school, at my heaviest, my thighs rubbed and wore out the inner fabric of my slacks. If ever I write a memoir, I plan to call it *I Could Never Wear Velvet*."

With intentional exactitude, I pointed out her title's hidden pun. "But you *could* wear velvet…*wear* it down to nothing."

Lydia reached to test some apricots in a bowl. She selected the softest one, her fingers rubbing the fuzzy skin. But I wasn't through with her yet. Continuing to speak as an expert, allowing underhandedness into my comments. "The flaunt of modeling was for Mom one long sad parade, grand-marshaled by advancing age. Like athletics, or ballet, the business of beauty grows harder as a woman matures. The poem about body parts extends the metaphor, pays homage to the models blindly seeking any attention they could get."

I realized too late my want to injure Lydia in some way, to infer her own aging vanity. I regretted it, but couldn't stop myself, going on to describe the woman in Harrisburg at the Italian lake. "Fox furs, netted hats, hair rolled like the forties. You could tell she'd spent hours in youth to acquire a sharp stylized look. One that took rigor to acquire. Now in maturity she was trapped in that stylized grooming of a younger self. And I believe Mom saw a shadow of herself in that woman, her own magazine glory, all those clippings, that woman's face frozen in a catafalque…like Eva Perón or Vladimir Lenin, or an Egyptian painting on a sarcophagus."

Lydia's horrified expression showed my cruel message had hit. I remembered Mom looking scared that same way. "Mom used to lecture and say—'recognize beauty by the effect it has on your own chemistry. Study the properties of beauty for what remains once the shock wears away.'"

Roberta knew I'd gone too far. To lower the pressure, she spoke up. "Look Lydia, I don't know what came over me. It's not fair for me to have dismissed Balenciaga. Of course, fashion can excite or disappoint."

Lydia nodded, her lips working to keep apricot juice from running down her chin. "No worry. You were right. Sometimes I just don't know when to shut up. Anyone can follow anything they like, even bind their feet if they want to!" Her gaze leveled.

A wicked silence followed. Buddy shifted back to my book. "These early ones. They just blow me away!"

Book Six

TRIANGULARITY

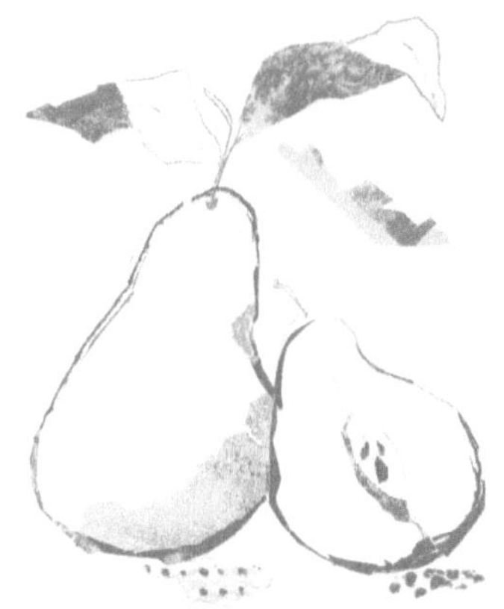

• • •

Later in the evening, working to refine my introduction to *The Galaxy of Love*, my cruel critiquing mood was still upon me. Capturing the right magnanimous tone after my harsh words to Lydia, seemed impossible. How could I possibly temper the pen from hurling negative acid to expound on the overwrought manuscript, how it held the curse of comparing the heavens to love, a perfect cliché for caution—how the muse, absent of restraint, turned fast to sicken with sweetness. But my publisher had already acquired the book and would be furious if he saw me treat the work as rancorously as my mood seemed bent on indulging.

I read the author's bio: *In his life, Mr. Aguillaro has worked as a grave-digger, dog walker, mechanic; he's adopted with his wife, three children from Asia, skydived, made snowshoes, learned crewel work, and raised Guernsey cows in order to make his own artisanal mozzarella.*

Try as I might I couldn't wrestle down my irritation. I seemed to be projecting my inner frustrations outward to anyone I deemed a worthy target. And here I was reading another oh-so-contemporary song-of-self, written to maintain the illusion that one could represent through irony, both victimized artist, forced to work at jobs deemed menial, but fascinating enough to represent the aggrandized voice of a renaissance talent. I studied the author's carefully curated list of *cute* jobs, none truly committed to for very long—like a politician photographed working at a hamburger joint—for an hour, who, unlike the other workers, has the luxury of not finishing the shift, and not showing up for yet another full day the next morning. This man had decided to put himself forth as a pillar of unique and fascinating virtue, yet he omitted that which probably couldn't be admitted even to himself—how in addition to baking his own crackers he also cheats on his wife, even as her family's money floats him to live in an elite neighborhood.

But is this form of modern elitism any different from the group of Academy poets that Buddy so loathed? They probably had more talent and potency? I felt pity and a wave of compassion for *The Galaxy of Love*'s author wash over me. In our world of overcrowded, over-entertained, attention-grabbers, where every act of reality might be *like* a scene in a movie or a tv show, this writer was desperately trying to stand out, was desperate to develop within a crowded space, one more kind of *otherness* - an individualist's persona, one unique, witty and interesting.

But my assignment was not to dissect weakness nor to express cruelty, and it could only be my current state of restless uncertainty, the frustrations surrounding a fantastical longing, that were stressing me to counter-judge this obviously suffering and misguided man. So, to dispatch an introduction to *The Galaxy of Love*, the best approach would be the development of a historical framework, one tracing Egyptian, Greek, and Roman romance accounts through the ages, up to the troubadours of Occitania. This benign subterfuge would help hide my knowledge of the author's weak function, behind what is many an introduction's typical mask—a display of irrelevant scholarship.

. . .

Across the terrace, hisses and shouted profanities signaled another fight underway. Awakened in a room pitch black, some furtive scuffling sounds could be heard. I lay on the chaise, a poetry manuscript still open on my chest. From experience, it was clear that partners pick their poison with great alacrity. But why on earth don't more quarreling couples just walk away from their bad investment—the worst of their vow. I weighed going over to pull them out of the ring, but interrupting the drama of Cupid tends to be a fool's mission, the peacemaker frequently belittled.

As a couple, they were under tremendous strain. The magic show had just toured four cities in nine days, with another ten days of bookings scheduled for cruise ships. When not on the road, Buddy sat with his typewriter on the terrace, writing new proposals and articles, also refining the pilot for the television pitch. From my spot above the terrace, it was easy to compare my own plodding routine against his irritating industry, and I came up short. Work harder, I vowed.

Something was thrown next door. A shoe, perhaps? More curses. More fumbling. Buddy could be heard hollering that Lydia should've married an eggplant, not a man. She hollered profanity back. To judge them was easy, lying in my bed alone, and it surprised me to find that the witness of their tumult came laced with a kind of envy. Too many years of solitude now stirred a yearning to do more than just listen to other people's problems, urges, and passions, as even in quarrel they sounded so amazingly alive.

His voice shouted again. "Small dogs and fleas are the only things capable of living with a prima donna!"

This was a case of two opposites, each wanting something difficult to define. As Blake wrote:

What is it men in women require? The lineaments of gratified desire.
What is it women in men require? The lineaments of gratified desire.

Buddy was now blubbering through his words. "What do you want me to do? What do you want me to *do*?" I'd never heard that before. In a strange twist, a feeling of sorrow and compassion awoke in me. Things grew calm. They came outside, the terrace chairs scraping the flagstone, the smell of sulfur blowing in the window from cigarettes being lit. She was first to speak, her voice fatigued:

"We've become generic."

"You mean a drug for poor people?"

"You needn't be sarcastic."

"Sounds like the wrong word, that's all."

"I'm not the wordsmith!"

"No, you're not. Maybe the word you seek is static?"

"I don't write poetry…"

"Neither do I, according to you."

"But I do have a long memory."

"Yeah? Well, me too. Every detail."

"Look Buddy, you brought it up. We weren't even married yet."

"You've studied too much acting."

"Stop hounding me! I work for a living."

"Did you take your medication?"

"Stop hounding. I've another rehearsal tomorrow. I can't stay up all night trying to pick the right damn word."

"All right, I get it. But I work too. Know how much time I've spent pitching your stuff? How do you think the television people got interested? While Garafallou sits around bullshitting, I bust my ass writing treatments. All to sell you and your talent. I've said it before, again and again: we'll get there. There's nothing you can't do."

"Oh, stop it! I can't take any more of your virtue."

"No, you stop!"

The chairs scraped. The terrace grew silent. I peered out between the vines and saw they'd both gone back inside. The remarks about medication again invited the question of just what she might—or might not—be taking.

• • •

Roberta let her kitchen be conscripted for the new shoot, providing a regal setting. "Can't beat those wall tiles," Buddy said. "And the light from these old windows is cash." To prepare the newer more deluxe menus, Pina and Lydia worked side-by-side to align appropriate recipes.

I happily waylaid my editorial work to come watch. "This session is bigger in scale," Buddy explained. "They're even sending a video operator! The editors mandated we feature fish. So, we got a bunch of mackerel that we're gonna broil, then drop in that clear broth. That one made with the local wine."

Buddy also explained Pina's cynicism was being brought into stronger focus, the hope being that she'd act not only as a comic foil, but also give voice to the many outraged Italian viewers, who might express indignation at having a foreigner exploit their cuisine. Utilizing Pina in this way was to beat objectors to their punch, maybe even making them feel superiorly included and understood.

On the second day, the team prepared Liguria's famous *langostinos*, for which American readers would be told to substitute southern crawfish or fresh Maine lobster. A third recipe involved dropping small fish into a deep fryer, illustrating the Ligurian version of *frittura di paranza*. The various recording devices captured all of these preparations for print and video.

Throughout the week, Pina never tasted a morsel of food, despite everyone's prodding. But on the last day, an enormous pink fish was poached, and of this beast, she accepted a nice hefty portion, yet in typical and stubborn forbearance, she packed her share in a container to be eaten at home out of our sight.

Completing the fish spectacular, the photographer departed, and order was restored to Roberta's kitchen. We congratulated one another with cocktail toasts and never-ending excitements over the miraculous potential of Lydia's transfer to television.

"Phil and I pass through Monte Carlo at the end of the month to meet our backer. We'll show him some tape—discuss costs and terms," Garafallou said. "He's now almost pneumonia free, but still ninety-two, so we must act quick if his haloed wings are to be clipped!"

Travel no longer merely an excursion, but a business necessity, Lydia and Buddy made numerous plans for overnight trips to Parma, Bologna, and Florence.

"We're still undecided about which foods to feature next," Buddy said. "But we're poring over every guidebook and brochure to pit the various regions of Italy against one another."

Again, Garafallou extended his invitation. "Corsica and Rome pair well. The rugged French Island offers a nice contrast to the Eternal City."

"There's no way we'd dare bring anything French into this," Buddy said. "We'd be shot."

In the evening I sat alone with Buddy over a bottle of scotch. "This is gonna be big," he kept saying as if to convince himself. "And to hell with waiting for some fossil in Monte Carlo! The necessary cash will be our own money. We're getting out of the salon biz, and we'll demand producing credits!"

• • •

Roberta invited me to lunch, served on her terrace beside her all-white garden. After coffee she presented the parcel we'd picked up from the post office so many weeks ago. I'd forgotten about it. The brown paper wrapping was already undone. I lifted the lid to find a shoebox full of black walnuts.

"Mother sends these from Oklahoma. The tree on our farm is a hundred years old and fifty feet tall, said to be planted as far from other trees as possible, so as not to poison them. In very hot weather, they also say the powerful scent can make even animals drowsy. As a girl, I sat under the branches and took deliciously dreamy naps. I recently read that scientists have determined that black walnut trees don't poison other trees, but are very thirsty, and somehow have the ability to grab any water first from other plants. But I still love the myth of the poison, the drowsy naps that myth conjured in my imagination, the intentional isolation of the dark walnut tree."

She unfolded a letter taken from the box. "Listen to this: *We've had very few bad nuts this year. Eat a couple each day, and maybe you'll remember your humble roots.* Can you imagine! First, I'm sent to a high-class finishing school in England…then they proffer humility, lest I've gotten the big-head and think I'm more than a farm gal from Oklahoma!"

"I wouldn't read too much into that. Parents are always afraid that by educating their kids they will lose them."

"Some parents want to lose their kids."

"Was being sent to board at Roedean a kind of punishment?"

"It sure felt that way, at first. But in truth, that school ended up saving me."

"Saving you? How so?"

"The schedule. The familiar pace. The form. They gave me continuity. Structure. A sense of knowing what was expected. And the other girls were hardly misfits. I mean it wasn't an orphanage. They had families, very regular ways—and most held a sense of certainty about them. I felt safe. Any family drama was muted. I guess I should tell you, my real father, like yours, disappeared when I was very young. I never knew him. Mother eventually married someone else, but by the time I turned eight my stepfather could not stand me. I used to stare across the dinner table at him—and found him so disagreeable. His life was spent pretending he was a developer of real estate deals—but the deals he made never materialized—and I knew he was draining Mother's money to maintain this façade of grandeur. He'd swagger and brag and drink, and hated me for being able to see that. In the end he squandered much of what Mother had. Meanwhile, I saw clearly the seething tension between us, and looking back now, I appreciate that she wanted to protect me from his sarcasm and ire."

"I guess in a sense your mother did save you?"

"In the only way she knew how."

"Picking an outstanding school."

"Yes and accepting the burden to pay the full price. So, tell me Walker, did your boarding school save you too?"

"My school was co-ed. And the entire first year was terribly awkward, as I saw myself as a misfit and still in deep grief. But then I too became acclimated and found myself settling in. I turned out to be a good learner. The only stigma was knowing that I was on a scholarship—which in my mind set me in another category from the wealthy kids. But still, the luck involved in being brought there turned out to be enormous. It gave me the wherewithal to travel with confidence, and feel at ease in many languages. So yes, I'd say given the circumstances my school did save me."

"If you look close, you'll see these nuts are different from the Italian variety, but can still make a wonderful version of Liguria's cream sauce."

"My Grandpa Gordon, on Long Island, grew walnuts. He'd dump them in a tub of water and throw any floaters into the compost pile. Later, I'd dig them out and crack them between rocks, the way they say the Indians did."

"In Oklahoma people put jumbos between two sheets of plywood and roll the car over them. Some go at them with dental picks. Our family always used a set of handmade nut forks." She lifted a canvas satchel and removed a small hammer. "This'll crack the shell open. In Tulsa they call that 'busting the seal.' The same phrase can also describe opening a pickle jar, while some studly guys use it to describe sleeping with a virgin."

"How refined."

She demonstrated the way the yellow handles of an electrician's side-cutter could be maneuvered to cut the cracked shell away, its extracted flesh tossed in a small bucket at our feet. As we worked, she asked about my upcoming lecture, and it was agreed we'd drive up together.

"It's part of a series. A trifle, really."

"No matter, I want to hear it!" Roberta paused, turning the pliers over in her hand.

"I've also been waiting for a right moment to speak to you about something else," she said. "I feel I owe you an apology."

"An apology?"

"Yes, for coming to your room that night."

"Oh, please. You're bringing up ancient history."

Roberta wiped her hands on a dishtowel. "It was childish of me. When I'm needy like that, I ought to be straight-jacketed."

"Please! I was flattered. I'm only sorry I wasn't up to it." Would now be a good time to admit my secret attraction to her lover? We traded implements, she taking the hammer, and I the yellow cutters. "You know, as a faux-debutante, I arrived late to practicality. My parents fought endlessly about money, and in a self-fulfilling prophecy, much of their accumulation did, in fact, evaporate. The rapidity of the loss shocked them. People who've lost their dough often look like people stepping out of a train wreck. My stepfather still reminds anyone who'll listen. 'It's not what you earn, but what you keep!'"

Another nut was turned on its end and gently hammered. I then picked out the kernel. "How many times a day must the average person think of money? Ten? Fifty? A Thousand? How many are frightened by it?"

"In my early days, I never gave a hoot about money. But by the time I attended Roedean we grew more fraught and soon thought of little else. Today I still live off a trust, otherwise, I'd never afford this house."

"As a boy, I used to complain to Russell, my stepfather, that we didn't live in a nicer neighborhood like Camp Hill, or on a horse farm somewhere. I cringe now to think of it. He'd just snort."

"Did your mother love Russell?"

"I think she respected him. For a broke woman at forty, a hardworking tax accountant was maybe better than she thought she even deserved. His kindness is what she appreciated most. At least, that's how I remember it."

And suddenly my head wagered on how much more I wanted to explain. "You're the first person I've ever told this to. It's just all so complicated." I recounted my blue house on Jefferson Street, the dark, ugly walls, and Mom's request to see them restored to brightness. "The tax man in Russell computed the cost of covering every wall in two coats of paint. The extra gallons tripled the cost. Forget savings. Conscious of not being more grateful, Mom couldn't bring herself to ask for one more room to be done. And so, my blue room was all that remained of my stepfather's misbegotten gift. Secretly, I would look at it and wonder—what if my skin held some other hue or value? Might my room have also then been repainted? The experience deepened something I already knew…that all pigmentation carries perceptions. Caste systems can uphold inverted bigotry, someone needing to denigrate the lighter boy, just as someone else might need to denigrate the darker."

Before Roberta could respond the kitchen door swung open, and Pina scrutinized us and our work. The cutters seemed to fascinate her and I offered them. She backed away, refusing to touch them, as if their blade might depend on voodoo. "Hurry, so the walnuts can be dried," she said, and returned back inside.

Alone once more, silence enveloped the terrace. My stomach already sensed something needing to be said. Roberta got there first. "Eligio mentioned you've been hanging out."

My head jerked. Then I quickly tried to look casual, staring down at my work, and the wood grain of the table. "What'd he say?"

"That you are innocent. That it's important to protect your privacy." Roberta then revealed that our hike to the tunnel had been reported, as well as our embrace. I wasn't sure if my emotional outburst was mentioned, but I was positively thunderstruck and felt my cheeks burn with furious shame. "Roberta, I am sorry…I don't know what to say."

"Just so you know, Eligio didn't rush over to gossip. It was I who brought it up to him. I did so because I sensed something unusual that night when we all dined together. Then Lydia said she'd recently found the two of you eating and drinking wine together, and the way she said it led me to speculate."

"She ought to mind her own beeswax."

"At any rate, it was me who asked Eligio. And just so you know, there wasn't the faintest trace of boast in him. He insisted we protect you…defined it as a *boy crush.*"

"That term is so juvenile."

"Maybe it is. I used to fall in love with all my girlfriends. We'd ride scooters wearing dungarees, while at the same time wearing plastic high-heels bought in the kiddie-section of the five-and-dime, then go click-clacking across the concrete sidewalk until a heel broke off. Then our walk would go crooked, as though living on the side of a hill. I wasn't exactly a tomboy, but a bit *scientific* maybe? I straddled two worlds. Catching frogs and salamanders, then playing nurse with a matchbox infirmary of potato bugs. And I also played mother, dressing cats in baby clothes, wheeling the imprisoned felines in perambulators. I suppose what any of us wants is to question what the world assigns us."

"No doubt, tomboys can disappoint parents—the same way delicate boys can?"

"Yes, but for us girls, boyishness is often a badge of honor. There's more acceptance for girls who want to act like boys. Women are also granted greater capacity to enjoy attractions to one another. Closeness threatens us less."

"Nothing brings more dishonor to a boy than wanting a dress. Maybe makeup is next, or disliking sports, or thinking athletic fields are for lunkheads."

"For we tomboys humiliation comes from being made to wear dresses! Mothers, aunts, or teachers scold us to cross our ankles, wear a bra, behave like little ladies. But despite this, I never needed to apologize or feel shame for experiencing a crush. And in time, I came to love dresses."

"Roberta, maybe Eligio told you? All we did was embrace and I was overcome with emotion. Any reciprocation from him was probably just a show of pity for my breakdown."

"Look, because it's you, Walker, I'm desperately trying not to take it personally. I even asked about your lecture as a way to let you know that whatever occurs, the future of our friendship is what matters most."

"I just wish I could justify or excuse it to you. To myself even. But I can't."

"Is there a larger question for you?"

"What?"

"I mean, whatever spell Eligio casts…do you hold similar feelings towards other men?"

"You mean, am I queer?"

"Or something in-between?"

It felt important to give Roberta as much truth as I could, in exchange for her honesty, perhaps as a kind of offering, a privation for my share of her pain over Eligio: "It's odd, but I've rarely felt the pressure of a sexual closet. I've never had to come out—because I was never really in. Maybe that's because I'm an orphan? There wasn't anyone too important to hide from. At the same time, I feel an inexplicable shame to have you ask me. I've always been able to explore anything I wanted, including a dress, or a triangle. Growing up, I was often called names or assigned words that didn't correspond to my experience. In the plant kingdom, a botanist will crave to conjure Latin names for genus and species, to assign no doubt as to which daylily or orchid one might be admiring. Which bindweed deserves to be poisoned. As a person, I somehow defy staying in a category for long, and over time my only consistency seems to be inconsistency. But then one day, I came to realize that there are over five billion people on this planet, and no two have the same fingerprints, or timber of voice. And we develop so uniquely, that we mourn the absence of each other's uniqueness when we die. One can't simply pick up a gardening catalogue and order another *Hemerocallis Candor.*

"And yet, one can sense how nervous it can make people, when some sad rag-a-muffin has not been assigned a label. I mean, without a label, that someone in a sense remains a stranger. And how people resent being denied the art of labeling—they rush to fill the void: brunette, Babylonian, beefy, brusque, overbearing, non-conforming, crazy, psychotic, racist, greedy. Yet, no one wants to admit that naming inherent traits as absolutes, clips all human people of complexity—including the person deemed the labeler. And aren't we all labelers? So, to realize our need to define absolutes, robs nuance…mutability…possibly…even freedom…for the labeled one as well as the labeler. To see the great variety of us is like having a dark veil lifted from one's vision. I don't expect you or anyone else to intuit what any of this means, for I as a poet, a hopeful describer of people and truth, am not very sure myself. Most readers will identify with certain tropes— but the best poets must pay attention to notice and describe fresh details—to see what people do. Actions are the gateway to sensing thoughts and feelings."

Roberta sat and seemed to be thinking. "And so…is all this complexity just a way to avoid telling me if you are or are not queer?"

The hair on my forearms and nape of my neck rustled at the word. "The term I prefer is *natural.*"

Roberta turned her head away. It astonished me to see her despair. "Oh, Walker, if this were happening with anyone but you…I'd feel even more agitated. Okay, I'll admit it. At first everything in me wanted to condemn you. I can be so incorrigibly jealous. But then I said to myself, don't interfere. Granting someone their fair share of life's experience is good for us all."

"Sometimes I believe that what I want isn't sexual at all, but rather something more like touch, validation or comfort. Perhaps to feel the warm skin of a father I never knew. Hugging in that tunnel…I felt feckless. But also flexible… fluid…stupid even. If only I could smokescreen all of it. As my *need* is just so humiliating."

"But that's what explorations are for. To move us out of comfort zones." Suddenly shy, I bent my face down to the task at hand and felt myself holding back. "Look, Walker, I don't need you to define what *naturalness* means to you. Do whatever you want…or must. But I will warn you. Eligio is elusive. And not always what he seems. It might end in bitter disappointment, even pain. Her voice began to break with emotion. Nonetheless, my hope now, is that you'll take the ride—whatever it turns out to be!"

It was my turn to sit in stillness, my thoughts turning, sensing how taking risks changes life. Yet, what of that girl whose brains floated in the water after a cliff jump? Had her risk been worth it? And suppose I too had died? Who'd grieve me? Roberta? Eligio? To be truly mourned, one has to have contributed something to the world. Breathing in, I found my courage. "Roberta, that night when you came over, the problem wasn't you. It was me. I'm what's called a slow warmer. I take more time in one-on-one situations. It might be gender confusion, guilt over Eligio, the trauma of my past, the intensity of being alone. I simply have never been able to figure it out."

"Another reason I should never have forced myself onto you."

"You didn't force anything. It's just that coupling stirs in me a sense of how lonely I've been. It awakens pain. Intimacy for me requires time, and that I allow for that time. That is my truth."

She looked across the garden. "I don't fully comprehend. But I want to. And it's a lot to take in."

"It's hard…I know. It boils down to circumstances that aren't chosen, but that get assigned, still to be judged nonetheless. For some, judgment can change sides faster than the weather."

The kitchen door opened, and Pina returned. Seeing the walnuts were finished and we were still sitting there talking, her irritated look let us know our delay was upsetting her schedule. She snatched the bucket, and raked her hand through the walnuts. I picked up a forgotten kernel, rubbed the last trace of oily paper skin away, before handing it to her as if it were a rare diamond. She scowled, as I knew she would, tossed it in with the rest and went back inside.

Roberta stood looking at the shells scattered about our feet. "You know, walnuts don't grow well in groves. Some *people* are like that."

"Most people need to belong to something, even if only to a small grove."

She came over and kissed my forehead. My face must've shown that same blank, faraway look she'd noticed before. She kissed my forehead again, then went to reach for the broom and began to sweep. After the shells had been brought into a neat pile, she returned, took my hand, and led me into the kitchen where Pina had spread the walnuts over two large baking pans. "Heat will cure them," she said, putting them into the oven.

A bottle of liqueur stood on the counter top, small shots already poured for each of us. "Here is something else you can make from walnuts." We tasted the liqueur, and Pina explained its recipe. "The kernels must be cut while still green. Exude the milk. Pour the liquid in a big glass jar. Add sugar. Wrap the jar in burlap, and place it in the sun. After a month, add grain alcohol and cinnamon. It's nature's best digestive."

Roberta lowered her glass and noticed her hands. "Oh, my Lord!" she shrieked. "Look! Walker, my palms have gone dark! Look!"

I glanced down and saw how my own fingers had darkened. "No gloves," Pina said. "Walnut juice dyes the skin."

Roberta and I began to laugh. I knew such heightened joviality could often be a reaction to the tension of pigmentation, the comic relief another chance to pretend that anyone could by choice or in the right circumstances qualify as an honorary octoroon, or a boy in a pink dress, our differences all accepted, unnoticed, unjudged, unimportant, and totally unrealistic. For once, I simply didn't care to analyze any of it.

Pina produced a can of abrasive paste saying it was derived from lava. "Don't worry, black soap will fix." At that, we laughed even harder.

• • •

In a field above the village a herd of goats grazed among the thin-stemmed wildflowers. I sat near them on a flat stone, notebook open, hoping to find pleasure in wordplay. *The soft sky suspends tranquility over the glassy sea.* Immediately, I mocked the pastoral conceit and crossed it out.

A few lines memorized in grad school came to mind: *Some creatures lull the rest with their notes. The repose is never complete.* I whispered on. *The wildest animals do not repose, but seek their prey now; the fox, and skunk, and rabbit, now roam the fields and woods without fear. They are Nature's watchmen.*

I hadn't thought of this in years, though the professor who'd supervised my dissertation taught me to appreciate Thoreau, especially his disquisition on civil disobedience. Down the ravine, the tin pan chorus of the goats demonstrated their own kind of disobedience. They nudged one another, bleating raw cries, then yanking tufts of grass from the dirt. I watched an elderly goat, as his masticating jawbone dripped green juice down his moving lips and into his beard.

I flipped the pages of my notebook back to a new poem begun a few days ago and read aloud:

Continental Shift

I sailed my country's coast for eight engulfing years,
but all her ports went dry.
Remapping those unmapped vows, continuing on in quest,
in search of warmth, a sweet berth.
The aching mind will give faith its challenge:
Leave home…take the boat out.
Go sail the high, wide seas—drown or find another
land to call home. You choose.

At sea, full sails snapping compass cupped in palm, neck craned across the
    curve,
that blue expanse so wide, my vessel but a small speck—
shark-bait or sea-dross—crushed by wind-force.
At night, the starlight, hope & heart in prayer: To die. To defy. To see.

Then one evening in shadow, a strip of grassy beach appears, alive with
    coco-scent.
Who knew such green sway held another culture, that a pair could draw
    such sweet life.
Amid the surf, reborn in cleansing waves, the aqua plage reveals:
What gift to know both shores. Communing with the new:
tomorrow's history passing that which the old, abandoned home
could not grow.

I contemplated how to cross out words and whole lines, when off in the distance, as if conjured by poetry, a moped was revving its engine. Lifting my head, I recognized Eligio's bike riding on the black road up through the valley, winding his way up, disappearing around olive trees only to reappear on one of the many bends. He approached the village, and gazed up to the meadow where I sat, revved again, and advanced until he banked over in a spray of gravel.

"Walker!" My name was spoken as if Eligio were making a great musical discovery. The openness of his face contrasted many men, who often are either too reluctant or too eager to smile. Removing his helmet, he cheerfully pushed his moped across the grass. "If a vision called 'romantic poets' was to be illus-trated, you writing in your book on that rock with goats and greenery, would be perfect!"

I got up to greet him, and we kissed cheeks. Eligio reached for my notebook. "May I?" He flicked the page back to my poem, then lowered himself, lips moving as he read. When he finished he reread the page a second time, now aloud.

"I've only just started it. It still has a long way to go."

"*Amid the surf, reborn in cleansing waves, the aqua plage reveals.* That's nice," he said.

"Again, I've only just started."

"I'm curious. Why did you use the French word for beach?"

"I thought it lent the sound of water to English readers, at a moment in the writing when something mystical may be occurring."

"Oh, I see. Yes. And might I have a copy?"

"It's a long way from done. But I guess so. Sure, why not? But now I'm already worried Lydia will see us up here."

"Surely, there's no law against two men reading poetry outdoors?"

"You are right…but…"

"But not to worry! We won't be here long. I've come to fetch you. Mama is expecting us for lunch!"

"Today? But when did this come about?"

"She's crazy to meet you."

"You've told your mother about me?"

"Just that we've developed a friendship."

"But I've not showered or shaved. I wasn't expecting this."

"No worry. Shower there. You'll be glad for a bath after the ride."

He motioned me to pack my things. "It will be fun. You'll love Mama. You'll see."

Still uncertain, I behaved compliantly and gathered my knapsack. Eligio had brought an extra helmet and following his instructions I put it on, and swung my leg over the vehicle's seat. He then got on and took my arms and encircled them around his ribcage.

Winding down the mountain, my torso leaned with his, first left then right, then back again, the warmth of his body, a tactile surprise, all of it an experience so surreal I wondered if it was really happening. The bike roared on in terrifying speed and exhilaration. My dazed mind split as if I were watching from a cloud.

. . .

On the outskirts of Chiavari, my nerves grew taut. Eligio's house was a two-family, split contemporary structure built on a slight hill, with a tall wooden gate opening to a garden. We entered what seemed a pristinely manicured emerald oasis, and a sumptuous, sticky fragrance met us at the door. His mother stood cooking apricot jam, a wooden ladle held at an angle to skim foam from an enamel kettle. She darted from the range, pearl earrings jiggling, and kissed Eligio's cheeks, then both of mine. Eligio made introductions, she took my hand, spoke in Italian. "Any friend of Eligio is most welcome." She hurried back to the stove. "Beware apricots that boil over too soon!" she said.

Her hair, bright with henna, was pulled in a rigorous chignon, a task that must rely on a certain amount of pain to fasten. Her martial build, like an apple on two sticks, was propped up by two tiny feet encased in patent leather slingbacks. A frilly cream blouse was trussed in an apron, her entire person as tidy as her kitchen. At the table, pits and peelings disappeared in a juice-stained newspaper, the careful folding worthy of a fine gift. She then tossed the whole package into the trash can without a spill.

Eligio bent to take off his shoes, and her free hand tested his hair. "A bit long, no? After dinner we trim."

"Walker needs a shower, Mama."

"Fresh towels upstairs. And we trim him too!"

A dizzy, reckless feeling encroached as Eligio brought me upstairs to his apartment. He left me outside the shower, saying he was returning back down to chat with his mother. A short while later, I stood lathering his sandalwood soap, warm water streaming down my sudsy skin, when the shower curtain gently pulled aside. Eligio stood on the mat quite naked. My eyes widened then burned with shampoo. "May I come in?" he whispered then put his finger to my lips for silence, stepped in and knelt. The warmth of his mouth on my genitals was a shock. My heart pounded with excitement and nerves, my penis growing. How outraged or curious some people might be, I thought, to admit all that the menu of human physicality could offer. And any male can choose. Some try column A, some B, some order *a la carte,* some choose but too fast. So many cosmopolitan temptations get assigned to big places, Rome, London, Singapore, Tangier, New York—then found just as easily in a quaint Italian town, or a Pennsylvania highway, or among some horny English actors working to convert *La Stalla.*

Eligio stood, took the bar of soap, turned me to face the wall and lathered my shoulders. I tried to imagine what could be more masculine. John Wayne? The Wild West? Football heroes? Firemen? Or the steel-hard phalluses of erotic fiction, those famously described members pushing in and out all night long, a trail of satiated women left in their stead. Were these fantasies what constituted real manhood? Eligio's robust soaping went down around my hips, around my buttocks, and then between my legs. The sensation of his hand exhilarated. For a moment, I wished Roberta were here to join us. Before I could weigh that, Eligio dropped back down to his knees and again forced my intense erection into his mouth.

"E-ligi-o-o!" We froze. His mother was calling up the stairs. "E-ligi-o-o!"

He called to her from behind the curtain. *"Uno momento, Mami!"*

We could hear her continue talking, but it was difficult to make out what she was saying. Like a startled gazelle, he yanked back the curtain, leapt out and, dripping water, cracked open the bathroom door.

"Momento, Mami. Momento!"

• • •

In the kitchen, they made a fuss, saying how good I looked in Eligio's tee-shirt and pajama pants. To deflect their attention, I praised the jars of apricot preserves, lined up on the counter in a gleaming row. *"Signora,* how fast you packed them!"

"Mama loves work," Eligio said. His mother sprinted to the oven like a runner heading for the finish line. "Look at her go!" In a cast-iron pot, a pork shoulder roasted in milk laced with the zest of a lemon, waited to be cut. Her playfulness turned serious, illustrating that the slicing of meat was no joking affair. "Our town is known for cod fritters and vegetable cakes, but Eligio ordered pork just for you!"

Her experienced hands laid the slices of meat on a platter. Eligio sidled over, shuffling his feet, and she, to my horror, fed him small, tender trimmings, his mouth chewing then remaining open and expectant for more. The sight of a grown man feeding from his mother's fingers as if he were a baby sparrow raised a tide of revulsion in me. Any romantic fantasy of him simply could not tolerate this. He was not some little bird, a sparrow, or wren. He was not an infant. In that instant, the opiate that had supplied my delirium, began to crash. It astonished me how swift an erotic attraction can de-celerate.

"Wait till Autumn, Walker. Mama makes our *mesciua* soup. It's to die for!"

Autumn! The mere thought brought sobriety. In fact, the more emphatically Eligio spoke, the more appalled I grew. Selling his mother with over-inflected excess, he reminded me of a carnival barker hawking phony kitchen gadgets. What happened to the suave Italian paramour I'd come to put stock in? Are we the only creatures capable of alarming ourselves by whom we might imagine we desire?

A bowl of small potatoes browned with grated parmesan accompanied the pork. Mama put heaping mountains on our plates, then poured more red wine from a jug.

"You see," Eligio said. "I told you. She's the best cook in all Italy."

His mother's eyes crinkled. "Only because I know his likes."

Eligio blew on his fork to cool the food then put it in his mouth with exaggerated gusto. It took but a short while, under Mama's watchful gaze, to empty our plates down to the porcelain glaze. Fearing she'd notice how stultified I'd become over her son, I followed Eligio and accepted her insistent second helpings. An enormous heap was put on my plate. "*Signora*, please," I said, only feigning jest. "Your eyes are much bigger than my stomach!"

"*Silenzio,*" she replied, voice stern with amusement. "Those lovely green marbles cannot gauge wrong! Eligio, doesn't your friend have beautiful eyes? Like green topaz."

Trying not to appear unappreciative, our plates emptied for a second time, and still Eligio's mother tried to serve more. Good God, woman! I thought. We may be pigs but we can't eat an entire pig! Together Eligio and I fended her off. She looked injured. "Maybe my cooking is not so good?"

"Mama! You know you make the best!"

With an uncertain expression, she rose, and began to dramatically clear the table, refusing any offer of help. Eligio stepped in her way. No doubt they'd played this scene since he was a little *bambino*. I joined in the work, piling cutlery on the counter over by the sink.

Once her mock tragedy had played out, she rejuvenated and opened the refrigerator for the finale; a tall, quivering, white-as-snow pudding. Eligio clapped his hands. "Oh! Mama's panna cotta!"

His mother poured raspberry coulis from a small flower-painted saucepan into a pitcher, that was placed on a tray accompanied by three crystal compotes. One held chocolate shavings, the second walnuts, and the third whipped cream. "Cream is not usually served with panna cotta," she said. "But as a little boy, Eligio got the habit!"

In a matter of minutes, the silky dessert and the extra cream disappeared from our dessert plates, the smoothness cooling our throats. Once more we ate seconds, while Eligio's mother began to discuss some new shirts she'd bought for him. The tone of her voice conveyed that the role as his dresser was as important to her as being his chef—clearly all of it on par with a religious vocation. "Please,

Eligio, you must try them on."

"Not now," he said, incredulous. "My big belly is too fat and full!"

"Nonsense!" she said. "You have the body of luck. It can eat all it wants."

Their talk shifted to the care of his wardrobe, particularly the handling of its linen, a discussion as serious as any biblical conference. She had washed and pressed a basket of clothes, and now as if it were some noble mission, she asked for permission to go upstairs to scout for other dirty garments.

"No, Mama, you rest," Eligio said, rising slowly to his feet and going upstairs. Mama undid her apron, and again looked forlorn. Apparently, not retrieving dirty laundry deprived her of a certain joy. After a moment she repaired her injury and girlishly signaled me to follow her into the drawing room, a petite chamber, its walls papered in wide sienna and black stripes, topped by a ceiling border of large pink cabbage roses. She plucked away some absurdly large fringed pillows, and by her insistence, I sank into the sofa as if it were a great stork's nest. A silver dish was placed before me piled with cream-filled chocolates, and she waited for me to bite into one. A gluttonous doge of Venice, I complied, but fortune smiled on me, when a merciful cocker-spaniel emerged from under the skirt of the couch, leapt up, and snatched the remainder. "Medici! Chocolate no good!" she scolded. "The dog…Eligio's. But he so busy…he live more down than up!"

I nodded. We sat in awkward silence. In Brooklyn, I thought, Eligio would be called a *Mammoni*—a guy who never marries or leaves mama, for fear of losing the goods and services she proudly provides. Outside the window, a sumac swayed in the hot breeze, its rounded form shaking fuzzy pale puffs. To make conversation, I told her I admired it. "Yes! The *parrucchino*! What good taste you have!"

Eligio returned, pulling a duffel bag. His mother received it as though it contained an offering of silk. I fought my increasing repulsion. With no small excitement for the laundress's tasks to come, she excused herself.

He came over to me, leaned on the arm of the sofa and whispered in a suggestive tone that we ought to now go swim in the pool. I resisted, warning that big bellies couldn't afford to get cramps.

"But she heated it just for us. I want her to come back and find us in the warm water."

"She'd find us boiled to death. Besides, I didn't bring a suit."

"No worry! You'll wear one of mine!"

. . .

In the pool, on my tenth lap, Eligio blocked my lane. "Hey there, Mister! Let's get you out of the water and dry you!"

I disliked being called Mister, as well as having my swim interrupted. I clung sidelined to the edge like a water bug.

He climbed out of the pool and squatted down to rub my shoulders. "Do you have something sexy on your mind?"

"No. No. Just my fatigue."

"Get out and I'll give your back a real massage."

As opposed to the unreal ones? His persistence won out and I complied to his wish that I pull myself out of the pool. But I sat on the concrete edging and refused the massage. I also declined to stand. It would've been better to appear nude than to be seen in Eligio's swimsuit, a skimpy patch of gold lamé sewn into a thong by his mother. In sewing Eligio's own suit, also a thong, she'd patterned a filmy white fabric that grew shockingly sheer when wet.

He sat beside me and the two of us stared in silence at the pool's lapping surface. How was it possible that my obsession with him had disappeared in such a hasty flash? The reversal was so swift and so complete, that even the intense gratitude I felt for his kind comfort in the tunnel was gone. And his fine manners now struck me as cloying and overdone. I surreptitiously turned to examine his profile. The line of his jaw was still fleshy but firm, the nape of his neck downy and soft. He had perfect skin, his lips elegant and wide. But the magnetic attraction they'd once generated was absent. He turned to stare back at me, and something about his eyes, their gentle calf-soft neediness, compounded my distaste. "Has your mother ever met Roberta?"

"That wouldn't be proper! Roberta is married."

"But it is okay to invite me?"

For a brief second his charisma flickered, but then his chin suddenly moved too close, and his mouth mashed his lips against mine. My feet churned the water as I wrestled him away. Had the world gone crazy? Was some edict decreed that men should start kissing other men whenever they felt like it? First the polygamist—now this? I looked around for a towel, but there were none in sight.

"What's wrong?"

"Nothing! I just prefer to be asked first, that's all." He looked at me with his ridiculous soft, wounded Mammoni eyes and any last chance between us faded with astonishing finality.

"Forgive me…how wrong I have been. But after our shower, I just assumed." He reached to place his arm around my shoulders. "You are now upset, my shy pet, not to be asked. And so, I the rogue bandit, must therefore come and *steal* another kiss!"

"No."

"Please!"

"No!"

"But the hour grows late. Many brave duels have been fought. And to kiss you is my reward!"

"Look Eligio. I'm just not into the naughty operetta thing." My words were a tactical mistake, for my objection only made him bolder.

"Aha! You dare deny me even one of your little sugar-coated kisses. And yet such sweetness makes Eligio so happy!"

"Look, stop, please! Too much sugar! And for heaven's sake cease speaking of yourself in third person."

He gripped me tighter. That determination caught me off guard, and in a stupor, I admitted his silly tongue. Wet and warm, it wiggled like a garden snake. My repulsion was now intense. I pushed him back. "Stop! We haven't even been tested!"

My lack of reciprocation confused him. "Oh, my little devil. Playing so hard to get!"

"No. I'm not."

"So hard. You want pursuit, like a lithe woodsman being chased over a field of clover!"

"No. You must stop!"

He paused, confused as to what game I might like to play. Then we sat in silence again, the weight of our potential losses beginning to settle. I was not playing hard to get. I had not been keen to come to lunch in the first place. And I'd not invited him into the shower. But this was not his fault, for I had led him on, and hadn't refused either. I shifted and felt the lamé swimsuit cut in all the wrong places.

His steady manner returned, but it now showed not confidence, as I'd always believed, but an obtuse stubbornness. Like the stereotyped Italian gigolo, he couldn't give up and a more serious version of his chase-game resumed. "Even before this abominable plague, many red-blooded men couldn't admit attraction," he said. "It seems naive, but even to whisper our desire can stir desire." Eligio placed his hand on my thigh and whispered. "We can go upstairs to watch something nasty," he said. "I've got some interesting material."

I shook my head.

"Maybe I can show you what fascinates me about erotic videos for straight men?"

I shook my head again. He ignored me and continued. "I'll be honest with you, I've always fantasized about what it would be like to make porn. What fascinates me in straight porn is the percentage of screen time given over to the male member. If male genitalia were censored, and the filmmakers showed only sexual parts of a woman, might straight men not miss a great deal of what they find arousing? I mean, such films are a business. No? So, profits depend on straight men becoming excited by what they watch. So, showing so many erections means that the sight of other men who are excited…is exciting. No? That means same-sex voyeurism arouses all men? No?"

"I guess so."

"I'm glad you see what I see."

"I get it. Maybe most men can only admit to being voyeurs—*à trois.*"

"But even if a woman's body *must* be present, it still means men get aroused watching other hardened men having sex…that such sights are a stimulant! There must be something animal in it. And not just for men who like other men, but for men who say they prefer *only* women! Otherwise, such straight-up fellows would become stomach upset at the sight of a hard phallus while watching the movie. They'd retch and vomit, and run screaming out of the cinema and up the street in disgust. Yet, I see no straight men screaming and running from adult cinemas. So…again, that means they must enjoy it! So much so, that they even pay more for it than for regular movies! And maybe *some*, even find the sight of the excited erection of another man *necessary* to get off! I think that Hans would agree. That word he uses…? Transference! Yes, penis transference might be the unacknowledged aphrodisiac of the entire porn industry! Still, I think if one asked most straight men, they would likely say that there is no possible way they would ever become excited seeing another man grow erect for intercourse."

"Maybe we're all just a bunch of knuckleheads."

"Knuckleheads?"

"Guys who sit in bars, punching arms, talking soccer scores, pussy, and Pontiacs."

"Pontiacs?"

"An affordable car."

"I see. But I also see, what is made *taboo* can bring desire. No? Just as you may find me to be *taboo*!"

"Or maybe it's just *natural.*" I glanced from the pool to the house and did a double-take. Only ten feet away, Eligio's mother was sitting in a lawn chair, her tiny feet perched on a needlepoint stool. How long had she been there? Had she seen our clumsy kiss? The shock went through my chest. Had she heard her son's desire to make a contribution to the phallic psychology of erotic cinema by becoming a filmmaker? I felt my ears go crimson and my shame turn to whispered rage. "Eligio…she's sitting right there."

"Don't mind Mama," he whispered back. "She sees all but constricts nothing. Perhaps tomorrow we can take her for a drive. We can go to La Spezia? She likes a public garden down there, with enormous flowerbeds and rare species. It was planted while the region was in Napoleonic euphoria! You can see all the way to the Apuan Alps!"

I forced a timid nod and wondered how even talk of gardens now seemed grotesque. And how many others had gone down that road to La Spezia with his mother? How many had been brought to sit butt-naked around this watering hole under her watchful gaze?

"I don't think I have it in me to go to La Spezia with your mother," I said. And finally, the diminishment of my ardor was felt. Eligio now sensed it as something substantial. Even his mother paused her knitting, and held her hand up to the sun. I wanted to get up and walk away, but to retreat in tiny swimwear after a big lunch was simply too humiliating. His mother sensed something amiss. She quickly folded her knitting and headed back indoors. Eligio began to recognize the shift inside me to be major. He stared petulantly at the small waves once more slapping the pool's perimeter. The motion hypnotized. "Evening is near," he said. "It's better if I return you, while light is still on the road."

"There's no need. I can taxi down."

"At least let me drive you to the station."

"All right." And so, I managed to stand and walk back into the house with as much dignity as I could muster. To put on my own clothes again was a blessed relief. Looking into the mirror, I also felt relieved that my hair hadn't been cut.

Back outside, with our final curtain well underway, Eligio's attentive mother was now nowhere to be seen. Again I wondered, in her time, how many had she seen come and go?

Eligio's torso on the back of the moped now felt like a sack of potatoes, no trace of thrill, and at the station, I quickly lifted off the bike. Under the circumstances I wondered why I did not feel some kind of sorrow. What I did feel was akin to burning a trunk of worthless confederate bank notes. "Look, I'm sorry," I said, and could think of nothing else to add. For a second we paused, took in the scene, both of us recording it for some future documentary drawn from memory.

"A fever broke," Eligio said. "That is all. A fever caught on a risk you sold yourself." He revved his engine, saluted with two fingers, and roared off.

Book Seven

TI VEDO

• • •

The train returned to Levanto too late to enjoy the prime dinner hour, and now the streets were crowded with people strolling about after exploring all the fine fare the town's many tables could provide. I took the quickest road leading to the outskirts of the town, then began my long walk up to our village.

Soon my collar was damp, and a warm breeze began to blow from the South, yet whenever I reached another shadowy green turn, chilly seams of mountain air crept up and out of crevices, like mortuary fingers caressing the back of my neck. *This is how Summer colds are born.* A bus shelter appeared and I debated whether to wait for a ride or keep walking. The shelter stood by a dilapidated apartment house, where more than three years ago, through a ground floor window I'd watched a woman wash her young son. After rinsing the boy, he'd been lifted to stand on a table, then wrapped in a thick towel and hugged. How I wish I could come clean like that. Once the boy was dried, a small girl in a flowered pinafore took his place, her hair brushed and secured with barrettes.

I pretended to study the bus schedule, but my true hope was to witness that maternal and domestic scene one more time. But tonight, the window blinds and shutters were drawn. How curious it is that people rarely reveal themselves to an expectant watcher—pay dirt for voyeurs is won in surprise. And yet, how much depends on the plan, or the patience, or the willingness to wait? I stepped back and saw the blue light of television screens flickering from behind the windows of many in the building. I averted my gaze to the garden, studying the beautiful shrubs growing pale flowers along a fence. As a soldier, did my grandfather ever travel here? Perhaps after Monte Cassino? Maybe his love of painting petals was born right on this very spot with these very blooms. I heard the bus rattling along over the cobblestones and flagged the driver.

Later, at two in the morning, I sat beside my window looking down across the valley toward Levanto. In the distance somewhere, a dog barked three times, that same fellow insomniac I heard so often. My bronchial tubes expanded, pulling in the same air sought by every desperate creature on the earth. On the other side of the terrace, the Swedes' house was quiet, any irritations silenced by sleep. Were Buddy and Lydia pressed warm against each other? What perversity to imagine those two coupling, one of them the rider, the other the horse? But which was which? I allowed myself to picture Buddy's palms flattening her breasts, Lydia leached of passion with the same contempt for sex with him, as for magic with Phil Filbertson.

The moon disappeared behind some clouds, and fat drops of rain plopped down onto our rooftop. In the distance the dark sea grew a gray haze from the moisture, and I used the quiet gloom to practice once more what I might say to Roberta about my reversal with Eligio. I pondered how so many relationships are coincidence, or convenience, or even the seeding of circumstance. A lightning bolt forked out its shock, and my thoughts glimmered like gemstones washed up on a beach, waiting for a night like this when a strange flash would reveal them to be hidden among the soft sea sand. Certain poems can sustain the same kind of shock, their gems patiently hidden among the library stacks, waiting for some patient reader's eyes to glitter them back to life.

I padded out to the study and inspected the watercolors still thumbtacked to the wall. I straightened them while wondering if the dawn would ever come. If only the pathways of youth could be re-trod with our adult vision; we'd now understand our elders, what it is to be busy with adult things, paying bills, aging, or cooking up something the young will one day yearn for. The fields and meadows encircling Harrisburg would still be devoted to farms, their landscapes belonging to any pair of eyes passing by. The wooden floors in the old grocery stores weighted with cans stacked in pyramids: cling peaches at nineteen cents, carrots and peas at eleven, and there'd be cans of string beans, creamed corn, a bin of iceberg lettuce, a few brands of cereal. In hindsight, people seemed naive, less jaded, but also perhaps holding more pride for personal character and skill. Men and women were sharp-eyed enough to spot a dress seam properly finished, or know when a metal wrench had been well forged, or how many months those planks in the lumber yard had been curing, or how long stewed tomatoes took, or what seasons did the gardens bear what crops, or how to recognize the cost of a horse by the quality of its teeth.

But such romance seemed to pass over the killers and the crooks. Or how even good-old-know-how couldn't withstand the mysterious threat of commerce, or things like Vietnam. That war certainly still loomed to disrupt any fantasy of rightness and heroic freedom. I remembered reading how following the Kennedy assassination a journalist had lamented: *Oh, we'll never laugh again!* Another countered: *We'll indeed laugh again, but we will never be young again.* Perhaps that's why America's grocers needed so long to remove those pastel portraits of that fallen president? And burying Dr. King, evoked the same feeling of lost youth, followed a few months later by RFK's killing, leaving thoughts of the future, of hope and of promise, in new heaps of absurdity, that time a place where even the smooth singing Rosemary Clooney came undone.

· · ·

The force of early morning sun lit the stone columns and finely balanced loggia of Roberta's house, a façade included and praised often in books of regional architecture. Beneath the overhang, I caught the scent of climbing roses, then knocked and waited as the great doors carved with garlands of bay leaves, angled open with the help of an eighteenth-century pulley system. I'd come to call on Roberta before morning coffee, to let her know my time with Eligio held no prize, no erotic daring, just the ridiculous laughable experience of spent infatuation. Did I really need the lesson on how these kinds of things can occur to any person at any time, through the tiniest of circumstances?

Roberta received me in her monogrammed robe, arms holding Apollo.

"I've come to say how wretchedly sorry I am."

She looked through me. "Am I supposed to find comfort in that?"

"No, I suppose not."

"These days there seems to be more truth than I can process." She hugged Apollo tighter, as though the dog were a teddy bear. "You can have that plump little bee and his free-love honey. I'm sick of being stung."

"I've come to tell you that I won't be seeing him again."

"Oh, stop." Roberta pushed her hair behind her ears. Looking for distraction, she placed Apollo down on the rug. "I'm working in the kitchen." I overcame my hesitation and followed her down the corridor leading to the back of the house. In the sink, a bucket of hot, soapy water had been filled. "Sometimes big muscle activity is the only thing to restore sanity."

"Big muscle activity?"

"Which means I'm going to wash the kitchen floor." Roberta added some lavender scented soap then twisted water out of a wet cleaning rag.

"I know this has been hard for you."

"Our headmistress at Roedean used to chant: 'Beware the pity.' She'd say, 'Life can't feel good all the time.' And I myself, refuse to be one of those ridiculous women who because of a man falls into drink and drugs, or one who hopes to cope by having her hair done, or even worse believes shopping is hope." She sank to her knees and began to scrub. "This morning I woke feeling very old. And that means—time to get busy—to let my muscles do some work."

"You still turn the heads of the men in town."

"So do Siamese twins."

I chuckled. It startled her when I went to the sink, took a spare rag from a pile, rinsed it in the bucket, and went to kneel at the opposite side of the room. I too began to scrub. Her face tried to hide its amusement, but I sensed my gliding the wet cloth around the metal base of the Irish cooker pleased her. She swished her rag in the lavender water, then slid over to a new section. "One can't expect hustlers to be heroes. And yet even hustlers aren't simply animals, but beasts of burden, come to learn the actual price of their human worth."

"Few of us are really seen for who we are, but in my limited experience of one-night stands, people most likely want you to represent whatever they project onto you. And that must be doubly true for hustlers who knowingly get paid to play a part in projection, as anyone who opts for sex with complete strangers must."

"Most hustlers only admit *that* in order to try and manipulate pity for their choice of trade."

"Eligio claimed to abide by certain rules, yet he never explained to me what the rules were."

"I know his rules. Mostly they concern logistics."

"For example?"

"Okay, like this. Does one rendezvous with a lover when it's convenient for your spouse—or for you? And is that time convenient for your lover? Next: are you permitted to sleep over? Can your lover phone? If so, what can be discussed in the spouse's presence? How might one avoid telling your partner more than he or she wants to know? Does someone feel upset if calls get taken in other rooms?"

"Oh, I see."

"Yes. Romantic pragmatism. I have a lot of experience there. Like if you in a rendezvous pay the expense of a hotel bill, does your partner accept the burden of such cost? If no hotel, then what about housekeeping? Do you clean the room after a visiting lover…and also before? And which pillows do you use?"

"I see. Who has to wash the sheets and towels."

"Exactly. Or even clean the toilet…or the shower drain."

"And who buys condoms or lubricant?"

"Yes, and where do you store them? And also, do you buy separate toiletries for each paramour? Not to mention extra precautions, birth control? Or now, with AIDS?"

"And lots of couples need childcare."

"And who's going to walk Apollo?"

"Or feed Grandma!"

"Ha! And what happens when you tryst…fall asleep…and forget the clock?"

"What if you're fatigued from lust and decline additional sex with your other partner? Can you explain the day's previous pleasure exhausted you?"

"I see. You've been satisfied elsewhere?"

"Yes."

"And how does anyone know when, or if, you plan to return or meet again?"

"I also presume multiple birthdays. Holidays? 'Do you mind, dear…I must pop in here to get an anniversary card for my lover?'"

"And one can't always like the person their partner sleeps with."

"No pre-approval allowed!"

"Nope. And you can't pick their cologne either." She scrubbed harder. "And so, if I may ask, did something happen to cure you of Eligio's mystique?"

"I saw him in another light…his natural setting. Much of my attraction turned out to be fantasy. When I divorced Chantel I felt something similar. A decompression of sorts."

"And now, I suppose you in reversal, are wondering what *I* could possibly have found attractive in him?"

"It did occur to me."

Roberta had the look of someone with a pebble in her shoe. "Nature is so vexing. I once read a book about a French woman…an architect. She felt like a receding shadow in the face of her husband's vibrant personality. The author, no doubt, had novelized her own life. Eventually, the character's husband moves them to Morocco for business, where she meets a wealthy Muslim businessman. An affair with him opens her to new strength. A ridiculous plot about colonial tolerance and religious difference ensues…and one day the man commissions her to become the first woman known to have designed a mosque, a project requiring them to question every tenet they've ever held. I pretended Eligio could be that kind of fantasy."

"But he's not Muslim."

"No,"

"Nor a businessman."

"Don't be caustic. Not when I'm so down. I'd hoped Eligio would be someone to help me resist all the *certainty* that is Hans. That somehow my marriage might alter itself. But instead, Eligio brought twice the misery. And I'm left to contend with what a taker I am, clutching, grabbing, wanting more, placing my comfort above that of others. I see now the way I've sedated every lover with my childish need. In times of discomfort, threat, or stress, I'll even behave wantonly for attention. Remember the day we lost Apollo…those men looking down from the promenade? I lied to you. I had indeed noticed them. What on earth was I thinking?"

"And so, now you wash the floor?"

"Yes. I'm thirty-five, and have designed no mosque…just another prison. So, I'm left to do whatever needs to be done. It's a comfort, for in every prison there's always a floor somewhere that needs a good scrub."

A shadow came over the open doorway. Signor Vescovi touched the brim of his hat and contemplated the scene of us in opposite corners, watching the wet tiles dry. "I bagged no rabbits today," he said.

Roberta twirled her finger in the air. "Lucky for the rabbits."

"Yes, indeed! But rabbits are always lucky, they can multiply overnight, and one can't worry over them too much, for which among us dies with all their clover eaten?"

Roberta tossed the scrub brush into the bucket, lifting it to the sink to empty the dirty water. "Please, come in. The floor is still wet in spots."

"I can visit from here." The barrel of his gun swung wildly as he recapitulated the disgrace of his ill-fated hunt: a lost shoe, dropped bullets, scores of runaway rabbits. As he spoke, Pina peered in from the dining room, a lemon-eating expression overtaking her face. Without a word, she left slamming the door behind her.

"Please, might I be permitted to ask? Just what is it between you and Pina?"

"I'd rather not say. It's a family matter. She might overhear."

"She's gone," Roberta said. "I heard her footsteps crunch out across the courtyard gravel. We won't see her again until this evening."

"All right then. I will tell you. Sadly, Pina was left bitter by an unfaithful husband."

"Oh," I said. "Well, we can understand that."

"The husband worked for Bene Piccolo. As you know, Bene and Mr. Garafallou produced Shakespeare tours in Italy. They starred Frances Leicester. Walker, when you bought *La Stalla*, perhaps you met Mr. Leicester?"

"I negotiated with him only by phone," I said. "The realtor was furious that I'd called him directly. Mr. Leicester had beautiful diction and agreed to our terms. He died in London ten days after the closing. The Bank of England auctioned his things, stage swords, trunks of velvet robes."

"Yes," Roberta said. "I remember, before the auction the Italian children tried on the Shakespearean capes and played Dracula."

"Yes, that was quite a day! But when the actors first came here, they needed to convert the mule stalls to make houses, so, Leicester and Bene Piccolo hired a university-educated man from Parma to oversee. Cousin Pina heard manual laborers were sought, and knowing I needed work, she coaxed me to come from across the mountains to help convert the stalls into the two houses. And so, for two seasons, while we were building, I came here and lived in Pina's house."

"That's why you know so much about *La Stalla's* plumbing!"

He nodded. "It took over a year to convert the stalls to make the houses. And once done, the actors from the troupe would stay there, every evening gathering on the shared terrace to recite speeches. That is why the terraces connect, they wanted to make a kind of amphitheater." Roberta and I stared in amazement.

"Pina was drawn by the sound of their speech. And on those joined terraces, a romance blossomed! One day Tibald, the scholar, now a construction overseer, decided he'd never return to his hometown of Parma, and instead would settle here, inviting Pina to marry. Bene Piccolo bought Tibald the house…where Pina still lives…as a wedding present. Now a resident of the village, Tibald began to work for Bene's theater as set-builder, stage manager, foreman, and sometimes just to stand on stage in armor when they needed a swarthy, muscular presence to play a guard or a soldier. When they weren't touring, and Leicester would go to England, Tibald looked after the properties. And the house's proximity was useful, for whenever Leicester *was* in residence, it was well-known that Tibald would be at his side.

"Pina's life grew difficult: two religions, one family, a husband often needing to be with his employer. The whole Catholic village against their marriage…for she converted to Anglican. Yet there's no Anglican church in Levanto, only an Evangelist one. She tried to go there, but found no comfort. So, most Sundays, she sat alone reading the Bible to herself…able to confide in no one. As well-educated men, Tibald and Mr. Leicester read scholarly books, and talked of them for hours. And then one morning at *La Stalla*, Pina found them in the same bed.

"To have a whole village cry, 'we told you so,' was not something she wanted to hear, so she kept to herself and sat alone in sorrow. But whenever she and I were together, she'd ask me: 'Do you think I have a good husband?' More than once I explained we must all adapt to the complexity that the universe has born in us…and these two men shared a *profundity* in their companionship.

"For her, it meant learning to balance an equation that she couldn't solve or understand. It didn't help that Leicester was older than Tibald. And no romantic lead. He played middle-aged, gentlemanly parts. Also, Leicester had an intellect and a vibrant social life that Pina could not compete with. When Leicester was in residence, the artists came and went. In watching that traffic, Pina saw how Tibald, a scholar, wanted to be among the learned excitement. She realized the situation would likely never change. One evening Leicester brought a group up from Monte Carlo, a famous German singer among them. Everyone called her *Angelo Azzurro*."

Roberta blinked. "You mean Marlene Dietrich?"

"That's her."

"Oh, I'd never have imagined her up here! There's a photograph of her hanging down at *Belacqua*. Her two eyebrows curved like arcs drawn by a compass!"

"It was said she needed money. When I saw her, she was plain, hair in a kerchief, a face without powder, just the flat planes of a Teuton, a typical German *hausfrau*. But she carried herself like a royal, sure of foot. One morning she came to buy eggs in a Chinese bathrobe, wearing nothing beneath. Women didn't dress like that in those days. In Hollywood, maybe, but not here. As Piccolo's friend, the singer knew whose bed Tibald slept in. Later, I learned Leicester actually sent her to meet Pina, thinking the viewpoint of a worldly woman might help. The singer got her eggs and offered to pay extra if Pina would brew her a cup of coffee. And so, I, who'd been asleep upstairs, awoke to the sound of grinding coffee beans. The actress spoke some Italian, but I was called down to help translate."

"Wait…you and Pina drank coffee with Marlene Dietrich?"

Vescovi nodded. "Was I not worthy?" His self-assurance grew from the awe on Roberta's face, realizing he'd underestimated the importance of the tale. "Pina and I never heard a woman talk like her. Cynicism, the dark voice, she drew no limit. I can still hear her saying: 'The marriage contract is the *lousiest* contract ever,' explaining how in business partnerships brief papers are drawn up to join—but the plan for un-joining runs hundreds of pages, with the hope that all consequences are clear, all possibilities accounted for. But no agreement for break-up accompanies the marriage contract. She called it *quatsch*."

"All this was spoken while you drank coffee?"

"Yes. And there's more. The actress pretended Pina was interesting to her, and she coaxed her to speak. Pina seemed grateful to finally tell her story, even if but to a passing stranger. The actress listened…as actresses do, then she spoke. 'Any woman grows despondent to discover the song of a siren has shipwrecked her sailor. But if the siren has the voice of a basso? Well! Only seafarers who've crashed vessels upon similar rocks can truly reckon it!'" Vescovi winked and continued. "The actress offered all kinds of perceptions. She said: 'Some creatures are born wilder than others…and to cage a wild thing is an impossible act.' The actress admitted to being wild herself! Despite all this, Pina remained tearful. And when the actress finished drinking her coffee, she paid for it, and her eggs, and offered up parting words: 'Some birds mate for life, some for only a season. In the end all remain true to their nature.' Then she left and went up the road, the sun shining through her Chinese bathrobe."

Roberta's face held a look of florid excitement. The story had burned too quick and too bright. "Did she ever return?"

"Never."

"And do you think Tibald loved Pina but for a season?"

"My God, he was no torturer of people. Not the kind to put a notch on his belt. He loved her for eternity!" Vescovi halted and unabashedly stared for emphasis.

Roberta grew impatient. "So what happened?"

"Who knows? Maybe, as Leicester hoped, that old German singer influenced her, but maybe not. Nonetheless, Pina seemed to arrive at some conclusion, deciding Tibald needed variety the way some men needed insulin or morphine. She began to think that if his divergence could be accommodated, his restored equilibrium would in time bless them both. I, on the other hand, being young and stupid, as well as loath to see her suffer, suggested an actress moving from theater to theater could find a way to ignore her marriage. But Pina, stuck in a village full of gossips? Well, no ordinary marriages can manage that. My anger toward Tibald grew. 'For Pina's sake, set her free,' I said. And via my scolding, he finally broached the subject of annulment. Pina became inconsolable. She refused to relinquish her vow. And blaming me as a bad influence, she threw *me* out!

"I was now without a home, and so Tibald lent me money to buy my house in the village. Signor Leicester lent it to him. When Pina learned that I would still be living here, assisted by Tibald no less, she grew outraged. That *contadina* pride of hers. And so, from those days to these, if she must address me, it's only with the curse of the devil." Vescovi tucked his gun under his arm with satisfaction. "So…that is that."

"Wait!" Roberta said "Did they stay together? Accommodate the openness?"

"Pina tried to love Tibald despite his libertine urges…and because he *needed* love. She has a weakness for men who are in distress. And if anyone finds a love that refuses to be shocked, that love runs deep. Think about it. What relief for

Tibald not to feel simply tolerated—but accepted. Someone intolerable, who's been graced with acceptance, will repay that gift a hundredfold. Tolerance for that which is unchangeable in another…is the greatest act of love."

"So…did their marriage succeed?"

"Sadly, no. Even they could not sustain it. Could you? I couldn't. Maybe intolerance explains why I'm still single. But they had tried. In fact, Pina conceived two children. Miscarried both. The village pronounced this divine judgment. And then one day, Tibald, convinced it was for her own good, did indeed depart. Pina took it hard, and never forgave my opposition to her genuine love."

Vescovi smiled, tipped his hat and moved to be on his way. Dumbfounded, we could barely bid farewell, and sat watching him exit down through the garden, stepping back over the boxwood hedge.

• • •

On the terrace of *La Stalla*, Buddy took lunch alone, as Pina watered the pelargoniums only a few feet away. The frenzied labor surrounding Lydia's cooking enterprise had grown, and their busy schedules left fewer chances for them, or for all of us, to gather and dine. When Buddy saw me, he grinned, then rested his chin upon his hand. "Can you cure a headache?"

"Wish I could."

"Every religion in the world thinks they hold the key to humanity, and yet the headache persists." A one-inch stub of cigar rested beside his plate. "A gift from Garafallou." His joy reminded me of how dogs proudly drag stuffed toys they're slowly destroying into view. Buddy stood and went to perch on the balustrade, one leg up, relighting the remains of the cigar. His thighs and rear had recently lost some of their thickness, probably from stress or the challenge of walking the hills.

"Remember in Harrisburg, religious people used to come to the door in serge suits and silk ties to spread the word? And ladies too, with great flowered hats. My father always wore them out with patience. I'd ask him why he didn't just slam the door and give them the heave-ho. His answer? That it injured salesmen not to feign at least some interest in their soap, and that even a tiny bit of listening kept their dream alive."

"Aren't scientists usually skeptics? Maybe he was unwilling to get blasted by some Bible thumper's threat of Judgment Day?"

"Dad sent a check to the atheist society every year in gratitude for getting prayer out of the schools. If churches were truly Eden, he'd say, then evidence not hypothesis would attract." Buddy relit his smoke and puffed. "At my college, the kids swallow Noah and his ark, and Jonah and his whale—hook, line, and sinker. They ignore it when I warn about seeking comfort in what isn't physically plausible…I mean what is within their own body's frame of probability. But they actually prefer believing they could live in the belly of a whale." He flicked a nubbin of tightly wound tobacco ash. It fell on his shoe.

"I guess that suspension of fact is not unusual at a Bible College? But I'd rather read a poem for comfort than hear a sermon."

Buddy looked at me with skepticism. "A love for poetry can't be taught. It's a dog whistle some hear, others don't."

"I disagree. Love of poetry *can* be taught. If words are well-used, then a blind boy can see the color wheel, and a deaf girl can detect Morse code."

"And what if my students can't do that? Is the poet to blame? Or does that imply I'm a lousy teacher?"

"Most schools wrestle the pleasure out of poetry. But a good poetry lesson can open a student's mind to the forces connecting the abstract and the concrete—how their inter-play works in the human brain. It's an important part of critical thinking."

Buddy puffed a smoke ring just as Lydia came out dressed for town. She glanced at him with annoyance. "You don't look old enough to smoke that thing."

"It's a Havana special. Beetle says they can't be bought in the States. I'm going to replace it for him, and buy another for myself as well."

"Why not just light a match to your wallet? I mean, eighty dollars for an oral fixation. That's what shrinks call it."

"Look, lay off, will ya? Don't I encourage your dreams and stuff? What about all those acting teachers?"

She brought a small compact from her purse and lifted her sunglasses to check her eyebrows. For a split second, despite her makeup, I detected a purple bruise at the left eye. The depth of their trouble sounded an alarm. All this time, I'd envisioned their combat as some sort of theater. No bruises. No marks. Was physical violence the new norm?

"Oh, I forgot my sun hat," she said, and hurried back inside. That small bruise now made me distrust his sinister side more than hers. How many in Harrisburg knew the advantages given him—family money, a father's influence admitting him to the *old* alma mater, landing him employment, membership in the *old* country club. He was far from the brightest, and ought to be thrilled to have a wife lead him on a fascinating trip to Italy. Why this need to fight?

"Headaches like this almost make me glad we don't have kids. Anyway, Lydia says she's too self-centered to be maternal."

"Lots of women say that. They change when it happens."

"She's been pregnant twice. Aborted both times. The first time she was only twenty-five. That's when I proposed. After the wedding, she said we needed to wait, that the world was in too big a mess."

"I'm sorry. I truly am. But this should remain private. It's between the two of you."

"Three years ago, she was pregnant again; we were both approaching mid-thirties, good money coming in. She said the timing was bad, that the salons had to come first. That was also after she was bitten by the acting bug. She said she had to focus on her new career. Imagine what would happen to my job if the folks at my college found out." His lips pressed into a thin line. "You've no idea how strict a Bible college can be. To get hired, you gotta sign an agreement to uphold their religious bull. And the students are more conservative than the teachers!"

"Is making someone sign a document about upholding faith even legal? Do they get government subsidies? Even federal tuition loans?"

Buddy shrugged. "It doesn't matter. I signed it. But working there with those pious religious shits, I'm becoming an atheist like my old man. Religious colleges have lost their moral vision. At Catholic schools most nuns and priests are retiring, taking rigor with them. The schools fall to a bunch of mediocre academics, or money-grubbing thugs who run things for their own satisfaction."

"So, to keep that job, you must pretend a belief in God?"

"Yup. Have to. And English departments don't flex the philanthropic muscle of law or business schools. In fact, now that the gifts from Dad's estate have diminished, the chair of the English department actually told me, landing a large donor was my only hope to survive. That if I didn't do some serious grant-writing, this trip to Italy would bring retribution."

"Maybe directly from God?"

"That's why Madalyn Murray O'Hair is my new antihero."

"Why did your dad endow a religious school in the first place?"

"Maybe he wanted to bait them? To prove hard-science preferable to blind-faith?"

. . .

On the day of my Genovese lecture, I was relieved Eligio didn't show, and also, glad Lydia and Buddy had absented themselves, claiming a meeting in Portofino with their magazine publisher, a woman stopping there for only one day on her way to Capri. After my talk some audience members gathered by the podium to introduce themselves and raise additional questions. A few held copies of my poetry books, which I gratefully signed. The agent who represented my last book stood waiting with Garafallou and Roberta. I thanked them for coming. "No problemo," my agent said. "Flying over here for this makes the trip tax deductible."

Later at a café near the lecture hall Garafallou by his questions showed that he'd been listening carefully. "What surprised me," he said, "was to hear you report so many writing gurus go on record to advise authors never write a novel with a writer as narrator!"

I let my agent answer. "We equate that to a walk in a lashing rain with no umbrella. Our sales departments say writerly voices hold little accord for modern readers."

"Ridiculous," Roberta said. "Thousands of books are narrated by characters who write."

"Mystery books can sell them," my agent said. "People love writers who solve murders. And romances also stand some chance."

"Yes," I said. "If the character who writes, also happens to be the richest woman in three counties, and is the most beautiful, wears exquisite pearls and stands by a grand staircase in the family ranch, backed by a family pedigree, and an idiosyncratic—yet modern—way of living. Otherwise, a wordsmith who narrates usually guarantees no book royalties, that ermine cape which already so few get to wear."

Garafallou pondered whether all writing might not, in one way or another, be a confession.

"I agree. I've always said all imagination is based on memory."

"That sounds like a topic for your next lecture!"

The bill came, and they treated me by splitting it. "For old times," my agent added, unnecessarily, implying our business partnership had no future. We left the café and bid farewell in front of a large discount store, selling mops and plastic tubs arranged out on the sidewalk. Roberta and I departed and Garafallou called after us: "Don't forget, Corsica is waiting and eager for this kind of conversation!"

The trains between Genoa and Levanto were frequent, our wait short. We boarded and took seats. Roberta then recounted how Hans had, by telephone, declared the timing of a Corsican trip to be bad. "He said: 'Any travel, for us, is at the moment out of the question.'"

"That's a shame."

"Him decreeing that, while saying '*us*' really irked me. But I'll claim the game."

"How?"

"Ignore him. I want to see Corsica. But I prefer not to stay at Garafallou's alone. So, I have a question: How would you feel about going along with me?"

My resistance lowered. "I wouldn't want Hans to think I'm stealing his place."

"His absence has already dismissed that. And traveling with you would be such fun!"

The train pulled into Rapallo, and on the platform waiting to board stood Buddy and Lydia. Through the open window I called back to them. They saw me waving and ran down the platform to board closer to the car we were in. They jumped on just as the train lurched onward, and soon came wobbling through our car's portal. "What're the chances we'd meet en-route!" Roberta cried. Together we flipped the back of the adjacent seat-bench so the four of us could sit facing one another.

"How'd your talk go?" Buddy asked.

Roberta jumped in. "He was wonderful. The place packed!"

"My old agent happened to be in Rome. He came up. Was honest enough to say attendance at my lecture makes his whole trip over from the States tax-deductible."

Lydia changed topics without acknowledging a word I'd said. "You oughta seen the crowds at the Portofino ferry," she said. "Whole town mobbed. They say Liz Taylor's there selling perfume. But forget her... I'd like you both to look at this." She held up a copy of *Hearth & Table* magazine with both hands. "This is a mock-up. The editor let us have it as a souvenir. We're to be the very next cover!"

Under the magazine's logo, Lydia and Pina stood holding the chestnut cake. Buddy flipped to the place intended for the article's placement. "Once the article is proofed and finalized, it'll be dropped into these pink boxes."

It was exciting to recognize ourselves in the photos, as we were that day, wearing the silly Easter-egg-colored jackets and vests. I'd deliberately stepped out of the frame more than once, but still could be found in far more shots than I'd realized. Eligio could be frequently seen as well.

Buddy pulled the edited text from a manilla folder. "Wait till I read you this! *Pina is an old-world cook, with taste buds so refined she can tell where in the region a tomato has been grown. In chewing but a single leaf of basil, she can specify the season's rainfall in the garden from which it was cut; the less water, the more pungent the herb. In these skills, Lydia is her match."*

"But that's ridiculous!" Roberta said.

Buddy laughed. "People don't read magazines for truth. They read to dream." He read the next sentence, a chestnut cake description, and we balked when he called it *delectable.*

"You said it was dry as sawdust!"

"Poetic license."

We studied the pictures, recognizing details of the kitchen. "It feels like a million years ago."

"The publisher has never done anything this fast. They've a new way of printing from a supercomputer." The last photo showed Lydia and Buddy toasting Prosecco with Pina, and behind them the miraculous view from *La Stalla's* terrace.

"I don't remember that," Roberta said.

"Oh, they used clip art to put that in, then airbrushed it. The publisher has a sparkling-wine account that he has to suck up to. Those aren't even our arms! They shot the background in the morning to capture the light, then dropped the whole image in."

Roberta was having none of it. "Is that even legal?"

"Enhancement makes it better. No different from the way Mona Lisa had her face altered. Soon they say the computer will be able to do it. And everyone will be able to alter their own image. It's the future!"

"But what happens to reality?"

"Technology just keeps improving it."

TRASFERIMENTO

* * *

Genoa, Italy

To prevent Hans from disrupting our travel plans, Roberta insisted we depart in secret. Toting two large valises we quickly boarded the train, and grew excited as it sped off toward Genoa. "If Hans suffers because I've declined his consent," Roberta said, "he can discuss it with his therapist. It's funny now, how when we met our sessions were endlessly about control."

"In couples counseling?"

"Not exactly." Roberta paused while we bought coffee from a cart pushed down the aisle by the food vendor. "Look, I'll tell you the truth in a moment. But only if you swear never to tell anyone. It's embarrassing."

"Well, only tell me if you want to." We waited until the coffee cart had gone on to the next car.

"Okay. Here it is. When I first met Hans, he was my shrink."

Eyes open, I tried not to stare.

"We fell in love."

"And?"

"He behaved appropriately. And I did too. Treatment ended at once. We waited months, then became lovers. But that's why he was so angry at the party the night after the theater. Lydia's questions were so dead-on, they felt threatening. He thought I'd told her."

"She has an uncanny ability to intuit the secrets of others. I won't tell a soul. But boy! We humans are all so damn unpredictable."

"Just imagine the glee Lydia would exhibit. Look how she dogged you about Eligio."

"Let me ask you this: do you think your care was compromised by these events?"

"No. Hardly. Hans insisted I find a new therapist and I talked about it with her. Not being haunted by a secret was beneficial. And speaking of such things, don't think I've stopped thinking on the question I asked that day we shelled walnuts."

"What Eligio represents to me on a larger scale?"

"You said women can admit more. Men usually must hide to remain men."

Her truth-telling encouraged me to put my well-practiced dodge of any closeness aside. "That's been my sense. In Philadelphia, I used to see married guys exit a pornographic theater called the Garden Cinema. I'd later see some of the same fellows at the university swim club, only a few blocks away. I noticed firsthand there were men who liked to watch other men, and some in turn liked to be watched while preparing to dip in the old L-shaped pool."

She laughed. "Isn't that the main attraction of sports?"

"But most men watch incognito. Or perhaps without sensing eros. In college, a suite-mate confided to a pugilistic crush. He'd go sit among the crowd at the Blue Horizon gym to watch a half-naked boxer named Ace Turner sweat it out as he trained for the Golden Gloves."

"So, are *you* like him? I mean by nature…would you rather *watch*?"

"What a question! Gee. I suppose. Sometimes. Some things. Are you becoming like Lydia—a miner digging out the privacy of others?"

"I'll ask in another way. Is there a long history of watching? I mean, women or men?"

"At an early age, probably due to Mom, I saw that being human was far more complicated for some than for others. Since then I've struggled to direct some childhood inhibition in my brain, a fear and longing to track who I might truly be, a search for something human that was missing or hidden from my perception of myself. And then I discovered the writer Montaigne."

"Montaigne?"

"Yes. A French writer. You see, Montaigne lost a very close male friend while only thirty. Apparently, he yearned for that friend for the rest of his life. In writing his essays, whenever he refers to the reader, it's said he really refers to that friend."

"Who was the friend?"

"Another writer, Étienne de La Boétie. Wrote about tyrants. How they strengthened when ordinary people ignored systems of power, mainly by being pre-occupied with diversions. The archetypes he identified included the courtesan, the cheat, the gambler, the drunk. In our time we'd probably add the pothead, the porn addict, and what you and I know too well—the hustler!"

"Ha!"

"Etienne was a libertarian, an early promoter of civil disobedience as preferable to nonviolent resistance. He argued that any human not too lazy to do so could withdraw his consent from any force or rule."

"Do you think that's true?"

"In some things, yes."

· · ·

We arrived in Genoa late, with just four minutes to board the *Côte d'Azur* express. From our train compartment, we watched the last of the city outskirts roll by, the apartment blocks growing massively clunkier and dirtier until they gave way to an industrial part of the coast.

"I'm having one of those train moments," Roberta said, her eyes transfixed. "Like in the movies. The tracks speeding along as time passes."

"I know that feeling. Lost in space. After Mom died, I felt it constantly. A kind of unaware melancholy." I leaned back to find Roberta staring at me.

"Walker, I see now how strange you must feel to have some family here in Italy. I mean Lydia and Buddy."

"Buddy isn't family. We did attend the same primary school, but his mother disliked the changes in public education and soon sent him to private school. A couple of months later, our paths crossed at a county-wide poetry contest. He said we couldn't sit together. His mother saw *mine* as trouble."

"Something to get snagged on?"

"Yes. The real test began when Mom mentioned she had stopped identifying as white."

"What? I've never heard of such a thing?"

"A liberal's conceit. Mom would recite poetic phrases. 'Defining kingdoms by any race polarizes progress.' Or she'd say: 'Ours is just another tint of skin.' My cousin Marvene thought that delusional, even nuts, and most certainly privileged."

"You mean nuts in that your mother even thought she could choose her identification?"

"Sure. Marvene called it *passing in reverse*."

"When was the last time you saw Marvene?"

"We send the annual Christmas card. But cultural differences have pushed us apart. I think my education is threatening. Marvene has accused me of being a snob…and also of somehow passing."

"So, you've not seen her after all these years?"

"No."

"Oh…I don't know how to imagine all these situations you're describing! And I'm beginning to see your mother as some kind of activist?"

"Not really. Just dangerously progressive?"

I longed to continue discussing what we had started, unusual for me, but Roberta excused herself. "I've got to track down that snack cart." Was she really feeling hunger or merely feeling the stress of my story? In a few minutes she returned with some red wine and potato chips to share.

"Your mother paid a terrible price for her views."

"She learned the hard way that defying one's race isn't as simple as changing one's hair color. That she thought she could imagine a different world, one where race was merely a bland fact, enraged any number of people on every side. But nonetheless she sought to change something, certainly for me, but often I think as much for herself."

We sat sipping and munching. "Do you think it's privilege? That a person thinks they can choose these things? Is that what upset people? I mean upset the people who *couldn't* choose?"

"Choice is an interesting idea. I think the Gordons, who acted as my grandparents, made existential choices about their lives, and their reactions to things. They did their best to accommodate Mom, knowing the rejection she faced for choosing their son to love. They were what I call *biblical* progressives. Theologically committed to the ideas of Christ. They believed there was freedom in Christ. Meanwhile, at boarding school, I saw many affluent students construct *mythical* backgrounds. Some claimed wealth, titles even, decadence or nobility, and no one took *them* to task. I myself used to pretend that I was the son of a diplomat. I've also seen upper-class kids wear sneakers with the laces removed, call each other *Dawg*, rhyme raps about life in prison—as if they'd been."

"Some of my clients pay people to invent a coat of arms. And in wartime the King of England declared himself no longer German. Simply snapped his fingers, and his German mother Queen Mary, and his German grandfather Prince Albert, were no longer the House of Saxe-Coburg and Gotha. They were suddenly the English-only House of Windsor. Roedean encouraged us to value that kind of royal license, to model ourselves on such imperious behavior."

"I've also seen UK folk all too happy to point out where on the food-chain the luck of personal lineage has placed each one of us."

"Our headmistress used to argue that the ancient caste systems of India, stood up well beside British rankings of class."

"She might be fired for saying that now! But class is a major part of the biases that get attributed to race."

"As an American, I didn't stand a chance! They even corrected me on how to pronounce Ar-kansas."

"When I was at college, a history teacher once upset her classroom by saying the globe is never without a slave. They accused her of trying to justify slavery. Yet Russell said the same thing dozens of times. He loved to tout how slavery was practiced by Africans long before the Europeans or Arabs took it up. To him,

Africa represented the primary source of everything."

"Slavery is still common to this day?"

"Look at communist China. We love to consume the cheap goods and labor of those workers. Many Western European industries have crashed since the Berlin wall came down…for the same reason. Markets are flooded with cheap communist goods."

"My Dad used to say trade deficits were what required foreign governments to keep investing in America. That they kept the banks afloat."

"That sounds plausible. Still, I've seen people hang flags on their houses, but then sell their nationalism if doing so saves them a buck."

"Who wants to pay five or ten bucks extra for an American hammer?"

"Nonetheless, Grandpa Gordon still thought America the land of salvation, and that to interpret or adopt mass suffering in order to become its victim, limited one's future."

"That sounds complicated."

"It's not so far from some of Mom's ideas."

"But that implies all anyone needs to do is step up and claim their prize, change their name, ignore the world's mirror?"

"Grandpa thought many raised with opportunity and privilege still clung to the past."

"But is that true?"

"He felt people avoided freedom mainly to remain eligible for whatever perks that might come from victim compensation, even if the perks were puny."

"I don't quite get that."

"It's the reversal of people who don't want change because they may not remain eligible for the big advantages they hold. He disliked working-class people who somehow managed to advance, access education, or opportunities, but still wanted to claim suffering. His point was that every life suffers something… no matter what one's heritage or class. He thought some who still claimed the victim's heritage had actually managed to assimilate quite prosperously—that they hadn't actually suffered enough!"

"Do you agree with him?"

"I can't blame suffering's claimants. Firehoses and police dogs aren't governed by some mysterious force."

"I'm sorry…but I think you lost me."

"I once knew a privileged woman—had a full scholarship to an expensive school, wrote an entire book romanticizing the plight of her homeland Sri

Lanka—a country she'd never been to! I mean at least Kipling *went* to India. Claiming *otherness* allows people to ignore how many of their own got burned—by their own—often at the stake—in the *name* of oneness. Marvene used to say the privileged students she saw at my boarding school had likely never *met* an attack dog. Some barely knew about the civil rights movement—or didn't think it involved them."

"And because of excessive money, it might not have."

"Right. Grandpa Gordon used to wonder how many generations of privilege would it take before the claim of victimhood was willing to be relinquished. But how do you get a leg up when the school you're assigned is inferior? Or too superior?"

"Don't you think people everywhere serve their own personal interests first...or those of their families?"

"There *are* theories about being a socialist at home but a capitalist in the street."

We turned our heads to the window as some green leafy branches went whizzing by, brushing against the glass. The spell of closeness she and I were coming to know, by talking openly, while in high-speed motion, remained. "As I said, some of my clients have enough privilege to create or modify a coat of arms. And at Ellis Island so many had their names or countries of origin officially altered. The privilege of power permits some to basically rewrite history."

"Mom used to say standards of variance vary, depending on *who* is seeking the variance."

"And Europe isn't as noble as people will pretend it to be. I mean someone not so many miles from where we are now lit the sticks around Joan of Arc."

"No continent on earth has passed the non-violence test for very long. To overcome power isn't as simple as Montaigne's friend implied. Ask any Greek about the Ottomans—or Smyrna. It was Turks and their munitions that exploded the Parthenon. And Chinese people certainly know what torture is. Just look what they did to the Koreans."

"Cruel wars span the classes of every global dynasty."

"Race is an easier caste to shout out than class—because to voice something against the upper-classes often illuminates the wealth and comfort of many of the *most* vocal upper-middle-class dissenters. Marvene showed me variations on this paradox. For one, if you look at students who descend from colonial rule—many thrive and bring diversity to Oxford or Harvard—but mainly because their Indian, Caribbean or African colonial educations prove far better than the education citizens who live in American projects get. And don't think the students from those old colonial systems don't come here and feel superior and look down on the Americans who can't complete an SAT. And yet, even coming from abroad, they'll *claim* ante-bellum slavery, Jim Crow and exploit common race to gain further advantage. They take advantage of America's guilt. My being admitted to boarding school is probably part of that."

"I suppose self-serving aggression has to be listed as part of our human commonality?"

"Maybe we need to admit that and temper it—to grant all to have the chance of choice. And I can't think of another country on earth that feels guilt the way Americans do."

"Most Germans I've met feel guilt. Their national pride committed atrocities."

"It's probably a noble characteristic."

Roberta poured more wine. "So, if I understand, one thing you're trying to explain is how the moral line between oppressed and oppressor is thin."

"Yes. How behavior imitates power without realizing it. One group who gains power behaves just as cruelly as another—as if in a mirror. For example, my mother's family knew well the story of Irish oppression. But then the poor, oppressed Irish blew up Viceroy Mountbatten…or should I say *Battenberg*? And how many ways are then wrought to interpret that violence? And of course, it's not fair to single out the Irish. Or the Germans."

"So, the old cliché is true? All power corrupts absolutely?"

"And therein lies the genius of Dr. King. His strategy brought more change more quickly to every class, and every race, than any radical since. His allies understood one part of education is to search for people's common ground—to awaken and uplift the moral conscience of everyone. To see our human similarities even as we note cultural difference. The genius of Dr. King was how he awakened people from every walk of life. I saw firsthand how Grandma Gordon, as well as my mother, tried not to judge people…even when people would defend their inertia. Even when people said: 'I did all I could…there were legal issues… I can't afford to lose a good paying job…my home, my family, my insurance.'"

"Don't you think blanket excuses or explanations avoid change?"

"Yes. Fear and a longing for safety keep people in stasis even for change they might be in favor of."

"There are sometimes prices in life that are unfair…and should not have to be paid."

"Do you think you've paid?"

"Hell, no. I haven't. My choice was to simply run away from my own face."

"And is that even a kind of choice?"

"Yes. In college, I enrolled in every world literature course I could, but… and this is a big but…*never* with the hope of finding my mother, or my two stepfathers, or my Aunt Greta, or even my biological father."

"In my life, I've never read a book with a character that seems like me."

"Neither have I. Yet I see myself in all of them. I've always longed to read stories about people who *weren't* like me."

"So, you could *find* yourself in their character?"

"Yes. We *became* all the characters we read about, no matter their age or cultural background. No matter how foreign the characters. And one gift of reading is to discover the human similarities between us and them. All literary characters, despite their differences, show us to ourselves. It doesn't matter where a novel is set. All know the same human problems: famine, war, greed, poverty, hunger, anger, retribution, joy, lust. So, reading *itself* then becomes the world's common ground."

"That sounds utopian."

"It is. Of all the global literature courses I took, or the African-American literature courses—none *ever* parsed out a text that told my story. But I already knew my story. Reading broadly was done to broaden my sense of myself, my own story, and to see how my story fits into the world of stories. I found personal value in Frederick Douglas saying: 'You have seen how a man was made a slave; you shall see how a slave was made a man.' Even though I was never a slave. Marvene and I used to like *The Jeffersons*, though we didn't find the zebra jokes they parlayed made for an enlightened family. During one phase of broadening ourselves, she and I became obsessed with movies where characters were referred to as in-betweens…*Imitation of Life*, *I Passed for White*, *Sapphire*, *Pinky*, almost always a beautiful woman in the stew. We imagined her suffering. We cried real tears for her plight."

"I used to love films where characters changed class: *To Sir With Love* or *Flamingo Road*. Yet, I never saw my own story there."

"A lot of people must've identified with something. Such movies were wildly successful with all races."

"I think I understand what you mean," Roberta said. "At least I hope to come closer to understanding."

"Baldwin, Hurston, Hughes, Wheatley, can expand the soul of anyone. And how many people will secretly cry over the painful poem Lucille Clifton wrote for Emmett Till. The boldness, going inside the head of a white sheriff's wife, an inversion of the minstrel practice. I used to like a novelist named Toomer… some still condemn him saying he tried to pass. But to me, his characters went beyond stereotypes because they *looked* beyond stereotypes. Grandpa Gordon used to say: people descended from slavery aren't always wise elders with tribal things to share. And they aren't always victims or tragic mulattos. And sometimes all people are racist bigots. Just look at how certain sons, dying of AIDS, are being treated by their churches…or the churches of their families."

She lifted the empty wine bottle and screwed the cap back on. "I like the idea that the act of reading itself becomes our common ground."

Our train talk suddenly exhausted us. We stared out the window as the train passed through the mountain tunnels linking Italy and Monaco. Later, as the lemon groves of Menton went gliding by, Roberta remembered the sandwiches Pina had packed. She brought them out, along with a thermos of cold tea, and we enjoyed them in silence, staring at the loops of electrical wire running up and down beside the track. "Do you think travel makes for common ground?"

"If a traveler is willing to let a trip take them out of their comfort zone. I mean, if we step beyond the Hilton, or the gates of some controlled resort. It's important to explore places we've never been. But it is a risk."

* * *

Nice, France

At the train station, we stood at the taxi stand, Roberta read me lines skimmed from a pamphlet on the Cote D'Azur: *Nice's station is Belle Epoque…style of Louis XIII…sometime during the First World War, the main hall was stripped of its chandeliers… No one remembers what became of them.* She shook her head. "At Roedean they used to warn us: 'Grandness always trades as a spoil in war.'"

At last, it was our turn for a taxi, and we drove along the promenade, following the curve of the famous stony beach. At the *Grand Hotel Majesca*, the owner welcomed us with a glass of champagne, saying a pair of rooms waited. "All the great and famous have stayed here," she noted. "Churchill, Lindbergh, Nehru."

We toasted to one another's health and then discussed what sights to see. "It's market day on Avenue Jean Medicine," the hotelier said. "And after that, don't miss the Roman ruins!"

Outside we followed the map she'd circled for us, and found the busy market with iced fish, meat stands, and stalls selling cheese from behind glass cases.

The fruit vendors had piles of clementines, and we bought a bagful, along with a tiny bunch of bananas from Tanzania.

After touring the afternoon away, we headed back down to the water, arriving in the early evening. At the boat basin we chose a restaurant facing the crowded dock, where all manner of vessels came and went. A few weatherworn boats floated by, but the majority were crusted in super, vain-glorious luxury, captained by sunburned older men, often accompanied by women who appeared surgically buxom and young. We dined alfresco on grilled Doré and Roberta made me laugh when she said she'd forgotten what it was like to eat a plate of fish that hadn't been photographed.

After our meal, strolling the old quarter, we spotted the owner of our hotel walking with a flamboyant woman dressed in a magenta taffeta suit with a matching purple turban. They entered a small museum open to the public for a reception. We followed to find sparkling wine being passed around in fluted glasses. The hotelier noticed us. *"Bon Soir!"* she called across the room. "How nice to find you are absorbing our city's culture! May I present, my friend Madame Dufresne."

Dufresne declined my handshake and instead put her palms together and bowed like a geisha. "Madame does *not* like to be touched." The hotelier smirked. "We've been pals for centuries and it's always been that way."

"True," her friend agreed modestly. "I'm like Howard Hughes, you know, germs, germs." Her vowels stretched to bizarre theatrical inflections, but were much more elegant than the strange hacking sounds of Phil Filbertson.

We sipped our wine and wandered the exhibit looking at intricate paintings of animals hidden in gardens, and staring out from thick forests. "Are you from Nice?" Roberta asked.

Madame Dufresne shrugged. "I suppose I don't belong anywhere." Her face seemed to grow sad.

The hotelier interceded. "Isabelle play-acts confusion. She's something of an actress, lives in New York, but summers here in Nice at her ancestral home. Her family were builders during the *Belle Epoque.* Her uncle's construction emporium, the *Palais d' Industrie* sat in a grand building, with two huge terra-cotta domes flying beautiful flags. The domes were removed in the 1930's and five floors of deco apartments were added to the stone base."

"Oh, please! *Must* you narrate all this?"

"She's one of those who desperately seeks attention, but then laments loss of privacy. She also claims small-talk bores her!"

"Such a magpie." Dufresne's voice was terse. "Why not also tell them the *Palais* was built on the backside of town for the convenience of the stones?"

"It's true. The *Chemin de Fer de Provence* is one street over."

"Why not also describe each stone brought down from the mountains, or better yet show some ancient sheets of inventory?"

"Acting outrage allows Madame to practice public rudeness. And while she may pretend to belong nowhere—wherever she *does* happen to be—she practices the snobbery of our most aristocratic French citizens. It's quite a show!"

We moved on through the hall, and the hotelier explained the paintings had been done by a Thai princess. "She and her bodyguard live in the *Alpes-Maritime*."

"I've visited her home," Madame Dufresne said. "Hundreds of shedding pets. One couldn't sit on the furniture, with all the hair."

Our hotelier stopped a waiter with a tray, to offer us more wine. Dufresne refused. "I never touch alcohol. You know that."

The hotelier sighed. "But how on earth do you get through the day?"

Dufresne chuckled. "Faith."

We finished at the art show and were invited to return with them to the hotel for a nightcap. At the bar, as an elderly man in a red jacket took our orders, Roberta studied the impressive monumental lobby. "The *Belle Epoque* must've been an enchanted time?"

Madame Dufresne shrugged. "The hand with the velvet glove must also wipe the bottom. No?" Her agility to shift with insouciance from empire to excrement astonished. When the drinks arrived, we saw she had ordered pear juice. Once more she criticized our alcohol infused cocktails. "You're poisoning your brains!"

"To know sobriety," the hotelier cheerfully toasted, "...one must know drink."

Dufresne dug in. "One day you'll discover *morality* is far more interesting than *mortality*."

"You think you can threaten me with death to get me to abstain to your degree."

Dufresne chuckled at her friend with mischief and to prevent further rebuttal, quickly turned to me, her tone that of an interrogator. "And? You? What is *your* occupation?"

"I thought French people didn't ask such things."

"Living in New York for forty years, I've learned not to waste time." I admitted to being a poet and an editor. "Oh. So, you set words as the gardener sets trees? The fruits of the universe determined by your spade, your eye, your prune? Without you, books go to seed? Words wait unweeded, unblossoming?"

"Sounds as if you might also be a writer?"

"Me? Oh, I've written, of course. But I hate books. Most simply have too much blah…blah…blah…In truth, I'm an *artiste virtuelle*." Her eyes shone with defiance. "But what most call art is for me *not* too interesting. Too many charlatans. Too many dabblers. Too many with no gift. Many let others do their work for them. Or worse, are those that still paint only masted ships!"

"Isabelle is *moderne*," the hotelier said. "She knew Warhol. And Dali too!"

"And what do you paint?" I asked

"Paint? Me? Why the future of course! Satellites! Mickey Mouse with wings!" Dufresne opened her handbag. "This morning I cut a poem from the newspaper. Would you like to hear it?"

The hotelier made a leery face, like someone about to be put in a stockade. "As a businesswoman, poetry is something I don't really get."

Madame Dufresne's quick non-sequitur brought her obvious glee. "Relax." She placed a pair of purple spectacles on her nose. "This is simple.

> *Vice is a monster of such frightful mien*
> *As to be hated needs but to be seen*
> *But seen too oft, familiar with its face*
> *We first endure, then pity, then embrace.*

"Simple! See? All you need do is define *vice*. Define it for yourself. Then the poem states how easily we grow accustomed to it. In other words, even something contemptuous can by familiarity become accepted." Dufresne put the poetry clipping away. "Art is like that. People follow trends. They mistake imitation for creativity. They copy, copy, copy. Meanwhile the art world is embracing shit. Everyone wants to be famous for fifteen minutes."

"We get plenty of artists and celebrities here," the hotelier said. "But it's business travelers who fascinate me most. Prideful, and thinking themselves invincible, thinking they've figured out some win over a system. I've met importers who scout the world for all that can be carried, bargain rugs from Nepal, boxed sets of clay ornaments from Xi'an, flip flops from Brazil. Self-admiring types owning empires, usually men, their spouses growing impatient with bellhops over luggage, or feeling under-valued, they'll brag to anyone in earshot how they only travel non-commercial airlines. Often their vapid children live on drugs, raise dogs, or ride horse believing they're dukes or duchesses. I've seen tycoons combat risk and loneliness with concubines kept near their factories, or CFOs who sleep with their overseas plant managers. Believing in their invincibility, nothing moral bothers them in the least."

"What you say can be true," Roberta agreed. "Many can *only* fall in love with people on their payrolls, guides or doormen or docents."

"Yes! They promise visas to the chambermaid, or that nice girl who seats them every night at the restaurant. Among the wealthy, once an excess of surplus is attained—the bottom line expanded to absurdity—the sense of absence or lack often shocks them. Suddenly they realize how dull profiteering has made them. But it's too late. As money-hounds, they're now embalmed and all the cash in the world can't buy what they've previously ignored—intimacy, originality, ethics, wisdom. These cannot be bought."

Dufresne interjected. "I always say, that's when they start buying art!"

"And when even art leaves them hollow, they come here, suddenly craving traditional places, daily routines honored not just for profit, but continuity. This hotel is but light sugar spun during eras of prosperity. If such buildings survive the intervening wars, in time their preservation becomes a symbol of all that's steadfast."

Dufresne sneered. "For Americans, Europe is a fantasy that soon becomes oppressive because of its mannered nobility."

"Yes. I think that's true. I decorate homes for rich people. When the golf course grows dull, or the newer one with a superior club house can't relieve insecurity or depression, they leave Terre Haute, Palm Beach, San Diego, Bryn Mawr, Dallas, come here to the South of France, or the Italian Riviera, or some other rich person's paradise. For some there comes a craving—a need for some kind of *spiritual* experience. They'll do up a house with a Zen view, or seek exclusive accomplishments, give money to a Guatemalan charity, strive for a horse show ribbon, take a walk on the Great Wall of China, maybe a partial climb of Machu Picchu, but only long enough to have their picture taken. Too much rigor, and they turn back! Some claim mindfulness, or to care so much about the planet they no longer eat meat. Others start eating only meat. Or swear to buy only fabrics of organic cotton or shades of one color. They hire decorators because they're too busy to expend effort. Walker suggests they're embarrassed to reveal their own taste."

"Buying becomes a substitute occupation," the hotelier said.

Roberta nodded. "On some owner's whim, we've built every kind of hideous and unused gazebo you can imagine. Or we buy ten thousand Spring bulbs for the gardener to plant, or we break down walls to remodel an ever-bigger unused kitchen or bath. Clutter gets cleared, but no sooner do people get decluttered than they go shopping again."

The voluble hotelier held up her hand. "But wait. Are we sounding too smug? Sanctimonious? Resentful even? The rich keep the world oiled. They extol self-confidence!"

Dufresne rolled her eyes. "No. They fabricate artificial attitudes, sell their sunny affirmations, or become absolute tyrants and bores."

Roberta looked intrigued. "So, Madame. Does money stand in for another kind of theology?"

I raised my glass. "My mother taught me wealth is in the soul. And I learned from traveling that it's best to keep only what's essential or exceptional."

Dufresne gave a thoughtful nod. "A good rule for art-making! But one has to learn how to figure out what is essential or exceptional, no?"

"You said yourself you hate books with too much talk."

"I do. Hate books that try to preach something. Some say virtue is a rarer act than vengeance. Do you as a poet attempt to do rare things?"

"I attempt. But who decides if I've succeeded?"

"A bored reader?"

"Ha!"

"This hotel is rare. And upon my death, it will most likely fall from French hands to Japanese, Indian, or Saudi owners. They say in another generation or two France will be a Muslim country."

An olive-green phone rang, and the bartender passed the receiver with great efficiency. The hotelier sighed, answered, then moved away, speaking with low-voice discretion that did not allow us to eavesdrop. She hung up. "Sorry, but I'm being summoned." Before her exit she signaled the bartender and he rolled out a cart draped in a pink cloth. The hotelier removed it to reveal a light supper hidden beneath. "Please," she said, encouraging us to partake. "Like MacArthur, I shall return!"

• • •

Madame Dufresne strode to the table and began filling her plate with salmon, asparagus, and crepes. "I've yet to be her guest when she isn't called away. Probably some potentate, checking-in ten days late, but still wanting the full treatment."

We joined her at the buffet. Dufresne pointed a serving fork at Roberta. "You must've inherited a lot of money."

"What makes you say that?"

"I've yet to meet a female decorator who doesn't have an allowance. Sister Parrish once told me aesthetics are the province of spenders, not earners."

"You're too clever by half. Yes, my work *is* also a bit of a charade. I live much of the year in Switzerland. People there don't even use decorators."

"Do you like angels?" Without waiting for a reply to another non-sequitur, Dufresne stood and insisted we follow to a large window facing the beach. "This is the Bay of Angels. From the word *Anglese*—because English people used to flock here. See how the water spreads the moonlight, and silvers the clouds as they mutate? Now, if one tried to paint that, those brilliant, voluminous moonlit clouds, nobody would believe it. Only a pink and gold sunset would look more ludicrous! But follow the horizon with your eyes, and between the ocean and sky, one can see a hint of the curve that gives credence to Pythagoras, Eratosthenes, Columbus—their convex proof. Now go off and try to paint *that!*"

"You spoke of angels," Roberta said. "Do you believe in them?"

"Of course!"

"And have you ever thought of starting your own religion?"

Madame Dufresne caught the jest, and with skill replied. "To start a religion, one must seek converts. And I don't like followers." She then twisted and rearranged the purple turban around her wiry hair. As we returned to the couches, a voice could be heard coming from the television behind the bar. The accent was unmistakable. Roberta and I looked at one another. "Oh my God…It's Phil!"

We rose and hurried to the set. The broadcast was a flashy Italian variety show. "My God, it's him!"

"Do you know Mister Phil Filbertson?" the bartender asked. He grew excited, as though the television had just sprung to life, and he was about to receive an introduction. His palms brushed back along the sides of his hair, and then he tweaked his tie. Awestruck at the image on the screen, we watched as a young girl in lemon-yellow tights, a corset, and bustle stood beside Phil, twirling a baton. The girl smiled at the camera and winked.

"Where's Lydia?" we asked in unison. The sarcophagus trick began. In disbelief, we watched the agile girl climb into the box. "She's barely legal!"

We stood mesmerized. After being wheeled around, sawn apart and reassembled, the girl stepped out to wild applause, and as the band played a rousing number, the audience clapped along. Metallic confetti snowed down as the host, all grins, dashed in from the wings to close the show. Speaking rapidly with force, loudness and energy, he extolled the show's upcoming promises, as tonight's guest stars strode out in evening clothes, to line up along the apron of the stage. The credits rolled, the camera dollying past the lineup of stars, and we caught a final glimpse of Phil waving a gloved hand, his expression both smiling and mystical. The host thanked everyone concerned, blessed the audience, then wished good night to the whole world, blowing us all a kiss.

"The son-of-a-gun has made it to television!"

"His second appearance," the bartender said. "The show is called *Extravaganza!*…and no one does it better!"

"Amazing!" Roberta said. "That crap looks so much more exciting on Italian television than it did in real life."

Madame Dufresne shook her head. "These shows hold no value. So unnatural and *so* ugly."

The hotelier returned and overheard. "Did I miss *Extravaganza!*? Oh, *merde*! It's such fun. An hour of instant cheer!" She came to the set and stroked it as though it were a caged animal.

Dufresne would have none of it. "Nonsense. Such artificial perceptions of reality corrode one's spirit."

The hotelier disagreed. "The more shows and programs people watch," she said, "…the more educated and interesting they become!"

The two women had obviously practiced this swordplay before, and now Dufresne grew haughty. "Not true! To recount to others some program one has viewed is like describing how much dust has collected under one's bed." She turned to us. "The paramount art of life is to make oneself interesting to others. Never should we utter the mundane. You as a poet must know this."

"Yes," I agreed. "Studying reality can seem dull at first but then some detail can become truly fascinating."

"I had an uncle who was education minister under De Gaulle, and he thought even card games displaced experience. That gambling was a kind of second-hand living. If my cousins and I played *crapette*, he'd pass through the room and hiss, 'You're wasting your *lives.*' And he was right! Who wants to dribble time away? It's doing that counts!"

"Oh, come now!" the hotelier said. "Don't be such a sourpuss. One can't sit at the loom weaving carpet all day. A good game of *crapette* invigorates the blood."

"But today everyone watches these programs instead of experiencing reality."

A strange affinity for Dufresne's position overtook me. "I've often thought that. It's like people who move into gated communities for safety, then sit inside watching endless movies about crime and lock-up. They come to believe being entertained-watchers grants them license to weigh in with stupid opinions. They think watching some program about crooks…they're now experts or can comprehend *real* experience of crime or victimhood. They imagine the show is their own life or has really happened to them."

"Precisely! Yet no tactile experience or labor has been exacted. There can be no substitute for living!"

The hotelier looked askance. "Why would I commit a murder when I can simply tune in and watch one instead?"

"Often what transfixes the mind isn't the content of a show…but the camera's constant motion. The eye never rests."

"Stimulating vision is most healthy for the eyes!"

Dufresne steadied her gaze. "Stimulation is *not* education. Put *le bébé* under a mobile and the movement will rivet the little beast. But the child isn't *learning* anything! The reason *bébé* is entranced and doesn't ignore is *fear*! If the tot were to look away, why, the dervish of motion might eat it! Tracking constant movement places rational thought on hold. The mind is kept busy worrying if we should fight or flee."

The hotelier submitted a blasé expression. "You can't convince me. After a long day, I love to put my feet up, turn the dial, watch color, music, beautiful clothes, dancing."

Dufresne smiled a fox's delight. "People who spend too much time in television's fantasy ought to be reminded of the reality of death."

• • •

Waiting in the cool dawn for the Corsican ferry to dock, a strategically positioned vendor sold us hot coffee and sweet rolls still warm from the bakery. Pulling the flaky layers apart, we ate, and between bites our astonishment over Phil's television appearance continued to fuel our conversation. We could hardly wait for our visit with Garafallou to ask him about the young baton-twirling girl.

"And what about that Madame Dufresne?" Roberta said. "She certainly was odious!"

"I rather admired her bluntness. She made the conversation jump."

"I found her argumentative. A contrarian."

"The Gordons had an old aunt we used to visit—also a contrarian. She lived out on Long Island, in Riverhead, and used to speak overbearing predictions as if they were truth. Things like: 'You'll never be as tall as that boy across the street…You'll never have your uncle's head for business…When you get older, you'll hate yourself for eating so many donuts.' Marvene used to say the old girl was a witch. Her talk of spells and augury did indeed frighten me, and because of her, I still harbor deep suspicion against chicaneries and false prophets."

"Does that include magicians?"

"Ha! Yes, I'm afraid so."

The overnight passengers began to stride down the gangway toting leather cases, baskets, and cotton beach bags, tanned faces glowing, all ready to be reabsorbed into the swirl of Nice. The boat held dozens of cars, but not having brought one permitted us to board first with the foot passengers. We hurried with them to outrush each other, scoping out the various lounges, until we'd secured a pair of seats beside a metal-rimmed window, horizontally striped curtains hanging limp on either side.

"I've a question about your family in Greenport."

"All right."

"When Cole died, did the bright story Grandpa Gordon presented to the world get challenged?"

"God, *no*. At least not that I saw. Grandpa deeply believed death was God's will. As a man who entered the work force *en-masse* after the acts of sixty-four and sixty-five, he intended to believe only stories of hope. He planned to retire by way of the great society with a thirty-year pension. Imagine, the ability of men or women like him *to* retire, buy a new car, take a trip, help grandchildren in college. Prior to that, secure jobs were rare, and Grandpa never seemed to falter in his marvel at that legislation."

"Your mother must have embraced his point of view?"

"Certainly. But pigment as class still made her crazy."

"What does that mean?"

"Skin shade became Mom's political cause, and Marvene was probably right, an appropriated cause to hide her privilege. She embraced the challenge—particularly toward perceptions, but she was also seeking to find some change within herself. Or some secret self."

"I guess we're all a mystery, even to ourselves. Are any of us what people assign us?"

"Nonetheless, she felt committed to let the world know race was not the most important characteristic of the two men she'd lived with—trying to dissuade those who thought the taboo of race to be their mutual attraction's only reason for being."

"Is privilege part of that too?"

"I always felt attraction for all of us is born of something else. Maybe acceptance for some secret suffering? A feeling of being validated or understood? I can only speak for myself—but can't figure it out exactly for them. Mom's dad was tough. But she seemed to have gotten around him. I've spent my life trying to understand it—as well as my grandfathers. One in South Central Pennsylvania, one in Eastern Long Island, both holding similar conservative views, both sitting on porches with pipes, reading evening papers, both eating ice cream in glass dishes brought by their wives."

"Did they ever meet?"

"No. Only in the intersection that is me."

• • •

After an hour at sea, the coast of France vanished behind us, any sight of land gone, Roberta went to the snack bar for coffee, and in her absence, all the talk of the past, unfurled my all too familiar melancholy. I retrieved my notebook from a bag in the overhead rack, and sat contemplating yet another blank page. Soon a drowsy, depressive impulse overtook me, but before I could nap, I heard Roberta return, holding a cardboard tray with two espressos, two bottles of sparkling water, some cookies and an orange.

"Had to fight for the orange," she said. "A delivery truck missed the boat and they cast off without re-stocking."

I watched her peel the rind, the thick citrus skin trailing into a single corkscrew. She went to the open doorway and threw the peel over the side of the boat, then leaned out to look as the peel was left behind in the water below. A breeze followed her back in, lifting her hair and scattering a newspaper about. I got up with some other passengers to help chase the broad sheets which made us all laugh. We slid the heavy door a bit more closed.

The orange slices perfumed the air, and she offered some to me. "While at the snack bar, it suddenly occurred to me, that you must get so sick of race and class as a topic."

"Yes and no." I nodded. "People love diversity talk."

"And you don't mind?"

"Sometimes I do. Where it gets me, is when I see how many fail to realize they'd be required to give up their own jobs to uphold the equities they spout. On the earth's ladder of inclusion, it's always another rung that's seen as needing to change or sacrifice. Unless there's incredible surplus, most grow mute if asked to actually giving up something. Though they have no trouble pointing out to others that they should."

"People work hard to gain status, friends, money, get promotions."

"Yup. And they want to keep them."

"I've also never asked what happened to the Gordons?"

"They aged out. I've been abroad for over fifteen years."

"That's the same gap as contact with Lydia?"

"Yes. The Gordons grew elderly, distracted with their own affairs. Marvene still manages a bank, and I sense her resent what increasingly appears to be my advantage. She doesn't see how she holds the true advantage—in that she *truly belongs* somewhere. I'm but an interloper…the Gordon family is genuinely hers. Funny, but recently I wrote a poem about the old days. How I once fell ill while visiting them, and stayed home from church with strep-throat."

"Can I read it?"

"Oh, no. It needs work."

"Please. Just read it *to* me, out loud."

"Maybe later."

She persisted until I flipped through my notebook and found it.

Baptist Hooky

On a cold-souled Sunday, too wet to walk to church,
Rainwater overspills our gutter,
the damp ranch house an ark. In the oven short ribs
braise in low-stoked heat,
and Mahalia's on the hi-fi, her contralto pushing
hymns to heaven: Oh, her God is so good.

Ma-hal-ia…mother…greeting…all,
arms uplifting her crepe-draped bosom,
God's supernal cheerleader
Florid in her orchid corsage.

She sings of no small glory—and the soul
itself rebounds. She sings of something bold,
and the walls come tumbling down.

Un-likes join: the breadline and the gravy train,
the headliner and the road to calvary,
her gospel, and the man who spins the record.

Who cares if the gospel don't sell as well as the blues?
Mahalia sings regardless. Mahalia sings for all.

Her songs set our Sunday table,
Her voice polishes our silver,
Her faith boosts our Sabbath meal,
knowing how this good-old, hard-sweet life
goes on and on.

Fighting fever, her singing cools my heat. The choral odes
call—even I too ill for a Sunday sermon,
hear that preacher's bark and drill—
I'm not forgotten and thus do not go un-paid.

An hour later, the family re-enters to gather round the table
praying once more—as mouths-water for the meat and gravy...
Another Sunday getting passed.

Roberta smiled. "You should publish that."

"It's not a poem I'd ever share publicly."

"But why not?"

"It only makes sense if you know my story. I'd have to explain the Gordons. Who they were in my life. How the poem marks one of my last visits. It could all be misconstrued as an appropriation. In my head, I'd hear Russell snickering."

"So what."

"The narrative brings me into the business of having to recant or defend my bio."

"So what."

"I've been at too many poetry slams where college-educated poets recite their suburban odes with black inflections borrowed from streets they know little about. Even for me to say the word 'bro' sounds artificial. And while one could argue that it's a kind of appreciation, I don't want to exploit the Gordons that way. And certainly no one wants to hear a guy who went to boarding school expound the virtues of Mahalia."

"I don't get that. Louis Armstrong didn't invent the trumpet. He just played it in a new way. Is that appropriation or appreciation?"

"That's different."

"How? Nina Simone, Ray Charles, Sarah Vaughn, they all played that European contraption, the piano. Do we denounce them for appropriation?"

"Maybe music gets through in a way language can't."

"Songs have lyrics. Poems can be music. And what about pasta?"

"Huh?"

"Noodles came from China…and have in five hundred years become Italian. Do we attack Marco Polo for *eastern-izing* the West?"

"Believe me. I get it! But you know some people hold fast that pasta comes from Sicily. And pasta simply proves why I'll never publish this poem. It's an invitation to an argument!"

"But your poem illustrates how lucky you are to have known two worlds."

"Russell would sure snicker at that. He'd say, 'Hell! I've only ever known two worlds!'"

"There's a line in there…something about unlikeliness coming together. What about that?"

"Should I then explain how my mother's father simply couldn't accept that the light-skinned black actor she married in New York was no singular mistake? That his girl held blatant preferences and appetites? That my presence is the proof of that. The poem is too narrative. Emily Dickinson never had to explain *her* poems as they reflected an interior experience, something every human knows."

"Okay…I think I'm starting to understand. You prefer not to burden your poems with defense. Or proof."

"Exactly. That proof intersects a failing of identity that I tried to explain to you before, an inability to form conclusions about who I might really be. And as the world of race continues to rely on categories, explaining, or even looking for these categories is, to me, the difference between literature and the social sciences. The corridors of social science can't allow *likeness*. Meaning…*that* which defines something of our *joined* humanity."

Roberta pushed the last remaining slice of orange in my direction. "I'm not sure what you mean by that. I'm not smart enough. I wish I were. What I infer is, you yourself might have spent too many hours looking at literature through the lens of the social sciences?"

"I abhor reading literature *not* as literature but as a social science."

"I still don't understand."

"Because the labels of social science are so external. Once the mind gets shackled to those labels, it's hard to throw them off."

"Can't the poem be read without explanation? Let the words speak for themselves? Does it have to be so difficult?"

"You're plenty smart. But these days to look at literature as simply literature, regardless of who wrote it—is to break away from a very strong set of mind-forged manacles. I can do it—but even in academia most don't get that they are shackled—let alone care to try to break free."

"Labels are but fashion. Didn't your mother say fashion was deadly? That it was the cause of the banal?"

"My love of literature is about appreciating the magic of well-placed words on a page. To read a riddle or spell through the experience of transmission. It's not necessarily the text, or the author, or even the story, but the transmission itself that is the pleasure. To be able to read and receive transmission is a sacred thing."

"The reader's art?"

"Yes, and Buddy is right. Literary criticism has become the province of social science. Speculating about the biography or biases or privileges or lack, or how their lot in life might be judged by today's standards. They seek to place limits on *why* someone wrote. They ask what their psychological intent expresses about them. And currently if the writer is poor or under-represented—or pretends to be poor or underrepresented—they're lionized and handed prizes—*no matter how good or bad their language on the page may be.* How this-or-that political power permitted such a limited record to be printed and preserved becomes the focus. By these *social* studies, the creator's background, history or class, becomes the focus—not the riddle, the spell, or incantation of the lettered symbols."

"So you think the text itself is being neglected?"

"Too often. And how to measure literary quality or value is strangled. In the social sciences, power and voice find it necessary to raise digressive questions, like what systems or what people did the Pharaohs of Egypt subdue to allow hieroglyphics to prevail? Such topics may be interesting in and of themselves, but I refuse to allow the changeable and obfuscating lenses of social science to eradicate the pleasures of language itself."

"You mean literature for joy, taken on its own terms?"

"Yes. And I don't give a rat's ass who wrote what, if the piece captures me in its spell. The ability to cast a spell is what holds me."

"The spell can exist in any language too, no?"

"Yes, it can. But the English lexicon is especially lucky. The power to know how to use a pen is also lucky. The power to decipher the code of that pen? Lucky! During the sixties, there was a movement to tell stories in lost languages, the native tongues of one's ancestors. That movement died fast. The vast English lexicon was simply too appealing and it holds the largest readership and market, and as most writers dream to be received in the widest arena, *voila!*"

"It almost sounds subversive."

"The sacred act of reading or writing *can be* subversive. Russell often spoke of concepts meant to divide—and language can be compliant and complicit in that too."

"Your poem unites the divide."

"But it fails to note how Marvene was raised to survive the divide of pigmentation in a way that wasn't required of me. She had to pay close attention to pigment to navigate the nuances and abstractions of caste. To ignore that danger could get her killed." I explained Marvene's visits to my boarding school allowed special permission for her to accompany me to class, and how when other students were nearby, she went mute. "One day we attended a lecture together at the library. A guest speaker talked about historical hindsight and how blindness worked to defy change. Marvene shed her shyness, raised her hand, and addressed the woman: 'Do you mean to suggest that some people hold superior moral tendencies?'"

Roberta's face showed its confusion. I tried to illustrate my point. "A girl from Singapore, her father a banker, raised her hand and said she knew she would have stood up to Hitler, and Stalin too, that she'd have chosen to be a freedom-fighter. The speaker nodded, 'Wonderful. Very courageous!' Marvene would have none of it. She looked at the girl and rolled her eyes. 'Historical judgment is easy,' she said. 'And convenient. That's your privilege talking.'

"Afterward, I can still see Marvene sitting at dinner in the cafeteria, sipping a lime soda, and in her point-of-view I could recognize the many things taught by Grandma and Grandpa Gordon, the AME church, the civil rights movement. She spoke with certainty. 'Your rich classmates show no hesitation to imagine themselves as individually strong, strong enough to face-off every kind of evil or horror wrought by man. They don't understand how many courageous people have made that righteous claim only to be corrupted or killed.'"

Roberta nodded. "Meaning it's hard for any of us to admit the worst of ourselves?"

"Or even consider it. Marvene was offended and furious to see how my fellow students actually *needed* to believe they were that superior kind of good. Spouting how they could *easily* stand up to wipe layers of dust off of thousands and thousands of years of cruelty. Many speakers we heard actually defined slaves as more virtuous than other people! As if suffering mutated or even gave birth to a separate and more advanced species."

"But maybe it does!"

"Maybe in some. For a time. But no human can separate themselves from humanity's entire history of oppression…greed, lust, envy…the possibility of Christ or Hitler is either inside all of us—or none of us."

"All of us?"

"What makes us think we're so special? You see, Marvene was raised in Grandma Gordon's house. She knew self-righteous talk was usually untested."

"The upside-down version of what your Grandma Gordon was saying means we can do evil as well as good?"

"Exactly. Most people have a psychic need to believe the best about themselves. Yet cowardliness can be practiced and upheld by anyone, even us! When AIDS fighters tell us that silence is collusion, or silence is death, more than once I thought of my own quiet cowardice over that."

"But I've also heard people say when in doubt, do nothing, or be *still* against *war*."

"But a pacifist's meekness can certainly permit a lot of evil. Just ask the churches of the world."

"How awful. For Marvene. For all of us. For your lovely poem."

"Now you know why I left America. Only to discover how the limits of our species span the globe."

• • •

News spread that the boat had failed to properly stock supplies, and though the maître'd of the restaurant's grand-salon assured passengers the delayed truck had only affected the snack bars, no one wanted to chance that the man might be lying. As a result, everyone was dining early, choosing from a substantial menu of moderate elegance pitched to flatter the discerning palate of French travelers. Having no reservation, Roberta and I sat at a round communal table with six chairs, one couple on the left, a single empty seat between, and to the right, a robust woman consuming a formidable caramel éclair.

"If you really want to see how well the French eat," Roberta said, "visit them on family occasions or on a holiday. Delicacies appear that they'd never waste on an American."

A steely, unperturbed waiter rose above the dining room's chaos and wrote down our identical order: scrambled eggs with truffles. The éclair-eater consumed her sweet in record time, received her bill, paid with cordiality, and left. The busboys instantly reset her place, and an elderly man with a waxed mustache received the chair. Uncharacteristic of many Europeans, he was immediately affable and volunteered his occupation and place of residency—a retired podiatrist from Rouen. "I hate dining solo," he said. "My wife died last year. She was always afraid to eat on ships. Couldn't stop washing her hands."

I nodded, recalling last night's odd dinner with germ-avoiding Madame Dufresne. The man ordered bouillabaisse, and it arrived just after our truffled eggs. He demonstrated his unique way of rubbing a raw clove of garlic on the hardened toast, adding dabs of rouille, and sinking it into the glistening saffron broth. We all wished each other *bon appetit*, and as we ate polite questions were posed. Discovering I was an editor, he grew animated. "Perhaps you've noticed how many stories that people tell one another, twist and wind around themes of unfair experience. But simply ask someone to tell a story of a time when justice was served and they fall silent."

"Maybe justice is rare?"

"Is it?" the man asked. "Would not justice and injustice be proportionate, leaning on each other like a house of cards?"

"What's unfair makes a better story."

"Perhaps. But so far no one can tell me why. Maybe to tip the hat toward justice means to forgo pity?"

"Perhaps."

"May I ask how long the two of you have been married?" He misread our confusion and gave a sly grin. "Oh, now don't tell me it's a honeymoon!" It disappointed him to learn otherwise. "Well, don't wait too long," he said. "Marriage is vital."

"I *am* married," Roberta said. "Which explains my ring."

"Oh, you are? But where is your husband?"

"Working."

"Ah, working…working?"

"He's a psychiatrist." Recklessly, Roberta admitted her main attraction to Hans these days was his absence. "He's from Zurich, a social scene similar to sitting on an ice floe in winter."

The man savored the last spoonful of his stew as he tried to comprehend the jest. "Why did you marry?"

Roberta blew on her coffee. "I don't know."

The man turned to me. "And you?"

"Divorced."

"Oooh." The sigh escaped him like a balloon. "That's the modern tragedy. A true tragedy." The man merely looked down at his emptied soup plate.

I teased him with flippancy. "The real tragedy was saying 'I do.'" The man did not laugh. "I always wanted to believe marriage was unending and whole," I continued. "Like the wedding ring itself. But divorce showed me the geometry of attraction isn't circular at all. It's more like parallel lines running adjacent to one another, each of us beginning and ending in a different place."

"Now that you explain it, my wife dying taught me something similar. I shouldn't tell you this," the man said. "But the best moments of my marriage occurred in sleep, arms folded over one another in that trusting way particular to lovers."

With our lunch plates cleared, the man insisted we partake in a cognac. After he gave a toast, his questions resumed. "Were you and your wife together long?"

"I met her working at a restaurant job one Summer. She came out of the changing room in her uniform, and my stomach dropped. I was about to start college, and I soon learned that the late teen years can be a fickle age. The energy of our physiological desire eventually wore out…and after five years of growing apart, we split."

"Tell me, did marriage grant you any insight to guide you from future mistakes?"

"Yes, I suppose. It taught me that without mental congruency, romance has a poor future."

• • •

Corsica, France

Our ship moored along the rugged coast of Ajaccio. Garafallou stood on the dock, his white linen trousers rippling in the breeze. We departed the port in a beautifully restored yellow Citroën by way of a road leading out of the city. A mountainous course wound through sedate villages with carefully pruned plane trees, their roots bulging into the roadway. Garafallou made light of our questions about Lydia leaving the magic act. "Bigger fish to fry…and we now have serious bids for the cooking show." He admitted to working diligently in helping her and Buddy sell the hair salons. "The money is desperately needed! Our angel in Monte Carlo is back under the oxygen tent."

"That new girl is *very* young."

"Such a talent! The magic show has benefited from the *Extravaganza* deal. With broadcast exposure, ticket sales are through the roof!"

"So, what happened to Lydia?"

"She simply told Phil her money would only be put into the cooking show. They locked horns. Again, she threatened to quit. This time he let her."

At a roadside restaurant with a wide valley view we stopped for dinner and ordered a sizzling platter of fresh sardines on a bed of wilted tarragon. Over the meal, we told about our lunch with the Rouen podiatrist.

"Boats are full of such codgers," Garafallou said. "Our seas perform a social function for the retired—widowers foxing around in plaid pants hoping for a widow in an argyle knit. They spend the night in a stateroom, and suddenly he's getting new dentures and trimming his nose hair, and she's braiding shells into her bangs."

As a second course, grilled flank steak over rosemary potatoes appeared, and Garafallou poured more wine. "My experience on such boats came from the uncle who raised me. Trained as a lawyer in Athens, he later made a fine living in diamonds. But with passing years, his vision faded, along with his ability to cut stones. A couple of expensive mistakes and his days as a diamond dealer were done. So, he returned to law—but found his legal judgment had also vanished. With ample savings, he decided to experience what he could of the sightless world. He brought me along as companion to navigate his blindness.

"Many voyages followed. The most memorable aboard a beautiful ocean liner. It was expertly appointed. The main dining room, trimmed in pecan, had bas-relief murals depicting huge jungle foliage, the tables beneath set with silver so heavy, the forks and spoons tired one's arms. A pastry chef, lured from Vienna, tantalized even those who ate no sweets with *schlag-sahne* cakes. On one of the lower decks was a great indoor swimming pool, the bottom lined with a mosaic of Neptune's chariot pulled by dolphins.

"On the third day a boiler exploded, and in gale-force winds, the sea a stomach-churning chop, our boat began to list. Lifeboats dropped, already struggling against the swells. Two collapsed and disappeared. Ours made it. In the distance, the great ship tilted, almost perpendicular to the water. It groaned, made a final roll, and, as if imitating a great Spermaceti whale, slid under. The long wooden vessels of our refuge fought against the ocean's treachery—one moment high as Mount Everest, looking across miles of seawater's range—the next plunging like a roller coaster, canyons of water on either side.

"Half a day passed before the seas calmed. Our lifeboats eventually met rescuers, but agitated by such loss, many survivors remained unstable. In the weeks to come, they with their lawyers, pored over all sorts of entries of ship's records, diaries, insurance lists, and freight documents, seeking proof of all that the brine had enveloped. Of course, there's always so much that can never be measured."

"How awful," Roberta said.

"Oh, my dears! Every voyage is a dare. I still imagine the ocean floor littered with beautiful things, all of them strewn alongside the pale bones of those who never made it." He leaned wearily on the table, paused then wiped a napkin over his eyes. Roberta patted the back of his hand, and we saw the Beetle was a man of unusual depth.

"Since that day, I've never packed a suitcase. Everything I need is bought *en route* or carried on my shoulder in a tiny overnight pack. And I've no small degree of distrust for the ocean and her wetness, so I always carry an extra pair of dry socks!"

Continuing South, our car passed lines of dusty cattle walking home in twilight, and municipal buildings with formal painted signs—schoolyards, bell towers, and churches defining citizen life.

In Propriano, we halted at a café for espresso, and took a walk to stretch our cramped legs. From the top of a hill, we studied stars in the evening sky, then headed back down, passing alongside a row of vacant butcheries and spotless bakeries standing in wait for tomorrow's customers. Automobiles, went whizzing past, tires screeching and headlights jumping as they rounded corners. At one alley, a French couple stood waiting for a tow truck. Their tires had been slashed. Naively, the couple had dared imitate the Corsican's privilege of parking on the sidewalk.

"Can't do *that* with a license plate from *Montpellier*!" Garafallou counseled and gave gentle condolence.

A few blocks away, the tires on our car stood intact, and we sighed relief. "I once drove a rented car with plates from *Antibes*," Garafallou said. "The locals mistook me for French, and, out of spite, stopped their cars in the middle of the road to chat with whomever happened to be crossing, while I waited behind them"

"But why the rancor? Isn't Corsica part of France?"

"Continentals who come to this island often portray arrogant subjugators. The locals contend themselves undervalued. They love to cite how the great conqueror Napoleon hailed from Corsica. Modernity brings no dearth of new resentments! A few years ago, an Italian company dumped toxic waste off the Corsican coast, creating red mud in the water. Fish and shellfish washed up dead. Some Corsicans deemed the French government hadn't complained to Italy with enough vigor. Taking matters into their own hands, a ship carrying toxic waste from Italy was bombed. Since the early seventies bombs and assassinations are not unheard of."

Some streetlights burned in the distance indicating we were approaching the outskirts of Bonifacio. "This is the southernmost town in Corsica, and the oldest," Garafallou said. When at last we arrived, his house showed itself to be a two-story stone dwelling, with a charming entrance illuminated by a pair of wrought iron sconces. He pointed out a torchlit path running toward to the back of his property. "If you wake up at night and want to take a dip, that route will take you to a private swimming beach."

We took our bags and followed him inside, then climbed upstairs, the bottle-green tiles lining the risers earning our praise, as did the quaint sleeping chambers with built-in beds, herbs hanging to dry from the ceiling rafters. Garafallou gestured upward. "There's lavender, rosemary, and the flat leaves of our noble laurel."

We were instructed to freshen up and then regroup in the main salon, where we sat on furniture slip-covered in creamy muslin, sampling brandy and tiny sugar crepes served by a housekeeper who was from Angola. Her name was Gwen, and she spoke little, mostly in Portuguese, which Garafallou translated. We soon discovered how exhausted we were by the day's travel and it wasn't long before we climbed the stairs.

Falling into the sweet-smelling bed assigned me, the house could be felt growing ever more still. I relived the night, weeks ago, when Roberta's svelte figure appeared at my bedroom door in a sheer nightgown. For the thousandth time, I also thought over my fixation for Eligio. Once more I saw the meat eaten from his mother's fingers, her cream chocolates, the ridiculous swimwear. What had I been thinking? Despite our travel fatigue, might Roberta pay a visit yet tonight? Might I visit her? And just what would happen if now I slipped from this bed to hers? My longing remained timorous, and the answer eluded, for sleep came and carried me away.

. . .

The Angolan woman set the breakfast table with cheese and toast and a plate of sliced peaches onto which she'd sprinkled a pinch of salt to exacerbate their sweetness.

"I've been on the phone all morning," Garafallou said. "The contracts for the sale of Lydia's hair salons have come through. A Korean buyer! And as a result, the cooking show will now be its own entity. Phil will no longer share producer credits. Top it off, my lawyer just sent an acceptance proposal from the television people. The cover story on *Hearth & Table* did the trick! Once the cash is wired, they'll set-up the first filming. I hope you're prepared to see your property values double or triple."

"How's that?"

"Your village is the backdrop for our location. If the show's a hit, it'll become a household name!"

"But that kind of tourism will kill us," Roberta said.

"Nonsense! Look what Bardot did for San Tropez! You'll cash in and buy an entire town somewhere else." Garafallou put two peach slices on his bread. "One can't build a life on nostalgia or succumb to homesickness, or you'll scratch for the past like a dog with fleas."

After breakfast we took the car and drove through Bonifacio, arriving at the famous citadel. At the foot of a rampart, a young man in traditional folk costume, a sheepskin vest and a loose cloth cap bunched to one side, sat waiting. It turned out Garafallou had hired him as a private guide and now apologized for our tardiness. The man gave a nod of disdain, stubbing his cigarette onto the sole of his boot. He pocketed what remained of the butt for later.

"Êtes-vous français?" he asked me point blank.

"No. American."

The young man switched to clumsy English. "You do not look American." He then welcomed us with a matter-of-fact delivery and led us on. We'd only gone a short distance before he began to seek our opinions of the French. "Brutal colonizers. Don't you agree?"

"Hmm. Perhaps no more than other countries."

"One could spend lifetimes studying their frustrations…their wretched penal colonies."

"*Most* countries fail the prison test," Garafallou said.

"France *refined* prison. Designed the destruction of mercy. When set beside that system, the Louvre, the ballet, even Lascaux—all taint." The young man touched one nostril knowingly. "What pride, their contribution to the world— three hundred cheeses! Escoffier cuisine! The penal colony!"

"Please," Garafallou said. "We've *not* come to dissect the French."

"The only arena the French excel par excellence is rudeness…provided you omit venery!"

"Please! We merely wish to see the citadel."

The guide looked miffed. "You must admit their aesthetic refinement, so admired, are but an obsession with object and scale. A garden with five hundred meters of box hedge, clipped during hideously corrupt monarchies."

"I'm afraid you've caught us on a day when we simply aren't in a political frame of mind!"

"Very well…I see. Give me liberty or give me death—merely symbolizes *moods* to you." The guide turned, and brusquely marshaled us through a portal, before speaking in a bored, mechanical way, his voice laced with sarcasm. "Bonifacio is really the drowned ravine of a fjord. The citadel is ancient and faces South toward Sardinia."

Further sizing us up as we studied the citadel's site and its grounds, he suddenly asked my occupation. Garafallou answered for me, saying we all worked in the arts and writing. Literature renewed the man's test. Because I resented having my liberty be written off as a *mood*, I took the bait, noting my respect for Descartes and Stendhal.

The man bristled. "Ha, Stendhal is absurd!"

"What about Balzac, Proust, Molière?"

"What is Molière—or even Voltaire—next to Shakespeare?"

Garafallou grew cross. "Too bad you weren't around in 1066," he said, crisp as toast. "Your wit might've prevented the Norman conquest."

"Do not mock me!"

"But how can you indict a whole people with jingoism? French philosophy is world-renowned. Diderot and Rousseau laid the groundwork for the revolution."

Roberta joined the fray. "I've always admired Joan of Arc, Charles de Gaulle, Madame Curie…the great French painters Monet and Seurat."

The guide sniffed. "People love their impressionists…the colors so vibrant over a *couchette!* But can they compare to Velazquez? Rembrandt? El Greco?"

Garafallou granted all the courtesy he could muster. "So, you prefer Spanish painting, and therefore are willing to accept *their* dictators, and monarchies?"

The guide scowled, as if our group had begun to exude a Camembert odor all its own. Like an automaton, he resumed describing the bay as the island's earliest route. "Corsica has a nickname: *L'Île de Beauté*. We have some prehistoric sites. One cave outside the city holds a hideous old mademoiselle carbon-dated to 6570 BC. While this fortress was begun in 870, perhaps on the site of pre-existing forts. At one time, the citadel was administrative quarters to the French Foreign Legion. The wind across the strait over the centuries carved out the cliffs, and legend says, in 1420, the steps were built in a single night by Aragon forces trying to win the town."

The infuriating man resumed his attack on the French. "They don't bathe properly, they piss in the streets, Belgians have better food, and God-forbid you own or share property with them. They'll dishonor themselves to ignore, dispute and cheat you wherever they can."

Garafallou's annoyance at the acrimonious diatribe did not hide itself. And seeing that, Roberta tried to placate with flattery. "You mentioned food. Well, nothing anyone eats can compare to the Corsican grouper!"

"So open-minded, *you* Americans. Absurdly open-minded. Since your Mr. Truman entered the Cold War, you've become warriors forever in a state of meddling. Your missile, and prison-builders grow rich, your ethical culture crumbles."

I stupidly weighed in. "Penitentiaries are global. They reach back to antiquity. The slave trade has its parallel in the pyramids, or galleons rowed by captive oarsman!" The guide dismissed me with the back of his hand, an effrontery that brought hot irritation to my cheeks. Was this some kind of joke?

Roberta came to my rescue. "At least our country fought a civil war to try and free slaves. Has any other country on earth done that?"

Now Garafallou stepped in. "My good fellow…with all due respect, I know the citadel well, and prefer to shepherd these guests myself."

The man shrugged. But then, in a buffoon's attempt to keep a patron, he warned, "The path is steep. Cut right into stone."

With a spirit fine as any general, Garafallou stood his ground. "I'm well acquainted."

The guide stomped off in a huff and we watched him go. "That man is crazy. A village idiot in a government post." Garafallou turned to lead us along the precipice. "Within these medieval spaces, the eyes of many a knight have kept watch." He pointed across the treacherous strait, where little shapes sparkled in the sun on the opposite shore. "Those are windows. The Sardinian village of

Longonsardo. Legends say criminals used to cross and hide there, staring back at Corsica, counting the days, months, or years before their crime's statute-of-limitation ran out so they could return home."

A forceful gust whipped against us, rustling loud as a birch forest and drying our lips. Roberta and I looked down at the waves breaking far below. "That guide is wrong about these steps," Garafallou said. "They're known to have existed before 1420, probably carved over decades by local monks. There are accounts of citizens using them to carry water up from a well."

"It's so very hot."

"Yes!" Garafallou said. "I wish we'd thought to bring water." Turning away from us, he stumbled, and teeter-tottering like a surfer, rode the wave of imbalance, both hands extending to steady himself. He reached down toward his feet, the vents of his blazer flipping to show its paisley lining. Then all balance went. In a flash, he was gone over the ledge.

Eyes wide to the sudden disaster, we flattened ourselves to the ground and inched forward on elbows to face the wind. Garafallou lay twenty feet below on the only thin ledge, clinging to a patch of weeds. Roberta leaned out with the agility of a gymnast, the pointed collars of her blouse blowing up. "Don't move," she cried.

His hand reached down toward an ankle. "Please!" he called, neck craning, mouth open, pink tongue visible. "Go find help!"

Thunderstruck at his precarious plight, I retraced our route along the pass, then ran back through the portal. I ran faster than I ever knew I could, yelling for help. From the far side of an ancient drawbridge, two guards came to flank me. In full panic, I reported the disaster. "Please, hurry! It's very dangerous!"

More men rushed over, quickly designating a pair to be assigned for return to headquarters to radio for help, the others were told to follow me. At the cliff, Roberta was still lying on the ground, Garafallou, huffing and puffing down below, staring up in shock, leg lying limp and swollen. His face was coated in sweat, and edgeless like a plaster statue left out in the rain.

"Please, help," he called.

"Hang on to the weeds," a guard called down. "And be still. A few inches more and you'll go straight to the rocks." The man tied a piece of rope to a water bottle and lowered it. Garafallou managed to grab hold and soon gulped in the way of a thirsty calf from a milk bottle.

After an eternity, a small team of men arrived, wheeling a thick metal contraption. It astonished me to see the annoying harlequin guide among them.

In place of the folk costume, he now wore a tee-shirt, printed on the chest with a giant lollipop. The man glanced down on Garafallou, and, to his credit, restrained from comment. He actually seemed to have been transformed into a very concerned rescuer. One of the guards, a mountain climber, said it was lucky for us that he owned the elaborate metal hoist and always carried it in the back of his van, though the rest of the men had apparently never used it.

"Can't you call a helicopter or something?" Roberta asked

"Too risky. The cliff leaves no room."

Half an hour passed while the metal framework was secured, several large boulders pried loose and rolled in place for ballast. Like politicians voting on an unpopular bill, the men argued the whole time, until at last, the moment came to lower a wooden seat and harness. The owner of the device called down, instructing Garafallou on how to tuck the board under his legs before buckling himself into the harness. Horrified, we watched from the sidelines, everyone clearing back to allow the pulley system to do its work. The device began to tilt. The man hollered at the men to use an iron rod and leverage over some additional boulders.

In what seemed a lifetime, Garafallou, ascot flapping in the wind, started his ascent, suspended over the drop, reminding me once more of a young animal, this time a baby elephant in transfer to a cargo ship. The men took turns cranking the stubborn handle, and in fifteen minutes, the seat was nearing the ledge. We held our breath. Two men, tied to safety ropes, leaned out to grab hold. Slowly the arm of the contraption began to swing back over to solid ground. Garafallou landed, tears of tension streaming down his face. Buckles unfastened, the men transferred him to a stretcher, heaving the wooden handles up on their shoulders. From above, Garafallou christened them his honorary pallbearers.

Back at the citadel, a military doctor examined the tumescent ankle, now twice its normal size. The exam room's door remained open with military indifference, permitting anyone passing in the corridor to catch a glimpse of a tremendous wine-colored bruise already staining Garafallou's backside. Luck prevailed once more; the bone had endured a serious fracture but no break.

Garafallou refused transfer to a hospital, and the doctor, in botheration, bent over the leg to fashion a splint. As he worked, Garafallou sipped from a boxed pineapple drink. Roberta and I were now brought to wait in a small office off the main lobby where a young soldier brought us coffee. Through the window I could see the parking lot, where the guide who'd been so abrasive now worked as part of the team loading the metal framework back into the owner's van. "What's the deal with that guy?" I asked the soldier.

"Who? Storch? Oh, he's all right. Just a bit unpredictable."

"From here he looks like a good worker, but he certainly wasn't helpful to us."

"He's a fine worker but no diplomat. He has trouble making friends. Suffers from Asperger's. A very rare thing here. Some government program placed him here so that he won't become too isolated by his illness."

"He was very rude."

"Oh, I am sorry. Did he go off on one of his *Damn those nasty French* tirades?"

"Yes!"

"Oh, Storch! He just can't control himself. Funny thing is, he's not even Corsican. Hails from Nimes. As French as they come. Very well-educated too, but completely obsessed with penal colonies."

. . .

An hour later Garafallou was rolled out to the Citroën, and Roberta climbed behind the wheel. The doctor, various soldiers, and our former tour guide Storch, giant lollipop on his tee-shirt, stood transfixed as Garafallou willed himself out of the wheelchair and into the passenger seat. He stoically smiled through gritted teeth, waving to his rescuers like the emperor of a small country. Only Storch waved back.

Roberta pulled away, and soon we were headed out onto the main road. Garafallou rejected any notion for the Citroën to return home and instead commanded us to stop in a small village at an outdoor restaurant. Calling the waiter over to the car, he pointed to his splinted ankle. "*Monsieur,* I need courage!"

Dumbfounded diners stared as the waiter hurried to bring a shot glass and a bottle of cognac, served through the window. After the third snort, Garafallou bought the remainder of the bottle and led us on.

"That guide and his ridiculous nationalism are to blame! Flags and folk costumes are used to herd patriots…just as fodder is used to herd sheep. It never ceases to amaze how fear…backed by an anthem…can rouse a populace to many ill agendas. That man ought to stand before a firing squad!"

"I was told he's afflicted with Asperger's. That he's part of a program to place those with illness in the workplace. Actually, he was quite a big help in your rescue."

"I don't give a hoot. Such nationalism is divisive."

"But by giving him a job in Corsica, the government is practicing inclusion."

"If solidarity requires inclusion for mental incompetents—then screw solidarity. Besides betraying the very word—that man's bias is just another joke. A way to keep poor working people from true unity."

"Isn't that true of all biases?"

Garafallou drank from the bottle. "True unity terrifies the elite. The rich find as many ways to isolate and divide as many people as possible, so that *they* own the earth. And workers who *do* unite are labeled communists—or worse."

"I still say that tour guide turned out to be okay in the end."

"Look Walker, you weren't the one lying on that ledge! I tell you if such madmen are to be accommodated—they ought to come with warning manuals. Don't forget what he said about Stendhal."

"Please, you guys," Roberta said. "I'm trying to concentrate on the road. All this angry talk is more than I can listen to right now. Especially after the morning we've had."

Garafallou patted her shoulder. "Yes…of course. How inconsiderate of me! You're in no *mood* to discuss economics." We drove on in silence, the liquor bottle emptying. Garafallou grew calmer, and then spoke again in a softening voice. "We just saw how terribly the *people* failed in Moscow. That big symbolic wall in Berlin struck down! But is capitalism a better control?"

Roberta and I did not answer but Garafallou continued. "In the world of religion, unity is often the message. But try talking unity with regard to economics…and you're made to sound like an evil anarchist."

"You're preaching again," Roberta said. "Please…can we discuss this later?"

"Oh sorry! I'm a bit tipsy. That always puts me in a mood to speak to the already converted!"

Roberta used humor to soften her chastisement. "Listening to the two of you go on is like being in a gulag on wheels. Forced to endure absolutes about jingoism while trying to drive—that's another thing the dividers want!"

Garafallou waved the bottle. "An excellent point."

• • •

Traffic thinned as we neared the coast. At the next intersection Garafallou grew alert. "Turn here toward the beach called Paraguan. You'll find its shore pristine, the water clear." We parked among other cars in a pine scrub, and a wooden chair taken from the trunk made a new throne. Entreated by Roberta, some boys playing volleyball came to help, and Garafallou found himself once more aloft, the players staggering to carry his weight. At a reasonably flat piece of sand among some contorted outcroppings, they lowered him under the shade of a twisted old tree.

"The water looks delicious," Roberta said. She wrapped a beach towel around herself, slid out of her dress, then wriggled into a swimsuit. Other women lying about were sunning topless, but Roberta wore a one-piece, and her confidence as she walked down to the water heightened her attractiveness.

A dozen private boats lay anchored out beyond the shallows, and occasionally someone jumped from the vessels to swim toward the shore. I followed Roberta into the glittering sea and we floated toward the bobbing boats, out to a place where we could stand shoulder-deep. We moved a bit further, treading water and breathing a sigh of relief to be free of the car and our earlier ordeal.

"Imagine what today would've been like if Lydia, Buddy, and Hans had been here to devil us," I said.

"I hope I wasn't too forceful with *my* irritations in the car," Roberta said, eyes squinting in the sun.

"Not at all."

"I get irritated with all this talk of unity. It sounds good, but it also sounds too perfect. I remember hearing such slogans in the sixties. *Smile on your brother,* and all that. But real change is slow—it only seems to come in rapid bursts. If forced it can create chaos and violence."

"Any change stirs fear. Speed brings uncertainty…that can induce people to unleash the depths of hate living inside themselves. I've seen that hate is possible from all sides."

"As you said, justice can have a steep price. Oh, but Walker, I don't think I'm stupid…but I can't yet comprehend all of your family's many moving parts. They're so disparate. So unlike anything I've ever discussed. I don't know if I'll ever be able to fully understand your mother. I'm so nervous that I'll get it all wrong."

"Maybe all you need to know is this—any forced cheerfulness or coping skills are a facade. And no matter how much hope Mom tried to present, or how much pain she hid, her bold choices brought chaos onto me. Not only did I swallow her pain, but it became mine. And yet despite that, I have to admit the world I live in is a better one than the world of fifty years ago."

"But surely the world has grown worse for some?"

"In television I've heard people argue that nowadays even most inner-city projects have air-conditioning, running water, refrigerators, central-heating. A hundred years ago the richest tycoon didn't have those things."

"But these advances in comforts haven't necessarily delivered happiness."

"I think to be human is to always want more. Or at least to be eligible for everything that you imagine everyone else has or is."

● ● ●

That evening, in a Morris chair brought from another part of the house, Garafallou poured drinks, and we watched Gwen, the Angolan woman prepare a stew of wild boar with minced carrot and onion. Roberta fractured a bit of Portuguese, to ask if she had any children. Gwen grinned with pleasure at the attempt to converse, and in a sonorous voice, said there were three. She put the same question to Roberta. Their eyes met. Roberta shook her head.

Garafallou grew blunt. "Except for Gwen, all of us at this table have no heirs. That absence will render our funerals barren," he said. "Even death by hemlock won't guarantee citizens to stream by our coffins."

"That's cheery," Roberta said.

With meticulous movement, bracelets jangling on her arm, Gwen ladled flat broad noodles and stew into flower-painted soup plates, noting the boar was hunted locally. At the table, she sat next to Garafallou, and it was interesting to see, neither in behavior nor speech, did she subordinate to his bluster. Our long day, with its near-fatal cliff fall, salt water swim, and high season sun, was concluding here around the warm closeness of a kitchen table. Our soup plates were polished with bread as the last of the wine was drained from the bottle. Roberta and I then rose to help Gwen with the dishes.

Garafallou intercepted me, saying he needed my arm to lean on in order to get to the courtyard. Once outside he admitted: "Gwen won't permit cigars in the house, even with my ankle. When she began to reside here, I put cigars on my list of sins."

"Did you really make a list?"

"Still do. Any couple embarking on romance ought to make a list. Self-evaluate the flaws. Own up to them. It was Gwen's idea."

A thunderbolt struck inside my head. Gwen and Garafallou's forthrightness represented more than I'd perceived. They actually lived in romantic partnership! After sleeping under their roof, not to have considered it sooner, embarrassed me. How easy it was to assume Gwen was simply the housekeeper, and all the while discussing disunity and so many unlikes! How smug to think I'd been raised to never make assumptions like this.

"Gwen recognizes that to self-admit one's own weakness gives strength. As you saw today, I'm too fat and wobbly to stand on a pedestal. She and I met in maturity, both fairly set in our ways. Such a list is probably harder for younger people who don't yet see the patterns of their mistakes. The point of the list isn't for the heat of passion, but for when the heat of love cools—as it inevitably can. Young people often don't believe that love might cool or vary in its temperature.

They cannot see all feelings come and go like flocks of birds, or rainclouds, only to return later.

"The truth in advance becomes an offering: 'Here are my limitations. I acknowledge these as the worst of what I know myself to be—what I know myself to do.' Gwen and I discovered that presenting our unpleasant truths for weighing in advance of trouble provided a kind of freedom. Of course, you must then also ask your potential mate—can you live with these flaws of mine—that you now have been warned about?"

"Was it difficult?"

"Conduct your own experiment! See if self-honesty is a curse or a bar of gold. No one necessarily wants to say I've a temper, am stubborn, often grouchy, have peculiar habits, am even too fond of a bargain! My own biggest insight came in realizing that if my feelings get hurt, I behave like an old dog and crawl under the porch."

"Retreat to lick your wounds?"

"Yes, but here's the twist. I lick my wounds for but a short spell. And then if Gwen doesn't get a stick and come round to coax and poke me out, I'm twice as mad for being ignored!" Garafallou's face assumed a shy smile. "Finally comprehending and articulating that embarrassing little peccadillo meant I could understand and admit my own wayward wiring. Only then was it possible to honestly ask Gwen the big question: Can you live with that?

"Gwen's acceptance of what I find repugnant in myself came as one of my life's greatest gifts. Now on a day of rare disagreement, she'll eventually say, 'Are you under the porch?' What a jubilant phrase toward armistice, for then I can say: 'Yes…*and where the hell have you been?*' And if on a day she's upset—her wants are her own. She likes cooing and having her hackles smoothed through gentleness."

"Signor Vescovi, the man with the ice in our village, said granting tolerance for that which in a partner stirs self-loathing—can be a great aphrodisiac."

"Oh, that's good! I suppose foibles accepted bring greater security than romantic ideals or fairy tales? I detest sentimentality even as I'm prone to it! Our planet is full of people who run around declaring love for one another. I love you. I love you! People say it so often it becomes rote. And so, I now confess to Gwen my feelings of love only at the moment…whenever they might emerge. I express each love sensation as something new, fresh and of this moment as love decides to reveal itself! Does that make sense?"

"I think what you mean is you are genuine to love. Just as you may be genuine to other feelings—sadness, joy, anxiety."

"Yes. Love may be a permanent declaration—but the feelings of love wax and wane nonetheless."

Gwen opened the door and stepped out. She moved about the patio, extinguishing candles. Exhaustion suddenly enfolded me in a quivering yawn. She came to stand by Garafallou's chair and straightened his collar.

"I have feelings of love for you," he said. "But don't worry dear. This too shall pass." He translated to her in Portuguese, and her reply showed repudiation.

"She's claiming to be the one who taught me that phrase!"

Gwen whispered something else to him.

"She's explaining the rules of a host," Garafallou said. "Apparently letting guests sleep is some kind of credo?"

She and I helped him out of the chair and amused, we joined in hospitality's last-minute charade—always some kind of advice on cooling, extra blankets, gratitude, praises, towels or where to find the toothpowder. We bid good night as happy friends do, the promise of sleep already lulling.

• • •

Gwen's day to volunteer at the town health clinic meant she couldn't host breakfast, so we made the half-hour drive to Porto-Vecchio. At a café, warm bread, red jam, and dark coffee brought us pleasure. That mood ended abruptly, for upon returning to our parking spot, we found the back tires of the Citroën sat withered from slashing.

"Hooligans!" Garafallou shouted.

The morning unraveled into finding a repair shop, and negotiating terms far from fair. "Cut rubber must be a boon to your gross domestic balance," Garafallou griped to the owner of the chosen garage. The old man toasted him from behind the cash register with a glass of Chinotto.

"Now, you two, go stroll about," Garafallou generously commanded us. "I'll handle this merry inconvenience."

We followed his orders, and went a couple of blocks, but his abandonment didn't sit right, and in a short while, we returned. Already the garage owner had provided an ottoman for Garafallou's leg made from a wooden crate and a pillow. The man insisted we join them in a drink, and procured a bottle of Napoleon brandy from a file cabinet. He asked Roberta to pour, saying he'd recently lost his sight. "That's why I no longer make engine repairs."

With gracious intonation, Garafallou told the man about his blind uncle. "Through his loss he came to study Braille's reading system and believed it to be one of the noblest of all inventions."

The garage owner bared some stained but still strong teeth. "I'm too old to learn."

"Don't be silly! My uncle was eighty when they taught him. Anyone can master it. Why, in Paris, legions of blind men and women used to turn out for the anniversary of Braille's birth. In fact, one morning in Athens, I read in the newspaper how Braille's remains were to be transferred from a cemetery to an honorary grave at the Panthéon—a national tribute planned. Though we were in Greece, my uncle insisted we book passage to France and pay homage."

The old man looked perplexed. "I thought the Panthéon was in Rome?"

"There's a newer one in Paris. Have you never seen the City of Light?"

"I've never been off this island."

"Well, nevermind. At the ceremony, we stood alongside a reverent crowd in the Place du Panthéon, the mausoleum's great columns swathed in blue, red and white fabric to echo the flag, all of it designed to enhance the visual beauty of the Panthéon's grand scale. I described every detail of the decoration to my uncle, and he said: "Imagine the many workmen who've been hired to unfurl the bolts of fabric, the dozens balancing on gigantic ladders, holding scissors, sewing needles, hammers, and tools. A thousand aesthetic decisions made. All that hand-eye coordination, but for a baseless pageant, as it will go unseen by most of the crowd!'

"For my uncle, Braille's genius meant the blind could now read in solitude, their rumination no longer bound to the voice of a reader. Imagine the dark eyes now traveling unchaperoned through the libraries of the world, visas stamped to commune in privacy with scribes both living and dead! Have you noticed the most expressionistic funerals transpire when the departed have freed their mourners of something? Braille's mourners crowded his bier, their heart's gratitude expressed through touch. Yes, their hands swept over the brass and polished wood coffin, as if the corpse of Braille could read their fingertips from within."

The owner of the garage inclined his head and lifted his glass. He told of a Sardinian woman he knew who made peace with death by giving herself a living funeral. "She desired to leave a beautiful corpse and lay un-departed in her coffin, still young and vital, for whatever friends and family members could be persuaded to come by and pay respects."

Garafallou toasted. "Splendid…really, splendid! To experience the ceremonies of death while still living. And why wait? Just think of the people through the ages who sat for portraits, posed for statues, saw to it that the chisel left their philanthropic names on buildings. Aren't these also tributes to the un-departed?"

The garage door opened, and the face of a raw-boned mechanic looked in, puzzling our group. He then quietly clanged two wrenches together. "*Monsieur*, the car is fixed."

. . .

The drive to the house passed through the rugged scenery and was notable in that for once none of us offered words. Crime can leave even the most beautiful landscapes crestfallen, and the tire vandals had robbed something not just from us but from Corsica. That evening no one cared to cook, so as a group we boiled eggs and ate them with tinned sardines and crackers.

Garafallou placed his forearms on the table, studying the newspaper. "With this ruined ankle stomping around Rome with you two gazelles is out of the question. But an overnight boat trip is a pleasure you still should not miss!" Calmly, he checked the schedule of passenger boats and circled several. Gwen took the list to the hallway phone and dialed, reporting after numerous calls that boats could be had, but none with un-booked bedchambers.

"Can't leave you sitting up all night on lettuce crates," Garafallou said. He insisted Gwen call an acquaintance of theirs with a brother who captained a commercial fishing trawler.

Gwen made the call, "He's scheduled for Livorno," she said, reporting the vessel still had two sleeping berths.

Garafallou delighted. "This'll be much more interesting than the ferries."

"The boat sails in just two hours." Gwen urged haste and we began to pack with speed, while she ran to the butcher, returning with an exquisitely browned capon. "I can make breast meat sandwiches, wrap them in wax paper? Or cut the whole bird into pieces to pack as a cold meal?"

"There's no time," Garafallou answered. "Meals are offered on the boat." The capon went into the fridge, knife and cutting board abandoned in the sink.

Gwen took the Citroën's wheel, Garafallou the passenger seat, and we piled into the back with our bags. After some detours, the vessel was found along the wharf, but the boat's owner shook his head sadly, saying with apology, our beds had accidentally been given to someone else. As captain, he was authorized to offer a reduced rate if we'd be willing to sleep in deck chairs. We looked at one another and laughingly agreed to the terms, literally counting our cash on the head of a barrel.

The deep horn of the trawler sounded its imminent departure. Eyes welling, we bid goodbye to Garafallou and Gwen. As we hugged, Garafallou whispered in my ear. "Use this trip wisely and well. You're both ripe for picking…don't miss your chance."

We waved madly, as the boat's wheezy engine pulled from the dock, smoke suspending over the dusky shoreline. All of us knew some great piece of life was passing by, forever to be remembered as that Summer we went to Corsica. Gwen and Garafallou stood arm-in-arm, shrinking ever farther into the distance, until all that remained were two tiny specks. Soon they finally vanished, and we moved away from the railing to a pair of creaky deck chairs, the shadowy night sky escorting us along the eastern coast of *l'Île de Beauté*.

* * *

At 8:30, a sailor sounded the dinner bell. The meal room held a huge table set for thirty, a single seating, mostly crew. Two rumpled students came late, blonde dreadlocks hanging down toward their dinner plates.

"I think they're sleeping in our beds," I whispered.

"Maybe, they'll jump ship."

A kitchen worker came out to offer either grilled scorpionfish with citrus chutney or beef cutlets in a Barolo sauce. We chose one of each to share. The meal exceeded the quality of food on the ferry, the dessert an icy tangerine sorbet, each portion inexplicably re-packed back into its scooped-out rind.

By the time the boat docked in Bastia, the sea was pitch black, a band of moon cutting a swath of light across the water. Sailors rapidly took on some cargo, and we pushed off again, the town and the yellow glow of her streetlamps quickly receding.

"It's time to explore alternatives to these chairs," I said, and we climbed a narrow ladder to an empty upper deck. From the high vantage point, the ship's prow could be seen slicing through the dark sea. Beside us, a raised metal platform ran down the center, large domed rivets spaced evenly along both sides, all of it lustrous under coats of glossy white enamel paint.

"Metal makes a hard bed," Roberta said. "But lying down is preferable to sitting up in those chairs." She stretched out on the platform, hands folding over her abdomen. I settled in beside her, and soon felt the warm tropical air caressing our skin. In the inky sky above, thousands of stars shone astonishingly bright and sharp. She turned onto her side, and I turned as well, spooning back to feel her body heat against my spine, thinking of how as a young boy I used to swim in the warm waters of the Peconic Bay in hot July. Somewhere far beneath the waterline, the boat's propeller churned vibrations that pulsed through the core of our bones.

How mesmerizing to think that tons of steel floated beneath us with no connection to sky or earth. I imagined sailors sleeping on the decks below, tilting in hammocks, first to port, then starboard, heads and hearts, livers and kidneys, all joined in a rhythm like ours, the whole vessel sharing the same gravitous motion of the sea.

"This trip feels like it's shaping me into a different person," Roberta said, her voice soft as she snuggled closer. "And I keep thinking of your mother…how beautiful she looked in those magazines. She must have traveled too?"

"As a model. A few trips to Europe. Later, when we had no money, she said she did not miss taking trips. But I doubted her."

"Would now be a difficult time to tell me?" Roberta whispered. "I mean the story of how she died?"

The question shocked me out of my trance. I knew Roberta intended no cruelty, but my body began to shiver as if in the grip of sudden flu. She held my bent arms close to my chest, as if she could sense my intense insecurity, the concealment of which was one of my life's greatest accomplishments. I tightened my arms in need for her. "Don't fear," she whispered. "I'm here."

Above us, a few wisps of clouds now trailed, and Roberta's warmth comforted yet somehow I still felt a lingering sense of nausea rise. A series of foggy but familiar mental obstacles, a gray mouse turning corners in its maze, the map of an old railway line branching off from some central point into greater and greater obscurity. My shaking eased. "Okay," I said, with quiet intensity, willing my voice to strip itself of emotion. "Whenever trying to talk of this…my vocal cords fail. I mean…they just stop working. Even if I want to talk…no sound comes out. But I'll try now, for you. Okay, it starts with Coleman Gordon. I can talk about that. They separated and he went to Hollywood. It only took three weeks for him to get his lucky break, a big prime-time detective series. After signing the contract, he called Mom to say he was sending for us. We'd make a new start. Overnight, problems of money that had come between them vanished. She packed, sold our furniture, and broke our apartment lease. The series started shooting and a few weeks in, traveling South on the Pacific Coast Highway, Cole died in a head-on car crash. Later, I heard a young man in the passenger seat also died, a fellow dancer. A blonde."

Roberta's voice sounded barely audible, but I felt her warm breath against the back of my shirt. "Oh, how terrible."

"The production shut down. A few weeks later, they re-grouped, my father's part cast with another actor. The show went on to run for seven years. All the leading actors grew rich with remuneration. As a boy, I'd secretly stay up late to watch the show in reruns, hoping to hit the night when one of the three original pilot episodes might air…all that was left of the man who'd acted as my father. On the few nights when I managed to see him, it was like watching a ghost." I felt Roberta's grip tighten once more.

"With his death, New York became a treachery for Mom. Not just its expense, but because whenever she went out, the chance to run into someone from her glory days threatened."

Again, I stifled a wave of nausea rising from somewhere deep within me. It did not abate but I dug my fingernails into my palms and pressed on. "So, we moved to Harrisburg, missing the funeral of Mom's mother by a few days. People she knew from childhood might've pretended to overlook the color of the man she married— now deceased. Things like that happened in New York, they'd say, showing the pride of their own liberalism or some Christian acceptance. But she'd returned too late for her own mother's funeral, and that became the substitute judgement—perhaps because its diversional story couched other cruel retributions. And…Mom… well she couldn't face it. Palmyra and the past proved too poisonous to mix with all her grief. I'm not a man who believes talking about the past brings catharsis, so, I've never told all of this…but it seems important that you understand. During her final days, it was difficult for me to even be in the same room with Mom."

Roberta exhaled. "She was in descent?"

"Yes. And when she died…her life remained, for me, a riddle sadder than any other." Involuntarily, I pressed my back into Roberta, allowing my hand to brush a thigh, our eyelids sensing flutter. I felt myself alongside her, and held by her, relieving something complex or convoluted, that in speech I thought could never be explained.

We lay thinking for a while, listening to the engine, and I had the tremendous feeling of being carried out of myself and into the night sky. Then she whispered something that puzzled her: "Do you reason your mother felt her own worth to be unsustainable?"

"Yes. And to this day…I feel in some way I abandoned her."

"Walker," she whispered her compassion. "Children have no agency against adult problems. It wasn't abandonment…it was survival."

"I've spent my life pretending I'm someone else. That I'm rich, sophisticated, intellectual. But I'm lost to myself…I've dressed like other people, followed their speech, their accents, their habits. At times, I wanted to be Mom… to feel the power of pretty."

Roberta maintained her whisper. "I think I understand."

"For years traveling kept me in motion…but the one I was eluding was me! Even in a jungle, where I knew the world was a maze of patterns and perfect geometry…that must yield to imperfection and die. I could not find the pattern that was myself. So here in Italy, I still live in search, and seem to fit into some familiarity…but I remain an impostor…pretending a life…afraid to be found out…continuing to pretend."

"Maybe imagination forms us…more than our facts. Or our faces."

Silence ensued and we held onto one other, once more sensing the ship's gentle sway, port to starboard and back again.

*   *   *

The vessel's great horn mounted above our heads, blasted an alarm so jarring we sat up ready to battle the dawn, our muscles more than sore from lying on the metal slab all night. We stretched our backs and saw in the distance a daunting brick fortress. Roberta read from a guidebook: *The English call the city 'Leghorn.'*

"Really? A curious habit they have…using exonyms for foreign cities and countries."

"Probably sailor's slang…all countries do this to each other. I think? *At one time, the sea had been Livorno's gateway, and approaching through the harbor, layered fortifications protect the coast in order of their centuries, the oldest closest to the shore.*"

In minutes, the pink horizon gave way to clouds, and a sailor climbed up, urging us to ready for port. We went down and stood at the railing to watch the well-ordered crew do their work, mooring lines, as lazy drops of rain plopped onto the oily surface of the water around the pilings, the rings shimmering iridescent green and purple, like the wings of a dragonfly.

Roberta continued to read from the guidebook. *During the Renaissance, Livorno was known as the ideal cosmopolitan city. A trade port, its importance brought many nationalities.*

"Garafallou spoke of a tremendous Greek community."

One of the hills has a church dedicated to the patron saint of Tuscany. People still make pilgrimages to pray there.

Off the gangway, we hauled our baggage and made straight for a railway station, eager suddenly for more adventure. Inside the terminal, the 7:04 Roman express was already boarding, and another ticket-buying frenzy ensued. "Roma—here we come!" Roberta said as a winking joke to the man behind the brass-grilled window.

"The train's almost full," he replied with no animation. "Only three left." He adjusted pale shirt cuffs that showed two inches below the sleeves of a merino cardigan. A maddening amount of time was then used to print and stamp the necessary paperwork, his Italian officialdom engaging no haste for the whims of foreign travelers. Staring daily through the counter's metal bars, into the faces of those excited by travel, I imagined him only half-satisfied with life, perhaps a nice wife at home holding a plate warm for him on the back of the stove.

With tickets finally in hand, we sprinted through the early morning rush-hour, Olympic runners heaving luggage, wishing we'd followed Garafallou's mode of travel—just a passport, a toothbrush, and a belt full of money. The conductor blew the whistle, and we jumped aboard just as the doors closed, iron wheels screeching metal against metal. Once we found our seats we began to laugh uncontrollably.

• • •

Rome, Italy

The rain followed us from Livorno, and the Roman sky grew darker and heavier. Gallons were coming down and the wet crowds waiting for a taxi were impossible. We decided we'd pause to regroup at a café, finding a round table of blue-veined stone that reminded me of the earth as seen from outer space. Ordering tea and buttered rolls, we sequestered by a window with our baggage to wait out the absurd downpour.

Roberta leafed through her guidebook and I, absentmindedly stared at the pages of *The Herald Tribune*. At the entertainment section my blood ran cold. "My God! Look at this!" I pointed to a bolded headline: *American Actress Now Cooking with Magic!* A publicity photo of Lydia holding a wooden spoon accompanied the article.

"You've got to be kidding? That's insane!"

A second photo showed Lydia laughing as she pressed her hands against the sides of her breasts to heave her cleavage forward. "Listen to this caption: *Still upset she hasn't yet gotten pinched in Italy!*" I read the opening sentence as the writer described Lydia's hosting the cooking show as a combination of luck and happenstance.

Roberta took over reading: *Lydia was literally walking down a street in Genoa, thinking of Anna Magnani in* Open City, *when a producer spotted her and asked her to audition.*

"What bullshit!"

"How shameless! She's never even seen a Magnani film!"

The article told how Lydia had once performed in *a rather horrible magic act,* but no mention of Phil Filbertson was made. "An admonitory snub!"

"What crap! And besides with her fine clothes she looks like Agnelli's niece or something. She's too chic to get pinched. The men thinking her well-connected would be scared to accost such a bitch."

The next paragraph explained how strict her exercise regime had become since the launch of the cooking show, and she bragged about how, if nothing else, she at least still had *slim calves.* "Maybe streetwalking helps? Mama Roma *was* a hooker."

"It shows such desperation," I agreed. "And I'm glad we're not in the village. Can't you just see how having her picture in the paper will delude her into thinking she's famous…like *Garbo,* unable to cross hotel lobbies without pandemonium."

"And yet, I hope you'll forgive me for saying this, despite the ridiculous hyperbole, or maybe because of it…I have to admit she *is* pretty entertaining!"

"I know. I thought so too."

Outside the window, the rain softened to drizzle, leaving the gray-green cobblestones slick. Again, I remembered Lydia's young speeches in public bathrooms, trapped between her mother's frilly department store fantasy and her father's bloodstained apron from the Swift's meat-packing plant. We finished reading and realized it was almost noon. "Our *elevensie* tea is over," Roberta said. We paid the bill and left to chart our new course.

The cab dropped us in front of a mid-tier hotel a short walk from the Spanish Steps, just as the deluge began again. We ran inside and a woman's voice, both lyrical and commanding, called from behind the check-in desk, ordering us to keep her floor dry. She told us to shake our excess water onto the welcome mat before advancing. Under her gaze, our drip-drying dance was performed, until she deemed us dry enough to cross a lobby of beige marble, set with old veneered furniture, stale with wax. Above us four crystal chandeliers made shadows on the molded faces of chipped plaster cherubs. The desk clerk had a strong Roman profile that balanced a pair of eyeglasses with gold coins welded on their hinges, a lurex sweater of gold metallic thread, and a collection of gold necklaces.

Roberta spoke under her breath. "Romans sure do gild-the-lily."

Hearing we expected two rooms, the woman dismissively informed us there was but one. Our protest met perfunctory bluntness. "One room. Or another hotel." Disinclined to drag ourselves back out into the rain, Roberta answered for us. "Fine. We'll stay."

The woman spun the guest book in an artful manner, and another round of Italian administrative tedium ensued. We signed the registry, and I wondered if Garafallou had possibly arranged the mysterious room shortage? The woman palmed the desk bell mercilessly and called. "Costanza! Costanza!" A tall teenage girl came scampering, took our things, and escorted us to a minuscule elevator. We crowded in, the bags set on end. As we ascended the girl explained in great detail how the ring of gray rubber encircling the key's bulbous wooden fob was a great invention, used to soften the banging echo in the hallway as the fobs dangled against the wooden doors.

Stepping off on the second floor, the girl unlocked a plain room with one king-sized bed. After parting the curtains, she opened a pair of glass floor-to-ceiling doors showing a small balcony beyond, set with two blue chairs. She then curtsied for her tip and exited.

Left alone, shyness immediately descended. Mechanically, we unpacked like new college roommates or two business associates in town for a sales convention. Roberta announced she'd like to shower away the grime of our trip. To afford her space, I stepped out onto the balcony. A small public square lay below, and at the shop on the corner, a florist in a gray lab-coat stood shaking raindrops off a bucket of voluptuous white chrysanthemums. On the left side of the square, a striped awning sheltered a local chess club, six players riveted, around their feet the wet pavement littered with burned-out cigarette butts. The three pairs displayed the same concentration as chess clubs anywhere in the world, be they Italian, Peruvian, Irish, Indian or those I remembered seeing as a boy in Washington Square. Who originally devised the age-old game? A mathematician? Someone with a jousting, military mind? A pawn?

Patches of blue sky opened, and a group of Italian women arrived, removing rain bonnets to spread on the bench seats, as they petted and fussed over two small dogs. No sooner had they settled in than one of the women leapt to her feet and slapped her forehead. With great drama she announced having forgotten to pick-up a husband's prescription. Umbrella quickly stashed in handbag, she scurried away, pebble gravel crunching under her shoes. The other women watched her go, until one brought forth some photographs and passed them, a niece's wedding narrated with hand gestures of exacting detail.

I pondered their joint respectability. It was likely they'd each had similar weddings, and spent lifetimes pursuing parallel courses, daily meals, schooling children, paying all manner of bills, satisfying or staring down the whims of a husband. I imagined the comfort of like-minded peers, their sense of permanence. Yet amid conformity, each must also hold some unique attribute—a love of music, Chinese puzzles, Cicero's philosophy, naked dancing, or a preference for certain perfume? Was this respectable seniority a worthy prize for a life of public respectability? *Roberta must be standing naked on the other side of the bathroom door, and if it were to open, might we both stand naked under the showerhead?*

A pair of swallows darted down between the trees, and my attention wandered back to thoughts of chess, how the bishop and the Queen can both move on the diagonal, how the lowly pawn can become a Queen more powerful than the King, but it's *his* health that decides the win.

Dressed in a crisp shirt and twill skirt, Roberta emerged. "I left that blue scarf at Garafallou's. I'll have to call. He can bring it to Levanto."

"I'll bet Gwen's already got it packed for him to carry."

My turn to shower, and I lathered up my fantasy in reverse: what if Roberta opened the door? I let the hot water rinse my skin, then lathered and rinsed some more. Clean and scrubbed, I turned the water off. Underfoot, the thick plush of a cotton bathmat still held the dampness of Roberta's feet. Impossible now to imagine a time when I'd not longed for her. *Steady boy*, I whispered to myself, and bit the corner of my towel.

To complement Roberta's sporty look, I donned a green cashmere vest over a sky-blue shirt and felt her appraising eyes notice it right away. "The rain's dampness is lifting," she said. "Navigating the streets will be easier once the humidity dries out." I had to hide how even comments on the weather suddenly held an air of licentiousness. Better we leave this heated place at once.

In the lobby, the tall girl who'd carried our bags, now stood on a stepladder, arms uplifted, washing arched windows with a squeegee, the intricate streaks drying in the sun. An indulgent stare studied our changed wardrobe, for hidden clues as to who we might be, or what we might be up to.

Out on the walkway, the quickening pulse of Rome was felt hurrying by, and we moved along with it. At a jewelry store window, we glanced at expensive baubles, feeling men and women of all ages passing behind us with purpose and pace. "Why do some cities remain so alive while others collapse?" I asked.

"A city is only as vibrant as its mass transit. That's what gives it energy."

"I suppose that helps. Harrisburg like so many other nice cities in America used to have trolleys. And then when it fell to idiopathic crime and rubble, whole blocks were demolished. Many bought by one developer, who planted grass in the empty lots, surrounding them with white-plank horse-farm fencing—as if town and country were trading places. They've sat that way for years."

At a crossroads we came upon the column of Trajan, its carved stone procession of horses and soldiers corkscrewing up the cylinder. I read from our pocket guide: *Dates from 106 BC. Built to honor Emperor Trajan for his victory in Dacia...* "I think that's somewhere in Greece."

"Actually Romania."

Roberta was nobody's fool. We moved on, dancers intuiting the movements of good partnership. She, sensitive not only to rhythm but step, yet still noting some odd architectural detail, a bit of fresco painted under an eave, or the curve of a house's window trim.

Passing a confectionery, she suggested we test their gelato. A man with dark syrupy eyes waited on us. Declaring ourselves purists, we surprised him by picking but a single scoop each, for me—vanilla, for Roberta—*amaretto*. "Americans usually want to try them all!" the confectioner said. We smiled then walked on, eating the cold bites from square plastic shovels that latched to the roofs of our mouths. Our pace slowed, better to enjoy the treat, until we arrived at an ancient church, its courtyard open. Standing under the imposing portico, our faces tilted up to study the ceiling's medallions. I felt my toes curl in my shoes with unencumbered desire. I turned and in a soft-spoken whisper asked if I might kiss her. Her nod was subtle, and in the shadow of the overhang, she met my mouth and returned my embrace, the most sublime I'd known, our cold kiss perfumed with vanilla cream and almond liqueur.

"I never imagined anything so public," she whispered.

"I just couldn't take it anymore."

"Should we go back to the hotel?" she asked, then pulled back smiling.

I nodded.

We joined arms and with the drowsy sensuality of a morphine drip, moved on our way without worry. How good it felt, her nearness, her health, her reliability, our legs and hips stepping in unison. Hips and legs, hips and legs, motion matching motion, side by side moving through the cobbled street, as if attuned to the same limb-swaying samba.

The girl, still on the ladder washing windows, unable to contain herself, gaped at our return. We skipped the elevator to climb the stairs, and holding hands, we bolted. I felt excitement in my throat as though I'd just been thrown from the saddle of a horse. And so, in the mid-afternoon, we closed the hotel curtains, hurrying out of our clothes in the dim light. Once undressed I slipped naked between the cool cotton sheets, she stood next to my side of the bed, letting my hand trace the thin elastic waistband around her hips. "Nervous?"

"Yes—and no. You?"

"Beyond nervous."

I began to lower her garment, and she stepped out of it. Sliding into bed, her warmth was welcome. My hands drew along her form, the roughness of my palms lending an erotic touch in contrast to her soft breasts; fingers sensing around her nipples and then the cupped flesh. Skin like folds of silk, led my fingers along the same tingling places Eligio might have touched. Two defined by way of three, me and she and him, our triangle somehow meeting in permutable complication. *She is the greenest grass…through her I am the greenest grass.* The carnality, the press of hard to moisture, the response felt in each conciliatory moan, backs arched in motion, pelvis and pelvis, thighs and hips gripping our wild ride, at times softening, at times vulgar. The spell not only human but of the animal kingdom; her sweat a Sapphic sweet, our breath now panting to catch itself, breathing in and out as alive and ancient as Adam and Eve, mouths taking in air not only to receive, but to give, turning inside out, outside in, the dizziness of chemistry stirring ecstatic pleasure, any reserve or rational thought waylaid for the push to intense climax.

Exhausted and knowing nothing more could be done, we unlocked, the tissues of our cells cooling satiation—the trancelike state every lover knows, a zone without care for food, books, sight-seeing, or anything brought in from the outside world. Slumber moved toward us with sweet contentment, the air downed by a sudden chill. From the foot of the bed, we lifted the thick comforter and tucked it in about our sides.

• • •

Room service arrived, rolling in with a cart of hot coffee, fried eggs, toasted bread, some yellow cheese, and two mellow Anjou pears. Had there ever been a time when we'd known more hunger? Carrying our plates and cups out onto the balcony in bathrobes, we noticed above us the clouds shaping to present a most unusual sky…below, another chess tournament at play.

Later, at the columned portals of the Vatican Basilica, Roberta's hand in mine blossomed to a place of interassuredness. A long hour passed as we waited in line, and finally inside the museum, through a well-waxed corridor the length of a marble football field, we discovered walls covered floor to ceiling with paintings. Thousands of sanded boards and looms tacked with canvas weave, miles and miles of carved molding, hundreds of thousands of nails holding up a million pairs of painted-eyes, the bulk belonging to popes or men in the church hierarchy, in the costume of their trade and among the architecture of their day. Some portraits flattered, others not so much, the whole assemblage illustrating an appetite for power, and the nature of faith, to which so many humans aspire.

Like bags of breadcrumbs scattered on the vast waters of Western civilization, the pictures massed a gluttonous feast of visual religiosity, obedient in theme, a surplus of allegory and divine image rendered in materials corresponding to their age, the advancing technologies of earth, pigment, egg yolk, walnut oil, plaster, all traceable. At the end of the first hallway, already huffing and puffing, many groaned to find another repetitive stone staircase to climb, opening into yet another hallway extending in identical length to the one below. Another long walk, another turn, and the prodded flesh and bone of our visiting stockyard became part of the spectacle. In this artful purgatory, shortcuts along the corridor were not offered, just the hindrance of a never-ending trudge through art. Within but seconds our eyes scanned the jewels of a chalice, the whiff of a devotional, the grain of a wood panel, all space elbowingly overpopulated, and with no space for meaningful contemplation. Among us, the amateur photographers, fearful of passing over a masterpiece, shot indiscriminately, the frenzy of clicking often obstructing vision. *How many would rather photograph than see?*

Roberta defied the odds by utilizing specific observation, pausing before a plank of chestnut wood painted with a coven of cardinals seated in a formal chamber. "Look, beneath their feet," she said. "That black-and-white floor mirrors a checkerboard." Though the work dated from the Renaissance, she saw an almost modernist approach. "An early study in perspective." Her docent's ability to point out something notable, granted our eyes private exhibition, and yet still we found it hard to linger. In what seemed an eternity we fought weariness, moving along just as extras in silent films do, their black-and-white pageant passing before some camera to depict crowd scenes shuffling to a great dance or a masquerade-ball.

At last, we were shunted through the final chamber, an extremely petite hall famously known as the Sistine Chapel. The scale was diminutive compared to the titanic museum, and the contrast made a dizzying transition. It was difficult to take it all in. The other obstacle hindering movement were the exhausted patrons; many sprawled on the inlaid floors like walruses on a beach. So as not to step on someone's fingers or ankles, in moving along we could but make quick glances up at the renowned ceiling's finely embellished frescos. For a moment

I stood perfectly still, gazing up at the details along the border, then a colossal figure holding a book. Up through the depth of that space, I felt a strange sense of compression, countered by a sense of soaring, as though using a telescope to view postage stamps. The artwork's intricacy required study, yet leaning back cramped the vertebrae of the neck and strained the tendons of the shoulders, adding to the ache in our spines and legs. Many visitors, for ease, had rented rectangular mirrors, held against their hipbones, peering down toward hell to see heaven's reflection.

Beyond another pair of great portals, the outside world shimmered and beckoned, and many people, including us, were drawn toward the sunshine, passing through the exit like a turbid, muddy river might pass through a rocky narrowing. What joy to finally exchange the gray dust of the cramped space for fresh air and light, the streetscape alive and congested with ever more hordes of visitors stretching on into infinity. The quickest escape was to dodge between kiosks selling Vatican placemats, cast resin statues, and red socks inspired by His Eminence.

Once beyond the frenzy, our minds relived the magnitude of what we'd just seen. "Imagine," I said, "for centuries this geographical place through art, holiness, politics, money and violence…has exercised spiritual power over much of the planet."

We walked on, and she sighed. "It's strange to realize that Catholics would label *our* union a sin."

I took her hand. "Most people are sinners in the eyes of most religions."

"I do think the way Michelangelo rendered the reach of God was beautiful…his finger outstretched to offer life to Adam."

I stopped and stared like a man waking from a deep coma.

"Walker, what is it? Is something wrong?"

"I was trying so desperately *not* to step on anyone's feet or body, when I looked up…I forgot to look for Adam gaining life!"

Roberta laughed.

"It's not funny! That was probably my only chance to see the face of God!"

. . .

The bells of gastronomy sound a precise clang in the Roman stomach, often after its accustomed citizenry have taken an evening stroll. Roberta and I changed clothes for dinner and joined the parade. When our time came, we opted for a small, olive-painted restaurant, its window artfully arranged with a straw-lined wooden box full of small peaches. We ordered sparkling water, and the waiter recommended a Barolo, uncorking it at the table with a cheerful yellow and white napkin tied about the neck. The ruby wine held spice, and I stared wordlessly at a decorative mirror behind us, reflecting my own features, a pleasant and noticeable change. A tan? Tricks of restaurant lighting? I watched Roberta pinch lemon into her water, the carbonation fizzing, and then I realized her dress, its generous cuffs and open neck, had been worn just for me.

The waiter came, and we followed his advice: spaghetti with Romano and pepper, lamb chops, burning finger style, fried artichokes, and salad of *puntarelle*.

When he left, Roberta smiled. "I'm terrified you're going to discover my edges aren't as smooth as you might wish. That you'll see the things I long to change in myself…but cannot. Every lover I've known has wanted me to change."

"I share the same fear." We laughed at our mutual self-consciousness. I told her about the list of weaknesses Garafallou and Gwen had composed, and how when injured, Garafallou went like a dog under the porch, waiting to be lured back out. The waiter brought the spaghetti, his eyebrows wriggling like two caterpillars. Then, as if sensing our mood, his manner became discretion itself and he artfully moved away. We tasted the pasta, nodded to him that it was perfect, and launched our meal.

"Do we let Hans know?"

"That's Eligio's game," she said. "He defines mutability for his own comfort. His right…a basic need. Personally, I'd rather cheat. I know sometimes I'm quite capable of injuring others. In this case it might not even be cheating, for Hans doesn't seem to care."

"What Garafallou and Gwen have come to know seems different."

"You mean offering up the worst of ourselves?"

"They've done an experiment toward a kind of self-acceptance. Perhaps you and I could, at the very least, develop a mutual pledge?"

"Oh, and what would that look like?"

"Exclusivity?"

"But what am I to make of your predilections that involve men?"

"Why not just say what most men say when it's two women 'That's *hot!*'"

She looked away. "And shall I expect monogamy from you…despite my marriage?"

"Well, how about this? If what we've found can't be sustained…might we at least agree to tell each other…before we toss on to someone else?"

She took a sip of wine. "I can live with that."

"I wish to enter a congress with you. But without need for caution or distrust. And so, to sincerely try…I must require that you leave Hans."

Roberta's glass suspended in midair, as if she'd just swallowed kerosene.

"I wish I had a camera. Your expression is priceless. By that look…I take it you still love him?"

"You know better."

"All right, then, my dear, I'll confess…I have feelings of love for you!" Roberta continued to study my face. "But don't worry," I said. "This too shall pass!" More bashful feelings overcame us, but our meal continued with the sense that something here in Rome was going right in the world.

• • •

Back at the hotel, the night porter propped a little television on the desk, and in approaching we heard the familiar confounded accent that could only be Phil. He and his new assistant were in mid act. Tonight, she wore a shimmering pink dress and he the box-cut tuxedo. "I see what you mean," Roberta said. "Camera lenses make things look glossier, more important."

"They can also diminish and distort."

"But how many rehearsals did Phil and Lydia need for even minimal smoothness on stage? So, a new girl exerting less rigor to master the same tricks, grabs instant attention by being placed in front of a lens? As you said, Walker, some events grow larger in front of the camera."

"Like the weather, for example."

She laughed. "Or the anxiety of anticipating the weather?"

"Russell used to say even if the daily news was dull the announcers would read it off the monitor with the same solemn urgency whether it was an earthquake or a cat up a tree. He said those gliding voices were not meant to inform but to excite—as predictable as gameshows promising free money or appliances."

Back in our room, Roberta decided to take a bath, this time leaving the door wide open. I undressed down to my boxers, feeling for the first time an inviolable freedom as I lay back on the bed, her body clearly visible through the transparency of the clear shower curtain. Roberta, soap in hand, brought her face around the plastic edging and smiled, inviting me to join.

• • •

We slept late, then went shopping for fine leather wallets, taking lunch in a small restaurant, sitting beside an elegant man with a moustache, eating that Roman specialty, a deep-fried artichoke. The curled-back petals as he cut them into pieces, resembled a crisp golden-colored rose. The man was oblivious to us, or the room, and made increasingly appreciative sounds with each bite. Mmm… Mmm…Mmm…as if dining in his own home. We enjoyed his enjoyment, and then also ordered the artichokes.

In the late afternoon, we wandered arm-in-arm to the old city and somehow knowingly entered the coliseum. We'd passed it many times, but intuited we weren't yet ready to face what remained there to see. For the next hour we hardly spoke as if under a spell. At a flat graded spot, perhaps once a spectator's platform, we attempted to apply comprehension to the great panorama. Beige mountainous hills formed a mighty backdrop for the ruin, its enormity saluting all the losses which a walk-through antiquity can extol. Staring in awe, Roberta leaned back against my chest, the thin silk of her shirt pressing the softness of my sweater, our ribcages barely perceiving their joined expansion, the subtle unison of sync, expansion, contraction, expansion, contraction, until a set of rippling interruptions halted that predictable measure. I knew then that she must be crying.

All the greatness that the mind of man can conceive to build but not retain, was shamefully confronted in this mighty rubble. No doubt many men and women have over the centuries cried here, overwhelmed to recognize the failure of every great republic, all magnificence relegated to war, incalculable death, savagery, spent wealth, all of it lost to centuries of doubt and chaos, civilized nature left uncivilized by inevitable ruin. Instantly I recalled how, but a few months before, I too had sobbed uncontrollably in a train tunnel. That memory of my life's inconsolable fracture, of such deep grief, brought compassion for this expression from her. We both knew beyond the conquered stones loomed the inevitable day when the winds of destruction would come to blow the best of our own lives away.

The sun was sinking lower against the monstrous wreckage, and we remained emotionally disquieted, the deep scarlet sky transforming the ruinous earth back to shadow. Today, here, and in this time, I knew Roberta wept for our past, our present and our future—and for the chance of us. Her face, like the face of God, stayed hidden, tears the inevitable cleansing, painfully gratifying, a payment in homage, as we recognized now why we'd come here.

We also sensed our Roman holiday was nearing its end, and that too heightened the darkness falling yet again over this part of the world, darkening all across Pompeii and Calabria, across Padua and Venice, and over all the seas surrounding the Italian peninsula, its mighty schools of fish darting silvery and swift under the blackening water of yet another night. Then at last, came the time for us to usher away from the captivity of this pitiful wrecked arena, and together we ever-so-slowly emerged, stepping out of the past and onto the modern roadway.

A public bus sat idling at the curb. We boarded in silence, and paid our fare, like so many other pilgrims before us, then sank down to rest.

TURNCOAT

• • •

Levanto, Italy

Our train headed North through the sunny landscape, tall dark cypress planted to punctuate the views. At the dusty yards of Carrara, crates of marble were stacked to be shipped, and chiseled into bathroom walls, kitchen counter-tops, gravestones. After La Spezia, the rocky land turned to cliff, tracks curving upward toward the Cinque Terre. We entered the first of the dark tunnels, and I peered out to see if it were possible for a passenger to witness anyone hugging in the dark—no not possible—the train moved too fast. The black void opened to a brief and brilliant shock of intensely bright aqua water, then after a split second another black tunnel, then another shock of aqua blue, then black. The excitement of this contrast astonished us, our senses electrifying. We were almost there, our homecoming nearly complete.

By the station exit, we passed a newsstand with a color poster of Phil eating fire, with an ad announcing he and the magic show were to be the hour-long special of the week.

"More proof," I said. "On television, anything can rise."

Signor Vescovi met us in the village parking lot, and we stood admiring the familiar sight of the Ligurian sea. But travel to more metropolitan places had reduced the village to quaintness, our descent recognizing just how narrow its shrunken passageways were. More surprises waited as a media crew came walking upward, shouldering two large black cameras. "Television has infected us," Signor Vescovi said in Italian. "This morning, a reenactment of the magazine cooking was taped for viewers. Again, the plum tart, again, the chestnut cake, but this time without you or Pina."

"What happened to Pina?"

"The director found her difficult. She wouldn't comply."

"Comply with what?"

"The schedule, the direction, alterations to the recipe. She's been eliminated. Meanwhile, your cousin, done with work for the day, has gone to Rapallo."

"What's in Rapallo?"

"A party."

Inside my house, the desk sat overflowing with new brown envelopes. "Better get busy," I told myself, opening the windows and letting the breeze flutter the blinds. Staring out at the vista, I wasn't yet ready to return to daily life.

Though the race to find one another had certainly not gone to the swift, time and chance had nonetheless favored Roberta and I with partnership. I wandered down to see how the garden had fared in my absence, then sat on the retaining wall of the terrace and thought of the actors who'd once recited Shakespeare in this strange oratorium. How oddly wonderful to recite drama to a retaining wall, its mortared stone tangled with vines of muscadine. I stood and without deliberation felt my legs stride back in the direction of Roberta's house. She smiled and embraced me.

"I just had to see you again."

"And I was about to come to you."

"What're you so happy about?"

"I've just made a plan to leave for Zurich," she said. "To see a lawyer about a divorce. I leave in two days."

· · ·

That evening a production assistant working for Lydia and Buddy telephoned to extend an invitation for lunch at Santa Clara, a most elegant restaurant, chosen in part for its proximity to the cooking show studio. Roberta and I both accepted, thinking it'd make for a memorable reunion.

The next afternoon at half past noon, a suave man confirmed the reservation, then ushered us down three curved wooden steps, passing alongside a table dressed with wildflowers, green figs, and an exquisite ricotta torte elevated on a glass pedestal and topped with raspberries. We took our seats and admired the dining room, done in pale greens, signaling a style both formal and cool. Roberta's divorce plans had brought us closer, and yet we sat apart, having agreed to show no affection in public, nor speak of her decision.

Buddy entered, his face set so anxiously that anyone meeting him would grow anxious too. His features shifted when he saw us and his expressions in greeting seemed both genuine and manufactured. "Geez, I thought you two would never get back…so much hell has broken loose! I mean we are off and running."

Roberta complimented Buddy on a new shorter hairstyle, his sideburns now extending down from the ear line. "Yeah, I bought a trimmer and sheared it myself. Way cheaper than these fancy Italian barbers. But the plug can't fit American sockets, so one day when it's time to go home, I'll leave it for Pina. She can shave her legs, her poodle, or the whiskers on her chinny-chin-chin!"

We began to say we'd been startled by all the cameramen wandering about the village, but Buddy grew distracted and signaled the *maître'd*. The man came at once and it shocked us to hear Buddy request a larger table, no easy feat for an American. To our astonishment, the maître'd did indeed offer a better location, and after moving and settling once more, Buddy began to tell the story of the magazine conquest. "They bumped the planned cover, so they had to cough up two fees for the issue. Now, the editor had already paid us for feature…but not cover. So, I thought what the hell, and I gave the guy a piece of my mind. Guess what? They came through with more dough for cover. Called it a courtesy stipend. Now, Holy Toledo…it's one of the friggin' best sellers in that rag's history!"

"You've picked up a lot of lingo!"

"Yes, you hang around these mag folk enough, it's bound to happen. And now four episodes are in pre-production. The tart thing filmed yesterday, and post-production will be accelerated so the pilot for episode one can air sooner. Imagine: they don't even want to see how the first episode fares. You guys gotta come to the studio after lunch. We're shooting a segment on vanilla. Lydia's crazy busy, but dying to see you. I told her, just demand the afternoon off. We're footing the bills, so let that damn director get off his ass and go out and do some second-unit stuff." Buddy sounded jovial, but the fact that he was here and not at the studio gave the distinct impression of worry. Still, the clear blue linen of his collared shirt lent something appealingly sharp to his frame.

Lydia entered and stood waiting at the top of the steps, unblinking, her features perfectly still under full television makeup, her hair, a bright new shade of auburn. Being before a camera appeared to have heightened her artifice, and people stared as she was escorted down into the dining room. That attention lent Buddy pride. To improve the estimation of himself, he rose from his wicker chair like an actor in a play, and placed his hands lovingly on her shoulders, kissing both cheeks.

Lydia gave an obligatory smile. "Someone's working the room," she muttered between clenched teeth. Roberta and I then rose and exchanged affectionate kisses and Lydia welcomed us with squeals and unusual warmth. After we'd all settled back, she posed a few polite questions about our trip.

"We went to the Vatican and Walker forgot to look up and see God," Roberta said, still gleefully amused over the incident. I described the enormous crowds.

"Oh? If I saw that many people in one place I'd turn around and go home," Lydia said. "We used to have a hairdresser at one of the salons…poor guy raised Catholic. He was outraged that a church still denouncing fags…could have at the center of its most holy universe a pietà by a fag artist."

"I don't care about the background of who sculpted it," I said. "Christ's body is so tenderly rendered."

"Has his sexuality ever been proven?" Buddy asked.

"The hairdresser? He's openly gay."

"No, Michelangelo. I mean how do you document private acts? Historical sex?"

"I recently met a priest in Levanto who wasn't afraid to admit many in the church have their own strange histories."

"A progressive priest in Levanto?" Buddy said. "Can't imagine that."

"The hairdressing guy said electing a pope by chimney smoke, seems no different from a reliance on Eastern mysticism, or some other crap."

"Working at a religious school, I can say that stuff is the real world beyond twilight!"

"The guy at the salon said it's hard for that church to condone same-sex acts as natural because the holy lawmakers can only imagine it in the sordid way it gets expressed within their own orders."

"Speaking of twilight," Roberta said. "I presume you've seen Phil with his new assistant?"

"Please! Don't bring that up. She's jail-bait. When I quit the show, Phil had the nerve to call me an old mare put out to pasture! And where the hell are that girl's parents?"

I smiled. "Probably standing by an empty cradle."

"Who the hell cares?" Buddy patted her shoulder. "I mean who cares? We're off and running with our cooking pilot."

At that Lydia began to lament her fatigue. "You've no idea what scheduling lunch with you took. But say what you will, these Italians do understand time for food!" As if on cue a bottle of prosecco was opened and poured, and we toasted the show.

Lydia lifted her drink. "Come back to the studio this afternoon while we finish taping. You might get a kick out of it."

"I've already asked them," Buddy said.

"Wait'll you see my clothes! Gowns and furs. Some are vintage. The costume guy found a bunch of great stuff in a vault at Cinecittà. One cocktail dress, exquisitely cut by the Fontana Sisters in Rome, was sewn for the trousseau of Linda Christian when she married Tyrone Power."

"You wear evening clothes while you cook?"

"No, I wear the glamour stuff to go shopping, you know, buy ingredients.

We worked at the market hall three days ago, but to swing it we had to be ready to shoot at five a.m.! They had to open the market an hour early. They shot it so it looks like I'm stopping by to shop after a night on the town. But, Holy Toledo, I still haven't recovered from that lost sleep!"

We soon saw how rising above the rank of magician's assistant only brought new things to complain about. "When I'm not on camera, I spend hours planning menus," she said. "So he can approve and then pitch them." She stared at Buddy and paused. "Where on earth did you get that shirt?"

"From a shop."

"It's very bright."

"Can't always wear gray flannel." That his new feathers so affected his mate brought visible joy. Wearing something not preordained implied an emboldened rooster, one thinking he could suddenly crow and run the barnyard. Perhaps new interest in finery walked hand in hand with new romance? A roving eye? The shirt was a coup. Better check that. Appetizers appeared and the dramatic way Lydia passed them showed the dining table to be just another stage. "While you were gone, a publicity story ran in *The Herald!*"

"We saw it!"

Lydia nervously laughed. "*New York Times* did something too, but dryer, and above it all. To liven it, I told them about Genoa, a story about a swarthy guy slowing his Vespa, just like in the movies. I told them he pinched your ass Roberta, but ignored mine!"

Roberta looked shocked. "You didn't!"

"No worry. I never use anyone's name when I make stuff up." Lydia dabbed a crust of bread into oil, her eyes returning to Buddy. "When did you even have time to shop?"

"A sidewalk sale. It was an impulse."

Lydia reminded me of a spider spinning a web, waiting to snag him on some detail. "Can such thin linen even be ironed?"

"I don't know. But must you find fault with everything?"

Her upper lip showed disdain for his pushback. How funny that ill-paired couples can so often manage to act magnanimously in public to the envy of others, while their encrypted talk resounds with all that I hate about marriage, the brain a slice of gray meat shaved to transparency, a spouse holding every thought up to the light for scrutiny.

Lydia changed the subject. "We've been waiting for you for this celebration. As you probably heard, the salons have been sold! Eager Koreans who plan franchises. American brands bring a premium over there. First one's aimed for Seoul to add big-city stature. Then they'll open in other towns. Imagine our salons going global. The Koreans wired the cash. That money is now allowing us to produce the cooking show."

We toasted as other diners glanced. The waiter appeared, and Buddy, playing host, insisted on ordering for all. Astonishingly, his command of Italian had grown more vigorous since last we saw him. The restaurant specialized in fish, and he requested it be served *stile familiare* so the whole platter could be photographed. The waiter looked serious, as if what he was writing down were related to a mathematical theory in physics.

While waiting, we were able to talk a bit about Corsica, and Garafallou's near-death experience. "After what he's put me through!" Lydia said. "I'da just left his fat-ass hanging on a cliff."

When the first fish course arrived, our turn to talk stalled. We waited patiently while the poor cooling creatures posed for remembrance, each camera flash now earning glares from fellow patrons. Photo session complete, dining commenced, and even the way Lydia offered to pass the salt and pepper felt cloying.

"Where exactly did you buy it?

"Buy what?"

"The shirt, stupid."

"Some guy hawking from a rack rolled right out onto the sidewalk." His vague reply sounded too casual. He explained lately he'd begun to crave brighter colors. "Maybe it's all this sea and sky."

The rest of our lunch went by quickly, and after the waiter had cleared, a cart with a cornucopia of desserts was wheeled over. The owner, in a jacket and tie, came graciously up beside it, greeting us with great charm, selecting several delicacies to place at the center before us. Lydia pointed to her watch. "I'm afraid we can't dawdle over sweets, or we'll be late." The owner snapped his fingers and a second waiter rushed from across the room to take our coffee order. Somehow, the well-informed management had been made to understand Lydia to be the American in the newspaper with the new cooking show. Perhaps that is why they so willingly changed our table? In the kitchen doorway, some workers in white uniforms peered out to get a look.

"Might we have a photo of you to put on the wall?" the owner asked. Eyes glistening, he reached for his necktie, adjusting the knot, then knelt and placed his arm around both Lydia and Buddy as the waiter snapped the picture. Buddy turned to the owner. "Hey, how'd you like to teach television viewers to make gelato?" The prospect caused the man to laugh unnaturally, as if an incredible story had just been told. Astonishingly, he then insisted on picking up the check, something I couldn't recall seeing a European do for an American. "It would be a great honor to make gelato on television. What flavors?"

Buddy patted the man's arm. "It will have to complement whatever she's cooking. But we'll be in touch to work it out."

"Perhaps you'll also mention our menu on your show?"

"Sure. I don't see why not."

• • •

Back on the street, Lydia raged. "You've got to stop that!" she said. "I can't live up to all these promises."

"It's all part of the game," Buddy said.

She looked at him with exasperated contempt. "Well, that game is for me to play, not you."

"Yeah? Well, you forget. I'm a producer."

We hailed a taxi to bring us to the unassuming building housing the television facility on the outskirts of town. Once inside Buddy began to study the lighting setup for the studio kitchen and then let his displeasure be known. Lydia touched my forearm, her voice confidentially low. "Look at him. He gets all involved. A laughing stock. We're not even shooting there till later. I wish you guys could help me keep him entertained. Find something for him to do. How about calling your guy Eligio? Why don't you get him to rent you all some scooters?"

"Oh, not me," I said, fast as I could. "Work piled sky-high."

"And not me," Roberta said. I could feel her amusement at the suggestion. "I head for Zurich in the morning."

"What? We're taping a street scene at a sidewalk restaurant. I wanted you to be there. Can't you delay a few days?"

"Sorry…but it's important business."

Lydia turned to me. "Walker, can't you invite Buddy to go on some trip? Anywhere. I don't care. Just to get him out of my hair?" The stage manager interrupted, saying that the makeup artist was waiting. "We must get underway!" Lydia gave us an imploring look as she let the rather imperious woman lead her off to the dressing room.

Buddy returned. "Let's take folding chairs to the back and watch from there." Once seated, he opened a manila folder and flipped through a dizzying array of pot roasts, paellas, cakes, and cookies. "Stock pictures, we buy to transfer onto video, splicing them to mark transitions. Later, we'll go to the cutting room. I'll let you see actual footage."

Lydia came on the set, makeup and hair freshened, her costume now a tailored pantsuit. She occupied a chair before a matte screen and followed the director's instructions. Even from where I sat, I could feel her nerves. All the classes, amateurish productions, tours of magic and twilight, not to mention the mysterious medications, were once more being put to the test. The prop stylist arranged a vase of tulips at her side, until the stage manager yelled: *"Silenzio!"* To set the mood, an actor read as the voice to be dubbed over. His lines echoed Buddy's magazine hyperbole. "Lydia's palate is so discerning, she can tell if a vanilla bean had been harvested in Tahiti or Madagascar." Roberta exhaled incredulity at yet another claim of superhuman taste buds. The director lifted his hand, and the camera began to move on Lydia. "I inherited my vanilla taste from my mother, a large brown bottle always in our kitchen." She segued to a comic monologue about the badness of her mother's cooking.

"Cut," the director yelled. Then in an enthusiastic voice he added: *"Magnifico!"*

Lydia stood and the stylist rushed her back to the dressing room for another change.

"Is that it?" I asked.

"Yup. All that work and waiting—fifteen seconds of usable stuff. In the old days, they did it live! Even with costume changes."

The stage manager stepped forward to read instructions. "Now the camera will close in to show Lydia scraping tiny seeds from a vanilla pod." An assistant came and stood in the kitchen before the cutting board, an X of masking tape marking the floor.

"That young woman's hands will be used to look like Lydia's," Buddy explained. When the shot of the vanilla pod being scraped had finished taping, two stagehands brought forth a large fish and rested it on the counter. Lydia returned, wearing a frilly blue dress, and held her arms out perpendicular so the woman from wardrobe could tie an apron around her waist, the logo of the television production company printed on the bib.

The camera now recorded *her* packing the fish with rosemary, tying it with string, and placing it in a poacher. "Cut!" The director's voice sounded from a video booth. *"Magnifico..."*

A burly technician rushed over, saying they had to retake something. A discussion ensued over which direction the fish needed to be held while it was tied.

"This'll go on forever," Buddy whispered. "Why don't I give you a tour of the cutting room?" Obediently, we followed down a narrow passageway, turning a corner toward a red door. He unlocked it. "Come in! Come in!" he said.

At one of the cutting tables, he fiddled with some switches. A blaring violin solo sounded from the speakers. We held our ears. He found the volume and dialed it down. After a few measures, the full orchestra cheerfully joined, playing what sounded like a variation of Vivaldi. "It's our theme music. I'm not supposed to let anybody hear it, but you're family!"

The piece rose to crescendo, and the voice of a man spoke in Italian over the music. "The cuisine of Italy is an important sacred heritage forged by the hands of our perpetual ancestors." Buddy switched off the tape. "That's for the intro."

"What are perpetual ancestors?" Roberta asked.

"I'm glad you asked. When I first heard that line, I asked the same thing. The director laughed, said it means those who perpetuate." He shrugged then flicked another switch. Three electronic beeps were heard, then the announcer spoke: "An Italian kitchen is the center of an ancient culture and a legacy stretching both forward and backward in time."

Three more electronic beats: "A nervous chanticleer must learn about the power of the media."

"That's to go with shots of Pina's rooster." Buddy flicked the switch once more; the three beats sounded. "The seas of the world are where life begins." Three more beats. "The word gnocchi refers to a knot in a piece of wood. It is also a pasta prepared using one of the most honorable and earthly of foods—the potato."

Buddy motioned us over to a video monitor. "They can dub this crap in any language." The screen lit up, and Lydia, just as she'd told us, emerged from a limousine wearing an evening gown, indeed pretending to be on her way home from a night on the town. The silent camera followed her path through Levanto's familiar food market. "That dress is bugle beads," Buddy said. "Weighed a ton."

Men and women tended counters stocked with produce, pasta, cheese, eggs, and hams. "Getting those damn vendors to come in before sunrise was a major pain. The office of tourism had to be called." In the last shot, at a vegetable stand, Lydia clowned, suggestively caressing some gigantic leeks. Buddy ejected the video and popped in another. Here Lydia was in a fish market, sashaying in a sable coat past the mongers, their stalls piled high with tails and fins lying on beds of crushed ice. One seller demonstrated how to check for freshness, under the gills. Acting smitten by Lydia, he brought forth a basket of tiny, exquisitely grooved clams. "The voice of the dubbing guy will say there that the man was keeping the clams back, waiting for someone special to come along. You'll see, all this stuff will get cut and pieced together to make drama."

A familiar panoramic view appeared on the tiny screen. We immediately recognized the cobblestones of our village. "I thought you guys would like this!" The camera panned over Roberta's courtyard and loggia. "The beauty of your place was irresistible!"

"But I don't *want* my house on television!"

"Relax! No one's gonna bug you."

"That's what they told the peasants of St. Tropez the first time Bardot swung down the street."

The camera meandered to the front of Pina's gate. "Here's where Lydia's buying eggs." The old rooster stood warily on guard as she entered, eyes beady black, red comb jiggling. Lydia strode past the furious bird and knocked on the door. Pina opened, scrutinized the camera operators, then lifted her shawl to cover her face. "Had to stop there. The old gal wouldn't let the crew into her house!"

"Good for her."

"So, we're just gonna say she was out of eggs. We'd leave her out altogether, but that shawl bit, that's the kind of Italian stuff that people go nuts for."

Another cassette showed a montage of potatoes being harvested, then put through a commercial potato washer. A travelogue followed, featuring hikers on the Cinque Terre stopping to take lunch at a tavern. "This part is already edited for the gnocchi recipe. We'll probably cut more." Kaleidoscopic food close-ups began to twirl, then melted in a blank frame. "This stuff is for commercial interludes. There's tons more. We'll probably only use cut pieces."

Lydia appeared in the next tape, and for the first time, we heard her recorded voice. "Every good Italian chef knows where to check fish for freshness. Not the eyes! Not the scales! But here!" She lifted the gills. The segment ended with Lydia on a dock beside a gigantic tuna hooked to a mighty scale. She lifted the giant gills, making one final approving face for the camera. "Here the voice-over will say something about fish, like how freshness can't be overemphasized."

Buddy changed cassettes again. "This section needs fine-tuning." A shot of the market combined with a voice-over explained Lydia's intention to make a dessert for an important dinner party. "But there's a crisis! The mistress has used all her eggs!" The camera pulled back, showing Lydia investigating the stall of a poultry purveyor. The man humorously juggled tiny quail eggs. Lydia was encouraged to try the same maneuver with predictably ham-fisted results.

"These eggs are too small!" Her squeal sounded well-rehearsed. The purveyor quipped, "Tell that to the *quail*."

Buddy leaned over the monitor to eject the tape as the cutting room door opened. A tall, lean woman with acid-green eyeglasses entered. "How did you get in?" she said, voice full of outrage. "This room is off-limits. This work is not finished! You don't belong here! I'm the editor! I will report this!"

Buddy looked like a child caught red-handed in the cookie jar. He was quick to anger. "My wife and I pay the largest share. You all work for me!"

"That gives no permit for you to interfere with my job." The woman quickly assessed the various cassettes, but remained fixed.

"All right…geez! Calm down. We're leaving." We quickly followed Buddy from the room, his hands shaking as he closed the door. Walking back to the studio kitchen, his face twisted in fury as Garafallou appeared. "She's got no right to be territorial. None!" Buddy recounted the incident and demanded action be taken against the woman.

Garafallou nodded, expressing sympathy and waited until Buddy was calmer. "The best course for us all—is to let this go. You don't want to lock horns with her or the other backers. One of them is that woman's brother."

"What? You've hired people's family members? That's nepotism."

"She's very good. Trained by Visconti himself."

"Why wasn't I told? I'd have vetoed her and her brother for sure!"

"You were on the road. Besides, being invested at only 49 percent, you'd be shot down." Buddy looked like a man just hit in the forehead with a frying pan.

We re-entered the studio kitchen and Lydia glanced in our direction. She was now whipping egg whites. Roberta whispered to me, "I see she managed to find some chickens who did their job."

"Yes, another crisis averted."

The camera followed Lydia as she poured the frothy mix into a straight-sided ceramic bowl. Once full, the stage manager rang a timer, and on cue, she pulled a replica, already baked and cooled from the oven. The director yelled: "Cut! *Magnifico.*"

The prop manager took the dish and carried it to the dining table. Lydia removed her apron and went to stand by it. On cue, she lifted a silver spoon and portioned a helping, holding the plate up to the camera, calling the dish *"Affanato,"* her pronunciation strangely perfect. She took a bite, then gave the camera a final wink.

*   *   *

Roberta departed for Zurich, and the next day the Cinque Terre's world-famous temperate clime, pleasantly warm days and gentle nights, gave way to a highly unusual chill. It moved in suddenly and made the air too cold to dine on the terrace. A brisk wind forced Pina to close all of the windows, and my meals were now served by the stove in the living room. "You'd never know this is the fat season," she said.

That night, my stone house turned so dank I pulled out a sweater and a cashmere robe from storage, the whistling wind making concentration difficult. Huddled in the study, a manuscript on my lap, Roberta's trip to Zurich pressed loneliness, any sense of freedom spoiled. I envisioned her warm arms coming in from the cold doorway to embrace me.

In the morning, a strange mist rolled in off the sea, bringing foggy air too bracing to even consider a swim. I opened the door and saw Vescovi go by in the dim light. "You won't be needing ice today," he joked, and I could see his breath.

"Not a chance."

"Can't hunt either. No sense shooting in the fog."

Two more days of hermit's hibernation, no sun, no warmth, a nightly squall, and still no word from Roberta. I sat indoors for hours, the closed-up rooms feeling dark, as if the fog had managed to penetrate my very bones. Staring at the watercolor postcards grandfather had painted beachside, I noted once more all the evidence of his artistic change. The cold motivated me to continue on making tremendous headway in the manuscripts my publisher kept sending, the concentrated work now an avoidance for my own crazy moods. At last, the long-stunted introduction to *The Galaxy of Love*, was complete.

Making calls to various departments at the publishing house, I also asked Malcolm Rinaldo's office to inquire about our quarterly meeting in Torino. His assistant asked if Mr. Rinaldo might meet with me sooner rather than later. I agreed and arranged for an overnight mail service to pick up the finished projects. They'd get to Torino for review in advance of my visit, and that way, I'd not have to carry them on the train. The courier arrived, I signed his forms, and he departed. Almost immediately, there was another knock. I yanked the door open, thinking the courier must've forgotten something, but it was Buddy.

"Listen to that wind, man," he said. "Excruciating. A raw scream that sways every tree. Open your window, stick your head out into that cold. It's the suffering echo of all humanity…a wailing haunted chorus. Now, just close your eyes and try to sleep through that. See if you can!"

"It's just weather," I said.

"Drives me nuts! I called you a thousand times, but you haven't answered. Then I saw the courier come and go."

"I'm afraid I've become a mollusk sealed in my shell."

Buddy eyed me with injury. "Well, one thing being cooped up has done is inspire me to take stock. For the sake of poetic truth, I've been conducting a written inquisition."

"Of what?"

"Of myself!"

"Oh, no. *Ouch.*"

"Walker, you once told me you met a priest who spoke English. You were caught in the rain?"

"Oh, yes. Padre Vincenzo."

"I'd like to meet the guy."

"He's easy to find. I'll give you directions."

"No. I need you to take me. To keep me accountable."

"I'm afraid I can't." I then explained my pending trip to Torino and how I was still on deadline. "Besides, you don't need me to see the padre."

"If you don't come, I'll cheat. I'll go nowhere. This unceasing wind already has turned me around. I'm half-nuts!"

"Only half?" He didn't smile. "Okay, what if we squeeze it in early tomorrow before the filming of the street scene? I promised Lydia I'd be there. I leave for Torino the next day."

. . .

A mysterious fog at dawn tinged the walls lavendar, then chalky cold white. Reluctantly, I rose from bed, made coffee and, after hurrying to dress, sat in silent contemplation wishing for sun. The green canopy outside my window seemed to have been wilted by the cold. At seven, I forced myself onto the terrace. Buddy was already waiting there, both of us in sweaters.

Shivering, we hurried up to the early bus, and soon were winding down the mountain. The popularity of the early bus meant many more stops. Along the familiar bend, despite the cold, the woman who'd lost her baby to the bee sting boarded, a black knit sweater wrapped tight about her body. After scanning our faces, she stepped down and we moved on.

As we continued, Buddy grew sentimental. "You've always been a steadfast friend," he said. "I only wish I'd have been a better friend to you. I should've done more to advocate for you and for your mom."

"You were only ten. Besides, we didn't need advocacy. My grandfather on Long Island used to say too many helpers can rob a person of their own agency, keep them from finding their own courage."

"Well…I sure don't want to do that.

"Unelected leaders…or loudmouths we used to call them."

"I know the type. They always say we—and elect their own sorry asses to speak for all concerned."

In town, walking over the frigid cobblestones, we approached the church, and in the entrance corridor, spotted Padre Vincenzo right away, several rolls of pink toilet paper in his hands. He greeted us with enthusiasm, and after stashing the paper in a tiny bathroom, invited us to his office. "In this cold weather, a cup of hot tea will stand us good."

We soon were sipping tea from mugs, and I felt awkward to hear Buddy be encouraged to let his list of woes spill out in my presence. They concerned the usual complaints: money, lost hair salons, patent expiring on his father's epoxy products, inheritance slowing to a trickle. Finally, he spoke with restrained admonishment about Lydia.

"Not a supportive wife?"

"Pretends to be. But she can make me nuts."

"Can you explain?"

"Okay. So, like back in the States, once in a blue moon, my department holds a dinner where faculty bring their partners. She comes begrudgingly. Says the conversations bore her. I tell her that academics bore each other all the time, but we must endure. She can't. She's downright rude to my colleagues. Afterwards, she rails for hours about their ignorance. Meanwhile, she can't tell Helen Vendler from Helen Keller, or William Gass from William Tell. Forget stuff like scansion, form, or free verse!"

Padre Vincenzo's eyes shone mirthfully. "But you must have known from the beginning that she preferred hairdressing?"

"Well, you oughta see the dinner parties she drags *me* to! Producers sitting around talking about commercials. Who shot that spot for Chrysler? Who did the hand-held camera?"

Padre Vincenzo nodded. "I assume you took an eternal vow? But do you want to stay married?"

The remark startled Buddy. He thought for a moment. "I have so many questions about eternal marriage. I mean, what happens after death? Do we meet on some kind of cloud? And what about the over-married people…Liz

Taylor, Zsa Zsa Gabor, Artie Shaw. Do they reunite with all their exes?"

Buddy's seriousness brought Padre Vincenzo to rub his chin. "What we know of celestial kingdoms are fairy tales—ancient ones. And we accept versions of these stories depending on how useful they are. None of us can presume to unravel the mysteries. Nor can we define the reality of another. Sometimes my job as priest is to gently guide people back from a detour. As for material things, a walnut breakfast room, a cherry armadio, all can be regained. But a healthy life of respect, happiness, eternal love…not so easy. The natural person is present in all, and natural impulses adhere to laws of nature."

The padre looked long and hard. "Buddy your only crime is confusion. Anything else is forgiven."

•   •   •

Lydia stood irate in the cold weather fuming about a difficult morning. "And where the hell have you been?"

"Our bus got taken out of service." Buddy's adept lie impressed me, though it was doubtful she believed him. I was given a superficial hug, perhaps to convey to any of the crew who might be watching us, the closeness of our family ties. However, the moment was lost, as laying a camera track with stiff fingers at an outdoor location preoccupied the technicians.

Lydia moved on, telling us she needed to study her script and Buddy and I stood forlorn on the sidewalk, watching a large camera align itself from beyond a window. A storefront with a tiny kitchen had been converted to a studio, and on the other side of the glass, the elderly man who ran the take-out stand worked alongside his wife, expertly whisking garbanzo flour, olive oil, water, and salt. The hard-working couple were charmingly blasé about the chaos going on about them, remaining intently focused on their batter. When the right consistency was at last achieved, they poured their prize into an enormous black iron pan which was banged against the wooden counter top to raise up bubbles and settle the cornered edges. Together they then lifted the great iron beast and slid it into the oven.

Outside the shop, a wooden platform, built right onto the street, always occupied two parking spaces, and here patrons could eat their take-away at some small outdoor tables. Today, the forty cold metal chairs were filled with people excited to be working as unpaid extras. The set-manager came out, moved a table, and asked the lighting director to bring a lamp forward. Watching these changes energized the extras with the importance of television-in-the-making, carrying the hope of being seen.

"Now people," the stage manager shouted in Italian. "As you line up to go for food, bring it back to the table. But don't eat it! I repeat—do not eat it! Wait for instructions for when to begin. Once the direction is given then try to animate yourselves. Eat with fortitude! Remember the recipe is very rare…handed down for centuries…guarded under lock and key."

"Idiotic," a woman standing next to me muttered. "It's only garbanzo flour and oil. To say it's kept under lock and key implies we're thieves. That we run around stealing each other's recipes!"

Through a stranger's eyes, I recognized how scorn can question artifice, and deny its administrative control. I liked the woman immediately.

The director escorted Lydia back onto the set. She now wore a denim jumpsuit and stood adjusting a cap the color of cream. The crowd gazed as if at a goddess sprung to life. Lydia rehearsed the director's instructions of where to stand and move in line with the camera, and practiced walking a planned route among the tables to gush: "In Italy one must meet Italians!"

Even we skeptics had to admit she held charisma, and when she asked the group to repeat the name of the special baked chickpea flour pancake, they willingly and in unison shouted: *"Farinata!"* just as they'd rehearsed.

"Is that what it's really called?" I asked.

"Who the hell knows? I've heard it called *Socca*" the woman beside me said. "It's only common street food. All this hoopla is a travesty."

A second flat pan was pulled from the heat, the chickpea batter browned to perfection. A camera recorded it being cut, and a line was instructed to form. With over-emphasized spirit, Lydia went to work behind the counter, allotting shares of the pie onto sheets of cut paper, each patron receiving their portion rationed with a bit of the coveted crispy brown crust along the edge.

"Perhaps she's hoping for a franchise?" the woman said.

"Yes…maybe a line of salad dressings?"

The last of the pie was doled, and the stage manager explained how black pepper could be added to the crepe upon request. Lydia now moved among the tables humorously responding to those wanting a twist of peppercorns from a ridiculously large pepper mill provided by the prop department. On cue, Lydia then winked at the camera.

• • •

After four hours taping the cooking show's cheeky shenanigans, lunch was called. Lydia didn't want Buddy, as a backer, to be seen chowing down at the craft-service table, so she ordered us to eat at one of the nearby bars, while she stayed behind to study lines. Walking down the street, Buddy elaborated his dissatisfaction. "Every time her show-biz crew sees me—they laugh. A few have joked outright, asking how I put up with her. To them it's all a big joke. And I'm some kind of chump. Her frenzy and grinding the axe reminds me of when people back home used to call her Lizzy Borden. Do you remember?"

I shook my head.

"Well, all right then. But you can imagine. I mean, from the stuff you went through with your mother. That couldn't have been easy. Lydia says the guff toward your household was always coming her way too."

"She exaggerates. If she did suffer, Mom was the one who paid the ultimate price."

"Hey. I'm on your side, pal! I told her she'd no right to grind her axe at you."

We found a bar and ordered the special of the day, pasta with zucchini blossoms, served with a pitcher of local wine. As soon as we'd eaten, Buddy paid the bill, eager to return. We took a shortcut up a side street and came upon a very overweight woman seated outside her doorway in a plastic chair. She held a deck of cards in one hand and a cigarette in the other. "Fortune, misters?"

I declined, but perhaps feeling the influence of the wine, Buddy agreed. "Sure. Why not?" The woman smiled and clutched the armrests of her chair, lifting her girth in a way that sent several saintly pendants swinging over her cleavage. One gold strand held a single red stone cut in the shape of a teardrop. She parted a beaded doorway. "Come in."

The room smelled of turmeric and sour bread and she indicated one side of a banquette for Buddy, while I was directed to a green plastic chair in the corner. "I read palm, tea, prism, or tarot…"

"Palm," Buddy said.

She nodded. "A perfect choice for men of action. And good price. Only four-hundred lira." Buddy smiled, pulling out his wallet like a sucker, letting the woman see all his cash. She counted the bills, and satisfied, pushed them through a slot in the wall, then gently placed Buddy's hand on a small red velvet cushion. She sat contemplating as if his palm held a magnificent map of treasure.

"Such lines…incredible!" A stream of horoscopic phrases began: "Much turmoil coming. A future with less anger and frustration…more opportunity. You must pare down excess. Avoid rash decisions. Or adversity will test forbearance. Trivial issues can distract. A structure for goals must be sought. Something rocky is pulling your freedom." Her comments were so abstract and general, that like astrology, could apply to anyone. I chided myself for not being more adept at escaping this room.

"Anything about love?" Buddy asked, and for a second Roberta flickered in my mind's eye. I imagined her taking care of business in Zurich.

The palm-reader focused with intensity, then shook her head from side to side. "The palms have gone silent. In love, tarot holds the key." For a moment Buddy's desperation startled. "Please. Tell me. I need to know."

"If you want to learn of love…tarot is the way." The woman's voice sounded sleepy, as if continuing to reveal additional information was to her, a fact of indifference.

"Please," Buddy said. "Read the tarot."

"Tarot is four hundred." The blankness of her round face was more infuriating than if she'd been scowling.

"But I already paid."

"For palm. Tarot is extra."

Buddy, ready to be bled once more, pulled his wallet out. Again, the woman confirmed the count, and stuffed the bills into the wall slot. She then reached under her seat and brought out a scrap of fabric from a shelf beneath the bench. After untying a deck of cards, she cut three times, her rings flashing. Buddy drew a trio: emperor, fool, and tower. A pink plastic calculator materialized. "Year born? Month? Day?" She punched his answers in. "Hour?"

"I don't know."

Her features puzzled. Using this minimal information, she calculated some kind of equation and announced herself to be the cipher for love's mystery. "Like your friend…" She motioned to me. "You like the familiar, but you also like variety…*no?*" Her sinister voice held the taint of swindle.

"Yes, but too much choice, and I get bewildered."

"Yes. *Bewildered!* Caught in the riddle of the animal. You like the familiar… but only a cup full…then what you want becomes too wild?"

"That's true."

"You live happy…but unhappy."

"Yes! How amazing!"

"Your children will be a great monument to your days."

"But I don't have kids." He stared at her with imbecilic trust.

The woman frowned, studied the cards, and then reshuffled, thick fingers flicking new cards, eyes wrapping back and forth like a plow. "Just wait…I see you as a father of great potency!"

From the sidelines, I longed to intervene against this yellow-hearted fraud. His wedding ring had clued her in on marriage, but how dare she prophesize children when his two chances had already been taken? She could only guess at the impossible marriage, a crazed wife reigning like a sovereign he longed to depose, a love so perverse it might be Stockholm syndrome.

"You'll travel across a body of water!" The voices of sarcasm sparred in my head. Oh, yeah? The sea? A river? That trickle under the little bridge by the village parking lot? Maybe the sewer pipe gurgling below the curb?

"An explosion will soon sever you from deep inside yourself."

A hydrogen bomb? A firecracker? Flatulence? My distrust could no longer be contained. "Buddy!" He looked at me, but failed to see how serious I'd grown. "The time has come for us to go."

The woman looked at me with eyes hot enough to scald milk. *"Signor,"* she said. "Weep not. The blood of nonbelievers is mixed, and even you, so holy, can't hide the Judas kiss."

Judas kiss? Mixed blood? How dare this viper try to turn the tables on me. My annoyance broke. "What you forecast is poppycock!" I said, in a baritone worthy of Pyrrho. "Fate can always be nudged with nonsense if people just plunk down four-hundred for swindle."

The large woman uncoiled like a cobra about to strike with venom to the face. "To question tarot, you show the devil his own face! The tarot knows! If a man has not suffered in the exact way *you* have suffered, you suspect, find condemnation and intolerance."

"Buddy, please! Let's get away from this horseshit!"

He glanced with uncertainty at the corpulent woman, showing both loyalty and helplessness. "You are welcome to stay," the woman said, unaffectedly lighting a cigarette. I employed pressure for the last time. "Buddy, wake up!" Lost in the yearning for someone to tell him that which he needed to hear, he ignored me, and ceded his remaining chance to exit.

• • •

Deciding not to return to the set, why put myself in the position of having to explain to Lydia that her husband's disappearance was due to the enchantment of an obese soothsayer, I moved along Levanto's least desirable backstreet, dreary, cramped buildings placed too close to the road and too far back for any sea-breeze or view. Headed for our village, once again I felt frustrated and angry at being caught in the middle of their oppressive marriage.

Climbing upward, the pavement was ridiculously cold and the dense shade only made it worse. To warm myself I increased my pace, and at the upper roadway, saw the sky had darkened, a gentle drizzle already falling. Mountain climbers often die pushing on in conditions best avoided or waited out, and while this was hardly Mount Everest, I paused at the familiar bus shelter. Though chilled, my climb's exertion still brought sweat to my face and neck. I pressed a jacket sleeve against my wet brow.

In the misty rain, the familiar old apartment house glowed, and I moved to stand before its hedge of wet oleander, inhaling their apricot perfume. To my astonishment, the window where I'd once seen the woman bathe her children, was warmly lit, she herself visible through a scrim of mist and shower-steam fine as smoke. From this distance, the woman's skin appeared golden warm, and she became a moving sculpture, hand rising with a damp washcloth along her long neck and clavicle, anything shivery or forbidden dissolved in the atmospheric vapor. She unfastened her hair, then re-arranged it, the bobby pins bitten open and pushed back into place. Her figure turned and the light shut off, the frame empty, its picture stolen just like that.

Abandoning hope for the bus, I walked on, raindrops splashing my eyelids. A strange rapture, mixed with sensual freedom, suddenly surged through me, as long-held memories and dreams seemed to break apart and purge away. Like Roberta, I was also eager to abandon the past, the murkiness, the ache of misery, the longing for what could be known only in absence.

. . .

I sat up with insomnia once more, waiting for my friend the neighboring dog to sound his familiar three barks. Again, I pondered the woman in the window, and how that ache was an unrequited event, like spying a beautiful stranger, perhaps changing planes at an unfamiliar airport—Shannon—Bangkok—Nairobi—a stunning stranger in a soft raincoat whose beauty and manner you instantly fall in love with, only in a split-second to lose them among the throng of boarding passengers. Years and years later, you still think of that stranger, and of how exhilarating that love might've been, if only you could've found each other. Such reality was now manifesting for me in the full-rounded care of Roberta's touch.

In the morning, too restless to edit manuscripts, I wandered over and entered her empty house, staring up at the fresco in the unheated foyer. I was in an impulsive mood, and employed Signor Vescovi to help secure a ladder. He held it steady as I climbed the rungs, then gently handed me some soft cloths and a pail of clear water.

Once my balance was certain, he, cautioning me not to fall, went to turn on an electric heater. "I've never before seen a cold spell of this duration in Summer," he said.

"Cold or no cold, if Eligio can clean frescos…so can I!" Gingerly, I took the first swipe at the painting on the chilly plaster wall.

Vescovi stayed close, recounting his morning trip to town. "People lately talk of little but the losses inflicted on their livelihoods by the weather …lost crops, a stunted tourist season. But today, everywhere I go, the cooking show is the topic of discussion. The Milan newspaper says millions are set to tune in!"

"Millions? But that's crazy!"

"Most seemed to be fascinated."

"Do they appear excited?"

"Beyond excited. They've already seen the ads showing the streets and byways they know so well. Seeing their own faces or faces of those they know is an astonishment. Television somehow validates them."

"I saw that first-hand during the filming. They huddled at restaurant tables in the cold air, their daily lives gaining significance by having their likeness pulled through a lens—to be captured, framed, electronically preserved."

Our attention returned to the fresco: fourteen by fourteen feet, and dingy with age-old grime. I continued to wipe and after many strokes was delighted to see the leaves of a tree begin to brighten. Soon a rhythm developed, the routine of moving big muscles to work through my chill.

Over the next few days Vescovi would arrive after breakfast to steady my ladder as I went up or came down, and I'd clean for an hour, or until my arms were tired. I'd then go home and edit manuscripts. Wherever I was working, Pina brought pots of hot tea, and she seemed to have mellowed toward Vescovi, perhaps by our collaboration on the fresco. The hardest evidence for this was in her inclusion of an extra clean teacup on my tray for him. He and I drank sitting by the heater, or in the kitchen looking out over Roberta's terrace.

Section by section the fresco began to reveal itself, the brightening olive groves, beehives, and mules loaded with jugs of oil, their bold, clear colors traveling back through centuries of dulling. Vescovi stood guard, whenever I had to lean my body out to reach some dark image, restoring color to the indented parapet or rounded tower of Levanto's ancient castle. In one corner, a snake appeared sunning on a rock beside a half-domed chapel, its roof cut away to show a mosaic ceiling, all of it growing sharper and more intense. Cleaning the final portions of fresco demanded more breaks, and I wiped my face on a warm, damp cloth just to manage the task.

. . .

One morning, during an early break, I stood alone on the terrace, and glanced down the valley toward the goats. There, as if in answer to my prayers, the orange Bentley could be seen climbing around a bend. I ran through the village in my socks to meet the car. In the parking lot, Roberta pulled in and leapt out. We embraced not letting go. "Welcome home," I whispered. She held me tight. "What a relief to find you here."

Vescovi's sharp eye had also spotted the orange car, and after bowing, he was already reaching for her bags. We followed him down through the village in our well-worn routine. At the house, he and I brought her inside and proudly showed off the clean fresco. She stood before the vibrant sections I'd worked so hard on and was transfixed. I couldn't help but grin. "You taught me big muscle activity can help alleviate anxiety and worry."

We went out to the courtyard to show how well her blooms were surviving the chilly climate; the roses, from days of cool shade, seemed brighter than any of us had ever seen them, petals shimmering against the edges of cut-stone paving. Roberta waved up at Pina, who was by the upstairs window. She nodded and bowed curtly, her *incoscienza* prideful, trying to avoid the way so many other people went overboard in their emotional comings and goings.

We took lunch in the kitchen just like old times, Roberta spooning sauce from a dish of thinly sliced potatoes baked in cream. As we ate, Roberta filled me in on happenings in Zurich. "Hans and I waded through our suite of parlor games, and it's with the lawyers now. Our end is definite. I'm already moving on. Whenever I'm standing at an elevator or waiting for an egg to boil, I instruct myself to list all the attractive and benevolent qualities Hans brought to my life. If I can think the best of him, I hope to be free."

By afternoon, the cold that had plagued us for so many days began to shift aside, a long-awaited warmth returning. We lingered over coffee then returned to the foyer, once more studying the fresco, astonished by the difference between the cleaned sections and those still mired in dirt.

"It's not the best, is it?"

"No," I agreed. "But it did survive all the wars." We continued to look at it, noting the awkward proportions on the legs of a strangely formed ox.

"It's really pretty awful…isn't it?"

"Yes, afraid so…the darkness actually helped it."

"The sands of time don't necessarily honor only what's great."

We laughed for the first time in weeks, and at Roberta's suggestion, decided to take a siesta. The bed was now miraculously dressed as if Pina had comprehended fresh bed-linen might soon be needed. Between the crisp sheets, the ruby chandelier bathing the room in the pink fire of afternoon, we made love. Not willing to leave one another, and still damp with perspiration, we fell asleep in the warm bed.

. . .

By noon of the next day the mountain rocks began once more to bake in the sun, and as if to play a joke on us, the mercury suddenly bolted sharply to the red. On the second day the earth began to radiate, as if something molten from deep within its core were erupting. Pina went down into the garden, turned the hose taps on and watered the roots of fruit trees. Later, in the courtyard, she pulled and pulled on the rickety clothesline strung across the garden, its plastic now so soft that the metal wheel was hindered. She then placed clothespins on the limp sheets and pillowcases and left the linen to hang as listless as the sails of the ancient mariner's ship.

None of us could fathom the change in temperature. Days ago, our teeth had chattered from shivering, and now the heat made work difficult. Once more Pina left tea, only cold pitchers to keep us refreshed and hydrated. And for lunch we shifted back to warmer-weather foods. Signor Vescovi brought provisions up from town, shirt drenched in sweat, noting: "So much sun now, even the fish are getting freckles."

At the end of the week our anticipation began to mount as the premiere of *Cooking Magic* was scheduled to launch on Saturday.

"So, the big night is approaching," I said. "What's the mood in town?"

"It seems as if all the entire Riviera knows—and everyone is fired with wonder. They talk of little else."

According to the paper, a grand premier had been planned in Genoa, but in all the hustle and bustle no one had thought to invite us, and by the time they did think of it, Roberta and I decided we were just as happy to have each other to ourselves. We did however look forward to seeing the reactions of our local citizens, and at nine p.m., at a hotel bar set a block back from the beach, we sat together to watch the airing of the first episode.

The event turned out to be a television presentation of absurd, but unusually entertaining quality. The absurdity actually worked in Lydia's favor to overcome the seriousness of an American thinking she could poach cooking from Italians.

As Buddy predicted, its odd but familiar fragments dovetailed together, and the music of the theme song brought elegance. Lydia's market arrival by limousine, with the score's dramatic orchestration, elevated her bugle beaded dress, as it did with the rest of her regal wardrobe. The images we'd seen in the cutting room were spliced together in such a way to suggest the camera trailed Lydia not by technical planning and design, but by desire. Because the market had been staged before actually opening, workers pulled from bed an hour earlier than usual, the hall was unnaturally empty, the long-shots conveying the hush and respect of a cathedral. In that quiet, even the most dismissive vendor had their gaze subjugated, and we noted how the editor turned out to be worth her salt—having spliced the images of people's eyes in such a way as to always have them appear fascinated by Lydia.

As Buddy predicted, even the banal phrases and sequences had been interwoven to make a whole, with shots of the purveyors offering pre-arranged delicacies. Wherever she went, treasures were brought forth to be tucked among her purchases: bunches of fresh purslane, radicchio, small scallops, and raw chocolate, all saved for buyers of discernment, all angles slanted to suggest Lydia as truly magnetic and arresting, with a palate refined enough to earn such prizes. One vendor looked straight at the lens to convincingly say the words assigned to him. "Glamorous women, like good wine, are worth cultivating."

In the studio, the youthful hands mixed herbs in the bowl, keeping their secret of belonging to the assistant. The large fish was pulled from the hot oven perfectly cooked, to be accompanied by olives, onions, and roasted red peppers served as the tempting tapenade. Between each sequenced interval the whole frame spun, as a roulette wheel spins, but instead of red and black numbers, the imagery tempted gamblers to bet on a cornucopia of food.

In the closing segment, Lydia appeared in a gown of blue velvet—and after slaving in a steamy kitchen—who wouldn't want enough energy left to dress like a courtesan—moving gracefully to uncork wine and light slender candles, all one's tempting labors mouthwateringly sprayed by stagehands with glycerin to retain their shine for the camera. Even the gnocchi and the sprigs of asparagus were artfully arranged and brushed with dye to look greener than in real-life. For dessert, a single poached pear swimming on a plate of the finest melted chocolate, appeared in Lydia's hands, courtesy of the editor, the shot with the plate cut in to suggest the sweet treats of life arrived as if by *magic*.

· · ·

Vescovi stood on Roberta's terrace and gave a report on how the town was taking last night's program. "They especially enjoy the faces Pina makes behind the back of the American thief. A majority of the women say their own cooking is much better. Most speak of the ridiculous clothes. Some wonder how the publicity will affect the region."

I noticed that Pina was listening to him from an upstairs window, and seeing me look, her face grew lost in its work, the rickety laundry line rudely pulled, pausing only to snap clothespins off the sun-bleached linen still too full of heat to fold.

A few days later, the sound of a shutter banging woke us from the sleep of another warm *siesta*. It turned out to be someone knocking on the chamber door. Pina's voice could be heard. She was calling in a fever-pitch: *"Signora! Pronto Soccorso, Ospedale. Ospedale!"*

I slid on my boxers and opened. Pina marched right past me, crossed to the bed and handed Roberta a slip of paper. She jabbered on making wild, circular motions beside her ear. In spindly blue ink, the address and number of a Genovese hospital were written. We dialed and soon learned it was Buddy who lay in the hospital. Apparently, he'd suffered some kind of head trauma. Within minutes we were dressed, and still holding the scrap of paper, speeding up the highway along the coast toward Genoa. At the hospital, the atmosphere appeared surprisingly jovial, if a bit chaotic. In all the commotion, it was difficult to know who was a physician, a visitor, or a patient. At the entranceway, we passed two men tersely discussing the merits of alcohol, while a woman sat in a gold vinyl lounge chair nearby holding her stomach, intermittently screaming at the top of her voice: *"Aiuta mi!"* Some nurses leaned over the reception desk, laughing at a comic book, and one of them still giggling, casually directed us to the hallway of the *Americano* with 'the problem skull.'

Buddy's door stood ajar, a curtain blocking our view. Through a gap, we saw him lying naked, head thickly bandaged. We pulled the curtain back and entered. A state of shock descended, for on the other side, sitting fretfully on a chair in the corner, Eligio was found.

"What are *you* doing here?" Roberta asked.

The skin on Buddy's body was slick with sweat and I pulled the sheet to cover him. His eyes opened. *"Gira testa,"* he said in a faint voice.

"The injury makes concentration difficult," Eligio said. "It's dizziness. And on top of it, we can't reach Lydia. She's off cooking somewhere. Message after message spoken to a phone machine."

"But what are you doing here?" Roberta asked again.

He looked stunned. "I was with him, we were riding mopeds." The memory of my infatuation and our hike returned with excruciating regret. How could I have been so ridiculously smitten? Was Roberta experiencing a similar confoundedness?

"I can't believe how warm this place is," I said.

"The air-conditioner is broken."

A somewhat sturdy female doctor entered, and we introduced ourselves. Roberta, in her impeccable Italian, asked about a prognosis. The doctor answered in English, charmingly melodic. "He has concussion. Eighteen stitches to close the wound!"

Eligio hit his fist into his palm. "We were attacked."

The doctor, having already heard the story, was less interested in crime than in studying the CT scan. Roberta turned to Eligio. "Attacked? How? By whom?"

"I'm trying to tell you! Boys outside the city…they hit him with a pipe. By the time the ambulance came, he was already blacked out."

The doctor interceded. "Vicious youths can be found anywhere nowadays. You know boys…their minds…at fifteen, sixteen…with that age the brain still soft like a cheese." Her pager sounded, and she grimaced. Before departing, she insisted Buddy be taken for a Doppler. "When he returns, it's important that you keep him awake."

Two orderlies arrived, unlocked the gurney, and while wheeling him out gave us thumbs-up signs. Eligio, not knowing what to do, and probably not wanting to stay in the room with us, followed the procession like a loyal hunting dog. Roberta and I watched until the elevator closed. A feeling of life's consequences fell over us. We agreed Buddy was lucky to be alive.

An hour later, the gurney had been wheeled back and repositioned inside the cubicle. Eligio was still obediently at bedside and he startled when Buddy moaned, "It's so hot." In frustration, Buddy kicked the bedclothes off, his full nakedness once more on display. Eligio reached over and mopped his brow. "They're working to fix the air-cooling system."

Roberta now pulled the sheet up. "How do we contact Lydia?"

"I left another message…said to the office this was urgent. No one knows where she is. All they say is tomorrow she's scheduled to make sausage with sage." Eligio gently patted Buddy's cheeks to keep him awake.

"Tell us about the attack."

"*Finally!*" he said in an indignant voice. "At last, I am permitted to speak!"

We stared at him with a kind of astonishment and he calmed down. "Okay, so, there I was helping Mama in her garden…wheeling a bag of compost to her border…when Buddy rings up. He asks where there might be a good place to rent a moped. He said he was nervous…wondered if I might be willing to ride along. He claimed to get lost on his own. So, I agreed to show him Genoa. He comes up by train, and at a good price, we rent him a bike from the man at the petrol station down in the valley. All goes well. We ride to Genoa and tour the city. But by afternoon the hills and the unrelenting heat exhaust us. So, we ride outside of town to a flat area, an industrial zone, with many abandoned buildings. At some point we hopped off the bikes for a break, sitting in some long-forgotten square. It was an abandoned lot with what must have been a lovely pond, now overgrown with vines and weeds. Behind us, among some trees, a scaffold rose, around a building set to be demolished. We sat below."

Buddy's eyes opened and I saw his pupils were dilated. His glance turned toward Eligio. "Our bird friends watched us—didn't they?"

"Yes, yes they did." Eligio poured a glass half full of water and held it to Buddy's lips, waiting for him to take a sip. His gentle manner suggested he'd make a good nurse. "Buddy is correct, we did watch the birds, and at some point, I said we ought to plan a trip to take Mama to La Spezia. Oh! Ha-ha! That reminds me. I must tell you. Mama *loved* the cooking show! She adores poached fish. You know, she told me she dreams herself of what it must be like to cook on television. Do you think we might introduce her to Lydia?"

"Now's not the time," Roberta said.

"No! No! Of course. Not now! The paper said more viewers watched than could be imagined."

"Yes."

"Imagine how such popularity must feel!"

"We didn't come here to discuss the cooking show," Roberta waved her hand dismissively.

"No! No! But still…if there might be a chance for Mama to be on the program? How wonderful. I mean, she should be permitted to meet before other women start lining up. Tell her, Walker! Mama is a great cook, *no*?"

"Yes," I said. "The best in all of Italy. And she gives haircuts too. But right now, we need facts about what happened."

Eligio looked disappointed, his lower lip hanging petulantly. "Okay…so… Buddy and I watch the birds, and then we look up to find a gang of angry youths sits above us on the scaffold. They shout *'Bochinaro, Bochinaro!'*"

"Bochinaro?" Roberta asked.

"Faggot," Eligio said. "I know they intended these words for us…and I thought, *this* can't be happening. Our mopeds only yards away! But it's easier for one man to run than two. Our feet hold heavy like cement. I decide I must speak to the boys with great fortitude. To show a true strength. I decide it might hold them off if I mention family matters. I mean hoping to confuse them. So, I call up to them, the first thing that comes to mind: 'He's my cousin!' I say. 'His father just died! Have you no respect?' In anger, I wave my fist to dismiss them. And oh! Yes! Oh, yes! Puzzle my words those boys do! Suddenly these scrawny mutts are not so certain! To save face, a skinny one yells out that our grief ought to be taken to a cemetery. In the space of that sentence, I speak strongly and tell Buddy: 'Run for the bikes!'

"Infuriated, the boys begin to climb down the scaffolding. 'Liars!' they scream. *'Frocione!'* But we are getting onto the bikes with success! As we pull away one of those dogs picks up a length of pipe. The sorry creature hurls it like a javelin. It hits Buddy right above the eye. He loses control of his bike…blood suddenly pouring. But danger can make one desperate, and in a miracle, he corrects his steering and races away. I follow, turning to look only once, the boys are running now, scared and scattering like the boys who killed Pasolini must have run. Running to avoid arrest.

"We continue on until we feel safe enough to stop. Blood is all over Buddy's face from the wind and the ride. In my rucksack, I find napkins to put pressure on, then take off my tee-shirt and wrap him, ear to ear. A woman from a nearby building sees us from her balcony. It is she who calls police and the ambulance."

Buddy stirred. "Our mopeds…where are our mopeds?"

"Don't worry, friend. A decent guy in a passing grocery truck took them to Chiavari. He went many kilometers out of his way. I called the petrol man about your rental and they have already gone to Mama's to pick it up."

Reassured, Buddy closed his eyes once more. None of us saw the doctor return. "Please," she scolded from the doorway. "You are supposed to keep him awake." Eligio's mouth stretched wide with the furious look of a man falsely accused. "But I have been doing all I can."

The doctor took no notice. "Also please, not so many friends at once. Take turns."

Roberta nodded. "That ought to be easy for us."

· · ·

At a nearby panini restaurant, Roberta and I sat and discussed how we might locate Lydia. "What if it were one of *us* lying there?"

Roberta turned to the window. "That thought is more than I can handle."

Our sandwiches came, and we chewed in silence. Something besides the chaos of Buddy's ordeal seemed to be causing us to feel ill-at-ease. "Can I admit something," Roberta said. "I find it excruciatingly embarrassing to be forced back into Eligio's proximity."

"Me too. Couldn't he have found some other friend to get attacked with? And I keep wondering how on earth could I have ever written a poem to him? A concupiscent poem no less, expressing the sentimental stench of Cupid."

"Ha! But I feel shame too, imagining I myself could be his *only* valentine!"

In the hospital lobby, we passed the gift shop, a weekly television programming publication centered in the window, Lydia's face on the cover. "She's everywhere!"

Behind the counter, the clerk proudly held up her personal copy. She excitedly told us the featured star had just autographed it. "I've not caught my breath!"

"You mean she's been here?"

"Not ten minutes ago!"

In the corridor outside Buddy's room, nurses and aides could suddenly be found loitering nearby. We realized their aim was to catch a glimpse of the American star who cooked the big fish on television. Beyond the doorway, the curtain hung slightly to one side, and we could hear Lydia's nasal inflection. Roberta and I too paused to listen with the other eavesdroppers.

"He's not a beetle! He's a rat!"

Buddy's reply was barely audible. "But how can you? If you fire him, you'll need someone to take his place?"

Apparently mounting success as a culinary personality had granted Lydia some kind of new veto power. It surprised us to hear that she expressed no concern for Buddy's injury, or its consequence, but was instead describing her own travails with the cooking show.

We pulled the curtain aside, and Lydia jumped back with over-animated surprise. "Oh, goodness me! Look who's here! They said you'd gone to eat!" She hugged us. "Oh, how can this be possible? I turn my back five minutes, and he goes falling into the jam pot."

"Where's Eligio?"

"Haven't seen him. A nurse said he went downstairs to meet his mother." Tears filled her eyes, and she dabbed a tissue at her eyeliner. "Oh, how I hate being at the mercy of these Italian hospitals. I mean, can we engage them in serious medical talk?" Buddy gave a low moan. "Oh, please don't make those sounds," she said. "Stop it, please! Don't you see I need you to be strong? It's not helpful at all if you start sounding like you're all set for a coffin! With so much change happening," she said to us. "Change that will affect the rest of our lives."

"Change?" Buddy's voice was weak with distress. "You can't fire Beetle until I'm well."

"I can't wait for you to be well. I need you to first be one-hundred-percent. This was urgent."

"What are you up to? Please. I can take it."

"Always in a hurry! All right, then, if you can't wait. My big news has nothing to do with firing Garafallou." She gestured to us. "Roberta…Walker, you may as well hear this too. I'll tell all of you at the same time." She paused for dramatic effect. "Behold, I bring you glad tidings." Our mouths opened with disbelief.

Roberta spoke first. "You're expecting?"

"Yes! Blame it on Italy…the wine…that damn moonlight!"

Buddy looked astounded. "You mean now…after all we've been through?"

Lydia assured him it was true. He tried to speak, but his voice failed. "Take it easy, big boy. Hold your horses."

"My horses…can't…"

I decided to speak just to keep Buddy from trying. "Lydia…I'm stunned. How incredible!"

Buddy's voice forced a growl. "Oh, God…now I have to heal."

The doctor appeared and nodded at us with a professional manner. She went to Buddy. "The tests are returning good result."

"Please," Buddy gasped. "Release me. You needn't worry…my wife has come. She'll take charge…see…kit-and-caboodle! Oh, let me introduce…she's going to have our baby."

The doctor made delighted sounds and gave congratulations. "Now I must work extra hard," she said. "Your husband has suffered a nasty concussion. There's still one brain scan, the MRI, that's most important. He must stay overnight."

Lydia crossed her arms and looked straight at the doctor. "The people at my television station say Gemelli is the best. They say I should insist he be flown there. They say that's where the Pope goes. We need to transfer there for a second opinion, just to be sure."

The doctor appeared startled and her voice grew curt. "He can't be moved to another city. I don't advise it."

"But if the Pope goes there—"

"Your husband is *not* the Pope."

"I can go," Buddy said. "Look, I'm already stronger."

The doctor then diplomatically conceded that his wife, of course wanted what was best. But it was too soon for a move.

"Let me get dressed. I'll check out. I'm happy to heal…heal *really* fast." His voice ran out of strength. His head slumped back on the pillow.

"You see. He's not ready." The doctor's pager sounded again. "I must go." She went out the door, offering Lydia a few additional congratulations, this time more subdued.

After she was gone, Lydia lowered her voice. "That doctor has me worried. You know I'm not the kind to just toss off medical stuff, but what'll happen if he gets worse? And why is this hospital so damned hot!"

"The air conditioning is broken."

"See this place can't be trusted. If anything goes wrong, I'd never forgive myself." In strangely counter-intuitive movements, she extracted a tube of lipstick and a compact from her handbag. "He could die of heat stroke in this oven." Utilizing the mirror over Buddy's sink, she re-drew the red lines of lipstick perfectly. "Everyone says Gemelli is the place. If need be, I'll fly him to Rome myself!"

"We've seen the wound," Roberta said. "It's deep. It will require full-time care. He probably shouldn't fly right now."

"I can go," Buddy said, eyes flickering. "I just need a bit…more rest."

Lydia pouted and used her pinky to swipe the edge of her lipstick just as a nurse put her head around the curtain. "You must be tired. Why don't you take a break. We have an espresso counter at the end of the hall. It is delicious."

"Thank you. We'll check it out."

"I saw your show the other night. You were fantastic!"

"Thank you."

• • •

In the lower hallway, we drank our espresso as more nurses and other staff kept stopping with the sudden urge for a coffee themselves, peeking with awe at Lydia, offering inquiring smiles. Lydia basked in the attention. We eventually moved on and found an empty lounge and took some chairs. Roberta and I stared at the green marble floor, listening as Lydia narrated her recent life. "Just back from Stuttgart, signing contracts for a German version of the show.

Imagine, my voice is going to be dubbed—Fräulein Lydia! Yesterday, mind you now, I'm expecting. Morning sickness. Had to drag my ass out of bed to get the plane for Cristoforo Colombo—which was late. Then last evening, I posed for a photo session here in Genoa…drank an entire magnum of champagne with the photographer, shooting with dozens of white lights in a park under an Araucaria tree. This morning? Sick as a cat. A raging migraine. The car service came to take me back to Levanto, and I'm telling you, I had the most eerie feeling. Like a voice in my head. It said: '*Call him one last time.*' So back into the hotel I go, this weird force directing me. Finally, at last: '*Pronto!*' Pina in her crazy Italian picks up. Thank heavens I understand more than I used to. But through no small miracle the hotel manager came by and I got him to help translate. The old bat gave him the news. When I get back, she'll probably want a raise, or to discuss a new contract! Thank God I hadn't left Genoa yet. And I still can't bear to think of what could've happened. And now with our accelerated production schedule on top of it." She pulled the television magazine out of her bag. "Did you see this? I'm on the cover!"

"Yes, downstairs. The gift-shop window."

"This joint is so out of date they don't sell it. I had to give them some."

"The woman behind the counter was over the moon."

"Really? Well, maybe now they'll start carrying the damn thing. Look, I can't thank you enough for coming. And I gotta also thank Eligio. I mean, thank goodness he was there to bring him in. The truth is, lately Buddy can't be left unattended, or he gets into trouble." Lydia paused, suddenly preoccupied, staring down at the elevator banks. Eligio, as if hearing his name had just stepped off and was walking down the hallway toward us, an insulated food bag at his side. His brow wrinkled when he saw Lydia. Like a child, he pouted sympathy toward her.

Lydia's eyes narrowed and she spoke with distraction. "Buddy has that same shirt." I saw she was right, only then noticing Eligio was indeed wearing, worse for wear, the blue shirt Buddy had worn to lunch at Santa Clara. "Buddy has the same shirt," Lydia repeated, as a way of greeting Eligio.

"Yes, this is his. Sadly, it got very dirty." He held up the bag. "Mama just brought me a fresh one. I'm going to change."

Lydia's expression froze. The idea of Buddy's blue shirt being worn by another body, collar open, armpits damp, launched something unpleasant.

"Mama, almost had a fit just now when she saw it. She was dying to remove it at once so she could find a laundry. She is still waiting downstairs with the car."

Lydia looked stricken, imagining something which she really shouldn't. Yet apparently there was something in it that she *did* want. The infamous shirt brought opportunity. Incomprehensible opportunity. Eligio took no notice, but Roberta and I, like two farmers watching a twister form across a field, saw it develop.

"I'm so glad you're here," Eligio said. "We left message after message. They said you were cooking sausage with sage." We began to walk back to Buddy's room together as a group. "I really should go back down to tell Mama to park. I want her to meet you. She loved your show. It will be so nice for her to meet you!"

"Don't you want to see Buddy first?" Behind Lydia's smile, I could see the blue fabric was figuring a strange calculation into place. I knew her scheming too well, this would be an equation with its own private solution. A garment transferred from one body to another. Buddy's newfound interest in clothes. Moped riding. Could it indeed be? Chance and all its chaos allowed a convenient plot to bloom doubt in her mind. The pretext, the very excuse she'd been hoping for, without even really knowing it.

Her manufactured emotions shifted toward discomposure. Her right eyebrow arched with fierce intimation and already I sensed a high artificial drama forming; faces were about to be slapped, eyes gouged out, someone's tongue torn from its jawbone. I watched as the incredulity of her compressed moral burn heightened to living theater. Only I, or a geologist versed in plate tectonics, could comprehend it. We entered Buddy's room and the curtain rose on act one.

"Buddy, wake up." Her voice moved to a higher pitch. "Do you want to tell me what's going on?"

Buddy opened his lazy eyes and bewilderment crossed his face. "What's going on?"

"Well, mister? Why is that jerk wearing your shirt?"

"Jerk?" Buddy's voice was soft. "Why…his was covered in blood…my blood." Lydia looked down at the floor and tapped her foot. Maybe her recent success and the hangover from yesterday's champagne was adding fuel to her fire?

"His shirt was used as a compress. The emergency room threw it away. We have to buy him a new one."

Some misunderstandings resolve, others detonate. Here, the traded shirts pulled the pin on a grenade canceling all our previous lives. "That third-class prick will fuck anything," she said.

Buddy stared, blinked, then glanced desperately over to us. In the best of times, the idea of cheating is never good news for a married spouse, but Lydia's irrational and suspect calculation brought increasing emotion to burn. From the doorway, Eligio also stared. "What are you saying?"

Buddy turned to Eligio. "Gee...I'm sorry," he whispered.

"Don't you dare apologize to *him!*"

Buddy tried to lift himself onto one elbow but fell back. His glance turned back to us. "I think there's a misunderstanding—she has something wrong."

"You fool! Don't you get that as your wife...*I'm* the one who deserves the apology?" The notion that Lydia might resemble Anna Magnani came back to me. I saw it more than ever, her face flashing with emotion, like she might find a hammer and start pounding nails.

"You're a ridiculous woman," Eligio said from the doorway. "Too much—by half!" His mouth remained open in outrage. Indignantly, he held up the insulated bag. "See this? Mama drove all the way from Chiavari to bring food. Let us forget all this."

"Not on your life!"

"So, consider for a moment maybe? Your husband has feelings too? And I saved your husband's life, and stay here as a friend, and bring *homemade food.*"

"Buddy will only eat what I, or the hospital brings. Indigestion now could kill him."

"Mama's food does not cause indigestion"

"Oh, please. This whole conversation is so degrading! You think I'll just stand by for your nonsense?"

"Stand for what? Mama's cooking is the best. Better than yours. You stand over a simmering pot cooking pasta on television in a fine dress...but you wouldn't know what good is if it came and bit you on your seat!"

Lydia turned her venom toward Buddy. "Do you hear how he speaks? He shows no respect for me or for you!"

In frustration, Eligio's free hand balled into a fist. "Woman...you are a *crazy* one! I saved the life of your husband. Are you too stupid to see that? You should be grateful he didn't die!"

"Screw you!"

"Hospitals are no place for this nonsense." I said, standing up. But it was too late, Eligio had already turned and went heading down the hall. Roberta and I caught up with him, where he stood by the elevator rocking back and forth on his heels. "Crazy...crazy! She is crazy! We are not on trial."

The elevator doors opened to reveal a chubby fellow inside wearing the blue uniform of an air-conditioner repair company. Eligio got on, the quilted food bag swinging at his side. "Please, don't go," I said. "Buddy needs you."

I saw him try to reckon some kind of deformed loyalty, but knighthood's sword had already been drawn to defend his mother's cooking, and too many acts of gallantry were known to be costly. In that moment, he wisely reckoned the price was un-payable. Before any further peacemaking could begin, the elevator doors shut, carrying Eligio down to the lobby.

"What do we do?"

Roberta looked puzzled. "We should make sure Buddy is okay. Then get the hell out of here ourselves." In the unbearably hot hospital, we swam like fish trapped in a heated aquarium back up the hallway to Buddy's room. We entered, wanting nothing more than to swim for cooler waters, but found Lydia still chewing Buddy out.

"How could you?"

"How could I what?"

I finally stepped forward and tried to intercede. "If we could all just calm down, I'm sure we can work this out."

"You're a fine one to tell me what to do, Walker. You fell for the same hustle, and you too Roberta!"

The sound of my name reddened my face, instantly pulling me back in time, remembering how I used to imagine stacking gray metal boxes in my brain to safeguard against my older cousin's invasion of my inner thoughts and feelings. "Stop these accusations," I said. "He can't handle this."

Buddy propped himself onto one elbow. "Did you take your pills today?"

"Don't you dare ask that! You're only trying to gaslight me in public!"

"Stop it!" I said. "I see what you're doing. This is one of your schemes."

Buddy echoed weakly. "Yes. Please stop."

"Schemes! He's the one lying naked and broken in this inferno. He who has everything to lose!" She turned to Buddy. "How could you all let yourself be undone by a jackass? A gigolo who stands to lose nothing!"

The improbable ugliness of her attack sank into my bones. I reevaluated Buddy's carnal appetite and saw how Lydia had become a woman erecting a massive guillotine of falsehood to chop away her husband's head. "Stop." Buddy whispered in quiet desperation.

"Good God, woman." Roberta said. "Can't you see he's at a breaking point?"

"Fuck off, you snooty bitch. I'll say whatever I like! He's my husband. You think I don't get it? That I'm too stupid to see? That slick Italian leaves you all branded with his conman's pride!"

Buddy began to cry. "Please…don't you…I hurt."

"Oh you…oh-so tender! Well, if *you* suffer so much, then stop making *me* suffer! I know that guy's type. Whoring to conquer anyone stupid enough to play—or pay! Men. Women. Dogs! That's how these Italian cats measure their worth!"

Buddy looked like someone staked through the heart.

She continued to stomp. "You deny it to my face. You deny it just so I'll have your damn baby."

His tear-filled eyes looked up at Lydia, his whole nervous system seeming to catch up with the overwhelming forces of woundedness. "Lydia…please stop. You're sounding manic. Stop…please. If I lost you, I'd die."

Lydia's voice quickened, as if testing the rule of probability. She mocked his voice. "If I lost you—I'd die."

"It's our chance…a new beginning…" His voice choked.

"Go ahead, cry baby. Cry till the whole damn hospital hears you! Add another heaping helping to my humiliation!"

Roberta stepped forward. "All right, that's enough! Stop your shouting. It's better if you two discuss this alone. Walker and I are going to leave."

Lydia looked suddenly frantic, a dramatist with her theater in exit. She tried to compose herself. "Oh, dear…oh, dear…This is unfair. How could he drag you both into this."

"He didn't."

"He brought you up here."

"Please. All he did was ph-*o*-ne for help." For a split second, I heard for the first time, the rounded and supremely superlative tone of the Roedean "O." Laid onto Roberta's Oklahoma twang, it forced the notion of class and rank onto the situation. Lydia heard it too, and the sound of that absurd silk-stocking artifice was the thing that finally shut her up.

Saying goodbye proved difficult. We backed off the conflict, offering all the soothing platitudes and instructions that a hospital case requires, then we excused ourselves. At the nurse's station down the hall, a group of staff stood looking at the television magazine, the battling American wife still cooking on the cover.

Again, we waited for the elevator, and even with us in earshot the staff couldn't resist discussing the match. Their consensus seemed to be that whatever it was that Buddy was being accused of, his defense sounded weak. "Italian men grow more vigorous in denial," one woman said. Through what I imagined was based on Buddy's bleak lack of heaving, slapping or other masculine force, they deemed him guilty. We pushed the elevator button a second and third time, knowing the mistake the audience's perception was making.

How could anyone know how deeply a stranger's mind schemed? Still false accusations of sexual infidelity have served as an underhanded way for spurned spouses to win something for centuries. I began to see the reason behind this attack. Lydia intended to move on, not recognizing she was still performing like a fat teenager, grabbing for more than her share of the production company, and other assets. To satisfy the perpetual hunger of that adolescent pain, she needed *him* to be guilty.

* * *

Genoa, Italy

Almost a fortnight would pass before Roberta and I went to meet Garafallou in Genoa. We walked outside the train station along a row of evenly planted hornbeams, toward a trattoria we all knew well. Drinks were ordered and we perused the menu, all opting for the same thing: simple plates of spaghetti whisked with eggs and olive oil.

"The third episode ran last night. A tremendous audience! What did you think?"

"I wanted to hate it. But couldn't. She was wonderful—if limited."

"She makes good food look fun."

"And seems to be gaining confidence. Even Pina seems to be having a harder time upstaging her."

"It was wise to keep Pina on."

Garafallou laid all tact aside. "I'm sure you've heard Lydia has left Buddy." We nodded. "And no doubt, you've also heard I've been dismissed?" We nodded again. "But executive-producers who control fifty-one percent of the purse strings can't be so easily turned. For the moment, the producers have all agreed it's prudent to let the *chef de cuisine* revel in her mad powers. When the time comes, she'll discover my contract to be iron-clad. But the other investors, as well as the television distributors, are already fretting about their percentages and payouts…especially if she goes berserk. And they're worried about maintaining her image. So, Walker, they've asked me to come and deliver a message to you."

"Which is?"

"Already they're uncertain if Buddy, with his injury, can manage all that's required of a public husband. It's important that everything look normal—no marital trouble. To weigh the risks."

"For advertisers?"

"And potential advertisers. Household sponsors are suspicious of decadence and some already think there's too much glamour—that her clothes are too extravagant. Others say her humor is too irreverent. Their factories make nice, clean housewifely goods—pudding mixes, cooking sprays, floor waxes. It's a home-centered show—cooking with all that a hearth implies. Those who design the show have made it slicker, faster, more urgent, but certain sponsors feel it should work toward something less fast-paced, something more wholesome."

"So, the backers are nervous to find out what exactly has taken place?"

"Yes. Currently, Lydia shows up to tape segments of the show, but hardly speaks to anyone. Afterward, like a recluse, she immediately disappears. We hear she's accepted an invitation to stay at a villa in Rapallo, owned by an awful Belgian woman with a rich, moneymaking husband. The couple reign as a pair of social scavengers. They're hardly aristocrats, but like aristocrats they desire the social visibility delivered by hosting entertainment stars. And since they are piranhas, and don't know the bigger fish, to host even a burgeoning television star under their roof will do. They're what Stalin had in mind when he used to call people *ruthless cosmopolitans*! I give their hospitality a month…then to escape her they'll head off to Biarritz or the Bahamas, and say they must close the house."

"It's too bad the sponsors couldn't have filmed the scene in the hospital. It would play like Medea. Such real-life drama would tear the ratings through the roof."

"There are limits to what people will accept! Meanwhile the show is about to sign a licensing deal with an airline. In the sky, one has a perfectly captive audience. For airlines content must also be squeaky-clean, positively boring and family-rated. So, what, pray tell, can you as her cousin, tell me about what happened?"

"There's no reasoning with her when she's like this," I said. "She's made up her mind about something…I think she's wanted out for some time. If the two of them had some common purpose, work, politics, a hobby, that might save them. But they have *nothing* to fall back on."

Roberta spoke up. "Under these terrible circumstances the only hope was expecting the child."

Garafallou showed surprise. "A baby! Now? Really? Oh dear, that's bad timing."

"Use it for public relations!" Roberta said, with more than a hint of sarcasm. "Sell Buddy as a virile superman…a hyper-sexual husband and father. There are so many aftershaves or baby products that need endorsing!"

Garafallou looked intrigued. "And might a baby unify them?"

Roberta shrugged. "Children help couples sometimes. But they're just as likely to hinder."

Garafallou remained perplexed. "Bah! Knowing that a child is now involved, I think Buddy must've done something truly wretched to warrant this kind of wrath."

"You sound like the nurses at the hospital."

"Both of you were there, what did Buddy and Lydia say in there about his affair?"

"What do you mean *affair*? I resent the way Lydia's gossip and spin are being repeated as truth."

"I mean the thing with Eligio."

"We don't think there's been an affair."

"But Lydia claims he's cheated…that he's turned to men. She's despondent!"

"Walker and I suspect it's her bipolarity, or ADHD, or maybe a hellish host of other maladies. Whatever she takes the white pills for."

"Those mood swings. Grandiose and flagrant one moment—cruelly bitter the next."

"Pulling pre-baked dinners from an oven could make anyone crazy."

Garafallou pointed his finger at Roberta, as if to recognize a legitimate point. "You my dear, describe what may be an occupational hazard for televised cooks!"

I joined in. "Particularly those ignoring art, culture, accurate history, truthful science, or any other form of human intelligence."

Roberta refused to let him off the hook. "And you, Mr. Garafallou, are the one who produces this pap!"

He shrugged. "In our business, sometimes one has no choice but to defend the lowest denominator."

I agreed and dipped a crust of bread into a saucer of green olive oil. "What strikes me is how even in this modern age, the perception of an affair between two *men* is still enough to ruin lives."

"Men will say two women are hot. But have you ever heard a woman say that two men together are hot?"

Garafallou nodded. "Of course it's not news to discover that many men like to knock about a bit. We make no judgments. I lived for almost a decade in

England and saw every manner of upper and lower-class sexual escapade. Some British men donned frocks at any opportunity, while many women sported tweed trousers, ties, and vests! I've met eccentrics of every stripe. Lords and members of the House of Commons who spend their vacations in pin curls and opera pumps or trysting with boys in Morocco. Or they're chauffeured to the docks by limousine to pick up roughnecks—hoping to get a survivable beating! And afterwards, the majority will re-claim limp respectability with a wife!"

Roberta looked askance. "In Corsica, you claimed to have learned a lesson about nationalistic generalizations! Or should we sew up some harlequin pants for you to wear as a guide?"

Garafallou winced. "Hmmm."

Roberta was on a roll. "And let's not forget the wife, who in his lordship's absence, might sigh relief that he went *out* for sex rather than trying to hump *her* into the mattress?"

"Down girl! Down! You've gotten me! But may we at least consider the Anglo-fetishes I've mentioned might simply be due to the fact that the English are a sea-going people? Lots of *loneliness* at sea!"

"Lots of loneliness at home too, us poor women left to find our own pursuits?"

"Oh, by heavens! So, let her ladyship pay a master in a dungeon somewhere to assault her with clothespins. Why not?"

I couldn't resist joining the fray. "I wager that to get off—many *require* sex to be forbidden. And the religiously faithful have done a great deal for sex by constructing a sin out of it. I'll further wager that bad behavior is almost always more erotic than good."

Garafallou waved his hand. "And as the accusations against Buddy attest, perhaps none of us is who we say we are?"

"My God," Roberta said. "Can't you both see? She's simply tired of him. It annoys her to see he's gained a fat ass…that he wants credit for her success."

I nodded. "And he forever links her to a past she wants to forget—to Wormleysburg. His getting hit in the head with that pipe has become for her an unexpected poker chip. An escape clause. And now the poor guy seems like a man having a nervous breakdown. And I must admit—I feel for him."

"One thing Eligio said that is absolutely right. Hospital sickrooms are poor settings to confront suspicions of cheating."

Garafallou rubbed his chin. "Okay. Let me re-assemble this. You both say Eligio and Buddy were never paramours?"

"Not possible."

"It's absurd!"

"Buddy doesn't have that imaginative capacity."

"We heard him say over and over she was wrong. And we believe him."

"Buddy's too straightforward. He lacks guile."

"Maybe he was drunk? If it's not plausible, why would she even suggest it?"

"If he is fluid—he's not fluid enough! If some man-lust did transpire, he's the kind of guy who'd need to confess it."

"Maybe Eligio needed to prove something?"

"These claims have no legitimacy. And whatever Eligio's grotesqueries, he like Buddy, tends to pride himself on candor and sexual forthrightness."

"Exactly." Roberta agreed. "He might be self-deceptive, but he's no liar."

"So, you both say it's a falsehood then? Nothing went on between those two?"

I nodded. "Look, Buddy might be unchallenged in some fundamental human way, but if he is testing something, it's in the way that anyone might."

Roberta nodded. "Let's not forget, Lydia was the one who wanted us to keep him busy and out of her hair. In fact, it was she who suggested he go moped riding in the first place!"

Garafallou placed his hands on the table and leaned back. "If I am to understand this then, what you believe is that she *wants* him to have committed a breach?"

"*Needs* him to!"

"Then Lydia is no better than the hooligans throwing the pipe."

"She might be worse. She simply knows how to make her attack look like defense. Covert aggression. A classic cluster B pattern!"

Garafallou sipped his drink. "Let me step back a moment, I have to process. I guess none of these happenings need be the sword of Damocles. Yesterday, a wonderful street scene was shot—grapefruits and fondue exploited. And we also taped a beautiful scene on a boat preparing ceviche. In the new segments, Pina is restored to grant the viewers a counter-irritant and to grant sponsors some common grounding. She offers a series of finger-wagging gestures that she may not even realize are comic."

"The producers ought to recognize gossip is a form of publicity, right?"

"Speaking of producers, what do yours want from me?"

"Ah, Walker! Always a step ahead! Well, right now they worry. Lydia looks to be living on the edge and a brouhaha won't be tolerated. If marital trouble scorches paradise, they fear sponsors will run like lemmings."

"And what if, as a result of public scandal, toothpaste and tapioca start flying off the shelves?"

"Then even brothels are tolerable!"

"Well, we feel for Buddy. All he knows to do is beg forgiveness—or pathetically pray that she won't leave."

"As my family on Long Island used to say, too much virtue can hurt you."

"This can all be sanitized. How many of our viewers bow down before the marital shrine of wood and stone? Burned offerings left at the base of the vow, the spouse a false idol. We must promote the idea of true love." Garafallou took out his pocket watch. "Oh, goodness. Two-thirty already! And as a trio, we've solved none of the world's mysteries!"

Before departing, Garafallou directed his gaze at me. "My boy, the producers have implored that I deliver to you a message. Given their position, I can't refuse."

"I know what it is without you asking. They want me to pay a call on my cousin to try and persuade her to stop this nonsense."

"There again! Always a step ahead! Yes, the season premiere of *Cooking Magic* is for some, a huge financial risk. If for no other reason, the villa that the Belgian banker owns might be worth a look? No doubt there's a splendid garden, a pool." He handed a card with an address in Rapallo.

"Can you go tomorrow morning? I'll make sure Lydia knows you're coming, and that she's there to receive you."

"What makes you so sure she'll comply…let alone listen? After her attack at the hospital, I mean. Already I feel my nerves."

"She'll comply. Or the 51% will cancel her show."

Garafallou took out his camera. "Mind if I ask the waiter to take a picture of all of us for posterity?"

"Not on your life," Roberta said. "I'm also heading for divorce court myself. The last thing I need is a photo showing me with the two of *you*."

* * *

Rapallo, Italy

A house of excessive luxury is a fortress, and at the Belgian's villa multiple security cameras made sure their artichoke-embellished gates were well defended. The elaborate barricade parted its metal scrollwork electronically, and I felt my heartbeat quicken passing through. A path meandered between several ten-foot walls of yew hedging before the house and its impressive facade appeared, the inhabitants maybe hoping such grandness implied they could be mistaken for monarchs. A maid opened the door and led me into an antechamber of such gargantuan proportion that Palladio would have laughed.

Destruction of her personal life had delivered Lydia to this opulent setting, and she stood at the foot of a cut-stone staircase, as if the house were a piece of her heritage. A pale-blue, silk day-dress looked as icy as her double-air kiss, yet her perfume, a citrus and spice chemistry, was instantly identifiable. I suspected it to be almost the same as the one I'd bought so many years ago in Harrisburg at the fragrance counter of Bowman's. Could she have sprayed it on for remembrance? I thought about how Baldwin wrote that sentimentality could disguise the enjoyment of cruelty, and her current emotionality, with its furious assumptive aim of an easy divorce, was just that.

"Do you realize," Lydia said. "This is the first time we've spent alone since my arrival?"

"That can't be true."

"It is. Other people are always milling about."

Her comment suggested an exhaustive, long-owed bill was about to be presented for payment. In an adjoining sunroom, under a stained-glass dome, an elegant foldable table was set with china cups and plates. The maid brought hot water and tea was steeped. "Everyone has an idea about how I should proceed. The woman who owns this house is Belgian. She says find someone of my own to screw. My agent says divorce. You've probably come to say I should overlook and forgive."

"It's an option." I struggled to keep from showing any salesmanship. "Whatever it is, the two of you might benefit from sitting down to discuss it? Hire a marriage broker, if you must."

The tea was poured, a cup handed. "Walker, I've heard you say the things we do which can't be justified, often turn out to be our most important decisions."

"Did I? Well, all right…but maybe that's been taken out of context."

"No. It's been brought into context. This isn't the first time Buddy has strayed."

"Really?"

"I'm sure of it. He's always wanted to explore something. His need, and maybe yours too? To repair a hurt of some kind?"

It took me a moment to process her remark. I could feel myself grow more irritated. "Think about your career," I said. "You've worked at it all these years.

If you lambaste your husband in divorce, you might ruin your opportunities. It's very dangerous."

We looked out the window, and as if the heavens wanted to underscore my remark, a series of storm clouds came roiling across the horizon. Their rapidity, shadowing the garden, mesmerized us. "The newscasters say despite that cold spell it's now becoming the hottest Summer in history."

"Yes. Rain is badly needed. Do you remember…the clouds looked exactly that way the day we buried your mother."

To recall Mom's ghost, *della morte,* and mingle that with the spicy perfume was to imprint significance on the past. We sat and gazed toward the vastness of the darkening sky the way characters in an opera gaze across the footlights. I'd seen people grow emotional at dramatic vistas, eternity passing right before their very eyes, but it angered me that she was primed for such drama, pretending to be just that kind of oblique sentimentalist. She unfolded a lace handkerchief. "You won't admit it, or can't, but how you've wanted to put me in my place ever since I got here."

"Not so. Though you do seem intent to want to surface my collective horror. As if Mom's coffin were being brought up to lie exposed in a boggy cemetery."

"I didn't intend that," she said, blinking as she wiped her eyes. "But modern lives won't hold secrets."

"Perhaps. But literature has already served up all that's human ages ago. The writings of St. Augustine, Sappho, the Marquis de Sade, even Anne Frank."

Lydia took out a cigarette. "Buddy's chaos has built a shell around my heart. I've had to grow hard just to survive. Yet in your eyes, no matter what I say or do, you see me as a simple nincompoop."

"I've never used that word."

"You don't have to. You know damn well I've never read the memoirs of St. Augustine, or any of the others, and never will. But since we arrived, you've worked overtime to flaunt your smart brain. Yet, I make allowances for your intellectual put-downs because of your tender psyche. What you went through— pitiful face splashed all over the newspapers at such a young age."

"That's cruel. Yes, I've worked hard to educate myself. But I've not high-hatted you."

Lydia ignored my reply, which was infuriating. "I know why you're here," she said. "The producers think you can restore my happy private life for public viewing." Rain splashed at the window and the lights flickered. An edge shook her voice. "Once more, it's you, not me, who bypasses family loyalty."

There was something borrowed in what she said. Again, our words echoed to-and-fro, and came mimicking back, far from their intention when anyone first said them. "I don't know what that means…but it's not truthful."

"Oh, it's most true."

"You're being cruel. I know the accusations toward Buddy are much ado about nothing. Because I know you, and your scheming."

She studied my remark, any doubt as to my innocence revoked. "Look, why in God's name are you defending that SOB?"

The rain pounded the windows, the water streaming down the glass. On the patio, the dripping scalloped edges of an orange umbrella flipped up and down in a flag of warning, but the broach of feelings couldn't be stopped. "Lydia. You're hurting Buddy. And for good reason, he still loves you. Maybe we all still share some lost bond from our early days."

"Ho, ho, ho! What bond? And marriage as hope? That's all crap. The beautiful bride, those tantalizing portraits, black tie and white lace."

"But it's a particularly female fantasy. Newsstands carry no magazine called *Modern Groom*."

"No, men get their kicks in the pages of *Playboy*, hoping to get laid wherever they please without any consequence or guilt. Truth is, none of you bastards can be trusted. You think I don't know Buddy runs around saying I have no talent?"

"Because of him, you're becoming an amazing television personality. I've seen how hard he works with my own eyes!"

"Why can't you understand? I'm not staying married." The cutting way she shaped her words made reasoning difficult. "What's more, I plan to take everything he's got. Whatever money we've left, whatever furniture, and the apartment in New York too."

"But the apartment is his. He had it long before you married. No?"

"Look, don't show up here like some storybook prince coming to restore justice to the land. Oh Buddy…your poor little lamb! The two of you at least got your asses carted off to fancy schools. Going to freebie college. Getting a fine education! You've no idea what the rest of us went through. Back home, I was never even taught to chew gum!"

"You sound like a parody…some old Joan Crawford movie."

"That's exactly what this is!"

"Oh? And when did you exactly become such a moralist?"

"Don't you dare speak to me that way! You and your oh-so-precious mother! You don't know shit about life. I waitressed. Swept beauty shops. Learned to fix hair. The tragedy of an old, aging model is nothing compared to leaning over a sink, washing scalps every day. And you? You go out and run off just like your mother did, living the champagne high-life around the world. Well, pal—you don't know a thing."

"Stop."

"I'll stop when I'm good and ready. We all know your poor dear mother couldn't face up to getting old. Oh, the poor dear. One so pretty! One so sweet! So…she finally skates back to us lowly folk…gets one over on a foolish jerk, who puts a roof over her head and yours."

"You're the one who doesn't know anything! She cared about Russell!" I fought hard to stay polite, against my growing anger.

"Oh? And how lucky he must have felt to have that white piece-of-ass lying around his house, turning into a lush and setting the whole town on edge. And what did it get him?"

"Stop it."

"Head smashed to bits! For some whore."

"My mother was not a whore! She was always appropriate!"

"That's a myth you as a Mama's boy want to believe."

"She had the right to marry any man she wanted."

"And what about the ones she didn't marry?"

"Don't you dare! I told you; my mother was not a whore!" I could feel my voice tighten. "And she didn't believe every white person she encountered who disapproved or disagreed with her on race issues was a racist."

"At sixteen, your mother got pregnant."

"And where did you hear that? Gossip in some hair salon."

"You don't know the half of it."

"I don't believe you."

"They wanted her to abort, but the old doctor who used to fix girls in Harrisburg was dead. My mother tried to help. She and Aunt Greta brought her to a farm in Maryland run by Catholics. You know the rest!"

"I don't…And I don't believe you."

Lydia paused. "You must know."

"I don't. I swear."

Her voice lowered, and she spoke in a monotone. "In Emmitsburg, a few blocks from the Mother Seton shrine, that baby came out black as the ace of spades. Word got out. People were scandalized. At Pomeroy's they moved my grandmother off the main-floor so that the notions department wouldn't seem,

because of her relations, like an advertisement for trashy living. They reassigned
her to the credit department, where she sat for years at a desk before a pegboard
in a cramped backroom. Want to know how much needling and bullshit my old
man had to take at the meat-packing plant? Do you know how many friends and
boyfriends I lost because of her? How many parties I wasn't invited to? The baby
turned out to be sired by the son of a school bus driver. Your mother wanted to
marry him. Know what happened? To help her husband keep his job, that boy's
mother reined in her wayward son…sent him to live with a sister out in Detroit."

I lost my ability for speech. On some level I knew there must be some truth
to what she was saying.

"Your mother always wanted us to swim at the Y while she frosted cakes,
hung balloons, gave out party favors—as if enough pin-the-tail-on-the-donkey
would make us forgive the suffering she carried wherever she went. Well, screw
it! Where was she when even years later…we were still glared at all over town.
And where were you? Sitting on your ass in a boarding school. Or hiding out in
foreign countries. And now you try to come here to this house and judge me? So
smug and superior, running around like some sophisticate! Well, no matter what
you may pretend…you and your trashy mother are no better than the rest of us!"

"Enough."

"Yes, Walker, I agree. It is enough. You came to say what you were told to say,
and you have said it. And I said what I had to say as well. Now it's time for you to
go back to your little village and tend your own beeswax." She rose defiantly and
rang a small silver bell, any further offerings waylaid. The maid entered and was
instructed to show me out. I stood with wobbly knees. No farewell was offered.

*   *   *

Levanto, Italy

The train roared back down the coast through the evening rain, and I had the distinct impression that up until this moment, nothing of any real importance had
ever been observed by me. Throughout my life I'd missed all the proper clues, paid
attention to all the wrong things. I was blind to what I could not see, and blind
to my very blindness. What Lydia alleged turned over in my mind. Her words
had the ring of truth, but there was no one left alive to whom I could turn to for
certainty. Calibrating the rule of probability, my shoulders rested back against the
leather seat. Now I was left to fit the last pieces of a great jigsaw puzzle into place,
all its mysteries sorted by borders, color, image, to complete a full portrait of Mom.

And, so what? Some forty years ago? A youthful romance? Only sixteen! She'd crossed the forbidden bridge of race. And so what! But she must've soon seen that never again would she be taken for someone who *hadn't* crossed that bridge. Her need to break rules might've even developed from such unjust bias; wasn't that always the way? The forbidden always a stain? Or had she merely been sleep-walking across the span, too naive to realize that the tarnishing bridge had no return? Whatever the case, the shame waiting on the far side, might actually have held more freedom than the shame she'd left behind. Maybe scandal even explains her father's willingness to change his mind, granting her permission to leave home? What irony, for what did she go on to model, if not something glamorously wholesome?

How hard she must've tried to defy her critics, to reject their assignation as slur, an old-fashioned stigma—nowadays, as ridiculous as the Salem witch trials. Or so you'd think? I knew better. In many places, on either side of the bridge, slurs still held potency, even among those like me, a growing number, who'd never belong to either side. Perhaps my life *betwixt and between* was but an adaptation because *she* could never advance forward or cross back. And the great effort to connect me with my cousin, had indeed been a hope to grant me some family from her side, the bigger hope being that Lydia and I could share some accordance later in life. Perhaps recovering some family for *me* helped *her* overcome the people she'd had to leave behind, her own mother among them.

Arriving in Levanto, I taxied up to the village, where I rushed over to Roberta's house. "How did it go?"

"Couldn't have been worse." I told her of the things Lydia revealed.

The astonished expression on Roberta's features made me feel understood with no need to explain further. She touched my hand, our trust was intact. I shook out my head, swinging my face from side-to-side, and when I found some balance, I announced a decision. "To defy my coarse cousin…I'm going to help Buddy in any way I can."

The next morning, head wrapped in a bandage so big he found it difficult to use a pillow, we brought Buddy home, helping him to re-settle into the Swedes' house.

I preoccupied myself with work. It felt like luck whenever a fair stretch of time passed in literary focus, distracting me from the analysis of the facts that Lydia had shared. Then in a desk drawer I found by no accident, Lydia's letter, the one delivered by the postman more than a year ago. I pulled out the two sheets of tissued onionskin, recalling the wonderment my fingertips had felt touching the same paper, the same black ink as she had. On the front of the envelope a small blue rectangle phrased those two intoxicating words—*par avion*—used since the First World War, French designated the official language of flight for the postal union.

Written in loose cursive style, an apology followed her salutation, begging forgiveness for not responding to my two postcards. I'd sent them more than a decade earlier. I knew penning regret at the top of a letter, meant she'd soon ask for a favor, and after explaining her performance in a magic act, the request was articulated: *I hope to locate a suitable house or apartment to rent—and perhaps you might help me—a place preferably somewhere along the Riviera?*

I held the envelope up to the light of the kitchen door, the postage stamps, neatly pasted along one edge, became silhouettes, as light from the window filtered through the clear pane. Her only correspondence in fifteen years, and still so self-serving, the closing remarks only confirming my suspicion that she'd only longed to appropriate my life—to see Italy *through my eyes*. I had slit open the side with a fruit knife, and seeing that cut in the fold, a bitter sense of fatigue and numbness fell over me, unpleasant in a mournful past, like a handful of ashes brought to the mouth.

. . .

Lydia's revelations continued to bring to life the old excruciating memories of finding Mom's body, her bleak funeral, the aftermath of adolescence lost to sad depression, all the chaos that Lydia's presence stirred. To free myself of such terrible hauntings still felt too much like a betrayal of Mom. Yet ultimately, I'd land on the same two words—*so what?*

I was typing a cover letter to go to my publisher in Torino, when the telephone rang from the hallway. It was Buddy, upset, his voice breaking through my isolating barricade. "Please Walker, come right away. I need help."

"Be right over," I said, without a thought. I quickly crossed our shared terrace and entered his house, finding him upstairs sitting on the edge of the tub. For some reason he'd decided to remove the bandage, and had almost instantly bumped his head against the sharp edge of the medicine cabinet. The gash had re-opened and was oozing blood.

"Sorry to be bothering you. I didn't want to. I just don't know anyone else."

I studied the weeping injury and dabbed antiseptic. "This looks deep," I said, with impatience. "It might need more stitches."

"No," he said. "No way am I going back to a hospital."

It took time, but finally, I managed to dress the wound in a way that would keep it secure to his head. Buddy, his speech erratic, pleaded for me to stay and take a drink. I agreed.

Downstairs, he poured two glasses of Scotch. "What an awful time. At five a.m. the phone rang. She was in a rage because of morning sickness. I doubt she's taken her medication. A horrible conflict followed. Almost an hour! She finally hung up on me when I asked why in God's name was our baby being born into the middle of this."

"Remember, you once said children were resilient? In time it will be fine."

"Conception must've happened around the time you guys went to Nice. She was extremely pleased by the magazine article then, and in a happy mood. For almost a week, I could do no wrong."

"You two need to learn how to balance the rocky parts of one another."

"Without seeing her face to face? That's impossible." He tipped back his drink and wiped his lips. "Walker, I hope you don't mind my speaking to you about poetry when you've already done so much. But I've got the bones of something new. I've been staring at blank pages, trying to bring myself to a place of blankness before I begin so that the page and the pen are not being predicated on my personality. And still, it surprises me to see I can't avoid leaving a map of myself. Somehow something deep and personal about me always comes through."

"But, Buddy. All imagination is based on memory."

"Well, I've been trying to work without a memory. Yet, I write and read myself into the page no matter how blank I make myself. Might you be willing to read it?" He rose to pull a sheet of paper from a stack on the table.

"Buddy, you called me here to help you with a bandage," I said. "Now I feel like I'm being bamboozled into reading poetry. To giving you free advice."

Buddy curved his spine back away from the table, like a reptile eyeing a silver-winged insect, his gaze maintaining a fixed determination. "Maybe you're too big to mess with my stuff? Well, thank *you*, pal!" He reached for his drink and held it with both hands to steady himself. "But I say…you're supposed to be an editor. Why not just go ahead? Edit!"

After a moment, hoping to convey assurance, I practiced what I hoped were my most sincere facial muscles. "Buddy, I don't mean to be curt, but today, I've got my own work to do."

"You're just saying that. I mean, you're afraid you'll have to be blunt. That I can't take it."

"Okay. Maybe so. But it's not my job to fix your work. All I can tell you is to just keep going."

"Okay, well…all right then. At least I know where we stand." He took a sip of Scotch, eyes raw and sad. "That fat fortune-teller, she saw right through my dissatisfaction and nailed it. You remember? I mean her clarity shocked! How you didn't take to her is beyond my comprehension."

"I guess that's what makes horse racing. We each pick our own nag."

"Writing, producing, fortune-hunting. It's all a gamble." Buddy stared down at the glass in his hand, then picked up the bottle and topped it off. "What that soothsayer said is still true. I'm in search of something. A human contact. Some closeness. Today I told Lydia it might soon be time for me to go home. Then I found out she's demanding most of our possessions in New York, even the furniture from my family. She says the apartment in New York is now hers. So, I may have no home to go back to. Can you imagine bringing a child into this?"

"Look, Lydia's insecurity requires her to feel like she's won something—especially against men. It's essential for her mental state. She's always been that way. For this reason, she'll demand and try to keep more than her share. But you have rights too. Fight back!"

"At the hospital, when Lydia said you'd been hustled by Eligio, what did she mean? I mean I know Roberta was embroiled—but not you."

His question caught me off guard. "You bring that up now?"

"Walker, are you of the mind that everyone ought to be required to sleep with someone of the same sex at least once? I mean, to ease the pressure?"

"What? Hell no! I don't believe that. Nothing sexual should *ever* be *required*. And what would that offer people already preferring the same sex? Would they be asked to sleep with the opposite sex?"

"I hadn't thought of that. As always, you cut right to the heart of it. I guess my thinking is how to eliminate fears or regrets. Lose some of the burden we men carry around over our masculinity."

"Buddy, you need to find someone to talk to."

"There is no one."

"Then you must cultivate someone."

Like cracking ice over a frozen pond, frustration broke through and he slammed his drink down. "If I knew how to do that, I would," he said.

I wanted to leave and slam the door so hard the windows would shake, but instead I planted another expression on my face, one I hoped would suggest I'm a person able to manage compassion for another. "Maybe there's some poetry society you can join?"

"Oh, forgive me. You *are* so right, Walker. I must *indeed* talk to somebody."

His flash of sarcasm faded. "Please. I feel lost. I'm desperate. I mean, did you feel like that? Did something like that cause you to make a play for Eligio? I don't know what else to think."

"In hindsight it's clownish," I said. "And private. But I hugged him. I don't mean a normal hug. But a deep…not exactly romantic hug…but something akin to that? At the time, it felt so comforting, and I cried."

"That's it?"

"Pretty much."

"How did Lydia find out?"

"You know her. She allows no secrets."

"Walker, it's not in me to fight the woman I once loved. I told her private things. I trusted her. Now everything I shared long ago comes back to hurt me. Today on the phone, she brought up some of the things I confided. She'd never have known them except I once shared them openly. Now she's using my own confessions against me." An imploring look consumed him.

"Lydia can't abide patched up things. Especially friendships. She also stupidly thinks she's still irresistible. That everyone whom she crosses swords with will always come back."

"I wish I'd known you were so desperate for a hug, Walker. I would've gladly hugged you. Children get hugged and held all the time. Why not grown men? I don't mind giving comfort to a crying friend."

"Too bad I didn't ask. Maybe then neither of us would be snared in this stupidity." I stood up and went to the door.

He gulped the Scotch in his glass. "My head is killing me." He leaned back on the couch, then stretched out as though it were a sickbed. "I hope you believe me when I say I've never cheated on Lydia. Again and again, I've pledged my loyalty, like some fat foolish fly beating its head against a windowpane. And here in Italy, children seem so important, and yet my anger keeps ripening at her even as she is to finally bear children. Over so many years I have known hurt. Sometimes I think she's inhuman…miscarriages induced by a formerly overweight girl, afraid she'll once more lose her figure! It's so self-centered I wonder if she might simply be unfit…or ill."

"But now you both have this new chance! A new child! Things will smooth out."

"You are right. It's an incredible renewal of life—it's so beautiful—and doesn't that beauty come from somewhere beyond?"

Book Ten

TOLÉRABILITÉ

. . .

From the upper roadway, Signor Vescovi returned with a newspaper in his hand. "Look at this!" he said, pointing out a photograph of the athlete O.J. Simpson sitting in a white Bronco, holding a gun to his head. I read the account and felt sick. I invited Vescovi to come in, made some coffee, and for the next hour we sat watching re-runs of the drama on my tiny set. Did Simpson kill his wife? I remembered how Russell had been falsely accused of killing Mom.

As he prepared to leave, Vescovi's attention shifted to the outside, where Buddy sat dutifully at the table, writing in his notebook, shirt soaked in sweat. "Look at *him*! He's lost."

"Yes. He's evaluating his mistakes—struggling as poets do. In the art of writing, his agony may find its way."

Something about a morning spent worrying over the world's crime and cruelty, made me decide to bring Buddy some water and a sandwich. "The sun is turning you into a piece of snakeskin," I said, approaching with a tray. And it was true. His physical appearance had altered, body leaner and tanner, the large cotton bandage now wound around the entire top of his head.

"I wonder about the person who first selected that low reptile to represent ruthless humanity?"

"What?"

"The snake."

I poured water and handed him the glass. Without explanation, I dodged talk of reptiles and conveyed the drama played out on the freeway in Los Angeles. He gulped the water, listening. "You mean the football guy? Who ran up all those stairs in *Towering Inferno*? He couldn't save anyone…remember? The door was jammed with a whole wheelbarrow full of cement." I confirmed it was indeed the same guy and Buddy let out a low whistle. It surprised me when he showed no further curiosity, but then it was happening on the other side of the planet.

"You must move into the shade," I told him.

"Okay. But these rays of sunshine have helped me decide to believe in God again! I tell you, atonement is the only way to face regrets. And from infancy, after the second of my birth, I now see how someone had to make me their highest priority. Someone had to give up important parts of their own lives for my sake—crib linen, diapers, bath towels, talcum powder, nipples. That was just year one! The list is endless. People imagine that we as babies give hours of infinite pleasure to our families, but the burdens are rarely reckoned. Babies are preconscious. Adults conscious. Disappointed that infancy eventually ends, we can't forgive the world for failing to honor our every whim. And don't think I haven't thought about marriage counseling. But it'll be impossible to find any stuff like that here. Impossible with my bad Italian."

My mind imagined his crisis. Lydia was propelling her speedy attack as if on a horse charging toward the joust of his masculine pride. *Make no blame*, I told myself. And despite her brutalist strategy, might she be an abuse victim? The goings-on of his notebook might simply be a smokescreen, or the crocodile tears of a man who wants to reform because he beats his wife.

Back upstairs in my work room, I turned to a new page in my notebook:

In domestic disputes, I've always presumed the man to be in the wrong. In that case, Lydia is the victim. But how often have I seen her actually pro-voke men? At times, her blistering attitude seems to dismiss every construct of masculinity. Sexual negotiations between her and Buddy must be either a nuclear summit or a nuclear meltdown.

More disturbing is the way she takes pleasure and enjoyment in practicing cruelty. She has a pride in contempt, and insult. And yet, somehow, she is still the victim. By recognizing her tactics, am I blaming her? Or in taking her side, am I falling for some kind of formulaic bias? Violence is violence.

Still, there's a sinister side to both. They each picked the other for a reason. She, from an early age, a tough talker, bragging about putting any number of boyfriends through their paces. It was laughable—then. But now, since I'd seen it from the stage, that kind of comic smack-down looks like a dis-guise for insecurity, a pain so deeply imprinted that she simply has to win something against men—no matter the cost. That need means she'll put anyone's hand in the fire, including her own.

Belligerent provocation and grotesque aggression cannot compensate for weakness.

• • •

Pouring my first coffee of the day, I glanced across the terrace, startled to see Lydia on the balcony. Such sightings must be what birdwatchers feel in a wildlife refuge when a rare species flies in, that hidden bird who arrives at night to excite someone's binoculars at dawn with its brilliant plumage.

Lydia joined the breakfast table, and I bid good morning. She fiddled with the tie-string of a sequined hairnet poised around her head. "What brings you?" I foolishly asked, thinking pleasantry could put our difficult Rapallo tea-party behind us, not seeing how confrontational my question was until it was too late. She glared, eyes contemptuously neurotic. "I needed a bath."

"The water's pure here!" Buddy said. "Vescovi says they use infra-red. I mean, to keep it safe from germs. Not a trace of chlorine!"

Lydia did not respond but got up and went to place fruit, eggs, and buttered toast on her plate. Diligently Buddy worked a facade of cheer, born from too much sappy romantic magazine advice. The desperate enthusiasm of his voice brought to mind television commercials, the kind where a new wonder-drug suddenly relieves someone of long suffering and they're soon rushing outdoors to swing golf clubs or plant the garden with paper-whites, all life's tragedies and miracles compressed within a mere thirty-seconds. He pulled out a chair for her, using his grandest manners, the kind that suggested love, not medication, could tame what was wild in another. "You look beautiful," he said. "Wait till those Milanese fashion folk see you."

If Lydia had flown in on some conciliatory idea, the impulse hadn't lasted through breakfast. Some mistakes are un-adjustable, and as if to illustrate this, she rose after but a few bites, carried her plate to the trash bin and forcefully dumped most of her food.

Buddy pretended not to notice. "Maybe we can all go down to the beach later for a swim?"

No one picked up the cue.

Without a word, Lydia went back inside. "Morning sickness," Buddy whispered. "We need to find a way to engage her. A card game? Charades? Anything to draw her out."

"She hates cards."

"And probably charades."

He poured more coffee. "Boy, I'll tell you, it was a shock to wake and find her asleep beside me, the palm of her hand curved around my shoulder."

Back inside at work, I kept contemplating that vision—the middle of the night, a yearning for some sleep-weary touch, and such simple details sadder than any I could portray. For while Lydia might long to sleep with someone, it most likely wasn't him, and she was probably only here in obeyance of a command put to her by the show's producers.

The day grew hotter, and Buddy displayed himself on a lounger, body bent in segments like a broken toy. I looked down at him and the shimmer and glare of white light on the patio's limestone put pressure on my optic nerve. I lowered the blinds.

At lunch, Pina prepared tiny stuffed zucchini and a *tiella* of Swiss chard, and as we gathered to partake, she remained on the upper pathway, her broom sweeping against the steps. "How does she manage such physical exertion in this heat?" Lydia asked. "Drives me mad."

"I agree," Buddy said. "Someone oughta buy that broad a leaf blower."

After eating, I carried dishes into the kitchen and Lydia followed, as though to ambush. "Are you stalking me, cuz—or did you *already* poison the coffee?" She laughed as I hoped she would. "So sly and suave you are," she said. I employed her tactic, turned on my heel and left the invective in the kitchen.

The afternoon wore on, and I forced myself to fulfill my work obligations, interrupting only to bring Buddy more water. Between gulps, he claimed new clarity, his previous cognizance compounding, and showed me his notebook, each page divided into sections. "The method is Japanese. Every hour of con-templation is split into twenty-minute segments. In each segment I reflect back on a three-year period involving one person. You're supposed to start with your mother, then go in order from birth to the age of three, then later say age seven-teen to twenty, or twenty to twenty-three."

"Where'd you discover this?"

"In a psychology magazine. For each twenty minutes the article said to do self-investigation on three specific questions. I feel the energy within myself magnify and begin to heal with each entry!"

"What questions?"

"I'm on Lydia now. So, first, what did I receive from Lydia? Second, what did I give to Lydia? And third, how much trouble did I cause her?"

"That's rigorous. But there's no column for the trouble she's caused you."

"Ahhh! That column of grievance is already deeply understood, and unbal-anced. To restore balance, I must ignore the negative behavior of others. The point is to say good-riddance to any place in my past that still exacts fury, guilt, or some other exorbitant toll. It's about owning my part.

"The article says to record the contraries of life, enhances life. So, in each three-year period, I write down every time I've been rude, inconsiderate, lazy, bad-tempered, belittling—to really see reality. Because of this, I can even see and accurately appreciate the many times she and I in our journey together made love. In the beginning, sometimes twice a day. Later two or three times a week. Then over the years every few months. Here in Italy, lovemaking was brought up to a couple of times a week. But of course, with her nights away performing magic, that was inconsistent. Still, if I multiply the average rate of frequency by ten years, I estimate we've had close to twelve hundred couplings."

"My marriage lasted less than two years," I said. "I can't imagine being with one person so long."

"What I can't decipher is if sex was something I did for her, or she for me."

"Maybe both?"

"What amazes is how out of twelve hundred copulations, we've only had three pregnancies. Of course, we practiced control—diaphragm, calendar, rhythm, not to mention interruption."

"Buddy, I'm worried that spending so much time on these lists, could be like watching too many old movies? Or gazing too long at photo albums? A tax on the present—and a lien against the future." My look of creeping judgment was read.

"Walker, dear Walker, for many of us, time spent in movies was better than time spent in real life."

"Then you must build a better life." I glanced up and spied her at their upstairs window looking down on us. How strange to once more find myself being observed—and with Buddy, no less. And yet for her, being forced to engage a husband composing crazy and repentant lists, his lone figure baking in the sun, a ridiculous bandage on his skull, while in the midst of taping some new edition of her show, must be infuriating.

Dusk fell, and I went to take a shower before dinner. As I dried myself, the sound of talking pulled me toward the open windows. I saw them together at the table below, two martinis between them. How on earth had she decided to join him? Was it her idea? Buddy spoke in a solemn voice.

"Roberta is divorcing Hans…for Walker."

To overhear my name as subject, sharpened my attention. "Can't blame any woman for wanting out of that devil's pact. Maybe she'll straighten him out."

"Hans?"

"No, Walker. That chip on his shoulder. The melodrama, the mixing of races, his mother."

A long pause followed, then the sound of the glass rod stirring the martini pitcher. Fearing they might be able to spot me from such a close range, I stepped back and sank onto my daybed. "Everyone's excited tuning in to the show. Everyone's jealous of your clothes."

"For Pete's sake, why must you always go on and on about stuff like that? It makes me nervous."

"I'm just reporting how excited people are. Can't we celebrate that? Restore even a tiny bit of civility?"

"Don't patronize me."

"I'm just saying, everyone's excited."

"Don't you dare try to touch me!"

"I'm just trying to comfort you. I want to hug you the way I should have hugged Walker."

"What?"

"He needed hugging."

"Are you just *trying* to make me nuts? Can't you see I'm only here because the fucking producers insisted."

"Look-ey here. I *know* the idea of a baby frightens…"

Something slammed the table. "Screw your compassion. It's grotesque. You say you know, you understand. You don't know a damn thing and you never did! I'm not maternal, and you can't admit that. You won't admit it because *you* want to be a daddy! No matter how hard I try, you keep finding ways to drown me!"

"But we have a low average—out of twelve-hundred."

"What?"

"Out of twelve-hundred love-makings."

"What?"

"That's how many times we've had intercourse. I charted it. It's part of deepening my gratitude."

"You really *are*…nuts!"

"I'm trying to remake myself. To be worthy."

"Don't hand me that Buddhist bullshit!"

"I'm trying to be grateful!"

"That crap is for assholes. Privileged assholes too lazy for a more demanding religion! No one gives a shit about how spiritual you are!"

I wondered if the rest of the village was tuning in? Or were they over the centuries already used to a mule and filly braying at each other in the colt pen at *La Stalla*. In which case they might be saying, so what else was new?

"But, Lydia, I've changed."

"Don't you dare claim that with me! If it's true, I say bull! If it were true then why *tell* anyone? Only self-righteous nuts go round with the need to broadcast how spiritual they are. When people start talking about their Zen ways, I want to vomit! They're pampered assholes stressed by easy living! I mean, *why* tell? Why run around and talk about your mystical yoga practice? How much downward dog you do? Who gives a damn! So, you sit your fat ass on a rolled-up towel and meditate? So, the hell what! Good luck to *you*!"

Buddy waited for her to calm "You are *right*. That's why I've dedicated my life to giving up everything. So we can start again. I'm adopting voluntary poverty. The loss will be a great gain for us as a family."

"People only tell other people crap like that in order to manipulate them. They say that shit to get things! To get things off of others." Her voice was dripping with mockery. "Oh, do you go to church on Sunday too? Oh, goody…goody!"

"I'm not insane." His voice leveled. "And there *are* options."

"Like what, pray-tell?"

"If you'd be happier, and don't want the burden, I mean now with the show, we might hire a surrogate."

"Oh, boy! You just keep hacking away."

"Having our baby be born into a life of gratitude means everything to me."

"Oh? And is now the time when I too should be divinely grateful?"

From the upstairs window I listened with outrage at the way she was going to play it. Again, I saw how each had cultivated a perception of themselves as injured, using that excuse to justify the pleasure of their corrosive retaliation. I knew her game well, but now I saw how his game included piety. He needed her to attack, to ridicule his manhood and faith, to imply impotence or queerness, so that in injured righteousness he could prove her wrong.

"I just want to be with you."

"Get lost!" Her voice pitched high, just this side of out of control. "You like the *idea* of me. But you don't really *like* me!"

Buddy lowered his head and sounded a strange moan. It embarrassed me to hear it. The sound soon extended over several seconds until it grew to a wail of oceanic proportion. It then progressed to descending tetrachords, a vociferation, the sound of sackcloth and mourning veils, a dog howling over a haunted moon. The intensity of his emotion cast a spell, and seemed to have captured and captivated her. As if by a miracle, his voice now gave way to sniveling, sloppy sounds wet with saliva and snot. And yet, still, somehow, could it be that they were emerging? How damn confounding! What if mutual suffering turned out to be the very thing that united them again?

She pulled on a cigarette. He gently admonished her. "Smoking is bad for the baby."

"Buddy, why can't you get it?" Her calm phrase inverted and hung in the air. "It's over. You're dancing on a grave."

For an instant, by his silence, it seemed possible Buddy might spontaneously combust. "I don't understand."

"No. You don't. You never did. Nobody in this world gets everything they want!" Suddenly she was as detached from her words as a marble statue. "I went yesterday *and had it…*" I repeated those last words in my head, as often as he probably did. *Had it? Had it? Had what?* In a flash, the chilling reason for Lydia's return to the village grew evident. She wanted the pleasure of telling him their future had died. I saw then how out of his league Buddy was. She was by far, and forever would be, the crueler of the two. "How?" he asked, his voice still raw from wailing. A chair scraped and then the sound of a hard slap.

"Ow! *Oh, you crazy son of a bitch! My God! How dare you*! You fucking *sicko*!"

"No. It's *you*!" he shouted. "You're the crazy. You're the murderer!"

In Italy, and in many parts of the world, many might agree it's reasonable, under the circumstances, and maybe even correct, for a husband to slap his wife over killing their baby. That he hit her while she was inhaling a lit cigarette wouldn't matter. I imagined anyone who one day might hear her tell the story, would discover not only did he never worship or exalt her, but he was also a deceiver, a pervert, a full-fledged abuser.

I looked down to see Lydia had already fled the terrace. Buddy stood completely undone. He began shouting up at their windows. "For this crime…your worst *Mother's Day* is yet to come!"

· · ·

Roberta and I sat on the couch, sipping wine. "Walker, I feel so sad. I mean for Buddy—for them both…but for the baby most of all. But still, aren't you going overboard to take his side." She looked straight ahead, as if deliberating something. "People say we often partner with people who have our parent's characteristics. Do you think she's like his mother? Or that I'm anything like your mother?"

"That thought makes me dizzy. When Mom died, I remember it was like a terrible prison sentence being handed down. That I didn't matter. I couldn't escape. While you were in Zurich, a very similar feeling came over me."

She stared at the floral watercolors thumbtacked to the wall. "You never finished sharing with me about the day she died."

"I don't think I can."

"I understand. But please."

"I can't. It's too loaded. Talking about her end has never been easy—or cathartic. The words choke. Even now, I have to pause to keep my voice in control."

We sat in silence. I thought of the cliff I'd jumped that day I took the boat ride. Out of fear of being shamed, I'd forced myself to take a breath—then took the plunge. And while I had no epiphany, I also did not die. I decided I owed it to Roberta to tell her the truth. "I once saw a therapist who tried to help me wade through the feelings. Well more than one. And when the pain grew too acute, that particular woman said: 'Can you sit beside those feelings for a moment and see what they have to say?' I did what she asked. But no language came. Nothing. I was dead. Many feelings died with Mom."

"Would it help if you tried that now?"

"I don't know." *Face the risk head on. Avoid that huge chance for potential regret. Lying on your deathbed, you'll wish you'd spoken more truth. Start with the weather. It was chilly that day. Unseasonable. Summer's last breeze. Shorter daylight. Trees shivering away their yellow leaves. The riverbanks, muddy from recent rain, starting to dry out. A year or so since a hurricane called Agnes cried fifteen inches over our city, the Susquehanna flooding our downtown with seventeen feet of water. The last of the businesses tried desperately to scrape off the thick muck and grit. But many never reopened. Harrisburg was now a city forever leery of rain.*

I began to speak. "On Jefferson Street, our household furnace clicked on to run heat for the first time since May. That early season stale-dry warm air circulating with that dusty Autumn smell." Roberta looked at me with the pity I hated so much. I looked away and worked to locate where I was, to relax my vocal muscles, reconstructing phrases inside my head. Roberta offered no prod or prompt, just sat waiting for me to find my way. "This is the dead place," I whispered, and slowly breathed in and out, again and again, finally forming words from those inside my head. "I found Mom's body on the kitchen floor."

I paused, then waited until my voice returned: "I did not want to see this. I did not want to see my beautiful mother…her torso twisted…a bloody cut on her lip. I did not want to see that she was lying in the cold waiting for me to find her. No neighbors. No Russell. Just me. And eventually the mailman.

"It was the mailman who finally got the Howards to open their door. But they wanted no part. Mr. Howard told me to wait out in his workshop past the breezeway, next to his cinder block garage. On the strip of yard between our two houses a camera bulb flashed. A newspaperman caught the tragic face of *that* boy…the mixed one who'd just lost his mother. My face appeared on the front page of both the late and early editions. My stolen image used again and again for weeks." I paused and felt Roberta press my arm.

"In the newspaper the next day, a policeman named Lembur described the physical force Russell had waged during his arrest. He lied. It was Lembur's force, or really the counterforce of his badge, perhaps meant to demonstrate the way to handle anyone in that community who kills a woman of pale skin. The officer, in fear and fury, smashed Russell's face against the bar. That exploded the pulp of his right eye. Then Officer Lembur completed his arrest by knocking out two of Russell's front teeth. The force lodged them in his windpipe."

I paused, and stared ahead barely blinking. "Overnight, our small lives proved certain outcomes. The ideas people needed to preserve. The very ones we disclaimed. Difference. Bad outcomes. Unavoidable situations. That's how it goes. Him a sexual predator. Her, either whore or a victim—rarely both. As if she held no agency. As if her own self-centered independence might not have also injured him. If not physically, then mentally and emotionally? As though he, in his life, had never been kind to her, had never repainted the whole house, had never played catch with me." My voice almost broke. I paused to regain composure.

"The investigation measured, and spun whatever it needed to spin. Two men from the morgue arrived. That evening I was placed in temporary foster care. There, I happened to see the late news showing the gurney with a body bag, and Mom zippered inside, pulled out onto Jefferson Street."

Tears began to run down Roberta's face. At that, my voice clotted. She rubbed her eyes, but they kept streaming. Once more she cried for both of us. I wondered, as the psychologists on detective programs always imply, if the empathy of her listening and hearing would somehow help me.

"That night, I knew both my mother and Coleman were forever preserved inside the television. One in a body bag. One in a doeskin sportcoat. Maybe that's why I both crave and hate it so much. A week later, the police in Harrisburg apprehended a second man, a felon, fencing Mom's wristwatch. Upon questioning, he broke down, confessing he'd crowbarred the house. In the midst of a random burglary Mom surprised him. She tried to reason with him. Tried to barricade herself in the kitchen. The man needed her to stay quiet. Through violence his weak character changed forever…from common thief to murderer. And so, the police, first conclusion mistaken, found a stranger had killed Mom. Russell had indeed been at the bar discussing income tax, just as he and his friends had sworn.

"Russell was decent. But his vigor was gone. Stolen by a killer he'd never set two eyes on. Let alone a ballgame, or a UFO. In the paper, the police regretted that Russell hadn't cooperated, said by way of his force, sadly he'd slowed their investigation. The second man's trial went quick. No appeal. They sent him to Rockview penitentiary. A short while later, a gang, reportedly made up of inmates and guards of many races, shanked him to death."

We sat perfectly still side by side. The story finished. Unlike crime shows where the worst unfolds and a saxophone plays music of resolution. I felt no relief. My mind-forged manacles remained fixed. And then, like the day in the tunnel, my chance to grieve overcame me. Roberta moved close and kissed my cheeks, her tears mixing with mine.

• • •

After midnight, I tossed and turned. Roberta, wrapped in bedclothes, slept peacefully at my side. So as not to disturb her, I moved to the living room and sat in a midnight trance, studying once more the colorful floral post-cards thumbtacked to the wall.

My mind sifted the past, to my poor schoolmate Ronny Wilding, like me, his head stuffed in a toilet. Ronny's passivity gave his persecutors the foul proof they needed, that he was an object worthy of punishment. His gentle mother, every day, like so many other mothers, sent her boy washed and pressed out into the world, only to have him diminished by a gang of punks. I didn't want to think of that, or how his family eventually fled Harrisburg, going back to Frederick, Maryland. Yet I couldn't help but wonder what the cruelty of boys had meant to Ronny's later life. How did my silence help cruelty award its head-lock? To watch such acts and let them go uninterrupted meant I was willing to aid the brute forces directed at Ronny, or my own family, or toward myself.

I stared at the postcards in silent misery. *The wet eyes of the sentimentalist betray his aversion to experience, his fear of life, his arid heart; and it is always, therefore, the signal of secret and violent humanity, the mark of cruelty.* Does the act of looking at a tyrant's artwork amount to collusion? But isn't art—separate from the artist? The poem—separate from the poet? And what gives anyone the right to judge? Have they no compassion for the flaws within every artist? Within every soul?

Staring at the postcards, I saw again the face of every boy who took part in Ronny's attacks. Many also took part in my own conquering: the Bickford twins, stars of the athletic field, later bedding half the girls on the cheerleading squad. Henry DuMonte, a thug with fracturable hands, a few days after whipping Ronny with an electrical extension cord stolen from the a.v. department, he wrapped his muscular legs around a potter's wheel, crafting delicate soup bowls, looking so seductive and moody, that even the young art teacher bent over his curved torso to peek at his hind quarters. I imagined him as he might be today, standing with roughnecks David Moretti, Trent Hoffer, Kyle Latsha, all of them loitering outside a convenience store at Third and Maclay, an aging pack of menace, making the average citizen uneasy to stop for a carton of milk.

Would my own biography someday mar the poetry I conjured? Across the years, passive shame still transmitted huge waves of remorse. For the zillionth time, I thought of life's predicaments. To my young ears, the painter of these water-colored cards, once called my mother promiscuous. Spoken to me, her son, even after the tragedy of her murder. Surely, that cruelty ought to soften a hard heart, let it forgive a young girl's desire for the body of a bus driver's son, an attraction that set her on a course of unalterable judgement. My fists clenched. Cruelty. Unnecessary pain. In a sudden fit against nostalgia, I leapt up from the couch and tore the postcards from the wall.

One by one I crumpled them, then brought them to the kitchen, emptying their wreckage into the sink. I turned on the exhaust fan, opened the kitchen door, and lit a match, placing it against the paper edges, watching the slow red glow burn through the cards until it spread. For a moment I felt regret, but only for Aunt Greta, who had so faithfully saved her brother's cards, then entrusting them to me. I stood by the sink waiting and watching until the fire's rising flame peaked, and finally began to fade, until nothing remained of the old man's petals but smoke and ash.

Roberta stood in the kitchen doorway, horrified. "Walker, what have you done?" In her eyes, by this act of destruction, I was now a philistine.

"Is it a mistake to expect more from the work than the artist?" I asked.

"You can't *judge* that way. Destroying something beautiful because of something not to your liking."

"He may have been but a cipher for the brush. And his life's summary is now and forever sacrificed to the element of fire."

"I thought you stood against such destruction? You said all art was sacred. Remember how it felt to look over the ruins of Rome?"

"Not all art deserves to withstand the sands of time."

"That's what bullies say. I loved those cards. They connected me to you and your family. What about my feelings? And what about forgiveness?"

"I leave all that to Christ."

"Walker, what's gotten into you? You're the one who said Christ is all of us or none of us. Are we all murderers, then?"

"Stop repeating the stupid things I've said. My regret is already kicking at the ashes. Forgiveness for what is cruel…is a bitter pill. It's easier if some kind of justice has been served."

"But that's not really forgiveness."

"Huh?"

"Forgiveness is for when justice *hasn't* been served. And that may be a bitter pill, but you keep saying Buddy needs to forgive himself for being human. What about forgiving *yourself*?"

"Oh, please! Forgive myself for what? Apathy?"

"No, for being a child. For not being able to rescue your mother. For not being able to rescue Russell. For not being able to rescue yourself! For being human."

"Okay. So now you know some of the worst of me. Like the guy who smashed the Pieta with a hammer, I burn art in vengeance. So, tell me now, can you live with *that*?"

Roberta gave a long pause as she pondered the answer I longed to hear. "Yes. I can. But for selfish reasons. Because virtue is a rarer act than vengeance… And I want to strive for rare things."

• • •

It took several days before the shame over Roberta's reprimand of my pyrotechnic impulse began its slow abatement, and to allow that the acceptance she'd spoken of, was trusting, real and enduring, and that she was more than some idealized fantasy projection of a woman than perhaps I'd been assuming she might be. A sense of calm came over both of us—but it was short-lived. One evening while stopping in Levanto for a Campari and pizza, the television behind the bar, set to the evening news, flashed a troubling photo of Lydia across the screen. We moved closer and asked the bartender to turn the volume up. A videotaped clip began playing, the announcer saying it showed the star of *Cooking Magic* as she passed through the revolving doors of an abortion clinic.

Immediately, an atomic explosion flashed over the room. In that flash the looming dread could be felt as it X-rayed every tissue, organ, and marrowed-bone in our skeletal bodies. We somehow knew this was going to be bad. During the late-night news, Lydia was featured on every broadcast, and the next morning was front-page on every paper. At noon, Buddy came over hauling a large black plastic television with the help of Signor Vescovi. "I can't stop watching this mess. It's driving me nuts. Please Walker, would you be willing to keep my set here for a while? At least until my serenity is restored? Or this catastrophe blows over?"

I agreed and found a spot in the mud room where the unplugged set could wait out purgatory. That evening Roberta at Buddy's request, helped slide it into the living room and plugged it in. "Yours is too small," he complained. We learned then that the footage had been stolen from the abortion clinic's surveillance camera by an undisclosed party and sold to a reporter.

The popularity of *Cooking Magic,* a show enjoyed by so many, meant the induced termination of a baby was simply too big a story to be ignored. And after twenty-four hours, when the exclusive rights to the video expired, stations could broadcast Lydia's entrance to the clinic as often as they wanted. We left the television on and like Buddy grew obsessed, watching Lydia revolving through the doors of the abortion clinic over and over. The sad end for her and Buddy's unborn baby were spoken by newscasters reading from teleprompters in solemn tones, like a Greek chorus. The moving stasis vaporized reality, the walls, the windows, the kitchen chairs, the rooftop, the olive branches, all the surrounding towns and villages. We sat glued.

The next day another undisclosed profiteer sold Lydia's medical records, and they confirmed the clinic had indeed brought an end to her fetus. The trial by media now began to sing a more full-throated drama, bringing more stimulation and attention than any person ought to know.

At dinner, Buddy came over and we sat mesmerized by the many stations of news. So as not to miss a word, Buddy began raising the volume on the television until we practically had to shout at one another. We were done with our meal when Signor Vescovi stopped by bringing us some homemade brandy. He joined us and we also re-watched footage of O.J. Simpson holding the gun to his head. Vescovi shook his head. "My eyes feel like they are watching poison. Twenty-four-hours a day of news, that's a new daily right. Soon people will go to the television more often than the church."

"Hardly a bad thing," Buddy said.

"I agree, but I feel deeper callousness with each program," Vescovi said. "You'll see! We'll soon learn how the world buckles under the weight of this much fear."

Buddy left the table to use the hall telephone and we turned the volume down to mute. We could hear him dialing and re-dialing Lydia at the villa of the

Belgians. No answer. Finally, Roberta got up and spoke with the operator, who said the line was disconnected. That brought a tremendous distress. "How can I ever reach her?" Buddy cried.

I finally shut the set off. "This will soon fade."

"Yes. Don't worry," Roberta added. "The public will lose interest very quickly...very quickly..."

But the news did not fade. Over the following days every tabloid in Italy kept Lydia on its front page. And if little paragraphs in *The Mercury* had once made her heart palpitate, the avalanche of negative publicity must now be causing her a major coronary. As one salacious newscaster put it: "In seeking fame, this American cooking star has found infamy."

The producers of *Cooking Magic* released a statement, explaining their decision to suspend the show while an investigation was conducted into the serious moral charges against their star and her husband, a fellow producer. And so, *Cooking Magic* went on the ropes.

The producers continued to convene privately, measuring their exposure and the financial risks of a fifty-one percent share. They hedged their bets for solvency as a group, and without any input from Lydia, voted to exploit the exposé for all the cash they could recapture. They decided to sell program footage to the highest bidders and they rehired Garafallou as press consultant.

Every morning Buddy would come over and watch his own television for an hour or so, then he'd blubber endlessly about how the value of news was no longer its essence; news nowadays depended on the quantity of repeatable film footage that was available—which determined the top stories, no matter how insipid.

The Italian papers kept the brushfires burning with stories about the diminishment of family, the destruction of a marriage, the indifference to human life. Within a few days, the moral flame spread over the woods of France, then leapt the channel to the United Kingdom and finally the great Atlantic crossing was made to America. Every day swirled by uncontrollably fast, as outrage grew, and we tended Buddy, he still attempting to reach Lydia in every way possible. A camera crew stationed themselves outside the villa in Rapallo, and the attention-seeking Belgians, were shown being chauffeured out through their artichoke gates with grim faces.

"Probably going to Biaritz," I said.

To feed the blaze, the producers of *Cooking Magic* released ever more footage, hoping to recoup losses. The highest bidders aired their prime exclusives, then the rights reverted back to the producers, and the clips were repackaged, relicensed, resold and replayed until the number of people who'd seen Lydia's face worried in concern over a browning plum tart, juxtaposed beside her entering the doors of the abortion clinic, rivaled the audience for the football World Cup.

Taking in so much of the news, we grew disorientated. In the days that followed, the story seemed to keep growing. Between commercials there were news promos and teasers: *Tonight! Shocking new details about Buddy Landers, husband of the American star of Cooking Magic. Tune in at ten o'clock!*

Naturally we found ourselves riveted by the story about Buddy. The broadcaster explained last month's hospitalization in Genoa was for head injuries sustained under mysterious and suspicious circumstances. The woman on the balcony, who in the aftermath called the ambulance to transport Buddy to hospital, was now quoted saying two men on mopeds were involved. A new overhead surveillance clip had been procured. It showed Buddy, bloody and unconscious, arriving at the emergency room, to be wheeled on a stretcher inside, 'a mystery man at his side.'

The next day the story was enhanced by two new sources, the moped rental garage that showed his rental application, and the hospital registry, both signed on behalf of Buddy by Eligio, therein revealing his identity. A caravan of cameras was dispatched to Chiavari. Eligio's mother, her hair tied in a sleep net, opened the door to a public inquisition about the sexual relations of her son. "Do you think the world might wrongly be judging your son's same-sex liaison?" Startled at the firing squad of questions her sleepy eyes grew wide with panic, the cameras capturing her expression of disgust before she slammed the door with frantic agitation. At the end of the week a frenzied photo of Eligio's mother was shown on the cover of *The Inquirer*. Inside, the dawn raid was intercut with bloody ambulance photos.

The following Sunday we stumbled on a Danish current events program— where the newscaster focused on the same-sex equation: "With all their lurid angles and story twists—it's astonishing how in the world's media, the mere hint of male-pairing can still ruin a man. Would the story play so wildly if it was alleged to be two women?"

After denouncing the lies to us, Buddy fell to his knees praying, begging accompaniment to visit Padre Vincenzo. Hiding behind my all too real publishing deadline, I declined. Instead, I urged Buddy to get up and settle into one of the lawn chairs. Buddy's increasing agitation finally won out, persuading me to call Padre Vincenzo's office and see if a counseling appointment could be arranged. But a cleaning woman at the church office told me the Padre was filling in at a church in Sestri Levante, for a priest recovering from gall-bladder surgery. "Oh, please, Walker, can't we go there then? Please. You must help. I don't feel well. I'm desperate. I need a blessing."

. . .

To avoid the sleepy press, we took the earliest bus down to the village, the dawn light in Levanto reminding me of a clearing in a forest near a ski resort I'd once visited. At the train station, the ticket windows were closed and locked, with signs announcing: *No tickets. No trains.* In the packed hall we joined a group loudly expressing concerns at the manager's office.

"Please, *Signor*," I said, pushing forward to a man seemingly in charge of information.

"How can I get my friend to the priest in Sestri Levante?"

The man eyed the bandage on Buddy's head. "*Sciopero! Sciopero dei treni. É stato annunciato in anticipo!*"

"I don't care if the strike was announced," I said. "It's ridiculous! How are we supposed to know about a pre-announced strike? This man needs to see his priest at once!"

The man shrugged. "*Sciopero!*"

I led Buddy away. "Don't worry. It's no big deal. We'll just go back to the village and borrow Roberta's car."

"But the reporters will by now be roused from their drunken stupors," Buddy said. "They'll swarm us."

A woman holding a toddler on one hip tapped Buddy on the arm. "Within an hour," she said, "a boat at the dock will go up the coast. It will take you to your priest." We thanked her, and went out to hail a taxi.

Only by walking blocks away from the crazy station, frenzied by the missing railroad employees and their service, were we able to find a driver. The man reminded me of a cartoon character rushing his vehicle through traffic with alarming speed. By predictable coincidence, the vessel we'd come to board turned out to be the same one I'd taken cliff-jumping. The captain at the wheel grinned, remembering me. "Hope you won't try flying from high places today," he said in Italian. "For today mine is a commuter boat…the sea once more faster than trains…and a thousand times more beautiful than highways." The captain gestured reassuringly toward Buddy. "Bring your friend again another day, when his head is healed. He too can learn the cliffs hold great adventure."

"You know that guy?" Buddy asked, as we moved back in the boat. I gave an edited version of my cliff jump, leaving out the profligate polygamist, his two wives, his repulsive kiss.

The boat launched its motor, the blaze of humid air and ocean spray circulating around us. We took seats beside a well-rounded woman, straw basket on her lap exuding the scent of green onions and earthen potatoes. As we moved back from the dock a pair of flags began snapping overhead, and a young girl leaned against the wheelhouse, trying to hold down the pages of her book. I too had to hold my cap down.

Buddy shouted to the captain over the engine's roar, asking for our expected arrival time. "Time?" the captain yelled back. "What is time? On the drive to the mortuary…all lights go green!"

Buddy turned back with frustration, his voice still shouting against the engine. "How easy it would be if we could just go out and get one of those big twig brooms…and then just sweep and sweep all this nonsense away. I mean… just sweep and sweep the way Pina does…just sweep and sweep, then sweep some more—until this whole damn, wretched fiasco could be gathered and dumped into a dustbin."

The boat took more than an hour to reach Sestri Levante. Buddy wasted no time pulling me into a dockside café so he could order cognac. "I'm trying to face myself," he said, gesturing to his cloth-bound book of Japanese self-examination. "I don't know if I can handle this meeting…it feels too risky."

"Buddy, several years ago, I edited a book by a guy who spent years interviewing people on the psychology of nursing homes. He spoke to thousands of elderly folks in their final days. According to him…something like eighty-percent… admitted the same thing. How if they had life to do over again… they'd take more risk."

"Eighty-percent!"

"Yes, can you imagine? They'd played it safe…kept the awful job…the dull marriage…bought everything the insurance man said they needed, and now, chained to a walker, sitting in a wheelchair, tied to a bed, safety did them no good. You're in the midst of a change…and that's a risk. But you're doing the right thing."

Second drinks were ordered, and Buddy downed his. He pointed to my untouched glass. "You going to finish…?" I shook my head. He grabbed my cognac and swigged it down. "Oh…Walker, how I wish my poetry could satisfy me the way yours does you. You're so unconcerned about outcome, or fame, or career."

"Fame is a poor dream. Throughout the ages, the true hallmark of privilege has been privacy."

"And yet privacy can isolate. Ask any hermit."

"Or maybe ask God."

• • •

Inside the portal of a modest church, the confession was underway. A line of five elderly women waited to confess whatever their elderly transgressions might have been: Kicking the cat? Greed? Envy? Lust?

Buddy paused, terrified to proceed. "I'm evaluating," he said. "The risk is too great! Walker, I just can't handle it."

"Buddy, just take the leap and simply speak from the heart."

"Won't you come with me. Come help me take the chance?"

I goaded him to the line, the women ahead of him briefly turning to see who this character might be. In a hushed voice I gave instruction. "Look when it's your turn, just go in the box and pour your sorrows out. When it's done you may get a penance, and then you'll be clean—forgiven."

"I'm a coward. I've lost any boldness to face risk."

"We must each weigh our own risk. Just be brave. And I'll be back to get you in half-an-hour. I promise." I moved away from Buddy's confession without looking back, wondering how I had been able to sell confession with so much oil.

Outside, I ambled down the street and found a tiny park with two benches overlooking a coast of rocks. I sat and opened my notebook, feeling a light breeze cool my skin. Somewhere inside a neighboring house, I heard sounds of pillows being thumped, feathers aired of sleep, a funny hereditary link to the flock of sparrows swooping down from the olive branches to land in a patch of dirt near my feet. The birds cornered one another in games of give-and-take, restlessly flicking from branch to bush, then back down to the patches of bare earth. One pair sat among roots bathing their wings in the dust. Were these the same birds that visited our village? The same birds Buddy had watched with Eligio?

I uncapped my pen and soon succumbed to the trance of nib scratching paper:

To bird watch is a dependable kind of voyeurism. More interesting than Buddy's worries. Beneath those nerves lie terror and shame. Will he rediscover his boldness? Return unafraid?

Can language be a healing antidote for Buddy?

Garafallou is right: the architecture of the alphabet, its simple forms and patterns, invent configurations of music. Sonnets, the sestina, the villanelle, the multitudinous pliability of free verse—all forms adapting to discover that which best suits need. All to accommodate and organize the human experience. And yet like a boxwood parterre, the forms of the alphabet contain that which is wild, so that the structure of us, and the wild of us, inform each other. The garden honors that our human essence can never be contained.

My wrist-watch rang the alarm.

I must go now. How could my writing time already be gone?

Back at the church, Buddy stood near the varnished wood confessional, next in line to go in. He turned and I nodded to him, then took a seat in the last pew behind three kneeling women dressed in muted colors and gazing up at the cross. They fingered rosaries, lips murmuring as if chewing crackers, not caring that the lives of the saints left harsh evidence for prayer's outcome. The confessional door clicked, echoing across the marble chamber. A woman hobbled down the aisle on swollen legs. Buddy waved in my direction, then went in. I opened my notebook and once more began to record thought:

Mother, it seems sitting in this church I'm drawn to channel to you once more. It's a kind of lunacy to stand apart and declare one's private thoughts to a ghost. Is the long path of tragedy toward your murder—the reason I must write this? Perhaps like Montaigne and his friend, there's a tragic need to break our silence?

Crime bends the spirit the way polio or rickets bend bone. How can one convey the experience of murder or violent crime, its negative notoriety? The immeasurability pressures life. Too many words still unspoken.

Somewhere in the beyond, a wooden door banged. I looked up as a craggy-faced priest emerged from his side of the wooden box, a man older than Padre Vincenzo, clipped white hair under his cap, eyes hard as steel. His robes swirling the smoke of incense like floodwaters. He grabbed the doorknob and yanked the confessional open. His voice rose—indignant Italian turning to indignant English.

"You. You!…Go!"

My stomach kicked. Whatever the old man's racket, I knew Buddy was responsible. The man's withered hands now tugged a sleeve as he physically pulled Buddy from the confessional.

Buddy resisted. "But, I've come for guidance…"

"You seek none!" the priest said. "You wish only to condone sin!"

"That's ridiculous. Are *my* confessions not as worthy as your flock of housewives?"

In the various pews, the women held their breath, staring at the spectacle of their priest throwing an American tourist from the church. "I'm no infidel!" Buddy spewed. "I demand to see Padre Vincenzo!"

Buddy backed down the aisle, bypassing the astonished faces. One of the women standing in the last pew spoke with compassion. "Not here…gone… back to Levanto."

The priest spotted me as I rose from my seat. "You too…go!" He pointed castigation in my direction, playing his part for all he was worth. "We welcome no *deviati* here!"

"Let me explain," I said. "Please…I'm his friend…I brought him. He needs counsel."

"Hail! You *must* leave our holy place!"

I pulled my angry gaze away from the blazing eyes of the dogmatic priest, and saw Buddy had already gone. I hastened after and saw him jumping down some steps toward the market.

"Whatever I've done, I don't deserve being treated like sin incarnate!" he said, as I caught up with him. "*Octogenarians* are the only folk welcome in that church! *Young* people won't feast on *that gruel.*"

I fought to keep up. "Buddy! You already know intolerance is religion's great whip."

"Then all religions be damned! I should never have turned to bloody priests. Only a fool would take advice on marriage from bitter old men and virgin nuns—who've never done it. Dad was right! Madalyn Murray O'Hair was right! How dare they mix church and state! How dare these horrible people be granted our tax deductions! Taxes collected from hard labor. Everyone forced to pay for their deductions—including non-believers!"

We continued past the espadrille shops and stalls selling candles and wildflower wreaths, halting before a rotisserie full of fat yellow chickens. Buddy stared at the plump, glistening birds as they rode their hot carousel. Turning away with agitation, he looked into the faces of people going by. "You there! Tell me, what difference between these chickens and men of the church?" He squawked like a bird as though struck insane. "Behind which face might there be a *brain* that can open itself?"

People hurried to avoid the lunatic with the bandaged head. Dozens gathered to stare from a distance. Buddy's voice cracked like thunder. "If your churches are so powerful, let them support themselves without government aid! Haven't the histories of the Vatican…or your greedy monarchies not been enough to show you why it's important to keep church away from state?"

"Right-o, mate!" A merry English accent shouted from a shop doorway. "Prisons be built with the stones of law—brothels with the bricks of religion!"

"Right-o!" Buddy shouted back and raised his fist.

I grabbed his arm. "Buddy, you must stop!"

"I hope these churches take their government subsidies and go straight to hell!"

"Buddy! Italian churches might not get tax breaks. And if they do it's none of our business. Confronting these people won't resolve anything. That old priest is a fool. In a couple more years, he'll have ceased to exist."

Frustration twisted Buddy's face. "You know what I've gone through? Lists! Prayers! Lydia's hell-bent competition! Her insatiable thirst for attention! Our children. Now, I have *three* absent lives to mourn!"

"Buddy, you came to atone, not lacerate!"

More people paused to watch our dialogue, and I began to worry over how to get Buddy back to the village. Not wanting to risk another boat, I hailed a passing taxi. The ride from Sestri Levante would empty our wallets—worse than fortune-telling—but to escape this public spectacle was worth every penny.

• • •

We drove to Levanto twice daily—bringing up new journalistic waste. Buddy devoured every critical absurdity. Each volley caused a corresponding scrutiny of his own ethics. Public reaction to the constant replay of images seemed to be growing more vitriolic. In the press, editorials screamed how this despicable woman must be made to pay, that any good Italian must insist on it. The scandal sold papers, and every day, new reporters came to stake out Levanto.

I tried to reason with Buddy. "In Levanto—we might still try and see Padre Vincenzo."

He sat back and turned to stare out the window, then said he no longer cared to see any priest.

After weeks of hiding, dissatisfaction plagued Buddy. His point of view never expressed. Roberta and I turned off the television set about twenty times a day. He had not recovered from our trip to Sestri Levante and for the good of all, I unplugged the television and stored it in the mudroom, giving it a good sleep under some old quilts.

* * *

On an afternoon when the white roses were at their fullest and the garden seemed laced with snow, Buddy lugged five pairs of Lydia's shoes out onto the terrace to give them a polish. I urged him to come back inside, but he refused, insisting he wanted to be seen—that polishing her shoes was a way to atone. "An act of kindness done for someone once loved—is my *secret service*."

"But by not doing it in secret…it's *not* a secret."

"Is it wrong to expect credit for goodness?"

I suspected Buddy, with his multiple contradictions, might be high on something, and I asked how many painkillers he'd taken today.

"Not nearly enough." He lifted a single open-toed shoe and buffed the heel. "Let them see how my heart's been staked. No! Let her see."

I tried to reason. "But after what she's done, this talk flies out the window. Her abortions will easily win you a no-contest divorce."

"But I intend to honor my vow. To keep the moral code upon which it rests."

"Buddy. Do you hear me? Abortion means a *no-contest* divorce! By law she's reneged on her marital duty. You can keep the diamond ring. Bill her for the white dress. She can't just pick-and-choose which parts of a marital vow she wishes to keep. There are laws!"

"I will not bring the abortions up in court. I know she hasn't fulfilled her marital contract. I know I'd get to keep the assets and the apartment. I know that. But as you said, psychologically, even for mental stability, she needs to win something. She needs to win in divorce much more than I do."

"But she's had her win. You brought all the assets to the marriage. You told me she brought only credit-card debt."

"It's true. I even gave her free rent for years before we married, so she could go to beauty school and build the first salon business." Buddy stared out to the sea. "But there are times in life, when we can do *more* than we think we can do."

I could see his pendulum swing back and forth between secret gratitude and resentment. "And then there are times when we're *called* to do more than we *can!*"

"It's true, she aborted our children. And I know, because of that, our marriage can be easily annulled. I wouldn't have to give her a dime. But I won't do it! I intend to define my own character, to accept my share of the responsibility."

"But, too much virtue can in this case hurt *her*! She'll end up locked in the prison of her own greed."

"She'll handle it. Introspection is hardly one of her shortcomings."

"True."

"It's absolutely true. My wife has the psychic ability to overlook her negatives. She even claims them as a kind of hard-scrabble New England virtue!"

"New England? She's hardly New England stock. Her father's Polish."

"That's her Yankee claim. And intolerance is her proof."

Buddy's movements halted, punctuated by the thump of his shoe brush hitting the table. I realized something indiscernible was occurring. A seizure? A stroke? Then I saw what he'd already seen: far off in the distance, a photographer's telescopic lens aimed in our direction.

· · ·

In defiance, Buddy continued his self-examination in his atonement notebook, a lone farmer tilling back and forth across fields of white paper, the pen trailing memory with a sillion of black ink. His defiance made a great show of sitting outside behind a single linen sheet pinned to a rope he'd strung across the patio. Every few minutes, a breeze stirred, lifting the sheet. I'd never seen anyone look so pitiful.

How lucky I'd been to have had my back to the camera, for a tabloid printed a lurid picture of Buddy wearing Lydia's high heels on his hands.

Above it in caps the headline read:

JUST WHAT GOES ON BEHIND THOSE CHAMBER DOORS?
The secrets of a village!

At noon, Pina persuaded Buddy to move his chair into the shade of an olive tree, and we both coaxed him to hydrate and so he gulped liters of water. At one point he complained of being haunted by awkward nightmares, and said his esophagus burned acid. We could not keep the television hidden from Buddy for long. If he came inside, he'd fixate on it for any new item on the scandal. The bare facts were by now digested, so the stories grew more expansive. One tabloid in Britain related Lydia to Lorena Bobbitt, an American woman who'd sliced off her husband's penis. Bobbitt left the house with the misbegotten organ and threw it from a moving car into a meadow. After a massive search, the penis was recovered, packed in ice, and that night reattached in a surgery lasting nine and a half hours.

To pair Lydia and Lorena stories helped brand their connection as examples of American individualism gone too far. Some worried that Italy might soon see a series of copycat crimes, castrations and abortions reigning terror on the land. A pundit for *The Times of London* assured its readers that if this were truly something to fear, half the men in Italy would already be missing genitals. Offended Italian tabloids responded to the English snipe, accusing the writer of being himself *Bobittized!* And another vitriolic round began.

Buddy now grew obsessed with late-night television, and the Bobbitt story with the expected sequence of rehashed borscht-belt briss jokes, while Irish and Scottish limerick clubs penned odes: *She took his thick hobbit, and proceeded to bob it.*

Meanwhile an Australian comedy show featured a man dressed in Lydia's familiar *Cooking Magic* apron, placing, to great applause, a plastic doll in a microwave oven.

One daytime program from Holland was centered on a mock courtroom where three former boyfriends testified at the 'trial' of a woman described to be strident and irritating; the woman appeared in chains. The men acted as contestants seeking monetary damages for trauma. They told of incidents involving her and a vacuum cleaner cord, a head pushed underwater in a bathtub, numerous affairs, some leotards shredded with a knife. The fake-judge held her deliberations, noting while these men did experience something bad, it couldn't compare to the American cooking star's crime against her husband. "That woman refused to give life to their child." For a second example, the judge cited O.J. Simpson and his response to *his* poor wife. The audience booed and again my stomach twisted.

"But O.J. Simpson hasn't been found guilty yet," Roberta said.

Buddy looked bewildered. "Then why drive on a highway like that?"

Roberta sought to maintain her fairness. "Frustration at being misunderstood? Fear of being falsely accused?"

At the Dutch program's end, one of the men—the one who'd been with the violent woman longest—received compensatory damages. The audience cheered wildly at this.

"This is pure misogyny," Roberta said, and shut off the set.

"No," Buddy said. "It's truth. It also shows a bias against men! I wish there was a word like that."

"There is," I said. "The word is *misandry.* It's rarely used."

We turned the set back on and changed channels, stumbling across an image of Buddy clucking like a chicken and shouting in the middle of the street in Sestri Levanti. We soon saw it had been taken from a security camera mounted on some edifice. It shocked me to hear Buddy spouting the same lines I'd heard in Sestri Levanti. They sounded much more incriminating through the eye of television. "Behind which face might there be a *brain* that can open itself? If your churches are so powerful, let them support themselves without government aid! Haven't the histories of the Vatican…or your greedy monarchies been enough to show you why it's important to keep the church away from the state?"

"Right-o, mate! Prisons be built with the stones of law, brothels with the bricks of religion!"

"Right-o!" Buddy was shown shouting back and raising his fist.

Roberta stared at us, her mouth open and aghast.

"When did that happen?"

"After confession."

The papers repeated the image of the homosexual American husband clucking like a chicken with great zeal, as if an important psychiatric link between fowl and humankind had been made. Some suggested the Englishman quoting Blake had been planted, and that the whole operation was a plot by the Anglican church.

Lydia was featured on every evening news summary and her plight was covered in great detail by CNN. I turned to a large double spread story in *Match*— shocking exclusive: *Unaccountable circumstances and mad coincidences—Buddy Landers, husband of the American star of Cooking Magic was last month hospitalized in Genoa for head injuries sustained under mysterious and suspicious circumstances.*

The *International Herald Tribune* ran an opinion piece with an historical component written by a professor of sociology at the University of Maryland: *Gay exploitation myths were nonexistent in ancient Greece; in polytheistic culture, erotic encounters held no gender restriction; people there didn't divide their sexuality into homo and hetero impulses—they evaluated positive influences, mentorship, or worth. They developed the character of both people.* Readers polled to see if homosexuality brought down the Greek empire. A rebuttal: *Why could an inflated hyper-heterosexuality not save the Egyptians or Romans—or better yet, Holy Romans?*

Buddy was offended by a visual aid designed by infographic pioneer Nigel Holmes. It depicted him and Eligio on a rainbow timeline among famous same-sexers of history—Gertrude Stein, Oscar Wilde, Rock Hudson. Buddy was furious, saying he would sue the program and Mr. Holmes but nothing came of his threats.

Three days later, a knock at the door allowed the postman to deliver an ominous registered letter, envelope embossed with the Redeemer College crest.

Buddy read a summons to a mandatory meeting with the provost. "I refuse to go to Harrisburg just to get the ax," he said. "Hell just fire me and be done with it."

"How can they cut you?" Roberta asked. "The point of a college is to wrestle with alternate viewpoints."

"They're pre-wrestled. Scared of academia's liberal liberty! And whatever they think or do, I did sign their stupid agreement."

"Regardless—isn't there some kind of legal action you can take?"

"The cost of a good lawyer is beyond me now. We've over-extended for the cooking show. Besides, that school should have the right to define its environment. The only reason for their existence is not intellectual advancement but to uphold religion."

"Really? Why not call themselves a seminary then, not a college or university?"

"There must be someone you can appeal to," Roberta said.

"Religious schools are beholden to arcane beliefs. They can only survive by pretending faith has become a science. To maintain that they need to limit the curiosity of their believers. And any appeal for decency will be brushed aside, for what is human injustice compared to the suffering of Christ?"

"So, you must accept abuse in the same way it's been doled out to him… or by them?"

"Yes, one learns to shut up and not dare try and top the chosen martyr. Religious people have a perversive need to think they have something unknown figured out. They need to believe they are right. A single kindly priest like Padre Vincenzo, or a thousand like him…isn't nearly strong enough to go against the savage history of the faithful."

. . .

After weeks of being at the center of lurid news reports, our fellow villagers were by now quite experienced at the dodge. One Italian journalist understood this, and so she arrived very determined. Speaking to the camera in a fox-fur vest dyed brilliant turquoise, the journalist speculated the village's cobbled alleyways to be secret carnal places for many husbands and wives, an absurd and wrongful notion given what we who dwelled here knew—our village granted absolutely no privacy. The journalist tried to interview Buddy, but her knock went unanswered. She then wandered about, knocking on other doors. She was about to call it a day, when up the road, Signor Vescovi came walking, gun in the crook of his arm.

"Don't shoot!" she said, joking. Seductively, she touched his arm, as if he were a general just home from a long war. Her gentle questioning soon discovered Vescovi was a longtime resident who knew Buddy and Lydia, and her ramped up journalistic charm soon ensnared the ever-loquacious hunter.

In the days following, commercials began to air promoting a rare special program to include an interview with a local insider. A softly intimate male voice—filled with lubricious innuendo asked: *What happens when a widely known cooking personality becomes a cuckolded wife? What happens when a homosexual husband sires an unwanted child? What lies behind the never-before-told secrets of a scandalous village!?*

• • •

Beside an antiquarian bookseller I knew well, was a bar I also knew well, its walls varnished a rich black, its floor a crimson stone, with glazed doors paired across the front, and left open on nights like this to allow the ocean breezes. We sat down to drink and catch the provocative exposé. Anticipation cheered the shiny faces of the patrons, many regulars, and tonight our fellow viewers. It was interesting to see local interest so extremely piqued. I for one was glad to have escaped watching the program with Buddy. Roberta and I, to avoid having to react with control, snuck down to town. The television set behind the bar was tuned in, and the room hushed as the program opened to a cello solo, playing a melody, not so different from the violin solo for *Cooking Magic*. The cello stirred the emotions of gravitas, suggesting a consequential and human happening about to unfold.

A voice-over re-hashed the drama, speaking over the by now well-known moving images—familiar as the acts of certain well-worn plays by Shakesepeare, Moliere or Chekov: Lydia pouring a pan of chickpea batter, tasting a lemon tart, or pushing through the revolving doors of the clinic. The audience seemed to relish the familiar clips, just as they might await the appearance of Hamlet's ghost, the set-up for a vivid tragedy already underway. To keep things from becoming predictably static, there were also some never-before-broadcast photos, including stills of her in the Egyptian box about to be sawn in half by Phil.

Once the basics were established, the voice-over went on to explain a vicious attack on American Buddy Landers during a homosexual encounter in an abandoned park, all while his wife: "ignorantly prepared a fondue feast." A black-and-white film shot from a security camera mounted high above, showed Buddy arriving at the hospital, head wrapped in a bloody shirt.

The woman on the balcony, who had called the ambulance to transport Buddy to hospital, and had been quoted, was shown again—only now with full makeup and smartly coiffed hairstyle—her speech energized with dramatic excitement. "There were two men on mopeds involved," the woman said.

"And did you get a feeling that something special stirred between them?"

"It's very possible. I won't rule out that they might've been lovers."

A man wearing the uniform of an air conditioner repair company appeared on the screen. "I was on the second-floor roof, fixing the cooling system when they brought him in. I saw it all from above. For sure he's dead, I thought. But there was something furtive about the other guy…the way he moved…like someone up to no good. Later we rode the elevator down together and I felt lucky to be alive. I mean not to have had my throat cut, before the doors to the lobby finally opened." The man crossed himself. He described how much confusion and blood there'd been, ambulance drivers moving with great alarm. "My greatest hope is that this professor will recover and Genoa, our beautiful city, will not be further blemished."

The familiar hospital camera footage appeared and was paused, so that a red circle could be drawn on the screen highlighting the figure of the mysterious man. The program cut, and Eligio's mother was shown once more, followed by the photo as it had appeared on the cover of *The Inquirer*. The bar erupted in tremendous gales of laughter.

Another psychologist, this one from the University of Edinburgh, also contemplated the same-sex consequence. His thoughtful and measured comments were intercut with more bloody ambulance photos. Additional clips of Buddy's wife came next, Lydia baking cookies, and pounding dough to make gnocchi. Pina's face appeared scowling comically at her side. At the sight of Pina the laughter in the bar sounded anew.

The voice-over made another banal comment about the difficult and delicate requirements of marriage. There was a quick cut to Elizabeth Taylor addressing Richard Burton on a vintage talk-show. "Marriage to you ain't easy—baby! You know what I mean?"

There was a second cut to boxer Ace Turner leaving a courtroom hearing after divorcing his seventh wife. A group of reporters was gathered around him.

Later, he spoke in a private interview with Howard Cosell and his old swagger was once more on display. Facing the camera, Cosell framed the story: "In the final days of an ill-fated marriage, the purse to endure the ring is pre-spent… So, two spouses take to their corners, shadow box, crack knuckles, brew poison and wait for the bell to ring its final betrayal. Here all you well-intentioned types better step back beyond the ropes, and let the cops and lawyers take it. Marital divide can be a blood sport, as spurned lovers know where every tenderness lies, and are well-practiced in swinging wild, jabbing fast, and punching hard below the belt. Whatever it takes to punish the one who was once—but is no longer—the beloved."

The next segment cut to a German news program we'd not seen before. The Italian journalist's voice was spoken over the muted original German language broadcast. The German crew had been dispatched from Cologne, and they filmed a popular cruising area frequented by sailors near the naval base at La Spezia. Men could be seen running from the cameras—jackets over heads—unwilling to have families and crew-mates see them scouting for sex on television. But one man, in mascara and earrings, remained and spoke to the camera in Italian. "Without promiscuity gayness will be destroyed. Without anonymity the marriages of many who claim not to be gay will be destroyed." Some of the patrons at the bar grew angry at these remarks, and called the program sinful. Still they kept watching.

The camera crew next appeared inside Levanto's train station, and the Italian journalist explained the German news program had unveiled a sordid history of homosexual activity skulking its bathroom. "This is ridiculous," one man shouted at the screen. "This could never happen here." The journalist was then shown walking toward Levanto's Town Hall which she entered with the camera crew. Seated opposite the desk of the town's police chief, whom everyone recognized, the journalist conducted a brief interview. The chief's outrage was kept very calm and steady. "Such remarks are ridiculously Saxon, and they besmirch the character of our citizenry. Deviant behavior in public spaces is simply not tolerated on Italian soil. We are consulting attorneys and are prepared to prosecute these libelous remarks to defend our beautiful home." The bar patrons cheered.

Despite the bar's joviality, the voice-over continued to pitch melodrama. The journalist's voice returned with the grave tone that something substantial was about to occur. "The photos you are about to see, unearthed by our researchers, have never-before-been shown." The first image showed Lydia standing backstage at one of the magic show venues, her breasts being pushed upward while being laced like Scarlett O'Hara, into her corset and bustle. Someone had also unearthed the infamous handbill, and the camera moved in for a close-up of the pink sticker announcing: *Special assistance by Miss Lydia!* The journalist intimated that the act was based on some kind of domination of Phil. A shot of the cadaverous Phil smoking on a backstage stoop, was followed by the photo of him sitting beside Christina Onassis. The frame cut to footage of Phil speaking like a huckster, the interview shot long ago at a college campus in Dallas. "M-ees Lydia ee-s a femme fatale," he said. "One who'd g-eeve any man angina."

The music suddenly softened and the echo of heels was heard in the studio as the journalist strode up to a director's chair, now dressed in a conservative three-piece pantsuit. She took a seat and reading from notecards began to describe various popular reactions to the recipe-thieving cooking show, noting how the Vatican was said to be preparing a statement, and while justice was slow to adjudicate, it was moving quicker at the level of American academia.

The segment cut to a clip of an attorney for Redeemer College standing with the provost and a member of the faculty senate. As he read a statement, the attorney's voice was muted and the Italian male's voice was laid over in translation: "As a classroom leader, one is expected to shine God's light, a beacon of correctness, to the eyes, minds and hearts of future generations of scholars. Underhanded dealings or errant behavior of any kind are simply not tolerated. We're addressing this blasphemous situation with utmost urgency. We have grief counselors standing by, and prayer circles forming, for any student or faculty who may be suffering as a result."

The journalist alleged that alongside the College's general counsel, the popular mind can often also move quickly—if only to humorize and make light of truth. "Comprehension often shows its first opinion in the marketplace." The camera panned over a shop window displaying an array of popular gag gifts and tee-shirts with slogans and images, one tea towel showed a likeness of Lydia cooking heroin in a spoon captioned: *Cooking Magic!* The camera then zoomed in on another tee-shirt, this one designed around the logo of a pink triangle, images of Lydia, Buddy and Eligio at each corner, the slogan: *silence = bliss.*

After some commercials for lemon soda, breath mints and another for Lotto's mega jackpot, the orchestra returned with an interlude that faded to silence letting us know the program was about to resume. The journalist was back walking the narrow streets of our village. It was there, before a stone wall, that Signor Vescovi appeared in a Tyrolean hat, gazing out over the valley. The bar patrons recognized him and cheered. From a distant classroom, school children's voices could be heard raised in song of a cheerful melody. The exclusive interview allowed a snippet of village history, but interrupted Vescovi's sad story about the demise of the olive mills, cutting away to a makeshift studio we knew had been set up in the back of a truck. The odd pair sat in contemporary armchairs and the questions began. "Can you explain what the mystery man was like?"

Vescovi looked thoughtfully at the wall. "What was he like? Well, he resembles someone charming in manner."

"A matinee idol?"

"Hmmm? Well, perhaps. Since you say so, it would be rude not to agree."

"*Il diavolo?*"

Roberta grew angry. "Eligio…*Il diavolo?* That's ridiculous! She's leading the witness to say stupid things!"

"He used to borrow ice."

"Was that for cooling a fire of some kind?"

"No. For cocktails."

"So, there was a lot of drinking?"

Signor Vescovi's voice was cut-and-dried. "Some wine…Scotch…*Campari.* He and she often dined with a friend. Sometimes, I'd see him take a late meal on the terrace, a plate of cold beef tenderloin. Some cold fish."

"With the husband?"

"No, another man. A poet."

"Did you find that curious?"

"No, not really."

I found mention of the cold fish infuriating, but Roberta thought the oblique way Vescovi referenced me, as well as his ice cubes, was hilarious. My face grew warm as suddenly the world revealed its overcrowded state. And just what would happen if cameras had been in the train tunnel filming my emotional embrace of Eligio, or worse, had been poolside filming me as I stooped to pick up my flip-flops in a scrap of gold lamé? What would cameras make of Eligio's mother feeding her grown son pork from her fingertips? Pina sunning on her employer's terrace? And what about the night, like a fly on the window, when I spied on the woman behind the window washing her children?

The journalist gazed earnestly at Vescovi. "You seem very trusting."

"I like to think the best of people, yes."

She brought the tips of her fingers together to form a concerned and thoughtful pyramid. "Would you say the wife…is a victim?"

Vescovi shrugged. "People have done such things to one another since the dawn of time. It's merely human nature."

"Several domestic violence groups allege the mental anguish that, as a woman, the star of *Cooking Magic* has suffered is ample defense for terminating pregnancy." The journalist lifted a piece of paper and read: *One psychologist has noted—this husband was dishonest, and by his acts the green oasis of marriage has gone dry. No woman can drink from an empty well.*

Vescovi stared as if deep in thought. The journalist grew inquisitive. "And? What are you thinking about right now?"

"That modern modes of living aren't modern at all. Study the history books."

"You mean betrayal, seduction, men who love men? Do you think the husband did these things on purpose? Or is he simply lost?"

"He seems to want to atone for something. He writes his contrition for hours on end."

"That alone seems to reveal he has a guilty conscience."

"Perhaps."

"And what do you know of Miss Lydia's…of her special assistance?"

"Nothing. I hear that she's clever. That she can do magic."

"And even holding that curious talent, do you think Miss Lydia has a chance for happiness?"

Vescovi again shrugged. "Last time I saw her, she had a rather desperate look. At a glance, I sensed even then she was with child."

For the sake of viewers, the journalist knit her brow into a single mitten of concern. "That news ought to bring joy to any woman, *no*?" And as if her own stomach were suddenly distending, she nervously pulled down at her vest.

Vescovi gave a final shrug. "I feel sympathy for anyone living a lie."

The interview ended with parting shots of the village, one featuring Roberta's courtyard, and the last filmed from the distance of the roadway, to suggest the camera's departure. Roberta turned to glance at me with disbelief. "Well, at least he didn't bring Dietrich into it."

Back in the studio, the journalist was now seated in a broadcast chamber, a group of experts assembled on either side of a table. The camera panned around the guests, and the journalist introduced them: a professor of sociology, a professor of history, a corporate lawyer, and a psychologist. All of them were Italian, and each took a moment to read a brief statement they'd prepared. The journalist thanked them and said the discussion would now get underway. Before analysis by the experts could delve too deep, some bar patrons began to hiss and swear. "These are the educated idiots our universities vomit out," one man said loudly, and he was received with great agreement and ovation. Some patrons began tossing cashews at the screen, and the outnumbered barman wisely switched to a football match—a mighty roar of approval ensuing.

• • •

The breakfast table sat empty but for a dish of brown dates left from last night's dinner. I made the coffee, warmed some leftover bread, and opened a jar of lavender honey. For the rest of the morning, Pina remained unseen, her absence and lack of breakfast, peculiar. At lunch, for the first time since I bought the house, her ancient presence offered no food.

"Maybe she and Buddy eloped," I joked to Roberta. We waited until two o'clock, then strolled by her door, disturbed to find her rooster also missing. Had the old bird gone truant with Pina?

"The day before the program aired," I recalled, "she dead-headed roses on the lower terrace. After pinching the stems, she put a single fresh blossom in a jelly glass and placed it on the table in front of Buddy. The orange petals were just opening, and he stared at them all afternoon, praising their color, blathering on and on about the rose being the most difficult flower to paint. He believed that in offering the rose, Pina was letting him know the pain of limitation was understood—but that now was also the time for risk. Buddy claimed new ambitions were awakened by the rose, that he planned to learn not only Persian but Greek, and to visit Japan before he grew too old."

That evening, Roberta cooked a huge platter of chicken and rice with no assistance from Pina. Selfishly, Buddy spread the last of the butter on the last of the old bread, then recognizing his absentminded greed, fumbled to scrape some away, offering the pale, crumb-laden excess back to us. While we ate, Buddy turned the television on, and it wasn't long before we were stunned to see Phil Filbertson appear. We watched spellbound as he and his new assistant endorsed a line of reduced-fat yogurt, that made calories and waistlines *magically* disappear. The commercial unnerved Buddy. He fumed. "That smug bastard is the only winner over this. He positively beams in spillover spotlight. What a crook!" It made no difference that Phil had signed his yogurt contract weeks before the scandal, or that the costume designer had measured, cut and sewn the black-sequined suit with purple trim months earlier. We all recognized Phil's advantage, the razzle-dazzle of Italian spectaculars, cashing in to endorse a popular line of yogurt, all boosted by the old photographs of him with Miss Lydia.

After dinner, Signor Vescovi came up from the lower garden, the tree tops swaying in the evening breeze. Buddy glowered at him in a lemon-eating way—just as Pina might—and without a word, left the terrace.

"Your interview wasn't to his liking," Roberta said.

"Yes. It was terrible. They said they wanted me to speak about the history of olives in our region. For more than an hour I spoke about the Benedictine monks who planted the first tree in the twelfth century. I went into great detail about harvesting *Taggiasca*—how they are the best in the world. I showed them maps of how in olden days, mules climbed our cliffs. I even showed them an old photo of *La Stalla*. But in the end, they only used my remarks about Buddy. I betrayed him in five minutes, without awareness as to how the program might be limited. The camera lights seduced me to candor, it is true. A bad mistake! I hope in time my apology will gain acceptance."

"I'm sure he will come around."

Signor Vescovi bowed his head. "With old Pina gone, I guess you've lost your procurer? In the morning, I will go to town and stock your larder."

"Where do you think she is?" Roberta asked.

"Her husband had a niece in Pisa. I suspect she's there. Who knows? It's possible she's finally realized the cooking program has made a joke of her. Maybe she'll never come back."

• • •

In the days that followed, we learned that in addition to re-financing forty-nine percent of the cooking show's production while Buddy lay in the hospital, Lydia siphoned off most of the money from their joint bank accounts, leaving him a pauper.

With this discovery, Garafallou came up to the village to see Buddy. "Discrediting that brash American interloper," he said, "that *thief* of the Italian kitchen seems to be a national delight. I've spoken to Eligio and advised him to wait in seclusion in Chiavari. He tells me his mother is still smarting from her encounter with the press. Apparently, she's combed out her hair, and now paces the floor in wait for the ill-begotten day when her door will have to reopen to the cameras camped outside."

He flung a press kit onto the table. "Have you ever seen such a pack of lies!" I glanced at the index:

La Republica
Il Gironale
Italia Oggi
La Stampa
Corriere della Sera
La Verità
Librero
Stern
Clarín
Match
Enquirer
World
The Sun Star
The Daily Mirror
The New York Post
People Magazine
Time
Newsweek
Kerala Kaumudi

"If you look at these vile articles as a group—you'll see how imitative journalism has become. And they all have one dastardly thing in common—none of them have offered to tell *your* side of the story." In exchange for much-needed cash, Garafallou then suggested a live television interview be arranged for Buddy. At first Buddy was furious to be exploited in this way, but the fact of hardship made him vulnerable. And the longer Garafallou spoke—the more reasonable the idea sounded. Roberta and I thought he finally agreed not just for money, but because he needed to be made visible, and desperately wanted a program to tell his side of things.

Roberta and I agreed to drive Garafallou back down to the station. "It's odd," I said, in the car, "that Lydia herself has so far resisted speaking about the scandal? Is she panic-stricken?"

"No doubt," Garafallou said. "But we, as her producers, have also placed a gag order on her. If she violates that, she's liable for damages to us all." The ride ended with him imploring us to continue our good care of Buddy.

The next day the producers, to prepare Buddy for the interview, insisted Garafallou hire an advertising consultant, who turned out to be a man from Manchester, England, the only one they could find in the area who spoke good enough English—but he usually advised sports stars. "Dodge any questions like the bloody royals do. And if you have to say anything, turn yourself into a real ordinary bloke. Give only mundane details about your life."

On the morning of the interview, Roberta and I drove Buddy to Genoa for the taping.

"I feel like Howard Beale," Buddy said.

"Who?"

"That guy in *Network*. Who screamed out the window that he was mad as hell."

Roberta laughed. "To me the whole thing is like a film by Preston Sturges."

We spent the next few hours waiting expectantly in the green room for the program to begin. Buddy came out of make-up looking paler and flatter than I'd ever seen him, the bandage on his head now heavily padded. The stage manager came to explain the sequence and Buddy soon realized what the producer's real purpose in having him appear was. "I'm the chump," he told us. "They need me to create a forum whereby they can *then* plant an enormous public relations *lie!*"

Before we could ask any questions, the stage manager whisked Buddy away. Inside the studio, Buddy appeared like a man laced into a too-tight waistcoat, heart and stomach compressing with his every breath. He did as his coach advised and talked of dull things, the academic calendar: "Labor Day school begins, then exam week, then the holidays, then Spring break. Always the same."

Droning on about the poetic abstractions to be explored during his sabbatical, skin pasty, hair matted at the edges of his enormous bandage, he seemed full of self-pity, ridiculously so, and most viewers hadn't a clue about what he was talking about, except that he hoped to be able to work on a blank piece of paper and from a place of blankness, growing surprised when a glimmer of himself or his biography would mysteriously appear through the stylus. He described his austere Pennsylvania lodgings, close to campus and rented from a calico-clad widow in the town of Lemoyne. "On weekends I travel to New York for high culture. But I have a class Monday morning, so I return on Sunday night, driving on Interstate-78 which then turns into Interstate-81. I call those routes the highways of death. They are major freight roads, passenger vehicles wedged between massive trucks. In Winter, there's frequently but one degree between rain and slush, and sometimes there's fog. Railroads certainly knew better; they realize how important it is to separate passengers from freight."

Roberta and I looked at one another, registering astonishment that he was going on about the weather and driving on freight roads. He then described in great detail his school, and the actions of a particular department chair. "This woman is a big, blonde, overweight bully, who brazenly filibustered a faculty meeting where a vote to protect certain literary programs was to be taken. She was from another department yet acted to uphold a posse of male religiosity—once innocent altar boys—now just bitter old Catholic men. Her cruelty cost several people their livelihoods." He went on to describe another, "rather frosty" dean, who still swung his dull opinions and biased judgements even though he himself was already stepping down to join another school. "The guy was already leaving our college. So, to support heinous acts, when he didn't have to, means he *enjoyed* the power to destroy. If that's not parochial evil—then what is?"

Roberta looked at me aghast. "Does Buddy think describing morally corrupt deans will help viewers sympathize with him?"

"Or up his ranking at his school? That big blonde department chair will probably taste blood and come out swinging simply because he called her fat."

"I can't imagine him being coached to say this."

Finally, the subject the producers depended on him to present, was broached. The interview cut to a bogus doctor, seated in his office and wearing a white lab coat. The man explained Lydia's miscarrying procedure had been medically necessary due to complications that upset her health. Buddy returned to the screen, face red with guilt, and he confirmed the facts presented by the doctor had been kept secret. The interviewer then asked point blank if he'd prayed for guidance. Buddy nodded just as rehearsed.

"And what do you pray for?"

"For a true redeemer—to replace the one which the churches and sacred schools of the world have destroyed. Like the rather unaccomplished and cruel academic deviants whom I work alongside. We've all seen such terrible things done on behalf of Faith, the Catholics, the Protestants, the Jews, the Muslims, the Hindus, the Buddhists, Marilyn Monroe, Elvis, Zeus and Hera, Running Wolf, the tribal ancestors, and all the other abominations of the world!"

These last words were definitely not in Garafallou's script. In disbelief, I looked at Roberta. "Oh my God, he's slammed every faith on the planet. Now all hell will break loose!"

· · ·

Corriere della Sera, the largest paper in Milan, and one that had been covering the scandal since the start, now ran a headline screaming: *HERETIC!* above a photo showing Buddy with his overly-bandaged head. The editorial referred to him as not only "Anti-humanity" but "Antichrist." They also mocked his drive on Interstate-81, labeling him: "The *Auto*-Professor."

The voice of incrimination was imitated in papers around the world. And Buddy's claim to seek high culture in New York, was now twisted to sound like a euphemism for sex. Vituperation against him magnified; on the car radio, we heard confirmation of what the reporter who'd interviewed Vescovi had intimated, that the Vatican had issued a denouncement prescribing prayer for such a misguided and lost soul.

"Prayer's the *last thing* Buddy needs more of," Roberta said.

At dawn, I strained for any hint of sound from Pina, hoping to hear her in the kitchen making toast, or turning on the faucet somewhere. From time to time, I sensed rustlings, but these were ghosts. Roberta slept beside me, her pattern of breathing light, the pale cotton sheet folded neatly under one arm.

I forced myself to rise from the warm bed, the clay tiles feeling cool under my feet. I brewed coffee in the kitchen, and while it cooked, went outside. The brightness of the azure sea startled my eyes as it always did. Turning from the terrace to go back inside, I noticed a small calico cat huddling at the top of the marble steps. "Now, how did you get in?" I went up, unlatched the gate, and the cat bolted. Pausing to inhale some rosemary branches planted in a huge pot, I detected some small drops of black paint spattered on the stone walkway in front of the Swedes' house. Most were dime-sized, some smeared. Stepping back, I looked up. To the left of the copper downspout and above the windows, someone had painted the house in wild black letters: *Filthy amoral birds—fly home!*

My ears pounded. Were the vandals still nearby? The cobbled alley sat silent, every shutter bolted. I hurried back down and only then saw Buddy lying on the ground in the lower garden. He felt my presence as I neared. "Ever notice ants?" he asked without looking up. "Glanced from above, they seem easy to consider. Then get closer, and watch them long enough, and you realize that they're really human."

I'd hoped to prevent him from seeing the letters scrawled on the house, but was too late. "An obituary for our marriage," he said. "An epitaph written on an empty crypt."

"We must clean it at once."

"Even if we do...won't the culprit simply come and paint it again...or worse?"

"That doesn't mean we shouldn't try."

"None of this matters to the ants—and none of it should matter to us."

Signor Vescovi stepped over the lower hedge, carrying a large grocery box from town. His features twitched at seeing Buddy lying on the ground. "I bought milk, eggs, pasta, cheese, bread and vegetables," he said. "Might you also like one of my rabbits?" I interrupted him, pointing to the painted message. He startled then spoke to me in an aside. "Your friend seems to breed pestilence wherever he goes."

I whispered back. "It's not his fault. He's trying hard to redeem himself."

"I just saw a camera crew lurking. The longer the paint remains, the more likely they are to film it for television!"

I snorted. "Another entertainment disguised as investigative reporting?"

"I think many crave such programs for distraction—to avoid feeling the wretchedness of their own lives." Vescovi's newly acquired cynicism, showed the extent to which he'd come to distrust. I enlisted his aid to scrub the letters off the house, and he handed me the groceries, then hurried to fetch a ladder. Putting the groceries in the kitchen, I went back down to Buddy, coaxing him to abandon the garden. He slowly got up, brushed dust from his shirt and pants, and followed me. Back in my kitchen, the coffee had boiled and I poured us some.

"Such unfair symbols," Buddy said. "I mean the birds."

"Yes," I agreed. "And which are the most amoral? Peacocks? Starlings? Bower-birds and their sparkling stolen treasures?"

"Don't forget Pina's rooster." Buddy smiled for the first time in weeks. I too smiled, if only in the hope that by way of humor, he might find a healthy tool to manage this new insult. "Perhaps the Swedes will have to screen future tenants, leasing only to those with morally faultless lives."

"Or find those who at very least hide their flagrancy."

Through the window I saw Vescovi return, bearing the ladder, a wide piece of canvas and some large clips. A camera crew followed on his heels. I went out and began unfolding the fabric as Vescovi climbed up toward the roofline. Before any camouflaging could be attached, the filming began.

"Shame on you!" Vescovi yelled down from atop the ladder. "Just look at yourselves. See how such cruel messages seem to invigorate you! And perhaps it was even you who wrote this judgement—you television people, or someone you hired? And you, Mr. Cameraman! You film and film, take photo after photo to waylay good people with nonsense. Your entertainment prevents them from banding together—to ask the really serious questions. What is our national policy? Where do our taxes go? Power people don't like to explain! Or reveal that it is *they* who make the laws! They who pay your putrid salary!" His angry words had a strange, shaming effect on the crew, and they began to move away. Wow, I thought. *Any human not too lazy to do so…could withdraw his consent from any force or rule.*

That afternoon, Buddy stretched out on the Swedes' plaid couch, holding the envelope of cash the producers had given him in exchange for his interview. "I knew it! Fabricating the story of that phony doctor could only heighten my internal conflict." He spread the bills across his chest and stared at them. "All impotent men grow sneaky. If *really* weak, they'll besmirch the strong—or as impotent men do, they grow more dependent, spend *other* people's money, including that of a wife, an employer or other affiliate. And realizing how sterile he truly is, the impotent man will crave impossible ways to attain manliness, gain a false sense of potency. Usually he settles for self-righteousness—political clout—or grabs at filthy lucre."

Roberta and I assured Buddy he was not impotent, and went to the kitchen to prepare dinner. He remained on the couch, only putting the money away when we urged him to join us at the table.

Book Eleven

TELOLOGY

. . .

The sound of language carries fluency. A fresh spring babbling beneath the feet of all people, human voices streaming in a torrential flow, accessible to any child's ear, all learned in preconscious thought. Toddlers have merely to dip their tiny hands down into that cool word-spring and draw talk up to their lips and tongues. The modes of early speech bond a tribe, but later it is adults who assign meaning and challenge toward those bonds. Language, written and read, can twist as someone wants it and needs it to be, developing into libel, inference, sarcasm, metaphor, surprising revelation. And even *we* who claim nothing shocks us, can arrive at startling realities, or conflicts wherein our words leave us—as true shock erases speech. In shock the words of meaning lose out to bewilderment as language evaporates.

Our world turned silent over breakfast, sitting in my kitchen, when Signor Vescovi came up from town, and said everyone was talking about a missing man. Apparently, an odd sea-captain had appeared on the news, describing the disappearance, in a breaking story. Vescovi left, and between bites of toast and oatmeal, we went to fetch the set, startled to find Buddy had entered during the night and reclaimed it. Our mouths were left with words of speculation, disbelief, worry, but the limitations of narrative quietly overwhelmed us, for somehow, we already knew our time to once more imagine a connection to tragedy had come.

We could not finish our repast. Instead, we crossed the terrace and knocked on Buddy's door. It was unlocked, and as we had feared, he wasn't there. The television was also not there. Had we been robbed? We crossed the terrace again, and were about to enter my kitchen, when Roberta looked down to the lower garden and discovered the television. Somebody had taken the blunt edge of an ax and smashed the screen, and hacked the black plastic casing into big, fractured chunks that lay scattered over the grass. Had we really slept through such a racket? Stupefied by the violent act, Roberta shook with alarm, trying to decide what to do next.

Signor Vescovi returned. "I just heard more on the radio news. Tell me. Did Buddy ever go boating?" Vescovi spoke rapidly to explain how the broadcaster had said an American man had showed up at dawn to join the earliest cliff tour. Then the boat captain explained how there was something familiar about the fellow, that he might've even been aboard the boat before. At the cliffs, many passengers swam and climbed to jump from the brown rocks. The man joined them, but after jumping, his body never surfaced. Vescovi paused, and I showed him the destruction of the box below. His eyes widened and his hand lifted to rest on the back of his head.

. . .

Scuba teams were dispatched, and by afternoon they'd found a body at the bottom of the sea. A struggle to bring it to the surface ensued. Rather than wear a life preserver, the man had put on a photographer's vest, every pocket filled with stones.

The police arrived to investigate and searched the Swedes' house, finding what we already knew, the house was empty. The language in our heads disintegrated further, fractured by the sound of the single village chapel-bell ringing out across the valley. The clanging was wrought by Signor Vescovi, who, in his dismay and distress, had climbed the steps of the bell-tower to ring the death knell for Buddy.

Again, no one could reach Lydia, and so making the official identification fell to me. In town, leaving the office of a prefect, I was led to a small morgue room, the chamber glowing with eerie incandescence, too strong for moonlight yet not bright enough for even a dim bulb. It was a shock to encounter Buddy lying cold on a marble slab. I'd been warned to expect a gruesome sight, as more than a dozen crustaceans had been pulled from his face, something delectable attracting the creatures to tear and eat away from his unhealed wound. The strange glowing lamp tried to soften the horror, tinting the whole atmosphere to duplicate the hour of dichotomy, spacing day from night, sleep from wake, sun from moon. It sought to represent a time and place where living people typically never go—the world beyond twilight.

And Buddy had indeed suffered a sea change into something rich and strange, the flesh surrounding his forehead and eye sockets torn away, the eyes themselves missing, probably liquified into seawater. My stomach lurched. The suicidal expression confounds, for it recognizes all of us hang over an abyss, even those we think are impervious or imbued with strength. Any of us can find our fingers grasping at loose clay and stone, like failed jugglers, their caste's long tradition of being the lowest of the low, knowing too well the order of motion, how we must all bow down to respect that thief of Newton's apple—gravity.

The attendant quietly officiated over the various formal documents. I signed in solemn conduct, fountain pen scratching the parchment. After the paperwork was complete, the clerk whispered that I might like some time alone with my friend. I nodded. The woman left, her gray skirt rustling as she walked. I stood by the marble table muted in stillness, enduring the shock of meeting a corpse belonging to someone I'd known. With Mom there'd been too much confusion to study and comprehend her as a cadaver, and we'd not gone to the West Coast to witness Cole's remains. For both of these loved ones, their composition in the aftermath could be remembered by me mainly through televised images.

How is it that so many of us remove ourselves from handling the bodies of our dead, choosing not to anoint our departed loved ones with our own hands. Is professionalizing death something we require? Did the Egyptians hire others to anoint their beloved? Did professionals wrap the mummies found in the tombs? They must have. Or was learning how to wrap a corpse something everyone was taught, a task to be practiced whenever death came to call? To handle a corpse generates respect for the life now gone, resistance spent, all at peace, any effort now holding the chance to pass over, to say all is forgiven, to murmur speech that says: *Fear not…I'll look after you now.* Somehow, the act of tending a dead body brings connection, a transfer to accept the humble and tactile end of all life. It's impossible not to see our own skeletons mirrored in the joinery of any fragile body lying on marble. For me to comprehend this was ennobling, with reflection on how inert my own parents must have been.

Standing beside that marble table, I stared down at Buddy's torn and ruined features. His body, absent of vitality, was now but a chamber, plain, vulnerable and empty. The act of looking, blurred my vision. He, like my parents, wasn't coming back. A pitiful remorse stole through me, his sad mutilation due in some way to my terrible negligence. I should've praised him more. I should've stayed closer. I should've read his poems. How might my detachment have advanced his dance with death? Could I reconcile my ignoble coldness and criticism? The spurned responsibility burned my throat, and I found myself more upset than I could've imagined.

Aside from my own shortcomings, what else had caused the psychic injuries bringing about this catastrophe? Was it something he said to my cousin? She to him? That pair, like so many of us, were specimens in a petri dish, splitting apart, to wriggle further and further away, recreating independence as two individuals…and yet organisms un-joined all the time. It wasn't so unique.

I'd forsaken my marriage to Chantel, feeling quite lucky to have decided it was better to be the one moving out. That helped me move *on*. Unlike my cruel cousin, in uncoupling, I roamed freer for not having tried to appropriate the physical and intellectual property of an ex-spouse. I never tried to follow

Chantel to her new home, or disrupt her from dating someone fresh, nor did I ever gloat or stalk. I'd forfeited any right to see what our old life might one day look like. So, what if sadness at the loss of youthful love could sometimes twinge? Better to suffer and endure the loss, so in due time, a new life could spring, one in every way superior to the old.

After great pain, a formal feeling comes. How Buddy's sunbaked brain must've shadowboxed with that. Or even worse, wrestled with the platitudes of childhood, those long-prayed passages about peace and heaven that we in distress can't quite abandon or haze out. *After great pain, a formal feeling comes.* Is it possible for anyone to have written that line without personal knowledge of deep, personal pain? Such a right arrangement of words, carving across time, connecting people born centuries apart, that could only ever meet via squiggles of ink. The sacred food of a generative idea, its syntactical transmission, the voice of supernal law. Still, this poem was not spoken by Christ, Confucius, or Vishnu, but yet another kind of poet. One whose anguish rendered so exactly that which all who encounter pain might come to recognize. Are all humans capable of similar relational formality? Might the same chords sound across many mortal strings? Might the inability to control the pen as it dips into poetic form hold a clue as to why so many scribes succumb to suicide?

All human systems had failed Buddy. All prayer, all friendship, all art, all marriage, all churches, all books, all ink, all hope, and sadly all the colleges he knew. Through the cruelty and narrow mindedness of academic life, he'd come to denounce the piety he'd endured, bound by what he called the limit and liability of educational systems. His public shaming and despair, the split of ill-fit marriage, all had weakened Buddy's cell structure. This too happened all the time. How might the character of anyone bend under deviant salacious slander or a libel born of opportunistic shame?

Do people who admit the delusional lies that every human tells to themself, suffer a stronger urge to die? Wasn't confession supposed to renew? Or was an avoidance of facing lies—that which granted health? Maybe it's easier to simply do what so many do instead—wind down into drugs, alcohol, depression, overzealous activism, comic rants, brutal new lovers, lawsuits, blind religious crusades, wars, or trolling after any fashion or fad. Is it when all other options for life appear malignant, that some choose to kill their own bodies…death the absolute settlement?

The exposed bone at the front of Buddy's skull now brought forth the long-sought feelings of kinship he'd so wanted. We were fellow-mammals. This was the bond that only his *finality* delivered, and how terrible to incur this sense of union now—the very thing I'd begrudged him from exploring while he was alive.

Slice the skin and flesh off all our bodies and our universal human core reveals itself: *o skeletos*. A single cavity for heart and lungs, one space for cranial thought and feeling, the universal envy, greed, jealousy, piety, murder, joy, wonderment, generosity, these traits found on every continent, in every culture, anyone classified within our species. Our sins and virtues are *the universal*—our tears, our songs, our laughter. Unwrap a mummy, unwrap Howard Carter, unwrap Christ, or Emmett Till. Unwrap the ancient Corsican woman carbon-dated back to 6570 BC. Go to Ethiopia and dig up Lucy, dig up all the ancient bones of Liguria, or the catacombs of Paris, the Grand View cemetery in Palmyra. Dig up all the sacred burial spaces on the planet. Go to China, India, Japan, Africa. Unwrap all our cultural differences, our various garments and lodgings, our various musicalities, our languages, what we eat, how we sing, what we read, whom we pray to. Pull the skin from *any—body*, and as always there remains the self-evident essence of uniformity—the bleached coral of our bones.

The limits of language, the challenge of words, the conveyance of truth, the possibility to define the impossible—to declare, divide, express, unite. Mom and my first stepfather both died so young, and to this day I rarely pass a grave being dug without questioning how many molecules of them might rest within that dirt, that compost, those ashes.

How many inflections and word patterns disappeared with them? How many instructions or recipes? How many memorized songs and poems. And perhaps, that's why I still sometimes write to her. Why I record the things I am seeing or have seen. I never cease seeking to know them through language. Yet my true eternal longing remains a wish to once more feel the touch of a vanished tactile form. Perhaps they know somehow? I thought once more of Montaigne, of his friend's death, how he wrote essays addressed toward absentia for the rest of his life. Might Étienne de La Boétie know he was being contacted? Might he listen and reply?

And yet poor Buddy appeared not to have cultivated such a friend. During his lifetime, I couldn't conceive of him as a man worthy enough for such a focus. A man daring to discover himself as a poet nonetheless, a title we both claimed, though I was now a *failed* poet, for I had neither comprehended nor been able to identify, let alone describe, the true depth of *his* plight.

I saw how we were both seeking something lost from other men. Not carnal contact. But something even more intimate. The comfort of physicality, of knowing something tender can be carried within that which is male.

Peering down at Buddy's torn lips, made perfect and plump by their bruising, I fought revulsion. My eyes began to well in deep sorrow. Leaning over his face, I lowered my lips to his mouth and kissed his defacement good-bye. The cold, roughness of his peeled purple skin in parting, shocked me, bitten hard and wintery as any department store mannequin. I placed my hand on top of his. It too, felt stiff and arctic. Having no spirit left to guard, the body now an empty vessel.

It scorned me not to have let this masculine creature feel some comfort or hope from me. Not to have loosened my own early pain and competition. Not to have shared with another man in pain more of an audience…despite our very differences. In my failure to do more, to even capture and compose *his* failure, I'd let our entire species down. And so, it came to be. Buddy died alone.

• • •

At the morgue's exit, the kindly clerk offered me a tissue and a cardboard box filled with Buddy's personal effects. I took his watch and his wedding band, and went through the pockets of the photographer's vest he'd been wearing; they were empty, the stones removed. The pockets of his pants were also empty. The last item in the box turned out to be the blue linen shirt worn the day we'd all had lunch at Santa Clara; the infamous sky-colored garment that had also once been buttoned over Eligio's skin, and had instigated Lydia's false witness.

"I'd like to keep the shirt," I said. The woman handed it over, agreeing to dispose of the other clothes. "I'm sure this is a stupid question," I said. "But did the police find any money on him? He had just received a lot of cash."

"No, I'm sorry. This box is everything." The woman looked at me with pitiful kindness. "Please know we at the morgue didn't take it."

"No. Of course not."

"It is a sad thought—but we lose everything by the end—even our money."

I paused in the doorway and nodded to express my thanks. Craving sunshine and physical movement, my feet brought me outside in a daze, and I headed down toward the beach, a sense of consternation following. At the water's edge, I wrapped Buddy's blue shirt around my neck to ward off the wind, and to feel his presence. "I will look after you now," I whispered.

It startled me to discover our striped chairs and cocktail tables had been removed. "They were kept out longer than usual this season," the muscled man who rented them said. "But our Summer scorch is long gone, and the furniture is finally back in storage." I was tempted to tell him our friend had just died, the one with the dancing iguana swim trunks, but to say the words out loud would be unbearable.

Down at the shoreline I stood, still wearing trousers, socks, and shoes, the water's mimetic motion pulling sideways, a brown foam stubbornly clinging to the cold sand like old beer suds. In my mind I heard the refrain of a melancholy song. Yes, it was indeed a long way from May to September, and the days did grow short in November. And just how many Summers does a person get? Seventy? Eighty? How many Julys? I'd likely already used more than half of mine, and a sense of time passing deepened as I watched the last of the splashing children run shivering out onto the beach. Defeated and windblown, my bones damp in the late-day shadow, I went to our cabina, Palermo 36, to retrieve our leftover towels and swimsuits for the last time.

• • •

Planning even a small funeral was difficult. I telephoned Padre Vincenzo and asked him to officiate, but he said the manner of Buddy's death generated an unresolvable conflict within his church. "Few who wear our vestments hold a liberal view toward anyone claiming their own life," he said. "So, I must decline. My battles of defiance must be carefully chosen, and while I take any number of risks for the living—sadly, I cannot afford risks for the dead. Pressure from other priests would prevail, especially the old one Buddy confessed to in Sestri Levanti."

I felt my anger rise. "Can't you at very least give a nod to his skeleton?" Obligingly, he offered a prayer over the copper phone wire. My feelings turned to outrage. "I thought in your Father's house, all were welcome? And where is your God in all this? Why didn't he or his long-suffering son rescue Buddy in the hour of his need? Why is his end not seen as *their* failure…but as *his* sin?"

Padre Vincenzo remained silent.

"I mean, how can a religion stoop so low as to forbid the hope of its most enduring story—the promise of life everlasting? That's some kind of taxation without representation. How can so many minds be taught to think suicidal people, and those who knew them, deserve yet *more* punishment, instead of simply allowing Buddy to participate in the already impossible belief of ascent into heaven?"

And still Padre Vincenzo remained silent.

"I'm sorry Father…I simply don't know what else I can say."

"I understand why you are angry," he said at last. "It is not possible to unravel mysteries known only to God." He added that he himself expressed a declination for judgment. In frustration, I hung up the receiver without letting him finish.

Without a church, I, in desperation, turned to Signor Vescovi. "It is essential to find a secret place for a service, one that those vultures of the press won't discover."

By evening, he informed me of an arrangement he'd made to use the back room of a bar on the outskirts of the main road, a place frequented by local truck drivers needing liquid courage to navigate the treacherous mountains. I thanked him, then phoned Garafallou, imploring him to lead the ceremony. He honorably agreed to both give the eulogy and uphold the location's secrecy.

. . .

At noon, we waited outside the bar. The captain who'd ferried Buddy to the rocks came up the hill from the direction of the harbor, wearing a black turtleneck, his face somber. "Only the devil buries people so young," he said.

Four other local men and women arrived. Signor Vescovi knew them and had rounded them up. Among them, I recognized a stationer who often sold notebooks to Buddy, and an English-speaking woman who volunteered at the library. The final attendees to appear were some members of an historical society, who apparently liked to document undocumented funerals. Their leader whispered they'd come at the request of Padre Vincenzo, who swore them to keep the service's location secret. Garafallou turned to me. "Maybe the absent priest is reckoning some guilt by sprinkling a few faces from his flock?"

I nodded.

Garafallou brushed his left eyebrow. "How incongruent are those who attend burials. As incongruent as those who opt not to."

"Any sign of her?"

"Not yet. If she arrives, her love of drama will play the widow in full, coming in late—wearing some outlandish veil or costume." Garafallou took one more glance down the valley, then turned toward the bar. "Some of the producers explained her attendance could garner sympathy and win back favorable publicity. She seemed to relish that. But…then she learned no press would be here."

I refrained from admitting that I myself had last evening spoken to Lydia, pleading for her to attend and pay respects. To repeat her final words before hanging up was for me infuriatingly impossible: *If I do what you ask…then I'm as sick as Buddy.*

We waited a few extra minutes, but no latecomers were seen. Garafallou's face sank, miserably disappointed. "Well then…we better go in."

The bar customers glared as we pulled the door open, expressing the universal disdain barflies have for outsiders, especially those who lack their superior history of a pelvis perched year-after-year on the same padded stool. We filed behind the glass-in-hand drinkers to the back room, and I thought how their condescension would've been no obstacle for Buddy. He'd proven many times over that if one's cash rang good enough for the house, then given half-an-hour and enough bought drinks, the insolence of any drunk could mercurially transform to the cheer of a lifelong friend—though typically not the sort of friend one composes an essay or a poem to, nor the kind expected to attend one's funeral.

At a small banquet table in the back room, the proprietor carved thin slices of ham shank, his fingers holding a vice-like hand-grip screwed to the bone's end, and molded from pewter to resemble the head of a boar. When the man saw us, he quickly covered the operation with a white tablecloth.

Our delay could stretch no further, and Garafallou called the room to order, saying we'd come here to honor Buddy. "His dear friend Walker here, has frequently reminded me of an old saying: *God is either in all of us…or he's in none of us.* Our dear friend Buddy knew both sides of this coin—but he's left us to go on a quest to discover more. He might've loathed what life was preaching, but nonetheless how he must have also dreaded to die, for he went unspent.

"The human life is born into tragedy, and we've all known many funerals— for death exists in every life." Garafallou then began the tale of his own early loss, a boy and his blind uncle, passengers on a beautiful ocean liner. "Watching that ship go down, forever changed my life. As survivors on lifeboats, we were left to speculate about the *weight* of things. Cases of perfume from Grasse, oak-aged Napoleon brandy in cut glass decanters, crates of wedding porcelain from Limoges, with enough settings for a dinner for twelve…or twenty, thick amber bottles from Marseille, holding lavender shampoos, a doctor's wooden box packed with bromides and digestives. Between the cresting waves and the ocean floor, I still imagine these objects passing one another, just as people do, some in descent, some in ascent, some suspended, some falling fast, all dependent on weight, density, volume, circumstance.

"After a mile of sinking, the heaviest things hit bottom first. Imagine the luxuries of life clinking in a cloud of silt amid darting sea-creatures. Imagine the prayers of *every* faith deposited along the way. It is in this same manner that we are left to puzzle the downward drift of Buddy.

"To this day, I can still wake to dreams of the boat. And I can also still sense the warp and weft of packing: all the planning, the foresight, the hindsight, the fretful short sight; all the bother, burden, and strain, the cataloguing, ordering, and muscle effort to haul things of daily living around the world in the hope of feeling familiar in a foreign place; to fend off discomfort—or ensure life might continue to benefit from quality's excess."

As the eulogy continued, I turned toward the back of the room in hopes of finding that Lydia might have turned up. But my angry, long-hurting cousin was nowhere to be seen. However, in the shadow of the rear wall, I noticed another figure, small and almost unnoticed, swathed in a navy shawl. She was probably unable to comprehend a word of what Garafallou was saying, yet a radiant expression still lit her eyes. Her presence pulled deep emotion through the muscles of my own face. How Buddy would've liked that Pina had come home to attend his funeral.

"In the sea, we counted items once paired…now floating apart. A single green bedroom slipper, one taupe kid glove, one ruffled garter, one bright red woolen sock, one sheer stocking. And imagine…the lovers who drowned, desperate to remain in lock, their fingers violet with cold. Or worse, lovers torn apart, clinging to life rings, not knowing the fate of their mate, or doomed to die alone clawing at the waves, the pink membranes of their lungs gulping, the panic-stricken bronchioles thickening with green mucous and salt water.

"Can you imagine my poor uncle—*blind* to it all? To give some ballast, I described the debris tossing in the waves, so he could imagine the suitcases and trunks. Baggage split like clamshells, the delectable meat inside made of fine-milled suits, stitched baize tennis whites, dinner jackets, bed jackets, jackets of eccentric plaid, silk charmeuse evening gowns, iridescent taffeta, furs of chinchilla, fox, sable, all sopping up seawater.

"Imagine…crocodile cosmetic cases, ivory handled umbrellas, half-submerged chair cushions acting like great sponges, thimbled sewing kits, kitchen utensils. And all the un-thinkables: baby bottles, emery boards, douche pouches, prayer books, round boxes of fine rice powder packaged in Paris—now turned to glue. Palmetto fans, playing cards, the prayer card of St. Paul, and from the Pyrenees, men's toupees, woven from human hair, swirling in the water like the legs of some vain, lacy squid.

"See the parcels and well-wrapped packages, the wedding presents, a grandmother's chocolates from Brussels, a tooled leather coin purse to delight a favorite niece, a can of cherry tobacco to make a father merry, a papier-mâché letterbox inscribed with gold letters: *For Rita, our beloved Thea.*

"All of it toted, packed, and repacked for the road, heaved and stowed in luggage racks and baggage holds from Athens to Toledo, from Munich to Moscow.

I learned then that to purchase the world for remembrance—is to put a noose around the future. All these marvels are nothing compared to the sustainment of human life.

"Buddy's now among the treasures at the bottom of the sea…and his absence will continue to teach us how miracles don't come from staring too long at the sun…or by lighting all the candles in a dark church. His earthly physical demise illustrates how both *too much*—and *too little* light—can lead to blindness."

As the service closed, Roberta reached for my hand. I turned back for one more look, but Pina had already gone.

* * *

Under the bar's soft light, shots of whiskey and beer chasers were passed alongside little plates of fatty meat, the salt developing our thirst. I quickly downed a whiskey and Roberta hurried outside to search for Pina. In the sting of the drink, I felt every fury, past, present, and future, surge through my veins. That Pina managed to attend the funeral but Lydia did not, incensed me. My ice-cold, bellicose cousin and her ability to turn off human feeling, tempted me to want to pen a sour-patch valentine to her. But Lydia already dwelt in a pain so perverse—a nasty note might simply stir pleasure in her, the joy of causing invective in people she wished to irritate. My anger subsided, recognizing that to antagonize through such rude absence might possibly be her one true affirmation. In fact, it might provide the sole perceivable evidence of *her* mad existence.

The captain tipped back his third beer and wiped the foam from his mustache. "I am sorry, but I must get back to the ship." He gave me a hearty bear hug and before departing extended the last of his apologies.

Garafallou caught my eye, crossing from the other side of the room. "Walker, my boy, you look terrible."

"I'm upset she didn't show."

"Now's as good a time as any to say it—*to hell with her!* You must march on. It didn't feel right to announce this before the service—but Lydia's producers and the station are again standing by her. The tragedy of death exonerates her, and in sympathy and curiosity for whatever she is perceived to have endured—the cooking show will be restored. So, if *they* plan to march on, why shouldn't *we?*"

I looked at him with disappointment. "Oh yes, the show must go on!"

He returned my stare. "In publicity, one must sear flesh while the pan is hot. Can't buy this kind of widespread visibility." He took a fresh shot of whiskey from a passing tray. "Besides, Buddy would agree. He'd want the show to go on."

"Don't people always say that to justify the limits of their grief?"

"Next week…eight new episodes begin taping."

"And the cooking of Italy once more bares its heart, a comfort and a tradition—even an edible antidote for suicide?"

"Something like that. A press release will soon announce Lydia plans to cook either malfatti or pappardelle, while exploring the street foods of Rome. And at the end of the first new episode, she will prepare linguini noir as a secret mourning tribute to Buddy."

"Oh, please…spare me! That's the most disgusting thing I've ever heard."

"You're correct to question just how low it can go."

"And what, pray tell, will that be?"

"You mustn't forget, it was Buddy's curse—to not only *pet*, but also *pelt* a ferocious feline. And *that* may have also been his greatest pleasure. A public relations firm has now been hired to try and tame the tigress, prescribing and coaching the media recipe practiced by liars everywhere."

"Which is?"

"Tears, tears, and more tears. And they must be shed in public. You see, viewers crave to bear witness…to measure *shame*. In order to move on, and waylay their outrage, they must sense a comeuppance has been served. It's that which makes them feel included. To make a comeback via forgiveness, Lydia must be perceived as having sufficiently suffered. The PR people are concocting how abuse and treachery affected not just her health, but the welfare of their unborn. Even as we speak, she's being trained to look with sincerity at various announcers, her raw stare imploring viewers to rub salve over her broken heart. She's being booked on talk shows to showcase her contrition, the emotions acted to portray whatever the public needs to see and hear in order to forgive. Her eyes will stream tears, and viewers will be made to understand she wants nothing from them, only their unyielding hug of support."

"But then Buddy will be blamed for even the miscarriage."

"That's how you survive our electronic world. We've become a place of artifice, opinion, false impressions, and rarely is it able to portray justice or truth without slant."

"That's disgraceful."

"Yes, and that *is* showbiz. And these days fewer and fewer people care to demark the difference between reality and performance. Don't ever forget, television can sell pencil shavings as smoking tobacco! People want, even *need*, to believe the delusions of fantasy. They need escape. They need to believe their physical impotence can be made virile through passive means. So, exploiting injustice or some other low-ball truth must ape the wail of Medea."

"Oh, I get it. And once sorrow is established, Lydia will quickly shift to become a courageous survivor. Maybe you can even have her pen an essay for *The Menhaden Review* recalling or delving deeper into her abuse. Maybe she can claim a low clinical depression, a trauma, or even a sexual violation experienced in youth. After all, a claim of serious trauma does provoke leniency! And then after that, she can emerge ever-glamorous and cheerfully plucky, standing on the red carpet to inspire millions of fellow sufferers with her survivorship."

Garafallou stirred some ice into his glass and added a shot over the rocks. "How you do see all Walker! And through the lens of a camera lies sentimentality, a strong epoxy bonding traumatized strangers to the trauma of other strangers!"

I contemplated the remark, and felt my lips twist. "I'm disappointed in you."

His voice resigned itself. "Oh, me too! And that's why, once I've resolved the financial worry of the backers, I will be stepping down. After Buddy's death, I want no part of what's to come."

I turned away repulsed. Realizing the depth of my upset and my sarcasm, Garafallou now tried to soothe me. "Look at it this way Walker. I predict, in the long run, she'll fail. The show will run its course. In a few years, she'll try other shows, other jobs, other relationships. If encouraged, a truly dire prediction can be spun."

"Okay, let's hear it. Lay it on me."

"One day she'll fade, retire, adopt a series of devoted but browbeaten dogs. And should you or I come upon her name in print, or see her image, her face will be plastic, ironic, artificial, trying to resuscitate a phony *joie de vivre*. She might still hope to make herself relevant, delighting in the sound of her own voice, genuflecting to whatever advertising spin or bitch of gossip might accompany the attention. One day, menial work will become her lot. If it gets too rough, she'll take in lodgers, empty bed pans, do community service. By the time she passes sixty, she'll be pruning weeds on arthritic knees in some crumbling church border."

Garafallou's words took me aback. No matter. He was right. As with so many who yearn for more than their share—to linger longer on stage than any part requires—Lydia would *never* be satisfied. And should, by some chance, a curtain rise, a band magically appear to play an encore in her honor—no matter how much she might march, preen, or bow, the opus would now forever echo through Buddy's cold and empty tomb. By stealing his own life, Buddy had disrupted her billing, his final exit forever upstaging her act.

I studied the paneling on the walls, following the curvature of the wood-grain. "Do you agree?" Garafallou asked.

"Yes, maybe she'll also look into bathroom mirrors, talk to herself, give interviews, expand upon her former glory."

"All possible," Garafallou said, shaking my shoulder. "I've woven this bit of cruel prediction, especially to try and cheer you. So, smile, my boy!"

I felt myself go still. For a split second, I saw an image: the gurney holding Mom's zippered body-bag. A sudden spirit of compassion returned, compassion for all the contradictions found in every skeleton moving about in every room, including this one. "I wish you could have known her when she was young," I whispered.

"You mean what she went through?"

"What she overcame. How she tried. She tried so damn hard! And believe me, it was all hard. And weighing the challenges of her youth, I do hope your prediction will turn out to be *wrong*, and that these things will never come to pass."

"Well then, let's pray instead she finds peace, happiness, contentment."

"No matter what, I'll always love her. And you can go ahead and pray alone. For I've seen how those prayers turned out for Buddy."

Roberta returned, her face distraught. "I asked everyone in the street if they'd seen Pina. But she has disappeared without a trace."

Before we could discuss it any further, three members of the historical society approached, expressing great appreciation to Garafallou for his eulogy. One man, in a green moleskin hunting jacket, with deer antler buttons, spoke for the group. "As historians we're also intrigued by shipwrecks. Please, can you tell us more?"

"It is most difficult. Most difficult. Imagine passengers sitting on lifeboats, trying to steer small wooden rudders against raging gallons of…"

"Please, I don't like to interrupt!" The man acting as leader smiled. "But I'm afraid I should've asked our question with more exactitude. What we mean is, can the wreck be pinpointed?"

"Oh! You mean latitude and longitude…that sort of thing?"

"Yes." The man's mustache twitched. "For the sake of our report. Some idea of where the ill-fated ship foundered?"

"Ah yes…I see now. Well, it was off the coast of Sardinia," Garafallou said, staring down at a map the man was unfolding. More scholarly questions followed. The exact year? The name of the boat? The actual storm?

Garafallou took one look at the map, then realized the mistake of explaining faith to non-believers. "No, it wasn't Sardinia," he said. "It was really closer to Lisbon."

The map opened wider. Garafallou's mouth pursed as though chewing whale blubber. Then he altered the ship's final location yet again. "Actually, it happened down here," he said, and pointed to the bottom tip of South America. "In the dark, shark-infested waters off the Tierra del Fuego."

The group stared, dumbfounded. I knew as far as Garafallou was concerned, historians as a lot would never be objective. He did not seem to care in the least that an opinion of him was being revised. "I'm afraid I tested a Pear Williams cordial at the bar," he said. "And it must've been bottled too green. I'm sorry, but I'm sure you know unripe potions can fog any mind." Excusing himself, he walked away, his balance perfecting a comic wobble.

The leader of the society stood in disbelief. He then refolded the map, and the group placed their tiny teacups back onto a serving tray. "That's why we never drink alcohol," one woman said, with a confidential tone.

• • •

Like a fine chariot, Roberta's trustworthy orange Bentley carried us up into the hills, the late season burnishing the trees, the garden plots now emptied—their tomatoes, melons and figs all brought to market, the grapes pressed to ferment. Most agreed, due to the strange cool spell, the harvest had been only fair, but that in time the wine would prove itself. At the familiar bend, we passed the house of the woman still clinging to the ghost of her bee-stung baby; it was a relief *not* to find her vacant eyes staring their familiar sadness into our car.

Roberta remained steady, and on the next hairpin curve, I looked out to scan the horizon. To the South, once more I imagined the continent of Africa, and ruminated over how much of what I'd been granted had been born by the riches mined there? How much was real? How much utopian fantasy? For how many on that continent, and around the world, given half a chance, would still leap *at the chance* to take a slave?

Garafallou had predicted a dire future for Lydia, and as an astute observer of human truth, he might well turn out to be right. Yes, she might laugh again— but she'd never again be young.

And so, this lovely temperate day—would forever be known as the day we buried Buddy. My shoulders released to soften with acceptance. I suddenly felt the well-known resentments toward my cousin Lydia unclench, as if by miracle.

I knew then, that facing Buddy in the morgue had cured me of any lonely need to pursue people who were not available. The linkage I'd encountered upon viewing his corpse, now related me not just to him, but to the bones of everyone, wherever they might lie on the planet. Grind down the calcification, mash through the marrow, and only nature decides what can remain.

The car crested the last hill and was forced to halt for a herd of goats blocking the communal lot. The chaos left us amused and powerless, unable to proceed, watching the animals try to outsmart a shepherd's order being imposed. Roberta stared out the window and then posed a question—one that had floated delicately between us ever since the funeral: "Walker…do you think Garafallou is telling the truth? I mean…was he ever shipwrecked?"

Gazing out over the goats who'd begun to advance South toward a hollow of cypress trees, I took my time to construct a reply. "In life, I've never been especially fond of hecklers," I said. "Those too-eager-beavers wishing to expose the feats of magic. And while a warrant might be served on Mr. Garafallou—there are other, bigger trials against truth waiting to be heard. First, let's cross-examine the fig leaves and tablets of Genesis…then the animals walking two-by-two onto the ark, then question the hundreds of *talking* animals moralizing their way through the world's fables…then the mighty goddesses and warriors of mythic legends must be served, to account for wreaking havoc on mankind. I suppose television commercials ought to also deserve hearings, and the myths surrounding favorite celebrities and saints, not to mention the conclusions of bad or faulty science. Now, already there's quite a line in the docket for these trials. Meanwhile, as we wait for those court judgements to crawl through, I'm *perfectly* happy to let Mr. Garafallou hold me in his spell with any riddle that he chants."

Roberta rolled her eyes. "It was but a simple question."

"Well…let the man catalogue as many losses as he needs to. I say, let him contradict himself along with the rest of us. And now, it's *you* who must be asked to consider something. I mean, I've just declared myself a man with a deep and abiding need to believe in magic. It's among the worst sins I practice, and I'm truly sorry and discredited to admit it. And now I'm afraid you must decide… can you live with *that*?"

Roberta lifted her head and gave a curt smile. "Let me not answer in haste. I'll think on it and get back to you."

The shepherd encouraged the last of the goats and their teeming life-force onward, and with the roadway cleared, he turned back to us, lifting his twisted, crooked stick and nodding. We drove on into the parking lot amid the last of the clanking bells. This, the final act of our play, was permitting something abstract to resolve in me. I longed to ask if *this* was what an ending of happiness felt like. The silver of loss, melding with the gold of possibility, to mint a new and steadfast metallurgical luck.

Roberta turned off the car, and we got out to greet Vescovi; already searching the backseat, it surprised him when it and the car's trunk both proved empty, as we'd acquired no additional baggage. Walking single-file down through the village, my mind envisioned the many tasks and assignments waiting, the mountains rising above our heads, their rocky cliffs tunneled with all the realities of mass. Pausing before Roberta's fine courtyard, her soft hand touched mine. It was then we heard the familiar sound, that scrape of sedge grass, angled in cut and knotted to a wooden handle, that well-known rhythmic chore, a manual labor binding our bodies across the centuries. Roberta turned to me, and through her joy, I saw all we currently knew was but this day, a single day, waiting to be swept across the cobbles.

ACKNOWLEDGMENTS

The years have passed fast & slow, and the number of people who lend their talent grows long. Most know who they are—but by this message of thanks, seeks to trace the involved names, faces & hands.

Thanks to my parents.

Special thanks to Marie Ponsot, for showing up—her loyal acts guided by a poet's moral compass.

Special thanks to Bronson & Carl, International Books, London.

Special acknowledgement for a valiant executive production-director: Catherine Walker.

Special acknowledgement to executive editor: Eric Groff.

Special acknowledgement to Chris Mele for editorial analysis.

I especially thank a group of dedicated readers: Donna Bucher, Anita Williams-McGuire, Rita Andreopoulos, Linda Morgan, Sharon Stea, Cassidy Uptegraph, Susan Miller, LB Thompson, Tim Small, Rosemary Deen & Wanda Moore.

Also: Martha Sandlin, Christopher Hermelin, Isabelle Dufresne, William Finn, Nikki Moustaki, & Ryan Harbage.

Thanks to David Lehman, for unflinching collegial allegiance.

Certain thanks to insightful PEN colleagues: Hettie Jones, Fielding Dawson, Bayard Rustin, Gore Vidal, Susan Sontag, Zia Jaffrey, Joan Didion, & Larry McMurtry.

Thanks to the SAW writers for their inspiration: Jamie Stern, Kate Dehais, Marsha Loughrin, Howard Clyman, Katherine Sweet, Nan Lombardi & Catherine Woodard.

Special thanks to friends of the Foundry: Jill Rehman, a dean who modeled steadfast integrity & courage; Gail Moran, a skilled person with a trustworthy head & heart, Professor Tim Small, so deserving of the teaching excellence award, & also Richard Greenwald, for his vision & noble courage.

Thanks to the writers at The Holy Apostles Soup Kitchen Writing Program, where large portions of this book were drafted—at a church under the spirited &

clear-eyed Liz Maxwell; also many thanks to Sue Shapiro, Ron Mwangaguhunga, & the consistent excellence of Alice Phillips.

Thanks for inspiration & dedication from a wonderful group of artists, all of whom by their own practice have informed The Green Pear: Francisco Franklin, Kelly Castagnaro, Karen Good-Marable, Tamara Warren, Marsha Nall, Rachel Moldonado, Ayana Byrd, Stacy Leigh, Suzanne Kazenoff Rosenzweig, Audrey Matson, Gloria Joseph, Connie Aitcheson, Chris Majcherski, Meg Mcguire, Daniel Parsons, Gabrielle Burnham, Alexa Wilding, Justin Torres, Ayana Mathis, Eric Boyd, Kimberly Bunker, Metanoya Webb, Magdalen Pierakos, Amanda Harris, Anna Linetskaya, Minju Pak, Madeline Peale, Kody Emmanuel, Anname Phan, Terry Wells, Alyssa Proujansky, Scott Bremer, Audacia Ray, Julia Strayer, Kirsten Levingston, Marie Denoia, Lande Yousef, Stephanie Bulger, Tonya Leslie, Angelina Lim, Brian Morgan, Erin Rickard, Bernice McFadden, Sumitra Rajkumar, Gabrielle Don, Stephanie Sirota, Jamiyla Chisholm, Jason Burstein, Kourtney Fullard, Rita Hickey, Helen Hofling, Hanan Mahbouba, Maleka Fruen, Erica David, Amanda Wong, Nathalie Auerbach, Kristin Fahlbusch, Andrea Duncan-Mao, Alta Starr, Sally White, Ana Egge, Emma Harzem, Suzanne Grabowski, Justin Morris, Jeanette Topar, Ken Derry, Andre Tiernon, Sarah Trelease, Danyel Smith, Jay Edlin, Witold Fitz-Simon, Brian Pennington, Chin-Sun Lee, Christina Winters, Bessie Oster, TJ Wells, Ben Kendricks, Ennis Smith, Eliza Janney, Joy Baglio, Annette Herfkins, Supriya Pillai, Joyce Fuller, Emily Rubin, Carlos Dews, Gregory Andreopoulos, Zarines Negron, Sue Jaye Johnson, Kate Meehan, Andrew Cotto, Geoffrey Knox, Isaiah Gibson, Sophia Ripple, Tina Jacobson, Laurie Douglas, Steven Estok, & the late Thua Maad, the late Steven Hobbs, & the late Anita Williams-Mcguire.

Thanks to Kate Trimble, whose wit leads her intelligent sense.

Thanks to Maryanne Diemer for direction that is good & orderly.

Thanks to Annette D.—there from the start & ever onward.

A thank you also to many friends in Harrisburg who gave time & care to The Blue Orchard: Eric & Catherine Papenfuse, Carol Mace, Jim M. Munchel, Bev Beshore, & Pat & Henry Greenawald.

Also special thanks to the people of Harrisburg who continue to inform the second book of this trilogy: the Reverend Billy Gray, Chef Joseph Randall Jr., Laura (Pam) Randall, James S. Togans, Marshall Waters, Hariette Braxton, Mr. & Mrs. Horatio Leftwich, Millicent Hooper, Andy Robinson, Mrs. Helen McBride, Dr. Don Freedman, Dr. Claude Nichols, William Byers, Dr. Walter & Jean Kirker, Dr. Minster Kunkel, Dr. William Tyler Douglas Jr., Helen Oxley,

Barton Fields, Dr. I.O. Silver, Mary Scheffer, Howard Clemens Sr., Spencer Nauman Jr., Bob Nation, Louisa France, Garner Thomas, Mrs. Russell K. Patterson, FitzHugh Shelley, Fran Hasselman, Emily Rine, M. Harvey Taylor III, Cecil Franklin, Hon. William Lipsitt, Dr. Marilyn Mahon, Legree Daniels, Oscar Daniels, Dr. Wilson Everhart, Marianne Leitner, Mrs. Janet Essence Morrison, Mrs. Spencer Norman, Stanley Lawson, Sen. Roy Zimmerman, Judge Robert Woodside, Gladys & Lester Gross, Susan & Herman Gross, Mrs. Sarah Raffensberger, Elizabeth Raffensberger, Mrs. Freda Walls, Dr. Gerald G. Eggart, Robert Christ II, Eleanor Byers, Leslie McCreath, Margaret Bruchey, George Love, Ursula & Lish Crampton, Verna Eckert, Leila Washington, Raymond S. McGarvey, Paul Beers, Jim Rollins Jr., Lonnie Moore, Hazel Pannebakker, Virgie Hosler, William Goetz, & Mrs. Martha Gibney.

Jackson Taylor is a celebrated novelist and educator. His debut, *The Blue Orchard*, earned widespread praise for its painstaking research and powerful narrative. Beyond he page, Jackson has spent his work-life fostering a new generation of writers—directing the PEN Prison Writing Program and helping to launch and develop MFA programs at The New School and The Writer's Foundry.